KUSHIEL'S
AVATAR

ALSO BY JACQUELINE CAREY

Kushiel's Dart
Kushiel's Chosen

KUSHIEL'S AVATAR

JACQUELINE CAREY

To Brian,
Thanks for traveling on the Long Road! All best,
Jacqueline Carey

TOR®

A TOM DOHERTY ASSOCIATES BOOK
New York

KUSHIEL'S AVATAR

This book is printed on acid-free paper.

Edited by Claire Eddy

A Tor Book
Published by Tom Doherty Associates, LLC
175 Fifth Avenue
New York, NY 10010

www.tor.com

Tor® is a registered trademark of Tom Doherty Associates, LLC.

Library of Congress Cataloging-in-Publication Data

Carey, Jacqueline, 1964–
    Kushiel's avatar / Jacqueline Carey.
       p.   cm.
    ISBN 0-312-87240-2
    1. Courts and courtiers—Fiction.   2. Indentured
servants—Fiction.   3. Angels—Fiction.   4. Women—
Fiction.   I. Title.

    PS3603.A74 K77   2003
    813'.54—dc21

                         2002040941

First Edition: April 2003

Printed in the United States of America

0 9 8 7 6 5 4 3 2 1

Acknowledgments

I owe a debt of gratitude to all the people who have contributed to the success of the *Kushiel's Legacy* trilogy; to my first agent, Todd Keithley, whose belief in the books made this possible, and to my agent, Jane Dystel, whose continued support has seen the trilogy to its conclusion and opened doors beyond it. To everyone at Tor, and especially my editor, Claire Eddy, for her skill and passion alike.

And last, but never, ever least: To the readers.

Thank you.

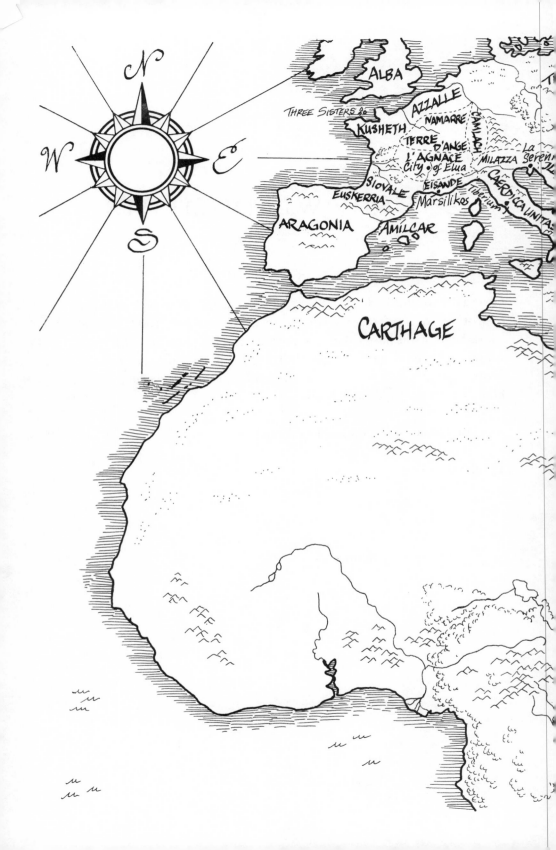

DRAMATIS PERSONAE

PHÈDRE'S HOUSEHOLD

Anafiel Delaunay de Montrève—mentor of Phèdre (*deceased*)
Alcuin nó Delaunay—student of Delaunay (*deceased*)
Phèdre nó Delaunay de Montrève—Comtesse de Montrève; *anguissette*
Joscelin Verreuil—Phèdre's Consort; Cassiline Brother (Siovale)
Fortun, Remy—chevaliers (*deceased*)
Ti-Philippe—chevalier
Hugues—attendant
Eugènie—Mistress of the Household
Clory—niece of Eugènie
Purnell Friote—seneschal of Montrève
Richeline Friote—wife of Purnell
Benoit—stable-lad

MEMBERS OF THE ROYAL FAMILY: TERRE D'ANGE

Ysandre de la Courcel—Queen of Terre d'Ange; wed to Drustan mab Necthana
Sidonie de la Courcel—elder daughter of Ysandre
Alais de la Courcel—younger daughter of Ysandre
Barquiel L'Envers—uncle of Ysandre; Duc L'Envers (Namarre)

ALBA

Drustan mab Necthana—Cruarch of Alba, wed to Ysandre de la Courcel
Necthana—mother of Drustan
Breidaia, Moiread (*deceased*), Sibeal—Drustan's sisters, daughters of
   Necthana

THREE SISTERS

Hyacinthe—apprentice to Master of the Straits; Prince of Travellers
Tilian, Gildas—assistants

LA SERENISSIMA

Benedicte de la Courcel—great-uncle of Ysandre; Prince of the Blood
   (*deceased*)
Melisande Shahrizai de la Courcel—second wife of Benedicte
Imriel de la Courcel—son of Benedicte and Melisande
Severio Stregazza—son of Marie-Celeste de la Courcel and Marco
   Stregazza; Prince of the Blood
Cesare Stregazza—Doge of La Serenissima
Ricciardo Stregazza—younger son of the Doge
Allegra Stregazza—wife of Ricciardo
Benito Dandi—noble, member of the Immortali

VERREUIL

Chevalier Millard—Joscelin's father
Ges—Joscelin's mother
Luc—Joscelin's elder brother
Yvonne—wife of Luc
Mahieu—Joscelin's younger brother
Marie-Louise—wife of Mahieu
Jehane—Joscelin's elder sister

Amílcar

Nicola L'Envers y Aragon—cousin of Queen Ysandre
Ramiro Zornín de Aragon—King's Consul, husband of Nicola
Fernan—Count of Amílcar
Vitor Gaitán—Captain of the Harbor Watch
Mago, Harnapos—Carthaginian slavers

Menekhet

Fadil Chouma—slaver (*deceased*)
Nesmut—harbor-lad
Raife Laniol, Comte de Penfars—ambassador to Menekhet
Juliet de Penfars—wife of Raife
Ptolemy Dikaios—Pharaoh of Menekhet
Clytemne—wife of Pharaoh
Rekhmire—Treasury clerk
Denise Fleurais—member of Lord Amaury's delegation
Radi Arumi—Jebean guide
General Hermodorus—enemy of the Pharaoh

Khebbel-im-Akkad

Sinaddan-Shamabarsin—Lugal of Khebbel-im-Akkad
Valère L'Envers—wife of the Lugal; daughter of Barquiel L'Envers
Tizrav—Persian guide
Renée de Rives—member of Lord Amaury's delegation
Nicholas Vigny—member of Lord Amaury's delegation
Nurad-Sin—Akkadian captain

Drujan

The Mahrkagir—"Conquerer of Death," ruler of Drujan
Gashtaham—chief Skotophagotis
Tahmuras—a warrior

Nariman—Chief Eunuch of the zenana
Rushad—Persian eunuch
Erich—Skaldi prisoner
Drucilla—Tiberian prisoner
Kaneka—Jebean prisoner
Uru-Azag—Akkadian eunuch
Jolanta—Chowati prisoner
Nazneen—Ephesian prisoner
Jagun—chief of the Kereyit Tatars
Arshaka—Chief Magus

Jebe-Barkal

Wali—river guide
Mek Timmur—caravan master
Zanadakhete—Queen of Meroë
Ras Lijasu—Prince of Meroë
Nathifa—sister of Lijasu
Tifari Amu—guide
Bizan—guide
Nkuku—bearer
Yedo—bearer
Shoanete—Kaneka's grandmother, storyteller

Saba

Hanoch ben Hadad—captain of the militia
Yevuneh—widow, sister of Hanoch
Bilgah—Elder of the Sanhedrin
Abiram—Elder of the Sanhedrin
Ranit—woman of Saba
Semira—woman of Saba
Morit—woman of Saba, astronomer
Ardath—daughter of Yevuneh
Eshkol ben Avidan—soldier

Others

Evrilac Duré—Captain of the Guard at Pointe des Soeurs

Guillard, Armand—men-at-arms at Pointe des Soeurs

Bérèngere of Namarre—priestess of the Great Temple of Naamah

Eleazar ben Enokh—Yeshuite mystic

Adara—wife of Eleazar

Michel Nevers—priest of Kushiel

Audine Davul—D'Angeline scholar of Jebe-Barkal

Emile—member of Hyacinthe's former crew; chief among Tsingani in the City

Brother Selbert—chief priest in the Sanctuary of Elua (Siovale)

Liliane—acolyte in the Sanctuary of Elua (Siovale)

Honore, Beryl, Cadmar, Ti-Michel—children in the Sanctuary of Elua (Siovale)

Jacques Écot—crofter (Siovale)

Agnes—wife of Jacques (Siovale)

Kristof, son of Oszkar—head of a Tsingani kumpania

Cecilie Laveau-Perrin—adept of Cereus House; tutor to Phèdre and Alcuin

Roxanne de Mereliot—Lady of Marsilikos (Eisande)

Thelesis de Mornay—Queen's Poet

Quintilius Rousse—Royal Admiral

KUSHIEL'S AVATAR

One

İT ENDED with a dream.

Ten years of peace, the ancient Oracle of Asherat-of-the-Sea promised me; ten years I had, and in that time, my fortune prospered along with that of Terre d'Ange, my beloved nation. So often, a time of great happiness is recognized only in hindsight. I reckoned it a blessing that the Oracle's promise served also as warning, and let no day pass without acknowledging its grace. Youth and beauty I had yet on my side, the latter deepening as the years tempered the former. Thus had my old mentor, Cecilie Laveau-Perrin, foretold, and if I had counted her words lightly in the rasher youth of my twenties, I knew it for truth as I left them behind.

'Tis a shallow concern, many might claim, but I am D'Angeline and make no apology for our ways. Comtesse de Montrève I may be, and indeed, a heroine of the realm—had not my deeds been set to verse by the Queen's Poet's own successor?—but I had come first into my own as Phèdre nó Delaunay, Naamah's Servant and Kushiel's Chosen, an *anguissette* and the most uniquely trained courtesan the realm had ever known. I have never claimed to lack vanity.

For the rest, I had those things which I prized above all else, not the least of which was the regard of my Queen, Ysandre de la Courcel, who gifted me with the Companion's Star for my role in securing her throne ten years past. I had seen then the makings of a great ruler in her; I daresay all the realm has seen it since. For ten years, Terre d'Ange has known peace and abiding prosperity; Terre d'Ange and Alba, ruled side by side by Ysandre de la Courcel and Drustan mab Necthana, the Cruarch of Alba, whom I am privileged to call my friend. Surely the hand of Blessed Elua was upon that union, when love took root where the seeds of political alliance were sown! Truly, love has proved the stronger force, conquering even the deadly Straits that divided them.

Although it took Hyacinthe's sacrifice to achieve it.

Thus, the nature of my dream.

I did not know, when I awoke from it, trembling and short of breath, tears leaking from beneath my closed lids, that it was the beginning of the end. Even in happiness, I never forgot Hyacinthe. I had not dreamed of him before, it is true, but he was ever on my mind. How could he not be? He was my oldest and dearest friend, the companion of my childhood. Not even my lord Anafiel Delaunay, who took me into his household at the age of ten, who trained me in the arts of covertcy and whose name I bear to this day, had known me so long. What I am, what I became, I owe to my lord Delaunay, who changed with a few words my fatal flaw to a sacred mark, the sign of Kushiel's Dart. But it was Hyacinthe who knew me first, who was my friend when I was naught but a whore's unwanted get, an orphan of the Night Court with a scarlet mote in my left eye that made me unfit for Naamah's Service, that made superstitious countryfolk point and stare and call me names.

And it was Hyacinthe of whom I dreamed. Not the young man I had left to a fate worse than death—a fate that *should* have been mine—but the boy I had known, the Tsingano boy with the black curls and the merry grin, who, in an overturned market stall, reached out his hand to me in conspiratorial friendship.

I drew a deep, shuddering breath, feeling the dream recede, tears still damp on my cheeks. So simple, to arouse such horror! In my dream, I stood in the prow of a ship, one of the swift, agile Illyrian ships I knew so well from my adventures, and wept to watch a gulf of water widen between my vessel and the rocky shore of a lonely island, where the boy Hyacinthe stood alone and pleaded, stretching out his arms and calling my name. He had solved a riddle there, naming the source of the Master of the Straits' power. I had answered it too, but Hyacinthe had used the *dromonde*, the Tsingano gift of sight, and his answer went deeper than I could follow. He won us passage across the Straits when we needed it most and the cost of it was all he had, binding him to those stony shores for eternity, unless the *geis* could be broken. This I had sought for many years to do, and in my dream, as in life, I had failed. I could hear the crew behind me, cursing in despair against the headwinds that drove us further away, the vast expanse of grey water widening between us, Hyacinthe's cries following, his boyish voice calling out to the woman I had become, Phèdre, Phèdre!

It shivered my flesh all over to remember it and I turned unthinking toward comfort, curling my body against Joscelin's sleeping warmth and pillowing my tear-stained cheek on his shoulder—for that was the last and greatest of my gifts, and the one I treasured most: Love. For ten years, Joscelin Verreuil has been my consort, and if we have bickered and quarreled and wounded each other to the quick a thousand times over, there is not a day of it I would relinquish. Let the realm laugh—and they do—to think of the union betwixt a courtesan and a Cassiline; we know what we are to one another.

Joscelin did not wake, but merely stirred in his sleep, accommodating his body to mine. Moonlight spilled through the window of our bedchamber overlooking the garden; moonlight and the faint scent of herbs and roses, rendering his fair hair silver as it spread across the pillows and making the air sweet. It is a pleasant place to sleep and make love. I pressed my lips silently to Joscelin's shoulder, resting quiet beside him. It might have been Hyacinthe, if matters had fallen out otherwise. We had dreamed of it, he and I.

No one is given to know what might have been.

So I mused, and in time I slept and dreamed that I mused still until I awoke to find sunlight lying in a bright swathe across the bed-linens and Joscelin already awake in the garden. His daggers flashed steel as he moved through the seamless series of exercises he had performed every day of his life since he was ten years old, the training-forms of a Cassiline Brother. But it was not until I had risen and bathed and was breaking my fast that he came in to greet me, and when he did, his blue eyes were somber.

"There is news," he said, "from Azzalle."

I stopped with a piece of honey-smeared bread halfway to my mouth and set it down carefully on my plate, remembering my dream. "What news?"

Joscelin sat down opposite me, propping his elbows on the table and resting his chin on his hands. "I don't know. It has to do with the Straits. Ysandre's courier would say no more."

"Hyacinthe," I said, feeling myself grow pale.

"Mayhap." His voice was grave. "We're wanted at court as soon as you're ready."

He knew, as well as I did; Joscelin had been there, when Hyacinthe took on the doom that should have been mine, using the *dromonde* to trump the offering of my wits and consecrate himself to eternal exile. A fine fate for the Prince of Travellers, condemned to an endless existence on a narrow isle amid the deep waters that divided Terre d'Ange and Alba, bound to serve as heir to the Master of the Straits.

Such had been the nature of his bargain. The Master of the Straits would never be free of his curse until someone took his place. One of us had to stay. I had known it was necessary; I would have done it. And it would have been a worthwhile sacrifice, for had it not been made, the Alban ships would never have crossed the Straits, and Terre d'Ange would have fallen to the conquering army of Skaldi.

I had answered the riddle and my words were true: the Master of the Straits drew his power from the Lost Book of Raziel. But the *dromonde* looks backward as well as forward, and Hyacinthe's answer went deeper. He had seen the very genesis of the *geis* itself, how the angel Rahab had loved a mortal woman who loved him not, and held her captive. How he had gotten a son upon her, and how she had sought to flee him nonetheless, and perished in the effort, along with her beloved. How Rahab had been punished by the One God for his disobedience, and how he had wreaked the vengeance of an angry heart upon his son, who would one day be named Master of the Straits. How Rahab brought up pages of the Lost Book of Raziel, salvaged from the deep. How Rahab gave them to his son, gave him mastery of the waters and bound him there, on a lonely isle of the Three Sisters, condemning him to separate Terre d'Ange and Alba, for so long as Rahab's own punishment endured.

This was the fate Hyacinthe had inherited.

For ten years and more, I had sought a way to break the curse that bound him there, immersing myself in the study of Yeshuite lore in the hope of finding a key to free him. If a key existed, it could be found in the teachings of those who followed Yeshua ben Yosef, the One God's acknowledged scion. But if it did, I had not found it.

It was one of the few things at which I had failed utterly.

"Let's go." I pushed my plate away, appetite gone. "If something's happened, I need to know it."

Joscelin nodded and rose to summon the stable-lad to make ready the carriage. I went to change my attire to something suitable for court, donning a gown of amber silk and pinning the Companion's Star onto the décolletage, the diamond etched with Elua's sigil glittered in its radiant gold setting. It is a cumbersome honor, that brooch, but if the Queen had sent for me, I dared not appear without it. Ysandre was particular about the honors she bestowed.

My carriage is well-known in the City of Elua, bearing on its sides the revised arms of Montrève. Here and there along the streets, cheerful salutes and blown kisses were offered, and I suppressed my anxiety to accept such tribute with a smile, for it was no fault of my admirers that my nerves were strung taut that morning. Joscelin bore it with his customary stoicism. It would have been a point of contention between us, once. We have grown a little wiser with the years.

If I have patrons still, they are fewer and more select—thrice a year, no more and no less, do I accept an assignation as Naamah's Servant. It has proven, after much quarrel and debate, a compromise both of us can tolerate. I cannot help it that Kushiel's Dart drives me to violent desires; I am an *anguissette*, and destined to find my greatest pleasure mingled with pain. No more can Joscelin alter the fact that he is made otherwise.

I daresay we both of us know that there are only two people in the world capable of truly dividing us. And one . . .

No one is ever given to know what might have been.

Hyacinthe.

As for the other . . . of Melisande Shahrizai, we do not speak, save in terms of the politics of the day. Joscelin knows well, better than any, the hatred I bear for her; as for the rest, it is the curse of my nature and a burden I carry in silence. I offered myself to her, once, at the asking-price of her son's whereabouts. It was not a price Melisande was willing to pay. I do not think she would have sold that knowledge at any price, for there is no one living who holds it. I know; I have sought it.

It is the other thing I have failed utterly in finding.

It matters less, now; a little less, though there is no surety where Melisande is concerned. Ysandre thought my fears were mislaid, once upon a time, colored by an *anguissette*'s emotions. That was before she found that Melisande Shahrizai had wed her great-uncle Benedicte de la Courcel, and given birth to a son who stood to inherit Terre d'Ange itself. Now, she listens; now, I have no insight to offer. Though Benedicte is long dead and his conspirator Percy de Somerville with him, Melisande abides in the sanctuary of Asherat-of-the-Sea. Her son Imriel remains missing, and I cannot guess at her moves.

But my Queen Ysandre worries less since giving birth to a daughter eight years ago, and another two years later. Now two heirs stand between Melisande's boy and the throne, and well guarded each day of their lives; a more pressing concern is the succession of Alba, which proceeds in a matrilineal tradition. Unless he dares break with Cruithne tradition, Drustan mab Necthana's heir will proceed not from his loins, but from one of his sisters' wombs. Such are the ways of his people, the Cullach Gorrym, who call themselves Earth's Eldest Children. Two sisters he has living, Breidaia and Sibeal, and neither wed to one of Elua's lineage.

Thus stood politics in Terre d'Ange, after ten years of peace, the day I rode to the palace to hear the news from Azzalle.

Azzalle is the northernmost province of the nation, bordering the narrow Strait that divides us from Alba. Once, those waters were nigh impassable, under the command of he whom we named the Master of the Straits. It has changed, since Hyacinthe's sacrifice and the marriage of Ysandre and Drustan—yet even so, no vessel has succeeded in putting to shore on those isles known as the Three Sisters. The strictures change, but the curse remains, laid down by the disobedient angel Rahab. For so long as his punishment continues, the curse endures.

As the Master of the Straits noted, the One God has a long memory.

I felt a shiver of foreboding as we were admitted into the courtyard of the palace. It might have been hope, if not for the dream. Once before, my fears had been made manifest in dreams, although it took a trained adept of Gentian House to enable me to see them—and they had proved horribly well-grounded that time. This time, I remembered. I had awoken in tears, and I remembered. An old blind woman's words and a shudder in my soul warned me that a decade of grace was coming to an end.

Two·

YSANDRE RECEIVED us in one of her lesser council chambers, a high-vaulted room dominated by a single table around which were eight upholstered chairs. Three men in the travel-worn livery of House Trevalion sat on either side, and the Queen at its head.

"Phèdre." Ysandre came around to give me the kiss of greeting as we were ushered into the chamber. "Messire Verreuil." She smiled as Joscelin saluted her with his Cassiline bow, vambraced arms crossed before him. Ysandre had always been fond of him, all the more so since he had thwarted an assassin's blade in her defense. "Well met. I thought you would wish to be the first to hear of this oddity."

"My la . . ." I caught myself for perhaps the thousandth time; bearing the Companion's Star entitled me to address the scions of Elua as equals, a thing contrary to my nature and training even after these many years. "Ysandre. Very much so, thank you. There is news from the Straits?"

The three men at the table had stood when the Queen arose, and Ysandre turned to them. "This is Evrilac Duré of Trevalion, and his men-at-arms Guillard and Armand," she announced. "For the past year, they have maintained my lord Ghislain nó Trevalion's vigil at the Pointe des Soeurs."

My knees weakened. "Hyacinthe," I whispered. The Pointe des Soeurs lay in the northwest of Azzalle in the duchy of Trevalion, closest to those islands D'Angelines have named the Three Sisters; it was there that the Master of the Straits was condemned to hold sway, and Hyacinthe to succeed him.

"We have no news of the Tsingano, Comtesse," Evrilac Duré said quietly, stepping forward and according me a brief bow. He was a tall man in his early forties, with lines at the corners of his grey eyes such as come from long sea-gazing. "I am sorry. We have all heard much of his sacrifice."

They would, in Azzalle. It was there that we had come to land, D'Angelines, Cruithne and Dalriada, carried to the mouth of the Rhenus by the mighty, surging wave commanded by the Master of the Straits, the wound of our loss still fresh and aching. And it was Ghislain nó Trevalion who met us there; Ghislain de Somerville, then. He has abjured his father's name since, and for that I do not blame him.

"Be seated and hear." Ysandre swept her hand toward the table.

Although the realm is at peace, they maintain the ways of vigilance at Pointe des Soeurs; the Azzallese are proud, and wary of the fact that the rocky promontory lies close by to the border of Kusheth. Even in times of peace, it is not unknown for the scions of Elua's Companions to skirmish among themselves. Blessed Elua, conceived of the blood of Yeshua ben Yosef and the tears of Mary Magdelene, nurtured in the womb of Earth, sought no dominion here, where he was welcomed open-armed after his long wanderings. He made this place his home, and Terre d'Ange it was called ever after in his honor. *Love as thou wilt*, he bade us; no more. It is another matter among his Companions— Azza, Naamah, Anael, Eisheth, Kushiel, Shemhazai and Camael—those fallen angels who secured his freedom and aided his passage, and who divided the realm betwixt them. Many gifts they gave us; and dissension, too. Only Cassiel took no part, remaining ever at Elua's side, the Perfect Companion.

They are gone, now, to the true Terre d'Ange-that-lies-beyond. Once, and once only, a peace was made betwixt the One God and Mother Earth, that it might be so. Only we, their scions, are left to bear out Blessed Elua's precept as best we might—but we are his descendants and our story continues. And this, then, was the tale that emerged, told first by Armand, who had been on night watch when it began.

"Lightning," said Armand of Trevalion, "such as I have never seen; blue-white and crackling, my lady, great jagged forks of it, all coming from a single cloud, some ten miles from the coast." He shrugged his shoulders. "I cannot be sure, in the dark, but it is in that direction the Three Sisters lie; I am as sure as any man can be that the cloud overlay them."

"Surely there is nothing so odd about a storm," Joscelin said mildly.

Armand shook his head. "I have seen storms, Messire Cassiline, natural and otherwise. This is my third turn of duty at Pointe des

Soeurs. This was no storm, and I have never seen its like. It was a calm night, with the sky black as velvet and every star visible save where the cloud blotted them out. With each flash of lightning I could see the underbelly of the cloud, violet and black, shot with glimmers of gold. I stood on the parapet in the stillness of a spring night and watched it. Then I went to fetch the commander."

"He describes it truly," Evrilac Duré affirmed. "All around us was calm, but though the waves rippled and the insects sang at Pointe des Soeurs, we could see the skies split open and the seas in a fury about the Three Sisters." He folded his hands on the table. "I have seen many strange things, living on the Straits. No man or woman, Alban or D'Angeline, would deny it. Tides that defy the moon, currents that run backward, eddies and whirlpools and unbreaking waves. You yourself have seen the Face of the Waters, is it not so?"

"Yes." It is a thing, once seen, never forgotten.

"So it is told," Duré murmured. "But I have never seen the like of this, nor heard it spoken. For the better portion of the night it continued, striking ever faster as Armand and I watched from the parapet. Beautiful, it was; and terrifying. In the final moments before dawn there came one last burst, a flash so bright it fair washed the sky in blindness, and a great crack of thunder. And a voice, crying out; a man's voice, it seemed, but so vast it carried over sea and wave. A single cry." He fell silent a moment. "Then nothing."

"Woke the garrison, it did," the third man, Guillard, offered. "And me the first out the doors, with the sky greying in the east. I saw the wave come and break ashore, and what it left in its wake. Fish, eels, you name it; thousands, there were, flopping and dying on the stones. A great ring of a wave, like the ripple from a cast pebble." He shook his head. "All along the shore, as far as the eye could see, writhing and flopping. Never seen the like."

"So." I frowned. "You saw a cloud, and strange lightnings; then a wave, which brought many fish ashore. What of the isles? Did you attempt the Three Sisters?"

Trevalion's men exchanged glances, and Evrilac Duré's folded hands twitched. "We did not," he said shortly. "Our orders are to watch and report. I sent word to my lord Ghislain, and he bade me bring notice in all haste to her majesty the Queen. This, I have done."

He was afraid. I saw it in his eyes, the tight lines around his mouth. I could not blame him. Men of Trevalion had died assailing the Straits; a good many of them under Ghislain's command, some dozen years gone by. It was no fault of his, but the orders of the old King, Ysandre's grandfather, Ganelon de la Courcel. Still, they had died, and I could not fault Duré for fearing. I was afraid, too.

Ysandre cleared her throat. "I've already sent couriers to alert Quintilius Rousse, Phèdre. But he is away on excursion to Khebbel-im-Akkad, and not due to return until summer's end. I thought you would want to know. It is my understanding you have made quite a study of the Master of the Straits."

"Yes." I passed my hands over my face, wishing the Royal Admiral were not gone. Quintilius Rousse had been there, when Hyacinthe made his choice; moreover, he had a long-standing quarrel with the Master of the Straits. It was Rousse who had tested the defenses of the Three Sisters, year upon year. If there was any man fit to try them again, it was he. I had only useless lore on my side—and Joscelin, who was little help at sea, for my own Perfect Companion, alas, was no sailor and was more oft than not found retching over the rails.

"What do you make of this?" Ysandre's gaze was kind. She had known Hyacinthe, if briefly, and knew of our long friendship.

"I don't know." I raised my head. "The Master of the Straits said it would be a long apprenticeship. Mayhap it is only that, some phenomenon of power, a demonstration. But it is in my heart that it may be something more. With your permission, I would like to investigate."

"You have it." Ysandre bent her gaze on Evrilac Duré, not without a degree of asperity. "Messire Duré, I will not command any man of Trevalion to assail the Three Sisters . . . but I will ask. If Phèdre nó Delaunay wishes to travel thence, will you carry her?"

Evrilac Duré swallowed visibly, lifting his chin a fraction. They are proud, in Azzalle, and she had stung him. My Queen had learned some few things about manipulating people herself since first she ascended the throne. "Majesty!" he said sharply. "We will."

Thus were our plans laid. Ysandre dismissed the Azzallese to seek food and rest, leaving instructions with the Secretary of the Privy Purse that they were to be rewarded and our excursion generously funded. Joscelin and myself, she invited to take repast in the garden with her, which I was glad of, now being hungry for my interrupted breakfast.

The late morning sun lay like balm on the greening flora, twice the size of my own modest garden and three times as well tended. It was a rare moment of intimacy we shared with Ysandre over egg possets and the first early fruits of spring. There were few people in the realm that the Queen trusted implicitly. Of all the honors she has bestowed upon me, that is the one I cherish the most.

The Chamberlain of the Nursery brought Sidonie and Alais, Ysandre's daughters, to greet their royal mother as she dined, and I must confess it was a pretty sight. The elder, Sidonie, was a grave girl, with a straight, shining fall of deep-gold hair and her father's dark Cruithne eyes. I saw much of both parents in the young Dauphine, and less in her sister Alais, who was small and dark and prone to private mischief. It was she who clambered onto Joscelin's lap, butting her curly head beneath his chin. Joscelin laughed and let her toy with the buckles on his vambraces. He was good with children, better than I.

Ysandre smiled with a mother's resigned indulgence, stroking Sidonie's shining hair as her eldest knelt beside her, absorbed in winding violet stems through the wrought iron of a table-leg. "Alais doesn't take to most people thusly, my lord Cassiline. Mayhap you should consider fatherhood; you seem to have the knack of it."

"Ah." Joscelin slid his arm around the child, holding her in place as he reached for a dish of berries. "I've broken vows enough without insulting Cassiel's grace, my lady."

The Queen raised her fair brows at me, and I returned her gaze unblinking.

We had thought about it, of course; how not? But there was a truth to Joscelin's words, and a deeper truth I did not voice to Ysandre. I have an ill-luck name, given me by a mother who knew a great deal about Naamah's arts, and not much else. My lord Kushiel marked me as his own, and he has cast his Dart in places further and more deadly than I might have dreamed. Who is to say, if the dubious gift of an *anguissette* is hereditary? I have never heard that it is; nor have I heard it is not. I am what I am, and there is no point in regretting it. I daresay I would not have survived such adventures as have befallen me if it were not for my unique relationship with pain. *Lypiphera*, they named me on the island of Kriti; Pain-bearer.

Nonetheless, I had no desire to pass this dubious gift on to any child of my blood, and I had never invoked Eisheth's blessing to open the gates of my womb. It is harder to watch another suffer than to endure it oneself. There are forms of pain even an *anguissette* will avoid. This was one of them.

"So be it," Ysandre said gently, nodding at the Companion's Star upon my breast. "I always thought you were saving your boon for your children, Phèdre. A duchy, a royal appointment; even a betrothal, may-hap. I have given my word."

"No." I fingered the brooch and shook my head, answering with honesty. "There is naught that I need or desire, my lady, save that which is not within your power to grant." I smiled ruefully. We are gotten on the wrong side of godhead, we D'Angelines, and the One God has washed his hands of Blessed Elua's descendants; not even a Queen can alter that fact. "Can you bring the dead to life, or give me the key to lock the One God's vengeance? Aught else I might desire, you have laid at my disposal."

"I would that it was more. My debt to you is great." Ysandre rose and paced, pausing to gaze across the verdant expanse of her sanctum. No herbs here, but only flowers for her pleasure, lovingly cultivated by her gardeners. Near the gate, four of the Queen's Guard loitered at their ease, at once relaxed and attentive, while the Chamberlain of the Nursery stood by and servants in the livery of House Courcel awaited to attend her pleasure. The Dauphine Sidonie sat cross-legged on the flagstones, humming as she wove a garland, and young Princess Alais tugged at Joscelin's braid. "There is no news of Melisande's boy?"

"No." I said it softly, shaking my head, although she could not see. "I would tell you if there were, my lady."

"Phèdre." She turned around, eyeing me. "Will you never be done with forgetting it, near-cousin?"

"Probably not." I smiled at her, leaning over to pluck a handful of violets from Sidonie's lap and plaiting them expertly into an intricate garland. I had done as much when a child myself, attending adepts in the Court of Night-Blooming Flowers. "There," I said, setting it atop her head. The child glowed with pleasure, rising to run with careful steps and show her mother.

Some things a courtesan can do that a Queen cannot.

"Very lovely," Ysandre said, stooping to plant a kiss on her daughter's forehead. "Thank the Comtesse, Sidonie."

"Thank you, Comtesse," the girl said obediently, turning round to face me. Her sister Alais loosed a sudden chortle and steel rang as she hoisted one of Joscelin's daggers from its sheath. The guardsmen started to attention at the sound, relaxing with laughter as a chagrined Joscelin cautiously pried the hilt from her small fingers. The Dauphine Sidonie looked appalled at her sister's breach of decorum; Alais looked pleased.

Ysandre de la Courcel looked resigned. "Mayhap you have the right of it," she said wryly. "Elua's blessing upon your quest, Phèdre. And if you pass the Cruarch's flagship on your journey, tell him to make haste."

THREE

I HAVE known other losses as grave as that of Hyacinthe's sacrifice and some worse, in other ways. The brutal murder of my lord Anafiel Delaunay and his protégé Alcuin are things I do not forget, any more than I forget how my chevaliers Remy and Fortun were slain on Benedicte de la Courcel's orders, cut down before my helpless eyes for the sin of their loyalty.

Their loyalty to me.

But the awfulness of Hyacinthe's fate was unique in that it was undiminished by time. He was not dead, but doomed. For eight hundred years the Master of the Straits had ruled the waters from his lonely tower—eight hundred years! And Hyacinthe had made himself his heir. No amount of grieving could wash away his sentence, and I could never forget that while I lived and laughed and loved, he endured, isolated and islanded.

It took no more than a day to make ready to travel. For all that I maintain one of the foremost salons in the City of Elua, renowned for gracious entertainment and discourse, I have not lost the trick of adventuring. Joscelin, ever-prudent, had sent to Montrève for Philippe, my dear chevalier Ti-Philippe, to accompany us the moment Ysandre's courier had appeared at our doorstep. Left to my own devices, I would have spared him the journey; and I would have been wrong, for Ti-Philippe, the last of Phèdre's Boys, came pelting hell-for-leather into the City, a familiar gleam in his eyes.

"I owe the Tsingano my life as much as do you or Joscelin, my lady," he said, catching his breath in my antechamber. "And have nearly foundered three horses to prove it. Let your seneschal oversee the shearling lambs without me; I will ride to Pointe des Soeurs with you! Besides, you may have need of a sailor."

After that, I could not deny him. And Ti-Philippe had brought with him a companion, a stalwart shepherd lad from the hills of Montrève; Hugues, his name was, a fresh-faced boy no more than eighteen or nineteen, with ruddy cheeks and dark hair, eyes the color of rain-washed bluebells stretched wide at all he saw. Ti-Philippe grinned at me as young Hugues bowed and stammered, blushing a fiercesome shade of red upon meeting me.

"He's heard tales, my lady, like everyone else. Since you come too seldom to Montrève, I thought to bring him to the City. Besides," he added judiciously, "he's strong as an ox."

I could believe it, from the breadth of his shoulders. I *do* travel to Montrève, and make it my residence at least a few months of every year, but the truth is, my estate prospers without me. I have an able seneschal in Purcell Friote and his wife Richeline, and Ti-Philippe enjoys lording over the estate without me, playing the role of steward to the hilt and dallying with the eager lads and maids of Siovale. I have heard it said—for I pay attention to such things—that nigh unto a quarter of the babes born out of wedlock in Montrève are my chevalier's get. Well and so; I could not fault their mothers for the choice. He is a hero of the realm, my Philippe, awarded the Medal of Valor by Ysandre's own hands.

And I saw the self-same hero worship in young Hugues' grey-blue eyes, cast onto Ti-Philippe and reflected larger on Joscelin and myself. "Well met, Hugues of Montrève." I greeted him in formal tones, playing the role in which fate had cast me. "You understand that this is no May lark, but an undertaking of the utmost solemnity?"

"Oh, yes!" He gulped, stammering once more, color rising beneath his fair skin. "Yes, my lady, yes! I understand in the fullest!"

"Good." I pinned my gaze sternly on him. "Be ready to ride at dawn."

Hugues muttered some wit-stricken acquiescence; I don't know what. As I turned away, I heard him say in a stage whisper to Ti-Philippe, "I thought she would be *taller!*"

This, I ignored, though Joscelin's cheeks twitched with suppressed mirth. "What?" I asked irritably, rounding on him when we were in private. "Does my stature amuse you?"

"No." Joscelin disarmed me with a smile, sliding his hands beneath the mass of my sable locks. "He is bedazzled by your reputation and you would have to be seven feet tall, to match your deeds, Phèdre nó Delaunay. I'd need to stand on a footstool, to kiss you." He did kiss me, then, bending his head. I caught my arms about his neck. "A veritable Grainne mac Connor," he murmured against my lips.

"Don't tease," I begged, tugging at his neck. "I'm no warrior, Joscelin."

"Naamah's warrior." He kissed me again, loosening the stays of my gown. "Or Kushiel's. As well one of us knows how to use a blade."

That he did full well, Joscelin, my Perfect Companion. Like Ysandre, I owe my life to his skill with daggers and sword; many times over. All of Terre d'Ange knows of his match against the renegade Cassiline and would-be assassin David de Rocaille. I have never heard of another swordfight that brought an entire riot to a halt. If he is equally proficient with that other blade with which nature endows mankind, fewer folk know it. They would not expect it of a Cassiline Brother, once sworn to celibacy.

I hadn't, either. But I knew better now.

Joscelin's hands were gentle on my skin; it is seldom in his heart to be aught but gentle with me, though I am an *anguissette*, Kushiel's Chosen, and find pleasure in pain. But we have learned together, he and I, and he knew well enough how to make a torment of gentleness. The Cassiline discipline is a stern one. I felt it in the calluses of his palms, of his fingertips, as he disrobed me. With infinite skill he roused me, until I ached with yearning and begged him in earnest to make an end of it. When he entered me at last, I sighed with gratitude, wrapping my legs about his waist. Looking at his face was like gazing upon the sun; the love that suffused it was almost too much to bear.

"Phèdre," he whispered.

"I know." I buried my face against his shoulder and held him for all I was worth, memorizing the feel of him against me, within me, surging with desire steadfast as a beacon. He was the compass by which I had fixed my heart's longing, and filled with him, I was replete. I held him hard, my voice coming in gasps. There were tears in my eyes, though I couldn't have said why. "Ah, Joscelin! Don't stop. As you love me, don't stop."

I felt him smile, and move within me. "I won't," he promised.

And he didn't, not for a long, long time.

Thus did we make love that night, the last night of our long peace. I daresay Joscelin could scent change on the wind as well as I; we had been together too long not to think alike, and ours was a bond forged under the direst of circumstances. Afterward I fell straight into sated sleep and slept dreamlessly. Any tears I had wept, the night breeze had dried upon my cheeks, and I awoke to a clear spring morning.

No matter how dark the quest, there is a freedom in the commencing. Always, my heart has risen at the beginning of a journey, and this one was no exception. My competent staff had seen to all of our needs, and Eugènie, my Mistress of the Household, fussed incessantly over the provisioning of our trip. We would lack for naught.

My own fortunes had prospered in ten years of peace. My father, whom I remember vaguely, was a spendthrift with no head for money. Had he been more prudent, I would not have been indentured into servitude in Cereus House, first of the Thirteen Houses of the Night Court. As a hedge against fate, I have always invested wisely, aided by good advice from my factor and my connections at court and elsewhere.

Nor does it hurt to be the foremost courtesan of the realm. Betimes there have been outlandish offers for my favor—and betimes I have taken them. Naamah's portion I have tithed generously to her temples; the rest, I have kept.

Evrilac Duré and his men were well rested from their travel and faced the return journey with a better will than they had shown in Ysandre's council chamber. He raised his eyebrows to see our party assembled, for we numbered only the four of us with necessaries carried on pack-mules.

"Only four, my lady?" he inquired. "I thought you would bring a maidservant, at the least."

"My lord Duré," I said pleasantly. "We are travelling cross-country to a forsaken outpost to assail the Master of the Straits in his own domain, not paying a social call on the duchy of Trevalion. I have crossed the Skaldic wasteland in the dead of winter on foot, and been storm-blown to Kriti in the company of pirates. Will you not credit me with some measure of competence?"

He laughed at that, flashing white teeth; the Azzallese love a show of pride. And so we set out across the greening land beneath the auspices of spring. As the marble walls of the City of Elua fell behind us, I filled my lungs with great breaths of fresh air and saw Joscelin do the same. Guillard and Armand stole admiring glances in my direction as we rode, and young Hugues sang for sheer exuberance. He had a prodigious set of lungs in his broad chest, and his voice was sure and true.

"He reminds me of Remy," Ti-Philippe said at one point, dropping back to ride alongside me, a shadow of sorrow in his smile. "He begged to come. I couldn't say no."

I nodded, the old grief catching in my throat. Remy had been the first of my chevaliers, the first of Phèdre's Boys to pledge himself unto my service. I had watched him die. I was never free of the chains of blood-guilt, that awareness forged in the ceremony of the *thetalos* in a Kritian cavern. Nor did I forget the living, whose numbers are never given to us to know. Would he have sung so freely and joyously, this stalwart lad, in a Terre d'Ange ruled by Melisande Shahrizai? I believed he would not. I could never know for sure.

"I am glad you brought him," I said gently to Ti-Philippe, who smiled in full.

"He writes the most abysmal poetry," he said. "Much of it dedicated to you, my lady, these two days gone by. 'O lily-fair, with raven-cloaked hair; O star-drowned eyes, like night's own skies.'"

At that I laughed, as he had meant; to be sure, Hugues' presence lightened the journey and it passed pleasantly enough. We made good speed northward along the Aviline River and into the province of Namarre, thence turning westward toward Pointe des Soeurs. The sun shone brightly on our travels. In the vineyards, pale green tendrils were beginning to curl on the stands of brown, withered grapevines and the silvery leaves rustled in the olive groves. We saw Tsingani on the road from time to time, making their way from the early spring horse-fair at the Hippochamp in Kusheth; there was no mistaking them, white teeth flashing against their brown skin, their women wearing their wealth in gold coins strung in necklaces and earrings, or sewn into bright scarves, chattering in their own tongue mixed with D'Angeline.

Hyacinthe was a prince of his kind, his mother had always told him; the Prince of Travellers, for so they called themselves, doomed to wander the earth. I had believed it, when I was a child; when I was older, I thought it a mother's fond lie, for she was an outcast among her people, deemed *vrajna*, tainted, for having loved a D'Angeline man and lost her honor. As it transpired, it was the love that had been a lie. Hyacinthe's mother's honor had been lost in a careless bet, laid by a cousin who must needs then trick his headman's daughter into a seduction to settle his debt with Bryony House.

It was true, after all. Hyacinthe's grandfather Manoj was the Tsingan kralis, King of the Tsingani. And he had welcomed his long-lost grandson with open arms when he met him.

That, too, Hyacinthe had sacrificed. He had committed an act that was *vrajna* when he used the *dromonde* on my behalf, that gift of sight he had from his mother to part the veils of past and future. It is forbidden, among the Tsingani, for men to wield the *dromonde*. But Hyacinthe had done it, and the Tsingan kralis had cast him out once more.

These things I thought on as we travelled, remembering, and I saw Joscelin's gaze sober when it fell on the companies of Tsingani in their gaily painted wagons.

We avoided cities and larger towns, staying only in modest inns such as catered to couriers along the roads where the proprietors looked askance at my features and murmured speculation, but asked no questions. Twenty years ago, few D'Angelines recognized the mark of Kushiel's Dart; there had been no *anguissette* in living memory. Now, they know. I have heard it said that country lasses hungry for fame in Naamah's service will prick themselves to induce a spot of red in the whites of their eyes. I do not know if it is true; I hope not. They do not do it in the City of Elua, where any urchin in the streets of Mont Nuit would know it for a sham. I would have thought, as a child in the Night Court, I would rejoice to have my name regaled throughout the realm; now, a woman grown, I kept my mouth shut on my fame and thought of other things.

It took a matter of some few days to reach Pointe des Soeurs, where our company was greeted with a certain awe, part and parcel as we were of the legend over which they maintained a watch. Duré's men Guillard and Armand affected a careless swagger, relishing their role as escorts, and the commander himself, Evrilac Duré, cast an indulgent eye on their antics.

I think the garrison at Pointe des Soeurs was a lonely one, for the fortress overperches the sea and there is no village within ten miles' ride; they grew starved, there, for polite company and news of the broader world. Still, I do not think they were expecting such news as we brought and the men fell silent when Duré called for volunteers for our excursion.

"Are you feared?" It was stocky Guillard who challenged his comrades, jeering. "I tell you, the Queen herself, Ysandre de la Courcel, said to the commander, 'Messire Duré,' she said, 'I will not command any man of Trevalion to assail the Three Sisters . . . but I will ask.' What have we seen to fear, lads? Fish?" He thumped his chest. "I tell you, *I'm* going! *I'll* not be left behind to hear secondhand stories around the fire!"

After that, the volunteers came forward in twos and threes, until Duré had to turn them away. Young Hugues watched it all with openmouthed delight, his face glowing. I smiled at his pleasure, and wondered what we might find.

Following on the heels of an afternoon repast, Armand and Guillard showed us about the fortress and its grounds. Here, I was told, the wave had broken on the stony shores, bearing its stricken load of sea-life. I paced the curve gravely, examining the drying corpses of fish left lying on the shore. Atop the parapet, Armand pointed northwest across the grey rippling sea, toward where a faint shadow lay on the horizon, nearest of the Three Sisters. There, he told me, the cloud had hung and the unnatural lightning played, quiet now since their departure.

I listened well and nodded solemnly. High on the fortress walls, the cries of gulls resounded in the salt air along with the fainter sounds of Duré's men making ready a ship for the morning's sojourn, checking the rigging and tending to minor details.

"What do you make of it?" Joscelin asked that night in the spare chamber we had been allotted. He had his baldric in a tangle on his lap, oiling the leather straps against the salt tang of a sea voyage. I looked up from the Yeshuite scroll I was reading—the Sh'moth, chronicling the flight of Moishe from the land of Menekhet and the parting of the seas. My old teacher the Rebbe would have chomped at his beard to see me handling a sacred text bare-handed and familiar, but he was dead these seven years past, his weary heart faltering in his sleep.

"Nothing." I shook my head. "Little enough they have recorded of Rahab, and naught to do with Elua's get. A few similarities, mayhap. No more. You?"

Joscelin shrugged, looking steadily at me, his strong, capable hands continuing to work oil into the leather. "I protect and serve," he said softly.

Once, he had known more than I of Yeshuite lore; they are near-kin, the Cassiline Brotherhood. Apostates, the Yeshuites call them. Of all the Companions of Blessed Elua, Cassiel alone came to follow him out of perfect purity of heart, a love and compassion the One God, in his ire, forswore. Yeshuites claim the others followed Elua out of arrogance, defying the One God's rule; Naamah for desire, Azza for pride, Shemhazai, for cleverness' sake, and so forth. Kushiel, who marked me for his own, was once a punisher of the damned; it is said he loved his charges too well. Mayhap it is so—but Blessed Elua bid them, *love as thou wilt*. And when the One God and Mother Earth made their peace and created such a place as had never before existed, Cassiel chose to follow Elua into the true Terre d'Ange-that-lies-beyond, and he alone among the Companions acknowledged damnation, and accepted it as his due.

He gauged it worth the price. That is the part they cannot explain, neither Yeshuite nor Cassiline. I do not think they try.

I know more, now, than any Cassiline; and I daresay many Yeshuites. It was still not enough. Rising from the bed, I went to kneel at Joscelin's side, pressing my brow against his knee. He did not like it when I did such things, but I could not help the ache of penitence in my heart.

"I thought I would find a way to free him," I whispered. "I truly did."

After a moment, I felt Joscelin's hand stroke my hair. "So did I," I heard him murmur. "Elua help me, Phèdre, so did I."

$\mathscr{F}$OUR

Iп THE morning, we set sail.

It is not a long journey to the Three Sisters from Pointe des Soeurs. Nonetheless, a stiff headwind sprang up against us, making our course difficult as we must needs beat against it in broad tacks. The galley was a fine and suitable vessel with a shallow draught and wide decks, flying the pennant of Trevalion, three ships and the Navigators' Star. It felt strangely familiar to have the sensation of sea-swell beneath my feet, and I soon recovered the trick of swaying to balance myself with it.

Duré and his men were capable, and had they not been, I daresay Ti-Philippe would have filled any lack, for he scrambled over the ship from stem to stern in high spirits. He had been a sailor, once, under the command of the Royal Admiral, Quintilius Rousse. The awe-stricken Hugues trailed in his wake, fit as an ox, while my Perfect Companion leaned against the railing, pale and sweating.

As I have said, Joscelin was no sea-farer.

Despite our to-and-fro approach, it was only a few hours before the coast of the Third Sister grew solid on the horizon. I stood in the prow and watched the island grow larger in my vision, a curious reversal of the terrible dream that had awoken me little more than a week ago.

Intent and focused, I did not see that we were not alone on the Strait.

It was a cry from the crow's nest that first alerted me, but in moments, we could all of us see. There, across the surging grey waves, a fleet of seven ships was making its way, coming from the opposite angle to converge on the same point.

If you pass the Cruarch's flagship on your journey, tell him to make haste. Ysandre de la Courcel's words had been in jest—it was in spring that Drustan mab Necthana came to stay with her, and there was ever

a prize granted to the first person who spotted his sails—but there could
be no doubt of it. The lead ship bore a great scarlet square of a mainsail
displaying the Black Boar of Alba.

"Drustan!" I breathed, and ran to tell Evrilac Duré, abandoning my
vigil in the prow. He stared at me in disbelief, then looked and saw the
proof of his own eyes and gave orders to his helmsman to change our
course, making to intercept the flagship of the Cruarch of Alba. We
had to go to oars, beating across the choppy waters.

They saw us coming and halted, lowering sails to idle at sea as
Duré's oarsmen heaved and groaned, the other six ships dropping anchor behind the Cruarch's. I saw him at a distance, a small figure across
the waters, recognizable by his crimson cloak of office and the flash of
gold at his throat.

"Drustan!" Ti-Philippe said at my side, frowning. "What in seven
hells is the Cruarch of Alba doing making for the Three Sisters? He
ought to be headed for port, and the Queen's bedchamber."

"I don't know." There was a second figure beside him, smaller and
slighter. Not one of his warriors, I thought, gazing across the water. It
was not until we drew nigh that I recognized the figure as a woman,
and not until we hove to alongside them that I realized I knew her.
She was Drustan's youngest living sister, the middle daughter, Sibeal.

I saw him smile, dark eyes grave and unsurprised in the whorls of
blue woad that tattooed his face, raising one hand in greeting. "Phèdre
nó Delaunay, my brother Joscelin," the Cruarch of Alba called from
his ship, "well met."

His D'Angeline was excellent; it ought to be, for I had taught him.
I gripped the railing and stared at him, Duré's men murmuring behind
me. "My lord Drustan," I said in bewilderment. "How do you come
here, and why?"

Drustan mab Necthana nodded to his sister, who raised her chin to
gaze at me across the divide. She had the same solemn eyes as her
brother, seeming even wider-set for the twin lines of blue dots that
etched her cheeks. "Sibeal had a dream," he said simply.

It was only meet, after that, that our forces were conjoined. It took
some jostling and maneuvering to enact the transfer, but the seas became
oddly calmed and we managed without much difficulty. Some few of
Evrilac Duré's men joined us; most did not, with varying degrees of
relief, and Duré ordered the sea-anchor dropped. Drustan helped me
aboard his flagship himself, returning my embrace warmly when I flung
both arms about his neck and gave him the kiss of greeting. There are

few people I like better and admire more than the Cruarch of Alba.

And when it was done, we heard his sister's dream.

They are seers of a sort, the women of the Cruarch's line. When we arrived on the shores of Alba, it was Drustan's youngest sister, Moiread, who gave us greeting; there to meet us, she said, in answer to a dream. Moiread is dead, slain these many years ago by a Tarbh Cró spear at the Battle of Bryn Gorrydum where Drustan regained his throne. I saw that happen, too. Many more would have died, if not for Joscelin. The Cruarch has named him brother since that day.

"I saw a rock in the waters," Sibeal said softly, speaking in Cruithne. "And on it stood a crow. I saw the skies open and the lightnings strike, and the crow stretched out its wings in agony. I saw the waters boil, full of serpents, and the crow could not fly. I saw the skies part and a white dove fly forth and land upon the rock." She hugged her arms around herself and gazed toward the island of Third Sister. "I saw the waters rise and the serpents lash their tales, and the crow could not fly," she said. "I saw the dove land and open its beak, and vomit forth a diamond. And then I awoke." Her troubled eyes turned to me. "You have dreamed it too."

"No," I whispered; my hand rose of its own accord to touch the naked hollow of my throat. There had been a diamond, once. Melisande had put it there. "That is, yes, my lady Sibeal, I have dreamed. I dreamed of Hyacinthe, no more."

"Hyacinthe." She spoke his name with a Cruithne accent, a faint frown creasing the downy skin betwixt her brows. "Yes."

"They say," Drustan mab Necthana said, "that a fortnight past, lightning flashed and the seas rose. So I have come to see."

"My lord!" The words came out sharply. "It is not fitting, that you should risk yourself in this fashion! Even now, the Queen awaits you in the City of Elua. Let *us* go, my lord. It is what was intended."

Evrilac Duré shifted behind me; at either side I had Joscelin and Ti-Philippe, who knew the risks and counted them full well. Drustan mab Necthana, the Cruarch of Alba, merely gazed at me. He had been there, when Hyacinthe paid the price of our freedom. If he could have paid it himself, he would have. He had not forgotten any more than I had.

We had always understood one another, he and I.

"Then let us go together, Phèdre," he said quietly. "One last time. Sibeal has had a dream that is a riddle demanding an answer. This I must do."

Thus it was that I came to the island known as Third Sister for a second time, borne as I was the first, on the flagship of the Cruarch of Alba. Whether or not the Alban sailors were affrighted, I cannot say; they were men hand-picked by Drustan, their worth measured in the elaborate degree of tattooing that swirled their arms and faces, and they showed no fear as they hoisted sail. The D'Angelines onboard murmured amongst themselves as a sudden wind bellied our crimson sails, making the Black Boar surge and billow. Joscelin was pale, though whether with fear or seasickness, I do not know. Ti-Philippe's features settled into unwontedly grim lines as he cast his eye on the steep, looming cliffs of Third Sister. Young Hugues shuffled from foot to foot in an excess of excitement.

Drustan looked purposeful, and his sister Sibeal, serene. I felt sick.

I had forgotten how the island rushed upon one, how the ingress was hidden by high, steep walls. 'Twas a mighty wave had brought us the first time. This time, it was the wind that picked us out like a child's toy, bearing us into the cliff-flanked harbor. I had forgotten how the open temple sat atop the isle, the endless stone stair cascading down to a rocky promontory.

Where a lone figure awaited us.

Even at a distance, I recognized him. My mouth opened to admit an involuntary sound, squeezed out by the unexpected, painful contraction of my heart.

Hyacinthe.

He lifted one hand and the wind went still. Our ship drifted, born on bobbing wavelets toward the shore. He lowered both hands and a shuddering ripple arose in the scant yards that separated the ship's planks from the rock shore, the water heaving and churning. And he stood there, very much alone, clad in breeches and doublet of a rusty black velvet, salt-stained lace at his breast and cuffs.

I made a choked gasp and he gave a rueful smile, his eyes, Hyacinthe's eyes, dark and aware in his familiar, beloved face, taut fingers outstretched at the churning waves. His hair still spilled in blue-black ringlets over his shoulders, longer than when I had left him. Tiny crow's-feet were etched at the corners of his eyes, always wont to smile; his eyes, Elua, oh!

"Hello, Phèdre," Hyacinthe said softly. "It's good to see you."

His eyes went deeper and darker than ever I had seen, his pupils twin abysses, blackness unending. And around them his irises constricted in rings, shadow-shifting, oceanic depths reflected in a thousand wavering lights. I heard Joscelin's cracked exclamation, saw those unearthly eyes shift.

"And you, Cassiline." Hyacinthe bowed from the waist, ironically. "My lord Drustan." His voice changed. "Sibeal."

"*Hyacinthe!*" I breathed, nails digging into the railing. "Oh, Hyas . . . name of Elua, let us come ashore!"

He shook his head, locks stirring, fingers still outstretched at the sea and a crooked smile quirked his mouth. "I can't, Phèdre, don't you see? I don't dare. You're the only ones I've let get this close, and I wouldn't if I didn't trust you. Once you set foot ashore, the *geis* is invoked." He bowed again, this time to Drustan. "Half the riddle is done, my lord Cruarch; you have wed Ysandre in love, Alban and D'Angeline united. For the rest . . ." He shrugged. "I will not ask anyone to take my place."

I was weeping open-eyed, the tears running heedless down my cheeks. As if from a distance, I heard Drustan say, "There was a storm that was no storm, ten days ago and more. What does it betoken?"

"He is dead." Hyacinthe's voice was quiet, yet it seemed to come from everywhere and nowhere. It had never been so, in my memory. "The one you called the Master of the Straits. What you have seen is the passage of power."

"Then come!" I caught my breath, regaining control of my voice, and spoke fiercely. "Come with us! Let it be ended."

Hyacinthe smiled, and his smile was terrible, not reaching the dark-ringed abysses of his eyes. "Do you think I can?" he asked, and relaxed his fingers, making to step onto the surging waves that bordered us.

All at once, the world *lurched*. I can find no better word to describe it. While we remained stationary, adrift on the waters, and Hyacinthe sought but to take a simple step, the very mass of the world itself shifted in a nauseating fashion. And in that few feet of water, something changed, opening; an abyss deeper and darker than aught in Hyacinthe's eyes, a bottomless, sickening void around which my world suddenly pivoted and in its depths, a radiant and dreadful presence moved, a defiant, destructive rage. I thought, for an instant, that he had done it, had completed the step and bridged the gap between us . . . and then the world righted itself, and I found we were adrift still, the abyss and the presence gone and Hyacinthe bent over double on the shore, gasping for air. He raised his haunted eyes, and his voice, when he spoke, belonged to the Tsingano lad I remembered.

"You see?" he panted, sweat beading his brow. "It cannot be done. Merely to try is like dying. I ought to know, I've done it enough times." He straightened slowly, as if the motion pained him. "Let it be proclaimed," he said formally, "since you have come, that the Straits have a new Master. Let it be proclaimed that all who seek passage will be welcome. The Cruarch's truce holds. While Alban and D'Angeline find love in common, the Straits shall remain open."

"Hyacinthe." I felt Sibeal's gaze upon me and said his name like a desperate prayer. "Is there no way to free you?"

He looked up at me, almost close enough to touch, and the sorrow in his eyes was ocean-deep. "I have not found it, Phèdre. Have you?" When I shook my head in wordless denial, he gave his terrible smile, fine lines crinkling at the corners of his eyes. "Then let all knowledge of my curse be buried and forgotten. If you love me, Phèdre, let them forget. For you see, I am still young enough and new enough at it to scruple at passing it on to any other. While my will holds, no vessel shall be allowed to land on these shores." Hyacinthe spread his hands. "But I am getting older, you see," he said softly. "The Master of the Straits was Rahab's get, on a woman who was first-born to Elua's line. I am not him, with three parts ichor in my veins to one part blood, to endure eternity unaging." He swallowed, then, hard. "Let them forget. Then, when all I have known and loved has passed from this earth, when I am a withered husk, then when my scruples give way, I will have less on my conscience."

My dream came back to me with terrible clarity; the gap, the widening void of water and Hyacinthe receding, his boy's voice crying out my name in vain. "What is it?" I made myself ask, forcing my voice to steadiness. "Hyacinthe, when you tried to step off the island, there was a presence, in the water. Is it Rahab?"

"Him, or an invocation of him. Yes." Hyacinthe went still. Our ship bobbed gently on the water, lines creaking, wavelets churning and milling. "You do know a way."

"Yes and no." I took a deep breath and gazed into the empty blue sky. "There is a word. The Yeshuites claim the One God is nameless and unknowable, but it is not so. Adonai, they call him; Lord, nothing else. But He has a name, and it is a word, spoken, that all His servants must obey. Even Rahab." I looked at Hyacinthe. "That much, I have learned. But," I shook my head, "the Name of God eludes me. I do not have the knowledge."

Something moved in Hyacinthe's oddly changeable eyes; power, mayhap, stirring in the depths . . . or mayhap only hope. "You can find it."

"Hyacinthe." His name caught in my throat. "I've been looking, for ten years! There are Yeshuite scholars who have devoted their lives to it, going back in an unbroken line since before Blessed Elua walked the earth. I will never, ever stop looking, I swear to you, but after ten years, I do not hold a great deal of hope."

Hyacinthe looked away.

"Tsingano." Joscelin's pragmatic voice broke the silence. "You have the *dromonde*. What does the gift of sight tell you?"

"The *dromonde*." Hyacinthe gave him his dire smile. "I see an island, Cassiline; I see wind and sea. What do you think? I have seen naught else since I came here."

"What of Phèdre?"

The question hung in the air between them. The intense black pupils of Hyacinthe's eyes blurred, losing focus. "Phèdre," he whispered. In the old days, he would never speak the *dromonde* on my behalf. "Ah, Phèdre! It is a vaster pattern than I can compass. There are branchings beyond which I cannot see, and each one lies in darkness. Kushiel bars the path, stern and forbidding, his hands outstretched. In one hand, he holds a brazen key, and in the other . . ." His gaze focused abruptly. "And in the other, a diamond, strung on a velvet cord."

I touched the hollow of my throat.

"It is my dream." Sibeal's voice spoke softly in Cruithne. "It is as I have seen."

ꜰIVE

Iᴛ WAS a somber journey back to Pointe des Soeurs.

We parted ways with Drustan mab Necthana and his entourage at sea; they would sail east, putting in at the harbor of Trevalion, where Ghislain and his wife Bernadette looked for their arrival. Evrilac Duré's men were in restrained good spirits, uncertain what had transpired, glad of their survival. I leaned in the prow and watched the water part before us, thinking.

Joscelin interrupted my thoughts only once, leaning beside me. The hilt of his sword jutting over his shoulder cast a wavering cruciform shadow on the water below us. "I know of only one such diamond," he said softly. "Melisande—"

"*I know.*" I cut him off sharply.

What had Melisande to do with Hyacinthe's fate? Nothing. Of the many things for which I blame her, that is not one. Ill-luck, it was, a destiny laid down eight hundred years gone by, and my Prince of Travellers caught in it. I could not shake the memory of my final glimpse of him. Hyacinthe had raised his hands, and the seas had answered, a limpid, rising swell that caught our vessel and turned us, carrying us plunging through the narrow entry and into the open seas. I had seen his lips moving as he did it, uttering words of command.

How could he, who now held such power in his hands, look to me for aid? It had grown unreal to me in his absence, this role in which he was cast. Now, having seen, I doubted the measure of my own meager skills. In ten years, what had I found? A rumor, nothing more; a tale buried in legend. The Rebbe had told it to me long ago, before La Serenissima. Lilit, the first wife of Edom, had fled his dominion; the One God sent his servants to bring her back. She had laughed and spoken His name, sending them back.

Well and so; I had not lied, I have spoken with many Yeshuite scholars since first I heard that tale. There are branches of mysticism within the Yeshuite religion, and those that hold the five books of the Tanakh itself is but the Name of God written in code. To each letter of each word a value is ascribed, and the resonance of every word to words of like value studied endlessly. Yet I never met a one who claimed the Name of God was known.

Now, there are fewer Yeshuites in the City of Elua and elsewhere across the realm, and their thoughts turn ever northward. The exodus that began ten years ago has continued, and rumor comes from the far northeast that they are forging a nation in the cold wastes. Not all agree that it is this which the prophecies of Yeshua ben Yosef intended—my old master the Rebbe did not—but the dissenters grow fewer every year. What he feared has come to pass: The Children of Yisra-el are divided. Of those who remain, their eyes turn increasingly toward the future, and less and less to the past. And I . . . I am D'Angeline. When the One God sought to bid Elua to his heaven, Blessed Elua and his Companions refused. I am a child of Elua, Kushiel's Chosen and Naamah's Servant, and I have no place in such matters.

But for Hyacinthe.

There is a Hellene myth, which tells of a man who had leave to ask a boon of the gods. He asked for immortality, and failed to ask for eternal youth in the bargain. The mocking gods granted his wish to the letter. Never dying, ever aging. At the end, when he had shriveled to naught but a dry, creaking thing of sinew and bone, they took pity on him and turned him into a grasshopper. How long? The myth does not say. To this day, I cannot hear the grasshopper's song without a shudder.

We passed a quiet night at Pointe des Soeurs, and in the morning, took our leave of the place. Evrilac Duré offered to send an escort with us, which I declined, though I thanked him graciously for the aid he had already provided. We broke our fast at dawn, and were on the road a scant hour later.

Joscelin, having already ascertained my mood, kept wisely silent on our journey, and Ti-Philippe knew well enough to follow his lead. It was young Hugues, prattling endlessly about the encounter, who would not let matters be. "They say his mother was the Queen of the Tsingani, with gold on every finger and gold scarves for every day of the week, and if she cursed a man, he would fall down dead. Is it true, my lady?" he asked eagerly. "They say he told fortunes in the marketplace when he was but a boy, and Palace nobles would line up to wait their turn!"

"He stole sweets," I said shortly, "in the marketplace. And his mother took in washing."

"But they *say*—"

"Hugues." I rounded on him, drawing my mount up short. "Yes. Hyacinthe had the *dromonde,* and his mother before him. She told fortunes, and sometimes people gave her coin; mostly, they were poor. She ran a lodging house for such Tsingani as did not disdain a woman who had lost her *laxta,* her virtue, and she took in laundry and changed her profit for gold coin, such as you have seen around the necks of half the Tsingani women on the road. Do you think her son was marked for this destiny?"

Blood rose to his fresh cheeks. "I did not mean . . ."

I sighed. "I know. It is a splendid, terrible tale, and you have been privileged to see a glimpse of it. Outside Azzalle, I do not think they even tell it. But Hugues, never forget it is real people who live out such tales and bear the price of the telling, in grief and guilt and sorrow."

He fell silent, then, and lowered his handsome head, and I felt remorse for having shamed him. We stayed at an inn in the town of Seinagan that night, and Hugues excused himself from the common room to retire early. Ti-Philippe, offering no comment, accompanied him.

It was pleasant in the common room, whitewashed walls freshly scrubbed, a fire to ward off the evening chill of spring smelling sweetly of pear wood. "You were hard on the lad," Joscelin said quietly, not looking at me, running his fingertips over the sweating earthenware curve of a wine-jug. "He's excited, no more. He meant no harm."

"I know." I put my head in my hands. "I know. It's just that it *galls* me, Joscelin. To see Hyacinthe thus, and be helpless. It is a pain in my heart, and I take no pleasure in it."

"Would that I had been the one to answer the riddle." Joscelin raised his head abruptly. "Is that what you want to hear? I would that I had, Phèdre. Better for all of us if I had. If I could trade places with him and spare you this pain, I would. But I *can't,*" he said savagely. "I'm not clever, like you, and I have no gift of sight to aid me. Only these." He turned out his hands, palms upward, callus-worn. "It has been enough, until now." His expression changed. "And could be still, if you convinced him," he said slowly. "I do know the answer, don't I? I don't need to be wise or gifted, not anymore. All I need is for Hyacinthe to let me set foot on his shores."

"Joscelin, no!" I stared at him in horror. "How can you even think such a thing?"

"Ah, well." He smiled faintly, wryly. "It would solve your problems."

"Idiot!" I grasped both of his hands hard in mine. "Joscelin Verreuil, if you think for one minute I would grieve over you one whit less than I do for Hyacinthe, you are a blessed fool," I said in exasperation. "He is my oldest and dearest friend and I love him well, but you . . ." I shook my head. "You are an idiot. And if you think I'm going to walk into darkness without you at my side, an idiot thrice over. You're not getting out of it that easily."

His fingers closed over my own. "Then I shall stand at the crossroads," he said quietly. "And choose, and choose again, wherever your path shall lead. I protect and serve."

They were words that needed to be spoken between us, and in the morning I awoke with a resolved heart and made greater effort to be gracious to those around me. Thus we made good time on the road and returned the City of Elua to find the word of Drustan's arrival had preceded us by a day, brought by Azzallese couriers riding at a breakneck pace to receive Ysandre's reward.

The Queen heard our news with grave compassion, taking note of the passage of power and Hyacinthe's words thereon. I daresay she was genuinely sorry for his plight—but there are limits even to a Queen's power. Ysandre had a realm to govern and her beloved husband, the father of her children, was making his way to her side. There was naught she could do. If there had been, I would have asked it; would have spent the boon, long-hoarded, she had granted me with the Companion's Star.

But there was nothing.

As a matter of courtesy, I consulted with the Master of Ceremonies on preparing the way for Drustan's entry into the City; it is one of the great rites of spring nowadays, and I was there at its inception. Once, there were precious few D'Angelines who spoke Cruithne. Now, traffic is brisk between our lands, it is taught in many schools and Ysandre does not lack for translators. The children of the realm do not need my coaching to greet the Cruarch in his own tongue.

One distraction I had in the days before his arrival, and that was a cabinet meeting of the Guild of the Servants of Naamah. It is the only appointment I have ever sought, and I have served in the cabinet since the days of La Serenissima, designated as the Court liaison. They reckoned themselves lucky to have me at first—over a hundred years it has been, since a member of the peerage served on that Guild—but they did not always like the reforms I proposed. We voted on one that day that had Jareth Moran, the Dowayne of Cereus House, tearing at his hair in frustration.

"If we have sunk four thousand ducats into an apprentice's marque and training, my lady," he said carefully, "and he or she is found unfit to serve, we *must* have a way of recouping our investment! Elsewise we will be bankrupt."

"Then choose more wisely, my lord Dowayne," I said remorselessly, "or have more care with your adepts. For those who are reckoned unfit have no way of recouping their lives."

Jareth glared, but made no retort, mindful of my history. I had been a child in Cereus House, reckoned unfit to serve by virtue of the scarlet mote in my eye. It was my lord Anafiel Delaunay who knew it for the sign of Kushiel's Dart and bought my marque, training me in the Naamah's Arts as well as the arts of covertcy. And with the gifts of my patrons I earned my freedom, inch by inch, paying the marquist to etch its progress on my skin. For each assignation, I paid, and my marque is complete. It rises from the base of my spine to the nape of my neck, a briar rose wrought in black, accented with drops of crimson.

If it signifies that I am Naamah's Servant, it also announces that I am a free D'Angeline, with no debt owing to be possessed by another. It is hard-won, my marque, and I have used the stature I have earned along with it to enact changes. No more were the Thirteen Houses of the Night Court allowed to set marque-prices for children sold into indenture, such as I had been. Now, it was all apprentices, or such children as were born into the Night Court and freely raised therein. Anafiel Delaunay would not be able to buy my marque today as he had when I was ten.

That was my doing, too, and I reckoned it well-done. For all that my lord Delaunay owned my marque, he had been the first to teach me that it was wrong to treat people as chattel. He did not permit it, in his household. All Naamah's Servants must enter the bargain of their own accord, but I do not think the choice was made so freely in the Night Court as in Delaunay's household. Now, it is. The Queen herself, newly a mother when I proposed the reform, backed it wholeheartedly.

And I do not think the ranks of Naamah's Servants have dwindled for these measures; indeed, if anything, they have swelled since I rose to prominence.

"Naamah lay down in the stews of Bhodistan with strangers that Blessed Elua might eat," said the priestess of the Great Temple of Naamah with considerable amusement. "Not to fatten the wallets of the Dowaynes of the Night Court, my lord Jareth. We find this proposal meet. If an apprentice is reckoned unfit to serve, it is meet that the Dowayne of his or her House provide a means for them to serve out the terms of their indenture in the time allotted. No more, and no less."

"You ask us to find *employ* for persons unfit for Naamah's Service?" the Dowayne of Bryony House inquired. "It is unreasonable. We do not have the means to serve as a referral agency for failed adepts."

"Will you tell me Bryony House cannot find a half a dozen suitable clerkships for a trained apprentice?" I asked cynically; everyone knows the financial acumen with which Bryony's adepts are instilled. "I am *saying* that the system of indenture as it exists is imperfect. It allows legal means whereby an apprentice may become a virtual slave to his or her House."

There was a silence, at that; D'Angelines like to reckon themselves better than the rest of the world, for we are closer than others to our nation's begetting. Even the meanest peasant among us can trace his or her ancestry to Elua or one of his Companions, who gave us many gifts. We have not practiced slavery since Blessed Elua trod our soil. *Love as thou wilt*, he bade us; slavery by its very nature violates his Sacred Precept. And owing a vast debt against one's marque is almost as bad as being a slave, when one is prevented from receiving patron-gifts.

I have a *couturiere*, sharp-tongued and gifted, who was a failed adept, flawed by a scar that rendered her unfit by the tenets of the Night Court; fifteen years or more, it might have taken Favrielle nó Eglantine to make her marque on the commissions her Dowayne allowed her— meanwhile, her youth fled and her genius gone to make the marques of her erstwhile companions. It did not happen, for I used my own earnings to pay the price of her marque and buy her freedom. But there were others, and I did not have the means to save them all.

Even my freedom had been bought. That was Melisande's doing.

And the diamond . . . the diamond had been her gift.

In the end, they passed the measure by a slim margin, as I had gauged they would. The representatives of the street-guild had naught to lose, and the Temple of Naamah had endorsed the measure. It was the Night Court that stood to be inconvenienced . . . but not so greatly

that its Dowaynes were prepared to stand in opposition to the rest of
Naamah's Servants.

Especially me, the Queen's favorite.

Afterward, I spoke with Bérèngere of Namarre, the priestess of the
Great Temple, thanking her for her support in the matter. In a way, I
have known her since I was scarce more than a child; she was there,
as an acolyte, when I was first dedicated into the Service of Naamah.
When I was rededicated, it was she who performed the rites.

"There is no need," she said simply, folding her hands inside the
full, elegant sleeves of her crimson robe. "The measure was a good
one. You have done good things in this cabinet, Phèdre nó Delaunay."

"I have tried." I flushed at the compliment; one does, from a member of the priesthood.

Bérèngere smiled, her green eyes tilted catlike in their regard. I
remembered the taste of honeycake on my tongue, and her kiss; sunlight
gilding the pinions of my offering-dove as it beat its wings toward the
oculus. "Pride, they have in the Service of Naamah; pride and passion,"
she said, watching the Dowaynes of the Night Court leave. "I do not
belittle these things, nor begrudge them coin and glory. But the heart
of the matter is love." Her gaze returned to me. "There are a thousand
reasons why Naamah chose to lie with strangers, to give and receive
pleasure as she did. Devotion, greed, modesty, perfection, solace, genius,
atonement, mastery, desire . . ." She named the attributes of the Thirteen
Houses. "All of them are true, but the chiefest among them is love.
Always love."

"I know," I whispered. I did. I have loved all my patrons, at least
a little bit. It is not a thing I tell to Joscelin, who would not understand.
For all that he was a priest, once, he was Cassiel's, and such things
Cassiel does not comprehend. Naamah's priestess understood.

"They forget, in the Court of Night-Blooming Flowers," she said.
"All the great Houses. Cereus, Heliotrope, Valerian, Jasmine . . . even
Gentian, with their visions. They forget, or comprehend only a piece
of the whole. You remember. Always remember." Bérèngere of Namarre reached out with one slender hand, laying delicate fingertips
above my heart. "The true offering is given in love."

I shuddered under her touch with fear and desire, almost as if she
were a patron. "My lady," I said, making myself deliver the words
calmly. "I have been told my path lies in darkness. What do you see?
Is it Naamah's will that I suffer?"

She shook her head ruefully, hair the color of apricots shining against the silk of her robe. "I am a priestess and not a seer, Phèdre nó Delaunay. This, I cannot say. Only that your knowledge will serve you true, in the end, if you do not fear the offering." Withdrawing her touch, she folded her hands once more in her sleeves. "*Love as thou wilt,*" she quoted. "Even Naamah's Servants follow Blessed Elua, in the end."

It was not the most comforting of advice.

Six

DRUSTAN MAB Necthana came to the City of Elua.

There was feasting, and fêtes; Joscelin and I turned out to meet him, of course, a part of Ysandre's entourage. And I wore the Companion's Star upon my breast, and had Ti-Philippe in attendance with Hugues as his wide-eyed guest, and we pelted the Cruarch with rose-petals and sighed, charmed, with the others when the young Princess Alais hurled herself at her father at the gates of the City. She clung about his neck like a monkey, wrapping her legs about his waist, and Drustan smiled, burying his face in his daughter's hair and walking half the distance to the Palace, despite how his twisted left foot must have pained him.

Truly, it would have warmed a heart of stone.

It warmed Ysandre's heart, I know; and I could not find it in mine to begrudge her. No monarch has risen to the throne of Terre d'Ange under graver circumstances than Ysandre, and none has held it with more courage and compassion. If I seem to damn my lady Queen with faint praise, it is not my intention. I have cause to know, better than any, to what mettle Ysandre's spirit is tempered, and I could not ask for any finer.

No, my discontent lay with the shadow on my own soul.

It is no one's fault but my own that I underwent the ceremony of the *thetalos* on the island of Kriti, and came face-to-face with the chain of sorrow and suffering that had arisen from my actions. If I had not transgressed, I would have been purged of the knowledge and cleansed to face life renewed and forgiven. I know, for I saw what transpired in the heart of Kazan Atrabiades, who was my friend; friend and lover, and one-time captor. But I *had* transgressed, and I could not be absolved. The mystery into which I stumbled was not meant for me. What I saw, I must remember and endure.

So I had, for ten years, and the pain of that knowledge had lain buried. Now, Hyacinthe's plight had split the healed flesh and the scars on my soul bled anew.

I went, when I had the time, to my last ally among the Yeshuites, the mystic scholar Eleazar ben Enokh.

He is held in awe and disdain among his people, Eleazar ben Enokh. Awe, for he is among the last of his kind and his knowledge is prodigious for all that he is young to it; disdain, for he looks backward and inward, pondering half-forgotten mysteries while the rest of his folk look increasingly to the north and the future. It is with Eleazar that I began studying the Akkadian language; and that too, his people disdain.

They are wrong, I think—Eleazar thinks it too. There are few tongues older than that which is spoken among the scions of the House of Ur, whose hero Ahzimandias led his people out of exile in the desert to reconquer their ancestral lands. Khebbel-im-Akkad, they call it; Akkad-that-is-reborn. Once upon a time, they were near-kin, the Akkadians and the Yeshuites. The Habiru, they were called then, the Children of Yisra-el; their language is still called the same. But when the Akkadians conquered, the Children of Yisra-el were dispersed and flung to the winds, their Twelve Tribes disbanded, Ten of the Twelve lost and the purity of their mother-tongue diffused.

So it is said, at any rate.

When the empire of Persis arose and overthrew the Akkadians, the royal court of the House of Ur fled, deep into the Umaiyyat, where they were succored by the Khalifate of the Umaiyyat. And there, for a thousand years, they maintained their traditions and language unaltered, and nurtured revenge. It was in Eleazar ben Enokh's heart that somewhere in the deep past, Akkadians and the Children of Yisra-el sprang from the same root. El, their deity was called; El, that is: God, whose True Name is unknowable. Now the Yeshuites think less on the Name of God, having affixed their faith to His son Yeshua ben Yosef, and the Akkadians care little for El, having reconquered Persis in the name of Shamash, the Lion of the Sun, in accordance with Ahzimandias' vision.

But Eleazar ben Enokh, a Yeshuite who dwelt in the City of Elua, kept his heart attuned to his One God and courted Him with profound meditation, fasting and reciting hymns, composed in Habiru and Akkadian alike, seeking betwixt the two to find the original root words, the First Word of Creation that spoke the world into being—for that, he believed, was the Name of God.

I sat with him as he did, for we had become friends, Eleazar and I, of the unlikeliest sort. I knelt on mats in his prayer-room, *abeyante*, as I was taught long ago in the Night Court, sitting on my heels with the skirts of my velvet gown composed around me. Eleazar knelt too, and rocked, inclining back and forth and keening all the while in his strong voice. Betimes he arose and danced about the prayer-room, hopping and spinning, his spindling limbs akimbo beneath his black robes, head thrown back in ecstasy.

I daresay it looked humorous; I know his wife Adara smiled, ducking her head to hide it as she brought water and crusty bread bought fresh at the market into the prayer-room to make ready for her husband who would be ravenous when he broke his fast. To her credit, it never disturbed her that her husband kept company with the foremost courtesan in the City of Elua.

"Father of Nations!" Eleazar gasped in Habiru, "Lord of the Divine Countenance! Hear me, Your meager worshipper, and grant me the merest glimpse of Your throne! Ah!" He went rigid, kneeling, arms outflung. "Abu," he whispered, reverting to Akkadian, "Abu El, anaku bašû kussû."

God, my Father, let me come before your throne.

A look of bliss suffused his face, the straggling ends of his black beard quivering. I knelt patient and watched, while Eleazar ben Enokh descended slowly through the realms of Yeshuite heavens and returned to the here-and-now. I knew, when he opened his kind, brown eyes and shook his head, that he had returned empty-handed.

"I have no name."

The words were spoken with ritual sorrow. He believed, Eleazar ben Enokh, that he beheld the Presence of God in his transports, and that one day he might return with the Sacred Name writ fast upon his heart. I nodded in acknowledgment, bowing low before him.

"I am grateful for your efforts, father," I said formally. Eleazar sighed and sat cross-legged, his bony knees poking sharply into his robes.

"Yeshua have mercy on us," he said sadly, "but we have lost the gift of it since we followed the Mashiach. He sent His Son to redeem our broken covenant." He broke off a piece of bread and looked at it as if it were strange and wonderful in his sight, placing it on his tongue and chewing slowly. "It is said—" he swallowed a mouthful of bread,

"—that one tribe alone never faltered, that is the Tribe of Dân." Eleazar shook his head again. "Adonai is merciful, Phèdre," he said softly, "and to us He sent His Son, Yeshua ben Yosef. I catch a glimpse of His throne, of His almighty feet; no more. For the rest, there is Yeshua." He smiled, and joy and sorrow alike were commingled in his mien. "It is upon his sacrifice that our redemption now depends. I do not think Adonai will make His sacred name known anymore to the Children of Yisra-El. Perhaps He will do it for Elua's child."

"Elua!" My voice was bitter. "Adonai cared so little for his ill-begotten scion Elua that he wandered forgotten for a hundred years while Adonai grieved for your Yeshua! I do not think He will share His name with one such as me."

"Then perhaps the Tribe of Dân holds it in keeping." Eleazar ignored my sharp tone and scrubbed at his face, weary with long prayer. "If you can find them."

To that, I said nothing; every Yeshuite knows the myth of the Lost Tribes. Most believe, if they venture an opinion, that they went north, beyond the barren steppes, where Yeshua's nation is to be founded in preparation for his return. Whether or not it is true, I do not know. Only that in the writings of Habiru sages before the coming of Yeshua, the Tribe of Dân is never mentioned among the exiles.

"And mayhap Shalomon's Ring lies forgotten at the bottom of my jewelry-box," I said, "but I don't think so." Rising, I repented of my ill grace and stooped to kiss his cheek. "Keep searching, Eleazar. Your God is fortunate to be served with such devotion."

He nodded, tearing off another piece of bread and placing it in his mouth. I left him there, chewing meditatively, the remembrance of glory illuminating his narrow features. Adara showed me to the door, where I pressed a small purse of coin into her hands. "A token," I said, "in gratitude for your hospitality." So I said at every visit. Eleazar would never have taken it—or if he had, he would have given it away within the hour—but Adara knew the cost of bread and what was needful to allow her beloved husband to continue his contemplations untroubled.

"You are always welcome in our house, my lady." There was such gentle sweetness to her smile. "It tears at his heart to think how your friend suffers for Rahab's cruelty."

Such is the carelessness of gods, I thought as I made my way home. And we are powerless against it. Even here, in the blessed realm, where Elua and his Companions gave us surpassing gifts of grace and beauty and knowledge, begetting musicians and chirurgeons, architects and shipwrights, painters, poets and dancers, farmers and vintners, warriors and courtiers, there is no power to be found to thwart a forgotten curse by the One God's mighty servant. All the love in my heart was but a weak and foolish noise before the enduring force of Rahab's hatred. And why? Because the Lord of the Deep had loved a woman, and she had loved another than him.

Blessed Elua, I prayed, such things should not be. If there is a way, let me find it, for I do not think I can bear to live out my days with this knowledge. I do not think I can bear to laugh and make merry, living and loving while Hyacinthe raises wind and wave, gazes into a mirror and waits for time to make a monstrosity of him. Wherever the path lies, I will tread it. Whatever the price, I will pay it.

In a mood thus dark and foreboding, I arrived at my home to find Joscelin and Ti-Philippe awaiting me in the salon, their faces grave. Young Hugues was nowhere in sight, nor any of the house-servants. I paused, wondering at the way they stood shoulder-to-shoulder before the low table.

"What is it?"

Joscelin stepped to one side, indicating a sealed missive that lay upon the table. Hardly an unusual thing, for I received correspondence almost daily—letters, offers of assignation, invitation, love poems. "This came by courier from La Serenissima."

Allegra Stregazza, I wondered; or mayhap Severio? Both of them wrote to me from time to time, and Joscelin was not overfond of my friendship with Severio, having never *quite* forgotten that I had once, briefly, entertained his offer of marriage. For all that he had forsworn jealousy, even Joscelin was human. But that would not account for Ti-Philippe's countenance.

The pale vellum glowed against the dark, polished wood of the table, fine-grained and smooth, sealed with a generous blot of gilt wax. Kneeling, I picked up the letter to examine the insignia stamped into the seal.

My hands began to shake and I set it down, staring.

A crown of stars; Asherat's Crown, that adorns the Dogal Seal and the doors of the Temple of Asherat-of-the-Sea. And beneath it, etched in miniature, a device of three keys intertwined—the arms of House Shahrizai.

The letter had been sent by Melisande Shahrizai.

$\mathscr{S}$EVEN

TAKING A deep breath, I cracked the seal and opened the letter.

The room was deadly silent as I read. Joscelin and Ti-Philippe stared at each other over my head, neither daring to ask. It was short, only a few lines, penned in Melisande's elegant hand. I would have known her writing anywhere. I had seen it since I was a child in Delaunay's household, when the correspondence was lively between them, friends and rivals as they were. And I had seen it in the steading of the Skaldi warlord Waldemar Selig, when I realized with sinking horror the infinite depth of her treachery.

Now I read it in my own home, and when I finished, set down the letter and pressed steepled fingers against my lips.

"Name of Elua!" Ti-Philippe exploded. "What does the she-bitch want?"

I looked up at him, lifting my head, and answered simply. "My help."

"*What?*" It was Joscelin, incredulous, who snatched up the letter and read it for himself, passing it to Ti-Philippe and taking an abrupt seat in a nearby chair. He stared at me open-mouthed, shaking his head in unconscious denial. "Phèdre. No. She's mad. She has to be!"

Dear Phèdre, the letter read, *I am writing to ask your aid in a matter of vital importance. There is no one else I may trust. I swear to you, in Kushiel's name, that this is no ploy and poses no threat of harm to your loyalties. Make haste to La Serenissima, and I will explain.*

That, and no more. I heard a stifled expletive from Ti-Philippe as he finished reading.

"No," Joscelin said again, although I had not spoken. The color was returning to his face. "Phèdre, you can't possibly consider it. Whatever it is, it's bound to be a trick."

"No." I looked past him at the bust of Anafiel Delaunay which sat on a black marble plinth in my salon. My lord Delaunay gazed back at me, silent as ever, a wry tenderness to his austere features. I remembered how I had first met Melisande in Delaunay's gymnasium, how she had touched my face, and my knees had turned to water. She was the only one he had ever allowed to see me before I entered Naamah's Service. They had been friends, once; and lovers, too. He might be alive today, but for her treachery. So might countless others. I have never dared number those dead by Melisande's deeds. "She swore it in Kushiel's name. Even Melisande has rules."

"You can't think it."

There was a ragged edge to Joscelin's voice I had not heard in more than ten years. My eyes stung with tears as I turned my gaze to him, swallowing hard. "It's Sibeal's dream, don't you see, and Hyacinthe's vision. Joscelin, I don't pretend to understand. But I have to go."

He was silent for a moment. "You would let her put her leash on you again."

"No." I took back the letter that Ti-Philippe had thrown onto the table, running the ball of my thumb over the waxen seal. "Melisande remains under the purview of the Temple of Asherat. She's not free to make claims on me. And I will not offer what I did once before."

"Melisande Shahrizai doesn't need her freedom to make claims on you," Joscelin whispered. "And you don't need to offer. Do you think I don't know that?"

"Joscelin." I dropped the letter and rubbed my temples. My head ached fiercely. "What do you want me to do? Stay here and slowly go mad, thinking about Hyacinthe and spending my days praying some poor, God-ridden Habiru mystic will stumble across the Sacred Name? I don't want to see Melisande; Blessed Elua knows I don't want to *help* her! But there have been dreams and visions pointing the way, and I prayed to Elua to show it to me. Now my prayer is answered; a letter, like a portent. What am I to do? Ignore it?" I let my hands fall to my lap and shook my aching head. "I can't."

"I'll go." Ti-Philippe's words sounded abrupt. "The Tsingano said the path would be dark. Well, I'm not afraid of darkness." He cleared his throat. "I can't imagine we'll see aught worse than we've seen before, my lady. And I'm not afraid of your facing Melisande Shahrizai. Whatever it is between you, you've outfaced her twice before, and won." He glanced at Joscelin. "People forget that."

"I don't forget!" Joscelin raised his voice sharply. In the old days, they had quarrelled often; this was the first time since La Serenissima. "But I don't trust anyone's luck to continue forever, even Phèdre's. And if you think you have seen all the world holds of darkness, chevalier, you are sore mistaken."

"Just because I'm no Cassiline to spend countless hours meditating on the damnation of my—"

"Enough!" I cut them off before the quarrel could escalate. "Joscelin," I said, fixing him with my gaze. "I am going to do this thing. Is it your will to accompany me?"

His smile was tight as a grimace. "I have sworn it. To damnation and beyond," he added, casting a pointed glance in Ti-Philippe's direction. "Though I would sooner that than Melisande's doorstep."

"My lady, you would be better served—" Ti-Philippe began.

"No." I shook my head at him. "Philippe, I value your courage and your loyalty more than I can say. But if there is anyone I need at my side, it is Joscelin. You, I need here. I need someone I can trust to keep watch over my household and my estates. And I need to know," I said gently, "someone is here, safe and well, keeping the lamps lit for our safe return."

Now it was Ti-Philippe who had tears in his eyes. "My lady," he said, "you know I would face any danger on your behalf."

"I know. I am asking you *not* to, and mayhap it is a harder thing." I laughed. "Anyway, of what are we speaking? A spring journey to La Serenissima? We'll be there and back inside a month. A paltry thing, as dangers go."

"There are no paltry dangers where Melisande Shahrizai is concerned," Joscelin muttered. "Captive, or no."

Ysandre, predictably, was displeased. I had to tell her, reckoning I owed my Queen as much. She scowled at me and paced the pleasant bounds of the drawing-room in which we met, her mood and actions more suitable to official chambers. I stood patiently and waited out her anger, glad of Joscelin's solid presence at my shoulder. For some reason, she had far greater faith in him not to undertake anything foolish—a misplaced sentiment, in my opinion. Ysandre had not been there when Joscelin crawled the underside of a hanging bridge to the prison-fortress of La Dolorosa and assailed it single-handed with naught but his daggers. Well and so, if Ysandre de la Courcel thought a Cassiline less rash than a courtesan, let her. I knew better.

For his part, Drustan mab Necthana said nothing, only sitting and thinking, his dark eyes grave and thoughtful. He had sailed to the Three

Sisters on the strength of Sibeal's dream; he would not gainsay my going.

"Fine," Ysandre said at last, irritable, fetching up before us. "Go. I tried to dissuade you once before, and I was in the wrong; I swore I would not do it again. Only remember, Melisande played you for a fool the entire time, and it is only with Elua's blessing that we are not all dead of it. If you think this is aught different, you're making the same mistake." She looked curiously at me. "Do you even have the slightest idea what game she's playing at now?"

"No." I answered calmly, my hands clasped before me to hide their trembling. In truth, it was that very thing that terrified me. I had always known, before. I may have misgauged her moves—with, as Ysandre observed, near-fatal results—but I had grasped the nature of the game. Now, I could not guess. *I am writing to ask your aid . . .* That sounded nothing like Melisande; and that alone made me nervous. "When I know, I will tell you, I promise."

"Elua," Ysandre sighed, and took my face between her hands, planting an unexpected kiss on my brow. "I swear, near-cousin, you cause me more worry than ten Shahrizai courtiers and my daughter Alais rolled into one," she said. "My lord Cassiline, please do whatever it is you do to bring her back safely."

Joscelin bowed, the shadow of a smile at the corner of his mouth. I think sometimes they understood each other too well, those two. Drustan rose and came to take my hands.

"Necthana's daughters dream true dreams," he said. "My sister Moiread knew your voice before ever you set foot on Alba's shores. We will await your return."

So we took our leave.

We travelled lightly, Joscelin and I, making a straight course overland across Caerdicca Unitas. It felt strange, covering the same territory through which we had ridden ten years ago in Ysandre's entourage, desperate to thwart the last, deadly stroke of Melisande's scheme. Now, I was riding to her aid . . . because she had asked it. Passing strange indeed. It was on that journey that we heard the stories they tell of Ysandre's ride, the fell and glorious company of D'Angelines who passed like the wind along the northern route betwixt Milazza and La Serenissima. Joscelin and I heard them in the inns along the way, exchanging glances, remembering the metal taste of fear in our mouths, saddle-weary aches and the endless arguing of Ysandre de la Courcel and Lord Amaury Trente.

Of such stuff are legends made.

Naught of moment befell us in our journey and the weather held passing fair, with only a few showers of rain to dampen our spirits. The northern route is safe, now, as safe as ever it has been. Once, the threat of Skaldi raiders was prevalent, but now the southern border of Skaldia is peaceful, and a number of tribes have formed a loose federation, trading freely with the Caerdicci. It is Waldemar Selig's doing, in a way. Although his endeavor failed—Blessed Elua be thanked—he was somewhat new among the Skaldi: a leader who thought. He gave them ambition and hunger for the finer elements of civilization, and he taught them that together, they might achieve what they never could apart. Shattered by defeat at D'Angeline hands, the Skaldi have grown circumspect, and seek now to acquire through honest trade and effort what they once sought to seize by might of arms.

One day, I think, they may try it again. But for now, there is peace.

Of La Serenissima, I have written elsewhere at length. Suffice it to say that the city is unchanged. It is beautiful still, redolent with the light that reflects from the water of her many canals, and reeking too with the odor of those same canals. It is a city that holds too many memories for me, and few of them good.

I might have presented myself, under other circumstances, at either the Dogal Palace or the Little Court, and availed myself of the hospitality that would surely have been rendered me. Incredible though it seems, Cesare Stregazza is still Doge of La Serenissima. I think he must be nearly ninety years of age now, which is unheard-of for his kind. Members of the Stregazza family seldom enjoy long lives. I daresay he would remember me, since I saved his throne for him. It is his younger son Ricciardo who administers much of the daily business of the city, or so Allegra writes. I think he will succeed his father as Doge. I hope so, for he is worthy.

The Little Court is Severio's, now. It has been for three years. They do not call it that, anymore; the Palazzo Immortali, he renamed it, after his social club. There is still a D'Angeline presence there—how not, when Severio is grandson to Prince Benedicte de la Courcel himself— but it is no longer a court in exile. For all that his blood is a quarter D'Angeline, Severio is Serenissiman to the core. He married a Serenissiman noblewoman some years ago, a daughter of the Hundred Worthy Families, and seems content with his lot. She is not, I understand, entirely unamenable to rough play in the bedchamber; a fortunate happenstance, as I had cause to know. Severio had once been a patron of mine, and his appetites bore a keen edge.

I did not wish to intrude into either situation on this particular errand. There is a good deal of bitterness still over Prince Benedicte's betrayal and the plot laid by Marco and Marie-Celeste Stregazza—and D'Angeline influence is held much to blame. Unfairly, I think, for Marco Stregazza was the Doge's own elder son . . . but still.

The genius behind it was Melisande.

And I had ridden to La Serenissima in response to her request for aid.

In light of this fact, Joscelin and I took lodgings at one of the finer inns near the Campo Grande. La Serenissima is a city of trade above all, and there was nothing strange about a D'Angeline couple travelling there. The only strangeness was in my mind, and the echo of memory as I gazed from my balcony onto the bustling market in the square below, the morning sun glittering on the Great Canal and striking gold from the domed roof of the Temple of Asherat. Joscelin came to stand beside me and we looked, thinking the same thoughts.

"There," he said, pointing. "That's where the parrot-merchant's stand stood, from Jebe-Barkal. Do you remember?"

"The Yeshuite," I said. "The Immortali picked a fight with him, and Ti-Philippe had a bloody nose at the end of it." I frowned. "How did you end up defending the parrot-stand?"

"I don't remember." He leaned on the railing, bracing his arms. "Elua, but I was an idiot then! It's a wonder you forgave me."

"No." I curled my fingers about his forearm. "We were both idiots, and I was cruel. I was so blinded by my quest, I didn't care how much I hurt you. I taught myself to relish the pain instead. Call it an *anguissette*'s folly."

Joscelin gazed down into the marketplace. "But you were right," he said, "when I thought you were on a fool's errand. And I was too proud to admit how terrified I was of losing you. It would have been different if I had."

"Ah, well." I rested my head against his shoulder. "Elua willing, we are a little older now, and a little wiser. Whatever happens . . ." I drew back to look at his face. "Joscelin, you know I would never leave you?"

"I know," he said softly. "I do know it, Phèdre. But what lies between you and Melisande frightens me, because Kushiel's hand is in it. You are his Chosen, and he has marked you for his own . . . and I, I am only Cassiel's servant, no more. What is that, to one who was the Punisher of God?"

Alone among the Companions of Elua, Cassiel bore no gifts, no earthly power. No province bears his name, and he left no mortal lineage. Only the Cassiline Brothers, middle sons, sworn into fruitless loyalty. What was it indeed to the cruel and merciful might of Kushiel, lord of atonement, guardian of the brazen portals of Hell? It is not an easy thing, to be Kushiel's Chosen.

"Love," I said to Joscelin. "Only love. And if that is not enough, Elua help us all."

Joscelin shivered and put his arms around me.

EIGHT

WE PRESENTED ourselves at the Temple of Asherat-of-the-Sea.

If the priestesses there knew who I was, they gave nothing away. It was a piece of the oddness, to stand in the Temple proper and gaze at the vast effigy of the goddess. Carved of stone, Asherat stared across the open space unmoved, surrounded by leaping waves. Once, I had stood upon the balcony opposite and claimed her voice for my own, crying out to stop a traitor from being anointed her beloved, Doge of La Serenissima.

Now, a member of the Elect was summoned and came to greet us, her bare feet whispering on the floor, glass beads glistening on the strands of her silvery veil. Whether or not I knew her, I could not say. She bowed in acknowledgment, blue silken robes stirring beneath their netting.

"The Lady Melisande will see you."

Joscelin and I followed the priestess of the Elect, flanked by eunuch attendants bearing ceremonial barbed spears. I remembered how the Habiru lass Sarae had shot one with her crossbow, how Kazan's men had slain others scarce-awakened, and shuddered involuntarily.

That blood too was on my conscience; innocent blood.

Our path wound down many corridors, longer than it had when I'd visited with Ysandre. Even then, the priestesses of Asherat had treated Melisande like a Queen in exile. In ten years, it had only grown more marked. I do not doubt that they honored her claim of sanctuary out of genuine reverence. Nor do I doubt that the manner of it owed much to Melisande's wealth fattening their coffers. Ysandre had claimed her estates for the crown, when Melisande was first adjudged a traitor, but the profit in them had already been routed to the banking houses of La Serenissima. Like the adepts of Bryony House, the Shahrizai have always understood that money is power—even in defeat, Melisande had managed to preserve hers.

A double rap at vast doors with gilt hinges, opened from within by an acolyte with downcast eyes, and the soft voice of the priestess of the Elect announcing us in Caerdicci accents. "The Contessa Phèdre nó Delaunay of Montrève and Monsignor Joscelin Verreuil."

And with that, we were admitted into Melisande's presence.

Sunlight filtered into the salon, which adjoined some inner courtyard, lending the room a pleasant warmth. There were low couches and a table, set about with careless elegance as in any D'Angeline sitting-room, and flowering shrubs in pots, perfuming the air.

Somewhere, a small fountain played.

Melisande Shahrizai stood waiting.

The impact of seeing her hit me like a tidal sea-swell, stopping the very breath in my lungs. Long-buried emotions surged in me, foremost among them a bitter, abiding hatred. No one has ever betrayed me more cruelly or wounded me deeper, and I could not see her without remembering my lord Delaunay, his austere features ivory in death, dark blood clotting his auburn braid as he lay in his own gore. And even so, even with all that lay between us and the memory of her hands moving on my flesh, her voice at my ear, compelling my body's response while my heart cracked and bled . . . even so, there was desire.

Too much to hope that the years had been unkind to Melisande Shahrizai.

Her beauty, that had dazzled like a diamond's edge ten years ago, had only deepened, attaining a richer, more mellow resonance. Melisande had set aside the Veil of Asherat for our meeting and her features retained the same remorseless symmetry, pale and fair, eyes the hue of sapphires at twilight, her hair unbound in a rippling fall of blue-black waves, her figure statuesque nigh to perfection.

And yet . . .

When she spoke, her melodious voice was restrained, her expression grave. "Phèdre," she said. "I did not know if you would come."

I shifted on my feet, aware of Joscelin's presence at my elbow, his love a fierce dagger by which to fix the compass of my heart. "I wouldn't have," I said with a lightness I did not feel, "if it were only your request, my lady. But you see, there is a prophecy at work."

"Ah." One syllable; her expression gave nothing away. Melisande inclined her head to Joscelin. "Messire Verreuil," she acknowledged.

The last time they had met, he'd drawn his sword on her. There was no love lost between those two.

"Lady Shahrizai." Joscelin's voice was neutral, his bow punctilious. He had left his arms behind, this time. What was appropriate to the Queen's champion was not suitable for a private visit to the Temple of Asherat.

"Please," Melisande said, indicating the couches. "Be seated." She waited until we had made ourselves comfortable on one of the couches before taking a seat opposite us, thanking the priestess of the Elect and her attendants before dismissing them. They went, too, discreet as well-bred servants. "You are wondering," she said without hesitation, "why I have summoned you here."

The unseen fountain splashed quietly in the background.

"Yes," I said. "I am."

Melisande drew a deep breath. Her gaze shifted off my face, fixed onto some unknown distance behind us. "My son is missing."

I nearly laughed; I made some involuntary sound, I think. "My lady," I said, "you deliver old news. Your son has been missing these ten years now."

She looked back at me with a trace of impatience. "Not to me."

It took a full minute for her meaning to process. When it did, it felt as if the world had changed position beneath my feet. On the couch beside me, Joscelin stirred. "You are saying . . ." I swallowed, picking my way carefully through the words. "You are saying you don't know where he is. Your son."

"Yes." Melisande Shahrizai nodded. "That is what I am saying."

I did laugh, then; disbelieving. "Well and so," I said, getting to my feet unthinking to pace the room. "Your son, whom you have hidden from the world for ten years, is missing. And here you sit, surrounded by fountains and eunuchs. Well, you were warned, my lady; Ysandre de la Courcel herself warned you, ten years gone by. If you did not relinquish him into her custody, into the role to which he is entitled as a Prince of the Blood and a scion of House Courcel, you would make of him a weapon lying free to be taken up by whosoever would use him." I ran both hands through my hair. "And now it has happened," I said, my voice running on too fast. "Well and so, it has come to pass. What do you want of me, my lady? What do you want of me?"

Melisande looked at me without moving. "I want you to find him."

It brought me to a halt. "Why?"

"Because," Melisande said simply, "you can."

I laughed again, out loud, staring at her. "So? Why should I help you?"

Something unfathomable surfaced in her deep blue eyes. "The boy is innocent."

"No." I shook my head in denial, summoning a will I scarce knew I possessed. "No," I said more firmly. "My lady, forgive me, but it is not enough." I felt Joscelin's presence behind me, solid as an embrace. "As I am human, I grieve for your plight, my lady; but I am not your ally nor your servant to aid you in this matter. My loyalty is sworn to her majesty Ysandre de la Courcel, and there it shall abide." I steadied myself against the knowledge of Joscelin's love, my Perfect Companion, and spoke with confidence, sure in her inability to answer. "So I ask again, why should I help you?"

In the silence that followed, I felt my heart beat three times over, slow and steady.

And then Melisande shattered my will.

"You seek the Name of God. I can tell you where to find it."

I heard Joscelin's sharp, indrawn breath; I was aware, distantly, of my knees locking. I stared at Melisande's beautiful, implacable face. "You don't know it," I said, numb and stupid. "You can't know it."

Melisande didn't blink. "Thirteen years ago, Anafiel Delaunay began his investigation into the matter of the Master of the Straits. Do you suppose I never wondered why?" She smiled wryly. "I was wrong, at first. I thought he courted the aid of Maelcon the Usurper, to secure Ysandre's throne. It is what I would have done, what Lyonette de Trevalion attempted for her son Baudoin. Nonetheless." Her expression hardened. "I knew what he sought, and followed his path. When your Tsingano friend paid the riddle's price, I knew you would continue to seek the key to his freedom."

I sat down, feeling the same shock that echoed in my flesh resonating in Joscelin. "And you would have me believe you found it?"

"No." Melisande shook her head, almost gently. "Not the key, no. But I know where it might be found. You are too like Anafiel, Phèdre, caught up in academic pursuit. I taught him to use people; I thought I taught him well, when he set you and the boy Alcuin to espionage in the name of Naamah's Service. But I did not teach him well enough. Although he used you hard, still he disdained to buy the eyes and ears he might have done." She took another deep breath. "I didn't. And I've had a longer time in which to do it. You seek the Tribe of Dân, yes?"

"Yes," I said, sick at heart. Hyacinthe.

"Well," Melisande said. "I can tell you where to find them. If you will find my son, Imriel."

The blood beat in my ears, with a sound like bronze wings clashing. A red haze veiled my vision. Kushiel's face swam before my eyes, cruel and compassionate. *In one hand, he holds a brazen key, and in the other a diamond, strung on a velvet cord . . .* I felt, somewhere, Melisande's gaze upon me, watching and waiting. There was a hard pressure at my wrists, like manacles; Joscelin's hands, clamped hard around me.

"No," he whispered. "Phèdre, don't do this thing."

I blinked, and my vision cleared. Melisande sat watching me unmoving. "Why?" I asked. "Why me? Elua knows, my lady, you've spies to your name still. Deny it, and I walk out this door, no matter what bait you dangle before me."

"I have spies." A corner of Melisande's lips curled. "Do you think I wouldn't try that route first, Phèdre nó Delaunay? They have found nothing. Whoever took my son plays a clever game." She looked around at her gracious prison. "And here I sit, surrounded by fountains and eunuchs. If I were free . . ." She shook her head. "I cannot enter Terre d'Ange. Not openly. And it is there that the trail begins. I need someone to be my eyes and ears, following it. I need someone capable of playing as deep and well-hidden a game as whoever took him. There is," Melisande said, "only you."

I looked at Joscelin, who slowly loosened his grip on my wrists.

"Don't ask," he said. "I have sworn it. You know I have."

"I will do nothing to cross the will of my Queen," I said to Melisande.

"Of course." She inclined her head. "I am asking you to find my son. Has not Ysandre asked as much?"

"Yes." I held her gaze. "You know I would be bound to present him to her. It was ever her wish, to bring him into her household. Whatever you plotted . . ." I shook my head. "I will have no part in it. If he is found, I will send word, but it is to my Queen I will report."

She nodded. "I expected no less. Will you do it?"

I raked both hands through my hair again, heedless of disarray. "Do you swear to me," I asked in despairing relentlessness, "in Kushiel's name, in Blessed Elua's name, that you are not playing me false in any detail?"

"Would that I were." Melisande smiled with bitter irony. "I do so swear."

"I will do it," I said.

The soft splashing of the fountain mingled with Joscelin's sigh.

Nine

"HERE." MELISANDE'S finger indicated the Sanctuary of Elua on the map. I bit my tongue on an exclamation. She glanced at me. "Yes. That close."

For ten years, her son—Imriel de la Courcel, Prince of the Blood, third in line to Ysandre's throne—had been raised in a Sanctuary of Elua in southern Siovale, not three hours' ride from my own estate of Montrève.

"I told you we should have spent more time there," Joscelin muttered. I shot him a look of pure annoyance.

"No." Melisande traced a path northward from Montrève to another sanctuary. "You would go here, I think, if you went to worship, Cassiline. Landras is too far to ride in a day and back. I was careful in my choice."

"Under our noses," I said, awed by the audacious brilliance of it. "Or nearly. Where was he when we searched the Little Court?"

"Hidden in the rear of Elua's temple." There was no satisfaction in Melisande's voice, merely matter-of-fact disclosure. "Ysandre's men didn't search it, only asked the priest."

"Who lied for you," Joscelin said. "*Lied!* And then took the child across D'Angeline borders to be raised in secret in the Sanctuary of Elua?" He shook his head. "I don't believe it. Why? It doesn't make sense."

"Ask Brother Selbert, if you want his reasons." Melisande bent to smooth a crease from the map. "He did not believe my request violated any of his vows." She straightened and looked at Joscelin. Her deep blue eyes were clear and calm. "Messire Verreuil, Imriel *is* my son, and he has done no wrong. Ysandre de la Courcel has no claim on him and the priesthood of Elua does not answer to the throne of Terre d'Ange.

Although you may not like it, there was no wrongdoing in it."

"He *lied* for you!" Joscelin repeated, but Melisande made him no further reply.

I didn't question the matter; not yet. I studied the map instead, thinking. Truly, Melisande had chosen well in the sanctuary at Landras. It was far from any city and the sort of political intrigue that made secrets impossible to keep. A quiet, provincial sanctuary, given over in equal parts to the academic study beloved of Siovalese, descendents of Elua's Companion Shemhazai, and pastoral pursuits.

"How did it happen?" I asked Melisande.

She shook her head. "No one knows. The children—there were five who were wards of the sanctuary—had taken the temple's goat herd to spring pasturage. At dusk, only four returned. Imriel wasn't with them."

"Your son," I said. "A goat-herd."

"A lost prince raised in secret by the priesthood of Elua." Melisande smiled faintly. "Innocent of his origins, cleansed of the taint of his parents' sins. Terre d'Ange would have embraced him with open arms."

She was right; we would have. I shuddered and put aside thoughts of what more dire plans accompanied it. "The other four heard nothing, saw nothing?"

"No." Her expression grew sober. "They were spread out across the hills with those little pipes, you know, that shepherds carry, to keep in earshot. After he questioned the children, Brother Selbert turned out the sanctuary to search the hills by torchlight. A few stray goats, no more." She was silent for a moment, then continued. "They searched again in the morning. He thought at first that Imriel must gotten injured, or trapped somewhere—a steep gorge, a cave-in, something. But there was nothing."

"So he sent to tell you," I said.

"He searched the countryside first, questioning as best he dared to learn if a boy of Imriel's description had been seen in any of the villages, on any of the roads. When he was sure none had, he came himself."

"And you believe him?" I raised my eyebrows.

"Because he lied to Ysandre's men, you mean?" Melisande met my eyes, reading my thoughts. "Elua's priests are sworn to serve love, not truth. Yes, I believe him. I have not forgotten how to read the tell-tales of a lie, Phèdre nó Delaunay."

I blushed, although for the life of me, I couldn't have said why.

"And that's when you set your spies to searching for him."

"Yes." Her lashes flickered. "My spies."

"Who found . . . nothing?"

"Nothing." Melisande drew a deep breath and exhaled. "Not a hair, not a footprint, not a rumor or whisper of conspiracy. My son has vanished as if he never existed. You see why I ask your help?"

"Yes." I rose to wander the salon, frowning in thought; a bad habit and apt to cause unattractive lines. I would have been chided for it in the Night Court, but I didn't like the direction in which my thoughts were going.

"Did anyone else know your son's whereabouts?" Joscelin asked Melisande.

"No." It was unnerving to hear her voice without its honeyed menace. What I had taken for restraint was an unfamiliar undertone of grief—and even stranger, fear. I don't think anyone else would have recognized it as such. I did. "Some of the priests and priestesses may have guessed; I cannot say for sure."

"So someone *could* have known," Joscelin said, watching me pace.

"Yes." Melisande followed his gaze. "It is always possible. There is always danger. Phèdre, what are you thinking?"

My name from her lips. It still raised the fine hairs at the back of my neck. I paused before a pot of flowering almond, brushing the petals with my fingers. "That there are very few people capable of playing as devious and ruthless a game as you, my lady," I said. "How many, do you think, in Terre d'Ange itself?"

"A few, mayhap."

It was a generous estimate. "Your kin?" I asked.

"No." Melisande hesitated. "No one in House Shahrizai would have harmed the boy, whether they reviled me or no. He holds too much possibility for us. If any of my kin had found him, I would know. One way or another."

Now that, I did believe. I sighed, turning to face her. "There is one person who comes to mind."

"Barquiel L'Envers." Melisande's eyes met mine, and I knew we thought alike.

We are wary allies, Ysandre's maternal uncle and I. Once, he was my lord Delaunay's greatest enemy, and I was slow to trust him because of it. I did, in the end; I placed the fate of Ysandre's throne in his hands, and he acquitted himself heroically, holding the City of Elua

against Percy de Somerville's rebellion until Ysandre came to reclaim
it. Still, I cannot forget those other acts he committed to secure his
niece's throne, that were neither noble nor lawful.

"He wouldn't," Joscelin protested.

"He had Dominic Stregazza assassinated," I reminded him. "He's
as much as admitted it."

"Dominic killed his sister." Joscelin flushed. "I'm not saying it was
justified, Phèdre, but he had cause to seek vengeance."

"Barquiel L'Envers is ambitious and clever," Melisande said, "and
he does not scruple to do what the Queen will not. If word of Imriel's
existence reached his ears, I do not think he would lay it in Ysandre's
lap. I think he would take whatever measures he deemed necessary to
secure her throne for House L'Envers' lineage."

Although her voice remained even, her face was unwontedly pale.
"I don't think he would," I said. "Not that. But he is one of the only
people I can think of who would be capable. I will learn what I can."
I looked at her a moment without speaking. "You know there is a good
chance the boy is dead."

For all that I hated her, I made the words as gentle as I could.
Melisande's expression never changed. Given the same knowledge, there
was no possibility I could conceive that she had not already thought of.
"I know." The words fell flat into the air between us. "If that is so,
then whoever is responsible will be remanded unto Kushiel's mercy. I
will honor our agreement nonetheless."

Barbed words, double-edged. As I was Kushiel's chosen, she was
his scion. If it was murder, one way or another, it would not go unav-
enged. I sighed again, feeling the weight of this task like a millstone
around my neck. "My lady, I will need to speak to your . . . spies. The
other likely possibility is that one of them has betrayed you."

"No." Melisande's chin rose a fraction, eyes narrowing. "That
much, I have determined on my own, Phèdre nó Delaunay. It was no
one loyal to me. Those who are suffered enough when my cousin Marmion betrayed me. I will condemn no more to the Queen's untender
justice."

"You will hobble my search," I said.

"I will spare you wasted time." Her voice was implacable. "Do you
really think I would maintain allies I could not trust implicitly at this
point? This was planned from outside, Phèdre, of that I am sure. I have
named the price I will pay for your aid. Do not seek to bargain for
more."

"We could walk away." Joscelin leaned back against the couch, unperturbed.

"You could." Melisande eyed him, then looked back at me. "I do not think you will."

"No." There was no point in dissembling. I didn't bother trying. "But you have your bargain yet to fulfill, my lady. How shall it be done?"

"Ah." Melisande rose gracefully and crossed the room to open a low coffer. She withdrew a scroll-case of oiled wood and presented it to me. "Here."

I opened it and removed the scroll within, unwinding it on its spindles to find a document on finely cured hide, written in unfamiliar letters. An alphabet of broad vertical lines inscribed the hide, black and decisive, the text illuminated here and there with brightly painted scenes in miniature. Here a king sat enthroned, receiving a gorgeously dressed woman in audience; here, he gave her a ring. Here was fire and swords and devastation; here, two men raised their hands before an altar. Here, a temple in ruins; here, a river voyage. I stared at it and frowned, uncomprehending. "What is this?"

"The document is written in Jeb'ez. The *Kefra Neghast*, they call it; the Glory of Kings." Melisande stooped as I sat to study it, marking a point on the hide. "See, here; this depicts the meeting of Shalomon and Makeda, the Queen of Saba. And this is the ring he gave her, a token of remembrance."

"Shalomon's Ring," I murmured. Her fragrance was distracting.

"Mayhap." Melisande gave me a quick glance. "It is Shalomon, and it is a ring. Here, you see? This man is Melek al'Hakim, Prince of Saba, Shalomon's son, come to the temple to retrieve his father's treasure in time of war. He bears his father's ring. And this man . . ." She tapped the hide. "This is Khiram, son of Khiram, architect of the Temple of Shalomon." Melisande sat back on her heels, neatly as any adept of the Night Court, her dark blue eyes thoughtful. "Who was born of the Tribe of Dân."

"No." I spread both hands unthinking over the hide. "The Tribe of Naftali. So it is written, in the Book of Kings."

"The Book of Kings, yes. Not in the Paraleipomenon." Melisande used the Hellene word and a rare impatient gesture. "How do you say it in D'Angeline?"

"Chronicles," I said. "The *Dibhere Hayyamin*, the Acts of Days." I tried to remember, and couldn't. It might be so, that the Book of Chronicles ascribed a different lineage to Shalomon's architect. "My lady, what are you saying?"

"What I was told. No more and no less." Melisande regarded me. "That it is legend, in distant Jebe-Barkal, that Melek al'Hakim the son of Shalomon and Khiram the architect fled the fall of the Habiru empire over a thousand years ago. First to Menekhet under Pharaoh's aegis, then southeast to Saba. And the Tribe of Dân went with them."

"You read Jeb'ez," I said, incredulous.

"No." Melisande smiled. "I had the scroll translated. What I was told, I committed to memory." She straightened, standing. "Take it. You are welcome to do the same. And when you have come back to report to me what you have learned of my son's disappearance, I will give you the name of a man in the city of Iskandria, in Menekhet, who says he can lead you south into Jebe-Barkal, to the very place where Shalomon's son founded his dynasty."

I rolled the scroll carefully, mindful of crackling the glaze on the painted characters. "What makes you think I cannot find such a guide on my own, my lady?"

"You might," Melisande admitted. "Although onesuch is not so easy to find, for the empire of Shalomon's son is long fallen and its history forgotten. But you have given your word. And you are Anafiel Delaunay's pupil. I do not think you will go back on it."

"No." I placed the scroll back in its container. "Did you teach me to use people better than you taught my lord Delaunay, my lady, I would take this and be gone. But when all is said and done, I am not like you." I placed the lid on the wooden cylinder, sealing it with a twist. "You spoke the truth, when you said your son is innocent. For that, if naught else, I will seek to learn what has become of him."

"Thank you." Melisande said it graciously, standing tall and straight. It gave me a strange feeling in the pit of my stomach, hearing those words from her. With nothing to resist, I didn't know what to do with my emotions. Joscelin swung himself off the couch in one seamless motion, assisting me to my feet.

"We'll come back when we've something to report," he said. "My lady."

Ten

SINCE WE had no reason to stay, we left La Serenissima in the same day.

For a long time, neither of us discussed it, speaking only of those pragmatic matters necessary for travel. I daresay I couldn't have borne anything more. My mind reeled, trying to make sense of what had transpired. I couldn't do it. It was too much.

"You did well." It was Joscelin who broke the silence somewhere outside of Pavento.

I turned to look at his profile, his gaze fixed on the road before him, hands competent on the reins. "Joscelin. I agreed to help her."

"I know." He glanced sideways at me. "And Elua help me, I don't know what else you could have done. You think she's telling the truth about this Jebean legend?"

"I don't know." I touched the scroll-case, lashed securely across my pommel. "She might be. It would be like her to have had this coin and withheld it for years."

"For what?" Joscelin's voice was curious. "I understand she was shadowing Delaunay, in the beginning, but what interest could the Master of the Straits hold for Melisande now?"

"What do you think Drustan mab Necthana would do if Melisande tried to put her son on Ysandre's throne?" I asked.

"Bring an army across the Straits and stop her."

"Yes." I stroked the oiled wood. "Unless the Master of the Straits barred the crossing. And for the price of freedom, he might consider it."

"Hyacinthe?" It was odd to hear him spoken of thusly. "Never."

"Never." I tasted the word. "Ten days ago, I would have said I would never have given my aid to Melisande Shahrizai of my own will.

And my never is a good deal shorter than Hyacinthe's, Joscelin." I remembered the despairing eyes of the Tsingano boy I'd loved looking out from the face of the Master of the Straits, immortal power trapped in a mortal body. In the back of my mind, a grasshopper chirruped a dry warning. "Now, no. In ten years . . . mayhap."

Our horses' hooves beat a rhythmic tattoo on the road while Joscelin considered my words. Travelling has its own pace, its own meter. "You're probably right," he said at length, and glanced at me again. "Still. It matters not, not any more. And I think you handled her well."

"I tried."

It was true, I think; I had done well. Once, only once, in my career as an *anguissette* in Naamah's Service have I given my *signale*, that password commanding a patron to cease, overriding all false protests and demurrals. It was to Melisande Shahrizai. I have had patrons more brutal, gleeful in their abuse, who left marks on my body that took many weeks to heal. I have never had any patron who played me with such consummate skill. But I had conducted myself well in her presence, yes. Apart from my initial shock at her request—and who would not react thusly?—I had remained in control, showing no sign of the weakness inflicted upon me by fate.

And now I ached with desire in every part.

Kushiel's Dart was pricking hard.

Joscelin realized it, in time. We had been together too long for it to be otherwise. Once, long before we were lovers, he had despised it in me. It was Joscelin who had been there the morning after that Longest Night, when I gave Melisande my *signale* and she strung her diamond about my throat. And it was Joscelin who had been there when I had awakened, sick and betrayed, after Melisande sold us into captivity in Skaldia. Even then, even in the depths of betrayal and self-loathing, I'd had no defenses against the craving she roused in me. She was a scion of Kushiel such as the world has never seen, and I was Kushiel's Chosen, the only *anguissette* born in living memory. We were connected in a manner nothing born of rational thought and the mind's volition could touch.

I could no more cease wanting her than I could stem the tide.

After that terrible second morning, I think Joscelin understood, at least a bit. And Skaldia . . . Skaldia changed everything between us. When did I discover that I loved him? I cannot even say. When I realized it, it came as something I had known for a long, long, time.

Somewhere, somehow, life without him had become unthinkable.

It didn't alter my desires.

To his infinite credit, Joscelin spoke no word of reproach but gave to me what solace he could that night where we took our lodgings. On the roughspun blankets of our rented bed, he laid aside his self-discipline and made love to me with all the savagery of his heart.

It helped, some. I clutched at his back, feeling his muscles work violently beneath his skin as he drove himself into me, burying my face in the crook of his neck as his hair fell in shining ribbons about us both and salt tears dampened my cheeks. It wasn't enough. Peerless warrior though he was, there was no cruelty in Joscelin. I ought to know; I loved him for it. Yet even as he stiffened above me on rigid arms, spending himself, and my ardent body responded, it wasn't enough. My skin craved the kiss of the lash, the bite of a keen blade. I longed to kneel in abject surrender, whispering obscene pleas.

I could not have been more miserable if I had.

Somewhere beyond us, Kushiel smiled pitilessly.

It would have been different, if anyone but Melisande had been the cause. This was a yearning that came upon me from time to time; when it did, we both of us knew it was time for me to take a patron. I can pick and choose, now, as I do thrice a year. Delaunay's *anguissette* no longer, I take assignations with only such patrons as I deem worthy. It galled my heart and filled me with self-hatred to know that now, even now, the mere sight of Melisande was enough to stir my darkest desires.

If I had not been what I am, if I had not known her as I do, I could never have thwarted Melisande's designs on the throne of Terre d'Ange. I know this. But why now? It served no need, no purpose I could discern.

Well, and who can discern the purposes of the gods? With an effort, I bent my mind from contemplating my inner woes and thought about our present dilemma instead. Imriel de la Courcel, a Prince's son raised a goat-herd, like something out of an old legend. The audacity of it dazzled me still. I was reluctant to confront the Duc L'Envers, though I could not help but hold him my chiefest suspect. He had saved my life, once, on the battlefield of Troyes-le-Mont—and he had saved Ysandre's throne. Still, Melisande was right. If Barquiel L'Envers learned of the boy's whereabouts, I do not think he would use the knowledge to enable Ysandre to fulfill her dream of ending the blood-feud that haunted House Courcel's lineage, bringing the boy into the fold. Barquiel L'Envers thought it was a weak and foolish dream. If he found the child, he might not kill him out of hand—Elua grant it were so—but he might well make him disappear.

And in my heart of hearts, I was not entirely certain he was wrong in his beliefs. Ysandre's sentiments were noble, but I was there when Melisande threatened the Queen with enmity should she take her son. I do not think Ysandre, who had long regarded Melisande Shahrizai her enemy, appreciated the difference.

I did. If Melisande threw away the stakes of her long game for vengeance, everyone would lose. Mayhap Ysandre believed her safely contained. I had thought so too, once, when Melisande was brought to justice at Troyes-le-Monte. She had escaped from there, and a good many people were dead because of it, some of them dear to me. I knew better.

So did Barquiel L'Envers.

Thus passed our return journey, pensive and unhappy. And I spent long hours too in contemplation of the Jebean scroll and the revelations contained therein, wondering if what Melisande speculated might be true. After so long, it almost frightened me to hope . . . and I am not ashamed to admit that the enormity of the tasks confronting me frightened me, too. I was not a child any more, rash and careless with youth's immortality. I was thirty-two years old, and I had attained a stature to which I had never dreamed of aspiring in my younger days. Foremost courtesan of the City of Elua, yes; but not a respected peer of the realm, bearer of the Companion's Star, the Queen's confidante, Kushiel's Chosen, to whom the soldiers of the Unforgiven had knelt. All those things, I was.

And it scared me to think of risking it all.

Jebe-Barkal. It was a place on a map, a parrot-merchant in the Campo Grande. I knew little more. Our critics claim Terre d'Ange is insular, and it is true. We ally ourselves with the Caerdicci city-states, with Aragonia, because they share our borders; now with Alba, because Ysandre de la Courcel wed the Cruarch and broke the Straits' curse. We guard our boundaries against the Skaldi, because they have sought to take what is ours; we make war and alliance with Khebbel-im-Akkad, because it is too great a power to ignore. So much, and no more.

It is changing, a little. Ysandre looks outward more than any other D'Angeline monarch in memory, forging ties, fostering exchange. It is in a small part due to me, I think, that we have formal relations now with Illyria, with Kriti in Hellas. And Ysandre does not fear to send delegates to Ephesium, to Menekhet, to Carthage, even to the Umaiyyat.

But still—Jebe-Barkal! It was, I reflected glumly as Joscelin and I crossed the border into Terre d'Ange, very, very far away.

Our return was met with ebullience on the part of not only Ti-Philippe, but my household staff as well. Eugènie, my Mistress of Household, has been with me for over ten years now, and I have grown to value her eternal concern as much as her efficiency. I remember the grace and loyalty with which my lord Delaunay's staff ran his affairs, and have done my best to achieve the same. If I have succeeded, much of it has to do with paying a good wage and treating everyone in my employ with fairness and respect, but much is also due to Eugènie's excellent supervision. One thing neither of us will tolerate is careless gossip. The only time I have ever fired anyone in my service was for indiscretion. It pained me to do it, though it was necessary.

After we had bathed and changed our travel-worn attire, Joscelin and I met with Ti-Philippe in the garden courtyard to tell him what had transpired. His eyes grew round to hear it.

"Surely you're jesting."

"No." I shook my head. "I am sworn to aid her."

"Well." He reached out and popped a candied almond into his mouth, chewing thoughtfully. "What will you do, my lady? And more importantly," he swallowed and grinned, "what can *I* do?"

"*I* will ask questions," I said. "Judiciously, of course. You . . ." I smiled. "You can find me a Jebean scholar, Philippe. I've a document I need translated."

He pulled a face. "Poking about in academics' dusty corners? Sounds dull."

"Mayhap." I shrugged. "It will likely take you to Marsilikos, though. I doubt anyone in the City Academy reads Jeb'ez."

"Marsilikos." It cheered him to think on it. Marsilikos is a port city, beloved of sailors, a meeting-ground of the larger world. If there was any scholar who studied Jebe-Barkal, it would be at the Academy there. "Can I take Hugues, my lady? He wants to see the sea again."

"Why not? If it comes to it. And Philippe, I want you to call on Emile, in Night's Doorstep."

"The Tsingano?" Ti-Philippe looked perplexed, and Joscelin shot me a curious glance.

"He was Hyacinthe's closest companion. The Tsingani should know. Besides, they go everywhere and they hear things. Ask him if he will call upon me." I don't know what made me think of it. A hunch;

a duty. It had been one of Hyacinthe's last requests, that I bequeath his mother's house and his own enterprise, a livery stable, to Emile.

"As you wish." Ti-Philippe reached out as Eugènie entered with a platter of tidbits of quail in puffed pastry. "Eugènie, my goddess! You read my mind, or at least my stomach."

"Leave be, Messire Chevalier!" She batted his hand away sternly. "These are first for my lady." The platter was lowered beneath my nose, and I knew I would have no peace if I didn't select a couple of morsels. If Eugènie was deigning to serve us with her own hands, she'd probably made them herself, too. She regarded me with disapproval. "You'll need to eat more than that if you're about to go gallivanting about the map again, running yourself into a ragged sliver, my lady."

I must admit, my lord Delaunay's staff never spoke to him thusly. Then again, my lord Delaunay was not an *anguissette*. I retrieved the silver tongs and took two more pastries. "I'm not going anywhere yet, Eugènie."

"No." She sniffed. "But you will. You've got that look again."

Joscelin laughed. "I didn't know you could tell, Eugènie."

"After ten years, and her like a daughter to me?" She cast an acerbic eye on him. "I don't forget, Messire Cassiline. And you ought not to laugh, stuck to her side like a shadow."

"Well." Joscelin was fond of Eugènie. "I've my vow to think of."

"Your vow!" She shook the serving-tongs at him. "I vow I'll warm your backside if you don't bring my lady home safe. And don't think I won't do it, Messire Cassiline. I've grown grandchildren as tall as you."

It made Ti-Philippe laugh uproariously as he leaned forward to pick her platter clean, and even Joscelin smiled, but I heard the genuine worry behind Eugènie's absurd threat. "I'll be careful, Eugènie," I said softly. "Whatever I do. I promise."

"You said that last time and it nearly killed you." My Mistress of the Household leveled a significant gaze at me, her figure broad and imposing in the dusk-lit garden. "Love means hearth and home too, my lady. Don't forget it."

"I won't." I watched her go, picking her way across the courtyard, vast figure swaying like a sea-born ship. It was a warm evening, and the scent of lavender and rosemary hung in the moist air. A new maid-servant, one of Eugènie's nieces, slipped into the garden with a lit taper, kindling the lamps that hung about in glass globes, casting a fairy glow.

I had musicians play when I entertained here, harp and flute and tambour.

Jebe-Barkal. My heart ached at the thought of leaving this place, this gracious home. Eugènie was right; this, too, was love. And yet even as I thought it, I ached elsewhere, with the soul-deep need of an *anguissette* that no kindness, no compassion could assuage. I was bound by my nature as surely as any patron's shackles. Melisande might as well have set her diamond lead about my neck, I thought, a bitter laugh catching in my throat.

"Phèdre." It was Joscelin's voice, quiet and familiar. "Go to the temple."

"Elua's sanctuary?"

"No." He shook his head. "Kushiel's."

ℰLEVEN

FOR ALL that I am Kushiel's Chosen, I go seldom to his temple. I, who feel the prick of his dart throughout all my days, do not require the aid of his servants to seek atonement. My lord Kushiel has always provided ample opportunity to his *anguissette*. I do not often need to lay my penance at his feet. For me, his altar is everywhere.

Only once before has Joscelin advised me thusly, after our escape from slavery in the wilds of Skaldia, and then, as now, I remembered what I so often forgot: that Joscelin was priest as well as warrior.

Now, as then, I listened. I went.

They asked no questions, Kushiel's priests, but only nodded to see me. Even if my face had not been known throughout the City of Elua, they would have known me by the scarlet mote. Kushiel's priests keep his lore sacred. Clad in stygian robes and wearing the full bronze masks of ceremony that hide even gender, they escorted me into the baths of purification and thence to the temple proper, the massive doors clanging shut behind us.

It is a simple space, high-vaulted, enclosed with thick stone walls blackened by generations of smoke rising from the candles that illuminate it. I made an offering of gold and poured incense on the altar-fire. A billow of smoke arose, stinging my eyes with musky fragrance. The face of Kushiel's great effigy swam above me, wreathed in smoke, stern and brazen, hands crossed on his breast bearing his rod and flail. When I had done, his priests helped me undress until I stood naked before him.

A sharp breath, indrawn behind a mask; I don't know whose. Even Kushiel's priests are not immune. I know what they saw, my bare skin glowing white by candlelight, the vivid black lines of my marque etching my spine, thorny and intricate, accented with crimson droplets. It was limned by Master Robert Tielhard himself, before he died; it is a crime now, to duplicate it for any but an *anguissette*. The Marquists' Guild voted it so.

And I am the only one.

I twined my hair behind my neck in a lover's-haste knot and knelt on scrubbed flagstones before the whipping post. Without further breech of protocol, a masked priest lashed my wrists to the post, tying them tight with rawhide thongs. My arms were stretched, pulling at their sockets, and my breath came quick and hard.

Then came the scourging.

They are masters of the art, Kushiel's priests—for an art it is, although ignorant people may believe otherwise. At the first stroke of iron-tipped lashes against my back, I cried out, jerking against my bonds. Pain, blessedly welcome, burst across my skin.

"My lord Kushiel!" I gasped. "Forgive me, for I do not know your will!"

The lashes of the flogger fell upon me again, too quickly for readiness; I discerned a man's touch in it. Streaks of fire laced my vision and my breath burned in my lungs, forced out in an involuntary cry. The rough wood of the whipping post pressed against my cheek. Again he struck, and again. Agony blossomed in me with an unbearable pleasure. I heard my own voice whimpering, and a priest's sibilant whisper above it, reminding me.

"Make now your confession."

"My lord Kushiel." Sunk on my knees, I craned back my head, seeing my own arms foreshortened and Kushiel's serene, pitiless face far beyond, floating in a haze of red. "Ah!" The iron-tipped lashes curled about my ribcage, biting deep. "The path is too dark, my lord, and I am afraid!"

No mercy. The flogger struck without pity, a whistling crack in the air, spattering wetness as it kissed my flesh. My head fell forward to hang upon my breast and I wept for shame.

"My lord Kushiel," I whispered, hearing my voice broken and small, clotted with tears. A shudder of release wracked my pain-stricken body as I uttered the fearful words. "I wish in my heart that I were no longer your Chosen."

There was a pause, the chastiser's rhythm broken . . . and then the air sung and the flogger came down hard, bursting against my lacerated skin in an explosion of pain. Once . . . twice . . . thrice, and it was ended, leaving me limp and gasping as I sagged in my bonds, feeling at peace.

"Be free of it," a voice murmured. I heard the sound of a dipper plunging, and then searing agony as saltwater was poured tenderly over my weals. Once more my body jerked and I flung back my head, seeing Kushiel's unaltered countenance through tear-streaked eyes.

It was done. I sank back onto my heels, lassitude infusing my limbs as the priests untied my wrists. With impersonal care, they helped me dress. The touch of my undergarments set off waves of pain.

To my surprise, one of the priests dismissed the others with a wordless gesture. When they had gone, he reached up and drew back the hood of his robe, removing his bronze mask. A mortal face, strong and stern, framed with iron-grey hair, regarded me.

"Phèdre nó Delaunay, Comtesse de Montrève." Unmuffled by the mask, his voice was deep and resonant. "I am Michel Nevers, foremost among Kushiel's priesthood in the City of Elua. I would speak with you."

"My lord priest." I curtsied, swallowing against the discomfort. "As you please."

The chamber to which Michel Nevers escorted me was dimly luxuriant, lit with too few lamps and hung about with tapestries. There were bookshelves on the walls, laden with well-tended volumes, the bindings cracked and much repaired. I saw a copy of Sarea's illustrated *History of Namarre*, that contains the story of Naamah's daughter Mara, Kushiel's handmaiden and, some say, the first-ever *anguissette*.

"Drink." The priest Michel poured me a glass of strong red wine. "It strengthens the blood. And you have need of strength."

Obedient, I sipped, and then drank deeper, tasting in the wine the bursting life of the grape, nourished by sun and rain, fed by dark earth enriched with death's decay; the soil of Terre d'Ange, moistened by Blessed Elua's own blood. Earth the womb that begot him, blood and tears the seed that quickened him. These things I tasted, and the violent death of the grape, the lusty joy of the commonfolk that crushed it, the vintner's careful lore, time and the slow wisdom of age transmuting it into wine, the oaken cask that warded it whispering of a tree's immense lifetime and the bite of the axe that made an end to it.

"You see." He poured a second glass and held it aloft, regarding it. "So much does it take to make a glass of wine."

"My lord." I set down my glass, wincing as my gown drew taut across my shoulders. "Do you seek to lesson me?"

"No." Michel Nevers smiled, unexpected and kind. "Only to remind you that, like the grape, we do not know to what end our brief lives will be transformed. You no longer wish to be an *anguissette?*"

"I am afraid." I folded my hands in my lap and met his gaze squarely. "My path lies in darkness, and Kushiel's Dart pricks me to unwanted desires. I wound my beloved with every choice I make, every breath I draw. Yes, my lord priest; I wish Kushiel would choose another. Have I not served him well? I have sworn this quest on my own honor, to free one who was a friend to me. Is it not enough? Must I be goaded every step of the way?"

He bowed his head, iron-grey hair falling over his brow. "You speak of Melisande Shahrizai."

"Yes."

The priest rose to survey his bookshelves, touching a few volumes here and there. "Throughout the history of Terre d'Ange, there surface tales of *anguissettes*. The lineage of Elua's Companions carries dangerous gifts, and none more so than Kushiel's. To impart suffering without compassion . . ." He raised his eyes skyward. "It is an abomination. Thence the need for an *anguissette* to balance the scales. To endure suffering untold, with infinite compassion—"

"Why me?" I interrupted. "My lord priest, I understand these things, to the best of my ability. Melisande Shahrizai is Kushiel's scion, mayhap the most deadly the realm has known, and I have played my role in thwarting her. Why? I've no divinely cursed lineage to boast of; I'm no Mara, gotten on Naamah herself by a condemned murderer. My mother was an adept of Jasmine House and my father was a merchant's son, spendthrift and foolish. I don't *want* to endure untold suffering with infinite compassion—"

"Phèdre." The priest raised his hand. "Forgive me. I did not mean to imply that such was your lot. Why you?" He shook his head. "I cannot say. We may spend many lifetimes upon the wheel of life before Blessed Elua admits us through the gates into the true Terre d'Ange-that-lies-beyond. Mayhap Kushiel in his infinite mercy allows you to atone for some crime that cannot be spoken. I do not know. I know only that he has chosen wisely, and if his touch lingers, his work is not yet done." Stooping, he kissed my brow with lips surprisingly gentle. "Kushiel's Chosen, Naamah's Servant. You bear the marks of both, and both you have served truly and well. Do not forget, they are merely the Companions of Blessed Elua, in whose bright shadow all of us follow—even Cassiel."

"It is hard, my lord," I whispered.

"Yes." Michel Nevers nodded, and I saw in his gaze something resembling infinite compassion. "It is."

Thus, then, my visit to the temple of Kushiel, and if I left it no wiser, at least I left it oddly comforted, both by the priest's words, and by the penance I had endured. The aftermath of pain left me calm and clear-headed. Although the yearning had not gone—it never left me completely—the tempest induced by my encounter with Melisande had subsided.

Joscelin tended to me that night, massaging unguent into the fresh weals. I lay content beneath his hands, enjoying the sensation, my head pillowed on my arms.

"All of this in love's name," he mused. "I don't pretend to understand it, Phèdre."

"No," I murmured, heavy-lidded. The unguent stung where the lash had broken skin. It felt good. "But you were right to send me."

"I know. I ought to, by now. How you and I ever survived one another is a mystery." In his voice was a fondness and humor no one else could ever comprehend save we two, whose love must surely make Blessed Elua smile. "Ah, well. You'll need to see the marquist, love." His fingertips traced a welt where it crossed the etched lines of my marque. "It will need retouching. Here," his fingers moved, "and here."

I shuddered under his touch, that transmuted pain into yearning. If we were ill-suited in the manifestations of our desires, still, there was an especial torment in knowing it, in the need to steal bliss by illicit means. Feeling my body grow languid with desire, I breathed his name, half-laughing as it caught in my throat. "Joscelin . . ."

"Do you want . . . ?" Joscelin whispered, one hand sliding over the curve of my buttocks.

"Yes." Rolling over, I drew him down to me. "Oh, yes."

TWELVE

In THE morning, I steeled my courage and presented myself at court.

I did not think Ysandre would welcome our news, and I was right. Her face went white and she paced the drawing-room like an angry lioness, lips moving in silent imprecations. Joscelin stood a step nearer to me than was his wont in the royal presence, and I was glad Drustan and Sibeal were there.

The annals of history will not show that Ysandre de la Courcel had a fierce temper. I have seldom seen her loose it unguarded, and never without provocation. It was a measure of her trust that she permitted herself to display it before us.

Nonetheless, it made me nervous.

"Who?" she demanded, halting with arms akimbo. "Who would do such a thing, and tell me naught of it?"

I opened my mouth, and closed it prudently.

"The Shahrizai." The Queen's lips thinned. "Will they ever be a plague on my reign? I will send for Duc Faragon . . ." She stopped, and I saw her remember. The last time she had summoned the Duc de Shahrizai before her throne, it had been because of her uncle Barquiel L'Envers' unorthodox meddling.

"My lady," I said. "Ysandre. Melisande is certain it was none of her kin."

"What do you think?" Drustan mab Necthana asked me.

"I think she is telling the truth."

"The whole truth?" Ysandre looked hard at me.

"Probably not." I shrugged. "One may assume it, with Melisande. But what she spoke was truth."

The Queen's sharp gaze turned to Joscelin. "What do you say, Cassiline?"

"Your majesty." He bowed to her with crossed forearms. "I concur with my lady Phèdre. Melisande Shahrizai is as dangerous as a viper, and twice as subtle, but I do not believe she lied."

"That child," Ysandre said, half to herself. "That poor boy. I warned her of as much."

Drustan was murmuring to Sibeal, clarifying the exchange in Cruithne. On her face alone I saw somewhat different reflected: hope, and a visionary's clear certainty.

"It was a true dream," she said in her softly accented D'Angeline when he had done. Her wide-set dark eyes turned my way. "You will find a way to free him."

Hyacinthe.

Jebe-Barkal.

"My lady Sibeal," I said. "I pray it may be so. But I have made a promise, and I must keep it. It may be that a child's life hangs in the balance."

"And it may be too late." Ysandre did not mince words. "Whosoever is responsible."

"I know." I met her eyes. "Still, I must look."

"Whosoever is responsible." She took a deep breath. "Whoever it is, they will face our justice, Phèdre, as surely as any criminal. Do you understand this to be true?"

"Yes, my lady. Ysandre." I knew what she was saying, and I bled for her. Ysandre de la Courcel was no fool. She had bethought herself of her uncle, and his ungentle methods.

"For so long as he lived," she mused, "this child Imriel de la Courcel has posed a threat to my throne and my daughters' inheritance. I have always known it. And I have always been prepared to deal with it, in my own way, in accordance with the dictum of Blessed Elua. I will show no clemency to any who seek to deal with it otherwise."

"I understand."

Ysandre raised her eyebrows. "You will, I trust, report to me before you do Melisande Shahrizai, near-cousin?"

"My lady!" I protested. "Yes. Of course."

And with that, we were dismissed.

In the halls of the Palace, Joscelin and I spoke of our meeting in low tones, offering courteous greetings to those nobles we passed. Only a few scant weeks ago, we would have numbered ourselves among them, D'Angeline peers who came to meet and mingle in the various salons, the Hall of Games, come for gossip and flirtation and such games of power as are played out in those elegant, marble walls. Now, it all seemed trivial.

"Did you see her face?" I murmured to Joscelin. "Although she did not say it, I think she bethought herself of Barquiel L'Envers."

"I saw." He paused as we drew nigh to the Marquis d'Arguil and his lady wife, a handsome couple in their forties, very much a la mode. Attending them a pace and a half to the rear was a Cassiline Brother, a young man in ash grey with a cultivated look of stern hauteur. "Well met, my lord," Joscelin said politely, "my lady."

"Comtesse!" The Marquise d'Arguil took my hands in her own, offering the kiss of greeting. "We invited you to our cherry-blossom fête, you and your gorgeous consort, and you were gone from the City, heartless creatures. You must promise to come to our next."

"I will try, my lady, but I make no promises." From the corner of my eye, I saw their Cassiline attendant make an ostentatious greeting to Joscelin, inlaid vambraces glittering as he swept his arms crossed before him and bowed. "Betimes my business requires travel."

Ten years ago, after Joscelin's duel in the Temple of Asherat, an unprecedented influx of noble-born families sought to revive the ancient tradition of sending their middle sons to the Cassiline Brotherhood. Even as the Queen had eliminated her own Cassiline Guard, it had become fashionable for minor royalty to hire them. I think the old Prefect, under whom Joscelin had trained, would have dismissed the majority of applicants on both sides out of hand. The new Prefect did not. Most of the would-be Cassilines never completed training, but a few stuck it out, and were now assigned to wealthy wards, sworn to protect and serve.

And all of them regarded Joscelin with a desperate mix of hero-worship and contempt. His defeat of the traitorous Cassiline who sought Ysandre's life was the stuff of enduring legend; but he had left the Brotherhood for my sake, and been declared anathema for it. Those who remain, honoring their vows of celibacy, resent him for it.

"Your business." The Marquis d'Arguil smiled knowingly. "Naamah's business, you mean!"

"As my lord says." I smiled in reply, laying two fingers over my lips in the gesture betokening discretion. Joscelin, unseen, rolled his eyes. "I will do my best."

We parted ways with cordial farewells, the d'Arguils' Cassiline guard making another ceremonial display, bowing low enough to reveal his hair clubbed at the back of his neck. He bore no sword, though, only daggers. Ysandre had forbidden it in the Palace. This time, Joscelin acknowledged him with a dour nod. The hilt of his sword, wrapped in well-worn leather, was visible over his shoulder, token of the Queen's trust.

"Elua preserve me," Joscelin said when they had left. "Was I ever such a prig?"

I took his arm. "Worse."

He laughed. "Well, mayhap. Remind me to have plans when next the d'Arguils invite us to a fête. Phèdre." There was a change in his voice, and I glanced up at him. "Had you planned on questioning L'Envers yourself?"

"I had." I gauged his thoughtful frown. "You think Ysandre will send for him?"

"Mm-hmm." He looked down at me. "He's her nearest kin. I think she'd confront him privately before accusing him for the world to see. How badly do you wish to ask him first?"

I thought about it. If Ysandre had a flaw, it was in her willingness to believe the best of people she loved. "Badly enough. Where is he?"

"Champs-de-Guerre." Joscelin raised his brows, offering an unspoken comment on Barquiel L'Envers' continued appointment to the role of Royal Commander. It had been a temporary thing, born out of necessity after Percy de Somerville's betrayal. But Ysandre had never revoked her uncle's appointment or named another commander. "It's less than a day's ride. We could arrive before she decides to send a courier if we left this afternoon."

"Well." I squeezed his arm gratefully. "It seems our business does require travel."

If I thought we would get away clean, I was mistaken. Ti-Philippe was awaiting our return, bursting with news. He could scarce wait for me to finish giving instructions to Eugènie to prepare an overnight travel bag for our journey to the training-grounds and barracks of the Royal Army.

"My lady!" he said, grinning fit to split his face. "You were wrong. There *is* a scholar at the City Academy who's studied Jebean lore, only she's a musician, not a linguist. Her father was a master drummer at Eglantine House fifty years ago; he travelled the world by sea after he made his marque, and studied in Jebe-Barkal many years. She made a fair-copy of the scroll, and thought she could have it translated on the morrow. And the Tsingano, Emile, he promised to call upon you in the morning."

"Tomorrow?" I pulled a face. "I've made plans to go to Champs-de-Guerre. Tell the Jebean scholar . . . what's her name?"

"Audine Davul."

"Tell my lady Davul that I will call on her on my return, and tell Emile . . . tell Emile I'll do the same."

"In Night's Doorstep?" Ti-Philippe sounded skeptical. I laughed.

"Why not? It's been too long since I had a drink at the Cockerel. It was my haven, once upon a time. Do you remember, we went there when first I brought you to the City. Mayhap I've been too long in rarified circles."

"I'll tell him." Ti-Philippe paused. "My lady, he said to tell you that Manoj is dead, and the *kumpanias* of the Tsingani speak the name of Hyacinthe, son of Anasztaizia, at the crossroads."

I went still, remembering. Manoj was Hyacinthe's grandfather; the Tsingan kralis, King of the Tsingani. Anasztaizia was his daughter, Hyacinthe's mother, betrayed and reviled by her own people. It would mean more than words could say to Hyacinthe that the Tsingani had not forgotten him, the Prince of Travellers, that he was remembered as his mother's son. "Tell him . . ." I said softly. "Tell him I am grateful for the knowledge."

"As you wish," Ti-Philippe said, keeping his reservations to himself.

With our affairs thus in order and Eugènie's admonitions ringing in our ears, Joscelin and I took our leave once more, and the white walls of the City of Elua fell behind us as we headed northward toward the Champs-de-Guerre. I told him as we rode what Ti-Philippe had related to me. Unlike my chevalier, Joscelin understood. He had been there, when Hyacinthe made his choice, turning his back on the inheritance that awaited him to lay the gift of the *dromonde* before me and assuage my terrors.

"The Prince of Travellers," Joscelin said, shaking his head. "Do you know, I truly never believed him before that? Until we met the Tsingan kralis himself, I thought it was just another damned Tsingano lie."

"So did I," I murmured. "Elua forgive me."

"Well, I'm not sure even Hyacinthe knew the truth of it until then." He jogged his mount alongside mine, eventually glancing sidelong at me. "Master of the Straits. It's hard to think of him thus. You do know she's in love with him?"

I gazed at the road before me betwixt my mount's forward-pricked ears. "Sibeal?"

"Mm-hmm."

I thought of the hope that had shone in her face, in her soft-spoken words. *You will find a way to free him.* I wondered if Hyacinthe knew, and what he felt about it. I wondered what I felt about it. But all I said aloud was, "I know."

Thirteen

WE PASSED the night in a pleasant inn, enjoying our evening meal in an open-air courtyard and conversing with other travellers. In the morning we found our mounts well rested, coats curried to a high sheen, led out to the roadside mounting-block by a country lad, his hands and feet too large for his gangling frame. He blushed and bowed when Joscelin gave him a silver centime, stealing glances at me beneath lashes as long as a girl's. One day he would break hearts, I thought, but not yet.

And then we were on our way again, riding down tree-lined roads through the fertile heart of D'Angeline farmland.

The sun was not yet high overhead when we reached Champs-de-Guerre, those broad green fields where the standing army of Terre d'Ange trained and was barracked. Inquiring at the officer's quarters, we were told that Duc Barquiel L'Envers was reviewing a corps of infantrymen on the main field.

"Shall we wait?" Joscelin asked. "They'll break soon enough for the midday meal."

"No," I said decisively. "Let's meet Lord Barquiel on the field."

An obliging lieutenant directed us to the place, though I reckon we'd have found it by the noise alone. It was a vast field, green turf churned to muddy collops by a thousand booted feet, with the grunting of men at strife and the clash of armor against armor and sword on shield resounding in the sunlit air.

'Twas easy enough to pick out Barquiel L'Envers, striding alongside the skirmish, a surcoat of L'Envers' purple over his steel-plated armor, shouting exhortations at subcommanders and infantrymen alike. I drew rein on my mount and Joscelin followed suit.

Presently Barquiel noticed, and gave orders to his standard-bearer to signal the practice ended. He himself came striding over with a grin.

"Well, well, well." Planting his feet, Barquiel L'Envers cocked his head at me. "Comtesse Phèdre nó Delaunay de Montrève. To what do I owe this unexpected pleasure?"

"Your grace." I inclined my head, still seated in my saddle. Sunlight flashed on the Companion's Star pinned at my breast, an unsubtle reminder that I had leave to address him as an equal. "There is a matter I wish to discuss with you."

Beneath his turbaned helmet, an affectation from his days as the ambassador to Khebbel-im-Akkad, Barquiel L'Envers raised his brows. "Is there, indeed? And what does my lady Comtesse offer in exchange for free range to my thoughts?"

I sat back, nonplussed. "What does my lord Duc desire?"

If it was an assignation, I had no intention of granting it; but Barquiel L'Envers was too clever for aught so obvious. His violet gaze, so like his niece Ysandre's, moved off me and onto Joscelin. "There is a myth," he said casually, "popular among my men, that a bare-headed Cassiline with a sword and vambraces can defeat a soldier in field armor bearing sword and shield in open battle. I say it is romantic folly. What do you say, Messire Verreuil? Shall we put it to the test?"

"Your grace." Joscelin's voice was mild. "I cannot claim that honor. I have been declared anathema by the Cassiline Brotherhood."

"Ah, yes." L'Envers smiled. "The Queen's Champion, Lady Phèdre's consort, the eternal apostate. And yet, Messire Verreuil, when people say *The Cassiline*, they speak of you. Will you not cross swords with me?"

Joscelin and I exchanged a glance. No words, not even a shrug were needed; we knew each other's minds, and the decision was his. "As you say, your grace," he said to L'Envers, "I am Cassiel's servant still in my own way." He shook his head. "And as such, I draw my sword only to kill, my lord. I will not draw it on you."

"A convenient prohibition," Barquiel L'Envers observed to his men, who had drawn nigh and watched with interest.

"My lord L'Envers." Joscelin dismounted with grace, handing his reins to a startled soldier. Facing Barquiel L'Envers, he bowed with Cassiline precision, daggers ringing free of their sheaths as he straightened. The ghost of a smile hovered at the corner of his lips. "I said I would not draw my sword. I did not say I refused your request."

A great cheer arose from the gathered infantrymen, who hastily arrayed themselves in a vast semicircle, clearing space for the combatants. Someone's squire ran pelting off the field to alert the encampment, and one of the subcommanders pounded another on the shoulder with glee. Barquiel L'Envers' eyebrows disappeared beneath the edge of his helmet in patent disbelief. "You propose to fight me with your *daggers?*"

"Your grace wished to fight a Cassiline," Joscelin said. "*The* Cassiline?"

There was a pause, and then L'Envers laughed aloud, slapping a hand on his thigh. "So be it, then! Till first blood, or the other cries yield, whichever comes first. Anton, my shield!" He grinned, showing white teeth, and shook his head. "Naamah's tits, but you've got balls, Cassiline. I almost like you for it."

Joscelin smiled politely, crossed daggers at the ready.

It could have been worse, I will say that much. L'Envers wore a foot-soldier's training gear of cuirass, greaves and gauntlets, and not full armor. Still, the tall, kite-shaped shield into which he slid his left arm would afford a good measure of protection, and his longsword had three times the reach of Joscelin's daggers. Cold steel, these weapons were, and honed to a killing edge. I sat my mount in quiet fear, putting a serene face on it as the Duc L'Envers hoisted his shield, testing its weight, and made a few passes with his sword. All over Champs-de-Guerre, shouting echoed, and the sound of running feet and pounding hooves as the ranks of our audience swelled. An impromptu honor guard formed itself around me, soldiers jostling to fend off their comrades. L'Envers' squire adjusted the cheekplates on his lord's helmet, tightening the strap beneath his chin.

"Shall we begin?" Barquiel L'Envers inquired.

Joscelin merely bowed.

The fight began slowly, both combatants circling for advantage. For all his arrogance, Barquiel L'Envers was a veteran of countless battles, not to be goaded into rash action. He made a testing thrust with his sword, eyes narrowing as Joscelin deflected it easily, his steel-clad left forearm sending the blow wide as he stepped inward and turned, bringing the right-hand dagger up with deceptive speed. It glanced off L'Envers' shield, which he swung in to cover his exposed side. Joscelin shifted backward, weight on his rear leg as he brought his daggers back to their crossed defensive pose, turning to meet the next attack.

I knew by heart the steps he took, the graceful, flowing turns of the Cassiline forms, daggers weaving an intricate pattern of bright steel. I had seen him perform them a thousand times and more, alone in our garden. Barquiel L'Envers sidled warily around him, leading with his shielded left side. Without warning, his sword-arm snaked forward in a low, lateral stroke aimed at Joscelin's midriff. I gasped out loud . . . but Joscelin was already moving, turning to his left, dagger sweeping down to intercept, catching the deadly edge between the curved quillon and the base of the blade, his right elbow rising as he turned to land a jabbing blow at L'Enver's throat.

Barquiel L'Envers coughed, eyes watering; I daresay the blow had bruised his larynx. "You wouldn't try that against a man wearing a gorget, Cassiline," he said in a strained tone.

"No, my lord." Joscelin smiled slightly. "I would not."

Catching his breath, L'Envers launched a flurry of an attack; short, quick blows that pressed Joscelin hard and left no opening for him to close. I watched it with my heart in my throat, for any number of them might have been deadly had they landed. To this day, I honestly do not know if the Duc could have pulled his stroke short if Joscelin's guard had faltered. Blessed Elua be thanked, it did not.

But if it became clear that Barquiel's sword could not penetrate the flashing circle of Joscelin's daggers and vambraces, it was equally clear that Joscelin could not get within reach of the Duc's longsword and past his shield. Around and around they went, churning the muddy field to mire, while the murmur of wagering rose among the watching army and cold sweat trickled between my shoulderblades.

At last, Barquiel L'Envers stepped back, setting his shield high and lifting his sword overhead, stepping up hard and fast to bring it down in a swift blow aimed at the top of Joscelin's head. In a single, blurred movement, Joscelin raised his crossed daggers to catch the blow, pinioning the sword between his own blades. For a moment, they were locked thusly, straining—and then L'Envers brought his shield up with a fierce jerk, driving it into Joscelin's unprotected face.

Joscelin staggered backward, twisting away from L'Envers' sword, and the soldiers surged forward. Unnerved, my mount shifted restively, tossing its head and blocking my view. By the time I got her under control, the two men had closed again and were grappling. Joscelin had L'Envers' sword-arm pinned low, blade caught in the curved quillon of his dagger; L'Envers pushed hard against him with his shield, striving to bring it up under his chin. Their legs were braced, feet struggling for purchase in the slippery mud.

It was Joscelin who faltered. I saw it, as they heaved and strained, saw his left foot slide, almost of its own volition, saw his left knee buckle. Overborne by L'Envers' shield, their blades entangled, he went down. With a crow of victory, Barquiel L'Envers wrenched his sword free and leveled the blade, tip pointing at Joscelin's throat. "Do you yield, Messire Cassiline?"

On his back, Joscelin put up his hands. "My lord, I yield."

The army roared its approval and I let out a sigh, glad it was over. Barquiel L'Envers chuckled and handed his sword and shield to his squire. Removing his helmet, he tucked it under one arm and extended the other hand to Joscelin, pulling him to his feet. "Well fought, Messire Verreuil, though I daresay your lady won't thank me for the condition of your attire. Still, you've earned her the right to her questions. Shall we retire to my quarters? I'll give you a proper welcome and see if my valet can't do something about that mud."

And with that, we were adjourned.

The Royal Commander's quarters at Champs-de-Guerre were spacious and well appointed, though not luxurious. A scattering of Akkadian pillows and carpets gave it Barquiel L'Envers' stamp. No sign of a woman's hand was in evidence. In all the years I have known him, I've met the Duc's wife only once. A strong woman in her own right, she seems content to run their ancestral estates in Namarre while her ambitious husband plies his skills elsewhere.

True to his word, L'Envers made Joscelin the loan of a pair of clean breeches, sending his mire-sodden doublet and hose with his valet. A repast of cold chicken was served, along with salted melon slices, crusty bread and a sharp white cheese. Afterward, Joscelin sat cross-legged on the floor in his linen shirt and borrowed breeches, methodically cleaning mud from his weapons and gear while I spoke to Barquiel L'Envers.

"My lady Phèdre." Still pleased with his victory, the Duc was in an expansive mood. "What is this matter you wish to discuss with me?"

"Your grace." I inclined my head to him. "What do you know of Imriel de la Courcel?"

"Melisande's boy." L'Envers shot me a shrewd glance. "Why? What do you know, Comtesse?"

I shrugged. "You have looked for him, my lord. I know that much."

He pursed his lips and stared into his wineglass, deciding how much to tell me. "Yes," he said at length. "I've looked." He set down his glass and looked frankly at me. "Your methods differ from mine, *anguissette*; on that much, we are agreed. The last time we failed to trust one another, we nearly gave the realm into Melisande Shahrizai's hands.

If I tell you what I know, will you return the courtesy?"

The sound of Joscelin's movements paused, then continued. "I will," I said.

"All right." Barquiel L'Envers drew a breath and ran one hand through his fair, short-cropped hair. "You know I've ties to Khebbel-im-Akkad, and to Aragonia. I've had agents search for word in both places, high and low; and from thence, Ephesium, Carthage and the Umaiyyat. No one has found a trace of the boy. I trust you've implored your connections in La Serenissima, Hellas and Illyria to do the same?"

"Yes." There was no strain in his voice, no flicker to his eyelids, not a single one of the tell-tales of a lie. "And I have sought rumor in Terre d'Ange as well."

L'Envers nodded. "As I thought. Anafiel Delaunay trained you well. If it were anyone close to Ysandre, I trust you'd have found them in ten years."

"It wasn't."

He stared at me. I saw his pupils dilate as comprehension dawned. Fear and excitement look much the same at close range; I wasn't sure which it was. "You know." He caught his breath in his bruised throat, coughed impatiently, closed one hand hard around my wrist. A few feet away, Joscelin unobtrusively readied his daggers. "You know!" L'Envers' eyes gleamed, his lips parted in a eager smile. "Who is it?"

"It doesn't matter, my lord," I said, ignoring his grip. "The boy is missing."

Letting go my wrist, Barquiel L'Envers swore a stream of invective filled with heartfelt passion. On the floor, Joscelin relaxed and continued cleaning his gear. I waited until the Duc had finished, and then told him an abbreviated version of Melisande's story.

"And you thought I had done it?" he asked when I was done.

"My lord has the means and the wits," I said diplomatically. "It occurred to Melisande as well. And," I added, "I suspect you'll be hearing from the Queen."

"A dubious compliment. I'll take it as such." Barquiel L'Envers grinned and shook his head. "Elua's sanctuary! I thought she must have spirited the lad off to Skaldia. It's the one place we've no means of searching, and like as not she's still got ties there from Selig's day. I never dreamed she'd allies among Elua's priesthood."

"Nor did I, my lord," I said. "Nor did I."

Joscelin, scrubbing at the buckles of his vambraces, made a sound of profound disapproval.

"Well." L'Envers glanced reflexively in his direction. "If she's out-smarted you and me, my lady Phèdre, it seems she's outsmarted herself as well. I'll not pretend I'd be sorry to hear of the child's demise. Innocent he may be, but while he lives, he's a weapon to be used against the descendents of House L'Envers. And I mislike not knowing whose hand might wield him," he said, looking back at me. "Has Ysandre summoned the priest responsible?"

"Not yet."

"She will." He leaned back in his chair. "It may take her some time to work up the resolve to confront the priesthood of Elua, but she'll do it. I know my niece."

I nodded, taking his words for warning. "Duly noted, my lord. My thanks for your candour."

"Ah." L'Envers grinned at Joscelin's bowed head. "You paid a fair price for it. I trust you're satisfied I was not less than forthcoming? Or do you require me to swear on it . . . by the burning river?"

I flushed as he spoke the ancient password of House L'Envers, the vow that binds its members to truth and succor. It was with those very words that I had charged him to defend the City of Elua against the traitorous Percy de Somerville, words given me in trust by his kins-woman, Nicola L'Envers y Aragon. "Would you so swear, if I asked?"

The Duc's gaze never wavered. "I would."

"No," I said. "I believe you."

It was late afternoon when Joscelin and I took our leave of Champs-de-Guerre, reckoning we could make the City of Elua by nightfall if we rode without stopping, for the days had grown long with the coming of summer. Barquiel L'Envers' valet had done a good job of cleaning Joscelin's clothing, now dry and only slightly stained. He was in good spirits despite his loss.

"If it wasn't L'Envers," he said, speculating aloud, "then who?"

"I don't know. You think he was telling the truth?"

"As surely as you do." He glanced at me. "It increases the odds that the boy's alive. L'Envers is right, he's a dangerous weapon for someone's hand."

"I wish I could think of whose." I sighed. "You know we're going to have to go to the Sanctuary of Elua in Landras and ask questions before Ysandre decides to summon Brother Selbert."

"Mm-hmm."

"Joscelin?" I looked at his calm profile. "You let him win, didn't you."

The corner of his mouth lifted in the hint of a smile. "What self-respecting Cassiline would do such a thing?"

I raised my brows at him. "Only one."

Joscelin laughed and made no reply.

FOURTEEN

UPON RETURNING to the City of Elua, I sent word to Ysandre, reporting briefly on my meeting with her uncle the Duc L'Envers and asserting my belief in his innocence. I stated also my intention to travel to Siovale, to the Sanctuary of Elua in Landras, in order to question the priests there about the disappearance of Imriel de la Courcel.

Well and so; if Ysandre wished to forestall me, let her do so. Until she did, I would pursue my inquiry in my own fashion.

First, though, I kept my postponed appointment with Audine Davul at the City Academy.

I have been there many times, but seldom to the Musicians' Hall, where I was escorted past various salons from which issued sounds both melodious and cacophonous. Students of all ages were intent upon their lessons, learning to play harp and lyre and mandolin, tambors and timbales, flutes and pipes—and of course, the drums. Audine Davul's quarters held more drums than I ever believed existed, great and small, low and squat, tall and narrow, goat hide stretched taut over bases of wood, copper and ceramic, steel kettles struck with tiny mallets, hand-held rattling drums. And each one, I was told, had its own voice.

An intent, wiry woman in her forties, grey-eyed and honey-skinned, Audine Davul was the product of her D'Angeline father's liaison with an Ephesian dancing-girl. When her mother died in childbirth, her father had taken her with him on his wanderings, paying passage aboard ship with his drumming, entertaining crews and setting the beat for the rowers. It was said that an oarship had wings when Antoine Davul gave the pace. From the time Audine was five until she was fifteen, they had lived in Jebe-Barkal. She grew up speaking and writing Jeb'ez while her father studied the "mountain-talkers," the percussive language of the great hollow log drums used in the highlands of Jebe-Barkal.

Audine Davul had translated the scroll Melisande had called the *Kefra Neghast*.

"Yes," she said, indicating the vellum parchment she had prepared. Not only was a translation in D'Angeline neatly transposed beneath each line of Jeb'ez, but she had included phonetic markings to indicate the pronunciation of the unfamiliar script. "Your information is correct; this is the story of Melek al'Hakim, the Prince of Saba. One does not hear it so much, any more."

I held the precious document gingerly, scanning the text. "It's true, then? He was Shalomon's son?"

"True." The music teacher smiled, turning calloused palms outward. "What is true? It is true that this legend is told in Jebe-Barkal, where the inhabitants of Saba fled after quarreling with the Pharaoh of Menekhet, and ruled for many years. I have translated the words truly as they are written. No more can I tell you, Comtesse."

"Thank you." Until that moment, I hadn't dared believe with a whole heart. Putting down the parchment, I flung both arms about her neck, impulsively kissing her cheek. "Maîtresse Davul, thank you!"

She laughed, returning my embrace. "Now the Academy will talk, saying I have known the favors of Phèdre nó Delaunay." Faint lines crinkled at the corners of her eyes. "And mayhap it will bring more students to study drumming."

"I hope it does." I accepted the scroll-case she handed me containing the original Jebean manuscript. "You've never been back to Jebe-Barkal, have you?"

"No." Audine Davul shook her head. "My father's feet followed a rhythm only he could hear. I did but follow him. When he brought me at last to Terre d'Ange, I knew I had come home. I have brought his rhythms with me to the City of Elua. I do not wish to leave it."

I laid a purse on the table before her. "Please accept this with my thanks for your excellent work. With your permission, I'd like to talk more with you about Jebe-Barkal some time. I'm only sorry my schedule precludes it now."

She bowed from the waist, smile-lines deepening. "As you wish, Comtesse. I am not going anywhere."

I envied her that, I thought in the carriage during my homeward journey. Strange, how her father's wandering urge had grounded itself in his half-D'Angeline daughter. Strange, that the child of a former adept of Eglantine House and an Ephesian dancing-girl should make her life in the arcane pursuits of academia. I thought about my own parents—my beautiful, languorous mother and my foolish, spendthrift father—and wondered for the thousandth time if they had ever known what became of me, if they had ever linked the Comtesse de Montrève, Delaunay's *anguissette*, the Queen's confidante, with the flawed, pretty girl-child whose marque they had sold to the Dowayne of Cereus House. They surrendered all claim on me to the Night Court, and until I was ten, I knew no other life. I never saw my parents again.

It was not a bad life, on the whole. Each of the Thirteen Houses has its own specialty, and in Cereus, it is appreciation for the transient nature of life and beauty. The adepts were kind enough, and I learned a reverence for Naamah's service. Many of the graces I carry, I learned in Cereus House. But their lives are given wholly over to entertaining patrons, and mine . . . mine has encompassed a great deal more. I cannot help but wonder if my parents ever knew.

If they did, they kept silent about it—and because of that, I think mayhap they no longer live. A good many people died during the Bitterest Winter twelve years ago, between the sickness that ravaged the land and the Skaldi invaders who did the same. I like to think they would have come forward if they had been alive afterward, when my name was first spoken in the City of Elua by poets as well as patrons. My mother wept the day she abandoned me to the Dowayne's care. I remember that she wept. I wondered if she would have marveled that a child of their loins should become an adept in the arts of covertcy. When all was said and done, I was Anafiel Delaunay's creation more than theirs.

I thought about Melisande Shahrizai's son, raised by Elua's priests. I wondered what he was like.

If time had permitted, I would have spent every waking hour of the next days poring over Audine's translation of the *Kefra Neghast*. Unfortunately, it didn't. Loathe though I was to admit it, Hyacinthe's plight was the less urgent of the two. Like the drumming-mistress, he wasn't going anywhere. Imriel de la Courcel was another matter.

Once again, Joscelin and I made ready to travel.

Since no word had come from Ysandre, I took it as a hopeful sign and gave license to delay our departure a half-day to keep my other postponed appointment, journeying to Night's Doorstep to meet with Hyacinthe's old companion Emile.

It is in truth the most disreputable district of the City of Elua, a warren of taverns and inns and gambling-houses at the base of Mont Nuit, the hill on which the Thirteen Houses of the Night Court are

located. If it lacks the sophistication of the Night Court, it makes up
for it in bawdy enthusiasm, and for countless years, it has served as the
slightly dangerous playground for the daring nobles of the City. The
denizens of Night's Doorstep know a thousand ways to fleece the pockets of the D'Angeline peerage.

Hyacinthe, my dearest friend, had been one of them . . . and it was
because of this that I regarded Night's Doorstep, that cut-rate antechamber to the civilized pleasures of the Night Court, as a sanctuary.
It was where I went when I escaped the rigors of Cereus House, and
later Delaunay's. My Prince of Travellers earned his silver telling fortunes to drunken nobles, using the gift of the *dromonde*; but also selling
information and trading favors, and, more pragmatically, running a livery stable and lodging-house.

It was the latter that he had left to Emile, chief among his cadre of
runners and assistants. Ti-Philippe had arranged the meeting ahead of
time, and we found a table held for us at the Cockerel.

"My lady Phèdre nó Delaunay!" Emile cried as I entered the busy
inn. He went down on one knee and spread both arms wide. "You
honor me with your presence!"

Ignoring the starts and murmurs from the throng of patrons, I
smiled and went to greet him, taking his hands in mine. "Emile. It is
good to see you."

"And you." He kissed both my hands and rose, no taller, but considerably broader than I remembered him. It had been eight years, at least;
I had visited only once since my time in La Serenissima. "Chevalier
Philippe, Messire Cassiline . . . come, sit, my friends! Let us speak of
old times and old acquaintances."

A space cleared around our table, leaving a respectful aisle about
us. I couldn't for the life of me have said whether it was due to my
dubious fame, my quick-tempered chevalier Ti-Philippe, Joscelin's Cassiline arms and dry, capable air, or if it was commanded by Emile's
presence. Clearly, he had prospered in Night's Doorstep, and was a
person to be reckoned with, at least in the Cockerel.

Once a jug had been procured and wine poured all around, Emile
leaned forward, bracing his elbows on the table. "You have word of
Hyacinthe?"

"I have," I said, and drawing a deep breath, I told him the story
of our journey to the Three Sisters, the passage of power from the
Master of the Straits, and the dire twist on Hyacinthe's curse.

When I had done, tears shone in Emile's dark eyes. "Ah! You break my heart anew. You may not have known it, Comtesse, but he was like a brother to me."

"I know," I said compassionately. "Emile, there is more, if you will hear it. I may have a key to unlocking this curse; or at least, I may know where it lies. It's a long, hard path, and there's something else I must do first if I am to pursue it. I know the Tsingani go everywhere, hear everything, more than the *gadje* suspect. Are you well enough connected to use their ears for me?"

He smiled a little to hear me use the Tsingani word for outsiders. "Well enough, I think. It is different than it was in Hyacinthe's day. The chevalier told you Manoj is dead? Now, the *kumpanias* interact more freely with those of us in the cities, and they do not despise the *Didikani* as they once did."

Like Hyacinthe, Emile was of mixed blood, D'Angeline and Tsingani—*Didikani*, they called them; half-breed. "So you hear things."

"I hear things." Emile rubbed his thumb and forefingers together as if holding a coin. "Sometimes I tell them," he said, then closed his hand in a fist. "Sometimes I do not. For you . . ." He opened his hand wide. "For you I will sing like a lark. What do you wish to hear, Phèdre nó Delaunay?"

"Any news of Imriel de la Courcel," I said. "Or a child matching his description."

There was a pause, and all of us—Joscelin, Ti-Philippe and I—leaned in close, but eventually Emile shook his head, regretfully. "No. I am sorry. It has been five years, at least, since anyone placed a wager in Night's Doorstep on the whereabouts of the missing prince. The gambling-houses will give you any odds you like, and laugh as they take your money. But I will listen." He glanced shrewdly at me. "A child matching his description, you say?"

"A child," I said, "gone missing from the Sanctuary of Elua in Landras, in lower Siovale. A boy, ten years of age, with his mother's eyes." I reached out and put my hand over his, closing his fingers. "And this information, Emile, is not to be sold at any price."

"I would not!" He looked hurt. "Hyacinthe was my friend, my lady. Anyone he befriended, Tsingani, *Didikani*, D'Angeline alike, he treated with loyalty. What do I care for missing heirs? I would not sell this knowledge for profit when you might use it to win my friend's freedom."

"Good." I relaxed. "If you hear anything—"

"If I hear anything, I will come to you." Emile drank off his wine at one draught and refilled his mug. "It is true, what I said. The story has grown slowly, but it has grown, and spread. Now Manoj is dead, and there is no Tsingan kralis. The *kumpanias* speak his name at the crossroads. Hyacinthe, son of Anasztaizia."

"He followed the Long Road to its end," Joscelin murmured unexpectedly.

"The *Lungo Drom*," Emile echoed, sighing. "Some of us walk the inner path, and some of us the outer. I do not know anyone who has walked a longer road than Anasztaizia's son."

None of us did. Ti-Philippe raised his mug. "To Hyacinthe."

"To Hyacinthe." Emile clinked the rim of his mug in salute, then surged to his feet, hoisting his mug in the air. "To Hyacinthe, son of Anasztaizia!" he shouted. "Come, whoever remembers his name, I'll stand a drink to toast the Prince of Travellers!"

The resultant roar was staggering, and even though I daresay half of them were cheering nothing more than free wine, it brought a lump to my throat. I remembered Hyacinthe holding court at the Cockerel, his face bright with mirth . . . and I remembered him on the island, despair in the shifting depths of his power-stricken eyes.

Whatsoever might come to pass, I feared the bold, merry companion of Emile's youth was gone forever.

I drank to his memory, and tasted the salt of my tears.

ꟷIFTEEN

"ꓒOW YOU remember why we don't go to Night's Doorstep more often."

"Shut up," I muttered, squinting against the merciless D'Angeline sun, which sent dazzling spears of pain into my eyes. My head was pounding like one of Audine Davul's drums, and I could have sworn my soft-gaited mare was clopping like a plowhorse.

"We could have departed on the morrow."

"I'm *not* losing a day to the Cockerel's rot-gut wine!" There had been a good deal of it after that first toast. Emile's largesse had flowed freely, and I'd felt obliged to stand a round afterward—it does not pay to be seen as stingy, when one has a reputation in the City—and between my private griefs and the public outpouring of nostalgic melancholy, I'd drunk enough to be sorry for it. With typical Cassiline restraint, Joscelin had abstained after the first toast and drunk only water.

"You look slightly green, Phèdre," he said, regarding me.

I opened my eyes wide enough to glare at him. "I'm *fine!*"

Despite my aching head, we made good time, and by the second day, I had recovered from the ill effects of too many toasts and we had passed from the rich fields of L'Agnace into the hilly terrain of Siovale. As always, something in Joscelin eased at the return to the province of his childhood, the set of his shoulders more relaxed, his smile coming quicker. I loved to see it in him, although it made me feel guilty for keeping him overmuch in the City. On the third day, we entered the winding mountain paths.

The village of Landras is located at the foothill of a mountain; the Sanctuary of Elua that bears its name, they told us there, lies beyond, over the peak and in the basin of a steep valley. Upon reaching it, we passed the evening in the village, enjoying the mayor's hospitality and relating in turn the latest news from the City to an avid audience. Siovalese are odd folk, most of them of Shemhazai's lineage, prone to pondering the vagaries of human nature and exploring the dynamics of the physical world. It is not unusual to find a sheep-herder eager to argue Hellene philosophy or a wool-dyer intent on building a better waterwheel, and they are keen to discuss politics as well. It reminded me with a pang of regret that I would have little time to attend to my own estates in Montrève this summer.

In the morning, we departed, following the narrow trail up the mountain, our pack-mules laboring under the tribute-gifts the mayor had pressed upon us to deliver to the sanctuary. The air was cooler in the heights, pine forests giving way to grassy plateaus. We picked our way around steep outcroppings of rock and sheer drop-offs. Joscelin's eyes sparkled, and he delighted in pointing out wildlife as we rode; ptarmigan and white-capped finches and shy ouzels, and once a herd of wild chamois, watching us with curious gazes.

"There," he said, pointing as we gained the summit.

The valley lay far below, a green swathe carpeted with blazing scarlet poppies and riven by a swift river. I caught my breath to see the grey stone buildings of the sanctuary itself and the rough-hewn effigy of Elua, seen in miniature from above. On the far side of the valley, winding trails stitched the mountains, leading to meadow plateaus and the peaks beyond.

"Goat-tracks," Joscelin mused, scanning the distant crags. "That's where it would have happened. No wonder no one saw anything."

High overhead, an eagle circled and gave its piercing cry; stooped, and dove. I thought of its prey and shivered. "Let's go down."

It took the better part of an hour to make our descent, even on horseback. Although I've seen my share of mountains, I let Joscelin lead, glad of his expertise. By the time we reached bottom, there was no doubt but that we had been seen and were expected.

"Welcome, travellers!" It was a young female acolyte who met us in the courtyard, fresh-faced and pretty. She made a formal bow, hands in the sleeves of her short brown robe. My weary mare lowered her head and blew a soft equine snort. "Ah, poor thing." The acolyte stepped forward, laying consoling hands on my mount's lathered neck.

"Sister priestess," I said. "I am Phèdre nó Delaunay de Montrève, and this is my consort, Joscelin Verreuil. Might we speak with Brother Selbert?"

The acolyte, who had lain her cheek alongside my mare's, glanced up with a start. "Oh! Oh yes, of course." She smiled. "He is expecting you, I think. At least he is expecting *someone*. If you will dismount, I will see to your horses, and he will meet you in the sanctuary proper . . . oh! And the mules, of course. You have brought us . . . what have you brought? Lentils, I think, and salted anchovies, ah! Thank you, thank you, my lady."

I watched her move among the animals and explore the mules' panniers as I dismounted. There was an old scar at her temple, a dented crescent, faded with age. "Is there someplace where we may wash the dust of our journey from our faces, Sister?"

"Oh!" She startled again, and laughed. "He has told me, again and again, and still I forget. 'Liliane, offer them water!'" Her eyes were as wide and guileless as a child's, and I understood, then, that she was a touch simple. "Yes, my lady, there is a cistern, there," she said, pointing. "And I am not a priestess yet. Only Liliane."

"Thank you, Liliane."

"You are welcome!" She beamed at us both, then added carefully, "And I will take good care of them, I promise. Your horses *and* the mules."

I didn't doubt it, for as she set off blithely across the courtyard toward the stables, our mounts and pack-animals fell in behind her unbidden, a string of tall beasts following nose-to-tail behind the bare-foot young woman in rough-spun robes.

Joscelin blinked. "Now there," he said, "is one truly touched by Blessed Elua."

The water in the cistern was bracingly cold and refreshing. We both drank deep from the dipper, then splashed it over our hands and faces. It was a narrow, arched passageway that led to the Sanctuary of Elua, cool and dark, opening onto the splendid vista we had glimpsed from above.

No longer small with distance, the statue of Blessed Elua stood alone in the field, tall and towering beneath the immense blue sky. His arms were outstretched, and bright poppies lapped at his granite feet. Stooping, I unfastened the buckles on my fine riding boots and unrolled my stockings. The soil was dry and crumbling beneath my bare feet.

"We have nothing to offer," I murmured to Joscelin.

He placed his own boots in the rack at the entryway. "We have ourselves."

There is a stillness that comes upon one in sacred places. Hand in hand, we crossed the field of wild poppies, crushing sweet grass and pale green leaves beneath our tread. Elua smiled in welcome as we entered his long shadow, a smile as sweet and guileless as his acolyte's. His left palm, extended in offering, bore the deep gash of Cassiel's dagger. It had been his answer to the One God's arch-herald, who bade him take his place in Heaven. Elua had smiled then, too, and borrowed Cassiel's dagger. Scoring his palm, he let his blood fall in scarlet drops, and anemones blossomed where it fell. *My grandfather's Heaven is bloodless: and I am not. Let him offer a better place, where we may love and sing and grow as we are wont, where our children and our children's children may join us, and I will go.* I knelt at the base of the statue with a wordless prayer, my skirts spilling in billows over the twining foliage, the petals of crimson satin with their velvet-black stamens, vivid as the mote in my eye. Bowing my head, I pressed my lips against the sun-warmed granite of Blessed Elua's feet.

"Phèdre nó Delaunay."

It was a man's voice that spoke my name, gentle as a breeze. Rising, I turned and saw him, Elua's priest, clad in blue robes the color of the summer sky, with the handsome, austere features of Siovale. His eyes, like the leaves of the poppies, were a pale silvery-green, and his light brown hair fell down his back in a single cabled braid.

"Brother Selbert," I acknowledged him.

"Yes." He smiled. "I have been expecting you."

From the corner of my eye, I saw Joscelin rise from his own obeisance, bowing in the Cassiline manner, crossed hands hovering over the hilts of his daggers. "Me, my lord?" I asked the priest. "How is it so?"

"You," he said. "Or someone. You are not the first." He cocked his head, and I heard in the distance the sound of shepherd's pipes calling and answering across the far crags. "Did the Queen send you?"

Beneath the shadow of Blessed Elua, I gazed at him, a solitary figure drenched in sunlight. "Whose emissary do you think I am, my lord priest?"

"Ah." Brother Selbert exchanged an enigmatic smile with the effigy of Elua. "As to that, I suppose you are Kushiel's. Come." He extended his hand. "We must speak."

So it was that Joscelin and I followed the priest across the field, as obediently as our animals had followed the girl Liliane. At the entryway, we paused to don our boots. Brother Selbert waited, patient and calm. Like the other members of his order, he went unshod, and his bare feet were calloused and cracked, engrained with the dust of a thousand journeys.

"Come," he said again when we were done.

We followed the priest into his private quarters, where he bade us sit.

"You are here about the boy," he said when we had done so.

I opened my mouth to reply, but it was Joscelin who spoke first, giving voice to his long-held anger. "How could you do it?" he demanded. "How could you betray the realm to aid, that . . . that woman?"

"Melisande." Brother Selbert spoke her name calmly, tilting his head. "Melisande Shahrizai de la Courcel." He smiled in reminiscence. "Why does it offend you, young Cassiline?"

Joscelin stared at him in patent disbelief. "Why? Where shall I begin, my lord priest? You are aware, I trust, that she engineered the Skaldi invasion? That she collaborated with the warlord Waldemar Selig? That she blackmailed the Royal Commander Percy de Somerville, wed Benedicte de la Courcel under false pretexts, suborned the loyalty of the Cassiline Brotherhood by—"

"Yes." The priest held up one hand, forestalling his argument. "These things she has done, Joscelin Verreuil. And not a one of them would have been possible had it not been for the greed, the fear, the unreasoning hatred, the hunger for vengeance, on the part of her conspirators."

The meaning of his words brushed me like the tip of a fearsome wing, and I shuddered. "You say she has not violated the precept of Blessed Elua."

"Yes." Brother Selbert bent his head to me. "*Love as thou wilt.* For good or for ill, Melisande Shahrizai alone has laid her plans out of love of the game itself."

"But," I whispered, "they are dire."

"They are." The priest nodded gently. "Such is not my place to judge; only the intent." There was a look in his silver-green eyes such as I had seen in Michel Nevers' in Kushiel's temple—a terrible compassion. "Thus are the gifts of Kushiel's scions, to see the fault-lines in another's soul. I can do naught, if it is exercised in love."

I swallowed. "Even love without compassion?"

"Even that." There were oceans of sorrow in Brother Selbert's voice. "I can but feed the spark where I see it. And I saw it, in the Lady Melisande's regard for her child."

"You lied to the Queen!" Joscelin protested in anguish.

"Yes, of course." The priest gave him a quizzical look. "The Queen sought to claim the child for her own ends. The ends are admirable, young Cassiline, and they are rooted in her love of the realm, her desire for peace. But they do not supercede the love of a mother for her child. The Queen did not know the child. He was the Lady Melisande's son. No matter what she had done, Elua's dictum made my choice clear."

"Elua's dictum." I pressed my temples. "Brother Selbert, you know it was Melisande's intent that the boy should be sheltered here, until he reached such an age where she might unveil his identity like some hero out of legend, staking his claim to the throne?"

"It was her intent." His eyes glinted the color of sunlight on the poppy-leaves. "He might have surprised her, in the end."

"He might have," I said, making my voice hard. "If he had not vanished. Thanks to your interpretation of Elua's dictum."

"Ah." Brother Selbert sighed. "And so we come to it." He spread his hands helplessly, his expression turning somber. "What can I tell you, my lady Phèdre? Even now, though I am racked by guilt and second-guessing, I believe I chose aright. If I were a vain man, I might think Blessed Elua mocked me for my pride—but Elua is not so cruel as to use a child to lesson his priests. Yet Imriel is gone, and I, I am left without answers."

I considered him. "You said we were not the first. Tell me about Melisande's emissaries."

"There were two men who came, bearing her token." He laced his fingers about one knee. "It was after I had gone to La Serenissima to bring her the unhappy news. They pretended to be from Eisande, though I do not think it was true. It is politics, that, and nothing to do with Elua. I will give you a description, if you wish, and the names they gave, although I think those too were false."

"Yes, thank you. They conducted a search?"

"They questioned me, and every other member of the sanctuary. And they searched the mountains, where it happened." Brother Selbert glanced toward the window. "I believe they searched in outlying towns as well, and questioned villagers." He shook his head. "We did as much and more. We combed the crags for days. Every cave, every cleft . . . I saw to it myself, and we gave her emissaries every aid during the duration of their search." His voice changed, a tone of ragged grief bleeding through his calm demeanor. "I pray you, do not mistake me, my lady Phèdre! If there were a way, any way—I would give my life in an instant if it meant Imri's safe return. When all is said and done, I do not believe even Melisande Shahrizai questioned my sincerity."

"No," I said absently. "She didn't. Your discretion is another matter."

"No one knew." The priest lifted his hands, let them fall back into his lap. "I cannot prove it, not now. They did not question it, when I took the boy to La Serenissima before; I let them believe we went elsewhere. After his disappearance . . . some guessed."

"You . . ." I paused. "You took the boy to La Serenissima?"

"When he turned eight." Brother Selbert nodded. "The Lady Melisande wished to see him. I swear to you, I protected his identity to the fullest of my ability. If anyone learned it, it was not through my carelessness."

"Huh." I was hard-put to imagine it was through Melisande's; and yet she had taken a risk, having him brought to her. A risk, I thought, that she had not seen fit to mention. "What about the boy? Did he know?"

"No." The priest's denial was firm. "Imri believed himself an orphan, that his parents had died of a Serenissiman ague aboard the ship that brought me home to Terre d'Ange, and bequeathed him to me as a ward of the sanctuary. No one ever had cause to doubt it."

"No one would doubt the word of a priest," I said. "Melisande counted on as much. She used you to her own ends, Brother Selbert."

"So she believed," he murmured. "And I, I believed Blessed Elua used me to his. Mayhap I was a fool. If so, I am punished for it now."

"Did Imriel not think it strange to meet his mother in La Serenissima?" I asked him.

"He never knew." Brother Selbert shook his head. "He was told she had been a wealthy noblewoman, a friend of his parents, who would stand as his patron when he grew to manhood."

"Still," Joscelin observed, breaking his silence. "He would boast of it. He was a boy! You lied to your colleagues, brought him to La Serenissima, and introduced him to this, this fantastic patron . . . what did you do, my lord priest? Bid him keep it a secret? A boy of eight? You may be sure of it, he told his friends the minute you returned."

"Not Imri." The priest smiled his enigmatic smile. "You didn't know him, Messire Verreuil! He believed the lady he met would be in danger if he breathed a word of it, and true enough it was. Ah, no." He shook his head again, his long braid stirring. "Imri would have gone to his grave with it, after that. Eight or no, he had that, that . . ." he searched for a term, "that streak of rash nobility which is the heritage of House Courcel."

I thought of Ysandre de la Courcel riding between two narrow ranks of the Unforgiven, parting the rebellious army of the Duc de Somerville, her chin raised, eyes fixed on the City of Elua. I knew what he meant. "And if he had half his mother's wits, my lord priest, he would have guessed his patron's identity."

"He might have," Brother Selbert allowed, "if he had known the story. But we had not yet reached current histories in our studies, and I was careful to keep that knowledge from him."

So the boy had truly grown up unfettered and free, believing himself a true orphan, Elua's child, attuned only to the gentle rhythms of life and worship within this sheltered valley. I sighed. Somehow it made my task all the more poignant. "When would you have told him?"

"Sixteen." The priest watched me. "That was the age on which we had agreed."

Sixteen. It seemed a long way off. "Brother Selbert," I said, gathering my thoughts. "I am sorry to put you through this once more, but if I might speak to the other clergy and your wards—most especially the children—it would be helpful."

"Yes, of course." He rose, smoothing his robes, then hesitated. "You never said if it was the Queen who sent you."

"The Queen," I said, "is aware of my visit. But, no. It was Melisande."

Sixteen

WHEN THE shadows in the valley grew long, we watched the children herd the goats down from the mountain. Once, there had been five; now, only four. They travelled in pairs, a brown-robed acolyte with both groups as they emerged from invisible plateaus to converge upon the narrow trail. Their voices rose clear and high-pitched in the thin air. The shaggy goats, brown and white with bells strung about their necks, wound their way down the track, picking their way surely on cloven hooves while the children scrambled behind, scarcely less agile. They fanned out as they reached bottom, long sticks in hand, prodding and deftly herding their charges across the wooden bridge that arched over the river. The acolytes followed behind at a slower pace, serene and watchful.

"And this is how it was the day Imriel disappeared?" I asked Brother Selbert.

"No," he said quietly. "Not entirely. We let the children go on their own, then, and the older ones might go alone, if they wished, to seek higher pasturage. Now, we forbid them to leave one another's sight, and an acolyte travels always with each group."

I raised my eyebrows. "Imriel would have been considered one of the older children?"

The priest's high, austere cheekbones flushed with color. "He . . . not exactly. But he was impulsive. Cadmar and Beryl are the eldest."

I picked them out by sight as they eased the milling goats into their paddock. A tall lad with hair that shone like flame in the slanting sunlight, and a dark-haired girl garlanded with flowers. The other two were younger, a boy and a girl who looked to be about the ages of Ysandre's daughters.

"Treat them gently, my lady Phèdre," Brother Selbert said. "Imri's disappearance frightened them badly, all the more so when Melisande's men came asking harsh questions." He watched gravely as they filed inside the sanctuary walls, laughing and chattering. "You see Honore," he said, pointing to the youngest girl, no more than six. "For a month, she refused to tend to the goats, for fear that whatever took Imriel would take her. And Cadmar . . . he puts on a brave face, but he will go near neither cave nor crag, staying only to the center of the trail. Ti-Michel has only just stopped waking in the middle of the night, crying for Imri, and Beryl, ah." He sighed. "Beryl blames Elua for letting it happen. I worry about her the most."

"You should tell them," Joscelin said shortly. "Tell them the truth. Fear and lies fester in darkness. The truth may wound, but it cuts clean."

"Mayhap you have the right of it, Cassiel's servant," the priest murmured. "I will think on it. Come, we will assemble for dinner."

In the Sanctuary of Elua, meals were a common affair, held in the great hall with its high stone arches. It was simple fare, but good—a pottage of lentils and onions, stewed greens and fish caught fresh in the river, with brown bread smeared with sharp goat's-milk cheese. The acolytes, of whom there were half a dozen, took turns at cooking and whatever chores were needful. Brother Selbert dined at a table with eight others, priests and priestesses alike, ranging from an elderly woman with a face so kind it made one ache to lay one's head in her lap to a young man whose vows had scarce left his lips.

Throughout the course of the evening, I spoke to all of them, and learned nothing of merit. I learned that Imriel had been a beautiful child, with blue-black hair and skin like ivory, eyes a deep and starry blue; his mother's son, though no one put the words to it. I learned he had been proud and kind and a little wild. I heard the story of his disappearance a dozen times over, and while the details varied slightly in the telling, the events remained unchanged. If their stories had been identical, I would have been suspicious. So it had been, when I had questioned the missing guardsmen of Troyes-le-Mont, who had concealed the fearful secret that Percy de Somerville had helped Melisande escape from that fortress. Ten years ago, in La Serenissima, the sameness of their story had given the lie to it. Here, it was obvious the denizens of the sanctuary were telling the unhappy truth.

From Brother Othon, the young priest, I learned how they had searched the mountains for days on end, finding no trace of the boy. Born and bred to Landras village, he had led the search himself, and his grief at his failure was writ clear on his features.

"How certain are you, Brother Othon?" Joscelin asked him in a gentle tone. "I do not fault your diligence, but the mountains are vast. I am Siovalese myself, and I know there are nooks and crannies of my childhood home of Verreuil that not even my brother Luc and I managed to explore."

"It is possible." The priest turned his failure-haunted gaze on him. "It is always possible. I still search, thinking to find his body lodged in some crevice where the lingering snows of spring have retreated at last, hoping to find him. But if he went of his own accord . . ." He shook his head. "He may have gone for days before harm befell him. We were slow in widening our search, sure that he was near. I cannot say."

And so I listened, and grew no wiser. They knew who we were, of course, priests and acolytes alike. I saw it in the sidelong glances, heard it in the hushed murmurs when they thought I was not listening. They are learned folk, Elua's priesthood; they knew well enough that Phèdre nó Delaunay was Kushiel's Chosen, the Queen's confidante. If they had not known before that their Imri was Imriel de la Courcel, son of Melisande Shahrizai, I daresay most of them had guessed it by now. But here, in Elua's sanctuary, no one spoke of it. And that, I thought, was wrong. Their silence was a canker of omission, blighting the serenity of this sacred place.

The only exception was the young acolyte Liliane, whose sweet smile fell like sunlight on all it touched; Liliane, and the children. I spoke to the latter after we had dined, when the wards of the sanctuary would have taken their studies in the library halls.

"The Lady Phèdre and her consort Joscelin want to hear about Imri," was all Brother Selbert told them before leaving us alone.

"Why?" the lad Cadmar asked bluntly when he had left, eyeing me with all the dour suspicion of his twelve years. "Who are you?"

"I am a friend of the Queen's," I said.

"The Queen cares what happened to Imri?" It was the girl Beryl who spoke, her voice sharp with disbelief. I looked gravely at her. She was the eldest among them by a year, budding into young womanhood, with black hair as fine and straight as silk, the tender beginnings of breasts and green eyes that held only scorn. I wondered if she was Brother Selbert's get. It was not uncommon for priest's children to end as wards of their sanctuary.

"Yes," I said. "She does."

The child Honore had clambered onto Joscelin's knee. He held her loosely, looking amused; I swear, I do not know why children adore him so. Most adults have the sense to find him distant and off-putting. "Imri taught me to climb trees," Honore announced, settling herself with a proprietary bounce. "He got me honey after Beryl told him not to. He was stung seventeen times and Sister Philippa put mud all over him."

"Be quiet, Honore," Cadmar muttered. "The lady doesn't care about that."

"Why not?" I asked, leaning forward and propping my chin on my hands. "I like honey. And I want to hear about Imriel."

"Imriel," Honore sang, bouncing on Joscelin's knee. "Im-ri-el! He made Cadmar angry, because he said he liked Beryl. Cad-mar likes Ber-yl!"

"Be quiet!" The lad flushed red to the roots of his fiery hair.

"Is this real?" Sturdy little Ti-Michel stretched his arms above his head to tug at the hilt of Joscelin's sword. "Can I see it?"

"Hush." Joscelin drew him onto his other knee, holding both of the young ones in place. "I'll show you later, if you like. Michel, what do you know about Imri? Were you there the day he went missing?"

"Yes." The boy's voice fell to a whisper, his expression changing to one of instantaneous distress. "He went . . . he wanted to find a higher pasture, past the rockfall. I played and played on my pipes, I did! Then he didn't answer, and I didn't, I didn't—"

"Ti-Michel came to find me, Lady Phèdre," Beryl interrupted him. "I was with Honore, in one of the lower pastures. We fetched Cadmar, and he and I looked as far as we dared, while the little ones watched the goats. When we couldn't find him, we went back to tell Brother Selbert."

"Did you go past the rockfall?" I asked her.

She paused, then shook her head. "Not then. It's a narrow ledge, and dangerous. There'd been another fall, we couldn't pass. Brother Othon worked to clear it that night."

"Cadmar was scared!" Ti-Michel slid down from Joscelin's knee, forgetting his distress, chin raised in challenge.

"So were you!" the older boy retorted. "*You* ran for Beryl!"

"Cad-mar was sca-red!" Honore sang, bouncing, then added, "Imri wasn't scared of *anything*."

"Is that true?" I addressed my question to Beryl.

"No." She gave me a cool look of appraisal. "Of course not. Nobody's afraid of *nothing*. But he was brave, for a boy." Her lip curled. "Braver than Cadmar. Imri liked to take risks, to see what would happen. And when he got hurt, he never complained. He was afraid, though. He was afraid of anyone seeing him cry."

"One time," Ti-Michel said, "one time I fell in the river, and Imri—"

"Oh, shut up," Cadmar said in disgust. "You could have walked out, if you'd stood up and stopped flailing around. It wasn't so deep."

"Imri taught us how to swim." Honore climbed down from Joscelin's knee and came over to stare into my face, clutching my skirts absentmindedly. "We took all our clothes off. I like to swim. How come you have a red spot in your eye?"

"Because," I said, touching her nose. "I was born with it. Why do you have freckles?"

The child looked cross-eyed at her own visage and giggled.

The words that followed were spoken in a half-whisper. "Mighty Kushiel, of rod and weal, late of the brazen portals, with blood-tipp'd dart a wound unhealed, pricks the eyen of chosen mortals."

I raised my head, looking at Beryl, who had gone pale and defiant.

"I know who you are," she said. "Brother Selbert thinks I'm too young to know, but I'm not. I hear them whisper. They are always whispering, since Imri disappeared. I see the books they study when they think we're not paying attention, the scrolls they hide. I know who you are. Why are you here? Why do you want to know about Imri?"

Joscelin and I exchanged a glance. "Beryl," I said gently. "What I have told you is true. I am the Queen's friend, and she does care about Imriel. If harm had befallen any of Blessed Elua's children, her majesty would want to know how and why. If there is more to it . . ." I shook my head. "It is not my place to tell you what Brother Selbert will not. You must ask him yourself. But if there is any knowledge you have that would help me to find Imri, I pray you tell me. I promise you, I seek only to aid him."

"No." Her shoulders slumped. "He's just *gone!* And Elua, Elua did nothing to protect him." A spasm of bitter grief contorted her features. "Brother Selbert says we are all in Elua's hand! Where was Elua when Imri needed him?"

In the silence that followed, Honore began to sob methodically, more upset by Beryl's anger than any true sense of divine injustice. Ti-Michel's lower lip quivered, and Cadmar set his jaw and looked sullen. I had done a poor job of heeding the priest's wishes. Joscelin moved to sit cross-legged on the floor, drawing Honore onto his lap where she soon quieted.

"Beryl," I said. "Elua cannot prevent ill things from happening. He can only give us the courage to face it with love."

"It's not enough!" she cried.

"It is," I said. "It's all we have."

Who was I, to teach theology to the wards of Elua's priesthood? And yet Joscelin had been right. It is a hard truth that lies at the center of faith. I watched Beryl measure that truth against the half-lies and omissions that had surrounded the disappearance of Imriel de la Courcel, and brace herself against it, drawing strength from its acceptance. Slowly, her shoulders squared and she sat a little straighter, fixing me with a direct regard. "And if I pray for him? Do you believe still that Elua will hear my prayers?"

"I do." I said it firmly, as if I had never doubted myself. Whether or not it would aid the missing Imriel, I did believe it would help Beryl.

"Then I will," she said.

Thus, for better or ill, was our encounter with the children of Elua's sanctuary. They were subdued when we took our leave, and I did not think Brother Selbert would be pleased, but there was a spark of new resolve in Beryl's green eyes, and I did not think it was entirely ill-done.

It was not until Joscelin and I were alone in our humble guest-chamber that I gave vent to my own frustrations.

"Name of Elua!" I hurled a down-stuffed pillow at the stone wall. "Brother Selbert, the priesthood, the acolytes, the children . . . they're telling the truth, aren't they?"

"Mm-hmm." Joscelin prudently moved the oil lamp on the bedside table out of reach of my swirling skirts. I paced the chamber in disregard.

"They're telling the truth," I said, ticking them off on my fingers, "L'Envers is telling the truth, Melisande's spies . . . Melisande, for love of Kushiel! Melisande is telling the truth. What am I missing, Joscelin? I cannot see the pattern here! Where's the lie? Who are we over-looking?"

"La Serenissima?" He fetched the rolled map from our travel-bags, spreading it on the narrow bed. "Selbert took the boy to see Melisande. Someone could have guessed."

"Severio would have told me if he'd gotten wind of it." I pondered the map, tracing a semicircle north of Landras. "If they'd made for Marsilikos, someone would have seen them along the way."

"Mayhap they didn't." Joscelin traced a ragged route southward. "Mayhap they stuck to the mountains."

"And crossed into Aragonia? L'Envers searched there." I thought about it and shrugged. "We could ride south, and inquire. We'd pass near to Verreuil, Joscelin. We could visit your family."

His eyes shone briefly in the lamplight, then dimmed. "I'd not want to take time from our errand. If we stop anywhere, it ought to be Montrève."

"It's no time to speak of. We'd need to take lodging somewhere." I got up and retrieved the pillow I'd thrown. "And Montrève's not on the way. Verreuil is."

"As you wish." He smiled with unalloyed pleasure, rolling the map. I was glad I could make someone happy.

SEVENTEEN

WE SAID our farewells to Brother Selbert in the morning, standing in the courtyard.

"I am sorry," he said, "that we could not give you the answers you sought."

"You have given us what you had, my lord priest." I inclined my head to him. "For that, I am grateful. It may be that the Queen will summon you to discuss your role in Imriel's disappearance from La Serenissima. I will speak on behalf of your intentions."

Brother Selbert swallowed, his throat moving visibly. "I never meant for the boy to come to harm. I thought . . . I thought he could grow up freely in Elua's grace, his spirit untrammeled by the machinations of politics."

"I know," I said.

"Tell them who he was." Joscelin adjusted the buckles on his vambraces, checking and settling his weapons. "It will help them make sense of it, Brother Selbert. And they should know that not even Elua's grace renders them invulnerable to the ill in men's hearts." He looked up at the priest. "Or the follies of pride."

"I will tell them." Brother Selbert returned his gaze unflinching. "Do not be quick to judge me, Cassiline. Can you claim to know the whole of Elua's will?"

"No," Joscelin said quietly. At the far end of the courtyard, the young acolyte Liliane emerged from the arch of the stableway, craning her head to smile at the morning sun, our mounts and pack-mules trailing after her like ducklings following their mother. "There are mysteries no one can fathom."

"Even so." The priest nodded. "And there are purposes too deep for us to grasp."

I could have sworn, from the sleek condition of their coats, their renewed reserves of vigor, that our animals had spent a month rather than a day basking in the sunlit paddocks of Elua's sanctuary. My mare frisked like a filly crossing the bridge, dancing and shying at the hollow echo of her hoofbeats on the wooden planks.

"Did you know Liliane was my mother's name?" I asked Joscelin.

"Really?" He looked surprised. "You never told me."

"It was."

So began our wanderings through the mountains of Siovale. We gained the lower pastures, where Beryl and Ti-Michel pointed us toward the rockfall of which they had spoken, a narrow ledge along a chasm, dangerous with overhanging crags. After making our precarious way past the cleared rockfall, we ascended to the further pastures, flat areas where the tall grass grew, perfect for spring grazing and fall harvest. There was nothing to see, but it gave us our starting-point.

We had marked the towns and villages searched on our map, and Brother Othon had left markers of his own along the mountain trails, scratching Elua's sigil onto rocks and trees in areas already combed. He was right; the search had been thorough. For two days, Joscelin and I rode in broadening arcs, keeping a keen eye out for Othon's signs. It reminded me of travelling along the Tsingani routes, searching for *chaidrov*, the secret markers with which they indicated their passing. We met a few folk along the way, shepherds mostly, who shook their heads, able to tell us nothing.

After two days, we ceased to find Othon's scratchings and I had begun to suspect that our search was fruitless. Still, we continued, until I was heartily sick of making camp in mountain meadows and bathing in icy streams.

"There's a village ... here." Joscelin glanced up from the map, watching as I struggled to draw a comb through my hopelessly tangled tresses. "We could make it by nightfall, and be in Verreuil by midday tomorrow."

"Let's do it." The comb stuck. I drew it out with a muttered curse. "I'm not going to see your family looking like I've been sleeping in a bird's nest."

He grinned at me. "You look like a maiden out of legend, fresh-tumbled by Elua."

"I feel like I've tumbled fresh out of a hedgerow," I retorted.

Joscelin laughed. "You still look beautiful. Come on, then. The village by nightfall, and we'll beg lodgings if they don't have an inn. I wouldn't mind a hot bath, either."

We made good time in the morning, reaching the deep divide that led southward to Aragonia—and then lost time in conversation with the merchants of a trade caravan, who had no news of any errant children matching Imriel's description, but a bitter tale of being cheated by Tsingani horse-traders. I held my tongue at their ire, though it galled me. It is true that the Tsingani take great joy in getting the better of the *gadje*, but it is equally true that most of the *gadje* bring it on themselves, seeking to do the same and making a virtue of it.

Afterward, we pushed too hard to make up for the delay, and one of the mules slipped on loose scree, straining a foreleg. Our pace slowed to a limping gait, and it grew obvious that we weren't going to make the village before dark. Joscelin rode ahead to scout out a campsite as dusk grew night, returning in good spirits.

"We're closer than we thought," he said. "There's a dairy-crofter's in the next valley. They make cheese to sell at market. I spoke to the husband; he said they'd give us lodging and fare for coin. And a hot bath." He grinned. "I asked."

"Elua be thanked!" I said fervently.

Darkness was falling by the time we made our halting way to the valley, and the crofter met us with a lantern, leading us to an unused paddock by the cow-byre where we could turn our mounts and the mules loose for the night, piling our saddles and packs under the shelter of a lean-to. He introduced himself as Jacques Écot and said little more, taciturn and withdrawn. I was surprised at his wife, Agnes, a petite woman with features that should have been vivacious, but for the sorrow that haunted her eyes.

It was only the two of them, alone in their croft. Agnes bustled about, heating water for the bath and laying out her best linens at the table, showing us to a neat bedchamber with whitewashed walls, a child's chest-of-drawers and a bed with a lovingly hand-sewn quilt atop it. I brushed my hand over the counterpane, wondering, but asked no questions.

We had our baths, Joscelin and I alike, and he lent a hand hauling water and emptying the tub. I watched the muscles bunch and gather in his forearms, remembering the first time I'd seen him perform simple menial chores. We had been slaves together, he and I, sold into bondage in a Skaldi steading. It seemed a long time ago.

Afterward we dined with Jacques and Agnes Écot, seated at the table in their cozy, rustic kitchen. Lamplight glowed warm on dishes of broad beans and ham, a purée of turnips, a pitcher of water drawn cold from the well. It should have been homely and charming, and yet a pall of sadness hung over that home, and I was oddly uneasy.

"It's no business of mine," Agnes murmured, pushing the food on her plate without eating. "But it is passing strange to find a fine lord and lady in the back hills of Siovale."

"Not so strange." Joscelin smiled at her. "My father is the Chevalier Millard Verreuil. Do you know of him? Our estates are near."

"Oh, yes!" Her face lit up. "He came to market once in town . . . more than once! He praised our cheeses. You have a look of him, now that I see it. He and those tall sons of his. What are their names?"

"Luc," Joscelin said. "Luc and Mahieu. My brothers."

"Luc and Mahieu," Agnes echoed wistfully. "They must be men grown now, with wives and children of their own."

"They are."

Jacques Écot's harsh voice broke the moment of reverie. "You're coming from the wrong way, if you're coming from the City of Elua." He looked me up and down. "And from your finery, I'd say you are."

"Messire Écot." I inclined my head to him, determined to take no offense. "You have the right of it. But more recently, we come from Elua's sanctuary at Landras, searching for a boy, some ten or eleven years of age, fair-skinned, with black hair and blue eyes. Have you seen anyone matching his description, alone or in the company of others? He has been missing for some three months now."

Agnes' fork fell with a clatter and the blood drained from her face. "Jacques," she whispered.

"Is this some jest?" The dairy-crofter was on his feet, hands balled into fists, sinews knotting, his mouth working with rage. "Do you seek to mock our loss?"

I sat very straight against the back of my chair.

"My lord crofter," Joscelin said smoothly, easing himself between us, putting his hands on Écot's shoulders and guiding him gently back into his seat. "I pray you, we meant no offense. My lady Phèdre speaks the truth, we do but seek a missing boy. Will you not sit, and tell us of your troubles?"

The dairy-crofter sat, obedient and dazed, passing one hand before his eyes. "Agnette," he murmured. "Agnette!"

I looked at his wife. "Your daughter."

She nodded her head like a puppet, face still white. "Our daughter.

Eleven years, going on twelve." She swallowed. "She went missing, my lady, some three months ago."

"Ah, no." I felt a wave of sorrow, gathering and breaking, too immense to be comprehended. "No." A sense of dread hung over me like thunder, and red haze clouded my vision. My ears were buzzing with a sound like a hornet's nest. I saw, at last, in the forming pattern, the thing I had been missing, the hand I had forgotten, awesome and implacable.

Kushiel.

It was Joscelin who drew the story of their daughter's vanishing from the dairy-crofter and his wife, though I daresay it was a familiar enough tale. The spring rains had been meager and she had gone with a portion of the herd seeking pasturage in the next valley. Sweet, pretty Agnette, with her mother's vivacious face, had never returned. Her father Jacques had sought her that evening, with the help of a lad they hired during the days, pushing his way among the lowing cattle with a lamp held high.

She had vanished without a trace.

Elua is not so cruel as to use a child to lesson his priests . . .

So Brother Selbert had said, and he had believed it; but it was not Elua who was once named the Punisher of God. It was Kushiel. And I knew too well his cruel justice to dismiss this as mere coincidence. *A pattern too vast for me to compass.* So Hyacinthe had said, reading the *dromonde* for me. Truly, it was. I had expected anything—*anything*— but this. I sat dumb as a post and listened as Jacques Écot warmed to his topic, his stoic demeanor forgotten in the passion of his grief. A bear, they had thought, or wolves—but surely creatures of the wild would have left traces, signs of passage, prints and struggle, bloodstains. No, he concluded grimly; it must have been human, whatever took Agnette. Tsingani, most like. Everyone knew the Tsingani were not to be trusted, that they would steal D'Angeline babies from their cradles and raise them as their own, given half a chance.

"They wouldn't," I murmured, but my voice went unheard, buried beneath the flood of anguish our inquiry had unleashed.

Somehow, Joscelin managed everything that night, hearing out their terrible story, making amends and apologies, pleading the travails of our journey and spiriting me away to our simple bedchamber. Agnette's chamber, I knew now, the counterpane stitched by a loving mother for the only child of her blood. I sat upon it, turning my dumbstruck gaze to his.

"Oh, Joscelin! What if it's . . . it's nothing to do with politics, with the Queen's kin, with Melisande. What if it's just. . . ." I searched futilely for words. "A bad thing that happened?"

"We will find out." He knelt beside the bed, eyes fierce, gripping my hands in his. "Phèdre, if someone is abducting D'Angeline children from their homes, we'll find out about it. We'll go in the morning to Verreuil. My father won't stand for this lightly, I promise you that! He'll give us every aid, put his men-at-arms at our disposal, rouse the countryside. We will find them."

I was shivering, to the marrow of my bones. I dared not think to what purpose the children had been taken, not yet. The rawness of the Écots' grief was unbearable. I do not know, if it had been my child, if I could have endured it. What did I know of a parent's suffering? It was that very fear had kept me from motherhood, and this bereavement was worse, far worse, than aught I had imagined. "These poor people . . ."

"I know." Joscelin wrapped both arms around me, warm breath against my hair. "I know," he repeated. "I know."

EIGHTEEN

A LIGHT rain was falling when we took our leave of the Écots' household. I sat my mare, raindrops glistening on my hair while Joscelin discussed treatment of our spavined mule with the dairy-crofter. We would move swifter without it, and they would gain a pack-mule in the bargain when it healed. I could afford the cost.

Agnes Écot lingered in the doorway and looked at me with eyes starved for hope.

"We will find her," I said to her as Joscelin checked the lead-rope on our remaining mule, preparing to depart. "As Kushiel's Chosen, I swear it to you. We will find your daughter."

Joscelin mounted his gelding without comment, swinging its head toward the west and Verreuil, and thus did we make our exit.

It was nearly an hour before he spoke of it.

"You shouldn't have said that to her," he said without looking at me. "What I said last night . . . you and I know the odds. I said it to give you heart. You made her believe, Phèdre. False hope is crueler than kindness."

"I know." I could not explain to him that the words had come from a hollow place within me, that I had not known I would speak them until I opened my mouth and the words had emerged. "Joscelin, I had to."

He did look at me, then, but offered no reply. Soon, our trail led back into the steep crags and gorges, rendering conversation impossible. Joscelin led and I followed behind the pack-mule's bobbing haunches, guiding my mare with care and considering the strange emotion that churned within my breast.

It was anger.

All my life, I have been marked as Kushiel's Chosen—and I have suffered for it, as have others, who have born the harsh brunt of my fate. And yet even as I have acknowledged the folly of my choices, the blood-guilt I bear, I have known, too, that each of us makes our own choices, and no one is free of responsibility for his or her actions. To believe otherwise is vanity. If I have questioned Kushiel's wisdom in choosing me—indeed, if I have prayed to be freed from the burden of my nature—I have never questioned his justice.

I questioned it now.

What had a dairy-crofter's child done, to be caught up in the terrible net of retribution? Nothing. What sins had her parents committed, that their only begotten should be used as an instrument of vengeance? Sold unripe cheese at market? I could not fathom it. Braced for intrigue, for plots within plots, I had found the last thing I expected: chance, cruel chance. If there were purpose behind it, it could only be Kushiel's doing—or Elua himself. I could not imagine a purpose so deep it justified this cruelty. And I was angered to the core of my soul.

The rain had ceased by the time we reached the top of a massif, a broad and windswept plateau, the mountains stretching below us in brown wrinkles. Joscelin paused to rest our blown horses. "Phèdre," he murmured as I came alongside him. "You said it yourself. Even Blessed Elua cannot prevent the world's ills. He can but give us the courage to face them with love."

I choked on a bitter laugh. "And what did the girl say? She was right. It's not enough."

"It has to be." He looked steadily at me. "It's all we have."

"This is Kushiel's doing." I brushed the tangled hair back from my face, gazing at the vista below, the distant blue mirror of a lake that marked the estate of Verreuil. "I feel it, Joscelin. I feel it in my marrow. I was a fool not to see it before."

"Mayhap it is so." His hands rested quietly on the pommel of his saddle, and his eyes were as blue as the lake. "Even Kushiel serves Blessed Elua in the end, and even he must use mortal means to do his bidding. And you are his chosen."

"Yes." I swallowed, remembering my pledge to Agnes Écot. "Come on. Let's go."

It was after midday when we arrived at Verreuil. I had been there before, but I forgot, between visits, the atmosphere of tranquil chaos that reigned at Joscelin's childhood home. It is a beautiful estate, sprawling along the shore of the lake—Lake Verre—crumbling in its oldest parts, the lines etched clean-graven and new where the family has expanded. We emerged from the dark shadows of fir trees to find one of his nieces at play on the forest's verge.

"Uncle Joscelin!" I caught a glimpse of an urchin face, smudged and wide-eyed, as the girl ran at him and heard Joscelin's laugh as he leaned down from the saddle, catching her in a hug. And then with a wriggle, she was gone, high tones setting the hills to ringing. "Uncle Joscelin, Uncle Joscelin's here!"

We hadn't ridden ten paces before the manor doors were flung open and its inhabitants spilled out into the courtyard; adults, children, a surge of barking hounds. Tears stung my eyes at the welcome. I hung back, letting Joscelin precede me.

"My lady Phèdre!" Luc Verreuil came over to grin up at me, two years the elder of Joscelin, and taller by as many inches. His broad hands spanned my waist as he lifted me from the saddle, sweeping me into a crushing embrace the instant my feet touched cobblestones. "Well met!"

"And you . . . you great lummox!" The air had fair left my lungs. I wheezed, greeting his wife Yvonne, tall and willowy, with fox-slanted grey eyes. "My lady."

"Oh, Luc, do let her breathe." Stooping, she smiled and gave me the kiss of greeting.

I caught my breath and turned to greet Joscelin's parents. "My lord Millard, my lady Ges, thank you for your hospitality. Forgive us for intruding, but we'd no time to send word."

"Nonsense." The Lady Ges smiled, warm and earthy, even as her husband bowed. "You're always welcome here, Comtesse."

"Thank you." I drew another deep breath. My lungs seemed to be functioning again. "I am sorry to say it isn't exactly a courtesy call, my lady."

Millard Verreuil gave me a speculative look. He was a tall man— all the members of Joscelin's family were tall—with the same old-fashioned beauty as his middle son. What he saw writ in my features, I cannot say, but he took it seriously. "We will speak of it inside."

I nodded, and then Joscelin brought his younger brother Mahieu to greet me, and Mahieu's wife Marie-Louise, and nothing would do but that I was reintroduced to their children and Luc and Yvonne's, and then his elder sister Jehane, visiting with a pair of teenaged sons who shuffled their feet and turned beet-red in my presence, and all around us was the milling presence of dogs, great hairy creatures that stood waist-high on me, as tall as everything else in Verreuil.

Somehow, the Lady Ges got us all indoors and managed to dispense with the children and dogs, assembling the adults in the parlour with light refreshments and wine. There was somewhat of her, I thought, in Joscelin's quiet competence, for all that he favored his father and had his father's reserve. I wondered, sometimes, what he would have been like had he grown to manhood in Verreuil, instead of being sent to endure the stern rigors of the Cassiline Brotherhood at the age of ten. I wondered too if he resented it. If he did, he never said so.

There was a scuffling and scraping of chairs as everyone present drew chairs around, the better to hear. The parlour of Verreuil had the gracious, lived-in comfort one finds in old homes. The furnishings were fine, but worn; the carpets threadbare in spots. Still, the wood was lovingly polished with beeswax and fresh flowers adorned the room.

The Chevalier Millard Verreuil took the place of precedence, seated in a stiff, throne-backed chair. I could not but help glancing at his left arm where it lay atop the chair's arm. It ended in a stump, hidden beneath the cuff of his cambric sleeve. He'd lost his left hand at the battle of Troyes-le-Mont, during the last, desperate surge of attack by a group of Skaldi invaders, cut off from their retreating army. He inclined his head to me, opening the discussion with formality. "How may House Verreuil serve her majesty the Queen?"

"My lord." I shook my head. "We're not here on the Queen's business, not exactly."

He blinked. "I thought—"

"Father." Joscelin leaned forward, elbows braced on his knees. "Do you recall the missing Courcel heir?"

"Melisande's child." The Chevalier said the words as though they tasted foul.

"Imriel de la Courcel," said Jehane, Joscelin's sister. "Son of Melisande Shahrizai and Prince Benedicte de la Courcel, brother of Ganelon, uncle to Rolande, great-uncle to the Queen. Missing since the attack in La Serenissima." She was the genealogist of the family, I remembered. I had not met her before. Joscelin had made a point of visiting at her husband's estates, but Ysandre had required my skills as a translator for an Illyrian delegation and I'd been unable to accompany him.

"Yes." Joscelin nodded. "He was at the Sanctuary of Elua at Landras." He ignored the indrawn breaths and murmurs of surprise. "Some three months ago, he vanished; disappeared, tending goats in the mountains. We thought it was part of a conspiracy, but last night . . . last night we learned of another missing child. A dairy-crofter's daughter, eleven years of age, stolen from a cow-pasture some miles outside of Harnis village."

"Bears," Luc said promptly. "Or wolves, like as not. They're bold in the spring, come calving season, and themselves still hungered from winter."

"I don't think so." Joscelin shook his head. "There would have been traces, remains, signs of bloodshed. The crofter searched, and so did the priests. They know mountains. This has an odor of human intervention."

"But who would do such a thing?" It was Marie-Louise, Mahieu's wife, who exclaimed aloud, paling. Plump and pretty, she contrasted with her husband, who was as tall as the rest of his clan and lanky with it. "And *why?*"

"We don't know," I said softly. I turned to Millard Verreuil. "That's why we've come, my lord. To ask your aid in scouring Siovale, at least the area between here and Landras."

"You shall have it." He sat upright in his chair, face fierce and bloodless with anger, eyes blazing like an old hawk's. "Name of Elua! I'll lead the search myself, and turn out the countryside. Every crofter, every shepherd, every small-holder—no, wait, I'll do more. I'll send to his lordship Marquis de Toluard, and see how many men he'll lend us for the task."

"I'll bear the message," Yvonne offered. "He's my mother's cousin, he'll listen to me."

"He'll listen anyway!" Millard Verreuil pounded the arm of the chair with his good right hand. "Elua's blood! No one of Shemhazai's lineage will rest while an abomination of this nature occurs in Siovale!"

The Lady Ges looked at me with worried eyes, her pleasant face furrowed. "You've no idea who might have done it?"

I turned out my hands. "None, my lady."

"Euskerri might have," Jehane said in her cool voice, thinking aloud, "if there was some gain in it, some way to force the Queen's hand in their quarrel with the House of Aragon." It was a quarrel of which I knew little, save that Euskerria was a native province of north-western Aragonia, annexed by the descendents of Tiberium who comprised the House of Aragon. She shook her head, dismissing the idea. "If they knew the lad's identity, that part might make sense, but not the crofter's daughter."

"No one knows mountains like the Euskerri," Mahieu observed, raking his forelock back from his brow. "And they're cunning enough to throw us off the scent by abducting a second child." Like his sister, he was of a scholarly bent, well versed in the history of the area.

"No." She frowned. "The Queen would have heard by now. Tsingani, mayhap. I've read accounts of D'Angeline children being stolen by Tsingani. Elua knows, there are enough of them that travel the passes between here and Aragonia. Tinkers and horse-traders, they say, but who knows what they might hide in those wagons?"

"*No.*" The sharpness of my own voice surprised me. I sighed, apologizing. "My lady Jehane, forgive me. But it is *not* Tsingani."

"As you say, Comtesse." Jehane looked at me with composed interest. "Near-sister, I should say. I must confess, you're not what I expected."

"Oh?" I raised my brows.

"No." A corner of her mouth curved in the familiar hint of a smile. "I expected a keen wit and a strong will. Joscelin wouldn't have fallen for less. And I know what you are. Still, I didn't expect you to ride out of the backlands of Siovale looking like one of the more delicate blossoms in the Court of Night-Blooming Flowers."

I flushed. Jehane laughed.

"Jehane!" Her father, already closeted with Luc and Joscelin, laying his plans for the search, turned to give her a look of reproach. "Be courteous."

She merely smiled, rose and stooped to kiss his cheek before turning back to me. "They'll be at it for hours. Shall I show you to your quarters? You look as though you wouldn't mind a rest before dinner. With your permission, Mother," she added.

"By all means." The Lady Ges, abstracted, gestured with one hand, counting on the other. "I'll be busy till nightfall trying to figure out how the larder's to provision this undertaking."

I followed Jehane through the rambling corridors of Verreuil to the rooms in which Joscelin and I had stayed before when we visited, clean and airy, with massive timbers supporting the ceiling and a window that looked out onto the mountains. It held, touchingly, some few items of Joscelin's childhood—a Caerdicci primer with a cracked binding, a book of verse by the warrior-poet Martin Leger, a child's miniature hunting-horn. Jehane lingered, picking up the horn and examining it.

"I gave this to him," she murmured. "For his ninth birthday. I had to beg the money from Luc to do it. I knew he'd only have a year to use it, before he was sent to the Cassilines. Does he speak of his time there?"

I sat down on the bed. "Not often."

"I missed him the most, I think." Jehane set down the horn. "Mahieu was too young, and Luc . . . Luc never said it, but I think he was glad it wasn't him. You know Father was furious that Joscelin broke his vows for you? It nearly killed him, when he learned Joscelin had been convicted in absentia for the murder of your lord Delaunay. He didn't believe it, but it nearly killed him all the same."

Joscelin and I had been enslaved in Skaldia when that had happened, betrayed by Melisande Shahrizai, though no one could have known it. It had been the logical conclusion, I suppose, when Anafiel Delaunay and his apprentice Alcuin were found slain in their home, while Delaunay's *anguissette* and her Cassiline guard had vanished. I remember how it grieved Joscelin, on the eve of battle, to think his father might have believed it. "I guessed as much," I said. "But he never said it to my face. He was always courteous."

"Courteous." She pulled a wry look. "Yes. Father is that. Well, he had the sense to realize that fate will out in the end, after Troyes-le-Mont. Mother was glad, though. She always mourned losing her middle son to the Cassilines." Jehane cocked her head at me. "You do love him, don't you?"

"Yes." I nodded. "More than I can say."

"Good." She dusted her hands, then wiped them on her skirt. "Keep him safe, will you?" She gave a self-conscious laugh. "It sounds foolish, I know. He with a sword at his back and daggers at his belt, knowing more ways to use them than I can count, and you . . . well. But he was my younger brother, once, and he's given his heart into your hands."

"I understand, my lady."

Jehane left, then, and I lay down on the bed. She was right, I was weary; more weary than I had known. Of a surety, travel takes its toll, but this was a weariness of the soul more than the body. The crofter's revelation had dealt me a blow. In all my careful efforts to unravel the mystery of Imriel's disappearance, it had never occurred to me that it could prove out to be a senseless crime. It was the last, the very last, thing I had expected; that anyone might have expected. All my wits, all my second-guessing and plotting, went to naught. Now it fell to Millard Verreuil and his compatriots to search out the truth by might of numbers and main force. If I was relieved to be free of the burden of responsibility—and I was—still, it left me feeling bereft and directionless, and very, very tired.

So thinking, I drifted into sleep and did not wake until someone shook me. I opened my eyes to find slanting gold rays of sunset filling the room and Joscelin seated on the edge of the bed, smiling down at me.

"You're not going to sleep through dinner, are you?" he asked. "I wouldn't blame you if you did—it's seven kinds of mayhem down there—but there are a few members of the family would be mortally disappointed."

"No." I yawned and sat up. "I'm coming."

Joscelin hadn't exaggerated. The dining-hall of Verreuil was nigh overflowing, full not only with his considerable family and their offspring, but the estate's eight men-at-arms and almost a dozen others, crofters and shepherd's sons in plainspun clothing, seated elbow to elbow with the minor nobility of Siovale. Millard Verreuil had wasted no time and stood on no ceremony. For all his formal courtesy, he was an egalitarian at heart.

All the talk was of the expedition to be launched in the morning. Yvonne had already departed with a delegation to the Marquis de Toluard, begging his assistance. Mahieu and Jehane had been busy in the library, gridding the region to be searched and copying maps, recruiting a number of the older children to aid in the endeavor. The Lady Ges and Marie-Louise had spent the afternoon supervising the harried kitchen staff, assembling packets of provisions for each of the parties. Small wonder, I thought, that dinner appeared to have been cooked in haste, the mutton roast charred without and rather too red on the inside.

Still, no one seemed to mind. I picked at my food and let the conversation wash over me, being gracious to those around me and ignoring covert stares from the newcomers. Jehane's sons begged permission to accompany one of the parties and were granted it; Luc's eldest daughter begged the same, and was sharply denied, for which I was glad. The lads were fourteen and fifteen, old enough to fend for themselves. The girl was scarcely ten.

"We'll leave at dawn," Joscelin said to me, his voice pitched below the clamor. "Mahieu and Jehane have established rendezvous points for the parties to meet on the third day, so if anyone's learned anything, we can proceed from there. Either way, we'll send a runner back to the manor. There ought to be word from the Marquis by then, and you'll be kept informed here."

"What?" I stared at him. "Are you mad? I'm going with you."

"Phèdre." His face hardened, white lines forming alongside his nose. "No. You'd only slow us down." He held up one hand, forestalling my outburst. "Listen, these men are born and bred to the mountains, and they know how to travel quickly and surely. I'm not even leading a group, I'm travelling with Reynard's party because I don't know the territory as well, I've been away too long. And you . . . you're staying at Verreuil."

"Slow you down?" I asked incredulously. "Joscelin, I crossed the Camaelines in the dead of winter with you!"

"Yes." His voice was taut and low. "Because we had to. This is different. Name of Elua, Phèdre! I don't have that many chances to keep you out of unnecessary danger. Won't you let me take this one?"

I opened my mouth to retort, and remembered Jehane, reminding me that I held her brother's heart in my hands. I sighed. Joscelin was right; there was no real reason for me to accompany them. If I wouldn't slow them down—and I might, a bit, it was true that he was better in the mountains than I—I wouldn't contribute much either. "All right," I said, giving way with ill grace. "I'll stay."

"Thank you," he said, meaning it.

Nineteen

MORNING DAWNED fair and bright over the mountains of Siovale, although the manor was awake and bustling long before. I felt displaced and underfoot with no role to perform. Joscelin was in the stables with Mahieu, seeing that all was readiness. Wandering down to the kitchens, I found Marie-Louise staggering toward the dining-hall with an immense pot of porridge.

"Here," I said, reaching for it. "I'll take that."

"Are you sure?" She rolled her eyes. "It would be a help. We've got every hand in there cooking, and no one to serve at breakfast. Mind, it's heavy."

"I've got it." I cradled the pot in my left arm, settling it on my hip. I learned how to serve at the table before I left the Night Court, and it is not the sort of thing one forgets. It made me smile, seeing the startled looks on the men's faces as I circled the table, ladling generous dollops of porridge into their wooden bowls. There is an art to table service; proper balance, unobtrusive approach, an elegant line. Out of practice as I was, I caught myself making a child's bargain in my head—if I make it around the table without spilling a drop, without a clink of the ladle, it means they will find them, Blessed Elua let it be so . . .

I was concentrating so hard I didn't see Joscelin enter and pull up a chair at the table, and startled at his amused features, inadvertently slopping porridge over the edge of his bowl. "Sorry! I didn't realize it was you."

"I didn't expect to see you here, either." He grinned and deftly spooned up the spilled porridge. "A fine send-off. Food that will stick to our ribs, and service fit for a king."

I shifted the heavy pot, feeling the warmth of it through my gown. "A baronet, mayhap. It's been a while. Everything's in readiness, then?"

"As ready as it can be." Joscelin took a mouthful of porridge and swallowed before continuing. "The horses are laden, and the sun's nigh cleared the horizon. Father's going over the search plan one last time with the party leaders. We'll be off as soon as we've eaten." He ate another bite. "I promise, we'll send word in three days at the latest; sooner, if anyone finds them." Mouth full again, he nodded with his chin toward the far wall, swallowing. "Why don't you set that pot down on the sideboard, it looks—"

His voice trailed off, and I followed his gaze instinctively.

Mahieu stood in the doorway, a peculiar look on his face. "Phèdre," he said in a strained voice. "There are these . . . these Tsingani in the courtyard. And they're asking to see you."

For a moment I stood frozen, staring at him, the pot of porridge in my arms. It was the scrape of chair-legs and a muttered expletive from one of the men-at-arms that brought me back to myself. "I'll be right there," I said, setting the pot down on the sideboard. Joscelin was already rising. "You." I pointed at the man who'd sworn at the mention of Tsingani. "Stay here. I don't want any interference."

He gave a brief nod, his jaw tight. It would have to do. I went out to the courtyard.

Although the sky overhead was pale gold, the cobblestones yet lay in the long shadows of the mountains. I needn't have worried about the man inside; already, people had gathered. Five men, Millard and Luc Verreuil among them, ranged in a semicircle before the Tsingani *kumpania,* swords half-drawn. I walked past them to meet it, Joscelin at my side.

It was a small *kumpania,* as small as the one we had travelled with from the Hippochamp years ago. There was a single covered wagon, its once-bright paint weathered, great splinters gouged from the wooden spokes of its wheels. Even travelling on the old Tiberian roads, passage through the mountains was not easy. The driver sat in the high seat, expression impassive. The women and children would be inside, hidden behind the closed curtains at the rear.

In front, two men sat on motionless horses, one a little to the fore. They were full-blooded Tsingani, with brown skin and liquid-black eyes, and both as tense as wires.

"Tseroman," I said to the leader, inclining my head. His shoulders relaxed a little at the Tsingani greeting, though his eyes were suspicious and watchful still. "I am Phèdre nó Delaunay. How did you know to find me here?"

"You have the mark. What Tsingani do not see, they hear. Your passage was noted." His voice was husky and accented. "I am Kristof, son of Oszkar. This is my *kumpania*." He bowed from the waist. The dust of hard travel lay on his black hair, his yellow shirt. "*Didikani* in Elua's City say the companion of the Tsingan kralis' grandson seeks a child."

"I do." My heart beat harder in my breast. "Have you seen him?"

"There." The Tsingano headman turned in the saddle, pointing unerringly to the south. "In the Pass of Aragon, before the leaves were full-grown on the beech trees. Two men and three children."

"D'Angeline children?" I asked.

Kristof nodded once. "A girl and two boys." He lowered one hand, palm downward. "So tall. They were not well."

"Sick?" I asked. "Injured?"

"Maybe injured." His gaze slid away from mine. "Drugged."

Somewhere behind me, Luc swore violently. I heard the sound of steel dragging against leather, and sensed rather than saw Joscelin turn, shaking his head in silent warning. Lines of tension showed in the faces of the Tsingani and the driver gathered his reins, but they stood their ground.

"You saw the child the *Didikani* described?" I asked Kristof.

"There was such a boy, a *gadjo* pearl, with black hair and eyes like the deep sea. Yes."

A shudder ran through me. "Kristof, who were the men? Where were they bound?"

Once again, his gaze slid away onto the distance. "We did not know, when we met them. It was spring. We only heard the words of the *Didikani* two days past. These men, they wished to buy our wagon." His mouth curled in contempt. "We did not sell it."

"Kristof," I said desperately. "Please. Who were they?"

He didn't answer me, jerking his chin at Millard Verreuil. "You, D'Angeline lord! Are you like the others, who say the Tsingani lie and cheat, and steal *gadje* children?"

"I have heard these things said," Millard replied steadily, returning the Tsingano's regard. "I have heard them said by members of my own household. I have not said them myself. If I have wronged your people with my silence, I am sorry for it. But it is the Lady Phèdre who asks, and I have heard with my own ears that she is quick to defend the Tsingani name."

"You." Kristof looked at me. "You travelled the *Lungo Drom* with Anasztaizia's son."

"Yes." I understood, then, the unspoken price of this information and spoke the words he wanted to hear. "*Tseroman,* I travel it still. Until Hyacinthe, Anasztaizia's son, grandson of the Tsingan kralis, is free, I walk the Long Road for him. He has seen it. And this one," I touched Joscelin's arm, "travels with me."

"If the *dromonde* has spoken, it is so." He drew a long breath. "The men were Carthaginian slave-traders. They were bound for Amílcar, in Aragonia."

"Carthaginian!" Luc exploded. "What would Carthaginians be doing wandering Siovale? If you're lying, Tsingano, I'll have your head for it!"

Kristof smiled with his mouth; his eyes were flat and black. "What do you know of trade, tall *gadjo?* There are people who will pay good money for a D'Angeline slave-child. If the Aragonese forbid it, Carthaginians are cunning enough for greed. Where better to hunt them? If one child disappears in the mountains, you *gadje* will say it is a wolf or a bear, or," he added, "filthy thieving Tsingani."

With that, he turned to go, his companion following, the driver twitching the reins and clucking to his team. I took a step after him.

"You knew. You could have reported it then, Kristof."

The Tsingano headman stopped, looking over his shoulder. "I knew," he said softly. "Who should I have reported it to? One such as him?" He nodded at Luc. "He will go to Amílcar, and if he does not find Carthaginian slave-traders, he will come looking for me with his sword in his hand."

"No." I shook my head. "The Queen's justice protects Tsingani as well as D'Angelines. I would stand surety for it with my life."

"It may. But Elua's City is far away, *chavi,* and even a Queen may believe a lie. It was not worth my life to test it. Perhaps one day it will be different, when we have a Tsingan kralis again." Kristof raised one hand. "Phèdre nó Delaunay. I will speak your name and remember it."

"And yours, Oszkar's son. May the *Lungo Drom* prosper you." I stood and watched them go, heedless of the muttering behind me. The sun had cleared the mountains and blazed full on the courtyard, splendid and golden. I watched the dusty little *kumpania* until they were out of sight around the first bend, then turned around to face the gathered inhabitants of Verreuil's estates. "Well." I considered them. At my side, Joscelin gave an inaudible sigh. "Who wants to go to Amílcar?"

It took only a couple of hours to make ready our departure, and most of that spent in arguing among the members of House Verreuil. For my part, I had my things packed in short order and used the balance of time to write a missive to Ysandre, couching recent developments in subtle language. In the end, it was Luc who accompanied us, along with two men-at-arms and a groom. It had been Mahieu's turn for adventure, by his father's reckoning, but he ceded his place to his elder brother. I daresay Jehane would have come—I saw the yearning in her eyes—but she was scheduled to depart for home in a few days' time. I half-wished she would throw caution to the winds and accompany us, for it would have been pleasant to have a female companion. Still, I could not fault her choice, and she would bear my letter to the Queen to the nearest Royal Couriers' waypost, for which I was grateful.

There was considerable debate over whether or not the word of the Tsingani could be trusted, which I ignored. Millard Verreuil decreed at length that the search would go on as planned, on a slightly smaller scale. It was a sound decision. Whether they believed Kristof's story was true or no, where there was rumor of slave-traders, there might be trouble.

Let them learn what they might. I was going to Amílcar.

I knew it was true.

Oh, Kristof might have left out details, and he might have been mistaken about the men being Carthaginian, although I doubted it. But I knew, in my bones, that it was Imriel he had seen. It had an awful symmetry that spoke of Kushiel's presence at work. It was as Hyacinthe had said. There was a pattern here, too vast to be compassed. No one can fathom the will of gods and angels as they shape mortal lives; I could sense the purpose in it, and pray it was less dire than it seemed. When Joscelin and I had stumbled unwitting into Melisande's conspiracy, she could easily have had us killed. She didn't. Instead, she disposed of us in another way, selling us into slavery among the Skaldi. We had survived. Imriel de la Courcel had a chance of doing the same.

I was going to Amílcar.

We set out ere midday, taking the high trails and shorter routes known to the Siovalese. On level ground, we could have covered the distance in a few days' ride. In the mountains, it would take thrice as long—and that only if the weather held.

No one spoke of the need for speed, though we pushed as hard as we dared. Three months and more gone by. The trail, if we found it, would be cold. I had hope of obtaining aid in Amílcar. Two years ago,

Ramiro Zornín de Aragon had been named King's Consul to the city, royal liaison to the Count of Amílcar. With Elua's blessing, his wife would be in residence, and Nicola L'Envers y Aragon was both a kins-woman of the Queen and a friend. If Nicola was there, I had no doubt she would do everything in her power to assist us.

That was the good thing about Amílcar.

It is forbidden to own slaves of Aragonian or D'Angeline birth in Aragonia, that much I knew. And it would be a bold Aragonian lord indeed who dared defy that edict. Terre d'Ange is their nation's greatest ally. Without our might at their back, Aragonia would be vulnerable to the empire of Carthage to its south. As it is, they enjoy an uneasy trade alliance. *What do you know of trade tall* gadjo? Enough, I thought, to know that illicit trade goes on everywhere. But if Carthaginian slavers were trading in D'Angeline children in Aragonia, they'd likely want them off their hands and out of sight as quickly as possible.

And Amílcar was a port city.

That was the bad thing about Amílcar.

On the third day, our course intersected the road through the east-ern Pass of Aragon and we were able to travel with greater ease, fol-lowing a great river basin in the shadows of towering peaks. Luc went fishing in the twilight as the men of Verreuil made camp that evening, setting lines in the swift-flowing river and catching several trout ere the light faded.

"Do you still remember how to clean a fish, little brother?" he asked Joscelin, grinning as he returned from the riverbank, gleaming fish dan-gling from his line.

Joscelin raised a laconic eyebrow. "I might."

I studied the translation of my Jebean scroll and watched from the corner of my eye, amused, as the sons of Millard Verreuil cleaned and gutted trout by the light of our campfire, a messy job at best. Luc jabbed his thumb removing a hook, swore, stuck his thumb in his mouth and yanked it out, swearing again and spitting at the taste of fish-slime.

"You shouldn't laugh, my lady," he said, aggrieved. "I'm trying to be gallant. Your consort there told me you like trout."

"I do," I said. "And thank you."

"You're welcome." Luc cast a disgruntled glance at Joscelin, who held up two fish without comment, neatly cleaned and deboned. "Oh, go ahead, you may as well do the rest. I didn't think anyone fished in the City of Elua."

"I don't." Joscelin started on a third trout. "I fish in Montrève."

"I should have guessed." Luc sat beside me, unselfconsciously rubbing his hands together to remove fish residue. "My lady . . . Phèdre . . . I meant no offense, back there in Verreuil. With the Tsingano, I mean. I wouldn't have harmed him, not really. Even if I was sure of a man's guilt, I'd still summon a magistrate and see him given a proper trial. I was angry, that's all."

"I know." I set the parchment aside. "Luc, I know. The problem is, there are others who wouldn't, and too many who'd remain silent to see it done. A Tsingano like Kristof isn't going to take a chance on which kind of man you are. I know their reputation. Some of it is deserved. Most of it isn't. I asked their aid. It took courage for Kristof to seek me out. It didn't help matters to have you threaten him."

"I suppose not," he murmured. "But how can you be so sure he didn't lie?"

I told him how to discern the nine tell-tales of a lie, watching his eyes widen.

"That's so . . . *complicated.*" Unlike his brother, Luc Verreuil was at heart an uncomplicated man. He rose, shaking his head. "I'll take your word for it, and stick to what I know, which at the moment is fish. Joscelin, since you're so fast with a knife, you can dispose of the offal. My lady Phèdre, if you'll forgive me, I'm off to the river to wash my hands and gather stones to build a cook-pit."

"Forgiven," I said.

When he had gone, Joscelin chuckled, wiping his fish-gutting blade on a handful of grass. "It's been eating him up since we left, you know. I'm glad he finally talked to you. Mayhap he'll actually think about what you said."

"Mayhap." I regarded him. "For all their energy and wit, members of your House don't appear over-quick to change their ways of thinking."

"No." Joscelin squatted on his heels beside the campfire, glancing to see that his brother and the others were out of earshot. "The old beliefs hold strong in the back-country. It comes home to me every time I visit. I love them, Elua knows, but . . . my childhood was a long time ago, and too soon ended." He stretched out his begrimed hands, contemplating the calluses left by dagger- and sword-hilt. "I held Verreuil in my heart," he mused, "and Verreuil went on without me, unchanging. It's I that has changed."

"Do you regret it?" I had to ask it.

"No." The firelight reflected in his eyes as he glanced at me, dispelled by a quick shake of his head and a half-smile. "Do you?"

"No," I said. "Not you. Never you." I brushed his forearm with my fingertips. "I didn't have much of a childhood either, not as people like your family would reckon it. But there was Delaunay, and Alcuin. Hyacinthe. I had love. And I have you. For that alone, it is worth the cost."

"Yes. Always." Joscelin gazed toward the south. "And there are worse ends to childhood than entering the Cassiline Brotherhood or Anafiel Delaunay's service."

I shuddered. "I know. Ah, Elua!"

"Melisande's boy." He was quiet for a moment. "Mayhap the priest was right to raise him as he did. At least he had joy in it. That's ended, now. Even if we find him whole and unharmed, it's a hard path he'll tread once he knows who he is. He's not like the crofters' daughter, to return to a loving family."

"Ysandre will see him safe," I said.

"She'll do her best, I know. Still . . ." Joscelin shrugged. " 'Twill be a hard path."

I thought about Imriel de la Courcel. What would it be like, at ten years old, to learn that everything you had believed about your life was a lie? To learn that you were a traitor's get, that your very existence was part and parcel of an unthinkable scheme, and people you'd never met would gladly see you dead?

"Poor boy," I murmured.

"Poor boy, indeed." Gathering himself, Joscelin eyed the pile of fish guts. "Ah, well. I suppose I'd best get rid of these, unless you'd care to do it."

I raised my eyebrows at him. "You're the one loves fishing."

He gave his wry smile. "That's what I thought."

TWENTY

İT TȮȮK nearly a fortnight to reach Amílcar. We lost two days to summer storms in which Jean-Richarde, the senior of the men-at-arms, deemed it unsafe to travel. I was impatient at the delay, but after seeing the torrential downpour swell the river until it overflowed its banks in a churning rage, lapping at the foot of the caverns where we'd taken shelter, I ceded to his wisdom.

We timed our arrival for the morning, taking lodgings in one of the better inns near the bustling harbor. Luc, who spoke fluent Aragonian, negotiated for our rooms. I understand the tongue, a little—it is a variant of Caerdicci, fluid and melodious, with lengthened vowels and a softly lisped 's' sound—but I am ashamed to say I have never studied it myself.

Once ensconced, I penned a swift note to Nicola L'Envers y Aragon, stamping it with the impress of Montrève's seal and sending it with Dolan, the younger of the men-at-arms, to the Consul's Quarters in the Plaza del Rey. When it was done, I ordered a bath and procured a laundress to press the creases from my best gown, such as it was—a silver-grey silk, the bodice finely embroidered with silver thread. It would do. I hadn't packed my garments with thoughts of a visit to the King's Consul of Amílcar in mind.

Nicola's reply, I thought, would come promptly if she was in residence; indeed, she was, and her response was faster than I had reckoned. No sooner had I finished applying a touch of kohl to my lashes and tucking my hair into a mesh caul laced with seed pearls, but a wide-eyed Aragonian lad knocked at the door, a servant of the inn come to announce in comprehensible Caerdicci that the King's own carriage was awaiting us below.

It wasn't, of course—it was the carriage of the King's Consul, but it was impressive enough, with a driver and a footman and the arms of the House of Aragon worked in gilt on the sides. Luc sat nervously on the tufted velvet seats, fussing with the curtains, taking up a good deal of space for one man.

"Elua, but it's stifling in here!" he said, tugging at the frogged closure of his doublet. His summer-blue eyes, so like and unlike his brother's, were wide and anxious. "Are you sure I'm dressed aright? I've never met foreign nobility before. Phèdre, what's the proper form of address for a lord of the House of Aragon? Should I kneel or bow?"

"The Lady Nicola is D'Angeline, and a friend," I reminded him. "And Ramiro is Consul, not the King himself. Just . . . pretend you're greeting the Marquis de Toluard, Luc. Accord them the same courtesies you would him."

"Tibault de Toluard would haul me off to the parapets to see his engineers' latest improvement on the trebuchet," Luc said glumly. "I don't think Ramiro Zornín de Aragon will do the same."

"No." Joscelin lounged against the padded seats, unconcerned. "He'll likely show you the latest game of hazard instead, and if you've not brought your dice, I'm sure he's a set to lend. Don't worry, Luc. You'll not embarrass Verreuil."

"I hope not," his brother muttered.

Amílcar is a pleasant city, though we saw little enough of it through the drawn curtains of the carriage, alighting in the Plaza del Rey. On one side of the square stood the Count's palace, a solid affair of grey granite with adornments of wrought-iron scrollwork. The quarters of the King's Consul faced it on the opposite side, a lower, more modest building. A pair of guards waved us through the archway into the courtyard, where we were met by a majordomo in the livery of the House of Aragon.

"Comtesse de Montrève," he said in fluent D'Angeline as I stepped from the carriage. "Messires Verreuil. The Lady Nicola will receive you."

We followed him into the marble foyer. It was cooler within than without, light filtering through fretted windows to cast complex patterns, date palms in vast pots lending a suggestion of green shade. He led us to the salon of reception, which had a narrow marble frieze about the walls depicting the King of Aragon pardoning a Prince of Carthage, much gilt trim and a carpet of a startling red hue.

"It's a bit much, isn't it?" Nicola L'Envers y Aragon smiled, coming forward to greet us. "I'm not allowed to make changes to the décor in the reception hall. Phèdre, my dear. Well met." A gold seal-bracelet tinkled at her wrist as she raised one hand to touch my face, giving me the kiss of greeting. "And Joscelin."

"My lady Nicola." There was a trace of amusement in his voice as he bent to kiss her.

"You must be Luc." Nicola regarded him with interest. "They breed tall in Verreuil."

"My lady." Luc blushed and bowed. Nicola laughed.

It was a familiar laugh, low and intimate, and one that set my pulse to beating faster whenever I heard it—even here, even now. But I have been an *anguissette* all my life, and I have grown accustomed to dealing with the distraction. "Nicola," I said. "I would that it were otherwise, but we're not here on pleasure. It's a serious matter."

"I assumed as much." She nodded toward a group of over-gilded chairs set around a low ebony table. Wine and olives awaited us on a tray. "Ramiro should be back before sundown. He's meeting with Fernan's Chancellor of the Exchequer to go over some accounts. Do you want to tell me now, or shall it wait?"

"I'd sooner you heard it first," I said.

Nicola listened without interruption as I laid out the story, her face betraying little of her thoughts. It was odd, seeing her in Amílcar, with her D'Angeline composure and beauty, clad in an Aragonian gown with a square-cut neck, her bronze hair pinned in an elaborate coif, stuck through with a pair of long hair-pins that sported the golden crown of the House of Aragon at the ends. Luc watched her raptly, unabashedly fascinated. I didn't blame him. I continued with my account, tracing our journey through Siovale. It was not until I related what the Tsingano Kristof had told us that Nicola reacted in astonishment.

"*What?*" Her violet eyes went wide with outrage.

"So he said, my lady," I said. "Carthaginian slave-traders, bound for Amílcar. Do you say it cannot be so?"

"I don't know." Nicola rested her chin on one fist, frowning. The dangling seal at her wrist winked gold in the slanting light from the high windows, the sun's rays turning lucent the cabochon garnet with which it was set. "No. I won't say it's impossible. Count Fernan does his best to see the harbor is patrolled, but there's a good deal of illicit trade goes on anyway."

"The harbor," Joscelin said. "What about the rest of the city? What if they were but passing through en route to Carthage?"

Nicola shook her head in dismissal. "If they were taking the risk of transporting D'Angeline captives to Amílcar, it would be for the seaport. There's no other reason."

"Can you help?" I asked her. "I've sent word to Ysandre, if it needs must go to a matter of state. She would demand Aragonia's aid. But it will be some time before a delegation could arrive, and every day we lose, the trail grows colder."

"Oh, I can help, all right." Her lovely jaw set and a look of cold determination settled in her gaze, familiar to anyone who knew members of House L'Envers. I'd seen it in the Queen, and Duc Barquiel before her. "You may be sure of it." Nicola picked up a small gilded bell from the table and rang it. A liveried servant entered the room in prompt reply, and she addressed him in fluent Aragonian. "I'm sending word for Ramiro to return posthaste," she added to us in unapologetic D'Angeline. "He's like to linger over his cups if I don't. It shouldn't be more than an hour."

"My lady Nicola." Joscelin stood. "With your permission, there are a few things Luc and I must needs procure at the market. Shall we return in an hour's time?"

Luc opened his mouth to protest, then thought better of it. Nicola looked at Joscelin, and what unspoken words were exchanged between them, I could not say. She inclined her head. "As you will, Messire Cassiline. I have given standing orders that you are to be admitted to the Consul's quarters."

"On the hour, then." Joscelin bowed and left, taking Luc in tow.

I watched them leave.

"He's learned a measure of grace," Nicola observed, refilling our wine-cups and sitting back in her chair, relaxed and less formal now that we were alone.

"He likes you," I murmured into my wine. "I don't think he wanted to, but he does."

"And why not?" She gave her cat's-paw smile, like unto her cousin Barquiel's, but more subtle. "I'm likeable enough, after all."

"You are." I lifted my head and met her eyes. "Truly, I'm sorry to come to you like this, my lady. It was never my intent."

"Phèdre." There was a mix of resignation and genuine affection in Nicola's voice. "Much as I would enjoy it, I never expected you to turn up on my doorstep on a pleasure-jaunt. I know what you are. I've known from the beginning, Kushiel's Chosen. It is folly, to make claim on one whom the gods have marked for their own. And unlike the others, I am no fool, to grasp at that which burns to the touch. What you have given . . ." she raised one hand, palm upward, the garnet seal dangling at her wrist, ". . . I hold in an open hand."

It reminded me of Emile, closing his fist in the Cockerel; it reminded me of Hyacinthe's vision of Kushiel, holding a key and a diamond in his grasp. It reminded me that I had known too few people in my life with the courage and wisdom to hold that which they valued in an open hand. It reminded me of why I had commissioned Nicola L'Envers y Aragon's garnet seal to be made in the first place.

"You wear it," I said softly.

"Yes." She laughed. "Ah, Phèdre! I always wear it. 'Tis the only one of its kind, after all. Aragonians may not know what that means. I do."

A cabochon garnet, as vivid a crimson as the mote in my left eye, bearing a single emblem carved in relief: a dart, exquisite in detail, from the sharp tip to the fine lines etched in its fletching.

Kushiel's Dart.

I have only ever given a lover's token once in my life, and that this seal, to the Lady Nicola. She was a patron, once; a friend, after. I have never forgotten that had I trusted to her advice, had I not been ruled by my suspicions, a good deal of harm would have been averted. It was at a time when Barquiel L'Envers and I were at cross-purposes to each other, both of us seeking Melisande Shahrizai, neither of us willing to believe the other. How Melisande must have laughed, safely ensconced in the Little Court of La Serenissima, watching us circle each other in mistrust! If we had shared information, if we had joined our forces, we would surely have found her sooner.

And my beloved chevaliers Fortun and Remy would not have died, nor many others besides. Imriel de la Courcel would not have been sent to the sanctuary of Elua, would not now be missing, stolen by slave-traders.

An outsider, exiled by marriage to the courts of Aragonia, Nicola had seen our folly. She had tried to tell me, though I would not hear it. And when I would not, she entrusted me with the sacred password of House L'Envers, the words which compelled aid in direst need. *By the burning river . . .*

Not even the Queen had broken with the protocol of her mother's House to trust me with those words. Only Nicola. It taught me something I never learned elsewhere. And some eight years ago, I returned the favor, giving her that which I never gave any other.

"I am glad," I said aloud, "that you value it."

"Ah, well." Nicola turned the seal-bracelet absently on her slender wrist. "I am glad, my dear, that you do not regret it. I am passing fond of your Cassiline, too, but he is a jealous consort."

"Joscelin . . ." I spread my hands, ". . . is Joscelin."

"Yes." She smiled. "And probably a worse torment to you than I could devise. Well, it must be hard on him, that you serve Melisande's will in this."

"Hard?" I pondered it, shaking my head. "Truly, Nicola, I'm not sure whose will I serve, anymore. What am I to make of it, when Melisande's will accords with Ysandre's? I am Naamah's Servant, twice-pledged—and yet Naamah has no role in this, none I can see. I am Kushiel's Chosen, yes, and Kushiel . . ." I shuddered. "Kushiel is architect of this horror, if I am no fool. Do I serve his will to thwart it? I thought, when I began, that it was my own will I served, my sole true goal to free Hyacinthe, my friend."

"And now," Nicola murmured, "you are not so sure."

"No." I drained my wine-cup and set it down. "Now that I have spoken to the warders and companions and parents of children, innocent children, who have suffered for Kushiel's justice, I am not so sure, not so sure at all whom I serve. There is something at work here. I do not know what it is."

A lesser friend would have spoken easy words of comfort. Nicola didn't. "I can make no promises, Phèdre. As you say, the trail is cold. But if it is to be found in Amílcar, Count Fernan's men will find it." Her smile this time was grim. "I don't care if it serves Melisande Shahrizai or the Khalif of Khebbel-im-Akkad. If there is trade in D'Angeline flesh going on in Amílcar, I will see it stopped."

"Thank you," I said simply.

Nicola shrugged. "This one needs no thanks. I have some influence. I am pleased to have a good reason to exercise it. They're few and far enough between as it is."

"Speaking of which . . ." I eyed her. "Will I find Marmion Shahrizai in residence?"

"Marmion?" Nicola relaxed again, looking amused. "No, Lord Marmion stayed at court, attending on the King. He has carved out a place for himself, and anyway, we quarrel if we are in the same place overlong, he and I."

I will own, I was relieved to hear it. 'Twas Marmion Shahrizai who betrayed Melisande, many years ago, giving her over to Quincel de Morhban, sovereign Duc of Kusheth, who brought her in tow to

Troyes-le-Monte. He paid for it in the end, for his ally, his sister Persia, had proved duplicitous, and Marmion had inadvertently—so he claimed—caused her death, his men-at-arms accidentally setting the fire that took her life. Whether or not it was true, I cannot say; of a surety, he was banished for it. I daresay House Shahrizai would have had his head, had not Nicola offered him sanctuary in Aragonia.

It was well-done, for whatever the truth of Marmion's crime, he had indeed been loyal to the Queen. Still, I was glad not to have to face him.

It was enough to have one Shahrizai in my life again.

TWENTY-ONE

In an hour's time, I told the story all over again to the King's Consul, Nicola's husband.

Ramiro Zornín de Aragon was a minor lordling of the House of Aragon, and a drunkard in the bargain. For all of that, I rather liked the man. He was good-natured and harmless, and capable of flashes of passion when prodded to it.

The rumor of Carthaginian slave-traders in Amílcar did just that.

I have no doubt Nicola would have urged him had it been necessary, but Lord Ramiro needed no prompting. Whether he liked a life of ease or no, he knew full well where his country's alliances lay, and knew too that his wife was cousin to the Queen of Terre d'Ange and his sons—two boys whom I never met—were half-D'Angeline themselves. By the time I'd finished the tale, he was already shouting for Count Fernan and the Captain of the Harbor Watch to be summoned.

It was rare, I gathered, for Ramiro to exercise the full authority of his role as King's Consul. He did it now, his narrow cheeks flushed with emotion, brown spaniel's eyes alight. Nicola watched him with affectionate pride; it had surprised me, when I first met him, that there was genuine fondness between them. In Terre d'Ange, she had spoken only of his shortcomings, but the bond went deeper than I had reckoned. Nicola was D'Angeline, after all, and no matter what the politics involved, none of Elua's children were likely to linger overlong in a loveless union.

And love takes many forms.

We had a hasty meal before the Count and his Captain of the Watch arrived, and then Fernan was there, black-bearded and broad-shouldered, slow to ire, but clearly unhappy at being summoned thusly by a man he regarded as the King's tame Consul. I saw him rethink the wisdom of it upon being introduced to me, and twice-over to meet Joscelin and Luc, the sons of Verreuil. Joscelin's cool Cassiline bow, crossed vambraces flashing, would have given pause to any man of sense, and Luc . . . bless his Siovalese heart, was an earnest specimen of all that is good and true in the old lines of D'Angeline country noble-dom, with his wide-set blue eyes and his father's courtesies on his lips in hard-learned Aragonian.

In time, between us, we roused the Count to full-blown anger. It took some doing, for he was a large man and stolid with it, secure in his holdings and misliking this sudden insistence on the part of the King's Consul. But he was a proud man, too, and the implications of our news cut him to the quick.

"Carthaginians," Count Fernan rumbled, switching to Caerdicci, a tongue we all held in common. "What do you say, Captain Vitor? Do we harbor Carthaginian slavers in Amílcar?"

Vitor Gaitán, Captain of the Harbor Watch, shrugged his shoulders. He was a lean man, with cheeks pitted by a childhood pox. "The lady's Tsingani may say so, but Tsingani lie. Give me your leave, my lord Count, and I will tell you ere daybreak."

"My leave." Count Fernan pounded one massive fist on the table. "My leave! By Mithra, you have my leave to turn Amílcar upside down!"

So it was done.

We rode out, that night, to see it done. Nicola, reckoning it folly to observe the rude proceedings, would have no part in it—and I did not blame her. It was an unpleasant business. Still, I had set it in motion, and I felt I should bear witness to it. Let us see, I thought grimly, how much bitter truth there is in the words of the lady's Tsingani; mayhap the Aragonians will not be so quick to condemn Hyacinthe's folk one day. We went with Lord Ramiro and an escort of his guards, as well as Jean-Richarde and Donan, the men-at-arms of Verreuil.

It was a night streaked with torchlight and steel, the air filled with the tang of salt water and the protests of desperate men. Captain Vitor's troops were ungentle, travelling in mass, rousting ship after ship in the harbor, turning out the inhabitants of dockside inns and flophouses and putting them to question at sword's-point.

I sat astride my steady mare, shuddering as three members of the Harbor Watch took to clubbing a poor Carthaginian sailor about the head and shoulders with the pommels of their swords on suspicion of lying. "My lady!" he shouted with a blood-reddened mouth, catching sight of me. "Gracious lady, I cry you mercy!"

Would that I had not understood the pidgin Aragonian he spoke— but I did. My ear was good enough for that. I turned my head and looked away, murmuring to Lord Ramiro, "Can they not question him more gently?"

To his credit, the King's Consul looked ill, though not so ill as Luc. "I've invoked Count Fernan's aid, Comtesse. I must let him proceed as he sees fit." He raised a silver flask and took a healthy swig of brandy, then passed it to me. "Here. It helps."

So we watched, and the methods of Captain Vitor and the Harbor Watch, brutal though they were, proved effective. One rumor, gasped from a split-lipped Carthaginian mouth, led to another. Under duress, an unspoken code of silence crumbled. Members of the Watch converged from every vector, bearing blood-stained scraps of gossip and hearsay. There was a man—no, two men, or three—who rented lodgings in the mean alleys, Carthaginians, yes, of a surety, eking out rent in copper coins, known to have met with the Menekhetan slaver Fadil Chouma, yes, known to buy opium in significant amounts . . .

Among all of us, I daresay it was Joscelin who bore the investigation with the most composure. While I averted my eyes and Luc leaned over his mount, retching, and the men of Verreuil breathed hard and grew pale, and Lord Ramiro gulped at his flask, Joscelin's features were set with Cassiline stoicism.

I had seen him look thus in the early days, when he escorted me to assignations.

By the time dawn broke sullen and grey, the smiling dolphins breaching in the harbor, blowing spume from their blowholes, Captain Vitor Gaitán had his answer. He grinned like a wolf as he led his men through the twisting alleys, his eyes gleaming above his pock-marked cheeks. A blowsy woman emerged on a second-story balcony, shrieking protests and imprecations as his men lent their shoulders to the door below. The Harbor Watch ignored her, heaving to with all their muscle. The lock burst, flimsy wood splintering around it.

We sat our mounts in the alley, watching as two Carthaginian men were shoved out into the grey light of dawn, blinking with shock and dishevelment, shackled half-unawares. Captain Vitor strode toward us.

"My lord," he said in Aragonian, bowing to Ramiro. "My lady."

He turned to me, and I saw in his fierce, pitted face a father's fury. "You will want to see this."

Needing no translation, I slid down from my mount, Joscelin an unthinking half-step behind me, following with his hands on his daggers as I raised my skirts and stepped across the threshold.

Inside, it was dark, and stank of cabbage and near-spoiled meat. There was a table and chairs, a few personal effects in the front room, an empty jug of wine tipped on its side. A member of the Harbor Watch sidled past me, a torch raised high. I saw the back room it illuminated, shrouded in darkness, reeking like a kennel. Two pairs of eyes, low to the ground, reflected the torchlight. I gasped, unable to help myself.

They were children, two of them, their fine-boned features marking them clearly as D'Angeline. A boy and a girl, ten or twelve at most. They clung to one another, scrabbling in the urine-fouled straw given them for bedding, pale-skinned with lack of sun, the irises of their eyes swallowed in the vast, dilated blackness of their pupils.

Behind me, I heard Joscelin utter a curse like it was a prayer.

Ignoring him, I knelt slowly, letting the skirts of my riding gown fall heedless over the filthy straw. "Agnette Écot?" I asked softly, keeping my gaze on the girl's face. I had seen, in her hollow eyes, her hungry cheekbones, an echo of the dairy-crofter's wife.

Pushing herself into the corner as hard as she dared, the girl nodded slowly; once, twice. Yes. The boy, younger, sought to press himself behind her, ducking his head, a tangle of hair like autumn oak-leaves falling over his brow.

Whoever he was, he was not Imriel de la Courcel.

"Agnette," I said in steady D'Angeline. "My name is Phèdre. I was sent to find you. These men are your friends." Sitting on my heels, I extended one hand to her. "You're safe now. Will you come out?"

A pause, then a flurry in the shadows, two heads shaking, lank hair flying, scrambling fear and mistrust. Joscelin took a step past me, squatting in the straw, the torchlight gleaming red on his polished vambraces. "Do you see these? No one will harm you further," he said, his voice flat and dispassionate. "In Cassiel's name, I swear it on pain of death."

With a sound like a sob, Agnette Écot flung herself at him, burying her face against his chest, slender limbs clinging to him monkeylike. Joscelin rose, straightening, with the girl in his arms, his head brushing the low rafters as he carried her out.

"Come," I said to the strange boy, my heart breaking at his wide-eyed terror at being left behind. He took my hand in a death-grip, letting me lead him from the Carthaginians' lodgings. No sooner had we reached the grey dawn-light of the alley than Luc stepped forth, his face haggard and drawn, and the boy fixed on him with a wordless cry, catching him about the waist, seeing somewhat he recognized in his kind, Siovalese features.

I stood in the street, my arms empty.

"So." Captain Vitor Gaitán sat his own mount, looking down at me. His men had the Carthaginians well in tow. "It is done. You have the children." He spoke Caerdicci with a sibilant Aragonian accent. "And the Count . . ." his gaze flicked toward Lord Ramiro, ". . . has his answer."

"*An* answer." Ramiro Zornín de Aragon drew up his cloak and his dignity. "We will not rest until we have a full accounting of how this came to pass."

Three children. The Tsingani had seen three. I met Joscelin's eyes, above the head of the girl he carried. "Agnette," I said gently, brushing her tangled locks. "Was there another? Was there a third with you, another boy?"

She muttered fitfully, turning her head. It was the other who answered, the other boy, whimpering in Luc's comforting arms. "Imri!" he whispered, jerking restlessly. "Imri!"

One of the Carthaginian prisoners said somewhat to the other, who laughed harshly, spitting on the packed earth of the alley. Although I did not understand the words, I heard the name Fadil Chouma spoken.

The Menekhetan slaver.

"My lord Ramiro speaks the truth," I said to the Captain of the Harbor Watch, speaking Caerdicci, light-headed with anger and despair. "We will have a full accounting. There were three children; three D'Angeline children stolen. Two, we have found. Ask these men: What have they done with the third?"

Vitor Gaitán inclined his head. "It shall be done."

TWENTY-TWO

İT WAS done.

It was done in accordance with Aragonian law, which is harsh and exacting. If I had known, at the time, what I was asking, I do not know if I would have had the stomach to ask it.

Count Fernan put the Carthaginians to torture.

And this, too, I made myself witness, for this too, I had caused to be done. It was carried out in the dungeon of the Count's keep, a room of dank stone and iron.

Nicola L'Envers y Aragon accompanied me.

It surprised me, a little; but it was a different thing, to watch a controlled proceeding, than to observe the mayhem in the harbor. Mayhap she feared to let me observe it alone; mayhap it was only that she had seen the children's condition when we brought them to the Consul's quarters. I do not know. I know only that I was grateful to have her there.

They had names, these men—Mago and Harnapos. First one, and then the other. One was held in chains, while the other was seated on a wooden stool, his ankles in stocks, as two strong men held his arms and the Count's enforcer lowered a burning torch beneath the soles of his bare feet. So did they make their confessions, and a fourth man recorded it all on a waxen tablet, his stylus scratching without cease.

It goes without saying that they screamed, though I will say it anyway. They screamed, as their skin blistered and blackened and split, and the torch sizzled with dripping fluids and the smell of roasting meat filled their cell. It took all the strength of the Count's men to hold Harnapos, the larger of the two, for his chest swelled and his throat corded like iron as he screamed himself raw. I daresay he nearly wrenched his arms from their sockets in his struggle.

My blood beating in my ears, I watched it all in a crimson haze.

Nicola translated for me, her low voice murmuring D'Angeline my only line to sanity. If the words caught in her throat, still, she kept on without faltering, and for that too, I was grateful. I do not think I could have borne it otherwise. For all that I have played at such things throughout my life, in the end, there is little resemblance between the emulation and the reality.

I have known the latter, too. And even I do not care to remember it.

Thus the Carthaginians' story: They had met a man in Carthage, the Menekhetan slaver Fadil Chouma, and fell to drinking pots of beer in a tavern. He told them there were buyers, mysterious buyers with a dire purpose in mind, that there was a fortune to be made for any man who might procure D'Angelines for sale in foreign markets. Mago was mountain-born. He had friends among the Euskerri. He had a map. He had a plan. They would meet in Amílcar.

It was as simple as that.

And Mago and Harnapos had travelled to northern Aragonia, plying on the trade-rights Carthage enjoyed, had evaded the sparse border patrols and gone into the mountains with their map and their plan, crossing into Siovale, picking their prey with cunning. Goat-herds, cow-herds, shepherd's children, picking those who would not be missed, those whose loss would be grieved in silence, abducting them in stealth—they used a leathern baton, Harnapos gasped, weighted with lead shot, to strike their victims at the base of the skull. Afterward, quick flight and a careful erasing of tracks, tactics learned from the Euskerri, and tincture of opium to keep the children compliant.

It was here that I interrupted, putting my questions, which Nicola translated, to the Count's enforcer. Where in Siovale? How many children? Where had they been taken? There was a pause, as one of Fernan's men retrieved the map. Mago pointed with a trembling finger, beads of sweat glistening on his face. Here, here and here. Yes, three children, there had been a third. A boy, yes, a flawless child, fierce as a wildcat, with black hair and eyes of blue, the prize of the lot.

And where was the boy now?

Neither wanted to answer, although I think they knew, then, that death was a foregone conclusion. I was unfamiliar with the laws of Aragonia, but I knew to read faces and I saw only death writ in the expressions of Count Fernan's men, and in the grave countenance of Nicola, who was wife to a King's Consul. Still, hope is tenacious, and men will cling to it against overwhelming odds. In the corner, Harnapos whimpered, rattling his chains. Mago slumped on the stool, sweat-streaked and panting, raising his head to meet my eyes.

He was a man, only a man, thoughtlessly cruel and greedy, reduced by his folly to abject pain, his ruined feet useless as lumps of tallow. Caught in the net of Kushiel's justice, he had walked into it of his own accord. And yet I had been in such a place, once, a terrible prison of stone, where humanity was stripped away by madness. Despite it all, despite his guilt, there was a spark of kinship between us.

One victim knows another.

What will you give me, his desperate gaze begged me, for the answers you seek? He did not speak my tongue, but he knew; he had heard my voice ask the questions.

I felt the presence of Kushiel, bronze wings buffeting—the Punisher of God, wielder of the rod and flail, despised, irresistible; ah, Elua! It was a storm in my head. Through the blood-haze that veiled my eyes, I saw the Count's enforcer nod, the men take Mago's arms, the torch lowered to his feet.

"Wait!" The word emerged harsh; I had spoken in Caerdicci unthinking. The Count's men knew it, and paused. "A clean death," I said, drawing a racking breath. "A clean death, if he answers it honestly."

It was all I had to give, and at that, not mine to offer. The Count's enforcer looked at Nicola. To her credit, she never paused, lifting her chin imperiously, addressing him in Aragonian. "The Comtesse of Montrève, favored of her majesty Ysandre de la Courcel, the Queen of Terre d'Ange, has spoken. The King's Consul of the House of Aragon concurs. Let it be so."

Mago exhaled, a long shuddering breath; the self-same breath, it seemed to me, that I had drawn. His hands, pinned by the Count's men, clenched and unclenched. Only a man, after all. I had no knowledge of his life, his history, the exigencies of a harsh lot that had driven him, had driven Harnapos, to commit such a vile act. His head fell forward, accepting the bargain. In a broken whisper, he told the rest of his tale.

Folly, nothing but folly. Although the Tsingani had refused them, they had procured a wagon in the end, smuggling the sedated children into Amílcar beneath the careless eyes of the Harbor Watch, who gave a cursory probe into the goods they carried. Thence to port, and the meeting ordained—the rest was but Menekhetan treachery, smooth-tongued Fadil Chouma and a ship bound for Iskandria claiming their agreement had been for autumn, not spring. He would arrange for buyers on the other end, yes, but it was a matter of some delicacy, they must understand. D'Angeline blood will out, and Terre d'Ange notoriously ferocious in its persecution of slavers, of course . . . Menekhet is far, but Khebbel-im-Akkad holds much sway, and the Khalif's son wed to the Queen's own kinswoman . . . perhaps he might take the one, yes, that one, peerless, that face . . . aiyee! And fierce, too, stronger than he looks, but Fadil Chouma had a buyer in mind; one, only one, mind, seeking somewhat special . . . another draught of opium, perhaps? Yes, a buyer in mind, and one fit to tame a mountain hellion, no, no names . . .

So much did I gather, piecing Mago's story together, leaving me sick with despair. "And you've no idea the buyer's name? The buyer in Iskandria?"

He didn't, nor did Harnapos. The Count's enforcer made sure of it, applying the flames over my protest. As much as they screamed and writhed, they knew no more; only that the Menekhetan had paid the purchase-price for the boy, less than they had agreed, promising to return in the fall for the other two if this deal went as planned, and meanwhile Mago and Harnapos left to care for a steadily weakening pair of D'Angeline children, keeping them hidden, keeping them silent, using the dwindling reserves of their money to buy lodgings, food, the opium that kept them sedated. No, they swore, both of them in extremis, they had left the children unmolested and intact, they were not such fools as to damage valuable merchandise, nor had they beaten them, no, not unduly, only enough to make them mind . . .

"Enough." I pressed my fingers to my aching temples. "It is enough. Let them give what information they may regarding Fadil Chouma and the arrangements for his return. I have no more questions."

Nicola spoke to the Count's enforcer, and I made no effort to follow the conversation. Kushiel's presence had faded, and I felt hollow, tired to the bone and ill with what I had seen. "It will be done," Nicola said to me when she had finished. Her voice was steady, lending me strength. "Fernan's clerk will see that you receive a full transcription of the account."

"Thank you," I murmured. "And the Carthaginians?"

"Execution at dawn. It will be public," she said, "but swift."

I nodded, and looked one last time at the men in the cell. "Then let us go."

Outside, evening sunlight gilded the Plaza del Rey. The fading blue sky seemed a vast openness, the salt tang of the harbor mingling with the fresh cool breeze from the north. Nicola shuddered, filling her lungs with clean air. "Elua! I'll not need to see the likes of that again soon."

"No," I said. "Nor I."

"It's a long way from playing with silken ropes and deerskin floggers," she mused. An involuntary shiver ran over my skin and I closed my eyes briefly, opening them to find Nicola regarding me. "Even after that, Phèdre?" she asked simply.

"Always." I gritted my teeth. "Always."

"Ah." For a moment, she continued to look at me, our escort of Lord Ramiro's men waiting at a polite distance. "Somehow, I understand a little better now why you chose to fix your heart on that damned Cassiline."

Unexpectedly, it made me smile. "It wasn't a question of choice."

"Nor for him, I suppose. Well, credit it to the wisdom of Blessed Elua." Nicola gathered herself with a shake. "Come on. I've need of a bath and a drink, and mayhap not in that order."

In the private dining-hall of the King's Consul, we found our companions well ahead of us. The remnants of an early meal were scattered across the table and the wine had flowed freely; for once, even Joscelin had drunk enough for it to show.

"I'm sorry," he said unevenly, greeting me with an embrace. There was a tension in his body that the wine had not dispelled. "Phèdre, I'm sorry, but I couldn't go with you, I couldn't bear to watch. I knew you were safe enough. I'd have gone, otherwise."

"I know." I found a clean glass and a flagon of brandy, and downed a measure, welcoming the burning heat of it in my belly. "It wasn't something you needed to see."

"No." His expression twisted, nostrils flaring. "But I was near angry enough to want to. And it frightened me. What did you learn? What have they done with Imriel?"

"Sold him." I poured another glass and curled myself into a corner of a dining-couch, letting weariness claim me. "Sold him to a Menekhetan slaver, bound for a buyer in Iskandria. How are the children?"

Joscelin sat down beside me, head in his hands. "Menekhet," he murmured. "Blessed Elua. They're sleeping," he added belatedly, nodding in the vague direction of the guest quarters. "Well enough, under the circumstances. Ramiro's chirurgeon examined them, and said they've taken no serious harm. Fear mostly, and lack of proper food and light. Opium sickness is the worst of it. It will be some days before they're fit to travel. Weeks, mayhap."

"Weeks." I watched Nicola, Ramiro and Luc in conversation. "We can't wait weeks. If we book passage tomorrow, we can be in Iskandria before Fadil Chouma departs. He said he'd return for the other two, though he may have been lying. As soon as the Count's clerk sends the description—"

"No." Joscelin lifted his head and stared at me. "Phèdre, are you mad? This has gone far enough. We found the trail here in Amílcar because of Nicola and Lord Ramiro's help. How far do you think we'd get in Iskandria, the two of us, alone? Neither of us even speak the language, and we've scarcely funds enough for passage." He shook his head. "No. Enough. We're going home to the City, and making a report to Ysandre. She's the Queen, Phèdre. If she wants to pursue it, she has resources at her disposal."

"I could find a factor in Iskandria willing to loan money—"

"No!" Across the room, Luc startled at Joscelin's raised voice. Joscelin sighed. "Name of Elua, you're like a bloodhound on the scent. Phèdre, listen to me. Luc's agreed to stay until the children are strong enough to travel, and Ramiro's offered his hospitality. Luc and the men of Verreuil will see the children restored. If this Menekhetan's coming back, they'll catch him here in Amílcar. You and I are catching a ship to Marsilikos, and going home."

"Fine." I closed my eyes, the warming heat of the brandy spreading lassitude throughout my limbs. I hadn't slept since the night before we arrived in Amílcar. He was right, of course; right, because he was Joscelin, and sensible when it came to risking my safety, and right for reasons both of us, in our exhaustion, had forgotten. "And then what?"

"And then we make our report to Ysandre, and it is in her hands," he said grimly.

"And afterward?" I opened my eyes to look at him. "I promised to return to La Serenissima, Joscelin, and report as much to Melisande. Do you remember what she promised in turn?"

He stared at me a moment, then began to laugh, the soft, humorless laugh of a man defeated by irony. "A guide," he said, pouring a tumbler of brandy and drinking it at a gulp. "The name of a man in Iskandria, who swears he can lead us to Shaloman's people in the south of Jebe-Barkal."

Hyacinthe.

Aware of the presence of an unseen pattern closing upon me, I nodded. "Even so."

TWENTY-THREE

NICOLA'S CHEEK, soft and perfumed, lingered against mine as we embraced in farewell. "Take care of yourself, Phèdre nó Delaunay," she murmured. "I would miss you if anything happened."

"I will." I smiled at her when she released me. "Come to the City, when this is all over. How can I believe you'd miss me, if I never see you?"

"Naamah's Servant, still." She laughed. "I come when I can, and you know it. 'Twas easier before Ramiro's appointment. I may have lacked money, but I had time in abundance. You have my letter for Ysandre?"

"Yes." I patted one of our bulging packs.

"Good." Her expression turned sober. "I promise you, the Harbor Watch stands on full alert. The Menekhetan will be in our hands before his foot touches shore, and a courier en route within the hour."

"Thank you," I said. "For everything. You may be sure, I will advise that Ysandre commend Ramiro to the House of Aragon for his aid as King's Consul."

"It wouldn't do any harm." Nicola watched Luc Verreuil enter the reception hall, a child holding either hand. "But it's not necessary, either." She turned back to me. "I hope you find him."

I opened my mouth to demur and didn't, saying instead, "Elua willing, he'll be found."

She smiled tenderly, lifting one hand to caress my face, the garnet signet winking at her wrist. "By the burning river, my dear. Keep it in mind, whatever your quest. It may come in handy again, one never knows."

"I will," I promised.

I said my farewells in turn to Lord Ramiro and Count Fernan, dourly proud of his men's performance, and then went with Joscelin to bid farewell to his brother and our foundlings, two very different children from those we had found only two days past. Neither was well— one could see the opium sickness in their pallor and trembling—but the worst of the fear had abated, and they stood without cringing or clinging.

"Agnette," Luc said gently, "Sebastien. Say good-bye to the Lady Phèdre and my brother Joscelin, who came all the way from the City of Elua to find you."

They did, in whispering voices.

"You'll be all right?" Joscelin asked his brother.

Luc nodded. "Donal's carrying word to Verreuil; he'll bring a party back to meet us, and Lord Ramiro will send an escort as far as the Pass. Father will alert the Écots, and they'll track down the boy Sebastien's family as well. From what we can tell, they tend sheep near La Crange. Mahieu will find them, like as not." He grinned. "Don't worry, little brother. It's been a right adventure, travelling at your side, and for once, I get to come home the hero. Yvonne's like to box my ears for it."

The boy Sebastien giggled at his words, and I relaxed a little at the sound. They would survive, these children; Blessed Elua willing. No child should have to endure the terror through which they'd gone, but they were young and resilient, and they had a chance to heal.

"Be well," I said to Luc, "and be careful. You'll send word as soon as you're home?"

"I will." He raised my hands to his lips and kissed them. "And I will speak naught but good of the Tsingani from this day forward, I swear it, my lady."

So did we bid farewell to friends, to family, to Amílcar.

It is an easy sail along the coast from thence to Marsilikos, and the summer weather held fair, hot and sunny, with enough wind to fill the sails and set a good pace. It was passing strange, after the arduous travel in the mountains, to find ourselves idle. Between bouts of illness during the first couple of days, Joscelin checked the condition of our mounts in the hold every other hour—no sailor himself, he was sure it was no fit means for horses to travel—but they bore the trip better than he did.

I spent the time doing what I had longed to do for many frustrating weeks, poring over Audine Davul's translation of the Jebean scroll, pondering the tale and its place in my studies of Habiru lore, memo-

rizing the written characters of Jeb'ez, sounding out the phonetic tran-
scriptions of the words she had provided, murmuring sentences over
and over to myself.

Joscelin, when he had gotten over the worst of his seasickness,
watched me incredulously. "You're trying to teach yourself Jeb'ez,
aren't you?"

"Mayhap." I raised my eyebrows. "You said it yourself, Joscelin;
we'd be helpless in Menekhet, neither of us speak the language. Shalomon's descendants may speak Habiru, but how am I supposed to travel
the length of Jebe-Barkal to find them if I can't speak Jeb'ez?"

He lowered himself to the sun-warmed deck to sit beside me. "Melisande doesn't, and she found a guide. He must speak Caerdicci, at
least."

"Hellene." I rolled the parchment and put it back in its case. "Hellene is the scholars' tongue of choice in Menekhet. She'd studied the
Tanakh in Hellene, didn't you note?"

"No." Shoving a coil of rope to one side, he leaned back on his
elbows. "I can't say that I did. Anyway, you speak Hellene. Mayhap
we'll get by in Menekhet after all."

"We might." I watched the blue waves pass the ship's railing. "But
it would leave us dependent on Melisande's guide in Jebe-Barkal. And
whether she's telling the truth or no, it's not an arrangement I care to
trust. I'd a hard enough time enduring my own ignorance in Amílcar."

"Well, add Aragonian to your studies," Joscelin said peaceably. "All
knowledge is worth having, isn't that what Delaunay used to say? If
Luc can master it, anyone can. It's near enough to Caerdicci, anyway.
I'll learn it, if you can't be bothered. Phèdre, what do you think Ysandre
will do?"

"I wish I knew."

"Barquiel will advise her to leave well enough alone," he said. "Like
as not, the boy's a pleasure-slave in some Menekhetan aristocrat's seraglio by now. He doesn't even know who he is. He couldn't have
vanished more thoroughly if he'd been slain."

"Yes," I said slowly. "So Melisande thought, when she sold you
and me to the Skaldi."

"True." Joscelin sat up, wrapping his arms about his knees. "And
it nearly killed us, or at least it did me." His face was quiet, remembering. "I would have died in Selig's steading, if you hadn't shamed
me into living. I wanted to. I was a man grown, with a Cassiline's skills
and training. How do you think Imriel will endure it? He's only a

child." He shuddered, his voice turning harsh. "You saw the others."

"I saw them." I had no answers. Imriel de la Courcel was strong, strong and willful. It was clear in all that was said of him, clear in the stamp of his blood lineage. And, too, he was Melisande's son. Whatever else one could say of her, there was no end of courage in Kushiel's scions. Would Imriel bend or break? I could not say. "Was it that which angered you so?"

"Yes." He rubbed his palms on his knees as if, even now, they itched to strike. "Do you remember . . . you said something to me once. It was in Morhban, after you'd . . . well. As we were leaving."

"I remember." It had been on our mad chase to Alba, to bring Drustan mab Necthana and an army of Cruithne to D'Angeline soil to face Selig's invading Skaldi. I had traded my favors to Duc Quincel de Morhban in exchange for passage across his holdings; a trade, I think, neither of us regretted. Joscelin had been less pleased. Although we'd not been lovers at the time, my *anguissette*'s proclivities offended his sensibilities.

"You tried to explain it to me—the pleasure, the *relief* in surrendering one's will to a patron. You asked me if I didn't feel somewhat similar when I gave in to defiance, when I fought against the Skaldi, Gunter's thanes, or Selig's, even knowing I would lose."

"And you owned that you did." I smiled. "I accused you of having a terrible temper."

"Buried under Cassiline discipline." Joscelin acknowledged it with a nod. "You were right, though I didn't want to hear it. Even so, I've never felt the sort of rage that could only spend itself in another's suffering. I felt it, the other day, when we found those poor children. I wanted to see the Carthaginians bleed for what they had done. It frightens me, Phèdre, to know that's in me."

"As it should." I touched his arm. "Joscelin, what's in you is no worse than what's in anyone else; a good deal better, rather. You're just more loathe than the rest of us to accept your own mortal failings. In the end, it's what you do with them that matters."

He looked sidelong at me. "I accepted you, didn't I?"

"Eventually," I said evenly. Joscelin laughed.

"Ah, well . . . the thing is, Phèdre, what would happen if I did give in to it? Such a rage, I mean."

"I don't know." I thought about it and shook my head. "Who can say? All I know is that if you ever did, you'd have a damnable good reason for it."

"I suppose." It relaxed him a little. "I hope it never comes to it."

Our voyage passed in like days, bright and idle. The Aragonian crew was pleasant and good-natured, and we dined some evenings at the Captain's table in his neat quarters. He was from Amílcar, an educated man who spoke fluent Caerdicci. He reckoned himself Count Fernan's man, but he spoke well of Lord Ramiro and his D'Angeline wife. Nicola, I knew, was a gracious hostess. I daresay Ramiro owed his present appointment to her skills, though to his credit, he seemed to do a fair enough job at it.

At length we arrived in Marsilikos.

If I had been less impatient, I would have paid a visit to Roxanne de Mereliot, the Lady of Marsilikos. She had been a friend for many years, and one of the few I trusted implicitly. But I was loathe to delay after so long on the road, through mountains and over sea. We had left one pack-mule in Siovale and the other in Amílcar; by now, we'd naught but our mounts and such baggage as they could carry. It would do. There were inns and villages all along Eisheth's Way to the City of Elua. If we hoarded our remaining coin with care, we needed to carry little in the way of provisions.

Travelling lightly and tarrying seldom, we made good time. It was a glorious summer day when we reached the City of Elua.

I hadn't realized how good it would feel to come home.

The white walls of the City glowed like a promise in the lazy afternoon sunlight and the guards, recognizing us, ushered us through the southern gates with a cheer. We had been missed. I saw even Joscelin smile, and raise one hand in salute, steel vambrace flashing. Truly, I thought, this has become his home, too. He has a place here, that no longer exists for him in Verreuil.

Word raced ahead of us, borne by one of the intrepid lads such as hang about the guards at the City gates, waiting for something of note to happen. I've no doubt Eugènie paid him in coin for the news, for by the time we arrived at my charming house tucked into the end of a winding street below the Palace hill, a joyous reception awaited us.

"Name of Elua!" Ti-Philippe was fair dancing with excitement. "It's about *time* you came back, my lady! Whatever missive you sent to the Queen, Court's been buzzing like a hive for a month and more, and her close-mouthed as a clam about it. You could have sent to us, you know. What is it? Did you find the boy?"

I opened my mouth to reply.

"Oh, let her be," Eugènie scolded, thrusting Ti-Philippe out of the way and coming forward to embrace me. "Come, my lady, ignore him. I've water heating for the bath, it will be done in a trice, and supper to follow. Julien's run down to the market to see if they've got fresh snapper yet . . ."

On it went, a litany of domestic comforts. I was home.

Ti-Philippe could wait; I had my bath first, luxuriating in hot water, fragrant with sweet oils, a handful of dried lavender floating on the surface and candles set about everywhere. When all was said and done, I was a courtesan still. Nicola was right in that. My bedchamber, I share with Joscelin, and no patron has ever seen it. But my bathing-room was my own.

Afterward, I lay on the massage-table and Eugènie's niece Clory rubbed my travel-weary body with an oil containing an infusion of mint, soothing and refreshing. I scarce knew the girl; she'd been new-hired in the spring. Not so new, now. It was I who had been absent.

"You've good hands, Clory," I murmured, eyes half-closed.

"I've been studying with a masseur from Balm House, my lady." Her voice was tentative, though her hands were sure, thumbs pressing hard into the small of my back, relieving days' worth of saddle-ache. "Aunt Eugènie said you would be pleased?"

"Your aunt is a wise woman." In the Court of Night-Blooming Flowers, Balm House is dedicated to comfort and solace. I sat up reluctantly. "Thank you, Clory."

She flushed with pleasure, holding out a silk robe in the proper manner. "You liked it? Master Lugard said a raw apprentice wasn't fit to tend to Kushiel's Chosen."

"What?" I looked over my shoulder, twisting my damp hair out of the way. "Well, the more fool, he. Listen to your aunt, child, she's wiser than him. I grew up in the Night Court, and I know how its servants gossip. I was one. Your skills are a welcome addition, but in my household, as Eugènie knows well, I value discretion above all else. Do you understand?"

"My lady." Clory bobbed a fervent curtsy, oil-slickened hands clutched together as if to hold something precious. "I understand, my lady. I would never betray your trust, never!"

"Good." I smiled at her, thinking to myself; child, Blessed Elua, I called her child! I never thought to hear such a thing from my own lips. "And the next time anyone dares suggest you're not fit to serve me, tell them I say otherwise."

"I will, my lady." Another curtsy, adoration in her eyes. "Thank you, my lady."

Ah, Elua. I sat before my mirror after dismissing Clory. My own face regarded me quizzically, fair and shadowed by candlelight, the dark pools of my eyes, a rose-petal of crimson marring the left, beautiful still, but not a maiden's anymore. A mouth made for love, the smooth curve of eyelid, brows arched like gentle wings. How long, I thought, tracing my features in the steam-misted glass, before it begins to fade? It is one of the ephemeral qualities most cherished in Cereus House— beauty at its fullest bloom, before the first sere kiss of frost. If I were an adept proper, pampered and cosseted, I might maintain it for years. On the road, the dark road that lay ahead . . . who could say?

"Phèdre." Joscelin leaned in the doorway. "Ti-Philippe's like to die of impatience if you don't come down to supper, and Clory's dropped a plate of sliced melon in Eugènie's geraniums. What have you done to overexcite the poor girl so?"

"Me?" I looked up at him. "Nothing."

"No?" He grinned. "It doesn't take much, with you. Come on, let's eat. I understand young Hugues has composed some few dozen poems in your honor, too. You'll not want to miss them."

TWENTY-FOUR

AFTER AN excellent meal—and indeed, a number of dubious verses—we talked long into the night, Joscelin and Ti-Philippe and I; I daresay we'd have stayed up until dawn, if not for the fact that Ysandre had left standing orders for me to report to her presence upon my return.

In the end, I went short enough of sleep as it was. Mayhap it was folly, but thus is ever the case in matters of love. I was reminded, with each homecoming, how precious was the life I had been given, how scant the time in which to cherish it. I was Kushiel's Chosen, yes; but Naamah's Servant, too. And she sees fit to reward her servants from time to time.

Moonlight filtered through the garden window into the bedchamber, the fine-spun linens soft and welcoming, scented with dried herbs. I dropped my robes standing in a square of moonlight, reached up with both hands to unbind Joscelin's braid when he had shed his own clothing. The tips of my breasts brushed his hard chest and his unbound hair spilled like flaxen silk over my hands, over his shoulders. I pressed my mouth to the hollow of his throat, tasting the salt of his skin, tracing his collarbones with my tongue.

"Phèdre," he whispered, lifting me onto the bed.

I used my art, yes; it was not the first time. I had, for this moment, a respite from Kushiel's unbearable presence, the demands of his choosing. It was a full moon that hung over my garden—Naamah's moon, a lovers' moon, round and silver. I let it take me, take us both, the tides of my blood matching its draw. A yearning of heart and loins, simple and sweet. I performed the *languisement* upon him until his phallus leapt like a fish on a line, taut and straining, a shimmering drop of seed forming at the tip.

And he—Joscelin smiled, heavy-lidded in the moonlight, infinitely patient with the long training of Cassiline discipline, raising me to capture my mouth with his, a languorous dance of tongues, his hands tracing my marque, molding my flesh out of Naamah's night, his fingers parting the petals betwixt my thighs. I sighed at the touch of his lips, his mouth at my breasts, suckling my nipples, his tongue tracing a path lower, probing the folds of my flesh to seek the hidden pearl.

Until I pushed him flat on the bed, straddling him, guiding his phallus into me with a shuddering exhalation, slick and aching with desire. Joscelin laughed softly, hair spread like moonlight on the pillows, hands on my haunches as I rode him, wave after wave of pleasure washing through me. "Some *anguissette*."

"Are you complaining?" I gasped.

"No." He sat up without dislodging me, arms coming hard around me. I wrapped my legs about his waist, taking his face in both hands and kissing him. "I take such gifts as they come," he murmured when I lifted my head, "and ask no questions."

Nor did I.

One day, mayhap, I will be wise enough to understand the ways of the gods. For now, it was enough to take what was offered, mercifully devoid of pain's cruel yearnings; pleasure, Naamah's coin, pure and unalloyed, graced with the presence of love.

Blessed Elua's presence. *Hold this near to your heart*, it whispered.

I did, and did, until we lay sated and exhausted, my head on Joscelin's chest, the soft breeze cooling our sweat-dampened skin. Still awake, he toyed with my hair as it mingled with his, lazily braiding our locks together. "See." He stroked the cabled length of it, sable and blond. "Dark and fair, intertwined as our lives."

It gave me an unexpected jolt of memory. I had done that very thing—twelve years ago, it must be—in Anafiel Delaunay's study, with Alcuin, who'd been nearly a brother to me; Alcuin, whose hair was as white as milk. I might have forgotten it, had Delaunay not entered in that very moment, bearing word that Melisande Shahrizai had come to offer me an assignation for the Longest Night.

And in the seeds of that offer lay betrayal and horror, the study turned abattoir, Delaunay dead and Alcuin dying, his white hair sticky with blood.

I hadn't known, then. How could I have known? I had no gift of the *dromonde* to read the future like an open book. I had merely startled at Delaunay's entrance, tugging my caught hair and feeling foolish.

This time, I took the omen to heart.

Beauty at its fullest bloom, before the first sere kiss of frost.

It needed no dream, no seer to give warning. Beneath the languor of pleasure, I felt the weariness of long travel in my bones, and a thousand miles lying before me . . . and in the distance, like hunting-horns blowing on the wind, the call of Kushiel's justice. *Hold this near to your heart.* Our twined locks, joined fates, lay quiescent on his chest. I gazed at Joscelin's face, relaxed and unguarded, as if to engrave it on my memory.

"Why do you look at me so?" he asked.

"Because," I said, "I love you."

Unsurprisingly, I slept overlong and woke to broad daylight and the Queen's summons waiting. At the Palace, we were met with alacrity and ushered into Ysandre and Drustan's presence.

Ysandre's face was unreadable. For once, she made no rebuke when I curtsied to them in greeting. Whether or not she was wroth that I had circumvented her authority, I could not say. She'd gotten the letter I had sent by courier from Verreuil, and I daresay she knew from my demeanor that the news was not good.

"Tell me," was all she said.

Drawing a deep breath, I did, leaving out no detail, with Joscelin supplying additional commentary. When I had finished, I gave her Nicola's letter. Ysandre read it without speaking, passing it to Drustan.

"I'm sorry, my lady," I ventured at length, unable to bear the silence.

"Don't be." Ysandre's gaze returned from the unknowable monarchal distance on which she'd fixed it. "You did well to find him. I'm grateful for it."

"Thank you."

"Mind you," the Queen's voice took on an edge, "I am not entirely pleased that you chose to question my uncle the Duc without my fore-knowledge, nor the priest Selbert, whose actions skirt dangerously close to treason. Still, I have learned well enough, Phèdre nó Delaunay, when it is unwise to interfere." I said nothing, and Ysandre sighed. "How is it that you never solve one puzzle without laying a greater one at my feet?"

"I'm sorry, my lady," I repeated.

"Oh, stop it." Ysandre rested her chin on her fist and regarded Drustan as he laid down Nicola's letter. "What do you say? How would the Cruarch of Alba handle such a matter?"

Drustan gave a wry smile at odds with his tattooed features. "What do you think, love? We are barbarians, after all. If a Prince of the Cullach Gorrym were stolen, the Cullach Gorrym would ride to war. It is not so simple in Terre d'Ange, and this thief is no rival tribesman, but a merchant from a distant land, with no idea of the value of his prize. You can hardly go to war against Menekhet over it."

"No," Ysandre said soberly. "Nor, I think, would Parliament support the notion. Carthage, now . . . blood will run hot over their crime. I will have no trouble, I think, recommending that we demand reparation from the oligarchy. It must be done, lest this should happen again; even so, what merit in it in terms of regaining the boy? The Carthaginian thieves are dead, Nicola writes, executed at the Count of Amílcar's command. You saw it done?"

It had been done. We had not watched it. I'd seen enough, even for my conscience.

"It was a public execution, my lady," I said. "Their heads were mounted on poles in the Plaza del Rey as a warning. That much, we saw."

"Unsubtle," Ysandre said. "Pray it proves effective. Still . . ." She shook her head, troubled. "Menekhet. They've little enough power, but it is an ancient nation, and cunning. Mayhap this slaver, this Fadil Chouma will return to Amílcar; mayhap not. I must presume the latter to be true, and proceed accordingly. There is our alliance with Khebbel-im-Akkad, but it is a tenuous one, and I suspect my uncle Barquiel would oppose me in this matter. It is his own daughter wed to the Khalif's son; without him, I do not like the odds of Akkadian support. If I offer a ransom for the boy's return—what then? Without the teeth of a threat, it admits weakness. In what risk do I then place my own people, my own children?"

"Treat it as a matter of trade," Drustan offered. He shrugged as she glanced at him. "A private matter couched in a greater, a Queen's whim fulfilled to grease the wheels of trade. If I have learned anything since Alba entered the broader world, it is that no nation disdains trade. Parliament may not authorize the threat of force against Menekhet— and I think you are right; for Melisande's son, they will not—but they would have no likely objection to a trade delegation. Especially," he added, "if your delegates bear an interest in Alban goods. Then it is the Cruarch's concern, and not Parliament's."

"A clever thought, for a barbarian." Ysandre's voice was soft. "You would do that?"

"Our goods, your delegates. Why not?" Drustan grinned. "We might make an exchange of it. Do you think you could persuade a few Azzallese shipwrights to winter in Alba?"

"I might." Ysandre smiled back at him. How strange it must be, I thought, to be wed not merely as husband and wife but Cruarch and Queen, trading men's lives and the wealth of nations as love-tokens.

I said none of this aloud, asking instead, "Who would you send?"

"Amaury Trente," Ysandre said without hesitation. "He'll argue against it, but he'll go in the end and I can trust to his discretion. Whatever transpires, I'd as soon this stayed quiet, Phèdre. Too many people would like to see it fail."

"Of course." I inclined my head. Her choice was a good one. I had ridden with Lord Amaury Trente on the flight from La Serenissima, when he served as her Captain of the Guard. For all that he would rail against the wisdom of it, he would do all in his power to locate Imriel de la Courcel and see him restored to Terre d'Ange. His loyalty was beyond question.

"What do you say, Messire Cassiline?" Ysandre asked Joscelin with genuine curiosity. "Is it wisely done?"

Joscelin bowed to her, his forearms crossed. "It is. Do you send to Verreuil, I give my word that my family's discretion will equal our own."

"I doubted it not." The Queen looked at me. "What will you do now?"

"Now?" I squared my shoulders against the burden of it. "I have some few things to be done in the City, my lady. There is a Yeshuite scholar I would consult, and some others. Then . . ." I drew a breath. "Then we ride to La Serenissima. I have a promise to fulfill, and a name to garner. Elua willing, we will be in Iskandria not long after Lord Trente."

"I thought as much." Ysandre's expression softened. "Ah, Phèdre! If you must do this thing, must you do it on Melisande's terms? Surely a courier could bear the news, and some other guide be found. I will not demand it of you, but Blessed Elua knows, if you are going to Iskandria, I would be passing glad to have your presence at Amaury's side. What do you owe Melisande, that you must deliver this news yourself?"

It caught me out; I'd not expected the offer, nor the question. They were looking at me, all of them, awaiting my answer. I felt my heart beat, slow and thudding, in my breast, the blood beating in my ears.

"I don't know," I said. My voice sounded small. I raised my hand unthinking, reaching for the diamond that no longer hung at my throat. "Forgive me, my lady, but I truly don't."

"So be it." Ysandre sighed. "You are bound on this quest to free the Tsingano?"

I nodded mutely.

"And you will go with her?" She bent her gaze on Joscelin.

"I have sworn it." His voice was flat.

Ysandre raised her brows. "Is there aught I may do to aid you in it?"

Joscelin shook his head. "Pray for us, your majesty."

"Wait. There is one thing." I met Drustan's eyes. "You will return to Alba come autumn? And Sibeal with you?"

"We will," he said slowly, catching the shape of my thought. "You think that the Master of the Straits will hear her?"

"I think he will." I swallowed. "They are seers alike, Anasztaizia's son and Necthana's daughter. I didn't understand it, when we met on the waters; her dream, that is. I see more clearly, now. If you . . . if you do not seek to land, but only to converse, I think he will allow it. And I might give her a message to bear. It is a long road, truly. We will be a year and more upon it. A word of hope . . . it might help him to endure."

"Speak with Sibeal," said Drustan mab Necthana. "If it be her will, I will see it done."

TWENTY-FIVE

Ì MET with Sibeal, Drustan's sister, in the Royal Mews.

There had been, I gathered, no few offers of lover's tokens or of marriage for the Cruarch of Alba's sister during her time in Terre d'Ange. Insofar as I heard, Sibeal had refused them all, with a serene grace against which no one could take offense. Instead, she preferred to spend her time in the unlikeliest of pursuits.

Currently, it was visiting the mews.

The Head Falconer, a slight, dark man with the aquiline features of his own charges, clearly adored her. He watched with doting eyes as she assumed the duty of feeding the fledglings, carrying a basket filled with gobbets of meat. Awkward and still partially down-feathered, the young birds craned their heads toward her with beaks parted, maws agape.

"Drustan said you wished to see me," Sibeal said in her soft Cruithne accent, setting down the basket.

"Yes." A bell rang beside my right ear, on the jesses of a perched hawk as it roused, then preened. I sidled to my left. "I have a message for Hyacinthe."

Her dark eyes were calm and unsurprised. "And you wish . . . ?"

"I wish you to bear it for me," I said firmly. The Head Falconer, clucking, hurried past me with gauntleted arm extended, untying the hawk's jesses and coaxing it onto his arm. It was not my choice of venue, but I had little time to waste.

"I do not think," Sibeal said reflectively, "the Master of the Straits wishes to let any vessel draw nigh."

"He'll let yours." I kept a wary eye on the hawk as the Head Falconer eased it onto a distant perch near the doorway onto the court-yard. "Unless I miss my guess."

"He might." The words were murmured, her head bowed. "I cannot say."

"You love him." I made the words blunt. It cost me, to say it; more than I had reckoned. It struck home in my own heart, and I saw her head rise, eyes startled. "He's D'Angeline, Sibeal, Tsingano or no. *Love as thou wilt.* I saw it, on Alba, all those years ago."

"Moiread." She breathed her sister's name; youngest of them all, slain in battle in Alba these many years gone by, a loss still grieved. "It was Moiread who made his heart glad. He might have loved her, and she him. Who can say? There was you, then and now. And I, I am only . . ."

"Alive." I said. "Alive, and in love. Well and so, Sibeal, we too are sisters in this, for he is dear to my heart. But Moiread is dead, and I . . . I have a long road to follow. Hyacinthe will understand that, if anyone will. Tell him I walk the *Lungo Drom* on his behalf, Joscelin and I. He was right about that. He saw it before I did. Tell him . . . tell him I go seeking the Name of God. Will you do that for me?"

"Yes. If he will allow it, I will tell him." Sibeal extended a hand toward one of the fledglings, stroking its half-grown plumage with one slender brown finger. "They are called eyasses, did you know? The young birds. Eyasses. It is a lovely word, I think."

"It is." I thought of the acolyte Liliane at the sanctuary of Elua, and our mounts following her in a line. I thought of the Battle of Bryn Gorrydum, where Moiread had died, and the black boar that had burst from the treeline there, giving the element of surprise into the hands of Drustan's forces. Truly, there were things in this world beyond my understanding. "Thank you, Sibeal."

"Come back." Her dark, visionary's eyes held mine. "It is what he would ask of you. However far you go, whether you find what you seek or no. Whatever is to become of us all. Come back."

A shiver brushed my skin, a touch of magic that was ancient when Elua was young. Earth's Eldest Children, they call themselves; barbarians, Drustan might jest, but they are older than we. "I will try," I promised, bowing my head to Necthana's daughter and taking my leave.

Joscelin was awaiting me in the courtyard—the weathering yard, the falconers call it, where the birds are trained on long lines. He had padding wrapped about his vambraced forearm, a peregrine's talons biting deep into the leather as one of the Head Falconer's apprentices instructed him. "Phèdre!" He grinned, hoisting the bird to display it. "What do you think? Shall we build a mews at Montrève?"

"Elua willing." I stood back a healthy distance, regarding the peregrine's fierce, round eye, its raptor's beak. I had seen that look on my patrons; I did not need to endure it from a bird. "We may build a bestiary, if you like, providing we return in one piece. Are you ready?"

With some reluctance, Joscelin returned the peregrine unto its keeper, and we departed. It was only one of several meetings I had arranged prior to our leave-taking, and 'twas the next I dreaded the most.

I have learned, in my trade and in my life, to deal with monarchs and their kin, with seers and scholars, priests and pirates alike. But if there is one person capable of striking fear into my heart, it is my *couturiere*, Favrielle nó Eglantine.

To be sure, she owed me a debt of gratitude; and never let me forget for an instant that it was a most unwelcome debt, no matter how much she prized the end result—which was, indeed, her freedom and her fame. If I had not paid the price of her marque to Eglantine House, she would have toiled in obscurity long into her middle years. Well and so; I do not think it was such a terrible thing to have done!

Nonetheless, Favrielle misliked the burden of gratitude.

"Short notice," she said in the antechamber of her salon. "What a surprise, Comtesse." As if I'd not gone to the trouble of making an appointment. "Are you in need of a gown for the Queen's piquet tournament, or is it some new patron you must now impress?"

"Neither." I strove to be gracious, ignoring Joscelin's suppressed laughter. "It's naught that requires your personal attention. I need two riding outfits, nothing more, fit for long travel."

"Nothing more." Favrielle nó Eglantine raised her brows, red-gold, like her mop of curls and the freckles sprinkled across her impish nose. On anyone else, it would have looked charming; Favrielle managed to convey unspeakable disdain. "All the world looks to Terre d'Ange to set the mode of fashion, and all Terre d'Ange looks to the City of Elua. And in the City of Elua, everyone looks to Phèdre nó Delaunay, the Comtesse de Montrève, because they know *I* clothe you, on the road no less than in the ballroom. Do not presume to tell me, Comtesse, what does and does not require my personal attention. So. Where do you travel?"

"La Serenissima and Menekhet," I said humbly. "And afterward, Jebe-Barkal."

"Jebe-Barkal!" It took her by surprise, but only for an instant. Favrielle's green eyes narrowed in thought. "You'll want somewhat light in weight, then, and none too close-fitting, but sturdy enough to wear. Light colors, too, but naught that will show the stain of travel." She nodded decisively. "Come. I'll show you some fabrics."

Casting a backward glance at Joscelin, I followed Favrielle into the depths of her salon; two floors, it occupied now, an entire building in the clothiers' district. The building, she owned outright. Her staff of drapers and cutters and embroiderers, seamstresses and tailors, watched us with amusement and an obvious fondness for the irascible mistress of their salon.

In the end, I chose two fabrics—a saffron wool, fine-carded and light as a cloud, and a raw silk of pale celadon green.

"You can wear it," Favrielle said critically, holding a length of the bolt near my face. "Although it's not your best color." She surveyed me, scarred lip curling. "I suppose I'll need to take your measurements anew?"

"They've not changed since you measured me last," I said with some heat.

"If you say so." Her eyebrows rose again. I sighed, and let her measure me anew, standing patient as the knotted cord was wrapped around my breast, waist and hips. Favrielle made notations on a piece of foolscap.

"Well?" I asked.

Head averted beneath the tumbled mass of red-gold curls, she hid a smile. "It seems your measurements are unchanged, Comtesse."

"I told you as much."

"You did." Without lifting her head, Favrielle made a rough sketch of riding attire in a series of swift, elegant lines. "This is what I'm thinking, do you see? Conventional, but with a looseness of drape that affords better motion and permits the flow of air. And an overgarment, broad-sleeved and hooded, that will keep off the sun's glare or the night's chill. Will it suit?"

"Yes." I looked at her handiwork and sighed. "Beautifully. How soon can you have it done?"

"Come back in two days for a final fitting." She sketched a fine border of embroidery, then looked up at me. The indirect light caught the genuine curiosity in her green eyes, showed plainly the scar tissue that twisted her upper lip. If not for that, Favrielle would have been an adept of Eglantine House, a Servant of Naamah in her own right. "Why Jebe-Barkal?"

"Because," I said. "There is somewhat I must do there. It is a debt I owe a friend."

"A debt." She cocked her head, lip curling. "You're very keen on debts, Comtesse."

Anger born of long frustration blossomed within me, and I met her gaze with a level stare. "Mock me if you will, but you are of Eglantine House, Favrielle, and trained there nigh to adept status. You know the art of telling tales as well as that of draping cloth; it was you who told me the story of Naamah's daughter Mara, the first *anguissette*. Do you know the tale of how a Tsingano half-breed called the Prince of Travellers became the Master of the Straits?"

For once, Favrielle nó Eglantine's regard held something in it that saw me as a fellow mortal being, and not an inconvenience and an unpleasant reminder of an unwanted favor. "I know it," she said softly. "I have heard it told."

"Well." I ran a length of cloth-of-gold between my fingers. "It is not ended. And that is why I must go to Jebe-Barkal."

"So." She bent over her drawing, adding an unnecessary fillip of embellishment. "Two days. And," Favrielle looked up, eyes gleaming, "you might pay a visit to the marquist, Comtesse. You've need of a good limning."

In her own infuriating way, Favrielle was right, of course; 'twas on my list of things to be accomplished ere we departed for La Serenissima. I thought on it with amusement and annoyance as I lay on the limning-table in the marquist's shop. It was an exquisite torture, the keen, ink-dipped needles piercing my skin, rendering the lines of my marque clean and bold. Whatever claim Kushiel may have on me—and it is a prodigious one—I am Naamah's Servant too, twice-pledged of my own volition. It would not do to set out on a journey of this magnitude with my marque ill-tended.

When it was finished, I regarded myself in the mirror of the marquist's well-heated shop, gazing over my shoulder. It was well done. The black-thorn vine designed by Master Robert Tielhard was immaculate against my fair skin, twining the length of my spine, accented by crimson petals. The marquist bowed, honoring the work more than the wearer. I paid him generously nonetheless. The Marquists' Guild tithes to the Temple of Naamah. A gift to one was a gift to the other.

Naamah, I prayed silently, do not forget your Servant.

There was a good deal more to be done, and much of it dull and prosaic. I met with my factor, Jacques Brenin, to discuss my finances.

We agreed on arrangements for the coming year—which is to say, I acceded to his suggestions, which were always good—and he gave me promissory notes for the Banco Tribuno in La Serenissima and a money-lending house he knew by repute in Iskandria.

I paid a visit, by day and sober, to Emile in Night's Doorstep. To him I gave my heartfelt thanks, and a purse of gold coin, which he made to refuse. "No." I closed his fingers over the purse. "Keep it, Emile. Half for yourself, or the *Didikani* of the City if you wish, and half for Kristof, Oszkar's son. Let it be known that it is out of gratitude, in honor of Hyacinthe, Anasztaizia's son. I ask nothing in return but silence."

"Tsingani do not meddle in *gadje* affairs," Emile said automatically, then grinned. "Not those who walk the *Lungo Drom*, any mind. So you found the missing prince?"

"I found his trail," I said. "And I will cross it again, Elua willing. But my duty is done to the best of my ability. It is Hyacinthe's quest I undertake now."

TWENTY-SIX

ON THE following day, I was no less idle, meeting with Audine Davul at the City Academy and listening spellbound as she told me aught that she might of Jebe-Barkal. In my ignorance, I had conceived of it solely as a desert land, like unto the Umaiyyat; but there were mountains, she assured me, and valleys dense with foliage, vast inland lakes and one of the most spectacular waterfalls in existence.

Our journey, as best I could guess, would take us through all these terrains and more.

"Show no weakness," Audine Davul cautioned Joscelin and me alike. "They are a proud folk, and capable of great generosity and great cruelty alike. These descendents of Shalomon of whom you speak—I know nothing of them save what is told in story. But in the north . . . Jebeans are jealous of their pride. Give every courtesy, and never reveal fear."

We thanked her, and Joscelin bowed deeply. I tried to imagine him showing fear, and failed. Then I remembered him in the hut in Waldemar Selig's steading where he had wished to die, enchained, his hands raw with chilblains, lank-haired and wild-eyed.

All things are possible.

Even the worst of things.

I'd made a fair-copy of Audine's translation of the Jebean scroll upon our return to the City of Elua and had it sent to Eleazar ben Enokh, my favorite Yeshuite scholar. It was upon Eleazar that I intended to call that afternoon—and I will own, it was an encounter I anticipated with some excitement. Ten years of my life I'd given to the pursuit of the Name of God. To be sure, I was a long way from finding it, but I looked forward to hearing Eleazar's thoughts with a scholar's arcane passion.

"I'll send the carriage back for you," Joscelin promised, dropping a kiss upon my brow. His mouth quirked in a half-smile. "I am eager to hear the shortened version of Rebbe Eleazar's impressions. I fear the full might of them would be too much for Cassiel's simple servant to endure."

"Liar," I said affectionately. He laughed and took his leave.

Within, I found Eleazar aquiver with excitement, sitting cross-legged on his prayer mats and slapping his bony knees, the translated *Kefra Neghast* on the floor in front of him. "Phèdre nó Delaunay!" he exclaimed. "What a treasure you have found! Come, and let us share our thoughts on this matter."

I took my place opposite him, kneeling, and opened the original scroll with its painted illustrations, weighting it carefully at the corners. "You think there is merit in it, father?"

"Merit, of a surety. It is a tale, is it not?" He shrugged. "You ask if it is true. Who can say? You must go and see for yourself."

"But you think it may be so."

Eleazar ben Enokh paused, then nodded. "I think it may be so, at least in part. Trade and war alike existed between the Habiru nation and Jebe-Barkal in the old days. This Queen, Makeda—" he pointed at the parchment, "—it is not impossible. Shalomon had many wives, including Pharaoh's daughter. The ring . . ." He tapped his lower teeth in absent thought. "Folklore says it bore the Name of God, and with it Shalomon commanded demons to build the Temple. What is the grain of truth at the heart of that pearl, eh? Perhaps with the ring of his father's authority, Melek al'Hakim commanded the architect Khiram, whose father was of the Tribe of Dân. His mother . . . ah!" His brown eyes glinted. "Perhaps she followed other faiths, yes? And Khiram's workmen also? Worshipping Asherat-of-the-Sea, and Baal of the high places."

"Mayhap," I said slowly. It made sense, though I was reluctant to own it. "Then you think it is a myth, no more?"

"Shalomon's Ring." Eleazar's voice softened, growing kinder. "Forgive me, for your scroll poses answers to mighty questions, and in my joy, I forget they are not the answers you seek. If you ask me, do I believe in my heart that Shalomon's Ring was inscribed with the Name of God . . . the answer is no, Phèdre nó Delaunay. I do not believe it. I have sought too long on the paths of prayer to believe the Word is writ on a mere gem." He leaned forward, touching the diamond of the Companion's Star on my breast. "Here is etched the sigil of Elua, yes?

It commands a mighty boon. But it is a human token, no less and no more, and it is the Queen who must answer to it, and not Blessed Elua himself. This I know to be true. So, I believe, of Shalomon's Ring."

I closed my hand over the brooch and stared at the scroll. "Then you do not believe this Melek al'Hakim carried away the Name of God?"

Eleazar shook his head. "I do not say this. There are paths of prayer the Children of Yisra-el have forgotten. It may be that Melek al'Hakim and the Tribe of Dân remember. And there is this," he added, indicating a line.

" ' . . . and Melek al'Hakim was anointed by Zadok the priest, Melek-Zadok he became, and with Khiram son of Khiram and his people who were of Dân, and twenty of the Tribe of Levi, that is, Aaron's line, they did despoil the Temple of Shalomon of its vessels and treasures, and fled amid the strife to Menekhet,' " I read aloud, then sat back on my heels. "What do you make of it, father?"

"Whatever Melek al'Hakim took with him, he had the priesthood's blessing," Eleazar said simply. "I do not know. Perhaps it was the Name of God. What other treasure is worth protecting more?"

"The Temple was built to house the Signs of the Covenant," I said.

"Yes." Eleazar nodded. "Moishe's Tablets, Aaron's Rod, and a jar of manna. So it is written, and it is written that the Ark which held them was taken to the mountains and hidden in the time of Judah Maccabeus." He shrugged. "Perhaps it is so. If it is, it has passed beyond mortal knowledge. But this object . . ." He pointed to the Jebean scroll, the original, where two men carried a cloth-covered chest on long poles. "It is shrouded, yes. And yet to my eyes, it looks very like that Ark which is described in the Tanakh. Do you not discern, here, the outline of two cherubim, facing one another?"

I squinted at it. "It may be so."

"It may." A grin broke over Eleazar's homely face, making it for an instant lovely. "Who can say, Phèdre nó Delaunay? It is a mystery, and one that we who follow the teachings of Yeshua ben Yosef have abandoned. Who needs the voice of Adonai speaking between the cherubim when the Mashiach has walked the earth, flesh and blood and somewhat more besides? Who needs the Name of God, when His Son has spoken the Word of redemption and pledged a new covenant?"

I thought of the terrible power and anguish caught behind Hyacinthe's eyes, of the yawning chasm that had opened in the sea between us and the awesome, wrathful *presence* moving in its depths. "Not all of Adonai's creatures accepted Yeshua's covenant with obedience, father. Rahab, who is the Prince of the Deep, did not; and it is Hyacinthe who suffers for it. If there is no power in Elua's lore nor in Yeshua's to turn him aside, if the Name of God is the only power to which Rahab must answer, then *I* need it."

"Perhaps it is so." Eleazar was silent for a moment. "You answer your own questions, and I can tell you no more. Is there merit in the scroll's tale? I cannot say. You must go to Jebe-Barkal and see. Only one other thing may I tell you, Phèdre nó Delaunay, one true thing." He folded his hands, his expression grave. "Adonai is beyond our mortal compass. To receive His Name, we must approach Him in perfect trust and love, to make of the self a vessel where the self is not."

"Eleazar." I swallowed. "I'm not sure what that means."

"Nor am I," he said gently, "though I have sought it these many years. I know only that it is true, for it was taught to me by my teacher and his teacher before him, as long as the Children of Yisra-El have endured. Although you do not worship Adonai, you are Elua's child, Phèdre, and as such know something of love. Perhaps the way will be revealed."

"Thank you, Eleazar," I said, rising from my kneeling position. "I pray you are right."

Well, it was less than I might have wished, but it was enough— enough to keep hope alive, at any rate. It seems strange to me that a people could be so dispersed, that so much of their lore and history could be forgotten, though mayhap it is unjust of me to think thusly. We are different, we D'Angelines, but what we have, we could lose as easily. Waldemar Selig's invasion had proved that much.

Yes, I thought, and how well would we endure then, trusting to the love of Blessed Elua to sustain us for a thousand years, keeping our faith? What tales would we still tell of Kushiel's justice, of Camael's might, of Eisheth's compassion, of Anael's husbandry, of Shemhazai's cleverness, Azza's pride and Naamah's generosity? Would we still admire Cassiel's loyalty, or reckon it folly? And Elua, Blessed Elua . . . what solace would we find in our wandering, misbegotten deity, whose sole province was Love?

I was ashamed, then, of my thoughts, and gave my blessing unto Eleazar ben Enokh. He embraced me at our parting, and his kind wife, Adara, did too. His parting words stayed with me, and I pondered on them. How could the self be where the self was not? In the end, it was like all mysteries: Unknowable. I would worry about that, I thought, in Jebe-Barkal.

"So?" Joscelin asked when I returned home. "What has the Rebbe to say?"

"Little enough," I said. "Less than I expected, though more than I might have feared. He says we must go and see for ourselves."

He nodded, accepting my words, his mouth twisting wryly. "Well enough, then. Melisande Shahrizai was right in one thing, at least. The scholar's art has taken you as far as it may. We will see what answers Jebe-Barkal holds."

It seemed soon, too soon, to be leaving the City of Elua once more when we had only scarce returned, but my business was settled and my affairs in order, my farewells said anew. We dined that night in the garden, a quiet meal, Joscelin and Ti-Philippe and I, amid a profound air of melancholy. Young Hugues sat some distance away, playing a sad, sweet tune on his flute. He was a better musician than poet, and the soft, piping notes rose plaintively in the twilight, born on the lingering scent of sun-warmed herbs.

Eugènie served us herself, as she had before, and if her expression was reserved, there were volumes of reproach in her eyes. I was torn in myself as I had never known, at once longing to stay, yearning to be gone.

"Let me go with you." Ti-Philippe came out with it at last, slamming his wineglass down on the table. Red wine slopped over the edge, staining the immaculate linen. His eyes glistened with emotion in the fairy-light of the torches. "Please, my lady. It's a dark road, the Tsingano said so himself, and already it has taken a branching you could not have guessed. Who can say what lies ahead? Can you truly afford to turn away aid freely given? Even a Cassiline can use someone to watch his back."

The sound of Hugues' flute halted. Joscelin regarded me without speaking, by which I knew he did not disagree.

I looked at Ti-Philippe's face, open and earnest. Of all of Phèdre's Boys, he had always been the most easy in his manner, the one least capable of hiding aught he thought or felt. He'd sworn his loyalty to me on a whim, a jest, so long ago—and yet he'd kept it, and proved it a hundred times over. I thought of his comrades, of Remy and Fortun, and how they had died. It had taken a half-dozen of Benedicte's men to bring down Remy, who had sung so sweetly and died cursing. And

Fortun, ah! My steady Fortun, who had almost made the door, a dagger to his kidneys and another to his heart.

These things I thought, and gazed at Ti-Philippe in the torchlight until his face wavered, and I saw him pale and dead, his throat gaping in a scarlet grin.

"No." The word came out harsher than I had intended. I shuddered, blinking. "No." I said it again, with gentle firmness. "This road is not for you, Chevalier."

What he heard in my voice, I cannot say, but it was enough. Ti-Philippe bowed his head, unruly hair shadowing his brow. His hand closed hard around the wineglass, white at the knuckles. "So be it," he said roughly. "My lady, I will keep your hearth until you return. But know that in my heart, I ride at your side."

On the marble bench where he played his flute, Hugues burst into tears.

So it was decided.

That night I slept, and dreamed again—the nightmare, the same I'd had before. It was the same to nearly every detail. Once again I stood in the prow of a ship, one of the swift Illyrian ships with its canted sail, my heart breaking as the stony shore of the island receded and Hyacinthe's boyish voice cried out across the widening gulf, "Phèdre, Phèdre!" It was his voice, alive in memory, the same that had greeted me in merriment, that had dared me to steal sweets in the crowded marketplace of Night's Doorstep, that had shouted warning when the Dowayne's men came to fetch me back to Cereus House, tinged now with terror and loneliness.

But the boy, the boy who wept on the shore and stretched out his arms in a futile plea, had skin the hue of new ivory and hair that fell in a blue-black shimmer, and his features were not those of Hyacinthe.

"I am coming," I murmured in desperate petition, thick-tongued and half awake at the greying of dawn, "I am coming." And then I woke and knew myself in my own bed, with Joscelin asleep beside me, peaceful in repose. While I am safe, no dreams trouble his sleep. I give him nightmares enough waking. I lay awake and stared at the ceiling, wondering to which boy I had spoken—the Hyacinthe-that-was of my memory, or Imriel de la Courcel, whom I had never met. The pattern of fate, like the Name of God, was too vast to hold.

Wondering, I slept and dreamed myself awake and wondering still, and knew no more until Joscelin shook me gently awake, and I opened my eyes to bright sunlight.

It was time to go.

TWENTY-SEVEN

WE WERE attacked by bandits on the northern route through Caerdicca Unitas.

It bears telling, for it served me a grave reminder of the limits of my own wisdom. I was so confidant in my own dire destiny, so sure I had done the right thing in forbidding Ti-Philippe to accompany us, that I paid scant heed to the normal dangers the road posed to a lone pair of travellers.

The new riding attire I'd commissioned from Favrielle nó Eglantine was all she had promised; fluid and comfortable, with an elegance of line and richness of fabric that fair shouted D'Angeline nobility. Of a surety, it did so to those who attacked us, reckoning a D'Angeline noblewoman and her single man-at-arms easy prey.

We were a day's ride west of Pavento when it happened. An irony, that; it is where Ysandre's couriers were slain, attempting to outrace Melisande's messengers many years ago. I daresay we had been more vigilant on our first journey. Still, it happened nigh too fast for thought, in a deserted stretch of road.

One moment, Joscelin and I were riding quietly side by side, trailing our newly acquired packhorses behind us; the next, some eight men had swarmed out of the hills.

They were Caerdicci, by the look of them, although some few may have had Skaldic blood. Poor and hungry, to a man; outcasts and brigands, with no armor and shoddy weapons. Two of them ran behind us, severing the lead-lines to our packhorses and claiming them. One was at my side before I'd scarce blinked, a grubby hand clutching my riding skirts while the other shoved the point of a dagger at my waist. Another held my mare's bridle. Joscelin's gelding reared, having once been battle-trained; he swore, getting it under control. Three men ranged around him with knives and makeshift spears and one notched sword, and their leader stepped into the road before us.

He held a crossbow, fine and new and gleaming, and I've no doubt it was stolen. Still, he held it cocked and level, pointed directly at Joscelin.

"Give us all you carry," he said in Caerdicci, speaking slowly and carefully, as if to a slow child, "and we will let you go unharmed. If you resist, your woman will be——"

And no more did he get out, for in a motion too quick for the eye to detect, Joscelin ripped one of his daggers from its sheath, hurling it at the bandit leader. The man's lips continued to move even as his hand rose, perplexed, fumbling at the hilt protruding from his throat, and his body slumped sideways.

In the instant of gaping surprise that followed, I clasped my hands together and brought them down hard on the head of the man whose knife poked at my ribs. He staggered and looked at me open-mouthed, but I had already set heels to my mare's flanks, hearing the ringing sound of Joscelin's sword being drawn.

"Cassiel!" His shout rose bright and hard on the midday air, the line of his blade arcing like a scythe as it sheared through flesh and bone, a spray of crimson blood following. His face was set in perfect fury. At a safe distance, I drew in my mare and sat her, trembling. Three men dead and another wounded, and he not trained to fight on horseback. He dismounted, stalking the remaining four. Seeing one retrieve the crossbow from their fallen leader, I drew breath to shout a warning, but Joscelin was already turning, braid flying out in a straight line, sword grasped in his two-handed grip.

The bandit closed his eyes and pulled the crossbow's trigger, whispering a prayer to any Caerdicci deities listening. There were none. The bolt flew and Joscelin's vambraces flashed, deflecting the quarrel. Cassiline Brothers actually prepare for such feats. He advanced, the backstroke of his sword perfectly level, catching his assailant even as the man fumbled to load another bolt. The bandit crumpled at the waist and lay bleeding into the dust of the road.

The others scattered. One of the packhorses balked and threw his head up hard, tearing the lead-line from his captor's hand; the other spooked. A pair of the remaining bandits waved their arms and shouted as they ran, endeavoring to scare it into the foothills. The wounded man followed at a hunched, limping run.

For a moment, I thought Joscelin would remount and pursue them, then I saw him gather himself. Thrusting his fingers between his lips, he gave the shrill, trilling whistle that summoned all our mounts. It is a trade-secret of Tsingani horse-trainers, though they taught it to us; more than that, I have sworn not to say. The errant packhorse came running, and my own mare's ears perked. I nudged her to a trot.

Joscelin stood in the road, breathing hard, blood sliding in crimson runnels toward the point of his lowered sword. "You're all right?" he asked without looking at me.

"I'm fine." I didn't wholly trust my voice.

He nodded, wiping his blade carefully on the roughspun tunic adorning the nearest corpse, and then, without warning, knelt in the dust. With his head bowed, he laid his sword down and crossed his forearms, murmuring a Cassiline prayer. The packhorses and I waited silently, while his gelding leaned in to whuffle his hair in curiosity. Joscelin's eyes, when he rose, were filled with anguish.

"It gets easier, you know." In one fluid motion, he sheathed his sword at his back and went to pluck his thrown dagger from the throat of the bandit leader, face averted from me. "Too easy."

"I'm sorry." There was nothing else I could say.

"I know." Cleaning and sheathing his dagger, he went about the business of splicing our severed lead-lines. "Give me a hand, you've a better touch with knots."

I worked without comment. When we had finished, we remounted and rode onward toward Pavento, where we sought lodgings for the night and reported the incident to the Principe's guard. No further hostilities troubled us that day or the next. If the local banditry had any network of information, I daresay word went out along the northern route that the pair of harmless-looking D'Angeline travellers were best left undisturbed.

On the next day, we reached La Serenissima.

Twilight hovered smoky and blue on the waters of the canals and soft roseate hues washed the buildings around the Campo Grande, here and there picked out with a brazen note of gilt where the sun's dying rays still pierced. Laughter carried over water, and voices raised in song. The painted bissoni and gondoli were out, young men of the Hundred Worthy Families courting and wooing in the ways of Serenissiman nobility.

It could have been my world. I even entertained the thought— once, briefly, for a heartbeat's space of time. Severio Stregazza, who is the Doge's grandson, proposed marriage to me in this city. His family would never have permitted it, of course. Still, he did not know it at the time.

I looked at Joscelin's profile, silhouetted against the deep blue of falling night.

I never doubted that I chose aright.

It made it all the harder to ask him what I had to ask, that night in the dining-hall of our elegant inn, the same we'd stayed in before. I'd no more inclination than I'd had the first time to burden any of my acquaintances in La Serenissima with this visit. The rooms were fine and the service well-trained; the food was outstanding for Caerdicci fare.

"Joscelin."

Amid the clamor of voices and rattling cutlery, he caught the hesitation in my tone. "What is it?"

I beckoned for the neatly-attired servant to bring more of the sweet muscat wine the inn served with its dessert course. He bowed, smiling with pleasure, and refilled my glass. I took a sip, and another, delaying. "I want to go alone tomorrow."

Joscelin sat unmoving, then blinked, once. Something hard surfaced in his expression. "To see Melisande. Why?"

"Because." I turned the delicate wineglass, watching the candlelight refracted in the fluted rim. It was exquisitely made. Serenissiman work, no doubt, blown on the Isla Vitrari. "What I have to tell her . . . it is about her son. And it is a matter between her and Kushiel. No one else."

"Oh, Phèdre." It was the sorrow in his voice that jerked my gaze back to his. "Do you have such a care for her pride? Even still?"

"It's not only that. Not pride." I shook my head. "Joscelin . . . you saw the children, the children we saved. And they were the lucky ones. I have to tell her that."

"It is Kushiel's justice," he said softly. "You said so yourself."

"Yes." I drained my glass and set it back. "Did you think it just, when we found those children in Amílcar?"

He didn't answer immediately. "It is not for me to judge."

"Nor I. But I think . . . I think there is no one in the world who despises Melisande Shahrizai with the same purity of emotion as you." My voice was shaking, a little. "And I think that when she learns that Kushiel has chosen to punish her by exacting payment for her sins from her son . . . I think that even Melisande deserves to hear it alone."

Joscelin's voice was harsh. "Do you think she would offer you the same compassion?"

To impart suffering without compassion . . .

"It doesn't matter." I swallowed, hard. "Joscelin, I am not easy in my heart with this. I have served Kushiel all my life, and never questioned his will. I question it now. I do not see that the end justifies the means. And I am made to endure pain, to revel in it, not to inflict it. To deliver this news with you glowering over my shoulder . . . I don't think I can do it."

"I wouldn't glower," he said automatically, then sighed, pressing the heels of his hands against his eye-sockets. "All right. All right, all right. Do as you must, and I will wait in the Temple proper." Dropping his hands, he looked at me with slightly bloodshot eyes. "Will it suffice?"

"Yes," I whispered. "Thank you."

"Don't." He shook his head. "I think your compassion is wasted on Melisande."

Thence the need for an anguissette *to balance the scales.*

"I know," I said miserably. "And mayhap you are right. But I can only act according to the dictates of my nature, not hers."

"Love as thou wilt," said Joscelin, and sighed again.

In the morning we went to the Temple of Asherat-of-the-Sea.

Poets and philosophers alike have written of the sense of strangeness that one encounters from time to time of a moment lived before; a place, a person, a chance word, that triggers something in one's memory that says, yes, I remember, that is how it was, that is exactly how it was. So I have read, but I have never encountered such a thing save that there was reason for it. I felt it that day. I had been here before, in this city built on water, beneath the great golden domes of the Temple. Full many a time had I met the blank stare of the great effigy of Asherat, towering vast and stony above the altar, carved waves surging at her feet.

I brought honeycakes, the first time. The second, I usurped her voice.

It was a bargain we had struck, the goddess and I.

And I had come with Ysandre, who had the right to order me because she was my Queen; and I had come, last of all, with Joscelin, as I came now, amid the priestesses of the Elect, with their whispering blue robes and the veils of silver net that hid their faces, glass beads shimmering like wire-strung tears, bare feet moving soundlessly over the floor.

"I will wait," Joscelin said to me, making a formal Cassiline bow, his hands clenched into fists beneath the steel mesh gauntlets of his vambraces. Amid the murmurous presence of the priestesses, the fierce soft pride of the Temple eunuchs with their ceremonial spears, he seemed an alien thing, hard-edged and masculine.

"I will return," I promised. He thought me a fool; I know he thought me a fool for my compassion. Was I? I didn't know. I followed the Elect priestess down the winding corridors, wondering. *What do you owe Melisande, that you must deliver this news yourself?* So Ysandre had asked me, and rightfully so. She was my liege and my sovereign, Ysandre de la Courcel; she had believed, when any other would have doubted. She had raised me up and given me every honor, given me the Companion's Star to wear at my breast, called me her near-cousin. When I thought of courage, when I thought of loyalty, it wore Ysandre's face as I had seen it on our return from La Serenissima, when she had parted the troops of Percy de Somerville's army and ridden without faltering to the very walls of the City of Elua.

And when I thought of love, it wore Joscelin's face.

Phèdre!

But there was Melisande's voice in my memory too, unstrung with shock, her beautiful eyes wide with fear after I had cracked open my skull against my cell in La Dolorosa. I had seen it, as I slumped to the floor.

A kiss, one kiss. It took all that I had to resist it.

She had only touched me once, since. And that with the point of a dagger. Joscelin's dagger. I'd have let her kill me, if she could. She couldn't.

It was the same, all the same. The gilt-hinged door, the priestess of the Elect giving the double knock and announcing my name in the soft, slurring Caerdicci dialect they use in that city. It was the same room, filled with slanting sunlight and the soft splashing of an unseen fountain. The sound of the door closing, leaving us alone, was the same. Even the fragrance was the same; a little deeper, in summer, of water and sun-warmed marble and flowering shrubs, and the scent, the faint, musky spice I would have known anywhere, could have picked blindfolded out of a crowd, the unique fragrance of Melisande, who stood waiting.

And the wave, the wave of emotion was the same, hatred and love and desire, cracking my heart to bits and grinding the fragments.

Only this time, I saw the fear in her eyes.

And this time, I knelt.

TWENTY-EIGHT

"TELL ME."

Melisande's eyes closed, lids dusky with blue veins, shuttered against the pain. I have done such a thing myself. I have seen it in others. I had never seen it in Melisande. I had been right to come alone. Her lashes curled like ebony wave-crests. I am D'Angeline. I cannot fail to notice such things.

"There was," I said, searching for words, "no conspiracy."

Her eyes opened. "What, then?"

I told her.

What I had expected, I cannot say. She bore it; she bore it well. I do not think anyone who knew her less than I—and who that may be, I do not know—would have seen her flinch, would have seen the awful comprehension that filled the deep-blue wells of her eyes. It struck her hard. Any mortal enemy she could have outwitted, outplotted. Not this. Not random chance, and the shadow of Kushiel's hand overhanging it.

"He is alive?" It was the first thing she said, the first she was able to say, forced between clenched teeth.

"I believe him to be so." The marble floor was hard beneath my knees, the discomfort of it lending me focus. "The Menekhetan saw his value. He paid in hard coin. By that token, I believe Imriel lives."

Melisande took a step, two steps. One hand reached out, entangled in my hair, wrenching my head upright. My neck straining, I stared upward, meeting her blazing eyes. I felt my breath shallow in my lungs, my heart beating fast and hard. I should have withdrawn from her, pulled away. To save my life, I couldn't do it. She had been my patron, once; the only one to whom I ever wholly surrendered. In a way I shuddered to acknowledge, Melisande's very touch was imprinted on my soul, and I felt her pain as my own. "You are sure?" she asked softly, searching my face. "You are very, very sure of this tale, Phèdre nó Delaunay?"

"The Carthaginians were put to torture," I whispered. "My lady, I watched it. I asked the questions myself. I'm sorry. But I am very, very sure."

She let me go and turned away. Bereft of her grip, I wavered on my knees. I gazed at her back, heard her murmur a single word. "Kushiel."

"Yes." My voice was hoarse, my throat thick with desire and compassion.

Melisande's head bowed. Whatever else one may say of her, she never lacked for courage. I knelt in silence, knowing what she knew. I have lived through the *thetalos* in the cavern of the Temenos. I know what it is to confront blood-guilt.

Never for a child of my birth. That I will never know.

"They will pay." Her voice was flat, her hands fisted at her sides. "The Carthaginians, the ones who began it . . . they are dead men."

"My lady." I cleared my throat, found my voice. "It is done. Their heads were adorning spikes in the Plaza del Rey ere we left Amílcar."

"So." Her shoulders slumped; only a fraction. It was enough. I saw. Straightening, she crossed the room and opened the coffer, the same one that had held the Jebean scroll. "I promised you the name of a guide."

I rose to accept it, unfolding in the single, elegant motion I was taught in the Night Court. Our fingers brushed as she handed me a scrap of vellum. I glanced down to see an unfamiliar name, an address.

"He hires out to guide caravans from Menekhet to Jebe-Barkal," Melisande said without inflection. "I am assured that he knows where to find the descendents of Saba. I cannot swear it is true, but my information is good. There is only so much I can do, here."

"Thank you." The words sounded stupid. I felt stupid. She gave a bitter smile.

"You have done what I asked, Phèdre nó Delaunay. I was not wrong to choose you." Her eyes searched my face again. "Tell me about the Queen's delegation to Iskandria."

I told her, and watched her pace, watched life return, her mind working as the first shock diminished, calculations moving behind her features. And Elua help me, but I loved her for it, a little bit. Even so . . .

"Melisande."

It stopped her. She turned to look at me.

I shook my head. "You cannot do it. I know how loosely this prison holds you; believe me, I know. It gives me nightmares. If you go to Iskandria, if you leave this place . . ." I paused. "I will know it. I am here against my Queen's wishes, against everyone's wishes. There's a death-sentence on your head, Melisande, should you abandon Asherat's protection. And if you do, I will be honor-bound to do what I may to see you thwarted."

"He is my *son!*" she spat, features contorting.

"I know." Although my voice shook, I stood my ground. "And I am Kushiel's Chosen, and in liege to Ysandre de la Courcel. I will go to Lord Amaury Trente, in Iskandria; I will go to Pharaoh, if I need. What can you do, now, that they cannot? Your resources are spread thin, and they will be spread thinner if you must needs evade capture. We have played this game before, my lady. Do you wish to set yourself against me?"

Melisande flung back her head, her bright, restless gaze raking the walls of her salon. Blessed Elua, even in despair she was splendid! I had not seen, until then, that it was a prison. I saw it, then, the subtle, gilded bars that confined her. She shuddered and grew still, contained. "You break my heart, Phèdre."

"Yes." A strange, dispassionate sense of calm overtook me. For once, at last, we stood upon even ground. I gazed at her, thinking on it. "You broke mine a long time ago, my lady."

"Kushiel's Dart." She came near and laid her hand against my face. "Naamah's Servant." Her touch was cool, her expression unreadable. "In the beginning, I thought you were a toy, no more; a dangerous plaything. I daresay even Anafiel knew no different, though he taught you well enough. Later . . . later, I knew better. A challenge, mayhap; a gauntlet cast down by the gods."

"And now?" I asked.

"Now?" Something stirred in the depths of Melisande's eyes, behind her face, beauty honed by grief, a vengeful cruelty. Our history was written there in all its betrayal and hatred and violent ecstasy. Dispassion shattered, a momentary thing, transitory and fragile. Her voice lowered, honey-sweet; how had I forgotten its power? "Now." My blood leapt in answer and my cheek blossomed with heat where she touched me. A familiar ache squeezed my heart, beat like a pulse between my thighs. I felt my lids grow heavy, my lips part. To feel it again, the heat of her, the press of her body, her breasts against mine, that cruel, expert touch; ah, Elua! I fought to keep from swaying forward. Melisande took her hand away. "Now, I don't know, Phèdre."

This time, her withdrawal hit me like a void; I nearly staggered against it, yearning toward her, the ache in my heart keening like a winter wind. I had done her a kindness, leaving Joscelin behind. She did me a kindness now and turned away, speaking over her shoulder.

"I never wanted a conscience. And yet it seems our lord Kushiel has seen fit to give me what I lacked at birth. If I have such a thing, it is embodied in you, Phèdre." Melisande turned back, her features composed, hands folded in her sleeves. "I have heard tell of Lord Amaury Trente. A capable man, it is said, and loyal to the Queen, but not, I think, a clever one."

"Clever enough," I replied unthinking.

One corner of her mouth curled. "He would have gone to the Duke of Milazza to raise an army if Ysandre had let him. It was you who suggested the Unforgiven, was it not? I heard they knelt to you."

It was true enough that I could not deny it. If Amaury Trente had had his way ten years ago, we would have led a foreign army onto D'Angeline soil. The Unforgiven ... yes. It had been my idea. And they had knelt. I shrugged with a stoicism I did not feel. "They gave fealty in Kushiel's name. They have much for which to atone."

"Enough that the Royal Army let them pass unchallenged." Melisande's face was still and calm, a cameo carved of ivory. "You threw coins," she said. Her brows quirked, a distant note of bemusement in her voice. "Coins."

We had; silver coins, bearing the profile of Ysandre de la Courcel, clean and fresh-minted. They'd arched in showers from the slings of Amaury Trente's men, fallen like silver rain. I remembered the soldiers' perplexed faces, staring, glancing from the unprecedented bounty grasped in sword-calloused hand to the woman who parted their ranks, her face in calm profile, riding inexorably toward the walls of the City of Elua. "Yes," I said softly. "We threw coins."

Melisande nodded, as though I'd said somewhat more. "And that was you, too."

No one else had drawn that line, made that connection. It was not a part of the stories, to credit me with the idea. I gazed at her. "In Illyria," I said, "it is unlawful for a coin to be cast bearing the Ban's image. I remembered. I have you to thank for my time as a hostage there, my lady."

"I thought as much. Kushiel uses his conscience hard." Melisande's regard was unchanged. "You are bound for Iskandria. The Menekhetans are subtle, and Lord Amaury Trente is not. You have a gift for knowledge, and are skilled in the arts of discretion. Whether or not you bear me hatred, my son is innocent of it. If you are bound to see me rot in this gilded cage, then I charge you with his welfare."

To impart suffering without compassion . . .

"You cannot." My voice *was* shaking. "I have done all I might. The debt between us is cleared."

"No." Melisande shook her head with terrible gentleness. "It will never be cleared, Phèdre nó Delaunay. We are bound together. Have you not realized as much?"

I looked away, remembering my dream, the boy who cried out with Hyacinthe's voice, Imriel's face, remembering the children in Amílcar, feral and half-blinded by torchlight. "What I may do for your son, I will, my lady. I would do as much for any child. Beyond that, I make no promises. The matter is out of my hands."

"And in the Queen's," Melisande murmured. She laughed. It was an awful sound, like glass breaking. "Who shall claim him in the end, my Imriel, and teach him to blame the mother who doomed him to such a fate. It is a bitter piece of irony that it is no fault of my own."

"I know," I said, holding her gaze. What else could I say? I did.

"Let him live to hate me, then; only let him live." The fear was back, naked and vulnerable. "I gave you a patron-gift to secure your marque. Will you not swear that much?"

To endure suffering untold, with infinite compassion—

I swallowed. "You ask too much. And I am a fool to listen. My lady, Melisande—there is no debt between us. Any debt I owed you, your betrayal rendered paid in full. I grieve for your son's suffering, but this was a simple bargain, and I have fulfilled it—"

"You are Kushiel's Chosen," she said abruptly. "This is his doing. Am I mistaken, Phèdre? You did not think so. Kushiel chooses to punish his scion. So it may be. But whatever I have done, my son is innocent. I ask only your aid in seeing him restored. You have a gift for such matters, as require the arts of covertcy. Is it so much to ask that you find it in your heart to ensure he does not suffer further for my sins?"

"No," I whispered.

Melisande's voice was quiet. "It is a small thing to ask."

And because I could summon no argument against her, because the pain of her loss was heavy within me, because I had seen the children we rescued in Amílcar, I swore it, like a fool, my heart filled with a swelling agony; though I still believed, then, that it was only a matter of overseeing the plans of Lord Amaury Trente, of ensuring that the boy Imriel was restored with Pharaoh's compliance to his proper place in the annals of House Courcel. I gazed into Melisande's deep-blue eyes and swore it. "So be it. In Blessed Elua's name, I promise. I will do what I can."

"Thank you," she said simply. "I will rest easier for it." She paused; her voice changed. "I wish you luck, Phèdre, in your own quest. The Tsingano lad . . ." Melisande shook her head. "He stumbled into an ancient curse. Even I could not have foreseen it."

"*He* did," I said, the words raw with emotion. It did not sit easy with me that she had exacted my promise when Hyacinthe's fate hung in the balance. "Hyacinthe saw his end. And he went to it unflinching; for me, for all of us. You set us on that path, Melisande, whether you knew it or no, whether you intended it or no. And you would have used him, if you could. The scroll, the guide . . ." I raised my hand, clutching the scrap of vellum. "You've had it all along."

"Not always." There was a curious frankness to her words. "I have few weapons left to me, Phèdre; what would you have me do? I did not make the curse."

I looked away, shaking my head. I would never, so long as I lived, understand her. "Nor did you make the slave-traders, my lady. And yet they have taken your son."

"Yes." The word dropped like a stone from her lips. I looked back at her, seeing her pale and steady. "Do not mistake me. I played a game and lost, and Kushiel has called the reckoning. Would you have me say it?" The awful knowledge was still emblazoned in her. "I will. I was a fool. I never believed Kushiel would exact his payment in innocent blood."

"No?" There were tears in my eyes; I blinked them away, laughing mirthlessly. "Oh, my lady, your games have always ended in the blood of innocents!"

Melisande stood very still, watching me, and what she thought, I could not have said to save my life. With terrifying gentleness, she took my shoulders, lowered her head and kissed me; softly, fleeting. A brush of lips, no more. It was enough. "You have always offered yours willingly, Phèdre. And that, my dear, is the difference."

When all was said and done, she knew me far, far too well.

I swayed on my feet, stung to the heart by the piercing sweetness of her kiss, understanding, at last, why Benedicte de la Courcel had been willing to commit high treason for her, why so many others had done the same.

Melisande smiled, faint and rueful, her eyes filled with infinite regret. "I have only done what I was born to do. If the gods did not want it, they should not have made me. It seems they repent of their error, since they have made you instead. You have your myth and your guide, Phèdre nó Delaunay. Go to Iskandria, and see my son loosed from the snare of Kushiel's vengeance. You have served your warning. I will heed it, and abide in this place. The stakes have grown too high. I am afraid of losing."

"My lady." I bowed my head, carrying the weight of her sorrow, her kiss lingering on my lips. I wanted to cry, still, and knew not why. "My lady, I swear to you, he will be found."

As she had at the beginning, Melisande Shahrizai closed her beautiful eyes. "Blessed Elua grant it may be so," she whispered, and it was the truest prayer I ever heard her utter. And then her eyes opened, and she spoke a single word. "Go."

I went.

TWENTY-NINE

JOSCELIN WAS waiting in the Temple.

He raised his head as I entered, and the sight of him was like a star in a dark place. I walked straight into his arms and felt them enfold me, walling out the world. Priestesses and their attendants paused, staring, as I leaned my brow against his chest. He held me close, resting his cheek against my hair.

"It is done, then?" I heard him murmur.

I freed myself reluctantly, taking his hands. "It is done. Thank you." I took a breath. "I have the name of a guide, and an address in Iskandria. We should see Master Brenin's man at the Banco Tribuno regarding the notes of promise, and book our passage. It would be . . . it would be wise to see Ricciardo Stregazza, too. I trust him to see the guard doubled on Melisande's confinement."

Joscelin raised his eyebrows. "You think she may flee?"

"I don't know." I shook my head. "It is in her heart to take matters into her own hands. I think I have convinced her otherwise, but I am not fool enough to trust her word in it."

"Then we will see it done," Joscelin said calmly.

We did.

It is a long sea-journey, from La Serenissima to Iskandria; the longest I have ever taken. Moreover, we were unable to book passage on short notice for a vessel with capacity for our horses, and must needs leave them in Ricciardo's care. This he offered graciously, and while I was sorry to leave them behind, I knew they would be well tended at his estate of Villa Gaudio on the Serenissiman mainland. It was pleasant to visit with Ricciardo's wife Allegra, with whom I had enjoyed a regular correspondence these ten years' past.

Most astonishing were their offspring, Sabrina and Lucio, whom I remembered as mere children. The former was a serious young woman of seventeen years, the latter a tall, ebullient lad of fifteen who chattered incessantly about which noblemen's club he would join when he came of age, reckoning the merits of each on his fingers.

"You've none of your own, then?" Allegra watched my amazement with gentle amusement. "They do grow up, you know."

"So I see," I replied. "It's only that it happens so *fast*."

She laughed, at that, and turned the conversation, telling me the latest developments in her sponsorship of the Courtesans' Scholae. It had been Ricciardo's project, in the beginning, but Allegra had been the true force behind much of it. In Terre d'Ange, Naamah's Service is a sacred calling. It will never be so in La Serenissima, where folk do not worship Elua and his Companions, but at least their status in society had risen since the Scholae was formed. There is strength in numbers and knowledge alike. Nothing will ever rival the elegant splendor of the D'Angeline Night Court, but the well-educated courtesans of La Serenissima were gaining renown throughout Caerdicca Unitas.

I was glad to hear it, since it was my idea.

We spoke of it aboard the ship, Joscelin and I, during the long, idle hours, after the worst bouts of his customary seasickness had passed. The duration was shorter this time. He was growing, I thought, more accustomed to sea-travel. Late summer was giving way to fall, but it was hot during the days. Our favorite time was evening, when the sun lowered beneath the distant horizon and twilight cooled the air.

"It was well-thought of you," he said. "Naamah must be pleased."

"Mayhap," I said, looking curiously at him. "You used to despise what I did, do you remember? Do you still think it wrong?"

"Wrong?" Joscelin shrugged. "I was taught as much, among the Cassilines; not only Naamah's service, but all of the ways of Elua and his Companions were folly. Cassiel alone stood steadfast to the truth, and one day he would guide Blessed Elua himself to redemption, whereupon all of Terre d'Ange would follow, both the earthly one and the true Terre d'Ange-that-lies-beyond." He smiled wryly, gazing out at the horizon where the first star of evening was emerging. "I did believe it, when I first knew you."

That much, I knew. "And now?"

"Now?" He turned his head to look at me. "No. Not when it is a contract entered freely in homage to Naamah, at least. That much, I have seen to be true. There are mysteries I may not understand, but I acknowledge them nonetheless. And my beliefs . . . my beliefs too have changed. Now I believe the greatest of heresies among the Brotherhood: That in the end Cassiel chose to follow Elua out of love. Not a love born of divine compassion, but simply . . ." he reached out and twined a lock of my hair about his fingers, ". . . love."

I sighed, and leaned against him. "I have always believed as much."

"You would," Joscelin said companionably.

"True," I agreed. A moment passed before I asked another question. "Joscelin, are you sorry we never had children?"

I felt his body stiffen slightly, then relax as I peered up into his face. "Honestly? Sometimes, yes." He stroked my hair. "I would like it, I think . . . I don't know. And yet . . ." He shook his head and looked away. "I have never lied to you. Whatever the truth of Cassiel's nature, I swore my vows in earnest."

"What you broke," I said softly, "you broke out of love."

"I know." He gazed at the fading glow of the horizon. "And I do believe it was in Cassiel's service still. But I spoke true when I said I would strain his grace no further. If a child of ours . . . if a child of mine was touched by Kushiel's Dart . . ." He shuddered. "Truly, some things are beyond enduring."

"I know," I said. "Love, believe me, I do know it."

"You alone are enough to nearly kill me." A hint of humor returned to his voice. "Ah, Phèdre . . . am I sorry for it? Yes, sometimes. I am sorry for many things, sometimes, and mostly they are things I cannot change, or would not if I could. Aren't you?"

"Yes." I watched more stars emerge as the sky darkened to velvet. "We would not be here, a thousand miles from home, if we had children."

"No," Joscelin said equably. "Probably not."

A soft, steady wind blew as the Serenissiman sailors moved about the ship's deck, kindling lamps fore and aft. Such frail sparks of light against the vast darkness, I thought, born aloft and lonely on the swelling breast of the ocean, while a canopy of brilliant stars spread overhead. I tried to imagine it, a life of domesticity and simple pleasures such as Allegra and Ricciardo Stregazza's family shared at Villa Gaudio, given deeper meaning by the good acts of charity and governance both had undertaken. It would have been that way with us. Joscelin had released me and his hands gripped the ship's rail, steel mesh glinting on their backs. I gazed at his profile, the cruciform hilt of his sword rising over his shoulder to blot out the stars. Would he be sorry to hang up his blades? I didn't think so.

And yet . . . somewhere, beneath this same night sky, stood a rocky isle with a high altar open to the winds and a single lonely tower, where my Prince of Travellers watched the sun set and rise, days turning to years, the slow advance of decrepitude and madness stretching into an infinite vista.

And somewhere, too, was a ten-year-old boy with eyes the color of sapphires, sold into slavery in a strange land. How they were linked, I could not yet fathom. I knew only that they were.

We belonged where we were, Joscelin and I.

So passed our journey.

For those who have not seen it, Iskandria is a splendid and enduring city, the product of many cultures. It is young as the Menekhetans reckon such things, for it was founded by the Hellene conqueror who freed them from Persian rule; Al-Iskandr, they called him, and crowned him with the horns of Ammon. It is his heirs who moved the seat of rule to his city, but within a generation of his death they ceased to rule in his name and took on the trappings of Pharaoh, wedding Menekhetan tradition with Hellene blood.

Like many other countries, Menekhet fell under the shadow of the empire of Tiberium; unlike many others, it retained its sovereign status, bowing to inevitability and paying homage in grain to its mighty neighbor. There was a cunning Queen who ruled as Pharaoh when Tiberium's might was at its apex, tricking the Tiberian generals into quarreling until their forces were spread too thin to seize the prize of Menekhet. My lord Delaunay had always admired her; Cleopatra Philopater, she was called. Afterward, Tiberium's difficulties in Alba began, and Menekhet was left untroubled.

It is different now, of course; it is the desert-riders of the Umaiyyat who threaten Menekhet's borders, and the vast power of Khebbel-im-Akkad. Menekhet walks a fine line between the two, placating both and maintaining its ties to the city-states of Caerdicca Unitas—especially La Serenissima, with its skilled navy—and to Carthage. We D'Angelines are newly arrived to this arena of politics, although not to be disdained; I daresay no one in Menekhet has forgotten that Terre d'Ange defeated the Akkadians in a sea-battle not twenty years past.

We entered the Great Harbour at sunset, and it was indeed a sight to see as we passed the offshore island which held the famed Lighthouse of Iskandria, a massive colossus thrusting some five hundred feet into the air, its white marble walls washed red in the setting sun. It is built in three tiers, and the base is as broad as a fortress. The ship's captain informed us it held an entire squadron of cavalry. I had to crane my head to see the top, where a plume of smoke unfurled against the sky.

To my disappointment, the beacon itself seemed dim and unimpressive in the gilded light, but the captain assured me that encroaching darkness would render it bright as a star, visible for many miles at sea. He pointed out the inscription rendered on the foundation stone.

"We are not near enough to read it, my lady, but it says, 'Sostrates, son of Dexiphanes of Knidos, on behalf of all mariners, to the savior gods,' " he told me. "The architect Sostrates was bade to inscribe the name of Pharaoh on the stone, but he carved his own, then covered it with plaster and chiseled Pharaoh's dedication atop it. In a hundred years, the plaster had chipped away and Pharaoh's name was forgotten. It is the clever architect's which will stand for eternity, and well it should, for the Lighthouse of Iskandria has no equal."

Joscelin smiled, the story tickling his Siovalese fancy; all of Shemhazai's descendents have a fondness for architects and engineers and the like, the cleverer, the better. I thanked the captain, who bowed and excused himself to oversee our entry into port. Although he had been exceedingly gracious, I was never fully at ease in his presence. Truly, it was through no fault of his own. The last time I'd been aboard a Serenissiman vessel, I'd come within a hair's breadth of being beheaded. 'Tis a hard thing to forget.

The sky was a vivid hue of purple by the time we made port, the unfamiliar shapes of date palms making tufted silhouettes above the roofs. Twilight brought little coolness this far south and the hot air was dense, rife with strange odors. I have travelled to many places, willingly or no, and thought myself immune to strangeness, but Iskandria was different, more alien than aught I had experienced. We had arrived late and, aside from our crew, the people in the harbor—men and boys, for I saw no women—were quick and dark, speaking no tongue I recognized.

It is one thing to travel to a strange place on foot or on horseback, observing the gradual change in landscape and culture; if I may say so, it is quite another to travel by sea, and find oneself arriving unceremoniously in a foreign city. I glanced at Joscelin, who stood on the quai beside our bags and trunks looking bewildered, and wished for a moment that we *had* brought Ti-Philippe. A former sailor and veteran adventurer, he would have spent his days aboard the ship gambling and swapping tales, and arrived fully prepared to lead us to the best possible lodgings that might be arranged in Iskandria.

"My lady." It was the Serenissiman captain, who approached with a bow, a smiling Menekhetan lad trailing at his heels. "Since you did not speak of your arrangements, I have taken the liberty of asking young Nesmut on your behalf. He is," he shot the boy a warning glance, "one of the most trustworthy of the young pups who hang about the harbor, and he speaks a little Hellene. He says there is a D'Angeline delegation lodged in the Street of Oranges, and he will procure a carriage and take you there for twenty obols. It is a fair price."

"We accept," I said, nodding to the lad. "Thank you."

He grinned, his teeth a flash of white in the gloaming, before dashing away. It reminded me with a pang of Hyacinthe's smile, the way it had been when he was a boy. In a little while, he was back, leading a carriage-horse, one hand on the bridle, all self-importance. It was an open-air carriage, plain but suitable. The taciturn driver perched in his seat and looked bored.

"Nesmut's a good lad," the captain said when our goods were loaded. "If you've need of a guide in the city, he'll serve. I've dealt with him before, and he knows I'll box his ears if I hear he's cheated a passenger of mine."

"Thank you, my lord captain," I said, with more sincerity than I'd evinced before. "Truly, I am grateful for your kindness."

" 'Tis naught." He shuffled and looked away, suddenly uncomfortable. "I've heard tell, you see. Sailors do. You're the one . . . you're the one that fell from the cliffs of La Dolorosa, and lived. They say Asherat-of-the-Sea held you in her hand and bore you up on the waves. I know . . . I know Marco Stregazza ordered you slain. I don't blame you for being uneasy with it. Still, I'll carry you anywhere you want to go. We're in harbor two weeks. You only need to send word."

What could I say to that? I thanked him for it again, feeling odd. At my side, Joscelin laughed softly. The boy Nesmut shifted impatiently, holding the carriage-horse's reins. "Gracious lord, gracious lady," he called in Hellene, "we go now, or you miss the supper hour, yes? Kyria Maharet, she will be angry."

Heeding his call, we said our good-byes and boarded the carriage; the Serenissiman captain bowed one last time and held it, low and sweeping. I didn't even know his name. And then the driver twitched his whip and we were moving through the warm twilight, the carriage-horse's hooves clopping on the broad, straight streets. Nesmut sat opposite us, wrapping his arms around himself and grinning. He wore a white garment like a tunic, ragged but clean, and his coarse black hair was cut like a bowl, falling into his dark eyes. I guessed his age at thirteen.

It is hard to get an impression of a city at night, but I gathered somewhat; Iskandria was a well-planned city, filled with elegant temples and parks, gorgeous palaces, and clean streets laid out in a grid. Nesmut raised his head and sniffed deeply as we turned a corner, waving one slender hand. "Street of Oranges," he announced. "You smell it?"

I could, a citron tang permeating the heavy air. A short way down, the driver drew rein before a low, arched doorway, twin torches burning untended in the sconces. Nesmut leapt down and dashed inside, barefoot and soundless. In a moment, he returned, grinning anew, flanked by a pair of well-muscled attendants.

"Gracious lord, gracious lady, you are here, yes?" He held out one hand expectantly.

I paid him in Serenissiman coin, having ascertained its relative value before I left; I am diligent about such things. He examined it carefully, biting down on the rim to be sure, reminding me anew of Hyacinthe. Joscelin supervised the removal of our belongings into the inn.

"It is good," Nesmut acknowledged at length, giving half the coins to the carriage-driver and tucking the remainder into a hidden pocket in his tunic. "I come in the morning, yes? Gracious lady, will need a guide to the city."

I began to demur, then thought better of it. "All right," I said in Hellene. "Thank you, Nesmut. I cannot promise I will need your aid, but I will pay you for your time nonetheless."

He grinned and made a surprisingly precise bow, then took to his heels. I watched his slight form recede into darkness, then followed Joscelin into the inn.

Beyond the broad, arched doorway, we were met by a solid figure of a woman in her forties, swathed in layers of silk. Her calculating eyes were lined in kohl, and her hair was caught in a neat bun at the nape of her neck, covered in an elaborate gilt cap. She placed her hands together and bowed, greeting us in flawless Hellene. "My lord and lady, I am Metriche. The boy Nesmut said you wished lodgings?"

"Yes," I said. "You have other D'Angeline patrons here?"

"Yes." Metriche bowed again. Her eyes were watchful. "Kyrios Trente and his party have taken lodging here. We are very near your ambassador's home. May I show you to your rooms? The supper hour," her eyes flashed briefly, "is nearly finished."

"Please," I said humbly.

Our hostess Metriche—Maharet, the boy had called her—led us to our rooms, which were gracious and well-appointed, cool in the evening air with a draft of citron coming from an unseen courtyard. "There is the ewer," she said, pointing, "if you wish to bathe your face. If you do not come to the dining-hall in a quarter of an hour, you will not eat."

With that, she left us.

I sat down on the bed and sighed. The mattress felt firm and pleasant, the cotton bedding exquisitely soft. After weeks aboard a ship, solid earth was unsteady under my feet. I welcomed the idea of sleep far more than sustenance. Joscelin poured water from the ewer into a marble basin, splashing noisily. "Ah!" He tossed his head back, looking unnaturally refreshed, in my opinion. "Phèdre, are you coming?" he asked, adding plaintively, "you needn't, but I'm ravenous."

"I'm coming," I said, and sighed again, hauling myself off the bed. I felt a mess, salt-stained and travel-weary. I smoothed my garments—I was wearing the celadon green silks—and silently blessed Favrielle nó Eglantine for her irascible genius.

The dining-hall was a vast open space with vaulted ceilings, punctuated by slender columns. Fretted lamps cast a gentle glow, and white-clad attendants moved on hushed feet. The whole of the space was dominated by a single table, where a large party sat, flanking a man who was obviously its leader. He sat with his head bowed, both hands fisted in his curly hair, while his companions sought to give him counsel.

It was not until we entered the room that he looked up and I recognized him.

"Phèdre nó Delaunay," Lord Amaury Trente exclaimed. "Thanks be to Blessed Elua! I thought you'd never get here."

ℭHIRTY

FADIL CHOUMA was dead.

That was the story that emerged over the course of an hour as the Menekhetan servants brought out plate after plate of rich, spicy food—grilled eggplant, broad beans, lamb with onion and parsley, pickled limes, chickpeas and sesame, fish in a sharp garlic sauce, all served with flat bread and a honey-sweetened barley beer.

Although I had not thought myself hungry, my appetite manifested unexpectedly and I ate with good will as Lord Trente told his story.

The delegation had had a swift, uneventful journey from Marsilikos and arrived a scant week before us. Raife Laniol, Comte de Penfars, was Ysandre's ambassador in Iskandria. He had bade them fair welcome and arranged for lodgings for the party with the lady Metriche. She was a widow of mixed blood, Menekhetan and Hellene alike; there was, I understood, an unofficial caste system at work in Iskandria, and native Menekhetans are reckoned of less worth than those descendants of Hellas.

Comte Raife had quickly grasped the sensitivity of the situation, and aided in negotiations with Pharaoh's Secretary of the Treasury, presenting the offer of Alban trade-rights as an alluring opportunity. Amaury Trente made a pretty presentation of the tokens they had brought: a chest of lead, brooches and armrings of intricate gold knot-work, and cleverest of all, potted seedlings of native Alban flora, for the Pharaohs of Menekhet were long known to be eager for exotic botany.

It had all gone remarkably well, and the delegation was presented to Ptolemy Dikaios, Pharaoh himself, who expressed his delight with the gifts and a keen interest in opening trade with Alba. Amaury Trente cited the interests of the Cruarch—linen flax, dates, wheat—mentioning as a casual aside a fancy of the Cruarch's to assuage his wife's whim, and retrieve a young D'Angeline boy mistaken sold into slavery in the city.

I have only the word of Amaury Trente and his companions by which to gauge, but I have no reason to doubt it. By all accounts, he managed it with a subtlety that would have satisfied Melisande. Pharaoh heard it with half an ear and waved his bejeweled hand, ordering his Secretary of the Treasury to ensure that this trifling matter was done, and returning to the more serious matters of flax and dates.

Well and so, it *would* have been done. The Secretary of the Treasury put one of his senior clerks on the matter, disdaining to sully his own hands, and the clerk found out the slaver Fadil Chouma's residence in the Street of Crocodiles. Invoking his master's name, he enlisted a squadron of the Pharaoh's Guard and presented himself at Fadil Chouma's residence, prepared to demand the return of the D'Angeline boy in the interests of the state, compensation to be, of course, negotiable, with death as an alternative.

But Fadil Chouma was already dead.

And the D'Angeline boy long since sold.

I understood better why Lord Amaury Trente clutched at his own hair. Although Chouma's household remembered the boy, there was no record of Imriel de la Courcel's sale—and Fadil Chouma had kept exacting records. There was, perhaps, a reason for it. Doubtless the D'Angeline boy was a piece of goods Fadil Chouma had sooner forget. It was Imriel, after all, who had killed him.

It was a fluke accident, in a way, although I daresay the boy intended it. It had happened in the kitchen—Chouma's women had cosseted the lad, owing to his beauty, and allowed him thence to feed him sweetmeats and the like—where Imriel had turned like a flash, faster than anyone could have reckoned, and seized a knife the cook had been using to debone a chicken. He sunk the knife into Fadil Chouma's thigh.

To be sure, 'twas no mortal wound; Chouma bellowed like a bull, the knife was removed and the wound bandaged. Imriel was beaten, and within two days, sold. Fadil Chouma, his mouth compressed in a tight line, would not say to whom. Already his wound festered. In four days, the leg was hot and rigid with swelling, red streaks making their way upward.

"He wouldn't let the chirurgeon take his leg," Amaury Trente said grimly. "I was told he died screaming, and I wasn't sorry to hear it. But no one knows what he did with the boy."

Our table had been cleared of dishes. The Menekhetan servants hovered nearby with pitchers of barley beer, clearly hoping we would retire for the evening. Amaury Trente and his delegates looked at me hopefully. I sat wondering to myself, what would Delaunay do?

"You believe Chouma's household was telling the truth?" I asked.

"I have reason to believe as much," Amaury said. "From my understanding, Pharaoh's guardsmen asked their questions at knifepoint, and none too gently. He sold the lad in a fury, and none knew where. The clerk, Rekhmire, went over his accounts in detail. Slavers pay taxes in Menekhet, the same as anyone else." He shrugged, his expression showing his distaste. "He'd an entry for the boy's purchase in Amílcar, sure enough, but naught on the other side of the ledger. It never mentioned he was D'Angeline, but the description matched and no mistake. Rekhmire's an industrious sort, especially when it comes to protecting the interests of Pharaoh's Treasury. He's pursued the matter in the last few days, made inquiry at the slave-auctions and among the libertines and pleasure-houses. Nothing. And believe me, my lady," he added grimly, "even in Iskandria, a ten-year-old D'Angeline boy would not go unremarked."

"No," I said. "I suppose not." What would Anafiel Delaunay do? All knowledge is worth having. Delaunay would analyze the situation, I thought. And derive . . . what? Weary with long travel and the soporific effect of a rich meal, I forced my wits to work. "Chouma," I said aloud, thinking. Fadil Chouma was a clever and exacting man. He had recorded Imriel's purchase; why not his sale? Mayhap because he sickened too quickly. And yet, he had concealed the information from his household, which suggested otherwise. Who knows what he had meant to do? But given the information at hand, I thought it unlikely that he intended to make a full accounting.

Why?

Political reasons, mayhap; surely, there was danger involved in trafficking in D'Angeline flesh . . . and yet not so much that he had feared altogether to record Imriel's purchase. No, it must be somewhat else. Why had he refused to divulge the boy's fate? The most obvious possibility loomed before me, sickeningly plausible. Imriel had stabbed the slaver. If Chouma had killed him in a fit of rage, knowing his household doted on the boy . . . then, he would keep it silent.

No. In an act of will, I rejected the notion, summoning the logic to justify it. Fadil Chouma was a slaver; a merchant. He had laid his plans too well and invested too much to dispose of valuable property out of anger. It had to be true, *had* to be, or all my searching was in vain, the bitter bargain, the promises made. Surely Kushiel's mighty justice must come to more than *this*, a small corpse mislaid, a blind alley in an unknown city.

It made me think of Amílcar, and the children there. A twisting alley, the darkened back room. I thought of the Carthaginians, poor stupid brutes, and Mago with his flame-ruined feet, screaming his lungs raw with his confession.

Fadil Chouma had a buyer in mind; one, only one, mind . . .

A merchant's ploy, I'd thought upon hearing it, to get out of a bargain he'd no intention of keeping. And yet . . . what if it were not? Fadil Chouma had had a buyer in mind. He'd hedged his bets, he'd recorded the purchase—but not the sale. Why? On a deep level somewhere below conscious thought, I felt the pieces of the puzzle fall into a pattern.

"Chouma was protecting his own interests," I announced. "He had a buyer in mind from the beginning, and whoever it was, it's someone dangerous. Dangerous to *him*; dangerous to be known, dangerous to be named. He was uncertain of the deal, which is why he recorded Imriel's purchase—but it happened, the buyer came through. He would have altered his records if he hadn't fallen ill." I blinked and realized Amaury Trente and the others were looking blankly at me. It had been a long time since I'd spoken.

"And so . . . what?" Amaury asked carefully. "What do we do about it?"

"Ask . . . what's his name? The ambassador?" My wits were dull with weariness and exertion. "Raife, yes? Raife Laniol, Comte de Penfars. Ask him, my lord. Pharaoh's a powerful man; powerful men have enemies. It's an ambassador's job to be able to name them. It will give us a starting point, at least."

One of the women among the delegates—Denise Fleurais—cleared her throat. "Ambassador de Penfars' knowledge," she said with a certain delicacy, "is confined to the upper strata of Menekhetan society."

"Hellenes," someone murmured further down the table. "She means Hellenes."

There ensued a discussion about the merits of Hellene civilization versus the native component. I listened with half an ear, watching the hovering Menekhetan servants, jugs of barley beer at the ready, waiting with well-concealed impatient for the D'Angeline guests to take to their beds. "Surely," I ventured, thinking about the polite brown masks of our servants' faces, "Ambassador de Penfars has contacts among the native Iskandrians as well."

A brief silence answered me.

"Not many," the Lady Denise said at length. She had auburn hair the color of new mahogany, and a shrewdness to her face which I liked. "There is the clerk, Rekhmire, or so we gather. But Ambassador de Penfars does not speak the argot of the land."

"*What?*" The word came out with more force than I intended, but in truth, it shocked me. Raife Laniol had been two years and more stationed in Iskandria; time and more, I reckoned, to learn the language. And yet . . . I saw from the delegates' faces that few of them shared my astonishment.

"Phèdre." It was Joscelin's voice, calm and thoughtful. "If you are right, then there is an avenue of questioning unpursued. Surely Chouma's household must share his fears. Who would be a client too dangerous to be named?" I looked at him and he shrugged. "No one asked them that, I'll warrant. But . . ." he plucked the cup from my hand, peering into the dregs of barley beer, "we're not like to get further with it tonight."

"Fairly said." I placed both hands on the table and pushed myself upright, tiredness dragging at me. "My lords, my ladies . . . let us adjourn."

No one gave argument, for which I was grateful. With a solicitous hand beneath my elbow, Joscelin escorted me back to our pleasant rooms, where windows were open onto the night breeze with its citrus scent. Once we were there, he leaned against a wall, watching me with faint amusement as I reclined on the comfortable mattress, my mind filled with thoughts that dispelled sleep.

"Well?" he said at length.

I sighed, propping myself on my elbows. "What would you have me say? That I am clinging to faint hope? That it is a crime that the Menekhetan ambassador does not speak the native tongue?"

He raised his eyebrows. "It's a start."

"Hyacinthe's plight comes first." I made my voice firm, trying not to think on the promise I had made Melisande. "We will see those arrangements made. Then . . . mayhap we will see what there is to be learned in Iskandria that lies beyond the Hellene stratum of Menekhetan society."

Joscelin smiled. "I thought you would say as much."

THIRTY-ONE

In THE morning, we reconvened over breakfast, which consisted of pungent bean-cakes, fried in oil and served with a sweet condiment of jellied figs, a strange but pleasing combination of flavors. Amaury Trente had already sent word to Ambassador de Penfars to arrange for an appointment. He was more optimistic than he had been last night; if nothing else, at least my suggestions had given him purpose.

Joscelin and I would explore Iskandria . . . and no matter what promises I had made to Melisande, I did intend to settle the matter of a guide to Jebe-Barkal first and foremost. Once the arrangements were made, I could dedicate my energies to aiding Amaury in the search for Imriel's mysterious purchaser with a clear mind.

True to his word, the boy Nesmut appeared while we were still eating, bright-eyed and cheerful. "You have work for me, yes?" he asked with a winning smile. "Gracious lord and lady need a guide to see the city? I show the best places!"

I took the scrap of vellum Melisande had given me from the purse at my girdle and showed it to him. "I am looking for a man named Radi Arumi, who resides at this address on the Street of Crocodiles. Do you know this place?"

Nesmut peered at it. "Gracious lady, I cannot read, but I know the Street of Crocodiles. If you tell me the number, I will take you there, yes."

After a brief negotiation, we were agreed.

The heat of the day struck us like a blast from a forge as we left Metriche's inn. It was hard to believe, I thought, that in Terre d'Ange, the fields lay in stubble and the chill autumn rains fell upon the land. In Menekhet, the sun blazed unceasing and the sky was a hard blue, copper-tinged with heat. Although the broad streets were swept clean, there was taste of dust in my mouth.

For all that, the city bustled. It would, Nesmut informed us, grow hotter yet; at midday, everyone retired to the shade until the worst of the heat had passed. It was well that we had risen early. He kept up a running commentary as he led us through the city, pausing to greet a half-dozen people on every block—servants, carriage-drivers, house-wives, water-sellers. Everyone, it seemed, had a good-natured word for the lad.

And all, I noticed, in Menekhetan.

"There is the Street of Moneylenders," Nesmut announced, point-ing. "If you like, I take you to a man to change your Serenissiman coin for Menekhetan, yes? Harder then for merchants to cheat you. I know a man who is fair."

I glanced at Joscelin, who raised his eyebrows. "*You* wouldn't cheat, us, would you, Nesmut?" he asked the boy in Hellene. "Because if you did . . ." In a movement too quick for the eye to follow, his daggers leapt from their sheaths and into his hands, crossed tips hovering under the lad's chin. "I would be very angry."

Nesmut's dark eyes widened. "Gracious lord!" he breathed. "Never!"

"Good." Joscelin put up his daggers and gave a cross-vambraced bow. A faint smile hovered at one corner of his mouth where only I could see it. "Then we will heed your advice. Thank you, Nesmut."

"Gracious lord," he said warily, pointing again. "It is this way."

It was well done of Joscelin, for the rate of exchange proved more than fair, and I daresay a good deal of it was due to the impression Nesmut conveyed of our seriousness. In short order, the transaction was done, and we left having exchanged our Serenissiman solidi for a con-siderable amount of Menekhetan coin. Nesmut led us to the Street of Crocodiles with a renewed air of importance.

The address Melisande had given me was in the jewelers' quarter and proved, indeed, to be that of a jeweler's shop. Tiny bronze bells rang as we opened the door, passing from bright sun into the relative coolness of shadow within the thick sandstone walls. To my sun-dazzled eyes, it was murky as night within the shop. I made out the angular figure of a man hunched over a worktable positioned in a patch of morning sun that slanted through a window. The figure's head lifted, and I heard a gasp; his hands moved in a flurry, overturning a number of cabochon gems on the worktable and laying them facedown before he arose to greet us.

"My lady." He addressed me in Hellene, placing both hands together and bowing deeply. His face, when he straightened, was filled with awe. "I am Karem. How may I serve you?"

"Karem," I said, blinking. My eyes were adjusting to the darkness. He was young, his beard still patchy on his chin, and clearly Menekhetan. "I am Phèdre nó Delaunay, Comtesse de Montrève in Terre d'Ange. I am looking for a man named Radi Arumi. Do you know him?"

"The Jebean." Karem's face showed his disappointment. "Yes, I know him, my lady; he rents a room in my father's lodgings in the back when he is in Iskandria. Wait here, please, and I will tell him you have come."

With another bow, he vanished out a rear doorway. Nesmut wandered over to a sitting-area to the right of the shop, low-slung leathern chairs arranged about a low table. He clambered into one of the chairs and sat cross-legged, quite at his ease. Karem was gone a long time. I looked at his worktable. Semiprecious gems lay scattered; carnelian, amethyst, chalcedony. I wondered why he'd overturned them. His jeweler's tools were works of art in and of themselves, tiny blades and picks and chisels, immaculately wrought, reminding me, with an uncomfortable shock, of Melisande's flechettes, those exquisite little blades capable of causing such exquisite pain.

When all is said and done, I am an *anguissette*. This is what it is to be Kushiel's Chosen. No purpose, no quest, can change the nature of what I am; for good or for ill.

After a while, Joscelin and I both took seats, waiting. And in time, Karem returned, with a second man in tow, of indeterminate years, black-skinned and leathered with exposure to the sun, an embroidered cap perched atop his wooly hair.

"Radi Arumi," I greeted him, standing and inclining my head. "In'demin aderq."

A grin split his creased face at my words, showing strong white teeth. "Ha! It is a dream-spirit that speaks to me in Jeb'ez," Radi Arumi said in pidgin Hellene. "Do I dream? My friend Karem dreams, and covers his groin with embarrassment."

I colored, although I daresay I grew no redder than poor Karem. "Messire Arumi," I said directly, ignoring it, "I am looking for the descendants of Melek al'Hakim, the Queen of Saba's son. And I am told you know where to find them."

"Ah." Radi Arumi sat down, eyeing me and my companions. He wore loose-fitting, brightly colored robes, frayed at the edges. "There was a man, a Hellene man, asking about such things, a year or more gone by. He served a mistress in La Serenissima, he told me. He wanted to know if the stories were true. I guide the caravans to Meroë. He wanted to know if I could guide him to the scions of Saba. I told him yes."

"You told him yes." It was Joscelin who spoke, shifting subtly in his chair to show the hilts of his daggers, his sword. "Can you?" he inquired.

Nesmut drew up his knees and looked from one to the other, bright-eyed with interest. "Yes, kyrios," Radi Arumi answered, giving Joscelin a seated half-bow. "Though it is far, far to the south, I can show you. But . . ." He held up one hand, pale palm outward, raising a finger. "It is a long journey, and difficult. Do you wish to make it?"

"We do," I said firmly, forestalling any other answer Joscelin might give. "We have some business to attend to in Iskandria, messire guide, but be assured, we are very interested in the descendants of Saba. Can you arrange to guide us there? We will pay."

Nesmut made a sound of protest. Karem, looking sullen, wandered to his worktable and pried at the edge of a cabochon gem, peering at its hidden face. Radi Arumi watched me through half-lidded eyes. "There is," he said presently, "a caravan leaving for Meroë in a fort-night's time. I have contracted to serve as their guide. Do you wish to go with them, I will accompany you, and from Meroë, we will set forth for Saba, where Melek al'Hakim's descendants endure. Does it please you, my lady? If it does, we will speak of money."

I glanced at Joscelin, who shrugged. "Yes, messire guide. It pleases me. Let us speak of money."

And so we did, in a polyglot of languages, for it would not do but that Nesmut, our self-appointed liaison, had his say, and Karem contributed, while Joscelin and I conferred in D'Angeline. It was an art, I realized in time, and part and parcel of making the deal. At some point, a tray of strong mint tea was served, sweetened with honey. We sipped it from small cups and made polite argument with one another. When it was done, Joscelin and I had signed on to accompany a Menekhetan trade caravan to the Jebean capital city of Meroë, and thence to pay

Radi Arumi a certain sum to lead us south to the descendents of Saba.

"May Amon-Re smile upon our endeavors," Radi said formally, rising and bowing. "I will await you at the Southern Gate a fortnight hence. We will leave ere daybreak."

So it was done, and it left us a full two weeks to search Iskandria for Imriel's trail. Although I kept my face solemn, I was pleased with the outcome. It was time enough, I thought. If it was not, no amount of time would suffice. I thought that, then.

"Gracious lady," Nesmut said tactfully. "The noon hour is nigh. Will you not take repose? There is a house nearby that serves a very fine beer, yes."

"Yes." I stood, stiff with long sitting, and wandered to Karem's worktable, attempting to see his handiwork. "Karem, these are very fine! What is this, a cameo? It's worthy of D'Angeline workmanship."

He moved awkwardly, interposing his body between me and the worktable, preventing me from seeing. "No, no, my lady is too kind," he murmured. "They are poor trifles; poor trifles, nothing more."

"Gracious lady." Nesmut, appearing at my side, tugged at my hand, looking at me with earnest eyes. "Let us go."

In the street, when the door to the jeweler's shop had closed behind us, he relaxed. I exchanged a perplexed look with Joscelin, who shrugged. The sun stood high overhead and the heat had intensified.

"Come," Nesmut said. "We will take repose."

The establishment to which he led us was thoroughly Menekhetan in nature; cool and dim, with thick walls to keep out the heat and high ceilings to diffuse it, and the same low arrangement of table and chairs, nearer to the cool tiles of the floor. We paused in the arched doorway. Several men seated within were playing a game with an inlaid board. They looked up, neither hostile nor welcoming. Nesmut spoke to the proprietor at length in Menekhetan. Eventually he nodded and waved us to a table, bringing a brown earthenware jug of beer and three cups.

The proprietor poured and the men resumed their board game, stealing occasional glances our way. "Nesmut," I said. "Are you sure we are welcome here?"

Draining half his beer at a draught, he nodded vigorously, swallowing and setting down his cup. "Yes, gracious lady. It is not a place for women, Menekhetan women, but I explained to Hapuseneb that you are a foreigner, and different. It is proper. Do not fear. I know much of the ways of foreigners," he added, boasting.

"And Menekhetans and Hellenes as well?" Joscelin inquired.

Nesmut refilled his cup. "Everything, gracious lord, that passes in the city. But you are going to Jebe-Barkal, yes?"

"Yes," I said. "In a fortnight." I sipped my beer and found it cool and refreshing, sweetened with honey and a trace of mint. "Nesmut, it is true, we do have need of a guide to the city, one who knows it inside and out. But our business here, it is a very delicate matter, and this guide . . . it must be someone whom we can trust, someone who can keep a secret."

His eyes had grown very round. "I can keep a secret!" he said excitedly, tapping his breast. "I can, yes!"

I shook my head. "No. Even a promise is not enough. It is too grave."

"I will swear it by Serapis, god of the dead." Nesmut shivered and knelt on his low chair, tucking his bare feet under him. "I will swear the most dire oath I know, gracious lady!"

I thought about it, and at length nodded, keeping my expression terribly serious. "All right, then. Swear it." He did, raising one hand and reciting a long oath in Menekhetan with all the gravity of his youth. "Good," I said when he had finished. "Nesmut, we are looking for a boy, a D'Angeline boy who was sold into slavery somewhere in Iskandria."

"Oh." Looking disappointed, he slumped back into his chair. "Yes, gracious lady. The one who put a knife in merchant Chouma?"

I raised my eyebrows. "You know about it?"

Nesmut sniffed. "Everyone knows. Rekhmire the clerk marched through the city to Chouma's house with enough men for an army. Everyone knows. Not," he added scornfully, "the lords and ladies, no. They are too busy aping Hellenes, courting favor. *They* do not care what Pharaoh's men do to a Menekhetan slave-merchant. *They* do not care that Chouma's third concubine will have scars."

"So much for discretion," Joscelin said to me.

"True," I said. "Nesmut, what else do people say about it? Do they know where the boy may be found?"

"No." He shook his head, concentrating on refilling his cup. The jug was empty; our young guide had a considerable thirst for beer. He glanced at Joscelin for permission before gesturing to the proprietor for more. "No, gracious lady, no one knows. But it is said . . ." He glanced sidelong at us and fell silent. The proprietor came with a fresh jug. Nesmut watched his receding back.

"Nesmut," I said gently. He met my eyes with reluctance. "Whatever it is you fear to say, I swear, I will never divulge that I learned it from you. I swear it in the name of Blessed Elua, and that is an oath no D'Angeline may break."

The boy stared into his cup, lowering his head until his hair obscured his face. "It is said," he murmured, "that the D'Angelines who came, the others, are looking for the boy. Why else would Rekhmire go to Chouma's house only then? So it is true. What is the name it is death to tell Pharaoh's men?" His voice dropped to a whisper. "Pharaoh."

It made sense, although I wished it did not. I should have thought of it myself. Terre d'Ange does not permit traffic in D'Angeline flesh. Of a surety, if Pharaoh had a fancy for a D'Angeline slave-boy, it would be a whim best concealed.

Fadil Chouma had a buyer in mind; one, only one, mind . . .

If Pharaoh had bought Imriel, it was done in secrecy, no doubt with Chouma's assurances that the lad was no one, a shepherd boy who would never be missed. I thought of the others, the children we found in Amílcar. It would have been true, had it been either of them. But no, it was Imriel, and now there was a delegation on Pharaoh's doorstep offering lucrative trade-rights, asking for the child's return.

"Elua!" Joscelin breathed. He looked ill. "If it's true, he could never admit it."

"No," I said. "He would give every evidence of cooperating. And I daresay it would be worth one's life to suggest a word otherwise. No," I sighed, "it's too late for diplomacy. We need to find out if it's true, first."

"And if it is?" Joscelin raised his brows.

"We'll have to steal him," I said. Nesmut let out a startled squeak. I glanced mildly at him. "I *told* you it was grave enough to warrant your oath."

From the look on his face, I daresay he agreed.

THIRTY-TWO

THE FIRST order of business was to determine whether or not Imriel de la Courcel was indeed housed within the Palace of Pharaohs.

After his initial shock, Nesmut proved a valuable ally; I'd not done ill in trusting him. The oath he'd sworn was a binding one, and Nesmut, balanced on the cusp of adulthood, regarded it with a boy's solemnity and a man's sense of duty.

Once he put his mind to the matter, he bethought himself of a considerable number of contacts within the Palace: a laundress, a cook's apprentice, a gardener, a beer-taster. The list went on and on. It was as I had seen that morning—likeable and quick-witted, the lad knew nearly half the city. And when he was not escorting foreigners about Iskandria, he ran errands and carried messages and gossip for coin.

So had Hyacinthe done.

As he became caught up in the spirit of conspiracy, Nesmut's eyes shone with eagerness and I had to remind him to lower his voice, to speak in coded reference to our plan. Whether or not any of the other patrons spoke Hellene, I did not know, but I was taking no chances. Elua, but he was young! It made me uneasy.

"No one," I instructed him, "is to take the slightest risk to gain this information, do you hear me? No one, and most especially not you." My lord Delaunay's voice echoed in my head. He'd said much the same to me, on numerous occasions. I'd usually ignored him.

"I hear you, gracious lady." Nesmut nodded vigorously. "No risk. Only to observe."

And that, too, rang familiar, with all the brash assurance of my youth. The irony of it was not lost upon me. Melisande Shahrizai taught my lord Delaunay to use people to his own ends; as he had used me, as he had used Alcuin, ruthless and guilt-ridden, honoring a vow the rest of the world had forgotten. He'd had little choice, for the doors of the society whose secrets he sought to penetrate had been closed to him.

As the doors to Pharaoh's secrets were barred to me.

And now I must needs use Nesmut to gain access to the lower echelons of Menekhetan society, to ferret out those secrets through the only avenue possible, in order to fulfill my vow to Melisande Shahrizai.

No, the irony was not lost upon me.

"Nesmut." It was Joscelin who changed the topic, a deliberate note of inquiry in his voice. I looked at him with gratitude, knowing full well he sensed my thoughts. "Why did the jeweler Karem turn over his work when we entered his shop?"

"Oh, that." The lad grinned. "Gracious lord, Karem makes . . . how did you say? Cameos? Portraits, yes, carved of Pharaoh's Queen for her admirers. For one of such beauty as my lady to gaze upon them . . ." He clicked his tongue and snapped the fingers of one hand. "The stone would crack with envy."

"Ah." Joscelin shot me an amused glance. "I see."

"It is well known," Nesmut offered helpfully, "that such things happen."

By this turn of the conversation, I gauged it time and more that we returned to Metriche's inn to confer with Amaury Trente. Indeed, Nesmut was filled with plans and ideas for undertaking his quest, and nothing loathe to part company for the day. We settled our account with the proprietor and Nesmut led us out the door of the beer-shop . . . only to stop dead in his tracks, one slender, brown hand flung into our path.

"*Skotophagotis!*" he hissed, flattening himself against the wall of the shop and urgently gesturing for us to do the same. Joscelin's daggers rang free of their sheaths and he went into an automatic crouch. Caught behind the two, I peered over their shoulders.

At the end of the street, which intersected a canal, a lone figure stood, clad in loose black robes, illuminated in the slanting afternoon sunlight. The sunlight glinted oddly upon his head, though I could not make out why; either his skull was shaved and oiled, or he wore some manner of curious cap. He paused, glancing this way and that, before proceeding, picking his way with a long steel-shod staff topped with an obsidian ball.

Nesmut sighed and relaxed as the figure moved out of sight, lowering his arm.

"Skotophagotis?" I said quizzically, even as Joscelin straightened and sheathed his daggers. It was Hellene, but no word I knew. "Eater-of-darkness?"

"Gracious lady." Nesmut shuddered all over. "Do not ask me. These things are known. Do not look on the Queen's portrait, lest the stone crack for envy. Do not cross the shadow of a *Skotophagotis*, lest you die before sunrise. Come, I will take you to Kyria Maharet's."

It must be, I thought, some priest of Serapis, the god of the dead. They are much obsessed with death, the Menekhetans, and spend a good deal of their lives in preparation for it. It was a cleverness of the Ptolemaic Dynasty to unite this worship with that of Dis, the Hellene deity. Now, I daresay, not even the ruling descendants of Hellas knew where one began and the other ended. They have become more Menekhetan than they reckoned, the Ptolemies. How not, in a thousand and a half years? But I, I had endured the mysteries of the Temenos on the isle of Kriti, and I knew some little bit about the living worship of its eldest scions.

Well and so; mayhap Serapis was like unto my lord Kushiel, who once maintained the brazen portals of hell for the One God of the Yeshuites. If it was so, I thought guiltily, I owed him a prayer. Only I was still wroth with Kushiel, the pattern of whose justice I had yet to decipher. If there was a greater purpose at work, I could not discern it.

With such thoughts did I occupy my mind until we returned to the Street of Oranges, and Nesmut remanded us unto the hospitality of the lady Maharet, or Metriche, as she would have it. He left us with promises to return in the morning, and with that I had to be content, wondering if my lord Delaunay had felt the same misgivings when I departed, full of cheer, to some violent assignation.

I'd have felt the same with Hyacinthe, if I'd known where the *Lungo Drom*, the Long Road of the Tsingani, would lead him. But I had been younger then, and more ignorant.

"You know who he reminds me of?" Joscelin asked as Nesmut took his leave, his quick grin flashing in the gathering twilight.

"Yes," I said softly. "I know."

"Well." He regarded me. "We need to talk to Amaury Trente."

At the dinner-table that evening, we found Lord Amaury full of his conversation with Ambassador de Penfars. There were, it seemed, numerous candidates for Pharaoh's most dangerous enemy, but Raife Laniol's favored contestant was one General Hermodorus; a cousin, it transpired, through the Ptolemaic bloodlines, and eligible for the throne should it suddenly become vacant.

"Comte Raife suggests," Amaury informed me, "that you and messire Joscelin might call upon the General, my lady. We cannot, without giving offense to Pharaoh, but you might. If it is remarked upon by the aristocracy, they will suppose that you are rivals to our mission, come to court Pharaoh's opponents."

"We will send a letter of introduction on the morrow, my lord," I said. "My lord Trente, I have heard another theory proposed today, from a Menekhetan source."

"Oh?" he inquired.

I saw the Lady Denise Fleurais, who had spoken of the divide between Menekhetan and Hellene society, take notice. And I saw too that the Menekhetan servant who hovered with a tray of fish was the same who'd attended us last night, lingering with the beer-jug. We had been speaking, in company, in D'Angeline. I continued in the same tongue without altering my tone. "My lord," I said, "there is a serpent in the corner."

A full half the company heard and startled, turning to stare; Joscelin was on his feet in an instant, a dagger in his hand, reversed for the throw. I kept my eyes on the Menekhetan and saw that he did not react to my words but looked instead at the reactions of our party, slow and perplexed, before glancing around.

It paid to be cautious.

"What serpent?" Amaury Trente asked, half-risen from his seat and irritable. "Which corner?"

"Forgive, my lord," I said. "I thought I saw somewhat in the shadows, and . . ." I nodded imperceptibly toward the Menekhetan, ". . . I needed to be sure."

Amaury sat, comprehension dawning. Melisande was right; he was not a subtle man. Then again, it is an eternal failing of those born to the peerage, forgetting that those who attend them hand and foot have eyes and ears and minds that think. Joscelin shook his head, sheathing his daggers and returning. I waited until the rest of our company was seated.

"It is believed among the folk of the city," I said in a low voice, "that Pharaoh has taken the boy for his own and plays a game of concealment."

It hadn't occurred to them; I saw it in their faces. I couldn't fault them for it. It hadn't occurred to me, either. If Amaury Trente was not subtle, he was no fool, either. He grasped the ramifications quickly enough, his expression somber.

"If it's so, we've lost the lad," he said grimly. "Ptolemy Dikaios could never own to it. And we've played our hand too close to the vest to threaten to renege on the deal over a mere slave-boy." He shook his head. "Ysandre was clear on that much. She doesn't want the boy's identity known. If we let slip his importance . . . Elua! He's a walking target, and she doesn't have the means to protect him. And if someone were to use him against her . . ."

"I know, my lord," I said. "Believe me, I do. I am doing what I can to learn if the rumor is true."

"And if it is . . . ?" It was the Lady Denise Fleurais who dared to ask it.

I looked squarely at her. "We will do whatever is needful. Naamah's Servants have always known that there are ways into any palace, and what was stolen, may be stolen back. If Pharaoh has not admitted the gain, he cannot acknowledge the loss."

"How would you—" Lord Amaury began to ask, then cut his words short. "No, never mind. We will speak of it later, if it comes to it."

"Thank you, my lord." I inclined my head to him.

Amaury sighed and fixed his brooding gaze upon Joscelin and I. "I'll speak to Raife Laniol again tomorrow and see if he thinks this rumor may have merit. Say what you will, Comtesse, but trouble seems to follow you like a lover, you and messire Cassiline here."

Neither of us disagreed.

It was not until we were in bed that night that Joscelin spoke of it. "What if it comes to it, Phèdre?" he asked, leaning on one elbow and gazing down at me. "Would you accept an assignation if needs be to gain access to Pharaoh's seraglio? Is it worth so much to you to see Melisande's son safe?"

I played with a lock of his hair, avoiding his shadowed gaze. I had not told him, yet, that I had made her a promise. With all that lay between us, all of us, it was too hard to say. "There need not be an assignation made in truth. It may be only a matter of convincing Pharaoh's attendants one such exists. I'd try that route first."

"And if more is required?" he asked softly.

"I don't know." I met his gaze, then. I had to. "Joscelin, he's a *child*. You saw the ones we rescued in Amílcar. This will be worse, much worse. Does it matter whose son he is? Naamah lay down in the stews of Bhodistan with common men when Blessed Elua hungered.

Should I—" my voice broke, "—should I scruple at less?"

He was silent for a moment, then shook his head. "No."

"It would fall to you to get him out whole and safe," I said. "By whatever means."

Joscelin smiled. "Do you doubt me?"

"No," I said fervently, wrapping both arms about his neck. I didn't, either. He had come for me on La Dolorosa, the prison-fortress no one could assail. Joscelin had done it, crawling beneath the underside of a bridge. If it came to it, freeing Imriel de la Courcel from Pharaoh's Palace was as naught to that. "Not for an instant."

"Then we are agreed." He lowered his head to kiss me.

I held him hard, praying it was so.

THIRTY-THREE

NESMUT CAME in the morning and informed us that the word had been spread and his contacts were keeping a sharp lookout in the Palace of Pharaohs. A friend of his mother's—the laundress—had a daughter who was responsible for polishing silver and gilt fretwork lamps within the Palace, and thought she might be able to secure an assignment within the concubines' quarters. Nesmut was bubbling over with excitement, scarce able to contain himself.

I cautioned him again in the strongest language I could muster, watching his eyes glaze even as he nodded obedience. Joscelin added his warnings to mine with a different emphasis, touching the hilts of his daggers and reminding Nesmut that we would know who to blame if our search was discovered. I daresay the lad took his words more seriously, looking warily at Joscelin.

It would have been amusing, had I not been so worried; like as not, Joscelin would sooner cut off his own hand than harm the lad, but Nesmut had no way of knowing it. And I must own, Joscelin could look quite dangerous when he had a mind to. Ten years as my consort hadn't dulled the edge of that implacable Cassiline discipline.

We sent Nesmut on his way with a bulging purse of coin; mostly coppers, and a few silver obols. He left at a trot, grinning broadly and fingering his jangling purse. I shook my head, feeling heavy-hearted, and went to pen a letter of introduction to General Hermodorus and his wife.

Afterward, since there was naught I could accomplish elsewhere, I accompanied the Lady Denise Fleurais on an excursion to the baths.

There are a good many bath-houses in Iskandria, and this one was recommended by our hostess Metriche as a suitable one, frequented by women of the middle aristocracy. It was built in the Tiberian style, with separate pools of water—cool, tepid and steaming hot.

'Twas a different world, there, from the one I had glimpsed with Nesmut yesterday. Here, there were no men save the attendants, quiet and unobtrusive. It was filled with women, young and old, chattering voices raised in a mixture of Hellene and the occasional word of Menekhetan. We bade the carriage-driver to wait and paid our fee, entering the bath-house. A bowing attendant handed us each a thick cotton towel and robes of fine-spun linen at the door to the changing-room.

It is the Tiberian fashion to commence in the cold waters of the frigidarium; a custom I have always found unnecessarily rigorous. We went straight to the caldarium, with its vast pool. It was here that the majority of patrons lingered. Conversation did not exactly cease as Denise Fleurais and I entered the heated bathing-chamber, but there was a lull, followed by a murmur of resumption. Looking at Denise, I could understand why. Her intelligent face had a high-boned beauty, and even wreathed in steam, her hazel eyes shone. The careless grace with which she had piled her hair atop her head, the way an errant lock coiled over one shoulder as she removed her robe . . .

We were D'Angeline. It was enough.

The tiles, emblazoned with fish, were slick beneath my bare feet, heated beneath by an unseen hypocaust. I slipped the robe from my shoulders and descended the steps into the steaming water, ignoring a collective gasp as I did so.

"It is your marque, Comtesse." Sinking into the bath with a sigh of pleasure, the Lady Denise glanced at me with heavy-lidded amusement. "They've not seen the likes of you before."

Betimes I forgot it myself.

A pair of Menekhetan noblewomen, giggling, dared one another to approach us. The braver of the two drifted near, addressing us in excellent Hellene. "Kyria," she said. "My friend and I, we were debating. Is it customary for D'Angeline women to . . ." she pointed at me with her chin, ". . . to so adorn themselves?"

I opened my mouth to reply, but Denise answered for me. "It is the marque of Naamah, who is our goddess of pleasure," she said with candour. "And the Comtesse Phèdre nó Delaunay de Montrève is sworn to her service. Do you not have such things in Menekhet?"

"No!" blurted the shy one of the pair, and they dissolved in laughter, clutching at one another. "It is true, then?" she asked. "Your gods demand you do service . . ." her voice dropped, ". . . in the bedchamber?"

I raised my eyebrows and looked at Denise.

"Oh, yes," she said blandly. "But only the most noble and beautiful, such as my lady Phèdre. You can see, can you not, that she is fit to serve only princes and kings?"

It seemed they could, from the merriment that ensued. One, greatly daring, asked if she might touch it; if one might, they all must. I endured it with good grace, standing waist-deep in the steaming water as tentative hands stroked my skin, tracing the elegant black lineaments etched the length of my spine, the cunning crimson accents. It is a unique torment for an *anguissette*.

"It feels no different!" the bold one said in astonishment. "I thought it would be raised, like a scar . . . Auntie, come here, feel, her skin is like silk," she added before switching to Menekhetan, beckoning to a veritable grandmother with wizened breasts and bright, curious eyes. All of them crowded round me, oohing and prodding.

"For this, you brought me here?" I asked Denise Fleurais.

"My mother was an adept of Bryony House," she said in D'Angeline, head bobbing low above the water, giving me her shrewd smile. "Amaury Trente may not care to guess how you might gain access to Pharaoh's quarters, but I can. If you mean to bring your Cassiline, you'll need to allay suspicion and let it be known it is a pearl of great price you bestow, worthy of guarding with the utmost care. To gain the upper hand in any trade, it is best to establish an outrageous value at the outset."

"Ah." I turned to face my admirers, inclining my head politely; curiosity satisfied, they acknowledged the tacit dismissal and withdrew, laughing and splashing as they went. "I have not made that decision," I said to Denise. "It would be premature to consider it."

"To decide, yes." She shrugged, cream-white shoulders rising from the waters. "Not to lay the foundations." She regarded me through the steam. "Her majesty assigned me to this delegation because I am skilled in matters of trade," Denise Fleurais said quietly. "Whatever transpires, she would not have the Cruarch of Alba make a bad bargain for her sake. And yet it is a merchant's gift to know the secret desire of her client's heart, and her majesty wants the boy, Imriel, restored to his place. I know this. I do not pretend to understand what desire motivates you, Comtesse, but you are committed to finding the boy. If you are willing to pay the price, do not disdain my aid."

Women's voices echoed over the waters of the caldarium, blithe and unconcerned. I looked at Denise, silent. I thought of the children we had found in Amílcar. I thought of Pharaoh, bejeweled and unknown. My skin still tingled from the touch of strange hands. I thought of Nesmut's valiant grin, that so reminded me of Hyacinthe. And I thought, too, of Melisande Shahrizai closing her eyes in pain, and of her lips on mine.

And of Joscelin. Always Joscelin.

"I don't know if I'm willing to pay the price," I said honestly.

"No?" Denise Fleurais smiled, sadness mingled with her shrewdness. "Most people don't, until the bargain is struck. I cannot answer for you. I do not bring the bargain, but only set the table for it."

Her words stayed with me as I went to submerge myself in the cooler waters of the tepidarium, and long afterward. I had thought of it, of course; the Lady Denise was right. But it had been a long time since I had sold myself for aught but love or the pleasure of Naamah's service. When I was younger, I thought, I would have done it unthinking. Now, 'twas somehow different.

Still and all, there was naught to be done and no point to agonizing over it until we knew for a surety that Imriel de la Courcel was held in the Palace of Pharaohs . . . and on that score, to my dismay, our investigation began to stall.

Nesmut reported on the following day, his expression glum. Despite an overwhelming eagerness to contribute to the search in covert defiance of the aristocracy, no one within the Palace had yet seen anyone matching the description of the D'Angeline boy—and, he assured me, they had a better idea what it meant now that descriptions of me were circulating, born of my encounter in the baths.

Against my own misgivings, I recruited Nesmut to aid us in searching General Hermodorus' house and interviewing his servants.

Our letter of introduction had been received, and an invitation to a dinner party with a few of their friends came in short order. Naturally, we accepted; and contracted Nesmut to serve as our torch-bearer for the evening.

Of that encounter, I will say little, save that it proved tedious in the end and unproductive. I daresay I met a good many Menekhetan malcontents that night, and they were eager to determine our motives for visiting Iskandria. I smiled and made polite allusions to the fact that Ysandre de la Courcel, the wise and gracious Queen of Terre d'Ange, wished it known that she had no interest in having a political say in the affairs of Menekhet, but only to trade freely with whosoever held power. Who knows? Like as not it was true.

Most of their questions, they directed toward Joscelin, eventually quizzing him on D'Angeline alliances and battle-tactics. What he did not know, he invented, describing fabulous war machines and siege-engines that I was fairly sure did not exist.

General Hermodorus himself was a bandy-legged man with a round belly and an intent stare, brows meeting over a beak of a nose; Horus, his companions called him, in a Menekhetan jest that eluded me. I neither liked nor disliked him. His wife, Gyllis, scarce spoke above a whisper, and I thought I might have pitied her if I had known her better. So we dined and made empty conversation, and my heart pounded all the while to think of Nesmut supping on bread and beer in the kitchen, making innocuous queries of the General's household staff.

I needn't have worried. Nesmut was waiting at the door as we made our farewells, carrying a fresh-kindled torch to light our way home. He met my eyes as he bowed, shaking his head imperceptibly, his expression disappointed. For all my fears, I cannot say I was surprised. General Hermodorus, whether he loved Pharaoh or no, did not strike me as a man willing to take risk for carnal passions.

So much for that thought.

Indeed, the only item of note in the entire evening passed nearly unnoticed, save by me; a small matter, scarce worth noting. One of General Hermodorus' serving-maids was Hellene and island-bred, got in some skirmish I could not name. I would not have known, had she not paused ever so slightly in laying a dish on the table before me, bowing her head as I thanked her. "*Lypiphera,*" she murmured in acknowledgement, moving onward.

Pain-bearer.

I had been called that only once before, on the island of Kriti, by slaves.

I do not know how they knew, then.

THIRTY-FOUR

A WEEK passed, and we were no closer to an answer; in another week, we must leave or forfeit our place in Radi Arumi's caravan.

Lord Amaury Trente was pulling his hair again.

Frustrated, I asked Nesmut to arrange a meeting with Fadil Chouma's widow and serve as translator. This, he did, and it too proved sublimely unproductive. We brought gifts of sweets and D'Angeline fabrics and jars of Menekhetan beer, spending a tongue-tied afternoon of pleasantries and abortive inquiries in Chouma's courtyard, where his wife maintained a stoic mien and his concubines giggled and whispered behind their hands—all except one, who hid her face behind a veil and said nothing. *They do not care that Chouma's third concubine will have scars*, Nesmut had said.

I cared. But Fadil Chouma's third concubine kept silent behind her veil. She would speak no ill of Pharaoh; nor would Chouma's widow nor his other concubines, for all their whispers. Nesmut only shook his head sadly. And the only item of note from that sojourn was that we saw once more one of the dread priests Nesmut so feared, walking boldly down the center of Canopic Street in the midday sun.

It is the broadest street in Iskandria, lined with immense effigies of Menekhetan deities whose faces bear a Hellene influence. This time, I saw the priest in advance of Nesmut's hissed warning.

"*Skotophagotis!*"

We who are D'Angeline are bastard-born of the One God's lineage, raised to respect the gods of all places. I stepped to the side of the street unthinking, and Joscelin followed suit, not going for his daggers this time. Nesmut crouched, baring his teeth as if in challenge. This time, I had a better look at the priest, until the chariot came. At close range he did not appear Menekhetan, I noted in surprise. No; his skin had a pallor theirs did not, and his square beard curled. This I saw, and why the sun glinted oddly on his head, for he wore a helm of bone, a boar's skull or somewhat like it curving over his pate, with plaques of ivory sewn onto it with gold wire.

And then the chariot came, advertising for the games held weekly in the great amphitheatre of Iskandria, the charioteer with green ribbons tied around his upper arms hauling on the reins and cursing. His team drew up hard, champing and foaming at the bit.

It was a pair of matched chestnuts. I remember it well, how they tossed their heads, spume flying, and the heat and the dust. I remember the hot stink of horse-flesh, and how the *skotophagotis* stood unmoving, hoisting his staff. In the midday sun, his truncated shadow lay cut like a knife on the road, jet-black and immobile, crossing the charioteer's path.

Nesmut made a keening sound, then bit the back of his hand to stop it.

The charioteer cursed in Menekhetan and flicked his whip.

And the *skotophagotis* bowed his head and stepped out of the way, sunlight gleaming from the yellowed bone that cupped his own skull. In a trice, it was over, and the charioteer plunging on his way, Nesmut tugging at my hand and muttering, "Do not look, do not look, my lady, do not cross his shadow."

It meant nothing at the time, though. That came later.

Lord Amaury Trente was in a foul mood that night when we dined at Metriche's inn, and for that, I could not blame him. There was no movement in the search for Imriel de la Courcel, and negotiations must carry on apace, lest we lose credibility with the Menekhetans. I'd scarce spoken to Denise Fleurais, who was the nearest thing I had to a friend among his delegates, these three days past. Ysandre would make no bad bargain on Drustan's behalf; that was sacrosanct.

To be sure, gossip had spread since our visit to the baths, and there was speculation in Iskandria that I would offer my gifts to Pharaoh to sweeten the deal; the offer, it was murmured, would not be unwelcome.

Joscelin had heard it by now, and what he thought of it, I could not say. I daresay he knew why, after our talk, though we did not speak further of it. I kept my own counsel. Not a single one of Nesmut's elaborate web of contacts could confirm Imri was in the Palace, and I had no intention of bringing my price to the bargaining-table if he was not.

"He wants to meet you, Phèdre." Lord Amaury hoisted his cup of beer and regarded it with disfavor. "Elua, what I wouldn't give for a glass of Namarrese red! We should have brought an extra keg. Any mind . . . it seems word has come to Pharaoh's ear, and he told Ambassador de Penfars today that he wishes to lay eyes on this treasure of D'Angeline womanhood. Especially since General Hermodorus has seen you."

I picked at the fish on my plate, separating tender flesh from a myriad of bones. "Well and so, he may meet me. If the ruler of Menekhet summons me before the throne, I can hardly ignore it."

"And if he asks more?" Amaury asked. "Comte Raife thinks he might. He has heard, it seems, something of Naamah's service."

At the far end of the table, Denise Fleurais coughed discreetly. I ignored it and met Amaury's eyes. "I am a free D'Angeline, and under no obligation to Ptolemy Dikaios. Does Ambassador de Penfars counsel that I should grant his request? Does he think Pharaoh will be struck dumb at my beauty and offer up the boy of his own volition?"

"No." Lord Amaury looked miserable. "But we're running out of options, my lady. And he thought . . . you are skilled in the arts of covertcy. Men talk, in moments of passion . . . Elua, I don't know! I thought, when you arrived . . ." He shrugged. "I thought we would have found him by now."

"So did I, my lord," I murmured. "So did I."

Amaury sighed and drained his cup, staring into its empty bottom until an attentive servant stepped up to refill it. I pushed away my plate of fish and glanced at Joscelin, who returned my gaze with an unreadable expression. The other delegates, less affected, laughed and conversed amid a merry clatter of cutlery. Someone, a minor lordling, was telling a tale of the day's events to an audience rapt with horror.

". . . dragged forty yards or better," he was saying. "By the time they cut the reins from his waist, his own mother wouldn't have recognized him."

"You should send a letter of introduction," Amaury announced in an abrupt tone, raising his head. "That much, at least. Raife Laniol's a fool not to have advised it sooner."

". . . matched chestnuts, the sweetest pair you've seen, with an arch to their necks to make a woman weep, I tell you, and the one with its foreleg dangling, I nearly wept myself . . ."

"Of course," I said absentmindedly, listening, "if you think it best. My lord Amaury, what are they talking about?"

"What?" Amaury Trente stared at me a moment, uncomprehending.

"Oh, that. A man was killed at the chariot-races, I believe. One of the charioteers. A terrible accident."

"Did he wear green ribbons?" My voice was unsteady.

"Green ribbons?" Amaury frowned, and asked; the question wended its way down the table and came back, the answer bedecked with a good deal of unnecessary detail. Yes, the charioteer had worn green ribbons, tied about his upper arms. Or at least he had, before. He'd gotten tangled in his reins and dragged, after the chariot had upset. Who could say what color his ribbons had been, once they were soaked with blood?

Either way, the man was dead.

It was then that a feather of foreboding touched me.

"My lord Amaury," I asked. "Who are these priests the locals name Eaters-of-Darkness?"

No one, it transpired, knew for sure; some had never encountered one and others, like me, had assumed they were Menekhetan priests, servants of Serapis, lord of the dead. I listened to them all, and learned little, beginning to wonder. Joscelin had seen the same thing I had. He listened too, and I saw on his face a steadily growing expression of disquiet that echoed what I felt. Somewhere, in these events, an unseen pattern was tightening upon us.

That night, I had another dream.

This time, it was different. I did not dream of the ship and the isle, but of Canopic Street, flat and bright-washed in the midday sun, dust lying heavy on the flagstones. A lone figure knelt in the center of it, a boy, his head bowed. A collar of iron weighted his neck, outsized and cruel, and his hair fell in black curls over his shoulders.

"*Skotophagotis!*" said a voice I knew to be Nesmut's.

I took a step forward, my feet as heavy as lead. A black shadow fell across the flagstones, fell across the kneeling boy. He lifted his head. A black bar of shadow lay over his face, cast by an unseen staff. He knelt unmoving, and I saw that a chain ran from the iron collar to his shackled wrists. Above the staff-shadow, his eyes were as blue as sapphires.

"*Lypiphera,*" he said to me in Hyacinthe's voice.

I woke up shaking and weeping, with Joscelin's arms around me and his voice, warm and alive, murmuring soothing things in my ear. He held me until it passed. My anxious heart slowed and my breathing grew calm. I freed myself from his arms, then, and went to stand before the open window, letting the night breeze dry my sweat-dampened skin.

"How long have you been having nightmares?" Joscelin asked behind me.

"Since the City," I murmured. "I dreamt of Hyacinthe, before it all began."

"You should have told me."

"I know." I turned around to look at him sitting up in the bed, his beautiful face somber with concern. "It doesn't matter, though, not really. I had nightmares before, too; before La Serenissima. I'm no seer. They never tell me anything I don't already know. Only things I don't want to admit."

"And what did this one tell you?" he asked, grave as a child. Joscelin would never laugh at my dreams, whether I told him or no. We had been together too long. I shivered and wrapped my arms about myself.

"I don't know," I whispered. "But I saw that priest's shadow."

"*Skotophagotis*." He said the word and fell silent a moment. "Phèdre, come to bed. I think this is a conversation better held in daylight."

I agreed wholeheartedly, crawling back into bed and into his arms. With my head on Joscelin's shoulder, I fell asleep at last. His eyes were still open when I did, staring awake at the ceiling, and what private darkness he saw, I could not say.

In the morning, we did not speak of it until Nesmut came.

He came at the tail-end of the breakfast hour, as was his wont, sauntering into Metriche's dining-hall. Taking a seat at our table—it was only Joscelin and me, Lord Amaury's delegation having departed already—Nesmut helped himself to a serving of bean-cake, amply spooning jellied figs atop it. He had, I noted, a new tunic, white cotton with a fine brown stripe, the fabric still crisp. Nesmut had prospered in our service. I felt guilty terminating it.

Nonetheless, there was the dream.

"Nesmut," I said, making my voice firm. He looked at me wide-eyed, his mouth full of bean-cake. "I have come to a decision. Our bargain is ended. I don't want you risking yourself or others in searching the Palace of Pharaohs."

"Gracious lady!" he said in dismay, curds of bean-crumbs on his lips. He swallowed, and began again. "Gracious lady, we have only begun to search—"

"No more," I said implacably. "Swear it. Swear it by Serapis."

Joscelin raised his eyebrows and shifted, showing the hilt of his sword to better advantage.

"I swear it," Nesmut muttered. With a sullen look, he raised his hand and rattled off an oath in Menekhetan. "The gracious lady is happy? You wish me to go?"

Guilty or no, I felt a great weight lifted from me. I fished in the purse at my waist for a silver obol. "It is not that I am displeased, Nesmut, only that—"

"Wait," Joscelin said mildly. He leaned forward. "Nesmut, my lady Phèdre fears to put you in danger; you, or anyone. It does not mean we have no need of your wisdom. Tell us this, if you may, and heed my lady's tender sensibilities well. Who is that man you call Eater-of-Darkness?"

Nesmut shuddered and glanced around, then lowered his voice in the bright morning light. "Gracious lord, it is a danger to name them! They are shades, priests of a kingdom that died and lives, Persis-that-was. In Iskandria, and all across the world, they go where they will. Akkadians hate them like the plague, so it is said, but even they fear to cross a *Skotophagotis'* shadow. Many have tried, and died for it."

"Like the charioteer," I said.

Nesmut nodded vigorously and reached for another bean-cake, forgetting his fear. "The gracious lady has heard, yes. We saw it, and he died, died before sunset. He was a fool from the countryside, and knew no better."

"Persis-that-was?" Joscelin frowned. "You mean they are descendents of the Persians?"

"No." Nesmut chewed and swallowed, pouring a glass of water. "That is, yes, gracious lord, they are of the ancient bloodlines, but there are many Persians in Khebbel-im-Akkad. The *Skotophagoti . . .*" he dropped his voice again, ". . . are of the kingdom that died and lives."

Joscelin raised his eyebrows at me and I shook my head. I knew something of Akkadian history through my studies with Eleazar ben Enoch, and a good deal of the language, but nothing of a kingdom that died and lives. Of Persis itself, I knew little, for that once-mighty empire was overthrown by Ahzimandias and the resurgent House of Ur some five hundred years gone by. The Akkadians were not merciful, doing their best to obliterate the remnants of Persian culture.

There is, of course, one story that lives in D'Angeline memory. It was the King of Persis who imprisoned Blessed Elua when he first wandered the earth . . . and it was Naamah who freed him, offering the king a single night of pleasure if he would release Elua. It is why we revere Naamah, and enter her service in homage.

I was disquieted by the thought.

"Nesmut," I began, but I never finished my question, for at that moment, Lord Amaury Trente entered the dining-hall, flanked by a pair of delegates, looking distractedly about the room.

"Phèdre!" he exclaimed, spotting me and hurrying over. "My lady, I'm glad you're still here. Pharaoh has sent word through Ambassador de Penfars. You are summoned to an audience," he said, adding, "Now."

THIRTY-FIVE

ONE DOES not ignore a summons from a sitting regent in his own capital city, free D'Angeline or no. I changed my attire, donning the one suitable gown I had brought, a deep rose-hued silk bedecked with crystal beadwork. It was a full year out of date, but Favrielle nó Eglantine had designed it, and the slim-fitting lines and the way an extra measure of fabric pooled at the hem were still being copied this year.

I'd brought it because it packed light.

"Very nice," Joscelin said in a neutral voice, watching me braid my hair into a coronet.

"He is Pharaoh of Menekhet, Joscelin." I fixed the braids in place with jeweled hairpins, turning my head to see them glitter in the room's dull bronze mirror. "Should I present myself before him in riding garb?"

Joscelin shrugged and made no reply. He had changed into a doublet and breeches of dove-grey velvet, the crest of Montrève worked small on the breast. If he'd worn his hair in a club at the neck, he could have passed for a Cassiline Brother.

I eyed him with resignation. "You'll not be able to take your blades into Pharaoh's presence, you know."

"I know. I'll leave them when asked."

It would have to do. I sighed and kissed him before applying carmine to my lips with a delicate brush. Mayhap it gave him dour amusement that I needs must dress my beauty in its finest rainment to meet a foreign sovereign, but he'd never been described as a treasure of D'Angeline womanhood, either. Whatever else transpired, trade negotiations with Menekhet were like to continue, and thanks to the Lady Denise's idea, I had a level of credibility to meet.

The Ambassador had sent his carriage, and Comte Raife Laniol greeted us himself in his courtyard, accompanied by his wife. He was a tall man with brown hair turning to silver, courtly and well-spoken. He was, I was told, an excellent Hellene scholar; well and so, I could admire that, though I thought him a fool for failing to learn Menekhetan. It is a scholar's weakness, to run narrow and deep. I rather liked his wife, Juliette, who had a grave loveliness that lit unexpectedly when she smiled.

"Comtesse," she murmured, giving me the kiss of greeting. "It is an honor to meet you. We would have had you to dine, you and messire Verreuil, only I feared to disturb your travails."

I assured her that it would be a pleasure, and then her husband held open the door of the carriage and we reboarded once more, all of us pressed close in the small space. Amaury Trente looked anxious, as well he might; although he said naught of it, I know he regarded the inspired plans to which I was prone with a degree of trepidation.

For my part, I felt only an unwarranted calm. I listened to Raife Laniol instruct us on the protocol of the presence, committing it to memory. We were to pause at the door to the throne-room, then follow three steps behind the Chamberlain upon being announced, preceded by the Ambassador and his wife. We were to make a full kneeling obeisance, and then stand with our eyes cast down until Pharaoh addressed us. Upon leaving, we were to wait for the Chamberlain to pass, and follow three steps behind, departing in the order of arrival.

There was more, too. I waited until he was finished. "My lord Ambassador, what do you know of these priests the Iskandrians call *Skotophagoti?*"

Comte Raife blinked, perplexed. His wife whispered in his ear. "Oh yes," he said, expression clearing. "It is some native superstition, I am told. Menekhet is like any place, full of its soothsayers and harbingers. Do they concern you?"

"They might," I said. "Where are they from? I was told Persis."

"Persis!" He laughed. "Someone has been filling your ears with nonsense."

"You have never heard of a kingdom that died and lives?"

"Ah." Comte Raife gave me a benevolent look. "It is Khebbel-im-Akkad you're thinking of, my dear. I am given to understand that the name itself means . . ."

"Akkad-that-is-reborn," I said. "Yes, my lord, I know it. This is something different."

He shook his head, bemused. "I think not, my lady."

And then there was no more time for conversation, for we had reached the Palace of Pharaohs. It is a gorgeous structure, to be sure, sheathed in white marble and jutting out into the harbor. Pharaoh's guards knew the Ambassador by sight, but they took no chances, peering into the carriage and confirming our identities, matching them against a list on a waxen tablet. Our entrance was authorized and we were waved through the gate.

Inside, the Palace was open and airy, with high ceilings and innumerable windows positioned to catch the sea breeze. Clearly, it was meant to be defended from without and not within. We were ushered into an antechamber where we were served a cooling drink of steeped hibiscus petals, and stoic slaves worked fans of massive palm fronds. Presently the Chamberlain came for us, accompanied by a pair of attendants. He was a tall, gaunt man with a slight stoop, and no trace of humor in his mien.

"My lord Ambassador," he greeted Raife Laniol in Hellene.

Comte Raife bowed. "My lord Chamberlain. You know Lord Amaury Trente, and his companions, Lord Nicolas Vigny and the Baron de Chalais. May I present the Comtesse Phèdre nó Delaunay de Montrève, and her consort Joscelin Verreuil?"

The Chamberlain's eyelids flickered. It is not done, in Menekhet, for women to take consorts as we do in Terre d'Ange—not openly, at least. "Pharaoh will be pleased," was all he said. "My lord Verreuil, will you consent to leave your weapons in our keeping?"

Joscelin gave a Cassiline bow in response, removing his daggers from their sheaths and unbuckling his baldric with practiced ease. One of the Chamberlain's attendants stepped forward, opening a length of the best Menekhetan linen to accept his weapons. The unadorned steel, oiled leather and worn hilts looked plain and utilitarian against the fine white cloth.

"Those blades once saved her majesty's life," Comte Raife said. "Guard them well, my lord Chamberlain."

So, I thought, he is not entirely unsuited to diplomacy. The Chamberlain glanced at Joscelin with a measure of increased respect. "It shall be done," he said, bowing briefly. "Now, if you will follow, Pharaoh is waiting."

We followed, Comte Raife and his wife three steps behind the Chamberlain, Amaury Trente and the delegates, and Joscelin and me at the rear. I kept my eyes downcast, walking at a measured pace, feeling the vastness of the throne-room echo on my ears. The air moved, fanned by slaves, scented with camphor and sandalwood. By the faint creak of armor, I guessed there were guards present, a dozen or more. I heard our names announced, and caught a glimpse of Comte Raife and Juliette making their obeisance, then Lord Amaury and his delegates. A male voice addressed them in pleasant tones, and another, a woman's, young and piping.

And then it was our turn. Approaching the throne, I sank to my knees, feeling the marble cool through the silk of my dress, bowing deeply and rising, keeping my gaze on the floor, conscious of Joscelin doing the same.

"Lady Phèdre." It was Pharaoh's voice that addressed me. I met his eyes. Despite his gilt-encrusted robes, Ptolemy Dikaios, Pharaoh of Menekhet, was only a man, of middle years, the gold diadem of his office set atop thinning hair. He smiled at me. "So this is the treasure of Terre d'Ange."

"My lord Pharaoh." I inclined my head. "Others have said it, not I."

"Oh, they've said well enough." He reached out to take the hand of the woman seated at his side; scarce more than a girl, really. "Do you not agree, my darling Clytemne?"

The Pharaoh's second wife and current Queen giggled. "It is true, then! My ladies said as much. Tell me . . ." She leaned forward, wide-eyed and curious. "Do you bathe in the milk of wild asses to make your skin so fair? I have heard it is so."

"No, my lady." I curtsied to her, keeping my expression serious. Well and so; this audience was not entirely what I had expected. Across from me, I could see Joscelin biting his lip and studying the floor. "I use a salve of wool-fat, from the first shearing, rendered with an attar of rose. It gives a marvelous suppleness. I am certain Lord Amaury could procure it if my lady wishes."

"Oh, yes!" Queen Clytemne clapped her hands together. Ptolemy Dikaios looked amused and indulgent. Amaury Trente looked dumb-struck, and hid it poorly. "Of a surety," the young Queen continued eagerly, "you recommend tincture of nightshade to give your eyes such luster, is it not so?"

"No, my lady." I shook my head and smiled gently at her. "It makes the eyes ill able to bear light, and I fear I would find myself blinded by your majesty's brilliance."

"Oh!" Clytemne blushed, pleased by the compliment, pink color

lending a moment's beauty to her sallow cheeks. "But your eyes . . ."
She leaned closer to peer at me. "Oh! You have the strangest flaw, Lady
Phèdre, a spot of crimson—"

"It is the mark of Kushiel's Dart," Raife Laniol, Ambassador de
Penfars, said smoothly, stepping forward to bow. "Or so we say, in
Terre d'Ange."

"*Mighty Kushiel, of rod and weal, late of the brazen portals, with blood-
tipp'd dart a wound unhealed, pricks the eyen of chosen mortals.*" The
words were spoken in Hellene, but their source was pure D'Angeline.
I saw Joscelin's head raise unbidden, his hands crossing unthinking to
hover over the hilts of his absent daggers. Ptolemy Dikaios was smiling
broadly. "Come, my lord de Penfars," he chided the Ambassador. "You
are a scholar. Tiberium may lay its claims, but all the world knows the
finest library is in Iskandria. For a thousand years, Menekhet has survived by its wits. Did you truly think I would entertain a D'Angeline
delegation without learning all I might? Did you suppose me ignorant
of the identity of your guests, who have dined with my dear General
Hermodorus?" Ignoring us for a moment, he turned to his young bride.
"Clytemne, my darling, you have seen the flower of D'Angeline beauty.
Now leave us to discussion."

With a show of reluctance, she climbed down from her throne, an
escort awaiting her. "You won't forget the salve?" she asked me hopefully in parting.

I looked pointedly at Amaury Trente, who startled before executing
a florid bow. "It will be my honor to execute the request personally,
your majesty."

And then we were alone with Ptolemy Dikaios, Pharaoh of Menekhet, whose intellect I feared I had greatly underestimated. He steepled his fingers, clad in a glittering array of rings, over his belly and
regarded us. "She had a desire to behold you, my lady, and learn the
secrets of D'Angeline beauty. We are grateful for your indulgence."

"It is my honor, my lord."

He waved one bejeweled hand. "Clytemne is a silly girl, but her
heart is good, and she brings to our marriage an allegiance with the
island of Cythera which I could ill afford to lose. For my part, I am
well-pleased. Tell me, is there aught I may offer in kind?"

I have served Naamah for many years, and I know a laden question
when I hear one. I knew it now. And I have studied the arts of covertcy
for nearly as long, and knew to read the shadings of tone, the unspoken
language of the body. *I know who you are,* said the silent features of

Ptolemy Dikaios, *and what you do. I know what you seek, and what you may ask. Do you dare?*

And I wondered how he knew and I bethought myself of Melisande Shahrizai, who had managed access, in her Serenissiman exile, to Hellene translations of Habiru texts, to rare Jebean manuscripts. Melisande, who had been on a moment's notice prepared to escape to Iskandria and pursue her missing son. It had not occurred to me, until now, to wonder why she was so certain of finding aid in the city.

And it had not occurred to me to wonder from whom. Melisande was never one to aim low.

"My lord Pharaoh," I said to him. "You know who I am. Do you know what I seek?"

Ptolemy Dikaios shifted on his throne, rings flashing. His features had gone impassive. "I know it does not lie within these walls."

I studied his face as if my life depended on it, and indeed, if mine did not, Imriel's might. He was concealing something. Knowledge, or the boy? If I was wrong, I lost my opportunity. I had to gamble. Pharaoh's face was smooth, sure of his unassailability. He would not be so certain if it was the boy. A secret alliance is much easier to hide than a ten-year-old boy. I thought of my dream, and the dark bar of shadow falling across Imriel's upturned face. Amaury Trente was staring at me, his lips moving silently, praying I would not do aught foolish. In truth, I could not say. "Then I will ask a question, my lord Pharaoh, as I perceive you are a scholar of the world." I drew a deep breath. "What is the kingdom that died and lives?"

The Pharaoh of Menekhet grew pale. "*Drujan.*"

"Drujan." I savored the word, along with the Pharaoh's pallor and the beads of sweat that stood of a sudden on his balding pate. "Tell me, my lord, what is this Drujan?"

One of his guards stepped forward, and a court soothsayer with a furrowed brow. Ptolemy Dikaios composed himself and waved them back. "Drujan," he said in a grim tone, "was once a satrapy of the empire of Persis. It is a kingdom, now, in the far north of Khebbel-im-Akkad."

"A kingdom?" Comte Raife arched his elegant silver eyebrows. "A *sovereign* kingdom, my lord Pharaoh?"

There was a pause. "Yes," Ptolemy Dikaios said. "So I believe it to be. The Drujani rebelled against their Akkadian overlords a score and ten years ago, and were crushed mercilessly. Every surviving member of royal blood was put to the sword, the women raped and slain.

And then . . ." He spread his hands, a powerless gesture for all the rings that adorned his fingers. "Eight years ago, something changed. What it was, I do not know, for the Akkadians are loathe to speak of it. But that is when the bone-priests came, the *Skotophagoti*. Sometimes alone, and sometimes with comrades, merchants and mercenaries."

"And you welcomed them, my lord Pharaoh?" I let a hint of polite disbelief show in my voice. "I have heard it said the Akkadians hate them like the plague."

"And fear them as much." He shook his head. "I never welcomed them. It is death to trade with them, death to house them, death to give them succor. That much, the Akkadians decreed. Such was the proclamation of Ishme-la-Ilu, who is Grand Vizier to the Khalif of Khebbel-im-Akkad, and I have obeyed it. The Drujani and their bone-priests are not welcome in Iskandria, nor anywhere in Menekhet. But . . ." he smiled tightly, ". . . it is also death to cross them, and not by Akkadian steel, no. Ignoble death, by a falling-sickness, by the bite of an asp, a runaway horse. Believe me," he added, glancing around. "I have consulted my priests, and I have consulted our great library. Neither have yielded an answer. There are talismans, prayer-scrolls . . ." He waved a dismissive hand. "Enemies of the Drujani bone-priests die anyway."

"So they go where they will?" I asked slowly.

Ptolemy Dikaios nodded. "We do as the Akkadians have bidden. Avoid them, and give thanks to all the gods that their numbers are few, and they offer no violence if unmolested." He gave his tight smile again. "Menekhet is ancient, Lady Phèdre, and she has weathered many storms. Whatever quarrel lies between Drujan and Khebbel-im-Akkad, we can outwait it."

"Yes, but now . . ." I was thinking half aloud. "My lord Pharaoh, what do the Drujani come for?" I paused. "Do they buy slaves?"

His face turned stony. "It may be, though it is forbidden."

"Of course," I said absently. "But if they did . . . if they did, would anyone stop them? Your guards? Would they be challenged at the gates of the city?"

Another pause, then he shook his head. "No. Not if a *Skotophagotis* was with them."

"And the punishment for a Menekhetan merchant caught doing business with a Drujani?"

Pharaoh met my eyes and answered softly. "Death."

I shuddered, and heard Amaury Trente utter a sound of dismay. It seemed strange and distant, for my ears were ringing with a bronze clash of wings and a haze of red veiled my vision. The unseen pattern was closing upon me. I saw through a skein of crimson Kushiel's face, cruel and smiling, his mighty hands. One, held close to his breast, held a key—the other, outstretched, offered a diamond, dangling at the end of a velvet cord.

"*Phèdre!*" There were hands again, Joscelin's, hard on my shoulders, shaking me. I blinked at him, my vision clearing, realized I was swaying on my feet. "Are you all right?"

"Yes." I gripped his forearms, steadying myself, and looked past him at Ptolemy Dikaios. "My lord Pharaoh, I crave a boon."

He made a slight gesture. "Speak."

From the corner of my eye, I could see Lord Amaury grimacing and Raife Laniol discouraging me with a discreet shake of his head. I ignored them both. "My lord Pharaoh, you know that her majesty has bade us seek a young D'Angeline boy, stolen by Carthaginian raiders and sold unwitting into slavery in Menekhet. You have aided us most graciously in this search. I ask that you aid us once more, and inquire of your Iskandrian Guard if such a boy was seen leaving the city in the custody of Drujani priests."

Ptolemy Dikaios relaxed slightly. "It shall be done," he said, and beckoned to a senior guardsman, resplendent in a white kilt and gilded breastplate, addressing him in Menekhetan.

"My lady Phèdre," Amaury hissed in my ear, one hand closing hard on my upper arm, "think what you do! You place yourself—"

"Shh." I waved him to silence, straining to hear the words Pharaoh spoke to the guardsman. He spoke with quiet discretion, but I have an ear for languages, and a memory trained by Anafiel Delaunay. "Amaury, did you give Pharaoh a description of Imriel de la Courcel?" I asked him in a low tone, speaking D'Angeline.

"A description?" He unhanded me and looked puzzled. "No, of course not. Pharaoh would not concern himself with such details. Even his Secretary of the Treasury didn't deign to hear them. I told the clerk, Rekhmire. No one else."

Raife Laniol, Ambassador de Penfars, glared at us both, put off only slightly by Joscelin's warning glance. I paid him no heed, considering the key Amaury had given me and what leverage it granted.

"It is done," announced the Pharaoh of Menekhet, putting an end to our covert squabbling. He looked at me with a cunning light in his eyes, a smile stretching his broad mouth. "It seems Terre d'Ange has a mighty interest in this young slave-lad, does it not? So, my lady, what boon will you grant me in return?"

Amaury Trente sighed and threw up his hands in despair, turning away. One of his delegates grinned. Juliette de Penfars gazed sympathetically at me, while her husband the Ambassador strove to put a good face on it. Joscelin . . . Joscelin merely frowned, like a man listening to the strains of distant battle.

"My lord Pharaoh," I said. "May I speak privately to you?"

Thirty-six

OF COURSE, he granted my request.

To this day, I cannot say whether or not Ptolemy Dikaios truly believed I would bed him for a trivial favor. Mayhap he did, or mayhap he believed I would reckon the price worth it to buy his silence in the matter of the D'Angeline slave-lad our Queen so ardently desired. After all, he knew his worth.

Either way, I disabused him of the notion.

"My lord Pharaoh," I said to him in his private reception-chamber, attended only by impassive fan-bearers. "This is my boon: In exchange for your aid, I will not tell Ambassador de Penfars nor Lord Amaury Trente that you have been in league with the Lady Melisande Shahrizai de la Courcel."

He looked at me for a long moment without speaking, reclining on a couch, head propped on one hand. "Now why would you say such a thing?"

"Because, my lord." I raised my eyebrows at him. "No one described the lad to you. And yet I heard you tell the guard he was a D'Angeline boy of some ten years, with black hair and blue eyes. Either you have seen the lad yourself . . . or someone else has described him to you. And I can only think of one person like to do such a thing."

At that, he had the grace to blanch a little. "You do not speak Menekhetan."

"No," I agreed. "I don't. But I listened to a young man in my employ translate those very words into Menekhetan for the benefit of Fadil Chouma's widow and concubines. I have an ear, my lord, for language."

"Indeed." After a moment, Ptolemy Dikaios rose from his couch and paced the room, his hands clasped behind his back. He regarded his couch, his impassive slaves, his frescoed walls. In time, he regarded me. "I have never seen this boy. Iskandria enjoys free trade with La Serenissima. This woman of whom you speak was wife to the sole D'Angeline presence in that city-state. Our acquaintance is of long standing."

"Her fortunes," I said, "have changed considerably from when first you knew her."

"Imprisonment." He waved a dismissive hand. "Or sanctuary, if you will. Yes. Even so, I am given to understand that her *son* . . ." he gave the word a subtle emphasis, ". . . stands third in line for the D'Angeline throne."

"He does," I said. "Which is why her majesty Ysandre de la Courcel would as lief see him safe. It does not alter the fact that his mother has been condemned for treason and is sentenced to die should she set foot from her sanctuary."

Much to my surprise, Ptolemy Dikaios laughed, and did more than laugh. It was a deep and considerable laugh, roaring from his gut, until his eyes watered and he must needs use the fringed end of a sash to wipe them. "Ah, Phèdre nó Delaunay! Why did your Queen not send you to begin with? We would have saved a tedious dance. I have heard of you, indeed I have. This woman of whom we speak warned me of your wits."

I waited for his mirth to subside. "I have other business in Iskandria. My Queen only wants the boy returned."

"Yes, of course. His own mother asks nothing more." He sat back down on his couch, sighing and dabbing at his eyes. "Oh, my! The gods themselves weep for laughter. You thought I had him?"

"Until today," I admitted.

"Would that I did." Ptolemy Dikaios heaved another great sigh and composed himself. "I'd have restored him, my lady, one way or another. I promised . . . our friend . . . as much, and she, I know, would not hold it overmuch against me had I sinned unknowing. A pity I did not, for she promised a formidable alliance should he take the throne. But no, my taste does not run to boys, not even D'Angeline boys."

"I would that it did, my lord Pharaoh," I said quietly. "If the boy were to appear, dazed and unsure, with some wild tale on his lips . . . there would be no questions asked. Only gratitude"

"You can guarantee that much?" he asked shrewdly. "You would swear to it?"

I thought of the brooch Ysandre had given me, the Companion's

Star, and the boon unasked. "Yes, my lord," I said to him. "I would swear to it. If it were true."

Our gazes locked, and it was the Pharaoh who looked away. "I spoke the truth," he said. "I've never laid eyes on the boy nor heard whisper of his existence until your Lord Amaury inquired. A letter came from La Serenissima, on the very ship that brought you, and I learned more. Believe me, I've conducted a search of my own, to no avail. And now . . ." He looked back at me. "If I were you, I would pray, to any god who would hear me. Because if there is any merit to your guess, if that boy's been taken by the Drujani . . ." He shook his head. "I cannot help you. No one can."

"Well," I said, light-headed with despair. "We will have to see. Do we have a bargain, my lord Pharaoh? My silence for your aid?"

He paused, and nodded. "We have a bargain. For all that it is worth."

It was then that there came a discreet rap at the door, and the Captain of the Iskandrian Guard entered with the news that would sunder my world in twain.

I had struck my bargain too late. Imriel de la Courcel was gone, far beyond the boundaries of any aid the Pharaoh of Menekhet might render. Once again, I was three steps behind, and only Kushiel knew into what dire darkness the path led.

Drujan, I thought, and shuddered.

Ptolemy Dikaios looked at me with pity. It frightened me more than I could say.

To his credit, Lord Amaury Trente received the news with fatalistic aplomb. "I knew it," he said glumly when we were able to reconvene and I gave the guardsmen's testimony verbatim. He put his head in his hands and tugged at his hair. "Blessed Elua, things *always* get complicated when you're involved, my lady! No chance, I suppose, that they're mistaken?"

"No," I said sadly, refilling his beer-cup myself. "I'm afraid not."

There was no great secret to it, when all was said and done. Sure that the boy was within Iskandria, no one had asked. Yes, Pharaoh's gatekeepers had testified readily, they had seen a Drujani party leave the city by the Eastern Gate, some five months gone by—high summer, it was—a *Skotophagotis* and three warriors, with a D'Angeline boy in tow. They described him readily: a face like a jewel, set in fear and anger, skin like milk, yes, and blue-black hair that fell in ripples, eyes the hue of twilight.

I rendered the translation exactly, lest Lord Amaury doubt.

He didn't, not really.

"So," he said, peering at me between his hair-clutching hands. "It seems I, at least, am bound for Khebbel-im-Akkad, to see how strongly the ties of marriage bind the loyalty of blood. Dare I ask you to accompany me, Comtesse? I would not presume, only . . . it is rumored that you have mastered the Akkadian tongue. And I fear I could use your aid."

I didn't answer, not right away. Our hostess Metriche, having heard that we had attended upon Pharaoh, had taken it upon herself to serve us with her own hands, that night. With a good deal of fanfare and many attendants, she brought a rack of lamb to our table, bowing her head and setting it before me. She had heard I'd merited a private audience. I gazed at her averted face, the elaborate gilt cap that covered the bun of her hair. I'd meant to buy one of those, to carry with me or to send to Favrielle nó Eglantine, who would find it of interest.

Radi Arumi's Jebean caravan left on the day after tomorrow, and our passage was already booked, a deposit paid for passage as far as Meroë.

In my vision, Kushiel had held forth the diamond.

Phèdre! cried the voice in my dreams . . . Hyacinthe's, or Imriel's? I was no longer sure. *Lypiphera,* it said to me, and the voice might have been Nesmut's, the soft accented Hellene tones. We had found him, Joscelin and I, on the quai; found him, and paid him for one last task, going back once more to the household of Fadil Chouma. I don't know why. We had the gatekeepers' testimony. But I needed to hear it, to be sure. "Ask her," I'd said to Nesmut. "Ask her if her husband knew a *Skotophagotis.*"

If Chouma's widow knew aught of it, she had hidden it well, shaking her head in horror at the very thought. It was his concubine, his third concubine, who hid her scars behind a veil, who fell weeping to the floor, covering her head. I had asked the questions as gently as I could, and Nesmut coaxed the story out of her. Between muffled sobs, she admitted it was so. That was the secret she had kept, even upon questioning at knife-point. Twice, she had seen Chouma speaking with a *Skotophagotis.* The first time, he had beaten her for it and threatened to kill her if ever she spoke of it. The second time, she had fled in terror from the bone-priest's shadow, and did not hear what had transpired. But there had been money exchanged, and Imriel was gone. She did not doubt the nature of the bargain.

I didn't doubt either, not really.

Fadil Chouma had a buyer in mind; one, only one, mind . . .

No wonder he'd sought to conceal it. My first guess had been right. It was worth his life to reveal it, in Menekhet. It was worth anyone's life. Pharaoh had uttered a decree of death for any merchant caught trading with a Drujani.

Radi Arumi's Jebean caravan still left on the day after tomorrow.

Amaury Trente was waiting for an answer.

I thought of Hyacinthe, and the terrible despair that lurked behind his eyes. How much worse would it become as he endured the slow death of hope? Another six months, another year—how much harder would it become? I thought of the children we had rescued in Amílcar, their stricken, haunted faces. How much worse had Imriel de la Courcel endured? How much longer could he endure it? Without me, Amaury would never have found his trail. And Amaury was bound for the intrigues of Khebbel-im-Akkad, without even the skills of a trusted interpreter. A capable man, but not a clever one; so Melisande had said of him. He would be dependent on Valère L'Envers, who had wed the Khalif's son. I did not think any daughter of Barquiel L'Envers would be eager to see Imriel found. Unlike Amaury Trente, I had the means to compel her aid. And unlike Amaury, I had the means to untangle the thread of truth from a skein of half-truths and evasions.

In Blessed Elua's name. I promise. I will do what I can. If I had thought it would come to such a choice, I would never have promised. But it had, and a child's life was at stake. In my mind's eye, I saw the shadow of the *Skotophagotis* and shuddered. Branching paths, Hyacinthe had said, and each one lying in darkness. I was afraid, I was very much afraid, that Imriel de la Courcel was already treading one. I did not think I could bear to see his face in my dreams for the rest of my life.

Hyacinthe, I prayed silently, forgive me for this choice I make.

"Phèdre?" Amaury Trente asked. "Will you go?"

I gazed at Joscelin, tears standing in my eyes. "I thought . . . truly, I thought we were done, here. I thought our path would diverge here, truly I did. Joscelin, beloved, if I told you I swore an oath, in La Serenissima . . ." I was shaking, I knew I was shaking.

Joscelin looked at me for a long time, and then rendered his Cassiline bow, correct and exacting. "I protect and serve, my lady," he said softly. "Is that what you need to hear? If you believe it needful, it is needful. Besides . . ." One corner of his mouth lifted in a smile. "I am not so overeager to see your Tsingano freed that I will not accompany you on this task."

I laughed through my tears. *Oh, Hyacinthe!* My heart ached, like a flawed vessel fired too hot. "Yes, my lord," I said to Amaury Trente. "I will go with you to Khebbel-im-Akkad."

So it was decided.

On the morrow, we went to the jeweler's shop to see Radi Arumi. There, the gem-carver Karem served us mint tea and we presented our plight to the Jebean caravan-guide, or at least as much of it as I deemed discreet. Radi Arumi heard us out with grave attentiveness.

"Understand, Kyria," he said with regret, "I cannot return your deposit to you. Certain arrangements have been made, provisions purchased, camels leased. You see how it is."

I allowed politely that I did, and speculated that the caravan-master would ensure none of it went to waste. After innumerable cups of tea and negotiations, it was agreed that a portion of the deposit would be refunded and we would forfeit the balance.

"Come again in six months, fair one." Radi Arumi grinned, his teeth a startling white against the lined darkness of his features. "I will be making ready another trip. If you are still wishing to go, I will be wishing to guide you!"

I had leave, thanks to my bargain, to peruse the royal library at will. In the days that followed, I used it to full advantage, little though it gained me. Of history, there was plenty. I learned that Drujan was a small province nestled alongside the Sea of Khaspar, warded by mountains to the east, north and south. Because it was easily defensible, it had a long history of fierce independence, although its satraps had paid homage to the Great Kings of Persis. I learned that it was a seat of worship for the ancient Persians, who called it also Jahanadar, Land of Fire, due to a phenomenon on the peninsula which jutted into the sea. There, at certain crevices in the rock, fire-spouts were wont to occur.

The Hellene philosopher Stratophanes saw these with his own eyes and gauged them to be a natural phenomenon, born of volatile gases trapped beneath the earth's crust. It was, he owned, nonetheless impressive. The Persians, who worshipped Ahura Mazda, the Lord of Light, built temples around them and tended the Sacred Fires.

Even the Akkadians, who destroyed so much Persian culture when they conquered, did not extinguish the Sacred Fires of Drujan, hailing it instead as evidence that the solar fire of Shamash had descended to earth to put the seal on their victory. The Persian priests—magi, they were called—were allowed to continue to tend their fires . . . only now they must do so in the name of Shamash.

So much did I learn, and then little more for a span of centuries, when Drujan, quiet for hundred of years, rose up in rebellion. At a guess, I would hazard that isolated Drujan, poor in natural resources, ignored by its overlords in favor of lusher lands, gradually returned to its old ways over the course of centuries.

Hoshdar Ahzad was the name of the leader who emerged, a prince of ancient bloodlines, and it was in his name that the Drujani took up their swords, slaying the Akkadian vizier and his garrison. All along the border, they rose up against the fortresses and on the peninsula, they took the fortified palace of Daršanga, where Hoshdar Ahzad installed himself as sovereign lord, and decreed the worship of Ahura Mazda restored.

Better for him, I thought, if he had kept quiet and seen to his borders first, for no sooner had the name of Ahura Mazda rung freely across the Land of Fires than the wave of Akkadian vengeance broke, drowning it in blood.

It was an Akkadian chronicle I was reading, and the author did not spare in his gleeful descriptions of the revenge they exacted, documenting atrocities that made my blood run cold. In Daršanga it was the worst. Hoshdar Ahzad and his family were taken alive. The self-styled sovereign was made to watch the rape of his wife and young daughters. When his cries of grief grew too loud, they cut out his tongue. His infant son was speared and spitted, his roasted flesh fed to the dogs. After that, they decided he had seen enough and put out his eyes. And while he wandered, blind and stumbling, mewling, the Akkadian general ordered a bloodbath. It was as Pharaoh had said. Lowborn or high, every man, woman and child of Hoshdar Ahzad's lineage was put to the sword. The stone floors of Darsanga were awash in blood and the corpses stacked like cordwood.

As a final touch, the Akkadian general gave his archers leave to use Hoshdar Ahzad for target practice, commencing with his limbs. It took him, the chronicler reported with pleasure, a long time to die.

I had seen enough, too. I shoved the manuscript away and sat in the cool, vaulted library, sickened by what I'd read. On the painted walls, Thoth, the Menekhetan god of scribes and scholars, strode serenely, ibis-headed, carrying a balance in one human hand. I had known the Akkadians could be brutal. I'd not known the extent of it. The diffident clerk who had aided me in my research approached with a bow and addressed me in Hellene. If the gods of Hellas had not penetrated the royal library, their language had.

"Do you desire aught else, gracious lady?"

"There is nothing further on Drujan?" I asked.

"Nothing." He shook his head. "That is the most recent. There is nothing further."

"Did you look for references to Jahanadar?"

"I looked in all the indices as you bid me," he said with inbred patience. "Drujan and Jahanadar alike, gracious lady. There is nothing further. These things the priests have asked, many times."

"The *Skotophagoti*," I said. The clerk was silent, but a sudden fear glimmered in his dark eyes. I sighed and rubbed my face, willing the vision of Akkadian bloodshed to dispel. "The kingdom that died and lives, they call it. Well, I have learned well enough how it died. What I want to know is how it lives."

"I do not know, gracious lady." The clerk's voice came out high and strained; he swallowed hard, fingering a talisman strung about his neck. "But I do not think it is the sort of thing scholars set to writing. Not if they are wise."

THIRTY-SEVEN

WE LEFT for Khebbel-im-Akkad.

It took a week's time to arrange transport and provisions for the journey, not to mention handling the ongoing trade negotiations. It was a good thing, after all, that I'd struck my bargain with Ptolemy Dikaios, for he proved unstinting in his aid. I daresay the price was worth it to him. With Imriel de la Courcel no longer a consideration, Menekhet had a good deal more to gain than Terre d'Ange in this exchange. If Amaury Trente knew Pharaoh had conspired with Melisande, he'd have no qualms in calling off the deal.

I had made as much clear to Ptolemy Dikaios, who understood; and understood too that there was little merit and much danger in continuing a covert alliance with Melisande Shahrizai. As far as he was concerned, her son was as good as dead, her chance of gaining the throne rendered naught. From henceforth, he vowed, he would treat only with Ysandre. I took a certain bitter pleasure in circumventing one of Melisande's last gambits.

Denise Fleurais would stay to conclude the negotiations, and probably, I thought, do a better job of it than Lord Amaury. Comte Raife was adamant in his insistence that Pharaoh would balk at dealing with a woman, but I thought otherwise, and for once, Amaury agreed with me—and as Ysandre had appointed him to head the delegation, the decision was his. The Lady Denise would seal the bargain and return with half the delegation to Terre d'Ange, bearing news of our quest.

She would also, we agreed, ensure the shipment of a gift of salve and other rare unguents and cosmetics to Pharaoh's Queen, poor, silly Clytemne. I felt a certain pity for the girl, and meant to see my promise kept.

Ptolemy Dikaios arranged a meeting for us with the Akkadian consul in Menekhet, one Lord Mesilim-Amurri. Although he looked down his nose at us at first, taking us for merchants, once he heard Ysandre de la Courcel's name, Lord Mesilim became very helpful, assigning four of his men to serve as guides and assisting us in plotting a course.

It was our intention to make for Nineveh, which had the virtue of being the nearest city to Drujan. More importantly, it was the city which the Khalif's son, Sinaddan-Shamabarsin, had been given to rule; the Lugal, or prince, he was called. And most important of all, the Lugal of Khebbel-im-Akkad was wed to Valère L'Envers, daughter of Duc Barquiel and cousin to the Queen. Hence, our tenuous alliance.

Odd to reflect, but I remembered when that union had taken place. Indeed, I'd been among the first to hear of it, from the lips of Rogier Clavel, a minor lordling in the Duc L'Envers' service. A besotted patron, nothing more; my lord Delaunay had used him as a stepping-stone to reach his old enemy L'Envers. And I had been . . . what? Delaunay's *anguissette*, nothing more.

It seemed so very long ago.

"Do you remember?" I asked Joscelin, aboard the ship which would take us from Iskandria to Tyre. "When official word of their wedding was released? It was just before you were assigned to Delaunay's household."

"I remember," he said, and was silent a moment. "That long ago?"

"Yes," I said. "Because it wasn't until after that Duc Barquiel returned to Terre d'Ange. And the first time you accompanied me, it wasn't to an assignation. It was to ask Childric d'Essoms to present an offer from Delaunay to the Duc, and ask a meeting."

"I remember." He smiled wryly. "He put a dagger to your throat. I tried to tender my sword to Delaunay afterward. He wouldn't take it."

"No," I agreed. "He wouldn't. And then Barquiel's men came and insisted Alcuin accompany them . . ."

". . . and you insisted on going, and Delaunay ordered me as well, and you and I and Alcuin ended up eating bread and cheese in the Duc's kitchen while he and Delaunay discussed affairs of state." Joscelin laughed. "Elua! Were we truly that young and foolhardy?"

"Yes." I leaned against him. "And you thought I was the most willful, depraved creature you'd ever laid eyes on."

"You were," he said companionably, putting his arm about me. "As I recall, when Delaunay threatened to sell your marque if you didn't stay put, you reminded him that Melisande Shahrizai might be interested in buying it."

I winced. "I said that, didn't I? I didn't know what she was, then."

"No." Joscelin looked at me. "But you do now. Phèdre, why did you swear an oath to her in La Serenissima?"

I was silent for a long while, gazing out at the ocean. It looked much like any other stretch of sea, interminable waves dashed by the wind into curling white crests. I should be glad, I supposed, that the overcast sky merely threatened rain. Though we were only going up the Akkadian coast, it was later in the season than sailors favored. "I don't know," I said finally. "It was only to help find her son. I never dreamed it would lead to this."

"I know." His voice was very soft. "And like as not, you'd have done it anyway. Believe me, love, I know how you feel. No matter whose son he is, he's only a child. I saw the ones in Amílcar, too, and it still makes my palms itch for the sword. But Phèdre, you swore it to *her*."

"I know, I know." All of that, my oath extracted, and she had still written to Pharaoh behind my back. Well and so; had I expected otherwise? He might have restored her son to her. And I, loyal to my Queen, would give him unto Ysandre's keeping. I had vowed to do no less, and Melisande knew full well that was a promise I would keep. I closed my eyes, feeling her fleeting kiss burn against my lips. "She said I was the conscience she never wanted."

"And you believed it?"

I couldn't fault him for his dry incredulity. I opened my eyes and gazed up at him. "Yes. No. I don't know, Joscelin. The priest of Kushiel, the last time I went—" I couldn't help a shudder of remembered pleasure, "—he reminded me, all the Companions, even Kushiel, even *Cassiel*, Joscelin, do but follow in Blessed Elua's shadow. I can only believe we do the same."

"Love as thou wilt," Joscelin murmured, "and pray like hell it is enough."

I nodded, my throat too tight to speak. I looked away and stared at the undulating waves until it passed. "What else can I do? I hate it that my heart should fall to my feet at the sight of her, but it does. It grieves me more than I can say that I have turned aside from my quest to free Hyacinthe, who has suffered so long. I am terrified of my dreams, I am terrified of the *Skotophagoti*, and I am terrified of the Akkadians, who are supposed to be our allies. And I am well and truly wroth with my lord Kushiel, whose justice seems to me to be monstrous. If I cannot trust in Elua's compassion . . ." I shuddered and did not finish.

"Phèdre." Joscelin put both arms around me and held me hard. "Hyacinthe has endured a dozen years, and he'll endure a dozen more if he has to. He's stronger than you credit him. He's like you, he's had to be. Your dreams are only dreams, no more, and the Akkadians, fearsome or no, *are* our allies. As for Melisande . . ." He shrugged. "Who knows? Mayhap you are her conscience. Of a surety, her son should not suffer for her crimes. Not this. No one should. It is a matter of D'Angeline pride to redeem him."

"Pride." I laughed, half in tears. "One of our sins, the Yeshuites would have it. Azza's sin was pride, though we all suffer our share. Joscelin, you've said nothing of the *Skotophagoti.*"

"Ah, the bone-priests." He smiled; I felt his mouth move against my hair. "I am Cassiel's servant, love, no matter what comes. If he does not follow Blessed Elua's unfathomable plan as surely as you pray Kushiel does, we are both lost. But while I have you to protect, I am not afraid to try my steel against any enemy, Eaters-of-Darkness or no."

I turned in his arms, and whispered, "Joscelin Verreuil, I would die without you."

"Probably." He smiled again. "Of melodrama, if naught else."

Against my will, it made me laugh; I struck at his chest with one hand, which he caught and kissed, and then he kissed me some more, until the Menekhetan sailors glanced sidelong and murmured and I had quite forgotten what our original conversation was about, or why I'd been so overwrought in the first place.

Our journey passed uneventfully and we arrived in Tyre, setting foot for the first time on the soil of Khebbel-im-Akkad. It was a mighty city once, in the old empires of Akkad and Persis, but it was sacked by the Hellene conqueror Al-Iskandr, and never restored to its former glory. It is still a thriving seaport, though, and we were able to find all that we needed for our journey overland within its walls.

Unfortunately, one of those items was a veil.

Amaury Trente had spent a good deal of time at sea in conversation with Lord Mesilim's men, one of whom spoke Hellene. The rules of conduct for women differ greatly in Khebbel-im-Akkad from elsewhere in the world; certainly from those in Terre d'Ange. I had known this, of course. I just hadn't reckoned on the rules applying to *me*.

"Highborn ladies do not show their faces in public," Amaury said adamantly. "Foreign or no. If you don't want to be taken for a commoner or a whore, you'll travel veiled, Phèdre."

"My lord," I pointed out to him, "my mother was an adept of the Night Court, and my father a merchant, and I am twice-dedicated to Naamah's Service. I am a commoner *and* a whore, and ashamed of neither."

"You are also the Comtesse Phèdre nó Delaunay de Montrève, counsel and near-cousin to the Queen of Terre d'Ange, and I daresay in Khebbel-im-Akkad, you'd prefer to be treated as such." He was right. I ceded the argument, and accepted the veil. There was only one other woman among Amaury's remaining delegates, Renée de Rives, a Baron's daughter who was the consort of one of the minor lordlings, Royce Guidel. They were young and regarded the entire outing as a lark, a chance to spend long months together without the intervening demands of Guidel's marriage. I am not entirely sure why Lord Amaury chose them, except that they were a charming pair, and Royce Guidel was reputed to be a good man with a sword.

At any rate, Renée de Rives grumbled nearly as much as I over the veil, and we befriended one another over the affair, which was to the good, since we were thrown together for much of the ride to Nineveh, surrounded by our escort of men. On the Akkadians' advice, Lord Amaury had spared no expense, and our company was richly caparisoned. The horses were very fine, tall and clean-limbed, with glossy coats. I grew quite fond of mine, which was a sweet-tempered dark bay with a white star. Our saddles were in the Akkadian fashion, which is to say scarcely saddles at all, but embroidered blankets with luxuriant silk fringes, a pair of long stirrups dangling on straps. The bridles, by contrast, were elaborate, with chased gold cheek-pieces and tall, plumed headstalls. It would have fretted my grey mare, but the bay thought himself quite fine in it.

After two sea voyages, it goes without saying that we were all of us considerably sore and stiff for the first few days, and I was passing glad that Lord Amaury had been profligate enough to hire a mule train and tenders, with servants to set up camp and cook and clean for us. The first part of the journey took us northward up the coast, skirting mountains and the harsh desert that lay beyond. Eventually, we forded the River Yehordan and made our way inland.

I could not but think of my Habiru studies as we crossed the mighty river, for it is one that features largely in their writings, a remembrance of home for those in exile. To be sure, the home for which they languished was a good deal further south, but it is the self-same river. This land was strange and harsh to me, with pockets of fertility clinging to the riverbanks and great stretches of arid soil between; still, I knew what it was to long for one's home.

We crossed the Yehordan and made our way through a low pass in the mountains, striking out across the vast untilled plains. It was an unmemorable journey and a miserable one, for the rains broke, washing across the hard-packed red soil. Our horses and mules slogged through red mud to the fetlocks, and all of us were splashed with it. It was winter in Khebbel-im-Akkad, and I cannot say I cared for it. The fine silk net of my veil clung damply to my face, making it hard to breathe.

"Take it off," Renée muttered, and I saw she was bare-faced beneath the hood of her cloak. "Who's going to care, in this weather? The mule-handlers? Let them talk."

It was still raining mercilessly when we reached the first of the two Great Rivers of Khebbel-im-Akkad, and crossing the Euphrate proved no easy task. Whatever other skills they might have—surely they are mighty weavers and horsemen—the Akkadians are no bridge-builders. Swollen by winter rains, the Euphrate ran too fast and too deep to be forded. Instead, we must needs cross it on reed rafts, drawn hand-over-hand along thick cables of rope.

After crossing innumerable seas, it seemed foolish to fear a river; but this river was like a living beast, turgid and angry. In the spring, one of our guides assured us with unwonted cheer, it would overflow its banks, depositing nourishing silt on the flood-plains, hailed by the Akkadians as a life-giver. Well and good, I thought, clinging grimly to the raft; I hope I am not here to see it. It was worst of all for the horses and mules, who must swim for it. I watched my poor bay, the bedraggled plume on his headstall nodding as he fought to keep his nostrils above water. The Akkadian raft-keepers clapped and cheered, shouting encouragements, seemingly unfazed by the crossing.

When all was said and done, we made it across safely, though considerable worse for the wear. Lord Amaury ordered camp made early that day, and we spent the daylight hours cleaning mud from our tack and clothing, and endeavoring to dry ourselves as best we might. Our guides assured us that crossing the Tigris would be far smoother. I contented myself with flapping my sodden veil in the air and glaring at them. Being accustomed to seeing noblewomen unveiled in Menekhet, they were undisturbed by it.

In all fairness, the following day dawned bright and cool, and I had to own that after league upon league of arid land, it was pleasing to see the rich flood-plains, cultivated mainly with wheat and barley, though it was off-season, now. There were roads, unpaved but smooth, and an elaborate system of irrigation ditches, siphoning water from the Great Rivers. We saw a good many more villages, too, and were able to purchase additional foodstuffs; milk and dates, and yearling kid. There were no inns, though, or at least none fit to entertain a company such as ours. Only in the cities, which were few.

And we had nearly reached Nineveh.

We saw it from the far side of the Tigris, a river twice as fast and half again as deep as the Euphrate—a solid city rising from the flood-plain, thick-walled and massive. One would not suppose a city built of red mud-brick to be impressive, but it was, a good deal more than it sounds. There is little else to build from in Khebbel-im-Akkad, and they have become surpassingly good at it.

For all that I doubted, our guides had spoken truly; there was a far better system in place for crossing the Tigris, a veritable floating bridge. It was built on the same principle, but much vaster, an immense platform of cedar planks, capable of holding a dozen horses and men at once. A complex system of ropes and pulleys was used to convey it from one shore to another. Why the Akkadians are so reluctant to span running water, I cannot say, but it worked well enough. We made the crossing in three trips and were deposited safe and relatively dry outside the gates of Nineveh.

"Right," said Lord Amaury, surveying his bedraggled company. "I think mayhap we should take lodgings for the night before presenting ourselves to the Khalif's son."

And with that, I did not disagree.

THIRTY-EIGHT

ONE THING I will say; Nineveh did not lack for luxury.

Amaury Trente saw to it that we were lodged in the finest inn, and it was very fine indeed. They had a dozen stablehands alone, and ample space to quarter our mounts. The rooms were generous, sumptuous with woven carpets and pillows, all wrought in intricate designs.

The only drawback was that the men and women were lodged in separate quarters.

"It could be worse." Renée de Rives, stripped down to her shift, flung herself on one of the overstuffed sleeping-pallets, stretching her arms indolently over her head. She looked at me under her lashes with a friendly smile. "And we could always entertain one another, Phèdre."

I smiled back at her and demurred. "Though you are kind to ask," I added.

"I'm not kind." Renée rolled onto her side, propping her head on one arm. "I'm dying of curiosity and insatiable desire, and it seems a shame to let these lovely beds go to waste. Is it because of Joscelin?"

I thought about it, sitting cross-legged on the pallet opposite her. "In part."

She made a face. "Phaugh! Why did you have to fall in love with a Cassiline, anyway? We're all the poorer for it."

I laughed. "Well, you may be sure, I didn't choose to. Did you choose in the matter of Lord Royce? It is always easier if one's beloved is unwed."

"And if I'd met him sooner, he might be." Renée laughed, too. "It's not the same, though, Phèdre. Everyone knows Joscelin doesn't care to share you. Royce, now . . . if I had the chance to share your bed, Royce would gladly push me into it! And I would do the same for him."

"Well." I rose, and stooped to kiss her in passing. "Mayhap he'll get his chance."

"Oh, unfair," she said, but she smiled as she said it, stretching and yawning. "Elua, you can't blame me for trying. If Joscelin is part of the reason, what's the rest? You never said."

"I didn't, did I?" I paused in the act of unpacking my trunk, holding up a creased gown and frowning. To be sure, it was a long time since I had engaged in casual dalliance, but I'd never denied its appeal. And if Renée was no one I would choose for a patron, it was hardly that she was undesirable. No, the lack of desire lay within me, a strange sense of waiting withdrawal. It was unusual, in a Servant of Naamah; in an *anguissette*, unheard-of. "I don't really know."

"Ah, well." Renée sighed, indolently. "I hope it passes."

Unwontedly fearful of what might follow if it did, I said nothing.

So it was that I spent the night chastely, and in the morning, Lord Amaury sent a letter of introduction to the Palace, addressed to Valère L'Envers, the wife of the Lugal Sinaddan-Shamabarsin. The reply came swiftly, an invitation fair blazing with eagerness. After some weeks in Khebbel-im-Akkad, I was hardly surprised. Luxury or no, Nineveh must seem like direst exile for a D'Angeline noblewoman. Visitors from home would be rare delight.

Our persons bathed, our attire cleaned and pressed, our horses groomed and gleaming, we rode in style to the Palace of Nineveh. Commoners in the street bowed low as we passed, touching their foreheads to the ground. I could tell the Akkadian nobles, even on foot, because they did not deign to notice us, looking only out of the corners of their eyes. We passed many temples of the lesser gods, and then the great ziggurat of Shamash, with the solar disk mounted at its apex. The god was represented as the Lion of the Sun, his leonine visage encompassed in a circle. Outside the temple stood a mighty effigy of Ahzimandias, three times again as tall as a mortal man. He gripped a spear in one hand—the Spear of Shamash, he was called—and his bearded face was filled with the same blank ferocity as the god's, glaring across the rooftops of the city.

I read the inscription as we passed, writ in Akkadian: "My name is Ahzimandias, king of kings: Look on my works, ye Mighty, and despair!" It gave me a shiver. After the chronicles I had read of the destruction of Drujan, I regarded the House of Ur with a certain apprehension.

The Palace of Nineveh was protected by thick walls and a cordon of guards, clad in long tunics over full armor, turbans wrapped around their pointed helmets. Here, no one got in until all our arms had been surrendered, including Joscelin's, and we were given an escort of guards. While marble was in short supply, the palace was tiled inside, cool and elegant, though rather dark.

I saw a good many servants hurrying about their business, but most of them were men—or eunuchs, I guessed, from their beardless state. Akkadians seemed to favor beards for men. There were no women, and I found myself relieved that Renée and I were veiled. Whatever status it conferred, I was glad of it.

At last we were shown to a small reception hall, and our chief escort presented himself briskly at the door, announcing us to a plump eunuch in rich robes, a gold chain about his waist, who bowed deeply and looked askance at the men in our party. The guardsmen drew back the doors, and we were admitted.

"Her highness the Lugalin Valère-Shamabarsin," the eunuch attendant announced in Akkadian, his voice high and resonant. We all bowed or curtsied low before the figure seated on the dais before us, glittering in jewel-encrusted robes, her face veiled and hidden.

And then the doors closed behind us, and the seated woman drew back her veil, reminding me, for a terrifying instant, of Melisande in the Little Court. But no; this woman glanced anxiously toward the door, making certain it was indeed closed, and I would have known her anywhere for a scion of House L'Envers, with those deep-violet eyes. "My lord Trente," said Valère L'Envers, descending from the dais to take his hands and offer the kiss of greeting. Beneath an elaborate headdress, her hair was the color of honey and she had her father's strong jaw, though prettier. "Well met!" Unerringly, she turned toward me, and I made a second curtsy, hastily pulling back my veil. "Comtesse Phèdre nó Delaunay de Montrève," she said, smiling. "Our houses have a long history together. It is an honor to meet you."

"The honor is mine, your highness," I murmured, as she bent to kiss me.

"And Messire Joscelin Verreuil!" Valère clasped both his hands in hers with unalloyed pleasure. "You've no idea how many times I've listened to 'The Cassilines' Duel' in the Serenissiman Cycle. It's my favorite part. I'm so pleased you're here."

"Your highness." Joscelin released her hands to give his Cassiline bow, vambraces flashing. "I am pleased it has given you pleasure."

"Indeed." Her smile turned rueful. "Though I fear it is not for my pleasure you have come, any of you. My lord Trente," she addressed Amaury. "Let us not stand on ceremony. I've enough of that. What brings you to Nineveh?" She saw him glance at the eunuch. "Burnabash is loyal to me, else you would not be here. Come, Lord Amaury. Out with it."

Taking a deep breath, Amaury Trente did. "As you are fond of the Serenissiman Cycle, your highness, you will remember that when we took possession of the Little Court of Benedicte de la Courcel, his infant son was discovered to be missing..."

He told the story in its entirety, or at least as much of it as he knew—Ysandre had told him only that I'd learned the boy had vanished from a Siovalese sanctuary and tracked him as far as Amílcar. Valère L'Envers heard it out in silence until he spoke of Drujan.

"Drujan!" She said the word like a curse, her expression hardening. "So that's why you're here."

"Yes, your highness." Amaury bowed. "I am here in the name of her majesty Ysandre de la Courcel, Queen of Terre d'Ange, to petition your aid in retrieving the boy from the Drujani, by whatever means you think best, whether it be trade or bribery or might of arms."

All traces of welcome and girlish pleasure had vanished from Valère L'Envers' features. Stiff in jeweled robes, she sat her throne like an effigy, only her lips moving as she said a single word: "No."

Blinking, Amaury Trente opened his mouth in protest, "Highness, you have my word—"

She raised one finger. "Hear me, Lord Trente. In the first place, I do not have the power to grant your petition. This is Khebbel-im-Akkad. I rule only over eunuchs and women in my quarters. I command no guard of my own, and have no authority to negotiate, save what counsel my husband will hear in private, and the fact that I am the mother of his sons. In the second place, I question the wisdom of this course of action you pursue. This *boy*, this Imriel de la Courcel, is a traitor's get twice-over, and the nearer he stands to the throne, the less I like it. And third..." She smiled humorlessly. "What do you know of Drujan, my lord?"

"Not much," Amaury admitted. "Only that its priests are feared, even by Akkadians."

"Jahanadar," I said. "The Land of Fires, sacred to Ahura Mazda, later to Shamash. Thirty years ago, it rose up in rebellion, under the leadership of Hoshdar Ahzad. Under the leadership of General Chus-sar-Usar, the rebellion was crushed, thousands slain and the entire line of Hoshdar Ahzad put to the sword. And then twenty-some years later, something changed, and Khebbel-im-Akkad will not speak of it, except to forbid commerce with the Drujani."

"Yes." Valère L'Envers gave another bitter smile. "That much, we may still do, at least for now. You've done your research, Comtesse."

I inclined my head. "Such as was available. Will you tell us of Drujan, highness?"

Her violet gaze, so like the Queen's, was unreadable. "Drujan has extinguished its Sacred Fires. Do you know what that means?"

"No," I said.

"Neither do I." Her voice was grim. "Nor do any in Khebbel-im-Akkad, save the Persians, who look askance and mutter of ancient prophecies. I cannot say if there is truth in them. Only that men die when the Drujani priests will them to do so."

"Drujan is sovereign?" I asked.

Valère L'Envers nodded. "For nine years. They rose up once more, fewer and twice as desperate, and slew the garrison—not just at Dar-šanga, but all the border forts. The Khalif sent a vast army. Three months later, a straggling remnant returned, bearing tales of poisoned water, rockslides, and wasting sickness."

"War is brutal," Amaury Trente murmured. "Such things happen."

"Yes." Valère looked hard at him. "Which is why the Khalif raised a second force, equipping them with the best mountain guides and a wagon-train of water, sending them into Drujan. Do you wish to hear what happened to them? They were trapped in a valley and slaughtered one another. Three survivors made it back, with scarce a set of wits between them. Under torture, all swore to the same story: In the night, the Mahrkagir and his Drujani army came down from the hills and fell upon them, cutting their forces to pieces. They fought back, fierce and desperate. And when dawn came, when the face of the Lion of the Sun gazed down into the valley . . ." She shrugged. "No Drujani. Only the Akkadian dead, slain by their own hands, brother against brother. The army had turned upon itself."

There didn't seem much to say to that. We all glanced at one another. Amaury Trente looked like he wanted to clutch his hair. Renée de Rives stood close to Royce Guidel, holding his hand in a fearful grip. The other delegates looked apprehensive. Only Joscelin's face was calm. I frowned, thinking. "The Mahrkagir, my lady?"

"So he calls himself, he who leads Drujan and sits the throne in Daršanga."

Old Persian is as close akin to Akkadian as Habiru. I sounded the word in my head, puzzling out the meaning. "The Conqueror of Death."

"Even so." Valère, pale-faced, nodded. "Now do you understand why your petition is futile? Even if I were inclined to grant it and beseech Sinaddan on your behalf, he will send no men of Nineveh into Drujan."

"Have you tried diplomacy?" I raised my brows.

"Diplomacy!" She gave a harsh laugh. "The Khalif sent an envoy, under a flag of truce, to discuss terms of peace after two armies were destroyed. The Mahrkagir sent their heads back in a satchel, eyeless and untongued. I do not recommend you attempt diplomacy."

"So you will grant us no aid, your highness?" Amaury Trente asked one last time, his voice torn between resignation and relief. I could not blame him for it. It was a hard assignment, and not, I surmised, one he welcomed. With Valère L'Envers' refusal, it was ended. As much as Ysandre wanted the boy restored, she would never ask loyal D'Angeline citizens to enter a violent, hostile territory to find him.

"No." Valère's tone softened. "Forgive me, Lord Amaury, but it is not possible. And I believe, in the end, it is the best thing for the nation."

It probably was, when all was said and done . . . but I had sworn a vow, and I was haunted, like it or no, by a vision from a dream, a pair of blue eyes raised in plea, the shadow of a staff falling like a bar across a boy's face. And I remembered too the light of the sun winking on the garnet seal Nicola L'Envers y Aragon wore at her wrist as she bid me farewell. *It may come in handy again, one never knows.* It was for this that I had come to Khebbel-im-Akkad. I sighed, and addressed Valère L'Envers in Akkadian, knowing the others would not understand. "My lady, I understand you have little aid to give, but I ask you none-theless to petition your husband on our behalf. By the burning river, I abjure you."

She went very still and stared at me, looking in that moment nothing like her kinswomen. "You would use the password of my House to command me?" she asked in fluid Akkadian.

"Forgive me," I murmured, "but I must."

Valère looked away. "My House," she said bitterly, "headed by my beloved father, who sold me into marriage to further his ambitions. You think I will honor its strictures?"

"I don't know." I kept my voice honest and level. "Will you?"

It was a long moment before she nodded, and she did it without returning my gaze. "I am D'Angeline, still," Valère whispered. "And I consented to this union. Very well; I will ask Sinaddan. And I tell you." She did look back at me then, tense and angry. "His answer will be the same. You have forced my hand to no avail, Comtesse, and I do not like it overmuch."

"I know," I said sadly. "But I had to ask."

Thirty-nine

Sinaddan-Shamabarsin, the Lugal of Khebbel-im-Akkad and ruler of Nineveh, threw a fête to herald our arrival.

It was Valère's doing and no mistake, but in truth, the Lugal was an unusual man, at least for an Akkadian. In the dozen years of their marriage, he had attained a healthy respect for the intellect of his D'Angeline bride and the mother of his sons. If he did not acknowledge it publicly, he was comfortable doing so in private, and had developed a certain fondness for D'Angeline ways.

Hence, the fête, which was attended by a select few Akkadian high nobles, and at which the women—all three of us—might appear unveiled without shame.

It was a very mannered affair and an awkward one, for among our number, none but I spoke Akkadian, and the Lugal spoke no D'Angeline, nor any other tongue we might have held in common. It is, I learned, despised as a form of concession, save among those few diplomats and envoys for whom it is a necessity. As Valère L'Envers did not deign to serve as translator, that duty fell to me.

Sinaddan-Shamabarsin—whose surname meant 'Exalted by Shamash'—was a handsome man in the Akkadian manner, some forty years of age, with dark, intelligent eyes and a neatly tended beard. His robes glittered with gold embroidery and a large emerald flashed on his turban, but he moved like a warrior despite it, fit and agile. He thanked Lord Amaury in courteous tones, which I translated, for bringing the Queen's greetings to her kinswoman in Nineveh, and commended at length the grace of D'Angeline artistry.

Lord Amaury, for all his discomfort, hid it well and replied in kind, which I also translated. He'd not been pleased when he'd learned what I'd done. None of the delegates were, a fact which Valère L'Envers perceived. When she broached her request, she presented it as mine.

"My lord husband," she said to him during the dessert course of candied rose petals and a sweet sherbet made of snow brought from the mountains, "may I presume to ask a boon on behalf of the Comtesse Phèdre de Montrève?"

Prince Sinaddan smiled at me. "For such a lovely translator, one may ask, my lady wife."

"It seems," she said deferentially, "that the Mahrkagir of Drujan has purchased a young D'Angeline boy, sold into slavery. Although I have told her such a thing is impossible, the Comtesse asks your aid in restoring the boy, my lord husband."

His face darkened, strong brows drawing together. "Alas," he said, regret heavy in his voice. "I would like nothing better than to try the strength of the Drujani, but it has been tried, to no avail. I will send no more of my people to die in that accursed land. I am sorry for your loss, Comtesse, and it grieves me to deny your boon. If it comfort you at all, the boy is not the only one. It is said that the Mahrkagir's vile priests have brought slaves from many nations for his seraglio."

Well and so; Valère had warned me. I had forced her hand in vain, and lost her goodwill in the bargain. "Do you know why, my lord?" I asked him. "Why does he assemble them?"

"I know what the Persians say." Prince Sinaddan looked thoughtfully at me. "Is your stomach strong, lovely translator?"

I could have laughed, at that. I didn't. "A man once tried to skin me alive, my lord Lugal. Is that strong enough?"

He did laugh, showing white teeth against his beard. "Aiee, Shamash! D'Angeline women are always full of surprises, is it not so? Well, you are here, so I suppose you may bear it. The Persians say the Mahrkagir has turned Drujan from the worship of Ahura Mazda, the Lord of Light, to Angra Mainyu, the Lord of Darkness." He shrugged. "It is an eternal battle between the two, they say. And it is written in their prophecies that Angra Mainyu shall be defeated, but he shall rule for ten thousand years before it happens."

"The Mahrkagir is willing to settle for ten thousand years," I said.

"Even so." Sinaddan nodded. "And to win Angra Mainyu's aid, he has extinguished the Sacred Fires, and raised up the priests of darkness. All things he may do to repudiate the Light, he has done. As for the act of love, which begets life . . ." He smiled grimly. "He has transformed it into an act of hate, begetting only death. These are the seeds he would sow in the nations of the world, enacted upon the flesh of its denizens. Hence, his seraglio. It is said the Mahrkagir searches," he added, "for the perfect victim, an offering beyond compare, whose violation will secure Angra Mainyu's ascendance." He shrugged. "It is folly, so claims the priesthood of Shamash, all folly and play-acting. But when the bone-priests of the Drujani walk the streets, they hide behind locked doors and pray."

My blood ran cold at his revelation; it was not, I supposed, the most dreadful thing that could be done. I have heard of worse atrocities, including those committed by Akkadians. But I am D'Angeline, and a scion of Blessed Elua, and I could conceive of no greater blasphemy. And too, I remembered the children left behind in Amílcar.

Fadil Chouma had sought one child; only one. Peerless; a *gadjo* pearl, the Tsingani had called Imriel de la Courcel.

And his mother had seen to it he was raised in perfect innocence.

"What does he say?" Lord Amaury placed a peremptory hand on my wrist. "Will he send men into Drujan on our behalf?"

Unable to speak, I shook my head.

"So be it." Amaury's tone rang with relief. "My lords, my lady de Rives, listen well! We have exerted ourselves at the Queen's behest, above and beyond the call of duty. Though I am sore grieved at our failure, we have come to the place where we can go no further. As I am entrusted with the Queen's command, I so decree it: Our quest ends here."

There was unabashed cheering. I do not think they lacked pity for Imriel's fate, but the fear of Drujan had grown strong. I looked at their happy, relieved faces. The Akkadians, thinking it a tribute, smiled with pleasure. Valère was whispering to Prince Sinaddan, explaining what had transpired. Renée de Rives was flushed and joyous, her youthful beauty like a candle in the feasting-hall. It was, I thought, passing strange that her offer had so failed to move me. I had never found surcease from my own nature before.

This is how it ends.

I looked at Joscelin, his quiet, capable hands curled around a cup of honey-beer, no rejoicing in his expression, only quiet compassion awaiting my reaction. I thought of my dream, my vow, the diamond held forth on Kushiel's hand. I wondered at the absence of desire within me, that terrible, waiting emptiness. And I felt the looming pattern that had hovered over us since that first awful moment in Siovale, when I realized that there was no intrigue, no plot, behind Imriel's abduction, come to a terrible fruition.

Branching paths, and each one lying in darkness.

It is said the Mahrkagir searches for the perfect victim . . .

What was Kushiel's Chosen if not that?

Ah, no, I thought; Blessed Elua, no! It is too much to ask; too much!

And even as I thought it, the emptiness was filled, a vast inrushing presence of joy and love and light, more light than I could bear. It swelled within me, lovely and unbearable. Filled with presence, I was vastened, conscious of an overarching pattern that encompassed all of life within it; all of love. Love, and all that it entailed; the complicated ties that bound us to one another, that begat life, loyalty, compassion, and sacrifice in its truest sense. I had not believed it possible, until then. I did not think it possible for a mortal being to contain such glory. What was it that filled me? Not Kushiel, no, nor Naamah, but Elua, Blessed Elua, the bright shadow whom they all followed, all of them, revealing at last the immensity of his plan, filling and surrounding me, golden and irresistible, filling my soul with radiant light, filling my mouth with the taste of honey, setting my heart to beating like a hummingbird's wings, yes, yes, yes.

No, I thought. Tears stung my eyes. No.

It is too much.

I drew in a breath and heard the air rasp in my lungs, and the presence eased, loosening its grip, beginning to fade like the dying strains of a beautiful song. Forgive me, I thought, desperately grateful, forgive me, Elua my lord, thank you for your compassion, for understanding, I swear to you, I will heed you in every action, I will pour incense upon your altar every day, I will say a thousand prayers in blessing . . .

The presence continued to fade, withdrawing in regret, all of it. *Farewell*, I heard, final and unarguable, *farewell*. And it was not only Elua, Blessed Elua, but the others, too—Kushiel, the bronze wings beating their last in my bloodstream; Naamah, her enigmatic smile fading.

All of them, leaving me forever.

And the dull grey emptiness waiting to take their place.

"All right!" I clenched my hands, nails digging into my palms, not realizing I'd spoken aloud. "I will do it."

"Phèdre?"

It was Joscelin's voice, low and concerned. I blinked at him through my tears, unsteady in my chair at the massive inrushing *presence* that filled me, vastening and painful, but there. I was not abandoned, no, and I was myself. "Yes?" I whispered.

"I thought . . ." His beloved face was perplexed. "You were just staring, at nothing, and for a moment I thought . . ." He shook his head. "I thought I saw the mark, Kushiel's Dart, the scarlet mote in your eye . . . it was disappearing, I swear it, shrinking before my eyes. I saw it dwindle to a pin-prick, and then . . ." Joscelin touched my cheek, wondering. "Then it returned."

"Yes." Giddiness and despair made my voice strange. "I suppose it did. Oh, Joscelin . . . you're not going to like this." Before he could ask what, I turned to the Lugal. "My lord Sinaddan," I asked him in Akkadian. "Would you perchance know anyone willing to guide us to Daršanga? Not as an embassy, but as merchants with human goods to sell?"

Valère L'Envers had already begun to smile, anticipating her husband's denial, when the Lugal of Khebbel-im-Akkad gave a thoughtful nod. "Yes, my lovely lady translator," said Prince Sinaddan. "As it happens, I might, for the right amount of gold."

Somehow, I was not surprised.

Thus ended our fête in Nineveh, with our entire company thrown into disarray.

It was Lord Amaury Trente who spoke most bluntly to me, once he grasped my plan. "You understand that I cannot countenance it?" he said, pacing and frowning. "It is little short of madness, Phèdre. If I had an ounce more sense, I'd have you clapped in chains."

"I understand, my lord," I said calmly to him.

He shook his head. "You know that the Queen would never permit such a thing? Name of Elua, I'm not even sure that Shahrizai she-devil would ask it of you!"

"I know, my lord," I said. "It is not Melisande Shahrizai who asks it."

Lord Amaury sighed. "All right, then; listen to me, Phèdre nó Delaunay. I have agreed to pay the asking-price of Prince Sinaddan's guide, who may I add, is a misbegotten Persian-born brigand who would sell his own mother for gold. He was one of the mountain-guides on the last expedition, and fled before the slaughter. And I have gotten Sinaddan to agree to send an armed escort with you as far as the Drujani border, which," he added, "I will accompany. From thence, you are on your own, provided—" He held up a cautionary finger. "Provided Joscelin Verreuil goes with you. Understand me, Phèdre. If the Cassiline does not agree to it, I will not let you go."

I nodded. "I understand, my lord. I am grateful that you are willing to take such a risk."

Amaury Trente looked sourly at me. "Make no mistake, I'm not happy about it."

Thus, Lord Amaury.

It left only Joscelin, who had not spoken to me for two days, not since he had divined the nature of my plan. What he did in that time, I cannot say, save that he spent a good deal of it walking the city of Nineveh. No one bothered him. Small surprise, with his grim expression and the sword strapped across his back, the daggers riding low at his hips. I waited until he came to me. There was a time he might not have done so. Ten years ago, in La Serenissima, he had walked out on me, and I'd not been sure he would return.

This time, I was.

I heard the shrieks in the women's quarter of our inn, and knew. No more, and no less. When he made up his mind, proprieties would not deter him. I looked at Renée, gazing wide-eyed at the door. "It is Joscelin," I said. "My dear, you don't want to be here for this."

She didn't argue, donning her veil hastily and slipping out the door past him even as he entered, oblivious to her fleeting presence.

"Phèdre," he said, a world of agony in the word; a single word, my name. It is an ill-luck name, I have always said so. "Do you know what you are asking?"

"Yes," I said steadily. "I am asking you to take me to Daršanga and sell me into the seraglio of the Mahrkagir of Drujan."

He turned away, hands clenched into fists; I heard the leather straps of his vambraces creak in protest. "A man who breeds death as another breeds life."

"Yes." My voice betrayed me by trembling. "Elua! Do you think I'm not terrified?"

"Then *why?*" Joscelin turned around, blue eyes blazing, innocent as a summer sky, filled with all the love and outrage in his being. "Blessed Elua, Phèdre, *why?* Do you care so little for me? Does Melisande's son mean so much to you? Is the desire that pricks you so unbearable? *Why?*"

"No," I answered, shaking. "No." I gazed at him, though it hurt to look at him. "Do you remember, on the ship, what we spoke of?

Joscelin, it is Elua himself who asks it of me. I swear to you, I would not ask this for anything less."

With a low sound, like an animal brought to bay, he dropped to his knees, hiding his face in his hands. "It is too hard," he said, his voice muffled.

"I know," I said softly, crossing the room and laying my hands on his head. "Believe me, my love, I know."

Joscelin's arms rose unbidden, holding me hard about the waist. "To damnation and beyond," he whispered, hot against my belly. "I have sworn it." The sound that caught in his throat might have been a laugh, or not. "As if I'd had the slightest idea what that meant."

"*Joscelin,*" I breathed. "It is taking my last ounce of courage just to contemplate this. Tell me now whether you will aid me or no."

On his knees, he looked up at me, blue eyes framed with tear-spiked lashes, an eerie echo of the face in my dream, though no shadow fell across it but my own. "I would sooner serve you my heart on a platter, love, but it is not what you ask. So be it. I will sell you to this man who calls himself the Conqueror of Death, and Elua help him afterward."

I could ask no more.

ꝂORTY

THERE WERE a good many tearful farewells before we departed for Drujan.

No one was happy with it, and I could not blame them, for once the moment had passed, I myself was riddled with doubt. I questioned my judgement some dozen times a day, seeking to rekindle that ineffable certainty that had assured me this was Elua's plan, the golden presence that had filled me and made me so cursed *sure*.

It never happened.

Baron Victor de Chalais would lead the delegates home, crossing the Great Rivers before the spring floods began. He was a good man and steady, and I was glad of it. Lord Amaury Trente, Nicolas Vigny and two others would remain, accompanying us to the border of Drujan with Prince Sinaddan's escort. There they would stay, for six months. If we were not back by then, they would reckon us dead or lost.

Renée de Rives fell on my neck, weeping hard and kissing me as she bid me farewell, leaving no doubt that she'd no hope of seeing me alive again. Despite the language barrier, the delegates had managed to get their fill of tales of Drujan; enough to render them certain that we rode toward our doom.

There had been a death in Nineveh, whilst we made our arrangements—a commoner, a potter, had been crushed by his own wares when a shelf had given way in his workshop, after he'd cursed a *Skotophagotis* who crossed his doorstep.

It was enough to fuel the fear.

Joscelin said little and sharpened his blades, working them endlessly with a whetstone, oiling his scabbard and sheaths and removing the last traces of rust from our rain-sodden journey to Nineveh. We had worked out a plan, such as it was. The Lugal's man, one Tizrav, would guide us to the palace of Daršanga. If we reached it safely, Joscelin would pay him half the agreed-upon price from his own purse. Our story was that Joscelin was a renegade D'Angeline lordling who had abducted a peer's wife—that was me—against her will. Having found the price of his escapade too steep, pursued by my husband's kin across several lands, he would be willing to trade my favors for sanctuary in Drujan, where no one would dare seek him.

A simple plan, and a good one. As a surety, Lord Amaury himself would hold the second half of Tizrav's payment, to be rendered only when the Persian returned from Drujan with the appropriate code-word. Joscelin and Amaury had agreed upon the word, and Joscelin would not give it unto the Persian until he was certain Tizrav had not betrayed us.

"What word shall we choose?" Amaury had asked, frowning.

Joscelin had looked at me. "Hyacinthe," he said.

It was only fitting.

There is a point where fear becomes so large it ceases to matter, and exists only in the abstract. I reached it, during those preparations. It was too vast to comprehend, so I went about my business. I met Tizrav, son of Tizmaht; he was not a figure to inspire confidence, a wiry, dirty man with one eye put out by a poacher's arrow, so he said. I considered it a good deal more likely he had been poaching. Nonetheless, the Lugal of Khebbel-im-Akkad vouched for him.

"Tizrav knows the mountains," he said. "He is a coward, but a cunning one, and he will not betray you, not where there is gold at stake."

I'd no choice but to believe him. "Are you willing to lesson me in Old Persian along the way?" I asked. "It is a long road to Daršanga."

"Of course!" he said, bobbing his head agreeably, grinning and fingering beneath his eyepatch. "Whatever my lady wishes. It is my milk-tongue; I speak it like a native! It is why no Drujani will trouble us, no, not when Tizrav is guiding."

I had my doubts; I had a thousand doubts. I kept my mouth silent on them. Joscelin looked at me without speaking and continued to sharpen his blades.

Ironically, Valère L'Envers forgave me for abusing her House's password and came to like me better once she thought I was marked for death. Having nowhere else to turn for it, I begged a favor and asked her to hold in safekeeping the Jebean scroll with the story of Shalomon's son, and Audine Davul's translation. Not only did she accede, but did me another favor unasked. "Here," she said, thrusting a coat upon me, a deep crimson silk lined with marten-skin. "It was a gift from Sinaddan, who had it in tribute, but the sleeves are too short and I've never bothered to have it sized. It ought to fit you well, Comtesse, and it will be cold in the mountains."

I tried it on, and it fit perfectly. "Thank you," I said softly, the silken brown fur of the collar nestled against my cheek. "My lady is kind."

"I'm *not* kind!" Tears stood in her violet eyes. "Elua, why couldn't you be different? I know your history! The Queen heeds you, my cousin Nicola dotes on you, even my father acknowledges your merit! Why do I have to be the one member of my House to send you off to die, and all for that viper's brat?"

"I'm not dead yet, highness," I murmured.

"No." Valère L'Envers turned away, fussing with her wardrobe. "But you may be soon, and I need to prepare for it. Well," she sniffed, "never let it be said that I allowed a D'Angeline peer to face death ill-garbed for it."

Favrielle nó Eglantine, I thought, would have appreciated her sentiments. I was not so sure Ysandre would. It hardly mattered, anymore.

We set off from Nineveh with a good deal of fanfare, and a special ceremony by the priesthood of Shamash. A fire was kindled at dawn and a brace of sheep sacrificed. I swallowed hard, seeing it; we do not do such things, in Terre d'Ange. Shallow golden bowls were placed beneath the gaping throats of the sheep, the blood carefully collected. Each Akkadian man on the journey placed his sword in the pyre, letting it glow red-hot at the edges.

When it did, each man quenched it in the sheep's blood, laying his blade flat in the bowl and uttering a declaration as the hot steel sizzled and blood-stink filled the air: "Mighty Shamash willing, let me next sheath my blade in the blood of my enemies!"

Well and so, I thought; they are not journeying into Drujan.

Joscelin watched the ceremony without comment, and uttered no prayer. His sword had been consecrated long ago, by his uncle, and his great-uncle before him, plain steel with a worn grip, oft-replaced. For him to draw it was an act of prayer. Until then, it remained sheathed. He wore a new coat, too; sheepskin, embroidered without, warm wool inside. I wondered if it were a gift or if he'd bought it. His hair hung loose, twined in small braids about his face, bound with bits of rawhide.

I'd not seen it thus since we escaped from the Skaldi.

It made him look . . . Elua, it made him look like a renegade D'Angeline lordling, fierce and desperate.

The priests of Shamash gave an invocation and finished, bowing deeply, dawn-light flashing from their gilded breastplates, inlaid with the Lion of the Sun. Prince Sinaddan's men bowed in reply, and the Lugal himself, on a balcony of the Palace, raised both hands skyward, hailing the sun. It was done. We were ready to depart.

"Blessed Elua," I whispered, stooping to touch the earth, the alien red earth of Nineveh, of Khebbel-im-Akkad, "keep us safe."

There was no answer, though I hadn't really expected one.

And thus we were on our way.

After several days, the plains gave way to lowlands, and then the lowlands to hills. Tizrav, grinning around his eyepatch, led us unerring to the shortest route. If he were going to betray us, I thought, it would hardly be here, in Akkadian territory. I rode veiled, surrounded by Joscelin, Amaury Trente and his men. The Akkadians made jests, none directed at me; fierce and bloodthirsty jests, hoping for battle.

So they might, I thought; they were young. It had been eight years since the Khalif had lost an army in Drujan, and dared not try again. These men were young and cocksure. Nonetheless, when nightfall came, they huddled close around the campfires, peering into their neighbor's faces and reassuring one another: Yes, we are men of Akkad, Akkad-that-is-reborn, we are brave and dauntless, and fear no shadows of the night.

"They are fools." Tizrav spat expertly through a gap between his teeth, making the campfire sizzle. He nodded companionably toward the Lugal's men. "Fools and children, jumping at shadows."

"Do you say shadows have no power?" Joscelin asked slowly, in fumbling Akkadian. He'd come late to the language, but his Habiru skills had stood him in good stead.

"Power." Tizrav grinned, showing his gap. Firelight played over the greasy leather patch that covered his missing eye. "What is power? These young fools surrender it with every heartbeat of fear. And so the shadows grow, and take on power. What is fear, but courage's shadow?"

"Common sense, mayhap," Joscelin said shortly, rolling himself in his blanket and making ready for sleep.

"You know better." Tizrav leered at me, despite the veil. "Light casts a shadow, the brighter the one, the darker the other. This is only fire, tame and kept. It will be different in Drujan. You will see."

I stared at him through my veil. "We are not in Drujan yet, Persian. Do you wish to forfeit your purse?"

"No." He shrugged unevenly. "Light, dark; it is all the same to Tizrav, if their gold is good. I have sworn my bargain and I will see you delivered. Lies, truth; I do not mind. Afterward . . ." He shrugged again. "You will see how great a shadow your courage casts. It is all the same to me."

The hills gave way to mountains, the air crisp and clear. It was here that we reached the outer boundaries of Akkadian rule, and bid farewell to our escort, who would remain, supplementing the garrison of an outlying Akkadian fortress.

After this, it would only be Joscelin and me and our guide Tizrav.

"I must be out of my mind," Amaury Trente said ruefully, embracing me in farewell. His breath made plumes of frost in the air. "Elua bless and keep you, Phèdre nó Delaunay."

"My lord." I was shivering despite Valère L'Envers' marten-skin coat. No matter where I went, it seemed there must always be winter, and mountains. "Why are you here?"

"Why?" He gazed across the foreboding landscape, an absent smile on his lips. "I don't know, my lady. Here is as good a place as any." He looked back at me then, and his expression changed. "I rode behind Ysandre de la Courcel into the heart of Percy de Somerville's army. You remember. You were there. She never looked back, do you know that? Not once. If she had, she would have seen me. I was there, and the Queen's Guard behind me. But she never even needed to look." He laid one hand on my shoulder. "If you look, my lady, we will be here. Right here, where you left us, guarding your back. Whatever fool's errand you're on this time, I reckon Terre d'Ange owes you that much."

"Thank you," I murmured, tears pricking my eyes. It was not enough, not enough by a long sight, but more than I could have asked. "I am grateful, my lord."

"Well." Lord Amaury smiled and withdrew his hand. " 'Tis little enough, when all is said and done. But if anyone's going to emerge alive from the heart of darkness, it's you and that half-mad Cassiline."

I swallowed. "We will try, my lord."

And then we were on our own.

ꝰORTY-OͶE

A DRUJAͶI border patrol found us the first evening.

It was twilight, just shy of nightfall, and we had made our encampment in a shallow gully out of the wind. Doubtless they were drawn by the light of our campfire. Tizrav had assured us it was folly to think we could cross Drujan in stealth. Better to allow them to find us, he said; we would die quickly, or not at all.

There were five of them, and they melted out of the shadows like apparitions, silent men on tough, shaggy ponies, armed with short, curving horsemen's bows. Joscelin was on his feet the instant they appeared, placing himself between me and the Drujani. Firelight glinted red along his vambraces, his crossed daggers. I wondered if he could block five arrows fired at once. I didn't think so.

"The wolves of Angra Mainyu are mighty hunters!" Tizrav greeted them in Old Persian. "Will you share our fire? We have beer," he added, hefting a skin.

"Why do you enter Drujan?" The leader lowered his bow a fraction. The others did not.

"Why?" Tizrav grinned. "This fine D'Angeline lordling has got himself in trouble and finds he has nowhere left to flee. Go and see, if you do not believe me. The guard at Demseen Fort has doubled and the lady's angry kinsmen are waiting. But my lordling here would sooner give her to the Mahrkagir if he will accept his sword in service."

The Drujani conversed among themselves in low tones, and my ear for Old Persian was not yet keen enough to decipher what they said. One of them laughed and rode forward. "Why should we believe you, Akkadian lick-spittle?" he asked, stroking Tizrav's cheek with the point of a nocked arrow. "Why should we ride to the border, when there is sport to be had here?"

To his credit, Tizrav did not flinch, even when the arrow's point scraped against his leather eyepatch. "My ancestors ranged these mountains when the House of Ur cowered in the deserts of the Umaiyyat. Do you disdain me for the sake of a line drawn on a map, son of darkness?"

Another of the Drujani spoke from the shadows beyond our campfire. I could not make out his face, only that he wore a girdle of bones about his waist, human finger-bones. Raising one hand, he pointed at me.

"Stand aside," Tizrav muttered urgently to Joscelin. "Stand aside!"

He paused, and then did, offering a sweeping Cassiline bow to the Drujani. Tizrav approached me where I knelt beside fire.

"Forgive me," Tizrav said under his breath, yanking back my veil.

The firelight was brighter without the sheer panel of silk before my eyes and I blinked against it, gazing up at the Drujani. Two of the riders startled; one laughed. The one who had pointed fingered his girdle of bones, and a slow smile spread across the face of the leader. It was not a pleasant smile.

"She is for the Mahrkagir?" he asked.

"I have sworn it." It was Joscelin who spoke in crude Persian, his voice raw.

The Drujani with the finger-bones murmured to his leader, who listened intently and nodded. The girded one, I thought, must be some manner of novice, an apprentice-priest. "The embers of despair gutter in your spirit, lordling," the leader said to Joscelin. "Is it as the goat-thief says? Are you willing to swear your sword unto darkness?"

I bit my tongue, longing to translate for him, but Joscelin understood well enough. The skin was tight over his high cheekbones. "Drujan died and lives. I am dead to my family. If I may live again in the Mahrkagir's service, his sword is mine." There was genuine anguish in the words. How much truth? My heart bled to wonder. I could not begin to reckon the price of what I'd asked of him.

It was enough to convince the apprentice-priest.

"Men will embrace anything to live," he said in a young, hard voice. "Even darkness. Even death. What of the woman?"

"You see her." Joscelin gestured at me. "As faithless as she is beautiful, a servant of our goddess of—" the word twisted in his mouth, "—whores."

It was the Habiru word he used, but close enough, it seemed. The Drujani conferred and settled on a translation, and the apprentice-priest laughed, high and breathless, before whispering to the leader.

Who smiled his unpleasant smile. "The Mahrkagir will be pleased," he said, putting up his bow. "You see, his mother was a whore." He jerked his chin at Tizrav. "We will believe you, lick-spittle, and ride to Demseen Fort to count the guards. If you are lying, we will find you and have much sport. If you are not . . ." He smiled again. "Well, *she* may pray that you were."

And with that, they were gone, melding into the darkness as swiftly as they'd appeared, only the faint rattle of a pebble dislodge by a pony's hoof marking their passage.

Tizrav exhaled with relief and picked up the skin of beer with both hands, drinking deep.

"Is it over?" I asked him.

"No." He lowered the skin and wiped his mouth with the back of his hand. "But it's begun, and we are still alive."

We were four more days in the mountains, and saw no further signs of human inhabitants; birds of prey, mainly, circling high above the crags, and on the ground, hares and sometimes martens, quick and darting. It was cold, though not so cold that the streams had frozen. Where we could not find water, we melted snow scooped from deep crevices. In the valleys, our horses pawed the hard turf and cropped at yellow grass, dead and frost-bitten, but nourishing nonetheless. Tizrav set snares in the evenings, catching hares when he might, and with these we supplemented our stores of dried foods.

On the journey, we spoke seldom. I rode without complaining, feeling I had no right. Tizrav, swathed in layers of felted wool, was scarce visible, his chin tucked into his chest, unlovely visage peering out beneath his thick woolen hat. Disdaining the cold, Joscelin rode bare-headed and silent, his mouth set in an implacable line.

"Did you mean it?" I finally asked him, two nights after the Drujani had come.

"What?" His tone was short.

"What you said." I hesitated. "That I was as faithless as I am beautiful."

"Ah," he said flatly. "That." He looked at me for a moment without speaking. "Mayhap. Phèdre . . . what you ask of me—I do not know if I can do it. All I can do is seek a way, and the way is cruel."

Would that I did not understand; but I did. "What have I done to us?" I whispered.

"I don't know." Bowing his head, Joscelin fiddled with a stiff buckle on his dagger-belt. "Do you want to turn back?"

I did. With all my heart, I did. "No," I said.

He nodded without looking up. "Then do not ask me questions I cannot answer. I am Cassiel's priest, and I have broken all his vows but one. You ask me to ride into the mouth of hell to keep it. I am doing what I can. Be satisfied, or be silent."

So it went between us.

On the fifth day, we entered the plains of Drujan. Mayhap it is a more welcoming place in summer; I cannot say. If it was less harsh than the mountains, it was more dire, for here people lived and labored, and here we saw the shadow under which they made their existence. The land is arable and there were villages, at the center of grain-fields and fit pasturage for sheep and goats.

We were not welcome there.

I saw it, on the faces of the villagers as we rode past, travelling now on the old roads, crumbling and still passable, that had once formed part of the mighty empire of Persis. They stared at us with hatred, and I did not even know why. In one village—it had a name, I suppose, but Tizrav did not know it—a woman stood beside the road, clutching her listless child in her arms, and watched us with hungry eyes, despair and contempt in her sunken gaze.

Too many fields lay fallow, dead and grey, naught of winter's doing.

Too many flocks struggled, slat-ribbed and gaunt, with staring coats.

"What has happened here?" I asked Tizrav, my voice shaking. "How can a kingdom that makes Khebbel-im-Akkad itself tremble come to such an impasse?"

The Persian shrugged. "You wished to come to Drujan, lady; the kingdom that died and lives. Behold, if you will, life-in-death."

I did not like it. *Turn back*, I thought; the words were on my lips, near to being spoken with every stride our mounts took. I did not utter it. I thought of that moment in Prince Sinaddan's hall instead, the slow, dreadful withdrawal of Elua's presence, and the emptiness that awaited. *Farewell.* And I gazed at their bitter, resentful faces, the starving Drujani, until my heart ached within me. They had not chosen this, I thought. What commoner ever does? Caught between the hammer of warfare and the anvil of survival, they endure; endure, and hate, seeing us ride of our own volition unto hell, on our well-fed horses with gold jangling at our bits, clad in silks and fur.

There were no fires, either. Jahanadar, the Land of Fires, lay sullen and bleak.

"Tell me of the faith of your forefathers," I asked Tizrav one night as we made camp.

He looked at me, his single eye like a cold ember. "My lady wishes to know?"

"I do," I said. "Truly, son of Tizmaht, I do."

He nodded, and swallowed, and looked away, then busied himself building up our campfire until it roared like a pyre, sending showers of sparks into the cold night air. "You see?" he asked quietly, watching the sparks ascend. "In fire there is light, warmth . . . life. It is Truth. Ahura Mazda is all these things; Lord of Light, the Truth." His mouth curved in a deprecating smile. "Good thoughts, good words, good deeds. It is the trifold way taught to me in secret by my father, and his father's father before him. And the fire . . . ah, the fire is proof, a living, burning flame set before us to purify the Lie."

In the heart of the fire, a pair of crossed branches crumbled, and the flames subsided.

"So." Tizrav's mouth twisted. "Darkness returns. Even the great prophet Zoroaster did not deny it would hold sway on this earth."

"Still," I said to him. "Morning will follow, and the dawn."

"Dawn, aye." He fed the fire and did not look at me. "The Lion of the Sun, the face of Shamash. The Akkadians have stolen the light of day, and named it their own. And Ahura Mazda made no protest, but let his people die beneath their swords. Do you wonder that the Drujani have laid claim to the darkness?"

"No," I said. "No, son of Tizmaht, I do not."

Tizrav shrugged. "My father was a fool, and his father's father before him. I place my faith in the only light that endures, yellow and unwinking: The bright sheen of gold."

To that, I had no words.

FORTY-TWO

THE *SKOTOPHAGOTI* knew we were coming.

That is not what they call themselves, to be sure, but it is the first name I knew, and the one that stays with me. After all, I have heard it in my dreams. We saw him at a distance, this one; he did not approach unseen. No, he came down the old royal road, the city of Daršanga rising behind him, its bulwarks and spires silhouetted against the wintry sea.

He rode a wild ass without stirrups or bridle, his legs dangling, and it would have been comical if it was not terrifying. Sunlight from the east gleamed on his boar's-skull helmet, and his staff of office lay athwart his ass's withers. I saw that he wore a girdle, too; finger-bones. I had not noticed, in Iskandria, that the *Skotophagoti* wore such things, but I had never been so close to one, either.

"You have come for the Mahrkagir." He pointed with his staff, lazily, the wavering ball of jet taking in all three of us. It seemed to linger longest upon me. I was glad I wore the veil, and did not have to meet his eyes.

"I have." Joscelin kneed his Akkadian mount forward, a long-legged black gelding with three white socks. His sword-hilt protruded from beneath the collar of his sheepskin coat and his gaze was as cold and blue as a Drujani winter sky. "Will he see me?"

The *Skotophagotis* merely looked at him, calm astride his ass, his shadow thrown before him, foreshortened and deadly on the old royal road, its fireclay bricks crumbling for lack of repair. "Yes," he said presently. "The Mahrkagir will see you."

We rode behind him into the city of Daršanga.

There was more life in the city than we had seen in the countryside and villages . . . more life, and more fear. How not, when we rode in company with an Eater-of-Darkness? People hurried to the sides of the streets as we passed, prostrating themselves before the priest, pressing their brows to the earth. The *Skotophagotis* took no notice.

Although there seemed no marketplace and no shops, there was trade of a sort, furtive and joyless; foodstuffs, mostly, a good deal of fish, and bread and oil. A man pushing a two-wheeled cart sold tallow candles; another, needles and skeins of thread. A cobbler sat on a wooden stool, measuring a Drujani soldier's foot for a boot. The soldier did not kneel, but bowed low as we passed.

Here and there, I could hear the sound of smithies at work, the ringing clangor of hammer and anvil, and the acrid scent of heated steel in the air. Daršanga might be poor and hungry, but it was able to feed its forges. It had the odor of war.

At the heart of the city, we passed a low plaza that might have been gracious, once. It had columns set at the four corners, but these had been toppled and shattered. In the center a marble-rimmed well was set nearly flush to the paving. A dome had stood over it, a hollow structure with three arched doorways. Now great chunks of debris filled the well and only the truncated foundation remained.

"It was a fire-temple," Tizrav said in a low voice.

Three elderly men crouched beside a scarred marble bench at the outermost verge of the plaza, clad in robes the indeterminate color of filth. Long, unkempt beards grew nearly to their waists, and the smell was fearful. I did not see, at first, the shackles that bound them; not until the *Skotophagotis* stopped before them, pointing with his staff. Then they moved, stiffly, going to their knees, and I saw the shackles at their ankles and the long chain leading to a mighty bolt sunk deep into the flagstones. All three made the prostration. The *Skotophagotis* nodded once and lowered his staff, riding onward.

"Who are they?" I asked Tizrav.

"They were Magi." His face behind the eyepatch was impassive. "Priests of the Lord of Light. Now they are beggars. It pleases the Mahrkagir to let them live and breed fear."

I looked behind me once as we left, twisting in the saddle. The Magi were huddled once more. They had made a den beneath the marble bench, blocking the wind with hunks of rubble and scraps of hide and blankets. At the furthest reach of their chain was the midden-heap, stinking of ordure. I wondered at their tenacity in clinging to life, for the conditions seemed unbearable. *Men will embrace anything to live,* the Drujani scout had said. Mayhap it was true.

And then we reached the palace.

It had been a pleasant structure in former days, charming and well-protected, seated on an outcropping of rock that overlooked the Sea of Khaspar. There had been a time, Tizrav had told me, when the Great Kings of Persis would use it as a summer palace, hosted by the Princes of Drujan, and they would hunt the length of the peninsula and ride hawking in the mountains. The windows stood open to catch the cooling breezes. The inner roofs had been tiled in blue and banners had flown from the towers.

Now the roofs were black with tar-pitch and the towers were barren, every window was barred and shuttered and the high walls bristling with battlements. The palace of Daršanga waited, weathered-grey and grim. I thought about the Akkadian chronicle I had read and how blood had run in channels down its halls. My mouth was dry with fear.

A squadron of Drujani soldiers met us in the front courtyard, armed to the teeth and clad in armor of boiled leather and steel plate, none uniform, all serviceable. They bowed to the *Skotophagotis*, making a corridor to allow us passage. The *Skotophagotis* dismounted, and we followed suit. Someone put a rope around the neck of the priest's ass, wary of its snapping teeth. Our mounts were led away to stable. No one asked Joscelin to surrender his weapons. The soldiers made jests under their breath, eyeing us with unpleasant interest. One rapped at the massive doors with the butt of his dagger, giving a password at the grate.

On the far side, a bar was drawn, a bolt thrown. The doors creaked open onto the darkness within.

"Come," said the *Skotophagotis* and strode inside.

I stood where I was, utterly paralyzed with fear. With a spat curse, Joscelin grabbed my wrist in a painful grip, dragging me after him as he followed the priest. It was dark inside the palace and my veil obscured my vision. I stumbled, tripping over the hem of my gown as I sought to keep up with Joscelin's long strides, filled with a terror so vast it seemed to stop my very mouth. At the rear, Tizrav hurried to keep up with us.

It was cold in Daršanga palace, cold and dark. At the time, I thought it was poorly built, or mayhap the city lacked for fuel. Now I know better. It was at the Mahrkagir's order, despising as he did light and fire. The torches in the wall-sconces were unlit, save every third or fourth one, shedding a guttering light. The walls themselves were bare, and no carpet adorned the floor. I saw dark stains in the cracks between the flagstones, and shuddered.

It is said that La Dolorosa, the fortress on the black isle of La Serenissima, is one of the most foreboding places on earth. Well, and I should know, having been a prisoner there. This was worse. La Dolorosa, for all its ills, is steeped in grief and madness. Folly was committed, terrible horrors, but it was the eternal mourning of Asherat-of-the-Sea that drove men to madness. Mortals are not made to bear the grief of gods.

The palace of Daršanga stank of deliberate human cruelty.

And it had invoked something worse.

I felt it on my skin, a crawling darkness, filling my mouth with the taste of foulness. I had not reckoned, before this, what it would be like to enter the stronghold of Angra Mainyu, enemy of life, Lord of Darkness. D'Angeline though I am, I have stood in the presence of other gods and known no such terror. Respect, yes; and fear. Never had I felt myself so utterly *despised*. It was . . . it was like nothing I can describe.

There are a thousand gods in the world; angry gods, vengeful gods, jealous gods. There are gods who delight in cruelty and mischief, gods who demand tribute in blood, gods who punish the weak and reward the tyrannical. Gods, yes; and goddesses, too. I know this to be true. There are gods who devour their young, gods whose followers sing as they slaughter, gods who raise the seas and shake the earth in their wrath, heedless of the count of mortal lives.

This presence was different.

It was all of these things at once; wrath, retribution, jealousy and hunger—Elua, the *hunger!* Demanding, unthinking, a bloodlust that could never be slaked, no, not if it devoured a thousand lives, a hundred thousand, for the fulfillment lay in the destroying and not the consuming. If the world itself lay desolate and barren, still it would howl for more, its maw agape, yearning and ravening. It was destruction, pure and simple, almost beautiful in its absoluteness.

And if it had been mindless, it would have been terrifying enough . . . but it was not. It was a presence that thought, cunning and aware.

"Angra Mainyu," I whispered.

"Ah." The *Skotophagotis* halted outside the doors to the great hall of the palace and looked at me with eyes slitted with thoughtful pleasure. "The lady senses his presence. Come, then, and meet his greatest servant, who shall become your Master."

We entered the hall.

It was dark, of course, and draughty. A sullen fire burned in the hearth at the near end and a few hanging lamps made pools of light in the air. The hall was vast, and mostly empty. A carved frieze ran the length of the walls depicting a tribute procession, but the faces were chipped and smashed. There were holes and blank spaces on the walls and furnishings where gilt trim had been stripped away.

A dais and throne stood at the far end of the hall, but no one was seated on it. Guards idled nearby, and a handful of men stood conversing. One was clad all in furs; the others wore long brocade coats over trousers and tunics. They fell silent as the *Skotophagotis* entered, and the guards straightened to attention, a giant of a man among them, with a chest like a bull, towering over the Drujani lord beside him.

They all bowed as the *Skotophagotis* approached.

All except the one standing next to the giant.

"Daeva Gashtaham," he said with interest. "What have you brought me?"

And this time, it was the priest who bowed, lowing his skull-helmed head, finger-bones rattling at his waist. "Mahrkagir," he said smoothly. "This lord of Terre d'Ange seeks an audience."

The Mahrkagir of Drujan wore no crown, no diadem, no badge of office; only black, unalleviated save for the worn silver brocade on his coat. Of average stature, he was unimposing in build, and he was young; younger than I had expected, scarce older than I. "Speak."

Joscelin released my wrist and bowed, crossing his vambraces. "Lord Mahrkagir." His voice was harsh, his words practiced. "I, Joscelin Verreuil, seek asylum in Drujan. In exchange, I offer my sword, sworn unto your service, and—" he said it without faltering, "—this woman for your seraglio."

The fur-clad lord laughed deep in his chest, and one of the others made a jest. Two of the guards laughed; the giant crossed his massive arms over his leather-clad chest. The Mahrkagir gazed unblinking at Joscelin. "Why?"

Joscelin conferred with Tizrav, who offered him words to say. "Mahrkagir," said the *Skotophagotis* priest Gashtaham. "This lordling had committed rape against this woman." He touched his ear beneath the boar's skull. "The night wind has spoken; her kinsmen gather at the border, with a company of Sinaddan's men from Nineveh, who rattle their spears and shout vain challenges."

"So." The Mahrkagir cocked his head. "One sword, and one

woman. I have swords, and men to bear them; I have women, and boys, too. Already I have paid dear for D'Angeline flesh, pure and inviolate. Why should I accept a lordling's cast-off? Perhaps this offer is not so sweet as the price on your head, Jossalin Veruy. After all, I have a debt to reclaim." His tone was mild. "Either way, Angra Mainyu feasts, and your futile hope will make the banquet sweeter."

Tizrav whispered urgently to Joscelin, who pushed him away. Tizrav stumbled and fell on the flagstones and Joscelin laughed, a terrible laugh, filled with despair, high and wild.

I knew, then, that I had driven him into the deepest depths of his own personal hell.

"You have no sword like mine, my lord, and no woman like this one." He yanked back the veil and twined his hand in my hair, jerking hard and forcing me to my knees. I went, the breath gasping in my throat, desire hitting me like a fist to the gut, awful and unexpected. "You see her," Joscelin said through gritted teeth. "This is no one's cast-off, but Phèdre nó Delaunay; Naamah's Servant, Kushiel's Chosen and the veritable Queen of Whores, my greatest passion, my sole downfall. I offer unto your keeping, Lord Mahrkagir, that which Terre d'Ange holds most precious. Do you say anyone will match her price?"

It was all there in darkling, twilight air of the hall, truth and lie woven together as seamlessly as a Mendacant's cloak, a polyglot mix of Habiru, Akkadian and Old Persian. The flagstones bruised my knees and my neck ached, wrenched back at an unnatural angle. I heard the scrabbling sound of Tizrav adjusting his eyepatch. I knelt at Joscelin's feet, the hem of his sheepskin coat brushing my cheek, his hand fisted in my hair.

And I felt the presence, not of Elua, Blessed Elua, but cruel Kushiel, beating in my blood.

I heard the Mahrkagir's footsteps.

He reached out to touch my cheek and his hand was cold, so cold. It was cold in the great hall of Daršanga. I felt his touch like fire, setting me ablaze between my thighs. At a touch, he knew me to the core. I shut my teeth on a moan. He was neither comely nor unattractive, the Mahrkagir, his features regular, clean-shaven. Only his eyes were beautiful; lustrous, long-lashed, the pupils dilated until the welling blackness wholly swallowed any other color.

Beautiful . . . and utterly, utterly mad.

"So this is what you offer." The Mahrkagir of Drujan raised his mad, beautiful eyes from my face to Joscelin's, showing even white teeth in a smile. "My lord Veruy of Terre d'Ange, I do believe I will accept it."

Joscelin let go his grip on my hair and I collapsed in a heap at his feet, dimly aware that he gave his Cassiline bow above me. "My lord Mahrkagir will not have cause to regret it."

"Let us hope not." The Mahrkagir looked down at me where I groveled on the flagstones. "Tahmuras, take her to the zenana."

FORTY-THREE

THE ZENANA, or women's quarter, of Daršanga palace was a world unto itself.

It was the Mahrkagir's giant, Tahmuras, who escorted me there. He said nothing along the way, and I would have wondered if he were deaf and dumb, were it not for the alacrity with which he had obeyed the Mahrkagir's command. Tahmuras strode down the halls, descending a stair, all but ignoring me as I stumbled in his wake.

Of what was befalling Joscelin and Tizrav, I could only guess and hope. I had made my choice and committed myself—and lest I forget, the awful pulse of desire, inflamed by the Mahrkagir's touch, throbbed between my thighs. I fixed my gaze on the broad back of Tahmuras, concentrating on following him. He bore no blade, but only a single weapon thrust through his belt; a morningstar, a spiked ball-and-chain mace, the steel rod jutting against his thigh. No scavenged armor would fit him, not this man. He wore a leather jerkin laced with crude plates of steel.

My mind was frozen, between fear and desire; I did not hear what Tahmuras said when he scratched for entry at the latticed door of the zenana. It was opened, I know, and I was thrust through it, given unto the care of the Chief Eunuch.

I began to realize the vastness of the zenana.

It had to be, to hold so many people; a large pool-room, honey-combed with darkness beyond. And it was warm, for a mercy. I sighed as the door closed behind me, feeling the warmth of the space seep into my bones. The Chief Eunuch surveyed me, pursing his lips.

"You see?" he asked in pidgin argot; a tongue that owed something to Persian, Caerdicci and Hellene alike; zenyan, it was called, but I learned that later. With a sweeping gesture, he indicated the room, the stagnant waters of the tepidarium, the surrounding couches on islands of carpet. "Here, you stay. Find a place that is empty."

"My lord." I swallowed and licked my lips, seeking my voice. "I speak Persian, a little."

"You do?" His brows rose. "Well, find a place. There are always some who have died. You should have no trouble making room."

I looked across the space, the knots of intrigue and scheming, like drawing to like. There were women, more women than I could have guessed at, from every nationality on earth. There were Persians and Akkadians with skin like old ivory; there were Ephesians with sultry eyes. There were amber-skinned Bhodistani and even Ch'in, whom I had never seen, with straight black hair caught up in combs and skin the hue of honey. There were Caerdicci of every shade and Hellenes, too; modest Illyrians, and there were Chowati, with light hair and slanted, pale eyes. There were proud hawk-nosed Umaiyyati maidens, and Menekhetans, too. Of a surety, there were Carthaginians and Aragonians as well, and Jebeans and Nubians with ebony skin.

And there were boys.

Not many; only a few, with terrified, defiant eyes, clinging to the couches of the women of their homelands. None of them were D'Angeline.

"I have heard there is one," I said to the Chief Eunuch. "A boy, so high . . ." I gave a vague indication with one hand, having no idea how tall Imriel stood, "from the same country as I. He would not speak your tongue, but he has blue-black hair and eyes . . ." I hesitated, ". . . the color of twilight."

"That one." The Chief Eunuch rolled his eyes. "The Shahryar Mahrkagir would have such a one from your country for his three-fold path. I would that the Âka-Magi had found a less troublesome one. Yes, he has been taken to spend time alone, for stabbing an attendant with a serving fork. You heard me, lady. Find a space."

And with that, he left me.

I made my way around the pool, the walls of which were coated with greenish slime. The water had a fetid odor. Stalwart eunuchs stood at guard around the perimeter of the room, their faces suffused with bitterness. I did not know why, then; now, I do. These were members of the Akkadian garrison that the Mahrkagir had captured. He'd had them all unmanned. A good many had chosen death instead. Those who hadn't, he'd set to guard his seraglio. And they did it, too, clinging to life, filled with rage.

It all served Angra Mainyu, who fed on hatred as surely as death, and longer.

Here and there I paused, asking in this tongue and that: Do you know of this boy?

They knew him; of a surety, they knew him. Children, I gathered, did not last long in the Mahrkagir's zenana, being altogether too fragile for his attentions. This one had lasted longer than anyone had bargained; it seemed the Mahrkagir wished him kept alive for some special purpose. With a slow-dawning sense of horror, I realized that they had bets on his survival.

It is a different world, and a harsh one.

I was new to it, then; I do not know if I can convey the sense of what it was to live there. It was not like a traditional hareem or zenana, no, where the lord's attention was sought and a matter of pride. Here, the lord's attention was death, or akin to it. Even so . . . how else to gain rank? Those whom the Mahrkagir favored had special privileges; private rooms, personal attendants. It won them pity and envy.

For the rest, they established their own hierarchy, based on force of personality.

"Speak to *him*," a Chowati woman said to me, deigning to understand my Illyrian, jerking her chin at a young man huddled in foetal position at the edge of an outer carpet. "*He* can tell you how the Mahrkagir treats with boys."

I tried to do so, crouching low before him, peering at his hidden face. He was Skaldi, I realized with a small shock, recognizing the cast of his features, the butter-yellow hair that curtained his face. I addressed him in his native tongue. He groaned and turned away, hands clutched over his groin.

"What is wrong with this man?" I asked one of the attendants, indignation overcoming my common sense. "Why does no one call for a chirurgeon?"

"He has been cut," the attendant replied, "and does not wish to live." His eyes glittered feverishly, and I knew by his accent he was Akkadian—that was when I began to understand, then, at least a little. "Do you blame him, lady? I do not. He is no longer a man."

I understood, though I didn't wish to. The Skaldi lad wanted to die; and I, I could not blame him. He was alone, the only one of his kind. It was not right, but there was no help for it. What fell on him would not fall on someone else, not that day. He was alone, and so was I.

So I sought an empty couch, and lay coiled onto my own perfect despair. I had attained my goal, the goal I never wanted, becoming a concubine of the Mahrkagir of Drujan. I had come a thousand miles to destroy the only true love I'd ever known. I had condemned Hyacinthe to age forever on his lonely isle. Of my own will, I had done these things. And for all of it, I had not found Imriel de la Courcel, whose face had haunted my dreams. It was fearful to contemplate what abuse he had undergone in this place, and I could only pray he had been spared the worst of it. What did it mean that the Mahrkagir kept him alive? For his three-fold path, the Chief Eunuch had said. I thought of the Skaldi lad and shuddered. If the Mahrkagir had a special purpose in mind, it could only be worse.

There was no comfort in the distant memory of Blessed Elua's presence. The gods are cruel, to lay such burdens on their mortal heirs. How can immortals reckon the cost to mere flesh? I did not know if I could endure this.

I slept, and prayed I would awaken elsewhere.

I didn't.

I awoke, stiff and sore, on a couch in the zenana of Daršanga, huddled in my stained travelling clothes and Valère L'Envers' marten-skin coat. Well and so, I thought; I am still Phèdre nó Delaunay, and I will be no less. The zenana was stirring, attendants bringing wheat-porridge on platters, and honey to a select few. Though I had no appetite, I made myself eat. Charcoal braziers were chasing off the night's chill, though the hypocaust which warmed the stagnant pool and the floors kept the zenana temperate. I thought with rue of my visit to the bath-house in Iskandria.

"Is it possible to bathe?" I asked the attendant when he returned. He stared at me a moment and jerked his chin toward the pool, clearing my tray. I shook my head. I had smelled that water, and I would have to become a good deal more desperate before I let it touch my skin.

Some women, I saw, had better luck; here and there, a few had small luxuries—a ewer of clean water, a comb, a bottle of scented oil. These held court on their islanded couches, sharing out their favors, combing one another's hair, lowering their gowns to dab scent between their breasts with the dispassionate immodesty of women condemned to live publicly with one another. There was no joy in it and little pleasure.

"You are new."

It was one of the eunuchs who addressed me, speaking in the zenyan argot; Persian, I guessed by his tone. He was young and slender, and had a gentle look to him.

"Yes," I said.

He shifted the tray he carried, balancing it on one hip. "If you wish . . . if you wish, I will bring you a basin, and soap."

If his hands had been free, I would have kissed them. Instead, I made myself incline my head and answer graciously. "You are very kind."

He went away. I sat cross-legged on my couch and watched the zenana. In the Night Court, pageants are often staged for wealthy patrons; the Pasha's Hareem was a common one, with scant-clad adepts reclining on cushions and disporting themselves in erotic play to the accompaniment of musicians. This was a dreadful parody of that sensual fantasy. The only pleasure I saw taken was in the smoking of opium, for there were water-pipes at many of the islands, and those women who smoked them fell back in heavy-lidded dreaminess. I saw one Ephesian woman tend to a crying boy of some eight years by blowing a thin stream of blue smoke from her own mouth into his. Presently he ceased to cry, and lay listless at her breast.

"It seems a kindness," I said aloud, watching.

"It is." It was the Persian eunuch returning, kneeling carefully to set a steaming basin of water on the carpet before my couch. "Until the Mahrkagir takes it away. Then they will suffer fresh torments and wish anew to die." He looked up at me. "I am Rushad, lady."

"Thank you, Rushad." Since there was nothing else for it, I undressed with the ease of long practice, kneeling opposite him in front of the basin. Rushad drew in his breath in a hiss, seeing my marque.

"What is *that?*"

"A sign that I am dedicated to the service of our goddess Naamah." I plunged both arms to my elbows in the steaming water, then took up the soap and began to raise a lather. "I am Phèdre nó Delaunay de Montrève of Terre d'Ange."

"Terre d'Ange," he repeated. "Yes. There is one . . . a boy . . . who looks like you, who has your . . . your beauty. But he does not speak our tongue. How is it that you do?"

"You have seen him?" I paused in the middle of my ablutions.

"Yes, of course." Rushad seemed surprised. "He is being . . . confined."

"For stabbing someone with a fork. I heard." I sat back on my heels, thinking. "Can you take me to him?"

"No!" He shook his head in alarm. "I would not dare. I am not like the Akkadians, who are unafraid to die. I have done you a courtesy. You must not ask such things of me."

"Why did you?" I asked him, continuing my bath.

Rushad considered, glancing over at the young Skaldi man I'd spoken to last night, who was now sitting against a wall, knees drawn up, his head low. "They say . . . they say you talked to him last night, to Erich. That you spoke in his tongue. He was my friend, before, although we could not speak, not even in zenyan. Now . . ." He shrugged. "He will not even try. I thought, maybe . . ."

"It is Skaldic," I said. "I think there is no trace of it in this . . . zenyan, you call it? Nothing he would understand. But he would not speak to me, either."

"Perhaps in time," Rushad murmured.

"Mayhap." Reluctantly, I donned my travel-stained attire. "I will continue to try, if you will help me find a way to the D'Angeline boy."

"He will be back in the zenana soon enough." Rushad fussed with the basin, avoiding my eyes. "You will see him then, if . . ." His voice trailed off. "Well, if you are here, you will see him."

With that, he left me.

If there is anything worse than terror, it is terror and tedium commingled. I sat on my couch, combing out my damp, tangled hair with my fingers, taking the measure of the zenana, of many dozens of lives condemned to spin themselves out beneath the vast, brooding shadow of the Mahrkagir's palace. How, I wondered, did they feel it? Did they sense it, the dire presence I had felt above? Did they know its name? Did they pray to their gods?

Some did, I know; I saw it, then and later.

There was a tall Jebean woman who told fortunes with bones, holding court on a carpeted island. Sometimes, with great ceremony, she would unravel a single crimson thread from her frayed garments and make a knotted talisman, handing it over in exchange for some small gift.

There was a Chowati woman who sat on the floor with her hands on her knees, rocking back and forth and uttering ceaseless prayers, eyes shut tight, diagonal scars marking her cheeks.

There were three Bhodistani who had plainly resolved to die, hollow-eyed, their skin touched with the translucence that comes of drinking only water and taking no sustenance. They had drawn their couches into a triangle and knelt facing one another, hands folded. I envied them their serenity. No one seemed inclined to stop them.

Of hope . . . there was none.

And not one of them, I thought, had known desire at the Mahrk-agir's touch.

I didn't like to think about it.

If Imriel had been here—if he had, then what? For all my vaunted skills in the arts of covertcy, I'd come here without a plan, placing myself in Blessed Elua's hand. The zenana was guarded, the Akkadian eunuchs wearing short, curved knives at their belts. Mayhap Joscelin could have fought his way through a dozen of them . . . but Joscelin could not aid me here. No, he was sworn into the Mahrkagir's service, surrounded by the men who had defeated and unmanned the Akkadians, clad in leather and steel plate, heavily armed. Even if he tried, they were enough to stop him; enough, and more.

And there were the *Skotophagoti*.

Blessed Elua, I thought, what have I done?

What have you done to me?

ꝶ·ORTY-FOUR

"You haven't wept."

The sound of a voice speaking Caerdicci—a civilized tongue, the scholar's language, nearly my milk-tongue—jolted me awake. I hadn't realized I'd been dozing. I stared uncomprehending at the woman standing before me, strong-featured and handsome. There was blood spattered on her woolen gown, which was cut in the Tiberian manner, a long shawl worn over it.

"Forgive me," I said, nearly stammering. "My lady . . . ?"

"Drucilla." She sat down on the far end of my couch uninvited, fixing me with a disconcertingly level grey-blue gaze. "It will do. You are D'Angeline."

"Yes." I sat upright, running my hands over my face. "Phèdre nó Delaunay."

"Phèdre." Drucilla nodded once. "That's an ill-luck name."

"So it seems," I said, eyeing her. She bore it with composure, only flinching a little and tucking her hands into the folds of her shawl. I saw before she did that the fourth and fifth fingers were missing the furthest joint on both hands. "Are you wounded, my lady?"

"No." She shook her head. "I have come from seeing Hiu-Mei, who is newly returned from his lordship's attentions. She is his favorite. In a fit of anger, he struck her face with a—" Seeing me blanch, she switched mid-sentence. "It is not my blood. I was a physician, once. I do what I can to tend to the living."

"Ah." I swallowed. "Truly, it is admirable, my lady."

"It keeps despair at bay," Drucilla said matter-of-factly. "One clings to what one knows, until . . . well." She glanced at her hidden hands. "Until one can cling no longer. They are speaking of you. I was curious."

I remembered the words that had awakened me. "Because I have not wept?"

"That, and other things. A guard said that you were not taken; you were brought. Others have been, but never one such as you. And now there is a D'Angeline lordling among the Mahrkagir's men, a leopard among wolves. There was a quarrel, last night in the festal hall."

My heart leapt in my breast. I schooled my voice to hardness, asking, "Is he dead?"

"No," the Tiberian woman said. "One of his lordship's Drujani soldiers is."

I looked away, hiding a profound relief. "You wonder that I do not weep. I spent my tears a long time ago. He told me my kinsmen would never cross the border into Drujan. I believe it, now."

"You'll weep," Drucilla said quietly.

It was truer than she knew. "What will become of me?" I asked.

She shrugged. "His lordship the Mahrkagir will send for you, when he is ready. It may be days, or weeks. Months, even. In your case . . . well. I do not think he will forget."

My blood ran like ice, and beneath it, somewhere, the awful stir of desire. "And then?"

"You will weep, and perhaps wish to die." It passed for compassion, in this place. "If you do not, if you survive . . . there are ways. Some few of us share what skills we have. And there are others, other . . . patrons, Drujani warlords and others, his lordship's guests." With a sweeping gesture, she indicated those women who enjoyed small luxuries. "It is another way to keep despair at bay. Not my way, but I have heard you bear the marque of one dedicated to your goddess of pleasure."

I nodded, understanding. "How is it arranged?"

"His lordship sometimes chooses to share his concubines among his allies. If they hunger for more . . ." She shrugged again. "The Akkadian attendants take bribes, sometimes. They have little loyalty for this service." She told me why, then.

Well and good; so the zenana was not impermeable, and I might hope to gain favor in the form of scented oils or dice or sweetmeats—or better yet, raw opium—if I chose to make myself available to any number of Drujani warlords. I kept my mouth closed, and listened to all that Drucilla had to tell me, which was a good deal.

I daresay it was a relief to her, who had not surrendered fully to despair, to speak to someone who had not yet abandoned all hope. Later

I learned that she took it upon herself always to speak to newcomers to the zenana. Most of them—of us—were victims of the slave-trade or conquests of war; some few were even tribute-gifts. Drucilla was an exception. Adventurous and independent, she had travelled from her homeland to see the sights of Hellas; falling in love with the country, she had set up shop as a physician in Piraeus. It was there that a *Skotophagotis* and a company of Drujani had taken fancy to the notion of a female chirurgeon as they set sail for Ephesium. And they had simply taken her.

It appalled me more than I could say, that the incursions of the *Skotophagoti* had grown so bold, that we had known naught of it in Terre d'Ange. Drucilla had cried out for aid. The Hellenes had turned a deaf ear. The Ephesian ship's captain had ignored her cries, though she pounded on the door of her cabin until her hands bled.

"Though they have bled more, since," she added with a crooked smile.

"The Mahrkagir?" I asked.

Drucilla nodded and looked away, knotting the folds of her shawl. "He wonders what I will do, when I have no fingers left to administer to the ailing. Fortunately, he does not remember to wonder it often. He is quite mad, you know."

"I know." I did. "Do you know why?"

"Perhaps." She bowed her head, loose locks of brown hair hiding her face. "He survived the purge, after the rebellion; Hoshdar Ahzad, do you know of it?" I merely nodded, not wanting to distract her flow of words. "He was an illegitimate son, bastard-born; his mother was a common street-whore, whom his father brought into the zenana and raised to concubine status." Drucilla raised her head, pointing toward a far wall, where the Skaldi lad Erich slumped. "It happened there. I had the story from Rushad . . . you know Rushad? One cannot be sure, speaking in zenyan, but he knows; he had it from his old Akkadian master, who commanded here years ago, until the second rebellion . . ."

A simple story, when all was said and done. The Mahrkagir, a boy of four or five, had survived the slaughter, struck a blow on the head and left for dead. Bleeding from a gash to the temple, eyes fixed wide, he had watched as the women and children of the zenana—lesser wives, concubines, his own half-brothers and -sisters—were ravished and slain, until the now-stagnant pool turned crimson with blood.

The corpses were stacked like cordwood, the Akkadian chronicler had said; in the zenana, they were stacked atop the still-breathing body of a boy of four or five, until they blotted out his vision. It was the giant, Tahmuras—then a strapping lad of fourteen, left alive by the Akkadians, who desired strong limbs to clean up after their massacre— who excavated him, removing corpses one by one, tearing him free from the womb of death.

"He protected him," Drucilla said. "He protects him still, night and day. It was the people who named him, so they say; the folk of Dar-šanga."

"The Conqueror of Death," I murmured.

Drucilla nodded. "No one knew what his mother called him, and he had no words, not after that. It was the blow to the head, I think. Ever afterward, his eyes remained dilated, and he cannot bear the light. It is said he remembers nothing, before his second birth. Only death. And he is mad. Wholly and completely mad. Of that, I am certain."

I could not speak for the awful pity that stopped my mouth. I swallowed, willing it to subside. "There is another boy," I said, my voice croaking. "A D'Angeline boy . . ."

"Imri." Drucilla folded her maimed hands in her lap, looking side-long at me. "You asked after him. I have heard it."

"You know him." Relief flooded me.

"He speaks Caerdicci. He was gently reared, once."

I thought of Brother Selbert and the sanctuary of Elua, nestled in the mountains of Siovale, where it seemed no harm could befall anyone. "Is he . . . well?" I asked.

"He is alive, and unmaimed." Her mouth hardened. "In this place, that passes for well."

I tried not to sound too eager. "I would speak with him, if it is possible."

"Not until Nariman relents," she said bluntly. "It may be days. He is Chief Eunuch here, and Imri's punishment is his province. I don't advise you to cross him. It is said that it was Nariman who opened the gates of the zenana, thirty years ago, to the Akkadian forces. It amuses his lordship to leave him in office. I cannot think why." Drucilla rose from my couch, stretching aching joints with a sigh. "Phèdre nó De-launay, do not expect too much of the boy. It is a comfort to have the companionship of one's homeland, but he has been a long time without it and cruelly treated in the bargain. I do what I may, but he does not welcome pity."

"No." I thought of Melisande's face when I had told her the news, the awful knowledge, the blazing fury in her eyes. "I don't suppose he would."

Drucilla left me, then, continuing on her rounds of the zenana; I watched, and saw that she was greeted with respect by some; by others, with indifference or disdain. She laid a hand on the shoulder of one of the three fasting Bhodistani. I could not hear what they said, but she merely nodded, sorrow in her mien, and went onward. She stooped to speak to the Skaldi lad, who turned his face to the wall. Nothing to be done there.

Someone scratched at the latticed door to the zenana—a Drujani soldier. A deathly quiet fell over the tepidarium. Nariman, the Chief Eunuch, conferred and stepped forward with a pair of Akkadian attendants. His keen gaze swept the room, and I saw many dozens of women suddenly try to make themselves invisible.

To no avail; Nariman pointed—there, there and there, and six women and one boy gained expressions of despair. One went wailing, and beyond the door, I saw the Drujani grin. The boy was Menekhetan, slight and stumbling; in silent anguish, I thought of Nesmut. The women whose couches he shared wept openly, covering their heads and rending their clothing.

No matter what, I thought, where battle prevails, women must grieve.

One of the Bhodistani had been chosen, a lovely woman clad in silks of crimson and orange. The warm hue of her skin and her long black hair reminded me eerily of my mother; there is Bhodistani blood, they say, in the veins of Jasmine House. The Akkadians stood by, waiting, almost respectful. Her legs gave way beneath her as she sought to stand, and one of the eunuchs caught her gently. Her companions, languid with the nearness of death, reached out to kiss her hand, tears in their eyes. Wavering on her feet, she gave them a lucid smile.

Blessed Elua, I thought, let me go as gracefully when my time to die is come.

And regarded the thought with horror.

Then they were gone, and the zenana buzzed with relief. They had gone, I knew from what Drucilla had told me, to the festal hall—to the Mahrkagir's entertainment. Some would return, depending on the lord's mood and that of his men. Some would not. I did not think the Bhodistani woman would, who had set her mind to die. I was not sure of the others, nor the boy.

Too restless to remain still, I got up and wandered the zenana. Since I had naught else to do, I sat for a while beside the Skaldi lad, Erich. "What is your tribe?" I asked him in his own tongue. "Where is your steading?" Wrapped in his own private misery, he rolled on his side, facing the wall and ignoring me. So I sang to him in Skaldic, the hearth-songs of his mothers and sisters, the songs I had learned when I was a slave—when I was first a slave, for what else was I now?—in Gunter Arnlaugson's steading, whence Melisande had sold me. I sang to him until I saw his broad shoulders shake with silent tears, and felt abashed. "Your friend Rushad is missing you," I whispered to him, then. "He does not wish you to die."

Erich the Skaldi made no reply or acknowledgment.

The effort made, I went upon my way, musing upon the strangeness of it all. It might have been day or night; I could not say. The rhythms of the Mahrkagir's whims dictated life in the zenana. If the attendants had not brought food at regular intervals, if they had not interrupted to fetch women and boys for the lord's amusement . . . who could say? There had been a garden, once, where the women of the Drujani prince might disport themselves—now it was barred, the rich soil tilled with salt, dead and barren, and strong timbers blocked the door, shutting out any glimpse of sky. The windows were shuttered. Day, night . . . it mattered naught. We lived here by lamplight, and the Mahrkagir's whim.

And I sang the songs of my captivity, the songs with which I had once bought passage across the deadly Strait, to a Skaldi lad, blood of my enemies, who was unmanned by the man to whom I'd prevailed upon Joscelin to sell me.

Truly, 'twas strange.

At the carpeted island of the Jebeans and Nubians, I paused. The tall woman who was chiefest among them stared up at me, hostile and demanding. A frayed cloth of intricate pattern sheathed her body, and she wore long pins of ivory thrust in her black woolen hair.

"Selam," I said respectfully, greeting her in Jeb'ez, bowing with my palms together.

She stared a minute longer, then laughed long and hard, saying something I could not understand to the others. "You think to speak Jeb'ez?" she asked me, then, in rude argot.

"Yequit'a," I said; "excuse me," adding in my best grasp of zenyan, "Only a little. I would learn more if you teach me."

All of them laughed at that, and not kindly. "You have opium?"

asked the tall woman, reclining on her couch. "Gems? Kumis? Sweet-meats, maybe?"

"No." I shook my head. "Forgive me, Fedabin," I said, according her the title the scroll granted to the Queen of Saba, "wise woman." "I will not bother you."

"Wait." Her voice stopped me as I turned to leave. I stood as she regarded me, a trace of curiosity emerging in her mask of indifference. "Why do you wish to know this, little one? You come here to die, gebanum? Understand? It is only when that matters, and how much you suffer in between."

"I understand, Fedabin." I inclined my head to her. "I would still learn."

Another of the women leaned over, whispering to the tall one; Kaneka, she called her. Kaneka listened with half-lidded eyes, then nod-ded, swinging herself upright. "Safiya has a thought," she announced. "For your courtesy, I make you a gift, a gift of knowledge." With one hand, she opened a woven pouch strung on a thong about her neck, shaking three unusual dice into her other palm. "You kneel, there," she said, pointing to the carpet. "And learn."

I knelt waiting. With great ceremony, one of the women brought out a tray of fine-combed sand, shaking it carefully until it was smooth, setting it down before me. Kaneka knelt opposite, her face as impassive as a warrior's, drawing a small circle in the sand with one finger.

"Days," she said, and drew another, larger, to enclose it. "Weeks." Glancing at me to make certain I understood, she drew the outermost concentric circle. "Months." Taking my wrist, she turned my hand over and placed the dice in it. "Hold them until they take on your heat."

The dice were amber, six-pointed, with eight facing sides, each one etched with a number of dots. I closed my hand on them. The Jebeans and Nubians had drawn around, watching intently; even a few other women had gathered.

"You see!" Kaneka raised her voice, addressing them. "In Daršanga, Death is a man, and Lord Death is always waiting here in the zenana. How long will he wait to summon you to his bedchamber? How eager is he to plant his iron rod inside you? If it be three days, will it be five weeks until he summons you again? If it be five weeks, will it be two months? It is," she said, looking at me once more, "the only question that matters."

Clutched in my palm, the octohedronal dice had grown warm. I gave them to her. Kaneka shook them in cupped hands over the tray, muttering a lengthy prayer in Jeb'ez. Opening both hands with a flourish, she cast the dice onto the sand.

Flawed amber glinted dully in the lamplight as they fell, one by one, within the concentric rings, forming a line as straight as an arrow—each face showing a single dot.

The taste of fear flooded my mouth.

Someone gasped; a number of women drew back. Kaneka stared at me, the whites of her eyes showing yellow around her dark irises. "You are marked for Death, little one. And soon."

I gazed at the unwinking line of dice, three single eyes on the sand. "Does it mean that is when I will die?"

"I'ye, no." Kaneka's voice was rough with fear. "It says that is when Lord Death will send for you." She pointed. "Day, after day; week after week; month upon month. No respite. When will you die?" She shrugged. "Like the rest. When he kills you, or when you can bear it no more."

"I see." I stood. "Thank you, Fedabin; amessaganun. If it please you to teach me Jeb'ez, I would learn it still, though I have nothing to trade."

Kaneka scooped up her dice and rose. "You are a fool, little one," she whispered harshly. "Believe, or not; the dice do not lie, and I have told you what any one of us would shudder to hear. Use the time left you wisely, and make peace with your gods while you may!"

"My gods." I looked past her at the watching zenana. "It is they who marked me, Fedabin Kaneka; not for death, but for pain. How shall I make peace with that?"

To that, she had no answer.

ꞯORTY-FÍVE

AFTER THAT, I was regarded with a certain fearful awe in the zenana.

It lasted all of a day until it changed.

It would have happened anyway, I daresay; the Mahrkagir would have sent for me when he did, Kaneka's prophecy or no, and there would have followed what followed. I am an *anguissette*. It could not have fallen out differently. The dice had merely ensured that I was already branded a target for fear and speculation. In a community ruled by dread, it is never far from thence to hatred.

Hiu-Mei, the Mahrkagir's favorite, had taken a turn for the worse. Drucilla tended her as best she might, but without medications, there was little she could do. It was not the blow to the face, I gathered, but a disease of long standing—a pox, one of the Illyrians swore, that men contract from congress with goats. The Tatar tribesmen whose aid the Mahrkagir courted were known to carry it.

Whether or not it is true, I cannot say; of a surety, the Ch'in woman was ill, a cause for bitter rejoicing in the zenana. Rejoicing, for any favorite was despised; bitter, for any favorite must be replaced . . . and the lot would fall upon one of us.

They looked at me and muttered about Kaneka's dice.

For my part, I felt numb and hollow inside. Blessed Elua's presence was long gone, and only his purpose remained, drawn with lines as straight and inevitable as the one cast by Kaneka's dice, leading to the Mahrkagir's bedchamber.

There was news, in the zenana; the Bhodistani woman was dead. One of the Mahrkagir's men—the wolves of Angra Mainyu, Tizrav had called them—had made a wager that given a choice between the point of a dagger and a morsel of food, the woman would eat. The Mahrkagir had taken the wager. She never flinched as the Drujani dagger pierced her heart.

It passed for entertainment, in the festal hall, and the Mahrkagir was happy.

I heard, too, other news; news of the D'Angeline lordling who never smiled, whose beauty shone like a star in the cold, dark halls of Daršanga. In the zenana, Joscelin was already coveted. It afforded me a certain bleak amusement. Otherwise, I felt nothing.

Rushad stole cat-footed to my couch, bringing a gift hidden in his right hand. "See?" he said, opening it to reveal a single pellet, dark and resinous. "Opium! If you take it by mouth, they say, the effect lasts longer, much longer, and the . . . the pain is not so great, it is as if it were happening in a dream."

"I see." I smiled and shook my head, closing his hands over his treasure. "You are kind, Rushad, but it is not needful. Keep it."

He looked at me with dismay. "The Mahrkagir has spoken of you. He will send for you tonight; I know it, everyone knows it!"

"I know." I frowned, listening to the sounds of the zenana. Someone sighed, someone cried out, the door to the privy closet closed with a bang. I thought I had heard a voice murmuring sleepily in Hellene, *Lypiphera*. Pain-bearer. It was my imagination, like as not. "I know, Rushad. But I cannot afford the luxury of waking dreams."

He went away disheartened. In truth, I was not sure of the wisdom of my choice. Of a surety, I had need of my wits . . . and yet. I had no plan; I had not even located Imriel de la Courcel. There was naught I could do. Even if I were able to speak with Joscelin—and I dared not risk it so soon—what would I tell him? That the Akkadian eunuchs despised their master and took bribes willingly? It was something, but not much. No more than he could learn on his own. Mayhap it would have been wiser to meet the Mahrkagir wrapped in a cocoon of dreams.

Or not.

I watched a Carthaginian woman draw lovingly at the mouthpiece of a water-pipe, limbs disposed in languor. Those who entered the world of dreams emerged only by force. It seemed a kindness, yes. *Until the Mahrkagir takes it away. Then they will suffer fresh torments and wish anew to die.*

I would have reason enough. No need to seek further.

So I waited in hollow despair, until the latticed doors opened and Nariman the Chief Eunuch conferred with the Drujani guards. The hushed and waiting silence fell as he returned. His pursed red lips quivered, and there was malice in his gaze as one plump hand rose, pointing first at me.

Even though I had expected it, my heart skipped a beat.

No one wept for me, as they had for the others summoned last night. Well and so; I was Phèdre nó Delaunay de Montrève, and I needed no one's pity. I rose from my couch with dignity, inclining my head to the Akkadian escorts. "Khannat," I murmured in their tongue, taking one's arm; thank you. I felt his body stiffen, rigid with unnamed emotion, and then he bowed his head once, briefly.

Five others were chosen, and a boy, the little Menekhetan who'd been summoned last night. He was still alive, his eyes more sunken and hollow than any child's ought to be. This time, the Menekhetan women on his carpeted island merely keened, low and agonized.

Thus were we summoned.

Our Drujani guards affected a careless demeanor, clanking in armor, talking over us as we ascended the narrow stair. I heard beneath their tone an undercurrent of excitement and knew why. I was something new; something different. My Akkadian escort's eyes gleamed in the darkness, mouth fixed in a grimace. At the top of the stair, we waited, while each one of us was searched for weapons.

Naamah, I thought, the prayer coming unbidden as I awaited my turn. Gracious lady, mistress of my soul, I have consented to this; consented, as you did, once upon a time. For love of Blessed Elua, you lay down with the Great King of Persis. Because Elua has asked it of me, I do the same, though Persis is fallen and the king who remains in this isolated corner of it styles himself the Lord of Death. My lady Naamah, if you have a care for your faithful Servant, ward me well in this place.

For an instant—only an instant—I thought I smelled attar of roses, and heard a sound like the quick, fluttering wings of a dove taking flight. And then it was my turn, and the hard hands of a Drujani guard patted me down, lingering on my body, his face leering before me.

It is an *anguissette's* nightmare. I kept my chin aloft, and betrayed no sign.

"Go on," he said to the others in Persian, jerking his head. "He's waiting."

And so we went, down the darkened hallways, a single torch lighting our way. Two of the other women wept and dragged their feet; one of the eunuchs—not my escort, but another—cursed and struck one across the back. The others walked with leaden steps. The Menekhetan boy straggled, his ambling path sending him wandering from one side of the hall to the other. The Drujani guards pushed him and laughed, making jests about wagering on where his next staggering step would fall.

"Enough!" I said fiercely, unable to curb my tongue. "Can you not see he is injured?"

"Shut up." The one with the torch thrust it toward my face, laughing when I flinched. "He entertained a few of the Shahryar's friends, is all. You'll be lucky if you can walk, you will, when his lordship's done with you!"

Shahryar; sovereign lord. Nariman had said it, too. They acknowledged him that in Drujan, the bastard-born son of Hoshdar Ahzad. I kept my mouth closed, fearing further retribution. With a sidelong glance at me, my Akkadian escort stepped to the boy's side, guiding him gently.

We were nearing the festal hall.

I could see it; the dull glow of a fireplace at one end and a few torches in between, much as the audience hall had been. It was different, though. That had been empty, subdued. We heard the roar from halfway down the hall. There were men here, many men, and drink flowing. I did not understand, at first, what it must be.

And then I saw the vaulted ceiling, rising to a sealed dome, and the low well beneath it, capped with rubble, and I knew. Men, elderly men, with white beards and filthy robes, waited on hands and knees, ropes around their necks, their faces a study in despair. They were Magi. I knew, I had seen them in the city.

This had been a fire-temple, once; the private temple of the princes of Daršanga.

Now it was the festal hall of the Mahrkagir.

Long, wooden tables had been set within the temple, and they were lined with men; Drujani, mostly, and some others with hard faces and slanted eyes whom I took to be Tatars, their expressions guarded and watchful. Starveling dogs scavenged beneath them for the remnants of the evening meal.

"My lords!" one of our guards cried in Persian, hoisting his torch. "I bring you tonight's offering, from the zenana of the Shahryar Mahrkagir!"

Someone shoved me hard, from behind; I stumbled forward, tripping on my gown and falling heavily to my knees. The men shouted and beat their cups on the tables, the sound dinning against my ears like the beating of distant wings; no dove's, these, but Kushiel's.

At the end of the aisle, in the darkness, a figure stepped forward.

I lifted up my head and met his eyes.

Fine pinpricks of light illuminated the silver embroidery that chased his black surcoat, and he was smiling, smiling as he extended his hand. His eyes, fixed on mine, were lustrous and black, utterly black, utterly mad. My blood ran ice-cold in my veins, heat blazing between my thighs. I pressed my brow to the cold stones, then rose. His smile beckoned me homeward. I took one step, then another, my legs belonging to someone else. Home. I put my hand in his; his fingers closed over it, cold and dry. A strange rill of energy surged between us. I tasted fear and desire, his mad smile, and lost myself in his dilated eyes.

Home.

In a dreadful parody of courtesy, the Mahrkagir escorted me to his table, seating me beside him. I sat facing the dim-lit hall, the savage, cheering men. Already the women who had accompanied me were circulating among them—ostensibly, to refill their cups with beer or wine or rankly pungent kumis, the fermented mare's milk favored by the Tatars. In truth, they were entertainment, there to be groped and fondled by any man bold enough to dare. One unruly group had the little Menekhetan boy atop their table, performing agonized back-bends and somersaults amid a gauntlet of naked blades; he had trained as an acrobat, once.

I sat and watched it in a state of shock, unmoving. The Mahrkagir smiled, one hand at the nape of my neck, and the icy touch of his fingers against my flesh held me riveted. I could feel my heart beating like a drum within my breast, my pulse beating between my thighs. *Blessed Elua, what have you done to me?* The Menekhetan boy whimpered, his limbs trembling as he sought to hold his pose. The Drujani laughed, two of them tossing daggers back and forth under his arched back. Elsewhere, one of the men moved his cup teasingly as an Ephesian woman sought to pour, forcing her to lean further and further over him; he bit her, then, on the upper curve of her breast, hard enough to leave the impress of his teeth. She cried out and dropped the pitcher. When it shattered, the Drujani laughed uproariously and pushed her to her knees, forcing her to lap the spilled beer with her tongue.

My gorge rose until I thought I might vomit, but the awful pulse of desire did not abate.

And there, a mere table away, sat Joscelin, surrounded by companionable Drujani. I do not know how he endured it. Even when he looked me full in the eyes, his face was absolutely expressionless. I have seen dead men who showed more emotion.

And I, who sat throbbing under the Mahrkagir's touch, did not blame him for it.

An unearthly howl split the air, and a blazing trail of sparks; someone had tied a firebrand to a dog's tail. I raised one hand to my mouth, smothering an outcry as the poor beast raced around the hall, sparks igniting its fur.

"Dogs," a smooth voice said at my shoulder, "are sacred to the followers of Ahura Mazda, because they are loyal and do not lie."

I looked up to see the *Skotophagotis*, repressing a shudder as I realized his torch-cast shadow fell over me. "Daeva Gashtaham," I said, remembering what the Mahrkagir had called him.

The priest inclined his head, light gleaming redly from the polished boar's-skull helm. "You have a keen memory." He watched as the burning cur went into throes of agony. The noise was horrible. "Duzhmata," he said in an idle tone, "duzhûshta, duzhvarshta. Ill thoughts, ill words, ill deeds; the three-fold path of Angra Mainyu."

"Go away, Gashtaham." The Mahrkagir spoke for the first time; his fingers caressed my neck. He smiled at his priest. "You brought her to me, now she is mine, and she does not need your counsel." He turned his smile on me and I stared at him, helpless. "She has ill thoughts already. I hear them, licking at mine, begging. Is it not so?" he added, asking me.

Hypnotized by my twin reflections in the black moons of his eyes, I whispered, "Yes."

"You are the first." He watched the priest take his leave with a displeased bow. "I have sent my priests, the Âka-Magi of Angra Mainyu, abroad, far abroad, to see if any god dare stand against them. In mighty Khebbel-im-Akkad, in Menekhet, in Ephesus, even in Hellas, their servants quail with fear, and my zenana grows. The lords of Ch'in and Bodhistan send careless gifts, thinking I may one day prove an ally. They do not understand I am planting the seeds of death in my zenana. But you, ah!" The Mahrkagir took my chin in one hand, studying my face, his dilated gaze lingering on my moted left eye. "You," he said, caressing my cheek, "are different. I feel it, I feel how the blood leaps in your veins to follow my touch." His hand trailed down my throat, cupping one breast. "Duzhvarshta," he murmured, pinching my erect nipple as hard as he could, fingers cold even through my gown. "Ill deeds."

A bolt of pain shot through me and I stifled a moan.

"Ill thoughts, ill words, ill deeds." He smiled tenderly at me, maintaining a pincerlike grip. The pain was like a red-hot wire; my hips moved, thrusting involuntarily. "You crave these things. I know. I knew it when you knelt before me. Phè-dre." My name was drawn out on his lips, and I whimpered in reply, my breathing shallow. "Your gods have chosen you for defilement. Is it not so?"

I closed my eyes. "Yes."

The Mahrkagir released me, and the sudden absence of pain was a loss. "For a long time, I sought one of your kind. Now, the gods of Terre d'Ange tremble with fear and send tribute to the altar of Angra Mainyu!" he breathed. I opened my eyes to see his face flushed and exalted. "Soft and weak, they may be, but gods nonetheless!" He laughed, then, free and boyish. "You are the first to be summoned," he said, caressing me lovingly. "The first."

Unruly as the hall may have been, it heeded its master. At some point, they had fallen silent and begun to watch what transpired between us. They could not hear what was said, but they had seen—seen what he did to me, seen my response. The men looked vaguely awed; the women had expressions of scarce-veiled contempt.

And Joscelin . . .

Joscelin.

In all the years we had been together, as consort and mistress, as lovers, as courtesan and Cassiline, he had never seen me with a patron— not truly, not as the *anguissette* I am.

He had now.

We stared at each other unblinking. It was Joscelin who looked away.

"Enjoy, my lords." The Mahrkagir rose to his feet, tugging me after him. With his free hand, he made a sweeping gesture, his black eyes wide and wild. "Tonight, what is mine is yours! Angra Mainyu has given me a sign. Let your deeds gladden his heart!"

And with that, he led me away.

Forty-six

I DO not like to speak of this night, nor of the many that followed.

I had thought, before Drujan, that I knew somewhat of the darkness of the mortal heart, mine own included. I was wrong. I knew nothing.

The Mahrkagir's quarters were cold and barren, like the rest of Daršanga, the walls stripped of adornment, booty piled in careless piles on the floor. His faithful guard Tahmuras escorted us there, taking up a post in the hallway when the doors were barred. I shivered in my gown—the saffron riding-attire that Favrielle nó Eglantine had made for me, in light wool for the Jebean heat—and looked about me.

Dirt and debris were mounded in the corners, and there were stains on the uncarpeted stone floor of the bedchamber. There was a flagellary . . . I suppose one would call it a flagellary. In Terre d'Ange, the implements of pleasure, violent or otherwise, are lovingly tended. Whips are cleaned and oiled, shackles polished, the mechanisms of stocks and barrels and wheels exquisitely maintained. Aides d'amour are kept in velvet-lined cases. Even Melisande . . . I remembered her flechettes, immaculate and gleaming, honed to a razor-blue edge.

Not here.

I gazed at the Mahrkagir's cupboard, a jumbled array of devices tossed here and there, leather dry and cracked, rusty iron, caked with black blood. And I bit my tongue to keep from weeping.

"Duzhvarshta," he said gently, freeing my hair from behind and running both hands through it. "Ill deeds. You understand?" He turned me around to face him, laying one hand over my groin. "Nothing that begets life."

I nodded, tears in my eyes. And to show I understood, I went to my knees before him, undoing the drawstring of his trousers and performing the *languisement*.

Whatever else he might have experienced in the worship of Angra Mainyu, I do not think it prepared the Mahrkagir of Drujan for the attentions of a D'Angeline courtesan trained by one of the greatest adepts of the Night Court. I felt his entire body shudder as I took him into my mouth. Unlike his hands, his phallus was warm; rigid with blood, erect and straining. A strange feeling of relief enveloped me as his hands clamped hard on my head, fingers tangling in my hair, forcing me. I plied my art with consummate skill, working with lips and tongue, the small muscles deep in my throat, grateful for his groan of pleasure.

Until he pushed me away, and I fell sprawling on the cold flag-stones.

"*I* decide," the Mahrkagir said, and struck me across the face with the back of his hand, so hard that my ears rang and I tasted blood. He smiled calmly, ignoring his erect phallus, so hard that the head of it brushed his belly, and struck me again, splitting my lower lip. "Do you understand?"

"Yes, my lord," I mumbled thickly, blood trickling down my chin.

"Good." He crouched over me and took my face in both hands, licking the blood from my chin and lip with one long swipe of his tongue. "Mm."

It shocked and appalled me more than anything I have known; and still, even now, aroused me. There are a thousand reasons I do not care to remember these nights, but that is chiefest among them, always. Not what he did, but how I responded.

"Ill thoughts," he whispered, and I could see my own blood spreading scarlet on his tongue as he said it, his left hand sliding beneath my gown, my undergarments. Cold, so cold! His fingers parted the folds of my nether lips, finding me moist and eager. "Ill words, whore of the gods." With a sudden thrust, he slid two ice-cold fingers inside me. I made a helpless noise and surged forward, meeting his hand. "Ill deeds." Deftly, his thumb penetrated me to the rear, and now with one hand, he held my entire nether region in a viselike grip. It hurt, and the force of my climax shook me. The Mahrkagir smiled tenderly at me, watching with his mad, mad eyes. "Now you understand."

I nodded dumbly, licking my split lip.

"Ishtâ." Murmuring a Persian endearment, he withdrew his hand from me. "I think you will become very, very special to me. Now take off your clothes."

That was the beginning.

There was more, a good deal more. Much of it hurt. It was not that he was particularly skilled in the arts of pain. He wasn't. I have known better—or worse, as it may be. I am not even sure myself which is true. *Your gods have chosen you for defilement*, he had said, and that was his gift. In time, he made me beg for what he did to me. Ill words. I did. I said all that he wished to hear. It was cold and dark and filthy, and I meant every word of it.

And then it got worse.

I did not see, at first, what he took from the cupboard, only that he handled it reverently. It had been some hours, I think, and my vision was blurred with exhaustion and tears, my body aching in every part from the violent commingling of abuse and pleasure. "You see?" he asked, stroking the leather straps, the thick buckles, showing me how the inside was hollow, lined with a cushion of oiled kidskin. Alone among the rest, this device had been tended with love. "A blacksmith made it for me. You see?"

I nodded dully, a knot of terror in my belly. I saw.

The Mahrkagir smiled, easing himself inside it, fastening the sturdy buckles. Man-shaped, the cold iron glinted, nubbed with hundreds of blunt spikes. It jutted from his loins like some terrible implement of war. "It is for you, ishtâ," he said fondly, stroking my hair. "All for you."

My lips shaped the sound of my *signale*, no; enough, no more. *Hyacinthe*.

He took me with it from behind, one hand shoving my face into the stained bedclothes. I do not have words to describe the pain of it. *How eager is he to plant his iron rod inside you?* More fool I, I had thought it a figure of speech. It wasn't. At the first thrust, I thought I would die, split asunder. My breath caught in my throat; I heard a mewling sound, unaware it was me. It was the sound of a dumb animal in pain. Surely now, here, there could be only agony . . .

Would that it were so.

Even this . . . even this. My body betrayed me, accommodating the agony, inner flesh torn, slick with desire and blood, accommodating . . . him, the dreadful iron reaving me in twain, all of it. I laid my cheek on the bedclothes, scratching roughly with the rhythm of his thrusting, staring onto darkness. Let him kill me with it, I thought. Let him. Pleasure mounted, inexorable, unspeakable. My fingers clenched on the bedclothes, clenched and released. A crimson veil fell over my vision. I could hear his breath, coming harshly now; he had released my nape, both hands clutching my hips, loins thrusting. The iron nubs . . . Elua!

What damage was it doing? I hoped he would never stop. I hoped I would die.

In the scarlet haze, Kushiel's face swam before me, loving and remorseless, bronze eyes heavy-lidded and downcast. In one hand . . . in one hand he held forth a diamond, hanging from a velvet cord. I stared at it, blinking, while the Mahrkagir labored behind me. Darkness surged in waves as Kushiel bent low over me, murmuring a tender benediction over my averted face, offering. The diamond dangled from his hand, refracting light from myriad facets, filling my gaze as the awful pleasure rose and rose. . . .

. . . until I breathed in, sharply, uttering a broken cry, and the diamond fractured; light, Blessed Elua, the *light*, dazzling, a thousand stars, drawn in through my gasping mouth, spangling the very blood in my veins, bursting inside of me, opening a window onto a universe more vast, more unfathomable . . .

The Mahrkagir groaned and stiffened, his entire body going rigid with the force of his climax. When it was done, he slumped over me a moment, laying his face against my back, my fair skin adorned with the work of a master marquist, striped by the weals of a crop.

"Phèdre," he murmured, withdrawing from me. "Ah, Phèdre!"

Empty of him, Kushiel's presence deserted me. I curled on my side, willing the last agonizing throbs of desire to fade. With all pleasure gone, the pain came in its wake, and it was formidable. The Mahrkagir sat beside me and stroked my face, delighted with himself, with me. "You love me," he said. "At least a little bit. Is it not so?"

"It is," I said wearily, unable to lift my head. "At least a little bit. It is so, my lord."

"I knew it!" He rose from the sleeping pallet, heedless of the iron phallus still jouncing at his loins, unbuckling its straps. "This," he said, raising it reverently, tasting the mingled fluids that darkened it with the tip of his tongue. "This will be for you and no other."

"As my lord wishes." I looked away, unable to watch.

Ignoring me, he went to rummage in a chest, throwing aside sundry gifts of tribute; pelts, gold chains, a box of Bhodistani spices. "Ah!" Pleased at having found what he desired, the Mahrkagir returned to the bed-pallet, clutching in one hand a carved jade effigy of a dog. "Here," he said, presenting it to me. "It is a gift, for you. From Ch'in, I think. Because you are my favorite, now."

I made myself kneel, dragging my aching limbs into position, huddling against the cold shivers that had begun to overtake me. "My lord is too kind."

"Yes." He smiled at the scowling jade face of the dog, its fierce features. "There was a dog tonight, do you remember it burning?" I nodded, unable to speak for the lump of horror in my throat. "This is so you will not forget."

"I do not think, my lord," I forced the words out, "that I will ever forget tonight."

"I forget things." The Mahrkagir's unfocused gaze wandered about the room. "Tahmuras said I had a dog, once. It was in the zenana, where he found me. Someone had flung it against a wall. It had blood on its jaws, though." He laughed. "I think it bit an Akkadian."

"You remember nothing from before?" I asked.

He shook his head. "Only the weight of bodies piled atop me. There was a woman's face, so close." He put one hand against his nose. "She had been strangled, and her eyes bulged in their sockets. I could feel one touching my cheek. Maybe it was my mother, I don't know."

A horrible wave of nausea and pity swamped me, making my heart lurch oddly. "When I was four," I said, "I was sold into servitude in a brothel."

"And you were born again as something else." The Mahrkagir's face glowed with understanding. "Something *more*." He held my face with his cold, cold hands. "Your gods were shaping you, Phèdre. There are forces at work here I dared not dream. But Angra Mainyu knew! Oh, he knew. We are alike, you and I. I summoned you, through the three-fold path. You were made for me."

I saw my twinned reflections in his gleaming black eyes, my face tear-stained, swollen-mouthed, nodding in helpless agreement. He smiled and released me.

"Tahmuras will take you back," he said, adding, "Don't forget your dog!"

And so I went, clutching the jade dog in one hand.

There was a passageway from the Mahrkagir's quarters that led to the lower halls outside the zenana. I walked with difficulty, bracing my free hand against the wall. Tahmuras waited patiently, watching to see if he would need to carry me; I daresay he'd done it often enough. My limbs felt leaden, as they had in my dreams, and my body ached in myriad places. I could feel my inner thighs sticky with blood, a dull agony between them. I clenched my teeth and ignored it, along with a mounting dizziness.

And then we were there, and Tahmuras scratched at the latticed door, and Nariman the Chief Eunuch received me, his small eyes alight with cruel pleasure. He had already had his orders. I hadn't expected that.

It was morning, and the zenana was already astir. I hadn't expected that, either. I stood wavering on my feet, praying I would neither vomit nor faint, while a hundred eyes stared at me with unalloyed contempt. They knew. It had been seen, in the festal hall; witnessed, and reported. I had committed the greatest blasphemy they knew—I had desired my own debasement at the hands of Death. Nothing else could be so foul.

"Here is Phèdre of Terre d'Ange!" Nariman cried in a high, triumphant voice. "The Shahryar Mahrkagir has chosen a new favorite." No one spoke. Nariman shoved me. "Go to your couch and get your things. Hiu-Mei's room is to be yours. She died," he added carelessly, "in the night."

I went, placing one foot in front of the other. No one met my eyes, not even Drucilla. I concentrated on the placement of my feet. It hurt to walk. I had not remembered that the zenana was so large. The stagnant reek of the pool made me feel ill. I stared at the tiled floor, the bare aisles between the carpets. Once, I drew too near someone's couch and saw a figure shrink, whisking back her skirts lest my touch contaminate them.

Blessed Elua, what have you done to me?

I paused for a moment, gathering myself, then continued. It must be near; surely, I had reached my couch! I raised my head to look . . .

. . . and saw him.

He was standing in my path, fists clenched, half-shaking with rage. A slight figure, standing no taller than my breastbone, his face white and bloodless, a shocking beauty. His eyes blazed like sapphires in that vivid, white face and his hair, lank and tangled, still fell with a blue-black sheen.

"Imriel," I said softly.

With a viper's speed, he darted forward and spat in my face, retreating before I could react, dodging around a set of couches.

Somewhere in the zenana, someone clapped; someone loosed a shrill laugh.

A warm gob of spittle slid down the side of my nose. I took a deep breath, fixing my gaze on my couch, a few yards away, Valère L'Envers' marten-skin coat tossed carelessly at one end. I took one step, and then another. The room reeled crazily in my vision. I saw the couch hurtling skyward in a smooth arc and understood that I was falling.

The last thing I saw before the tiled floor rose up to meet me was that someone had defecated upon my coat. Then darkness claimed me, and I knew no more.

FORTY-SEVEN

"THIS WILL hurt."

Drucilla's voice was impersonal, all of yesterday's—was it only yesterday?—warmth gone. I knelt without moving as she smeared a pungent salve on various weals and cuts. It stung like fury. "Camphor?" I asked.

"Camphor and birch oil, mixed with lard." She sealed the jar. "The Tatars use it on their horses, and themselves as well. It is the only thing I can get." A muscle in her jaw twitched with distaste as she nodded at my lower regions. "I should examine you. Women have taken septic and died before."

I let her, shifting to allow her access, gritting my teeth against the burn; Drucilla had not wiped the camphor liniment from her fingers. It felt . . . ah, Elua.

"It could be worse. Most are." Straightening, she did wipe her hands, as if she had touched somewhat foul. "Your . . . willingness . . . made it easier. You're already beginning to heal."

"I heal quickly," I murmured bitterly, leaning my head against the wall of my private chamber. It is true. It is the only gift Kushiel ever saw fit to give me.

Drucilla gave a brusque nod. "You bathed thoroughly?"

"Yes." There were some merits to being the Mahrkagir's favorite. Rushad had brought me a basin unbidden. I'd gotten him to boil the bedclothes, too; Hiu-Mei had died in them, infected by an unnamed pox.

"Then that is all." Gathering her things in a basket, Drucilla turned to go.

I struggled into my gown, watching her, suddenly, desperately bereft. No one else had even spoken to me; not even Rushad would meet

my eyes. I daresay Drucilla wouldn't have either, if she were not clinging to her physician's identity as her sanity.

"Drucilla," I said as she parted the hanging curtain of beads that
served for a door. She halted, her back to me. "Drucilla, I am an
anguissette. I was chosen by the gods to find pleasure in enduring pain."

She did turn around, then, still holding her basket, a frown creasing
her brows. "Why would your gods do such a thing?"

"To preserve balance." I held her eyes, keeping my voice steady,
trying not to betray the dreadful urgency I felt to make one friend, one
ally. "So say the priests of Kushiel, the god who has marked me as his
own. Because there are people born into this world—or made by it—
who lack all compassion, whose pleasure is only to own, to possess, to
destroy. To hurt." I thought of the priest, Michel Nevers. " 'To endure
suffering untold, with infinite compassion.' That is the balance, so they
say."

Drucilla swallowed; once, twice, and the blood drained from her
face. "Who *are* you?" she whispered, staring at me as if seeing me
anew. "And why have you come here?"

"I had a friend, once," I said slowly, praying I had not revealed
too much. "When I was a captive . . . another place, another time. He
was a Hellene man, a slave, a physician's grandson in Tiberium, freed
by pirates. And now you, here . . . a physician of Tiberium, captured
into slavery in Hellas." I looked at her, standing with her maimed hands
clutching the handles of her basket. "If I had an answer to your question, Drucilla, it might be worth my life to speak it."

"First do no harm." A measure of strength returned to her voice,
her frowning face. She set down the basket. "Whatever or whoever you
are, Phèdre nó Delaunay, know this. I am a physician. I have sworn
the sacred oath of Hippocrates, of which that is the first tenet. The day
I violate it is the day I die. I cannot promise you I won't, in this place.
Only that I will never do it of my own will."

I nodded. It was enough; it had to be. "I've come for the boy."

"*Imri?*" Drucilla's voice rose in surprise; her knees gave way and
she sat down abruptly on the bed, giving a startled laugh. "Are you
mad?" she asked, eyeing me with uncertainty, feeling at my forehead.
"It may be fever, or the violence done you . . . Phèdre, you would not
be the first to escape into fantasy—"

"No." I caught her hand. "Ask him, if you doubt; he will not speak
to me. Ask him if it is not true that he was raised by priests in the
Sanctuary of Elua, if he was not captured by Carthaginian slave-traders

while herding goats." I released my grip on her. "They took him to Amílcar, and sold him to a Menekhetan, Fadil Chouma. It was Chouma who sold him to a *Skotophagotis*, to one of the Mahrkagir's priests."

Drucilla's hand slid over her mouth, eyes wide with shock. "How can you know this?"

"I learn things." I thought, for some reason, of my lord Delaunay. "It is what I am good at, along with enjoying pain."

For a time, she sat saying nothing, knotting the folds of her shawl. "You have a plan?"

I shook my head slowly.

"You are mad, then." This time there was no uncertainty in her voice. "Who is he, anyway, that you would walk into the jaws of Death for him? He doesn't even know you!"

"I know." I shifted on the bed, experimenting. The liniment was doing its work. The sting was fading, and the pain with it. A few hours of sleep had done the rest. I was Kushiel's Chosen. I would heal, whether I liked it or not. "It doesn't matter. He doesn't even know himself. I have to try."

"You know there is nothing I can do to aid you." Drucilla held out both hands before her, worn and maimed, the tissue pink and scarred on the stumps of her fourth and fifth fingers. "This is all I have; this, and some Tatar horse-liniment."

"You have Imriel's ear," I said. "Convince him, if you can, to hear me. And you can look at me as if I am not something one finds on the bottom of one's shoe."

Drucilla nodded doubtfully, unconvinced of either skill. "What of the D'Angeline lordling?" she asked, standing to go. "The one who swore his sword to his lordship's service?"

There were limits to my trust. I was willing to risk my life. Not Joscelin's. I shook my head, letting a touch of frost into my voice. "His business is his own."

So passed my first day as the Mahrkagir's favorite.

That night, he sent for me again. I went, of course; I had no choice in the matter. My companions were different ones. The Menekhetan boy had died—of internal injuries, Drucilla thought. A chirurgeon might have saved him, though perhaps not.

It was different, this time. Word spread quickly in Daršanga, and anyway, they knew. Like the women of the zenana, they had seen it last night. I was different. I was Death's Whore. The Drujani greeted me with obscene cheers. The kneeling Magi lifted up their faces as I passed to stare at me with horror and disgust. The priest Gashtaham smiled to himself like a cat licking cream. The Mahrkagir . . . he was smiling, too, his manic smile, one hand extended as I went to him, black eyes gleaming. I took my place at his side.

How many nights did I sit there beside him, at the head table in the festal hall? I cannot say. I could not bear to count them. In truth, I am not certain which was worse, the bedchamber or the festal hall. What passed between us in private was horrible. I came to know, in that cold chamber, the lowest depths to which I was capable of sinking, the worst depravities. And the more I became the thing I despised the most, the more I craved them, the more I yearned for punishment and humiliation. It is not a place I willingly visit in my memories.

But the hall . . . the hall had Joscelin.

And that was harder to bear.

I had to see him, his beloved face as impassive as stone and twice as hard, and know that he was watching it all, hearing it all. I couldn't fail to see him in that dark, sullen hall, his fair hair gleaming, the proud, austere lines of his face, as splendid as distant mountains. And I knew, with every breath I drew, that he was living in hell.

He held his own among them, Joscelin did, although they tried him. A Tatar tribesman tried it that second night—ferocious, drunk on kumis and dangerous with it. I didn't see how it began, only heard the roar of approval when the fight was engaged. They cleared a space amid the tables, and the wagers went fast and furious. The Mahrkagir watched it with unalloyed pleasure, one hand on his wine-cup, one hand on me, eager as a boy for the spectacle. I watched it with my heart in my throat, digging my nails into my palms, my face expressionless.

The Tatar bristled with weapons, clad in furs and plated leather. In one hand he held a short spear, and the other a sword. Stamping his feet, he roared out a challenge in an unintelligible tongue. I never did learn to speak Tatar, or the myriad dialects of it. Joscelin merely bowed, crossed vambraces visible beneath the sleeves of his sheepskin coat. The hilt of his sword rode over his shoulder, untouched. He held his daggers instead.

"Will he win, do you think?" the Mahrkagir asked me.

"Yes, my lord." I kept my voice dull. "He will win."

The Tatar moved, feigning a drunken stagger. On crouched legs, Joscelin slid to his left, daggers held low. With near-sober aplomb, the Tatar cocked his spear and threw it, hard, at point-blank range.

Joscelin's daggers swept up, crossing, catching the spear in mid-flight, honed edges biting into the wooden shaft, its point mere inches from his face. The Drujani roared, loving it. When all was said and done, Joscelin Verreuil had never lacked a flair for the dramatic. I bit my lip to hold back the tears, terrified of revealing how much I loved him.

After that, it was a foregone conclusion.

A leopard among wolves, Drucilla had called him; I saw it, during that fight. With daggers against a sword, vambraces against armor, Joscelin toyed with his Tatar opponent, moving with grace through the elaborate Cassiline forms. After all, it was his strength—it is what they train for, this close-quarters combat.

And he smiled as he fought, a deadly smile. It is the only time I saw him smile in Daršanga. I do not know how many times he cut his opponent, glancing blows, pricking his thighs, slipping through gaps in his rough armor. Many. Enough that the Tatar began to stumble for pain and loss of blood, swinging his sword with comic ineptness.

It was cruel. The Drujani pounded their cups and shouted with approval; the Tatars merely grumbled. And Joscelin smiled up to the moment he slit his opponent's throat with crossed daggers, opening bloody gills on either side of his neck. The Tatar gaped like a fish, his mouth opening and closing, dropping his sword, dropping to his knees, hands rising in vain. The Mahrkagir was laughing, flushed, boyish and happy.

I had not thought, until then, what Joscelin would have to do to survive in that place, nor what it would cost him.

With studied care, he wiped his blood-stained daggers on the Tatar's furs, then turned to the Mahrkagir and gave his Cassiline bow, restored to impassivity. "Shahryar. This man doubted the skill of the wolves of Angra Mainyu." His Persian, I thought, had become good; quite passable. He had learned more than I guessed, listening to Tizrav's lessons on the road to Daršanga. Blessed Elua only knew what he had learned since.

"Do you hear that?" The Mahrkagir rose, a hectic gleam in his eyes, lifting his cup. "It is folly to delay, my friends! Angra Mainyu prevails, and his time is coming. Once the Tatar agree—Kereyit, Kirghiz, Uighur, all the tribes—and Daeva Gashtaham and the other Âka-Magi decree it is time, the forces of Drujan will sweep across the land and armies fall and the priests of foreign gods will quail before us! Is it not so? Already, there is tribute sent. Jossalin Veruy," he announced with a magnanimous gesture, "Bringer of Omens, I give you pick of any woman in the zenana! If none here pleases you, go choose another."

I heard my breath hiss between my teeth.

Joscelin stood unmoving. His gaze rested on me. "Shahryar Mahrk-agir, I have given the only woman worth having to you," he said in a flat voice. "After her, there is no other."

"Bring him a boy, then," the Mahrkagir said, laughing, to Tah-muras. "What do you say? Shall we give him the D'Angeline boy, whose suffering caught the ear of his fearful gods? Why not, now? Perhaps it is a fitting step on the three-fold path!"

Behind him, Daeva Gashtaham stirred. "Shahryar," he murmured in warning.

What it meant, I could not say; I was caught in Joscelin's gaze, unable to look away. For an instant, a brief instant, I saw something human surface in his eyes. Does he know? it asked me. Does Imriel know? I gave my head an infinitesimal shake in reply. If I could, I would have told him to say yes, to accept the offer, to tell Imriel who we were, why we had come. But all I could do was answer the one silent question asked.

"Shahryar." Joscelin interrupted with a bow. "I desire nothing."

The Mahrkagir shrugged, already forgetting the impulse. "So be it. See, Gashtaham?" he added to the priest. "All is well."

I exhaled a breath it seemed I'd been holding for ages, and the evening's amusements continued. I could have wept at the lost oppor-tunity, at the brief glimpse of my beloved in the stranger's face Joscelin wore. I didn't. I sat at the Mahrkagir's side and watched the unholy license my presence had unleashed. His decree of last night held; the women of the zenana were fair game. The men took them, right there in the hall, as shameless as dogs. There was a line forming behind the prettiest. No wonder, I thought, they despised me so.

After a time, we retired to his bedchamber.

My heart beat too fast, and there did not seem to be enough air in the cold, dark room. I knew, this time, what it was; I knew what to fear. It would be worse, this time, my flesh already torn and bruised. I could not help but look for it, sending fearful glances toward the cup-board. The Mahrkagir watched me, smiling.

"This is what you fear, ishtâ," he said, taking it out and pressing the cold, nubbed iron against my cheek. "This is what you crave."

It smelled like death and desire. "No," I whispered. "Not crave."

"You will." He took it away and put it back in the cupboard. I concentrated on my own vast relief and ignored the sickened twinge of disappointment. The Mahrkagir smiled and caressed my hair. "It is easy enough to destroy your body. It is harder to consume your soul. I will wait. And in time, you will ask for it. Is it not so?"

"No," I whispered again, and this time I knew it for a lie.

It did not matter; Angra Mainyu delights in lies. I felt the encompassing darkness of Daršanga revel in my unwilling desire; a god's amusement, boundless and incomprehensible. The Mahrkagir laughed, something ancient and untamed looking out of his black, black eyes, and only sodomized me quickly and brutally, sending me back to the zenana to curl on my bed in my private chamber, throbbing with unwanted, unfulfilled desire.

And cursing Kushiel's name.

ꜰORTY-EİGHT

İMRİEL DE la Courcel would not speak to me.

I tried approaching him on a number of occasions. Drucilla had tried, so she told me—speaking to him in Caerdicci, endeavoring to convince him to see me. Alas, she dared not reveal *why*, and Imri only made her a rude reply in zenyan and avoided her thereafter.

It is, I will say, a near-impossible task to corner an agile ten-year-old boy in a large, crowded space. I took some glum comfort in the fact that despite what he had endured, Imriel was hale enough to evade me. I daresay none of the others were; there were only two, now, and the Ephesian was lost in secondhand opium dreams.

I did not know, yet, how severely Imriel had been abused, nor what purpose the Mahrkagir had in mind for him; or had had in mind. I gleaned some hope from the fact that Gashtaham was unwilling to let him lend the boy. Mayhap . . . mayhap he had been spared the worst. Still, I could not know until I spoke to Imriel—and that, he refused to do.

How many efforts did I make? A dozen, at least, much to the amusement of the women of the zenana. In the end, I was always forced to give up the task. We were the only two D'Angelines and I was a pariah; to an extent, no one questioned my desire to speak with the boy. Only to an extent. If I had scrambled panting after him to the point of humiliation, they would have begun to wonder.

And my position was already precarious.

There had been no further incidents since the despoiling of my coat—which had scrubbed clean, more or less—but it was always a possibility. There was no logic to it. However bad matters grew in the festal hall, I had freed them from the Mahrkagir's attentions, which were more deadly; one might suppose they would be grateful for it. They were not.

"It is always so," Drucilla told me. "The favorite is always despised, and you doubly so."

And Imriel de la Courcel despised me most of all.

I did not blame him for it; I never have. Whether he knew it or not, the blood of two noble Houses ran in his veins, in all its attendant pride. Horse-breeders will say that qualities are transmuted in the blood. I believe it. Throughout his solitary travail, Imriel's pride and anger had kept him alive. And now, at last, to have a countrywoman appear only to prove the most craven and self-abasing of slaves—Death's Whore, the abject offering of weak gods, for so they believed me, in the zenana—no, I did not blame him.

I sought to woo him with kindness, instead, and when that failed, to catch him unawares. None of it worked, of course. If it hadn't been for the Skaldi, like as not I'd still be chasing him.

I'd caught him out as I returned from a trip to the privy closet, finding him engaged in an effort to pry a board from the door that led onto the barren garden. "Imriel," I said, blocking the foot of the low stair leading to the garden entrance. "I want only to speak to you."

Startling, he rose from a crouch to show me a feral snarl and leapt sideways from the low stair, sidling along the wall, eyes darting, seeking an opportunity for flight.

"Imriel." I followed him, watching warily. "Listen to me—"

Nearing the place where the Skaldi lad Erich slouched despondent along the wall, Imriel made his bid for freedom, lunging to hurdle the Skaldi's legs as if he were no more than a piece of furniture.

Without a word, Erich reached out a single, brawny hand, catching the back of Imriel's shirt and holding him fast. His eyes, grey-blue under a thatch of unwashed blond hair, met mine.

"Thank you," I murmured in Skaldic. He made no reply, turning his head to watch the boy, who was watching me. "Imriel," I said to him, speaking D'Angeline, knowing, at least, that no one else within a hundred miles would understand it. "I am Phèdre nó Delaunay de Montrève—"

Elua knows, he was fast; I'd seen it before, and I'd no doubt it took considerable speed to plant the knife in Fadil Chouma's thigh, not to mention the serving fork in the attendant. The Scions of Elua are gifted. But I am D'Angeline too, and if the blood that flows in my veins is not nobly gotten, it holds no less of the lineage of Elua and his Companions for it. My mother was an adept of the Night Court, and in Terre d'Ange, it means as much to be a whore's daughter as a prince's son. Even as his arm flashed out, I reacted, half-expecting it. After all, he was Melisande's son.

I caught his wrist, his clawed fingers reaching for my eyes, and held it, inches from my face. "Your mother sent me to find you."

For a moment he only stared, like an animal in a snare, trapped and vulnerable. And then rage suffused his features, vivid blood surging to stain his alabaster skin. "You *lie!*" he hissed, convulsing, tearing himself free from my grip, from the Skaldi's restraining hand. At loose, he spat violently onto the floor between us. "My mother is *dead!*"

"No." I watched him retreat, opening my empty hands to show I meant him no threat. "Imriel, I speak the truth. It is Brother Selbert who lied to you."

It stopped him in his tracks, and there was an instant of recognition. For a moment, we merely looked at one another. Then, with a low sound, Imriel turned and bolted, a rabbit fleeing the trap. I let him go, kneeling beside the Skaldi. "Thank you," I said gravely to him. "If there is aught I might do, aught that might increase your comfort . . ."

Without a sound, Erich turned away, facing the wall. I sighed, stooping, and kissed his brow, then returned to my chamber.

After that, Imriel shadowed me at a distance, warily curious. I let him. No matter what he had survived—and I shuddered to think on it—he was a boy, carrying a hurt and rage few adults could bear. If he were pushed, he would lash out; and if I pushed before he was ready, it would be I who suffered for it. One word of betrayal was all it would take. I would not risk it coming from the lips of a hurt, angry child.

One good thing came of the encounter, and that was that it restored the Persian eunuch Rushad's allegiance to me. His beloved Erich had reacted, had undertaken some action affirming life. It was enough, for him. He came to speak with me thereafter, and did me small kindnesses unasked.

"Drucilla said you were here, when it happened," I said to him one day, "serving the Akkadian commander. How did it happen, Rushad? How did the Mahrkagir rise to power? Who are the *Skotophagoti*, the Âka-Magi? Do they truly hold power over life and death?"

"You ask many questions, lady," he murmured, picking up the figurine of the jade dog and studying it. "I was a slave, only, tending to my lord's wife in the zenana. I know only what I have heard."

"What have you heard?" I asked, coaxing the story from him.

From what I gathered, much of the rebellion had taken place underground, as it were, among the lower echelons of Drujani society. Hoshdar Ahzad's family was slain, and most of the Old Persian nobles among them. The Mahrkagir, rescued by Tahmuras, was raised in secret, amid the legions of servants who attended upon General Zaggisi-Sin, the Akkadian commander of Daršanga; a strange boy, eyes all pupil, unable to bear the light, prone to laugh at inappropriate times. Still, he was Hoshdar Ahzad's son, and as he came of age, the stories circulated.

And they came to other ears. It was the priest Gashtaham who divined the signs, who determined what the Mahrkagir's strangeness portended. Somehow I was not surprised to hear it. A Magus-in-training, it was he who first put forth the notion of turning away from Ahura Mazda, the Lord of Light, to embrace the worship of Angra Mainyu.

"He killed his own father," Rushad whispered, dropping his voice even in the relative privacy of my chamber. "That is what they say. It is the offering, the glorification; vahmyâcam, they call it. The dedication to Angra Mainyu: to destroy that which is pure and good. To kill what one loves the most." He looked nervously from side to side, confiding, "He ate his father's heart. And he wears his finger-bones at his waist."

"I have seen it." I remembered, sickened. "And thus he gained power?"

"Yes," Rushad said, still whispering. "All of them. They called upon Death, and Death answered. Daeva Vahumisa ate his brother's heart, and Daeva Dâdarshi, his wife's . . . oh, there are many. And the people . . . the people were angry, because Ahura Mazda had not protected them. When they saw that the Âka-Magi held power, they followed. And there was a, a mighty rebellion. The Âka-Magi raised up the Mahrkagir, and the people followed. First . . ." he swallowed, ". . . first, they overthrew the temples. And then riders went out, all across the land, riders went out to the borders, the fortresses, quenching the fires . . ."

"They took the borders," I said. "And slew the garrison at Daršanga."

Rushad nodded, relieved at not having to explain it. "He laughed," he said. "The Mahrkagir laughed as he fought, spattered with blood from head to toe. No one touched him. The Âka-Magi would not let them, and Tahmuras protected him, Tahmuras and his morningstar. And shadows fled squealing along the walls, and Akkadians fought among themselves, and my lord Zaggisi-Sin died, choking on his own tongue, that someone cut off and shoved in his throat. And in the zenana . . ." He fell silent, looking at the wall. "They let me live because I was Persian. Sometimes I am sorry they did. I know . . . I know what happened thirty years ago, when General Chus-sar-Usar defeated Hoshdar Ahzad's forces. I have heard the stories, although I was not born, then. My lord . . . my lord was not like that. And his lady wife . . ." Rushad shook his head. "Well," he said. "They are dead, now. And the Mahrkagir rules. Soon," he added, "I think he will rule more than Drujan."

I thought about it, frowning. "Who rules whom, Rushad? Does the Mahrkagir rule the Âka-Magi, or is it the other way around?"

"Truly?" He shrugged, hugging his knees, sitting on my carpeted floor. "Lady . . . who is to say? The people . . ." He gave his nervous glance. "The people fear the Âka-Magi, and the soldiers follow the Mahrkagir. Both need the other. Who rules who? I cannot say."

"So the Mahrkagir does not possess the power of an Âka-Magus," I said.

"No," Rushad said simply. "He cannot, because he cannot make the vahmyâcam, the offering. The Mahrkagir remembers nothing of love, only death. Though he seeks, he has nothing pure to offer upon the altar. Nothing that is *his*. Daeva Gashtaham . . . Daeva Gashtaham says he is the doorway. The will of Angra Mainyu flows *through* him, to be made manifest in the Âka-Magi." Still holding his knees, he shuddered. "How fearful he would be if he held that power!"

Truly, I thought; fearful indeed.

And I remembered how the priest Gashtaham had smiled, like a cat licking cream.

It made my blood run cold to think on it.

Because my lord Delaunay trained me to seek answers, because he raised me to believe all knowledge, no matter what the cost, is worth having, I pursued the matter. It was not hard to do. In the festal hall, Daeva Gashtaham was ever at hand, the resident Âka-Magus of Dar-šanga, spreading his invisible cloak of protection over the Mahrkagir. In truth, he sought me out, hovering at my shoulder like a blowfly over a corpse. I do not know why. That it was part of his greater plan— yes, that I was coming to understand. But there was an attraction that ran deeper. It may be only that it pleased him to see me flinch when his shadow fell over my flesh.

Or it may have been something deeper, something the Drujani priest himself did not understand. I cannot say. It is a question for the theologians to settle, for I do not like to think on it. Nonetheless, I made myself speak to him.

The priest was sitting at my left side on the night that I chose, watching that evening's entertainment: an impromptu "chariot" race staged by a pair of the rowdier young soldiers, using the Magi—the true Magi, priests of Ahura Mazda—as horses. It was painful to watch, the elderly men scrambling undignified on hands and knees, lengths of rope between their teeth, filthy robes hiked up to reveal spindly, aging shanks. The soldiers trotted behind them, holding the ropes like reins in one hand, whooping, lashing the Magi with crops when they slowed.

"Ah, Arshaka." Gashtaham smiled, shaking his head, watching the eldest of the Magi scramble, tripping over his own beard. "Old man," he said, caressing the length of his jet-headed staff, "you should have had the courage to die."

Almost as if he had heard, the ancient Magus lifted up his head, gazing at Gashtaham. The priest continued to smile and stroke his staff, dark shadows pooling in the eye-sockets of his boar's-skull helm. Something in the Magus' gaze blazed, then quailed; lowering his head, he scurried forward, unsuccessfully seeking to avoid a soldier's boot planted between his scrawny buttocks. To my right, the Mahrkagir laughed, clapping.

"The Magus fears you, Daeva Gashtaham," I said in a low voice.

"Should he not?" The priest bent his smile upon me. It held no madness, only the promise of vile things wriggling in the darkness. "He was a wise man, once, the Chief Magus."

"And wise men fear." I held his gaze, quelling the urge to shrink away from it. "In Menekhet, they name you Eaters-of-Darkness; they believe they will die before sundown, if your shadow touches their flesh."

"You have borne its touch," Gashtaham said, "and lived. Do you believe?"

"I do not know," I said honestly. "In Daršanga, they say only that the Âka-Magi hold power over life and death. I do not know if it is true, Daeva Gashtaham."

"Ah." He nodded. "Then you shall see, since you asked it." Rising to his feet, he extended his staff, pointing across the tables, pointing to the open space beyond, directly at the second chariot-Magus as he crawled frantically across the flagstones of the desecrated temple, the rope bit between his teeth. I saw the Magus stiffen, rising to his knees, the rope falling as his mouth gaped wide, both age-spotted hands clutching at his robe over his heart. The soldier behind him cursed and whipped him about the head and shoulders.

'Twas to no avail; a deep tremor shook him, and his eyes glazed. His body crumpled sideways, making little sound as it fell.

"Death," Daeva Gashtaham mused, taking his seat, ignoring my horror-stricken expression and the rumbles of annoyance from the Drujani audience deprived of its amusement. "It is a constant presence among us, do you not think, Phèdre nó Delaunay? Every instant, waking or sleeping, we are but one step away from it, holding it at bay with each breath we take. You may have . . ." he reached out with one long finger to touch my breastbone, ". . . such a flaw in your heart, waiting to burst. Or perhaps you might trip upon your skirts . . ." he twitched the folds of my gown almost coyly, ". . . and fall upon the stairs, splitting open your skull. It may be a disease, yes; a pox, an ague, a wasting sickness. In the zenana, a woman coughs; is there death in her sputum? It may be so. Perhaps your horse will stumble, and drag you; perhaps a raft will overturn, and you will be swept away in the torrents. Or perhaps . . ." he smiled, and caressed my cheek, "it lies within."

I shuddered to the bone, and hid it. "You have made an ally of Death."

"I have." Gashtaham looked at me with something like regret. " 'Tis a pity you are a woman. If my apprentices were half so clever, I would be pleased. Still, you may serve your purpose."

What that was, I did not ask.

I was afraid I already knew.

ᏁORTY-ΠΙΠΕ

İ HAVE not spoken of the desire, nor how long I resisted it.

Mayhap it is that such a thing need not be said. At times, I kept it at bay; for long hours, sometimes. In the zenana, I relied upon my wits, constantly observing, gauging the ebb and flow of hatred, the secret alliances, the undercurrents of despair. Where the dim spark of defiance sputtered and refused to die, I took note, finding it in Drucilla's endless physician's rounds, in the bitter survival of the Akkadian warrior-eunuchs, in Kaneka's impromptu court of superstition. I found it in the dignity of the fasting Bhodistani, until they died; I found it too in individual women, here and there, especially the fierce Chowati. I found it in Erich the Skaldi's single gesture, and the fact that he had not yet abandoned life.

Most of all, I found it in Imriel de la Courcel, who was at odds with everyone and everything, and who continued to skulk at the edges of my existence.

I had a carpet set outside the door to my chamber, and there I would sit or kneel, watching the zenana. It drew comments, which I ignored. I could not afford to lurk within my walls and remain ignorant. I watched Imriel return time and again to the garden passageway, worrying at the boards. Like his mother, he despised his cage, and yearned for a glimpse of sky. When Nariman the Chief Eunuch was watching, the Akkadian attendants would pull him away. And he fought them, tooth and claw; it was one of the Akkadians he had stabbed with a fork. For all that, I saw, they accorded him a certain forbearance. It may have been due to the Mahrkagir's plans for him, though I suspected they harbored an appreciation for Imriel's defiant spirit.

Once, one brought him to my carpet, slung over his broad shoulder, spitting and kicking. It was the attendant from the first night—Uru-

Azag, his name was—who had guided the Menekhetan boy.

"Khannat, Uru-Azag," I said to him, bowing from my seated position. "Thank you."

Something glimmered in the Akkadian's dark eyes. "Yamodan," he replied briefly, shaking his forearm where Imriel had bitten him; you are welcome.

Imriel crouched, one hand touching the floor, regarding me warily. "Uru-Azag is not your enemy," I said to him in D'Angeline. "You do wrong to fight him."

"Death's Whore!" He bared his teeth in a snarl, black hair falling in a tangle over his brow. "Mother of Lies! I know who my enemies are!"

"Do you?" I asked. "So do I. Fadil Chouma was your enemy, was he not? He is dead, now; did you know it? You stabbed him, in Iskandria—stabbed him in the thigh with a carving knife. The wound took septic, and he died. I know your enemies better than you do, Imriel."

Alarm widened his twilight-blue eyes and his mouth worked soundlessly. Deprived of adequate words, he spat once more onto the tiles between us, and fled, overturning an Ephesian water-pipe in his flight. Muzzy curses followed him, which he ignored, taking refuge at the couch-island of some Hellenes, who were glad enough of a boy-child to stroke and pet, having none of their own. His eyes, his mother's eyes, continued to watch me, gauging my reaction.

Those were the good times in the zenana.

During the bad times . . . during the bad times, I was conscious of the desire. I remembered it, the blood-dark throbbing, Kushiel's brazen wings buffeting my ears and the light, the glittering light, the cold iron nubs rending my flesh. I wanted it again; Elua, but I did! When I was weak, when I let myself remember, horrified, the face of the poor Magus, seized in a rictus of death, I knew the chains of blood-guilt lay heavy on my soul. I had undergone the *thetalos*. I knew. And I saw Joscelin and his deadly smile, playing cat-and-mouse with the Tatar. My fault; my doing. And it seemed, at those times, that nothing would redeem me, that the only absolution I might find lay within the Mahrkagir's bedchamber, the dank air and his icy fingers digging into my flanks, oiled leather straps creaking as I welcomed the reaving iron into my flesh.

My title, my name, my very will . . . all laid upon the altar of destruction.

Only then would it *stop*.

In time, I asked him for it. No; that is wrong. In time, I begged. I do not pretend to be more than I am. There were times, in that place, when the tides of my soul ebbed, and I saw only darkness, only despair. You must make of the self a vessel where the self is not, Eleazar ben Enokh had told me, and this I sought; not in perfect love, but perfect self-loathing. Of a surety, he prompted me, the Mahrkagir, whispering in my ear as he used his rusted implements of pain, as he took me in some other orifice—do you not want *this?* He knew. There is a cunning in madness. As he whispered in my ear, Angra Mainyu whispered in his, and the dark wind blew through us both.

I begged.

And the Mahrkagir gave.

I was wrong, though; wrong about one thing. It did not make an end to it. For a time, it did; a time bounded by the endurance of my flesh—and his. Mad or no, the Mahrkagir was mortal. When it was over, it was over, and I was still alive, still Phèdre. Those are the times when I would lie shaking, curled on my side, throbbing with the aftermath of pain and fulfillment, and he would stroke my sweat-dampened hair as tendrils grew clammy on my brow, whispering endearments in Old Persian; ishtâ, he called me, beloved, smiling to see me tremble, srîra, beautiful one.

He was mortal, only a man, spent.

The Mahrkagir remembers nothing of love, only death . . . How fearful he would be if he held that power!

I remembered Rushad's words and Gashtaham's smile, and the Mahrkagir of Drujan caressed my quivering flesh, stamping it his, his own, every fiber of my Dart-stricken being answering to his icy touch, and I gazed into his black, black eyes, gleaming with madness and pride, and cursed the inevitable return of that flicker of consciousness within my skull, Delaunay-trained, proclaiming the awareness of *self.*

Because, knowing it, I could not fail to recognize the answering stir within the Mahrkagir himself; the tender line of his mouth, the lambency of his gaze, all announcing as loud as trumpets the dawning of that which he had never known, of that sacred mystery which is the province of Blessed Elua himself.

Love.

The only mercy was that he had no idea. I realized it the night he sought to scar my face, drawing the point of a rusty awl along my cheekbone. "Ishtâ," he whispered, watching me shudder and force myself to stillness. The point of the awl crawled over my skin. "Such beauty! It would be duzhvarshta indeed to despoil it."

Ill deeds. I closed my eyes, unable to bear it. Hot, stinging tears seeped from under my lids. I felt the awl, tear-moistened, tracing rusty patterns on my face, the tip prodding my cheek. Elua! Must I lose this, too?

When the awl clattered into the corner, I wasn't sure what had transpired. I opened my eyes to see his face, the wide black eyes bright with wonder. "I could not do it!" he said, gazing at his empty hands. A laugh burst from him, loose and free. "Do you know, ishtâ, I could not do it! How strange."

At that, I flung both arms about his neck and kissed him, all over his face.

In some ways, those were the worst times of all.

In the zenana, when I had nothing else to do, I would have my carpet moved so I could sit near the couches of the Jebeans and listen to their conversation, quietly shaping their words to myself. Kaneka and the others watched me with irritation, but dared not interfere. Imriel, as ever, lingered at a distance. I dreaded the day that the Mahrkagir would summon him to the festal hall. There had been a time in autumn, Drucilla had told me, when Imriel was a regular favorite; the Mahrkagir had kept him close by his side, and allowed no one else to touch him.

"Did he . . ." I had closed my eyes, ". . . *have* him?"

Drucilla was silent for a moment. "I don't know," she said at length. "I don't think so. But he wouldn't let me examine him, after. He might, now. But one day Gashtaham, the priest, came to the zenana. He spoke to Nariman. Since then, Imri has not been summoned."

"Do you know why?" I asked.

She shook her head. "The Mahrkagir was saving him for something . . . special. He was waiting for spring. Since you have come . . . Phèdre, I am uncertain. He has never favored *anyone* as he does you."

"I know," I murmured. "Elua help me, I know."

There was pity in her gaze. "It will not spare him, you know." She told me, then, of Jagun; a warlord of the Kereyit Tatars, fiercest of the lot, and like to return with the spring thaws, when the Mahrkagir's plans for conquest would be laid. And Jagun had a fondness for boys, especially Imriel, whom he had coveted with fierce desire. "He made an offer," she told me with reluctance. "The Mahrkagir refused, but—"

A boy of surpassing beauty, worth, mayhap, the allegiance of an entire Tatar tribe.

"Now he may be saving him for Jagun?" I had asked.

Drucilla had hesitated, then nodded. "I think so, yes. If you had not come . . . well, it may have been different. For a while, when he was summoned often, I thought Imri wished to die. Now . . ." Her mouth twisted. "Now he lives, filled with defiance. It will make the destruction of his hopes all the sweeter. The Mahrkagir," she had added, glancing at the Skaldi lad, "enjoys that. You would do well to remember it."

As if I were in danger of forgetting.

I knelt on my carpet, remembering what she had said, letting the distant Jebean words flow over me as I echoed them to myself, feeling sick at heart. Ah, Elua! It brought me hope to hear that Imriel might not have suffered what I had at the Mahrkagir's hands—but what a bitter jest that would be, if I had usurped his place only to condemn him to life as a Tatar's catamite. Spring. What season was it? Winter, still, I thought; I could not be sure. Days, nights . . . time was meaningless, in the zenana. Drucilla claimed to remember autumn, but she could not name the date. Time; a long time. She measured it by the healing tissue of her finger-stumps. It was as good a calendar as any, a fit one for Daršanga. I watched Imriel prowl the zenana, restless, drawn to the boarded garden-entrance, glancing over his shoulder for Nariman. One would know the season, I thought, in the garden, barren or no.

"Why?" It was Kaneka who stood before me, limbs akimbo, exasperated. Distracted, I'd not heard her rise from her couch. I swallowed, realizing that my voice had risen, still echoing their conversation.

"Yequit'a, Fedabin," I said politely. "I did not mean to disturb you."

"*Amon-Re!*" She said the god's name like a curse; a Menekhetan god, I thought. Strange, how the Jebeans had adopted the very customs and faith that the Menekhetans had abandoned. Kaneka looked at me, showing the whites of her eyes. "You see? Why, *here*, do you persist? Jeb'ez! Why do you seek to learn Jeb'ez?"

The Jebeans and Nubians were watching, whispering and laughing; I ignored them. Kaneka did not jest. It unnerved her. "Fedabin," I said in zenyan, looking up at her. I answered truthfully, clinging to the hope that lay within my words. "I want to learn Jeb'ez so I can seek the descendants of Makeda and Melek al'Hakim."

"You *what?*" There was disbelief in her tone.

Lifting my chin, I thought of Hyacinthe, framing my reply. "There is a man, Fedabin, under a terrible curse. He is my friend, my oldest friend." I told her, then, in Jeb'ez and zenyan, searching for words, laying out the story of Hyacinthe and the Master of the Straits, Rahab's Curse. And degree by slow degree, Kaneka's irate stance relaxed until she lowered herself to sit opposite me and listen with a bemused expression.

There was a good deal I left out—most of the Skaldic invasion, and the whole of my part in it. It didn't matter. It was Hyacinthe's story I told. It was enough. I was a bit player in it; an old friend, one-time lover, pursuing hope beyond reason, a key found in a Jebean scroll.

And yes, I left out Melisande, too. She was Imriel's story, now. If we lived, he would learn it. Not here, not the whole of it. There was only so much the boy could endure.

When I was done, Kaneka laughed.

It was not like before, harshly; this was deep and unfettered, and somehow wholly her own. She doubled over with it, tears of laughter gleaming like bronze against her dark skin. "Ah, little one! A face, moving on the waters; a whirlpool that speaks! And this man, with storms in his eyes, growing old without dying. It is a good story, truly."

"It is true," I said in a tone of offended dignity.

"Perhaps it is." Kaneka wiped her eyes. "Perhaps it is. So you seek the Melehakim?" I stiffened at the word, sending her into further peals. "Ah, my grandmother would enjoy you, little one! I would not have guessed it so. You tell a story as well as she."

"You know them," I said. "The descendants of the Queen of Saba."

"How not?" she asked, pragmatic. "My grandmother kept the stories for the village of Debeho. Well, then, little one, Death's Whore, if that is your quest, I will allow it. Eavesdrop if you will, and learn Jeb'ez. I will not dissuade you."

"Thank you," I said, inclining my head.

Kaneka looked at me strangely, fingering the pouch that held her dice. "You believe in this story, this curse."

"Yes, Fedabin." *Show no weakness*, Audine Davul had told us, speaking of the Jebeans. *Give every courtesy, and never reveal fear.* "If you do not believe . . ." I nodded at the zenana, ". . . ask the Aragonians and the Carthaginians here if it is not true that the Straits have been opened for the first time in eight hundred years, freeing traffic to Alba. They may not know why, but they know it is so. I know why. I was there."

"If you were *there*," Kaneka said, "and what you seek lies in Jebe-Barkal, why are you *here*, little one?"

Her tone made it clear she thought the question unanswerable. I held her gaze unblinking. It was not an easy thing to do, for she was an imposing woman and held the will of the zenana in her power, such as it was. "You are the only one here who claims her gods still answer when she speaks to them. Ask them, Fedabin Kaneka. If they answer, we will both know."

"Ah." A harsh smile curved her lips. "And what will you give me for it?"

"Nothing." I shook my head. "You asked the question, not I."

She glanced over her shoulder, only now becoming aware of the incredulous stares of her countrywomen, of much of the zenana. Our conversation had gone on too long, far too long, to be the denunciation of me that they had expected—indeed, Kaneka had sat at my carpet and heeded my story, had *laughed*. I saw her shoulders stiffen and her nostrils flare. "I do not need to ask! Everyone knows. The gods of Terre d'Ange are weak and craven, the last-born. While the elder gods seek ways to resist Lord Death, the spineless servants of Terre d'Ange send him tribute!"

There were shouts and clapping from the couches of the Jebeans. Kaneka had risen to her feet to glower at me in threadbare majesty. I remained kneeling, hands folded in my lap, and raised my brows at her. "So says the Mahrkagir, Fedabin. Do you accept his words as truth?"

Her anger held a moment longer, then passed; Kaneka sighed, her expression rueful. "Death's Whore," she murmured. "You spoke truly, little one, when first we met. Whatever else they are, your gods are cruel."

And with that, I did not disagree.

ꟿꟷFTY

İT BEGAꟷ when I got Erich the Skaldi to remove the boards from the garden door.

Not all of them, only the lowest two, making an opening large enough for an agile adult to squirm through. It was on a day when Nariman the Chief Eunuch was gone for several hours, meeting with the Treasurer of Daršanga to discuss the zenana's accounts. Little enough though we were given, there was still the matter of the kitchen's supplies and staff, water-bearers, servants who emptied the privy closet's chamberpots.

Imriel was haunting the door's alcove, as usual, worrying splinters from the thick boards. I watched the Akkadian eunuch Uru-Azag observe him impassively.

"Greetings, Uru-Azag," I said to him. "Tell me, what would happen if the boy were to succeed, now, while Nariman is not present?"

He turned the same impassive face on me. "He will not, lady."

"Nonetheless," I said. "If he did?"

The Akkadian shrugged and looked away. "The garden walls are high, and there is no door leading out. The windows of Daršanga are shuttered. No one would see."

"So he would not be punished," I said.

Uru-Azag's eyes glittered. Of anyone in the zenana, the Akkadians despised me the least, despising themselves more. Most of their companions, the soldiers of Zaggisi-Sin, had died—properly, in battle, albeit in the grip of a madness they could not comprehend. Those who remained, the attendants of the zenana, had chosen survival and paid the price of their manhood. "For a glimpse of sky?" he asked. "No. Not while Nariman is not present."

"Khannat," I said, inclining my head. "Thank you." And I went to see Erich.

Usually, I spoke gently to him in Skaldic, cajoling. This time, I merely stood over him without speaking. For a long while, he ignored me. I waited until he bestirred himself and looked up at me, blue-grey eyes blinking through his lank hair. In the alcove, Imriel crouched and watched, wary as an animal.

"Help him," I said to Erich.

I didn't think he would . . . and then I heard a sound, as he did. It was Rushad, on the far side of the zenana, stuffing his knuckles against his mouth to stifle an outcry as the Skaldi rose. He moved slowly, Erich did. For how long—weeks? months?—he had risen only to use the privy, and that seldom more than once a day. Hours of immobility had stiffened his joints. For all that, he was a young man, and strong.

There was a silence in the zenana as he mounted the short stair. I held my breath. At a single word, it would be over. Someone would betray us; someone would fetch Nariman. And then we would be punished, all of us—Erich, Imriel and me, mayhap the Akkadians, too.

No one spoke. I felt curiosity prickling on my skin, a stirring of interest, *life*.

For the first time, I remembered something of Blessed Elua's golden presence.

The iron nails screeched as Erich set to and heaved, muscles straining across his shoulders, the tendons in his arms standing out. The lowest board came loose, clattering on the tiled step. A breath of cold air swept through, fresh and clean, smelling of the sea. I fought an urge to laugh, or weep. Erich leaned his head against the rough planks, resting, drawing in the air in great gulps. Imriel, flattened against the wall, stared at the gap in starved disbelief.

The second board, better nailed, came harder. Erich loosened one end, but the other was fixed tight and flush and his fingers could find no purchase. Silent as ever, he shook his head.

"*Shamash!*" The curse came from behind me; I turned to see Uru-Azag snatch the curved dagger all the Akkadians wore from his belt. "Lady," he said, handing it to me. "Give him this."

Erich worked the thin blade under the board, prying down on the hilt. The wood creaked, and the nails gave—only an inch, but enough to get his fingers beneath the board. His strength did the rest. And there was the gap, large enough to admit a person.

"Tell him to dig out the nail-holes," a woman's voice said in zenyan. I turned to see a Carthaginian woman, and several others watching behind her. "My father was a carpenter," she said. "If he widens the holes, we can put back the planks and Nariman will not see."

I nodded, relaying her instructions in Skaldic. Erich worked the point of the dagger into the holes, enlarging them. Despite the cold air, beads of sweat stood on his forehead.

"Like so," the Carthaginian said, going to help him. Together, they fit the upper board back in place. It held. The lower board proved more stubborn, two of the nails bent. "Here," she said, passing it back, miming pounding with a hammer. "Someone. The nails must be made straight."

Taking the board gingerly, two Ephesian women laid it on the floor and began beating at the bent nails with the heels of their slippers. By now, nearly half the zenana had crowded around to watch. A Chowati berated them, attempting to describe a better method. One of the Akkadian eunuchs came over to kneel beside them, drawing his dagger and pounding the nails with the hilt.

"Rushad," I murmured, slipping through the crowd to find him. "Someone should watch for Nariman's return."

"It is already being done, lady." He pointed toward the latticed door, where two Menekhetans stood watch at careful angles.

A stifled cheer went up from the assembled group; the nails were straightened, and the board fit snug once more. To the casual observer, it looked unaltered. Erich removed the boards, and they came easily. He leaned them both against the alcove, and went back to take up his post once more, sitting with his back to the wall.

Everyone else stood staring spellbound at two feet of cold air and grey light.

Imriel, taut and quivering, caught my eye, and there was a naked plea on his face.

"Yes." I nodded. "Go."

Like a flash, he crawled through the gap. Now that it was done, no one else dared follow, awed by the audacity of what we had done. I stood irresolute, longing to go, but fearful of putting myself forward. Whatever had happened here, it was a fragile alliance. If they remembered how much they despised me, it would die an early death.

"Lady," said Uru-Azag, pointing at me. "Your place is second."

It was better, coming from him. It left me no choice. Walking slowly through the crowd, I mounted the stair, gathering my skirts about me. I had to duck low to clamber through the opening, and the rough planks caught at my hair.

And then I was through, and there was frozen earth beneath my knees, a dizzying sense of openness above me. I stood up, gasping, filling my lungs with searingly cold air. Elua, the sky! It was wintry and grey and utterly magnificent. At the farthest corner of the garden stood Imriel, arms wrapped about himself, teeth chattering, a look of pure delight on his face.

Others followed, after that; not many, when all was said and done. The Carthaginian carpenter's daughter came, and two Chowati. An Akkadian woman with haughty brows, but none of the eunuchs. I did not blame them. They had done as much as they dared, and more. One of the Ephesians poked her head through the opening and withdrew, shivering. It was cold, it is true, terribly cold. For once, I did not care, nor that the garden was completely barren. It was mayhap thirty paces on each side, a dry fountain at its center, stone walls thrice as high as a man's head encompassing dead soil and crumbling paths. I saw tears in the eyes of the carpenter's daughter as she stumbled across the frozen sod, gazing at the sky.

In that place, it was a paradise.

"Smell," said one of the Chowati, sniffing the air. "Spring comes behind the cold."

It put me in mind of Drucilla's warning, but even that could not dampen the exhilaration. All too soon, someone gave a sharp whistle—Uru-Azag, I daresay—and it filled us with urgent terror, setting off a scrambling race to return to the zenana. I made myself wait, going last. No one objected. For a moment, I feared that they would seal the boards and leave me—but no, there was Rushad on the inside, his eyes wide with fear as he extended a hand to help me through. Uru-Azag, his face oily with sweat, shoved the boards in place.

That evening, before the Mahrkagir's summons, Imriel came to my chamber.

He hovered inside the beaded doorway, uncertain and frowning in the light of my single oil lamp. I sat cross-legged on my bed, waiting. I lack Joscelin's gift with children, but this one, this child, I understood.

"Why did you say my mother sent you?" he asked.

"Because it is true," I replied. "She asked me to find you."

"No." Imriel shook his head, eyeing me suspiciously. "My mother is dead, and my father, too. They died of an ague aboard a Serenissiman ship and asked Brother Selbert to take care of me. I know, he told me so. Why would Brother Selbert lie? How do you know him?"

"Your father is dead, that much is true. But when you were eight," I said, ignoring his questions, "Brother Selbert took you to La Serenissima. And you met a lady there."

"No." A look of alarm crossed his face, and his mouth formed a hard line. "Never."

I remembered what he had been told; that the lady was his patron, and that she would be in grave danger if he revealed it. "It was partly true, Imriel, and the lie only to protect you. Brother Selbert believed his actions in accordance with the precept of Blessed Elua."

"Elua!" The word was an agonized curse in his mouth. "Elua is a *lie!*"

For that, I had no words; none that I could speak to this boy. Mayhap a priest or a priestess could have done, I do not know. I know none who have endured Daršanga. "She is your mother, Imriel," I said instead. "The Lady Melisande."

"*Why?*"

One word; a single demand. It is the question children ask most, I am told. It was a question of immense proportion, coming from Imriel de la Courcel's lips, and most of what it encompassed, I could not answer. I do not know the will of the gods. If Blessed Elua had willed Imriel's presence here, I could not say why. But Melisande Shahrizai, I knew, and it was to that I spoke. I had thought long and hard how I would answer this question without revealing the tale in all its horror. "Your mother did somewhat foolish, once, Imri," I said gently. "It is why she cannot leave La Serenissima, and it is why she has enemies. Because she loves you, she did not wish her enemies to become yours. And that is why she and Brother Selbert sought to protect you with a lie."

He looked away and I could see the shimmer in his twilight eyes, but his jaw clenched and no tears fell. I remembered the girl Beryl at the Sanctuary of Elua, composed beyond her years, speaking of Imri. *He was afraid of anyone seeing him cry.* My heart ached for the boy. "I don't believe you," he said through gritted teeth. "I don't believe you! Even if it were true, why would my mother send *you?*" His voice made his loathing plain. "Death's Whore!"

"Mayhap," I said, unflinching. "All the same, I found you."

And then Nariman came to summon me, and we spoke no more that evening.

It was a beginning.

*Ḟ*IFTY-O*N*E

THE *SKOTOPHAGOTIS* knew.

I was not sure, not until the night he urged the Mahrkagir to share me among his men. If I have not made it clear, I may say so now; Gashtaham was clever. Sometimes the Mahrkagir listened to him, and sometimes he did not. The priest had a knack of knowing when he was able to exert his will over the ruler of Drujan, and plying it expertly.

It was at one such time that he convinced the Mahrkagir to share me.

I could not hear what he said, not all of it. The priest murmured low into his lord's ear. I caught a word here and there, enough to gather the gist of it. I had grown haughty, over-proud, confident in the Mahrkagir's favoritism; I ruled the zenana like a queen, threatening to invoke my lord's displeasure on any who opposed me.

It was a lie, of course. Nothing had changed in the zenana except that I was viewed by some with wary skepticism instead of outright despite. The spirit of conspiracy that had opened the garden had not died, but it had returned to dormancy, waiting. And I had no plan to reawaken it, nor yet to make use of it.

"No favorite, my lord, but has known herself fit prey at the Mahrkagir's whim for the wolves of Angra Mainyu," the priest said smoothly. "It would be duzhvarshta indeed to shatter this hollow arrogance."

Restless with drink and boredom, the Mahrkagir agreed, a mad gleam in his eyes. "Tonight!" he shouted, banging his cup on the table. "Let it be tonight, then!" Grabbing my wrist, he rose to his feet, bringing me with him, holding my arm above my head as if to display a trophy. My lips formed a protest, but he was already addressing him. "*This* will be tonight's entertainment! Let the wolves of Angra Mainyu fight amongst themselves, and whosoever among you prevail shall have my lady Phèdre!"

They were on their feet, roaring, fierce, filthy warriors in piecemeal armor. It was all Drujani that night, no Tatars among them. I saw, for an instant, the dreadful shock register on Joscelin's face. "My lord, no," I whispered, even as the Mahrkagir dragged me by the wrist into the aisle between the tables, pushing me into a forming mêlée. "No."

After that, it was chaos. A Drujani warrior caught me in his arms, pulling me close and laughing; then another struck him hard atop the head with a dagger-hilt, and someone else grabbed me from behind. I don't know what happened to him. From the corner of my eye, I saw Joscelin borne down by a swarm of Drujani. One of them had leapt from the table atop his shoulders; he'd never even had a chance to draw his sword. I daresay he might have, that night. A pile of leather and steel and limbs writhed on the floor, giving evidence to his struggle. The others pressed close around me and I felt like Imriel, fighting with tooth and claw to keep them off as I was jostled and groped and snatched from one man by the next.

To no avail; a Drujani wielding a broadsword cleared a space around him and then flung down his blade, seizing me and bending me backward over a table, the heel of his hand under my chin. "Do it, Kishpa!" a voice behind him laughed. "We'll ward your back if you'll give us a turn!" The edge of the table pressed hard against my buttocks, and my neck was strained. Someone was holding my arms. Tears stung my eyes as he pressed himself between my thighs, fumbling at my skirts.

Then came shouting, and the sound of someone else waded into the fray. The pressure left my chin and my limbs were free. I straightened to see Tahmuras in the thick of battle, his morningstar a spiked blur as he whipped it in deadly patterns with effortless skill. Men yelped and dove out of the way. One was already down, the side of his head crushed and bleeding. Behind Tahmuras stood the Mahrkagir, unarmed, calm amid the chaos, his mad eyes watching. No one laid a finger on him; no one would dare. There was Tahmuras, for one thing—and a few paces away, there was Gashtaham, stroking his staff of office, gathering darkness around him. None of them seemed to care in the least that Drujani were being maimed or killed.

And I was still in the middle of it. A tall warrior staggered backward, knocking me half off my feet. Someone else lurched into my left side, and . . . how it happened, I cannot say. Only that I fetched up hard against Joscelin, who had somehow shaken his attackers and regained his footing.

I knew. Even before I saw, I knew. His hands closed on my upper arms, and I lifted my gaze to his face. Like the Carthaginian looking at the sky, I could have wept.

"Phèdre." He spoke quick and low in D'Angeline, his expression betraying nothing. "If I thought I could throw before the *Skotophagotis* killed me, I would perform the *terminus*. I don't. Blessed Elua had best make his will known fast, before I go mad here. I don't know how long I can endure this."

Elua's will. It was then that the first terrible inkling of suspicion dawned.

"I need time," I whispered. "I think . . . Please. A little while longer."

Joscelin said nothing, only released me and bowed, looking past me to the Mahrkagir. The fighting had settled. One man dead, and another dying; half a dozen others lay groaning. The Mahrkagir was smiling. "I changed my mind," he said calmly, taking my hand and leading me back to the head table. "Gashtaham, that was a foolish idea."

Like Joscelin, the priest only made a bow in reply, the girdle of finger-bones rattling at his waist. He had killed his own father and eaten his heart, and there was no annoyance at the Mahrkagir's rebuke in his expression, only the guarded satisfaction of a man who has confirmed a long-held theory. It made my skin crawl to see it, so I looked away. At the far end of the opposite bench, Tahmuras was wiping blood and bits of hair and flesh from his spiked mace. He gave me a long, measuring gaze, and there was hatred in his eyes.

He knew, too.

And he did not welcome the news.

That night, the Mahrkagir was zealous in his attentions and there was something new in his manner, heated and triumphant. With his hands and teeth, he tore at my flesh, leaving his mark on my skin. It was a conquest, not only of me, but of all others who sought to possess me, and his victory was in my yielding. I knew it well, for many of my patrons have been possessive. Whether he knew to name it or not—and I do not think he did—the Mahrkagir of Drujan had discovered the hot pleasures of jealousy that night.

It was what Gashtaham had sought to confirm.

Afterward, in the zenana, I asked Rushad how the vahmyâcam was made.

"As for that, lady, I cannot say. Only that the Âka-Magus-in-training makes a dedication of his offering, and they are linked in the sight of Angra Mainyu. After . . ." He hesitated. "It is done alone, in darkness. I have heard it must be done with bare hands, or with an iron knife. And I have heard the victim must be throttled with the girdle of a living Magus. I do not know."

"But the others, the other Âka-Magi, are not present?"

"For the dedication. For the offering . . ." He shook his head. "No. The pact is made alone. No aid may be given, no support. Only death and darkness."

I nodded. "Thank you, Rushad."

Outside Daršanga, spring was coming to Drujan. It was not often that Nariman the Chief Eunuch was absent from the zenana long enough for anyone to venture into the garden, but there were times. I went, when I could, and gauged the rising warmth in the air, the moisture of spring winds, wondering when the northern passes would thaw. And I gauged, too, the height of the garden walls. It was useless as a means of escape, leading only to the pitched roofs of the inner palace. A man with a grappling hook and a rope might be able to scale them, though. I wondered if Joscelin would dare.

Probably.

But I didn't think it was worth the risk.

It would have been a simple enough matter to get a message to him, if there was anyone summoned to the festal hall whom I dared trust. There wasn't, not yet. So I waited, living out endless days in my private hell. Drucilla tended my injuries without comment. Time and again, my flesh healed cleanly, only to be torn and ravaged anew. I grew inured to the pain. Not the nights of iron and blood—no, never that—but the inevitable dull aftermath. Ignoring it, I walked the length and breadth of the zenana, considering escape routes.

Unfortunately, there weren't any.

"You're mad," Drucilla said. "You'll get us all killed!"

"For what? Walking and thinking?" I cocked my head at her. "Drucilla, has anyone ever tried to kill the Mahrkagir?"

"What?" Her face went pale. "You *are* mad."

"They search us for weapons. Someone must have tried."

"Someone did," she said grimly. "It did not end well. Her punishment . . . well, there may be worse ways to die, but I cannot think of any. Ask someone else, if you want to know it; I do not care to remember. His lordship may be insane, Phèdre, but he's a trained warrior, and not careless with his life when his priests are not there to protect him."

Unless it was someone he trusted, I thought; someone he *loved*.

And the surety of it gripped me like a storm, until I had to bow my head in horror and weep, mumbling for Drucilla to leave me, that I needed to lie still against the pain. I lay curled on my bed, staring at the jade dog figurine on my shelf. Once upon a time, the Mahrkagir had been a boy with a dog. I did not know if I could do it. Blessed Elua, I prayed, is this your will? Might even he not be redeemed through love?

I already knew the answer. The boy with the dog had grown into a monster. And as much as it might pain him, as much as his black, black eyes might grow lustrous with tears, he would take the gift of *love* and offer it on the altar of Angra Mainyu. He would make me beg for death and grant it as a final, loving boon, whispering endearments as he ate my heart.

Unless I killed him first.

It terrified me even to think it, so I thought of other things instead, such as how we were to escape if I did it. And to that, I had no answer. If what Rushad had told me was true, the power of the *Skotophagoti*, the Âka-Magi, flowed through the Mahrkagir. Their powers would be broken with his death. Well and good; that left only the whole of the Drujani army.

If we could take Daršanga, I thought, we could hold it, at least for a while. Long enough, mayhap, to commandeer a ship and escape along the coast of the Sea of Khaspar to Khebbel-im-Akkad—or, at the least, to send word via the sea route. I did not doubt that the Lugal Sinaddan would descend upon Drujan in all haste if he knew. I could only pray it did not result in a second bloodbath like the one that had begotten the Mahrkagir.

Taking Daršanga was the only problem.

That, and committing murder.

I sat upon my carpet and watched the zenana on an afternoon when Nariman was absent, gauging its mood. They worked together to enjoy the garden, posting watchers, setting up a warning system. Not all, of course—many preferred the escape of opium dreams—but enough. I watched the blue smoke curling from an Ephesian water-pipe, and wondered how much opium was present in the zenana, and how much it would take to drug the garrison. I remembered the pellet Rushad had offered me, and wondered if it could be placed in the food, or whether it would dissolve in drink. Kumis, I thought, would mask the taste of anything.

"Watching and listening," Kaneka called from her couch. "Always watching and listening. You are not practicing your Jeb'ez, little one, though I gave you permission."

"Yequit'a, Fedabin." I bowed from the waist. "I was thinking of somewhat else."

"Your storm-lord?" She laughed, the others laughing with her.

"No, Fedabin Kaneka." On a whim, or something like it, I told the truth. "I was wondering whether or not opium dissolves in liquid."

Kaneka's brows rose. "Why such a thing? Will no one share a pipe with the Mahrkagir's favorite? Well, then, beg him for one, or eat it in pellets, if you will."

"It is a thing I wonder, that is all."

It bothered her; I saw the thoughts flicker behind her frown. "No. It must be brewed in water, to be drunk. The resin of the poppy must boil a long time."

"Ah," I said. "Thank you, Fedabin."

"Come here." Her tone was peremptory. I rose and went to kneel on the Jebeans' carpet. Kaneka stared at me with hooded eyes. "You did that," she said, pointing to the garden door, the posted sentries. "I saw. I watched it happen. The others, they forget. I don't. Why?"

"For Imri," I said. "I wanted him to see the sky."

"That boy." Her voice deepened. "He does not even like you."

It was true enough. Having dared two steps forward, coming to see me, Imriel had taken a large step in retreat, unwilling to accept the truth of what I had told him. I shrugged. "It does not matter."

"It matters in here," said Achara, one of the Nubians.

"He is only a child," I said, thinking of Melisande's words. *Let him live to hate me, then; only let him live.*

Kaneka laughed, harsh and dark. "There are no children here," she said. "Whose wine were you thinking to lace with opium, little one? Lord Death's?"

"No." I smiled at her. "There is a great deal of opium in the zenana, Fedabin Kaneka; enough to dull the wits of the entire garrison of Daršanga for a single night. I was only thinking, no more."

Something behind Kaneka's eyes closed, rendering her face mask-like. She looked at me without speaking for a long time. "Dangerous thoughts," she said at length. "And dangerous words."

"And even more dangerous deeds," I said softly. "Yes, Fedabin.

That is why I say they are only thoughts and no more. It would endanger the entire zenana to speak them openly, would it not? And to render them deeds . . ." I shrugged. "Of a surety, some of us would die. All, if we failed."

Her hand flashed out to grab a fistful of my hair, yanking my head forward as she leaned down from the couch until our faces were mere inches apart. I could see the red veins lacing the whites of her eyes. "I will not die for your dangerous thoughts, little one, do you hear?" she said, her breath hot against my face. I could smell the sharp sweat of fear on her. "No one here will! Hope kills in this place, and betrayal kills quicker. Only those of us who have learned to live with Death, to keep him at bay one day at a time, endure. Better for us all if you keep your mouth silent on these thoughts!"

"You will die here, Kaneka." With her face loomed over mine, I somehow managed to say it unflinching. "*When* is the only question that matters. One day, your dice will call your number, and your charms of thread and bone will not avail you."

Kaneka released me with a Jebean curse. "Not while you live!" she spat. "I do not fear Lord Death's men, grunting fools. Only him. And while you live, he will summon no other, Death's Whore! I know this to be true. The dice do not lie."

"My number," I said, "has already been called. Whose will be next?"

And with that, I left them, a low buzz of Jeb'ez following me. Amidst the angry reactions, I heard someone—Safiya, I thought—remark thoughtfully that it was known a cook in the zenana was enamored of Nazneen the Ephesian, and surely he would boil opium into a tincture for her sake. And then Kaneka ordered her to silence, and they spoke of it no more.

I went to my chamber and sat on my bed, trembling at the risk I had taken.

The little jade dog on my shelf stared at me with bulging eyes, reminding me that betrayal from within the zenana was the least of my fears. Kaneka spoke truly—in this place, hope could kill, and betrayal quicker.

But if I died in Daršanga, it would be at the hands of love.

I have known love in my lifetime; known what it is to love, and be loved. I had it first from Hyacinthe, my truest friend; from my lord Delaunay, who redeemed me, and from Alcuin, the brother of my childhood. Truly, it is in loss that we learn a thing's true value.

There are loves I have never known, whose lack I have mourned half-unknowing—for my parents, who sacrificed me on the altar of their own passion, for the children I dared not bear. But I have known the love of good comrades and stalwart companions, of a sovereign whom I admired and revered to the depths of my being.

I have known love in all its cruelty; so I thought, before this. Melisande's voice haunted my memory. *We are bound together.* When all was said and done, it was true; there was an inextricable link between us. But ah, Elua! There were blasphemies here such as she had never dreamed. Love may be cruel, but even its cruelties can be profaned.

And I have known love that defied all odds.

Thinking of Joscelin, my throat grew tight. His face, taut with despair, swam before my face. His part in this was harder, so much harder than I had reckoned. Already, madness nipped at his heels. I had asked too much of him, and I did not know how much longer he could endure.

All I could do was pray.

ℱiFTY-TWO ⊙

SPRIⅡG CAⅢE to Daršanga.

In the garden of the zenana, it brought a few pale seedlings, strag-gling, weedy things pushing through the crumbling soil in the corners where the scorched, salted earth was less barren. There was a slow-witted girl from the island of Cythera who tended them whenever she had a chance, crooning over them, bringing stagnant water from the pool inside in a tin cup to nourish them. I would have thought it more like to kill them, but they grew all the same, stubborn little shoots inching toward the sun.

Betimes, Imriel would help her, unexpectedly patient, and I remem-bered the simple-minded acolyte at the Sanctuary of Elua and her gift with animals—Liliane, who bore my mother's name. Imriel would have known her, of course, nearly all his life. I remembered how our mounts had followed her unbidden. And I remembered too how the *Skotopha-gotis* had ridden his ill-tempered ass without so much as a halter.

The gifts of Blessed Elua.

The power of Angra Mainyu.

One of these would prevail, here in Daršanga. And I, who bore this knowledge alone, shuddered under the weight of it. Weak and craven, Kaneka had called the gods of Terre d'Ange; last-born, spineless servants. Even Imriel despised them, and Joscelin . . . I did not know what Joscelin believed, not now. He had been Cassiel's priest, once. Now he lived the damnation he believed he had accepted when he chose love over duty.

All around me, the palace of Daršanga breathed darkness and ha-tred, the hunger of Angra Mainyu waking anew to spring and the pros-pect of new life to destroy. Its numbers were swelling. From all over

Drujan and elsewhere, the Âka-Magi returned to the palace, to the Mahrkagir. First there were three, in the festal hall, then five, then eight. The apprentices came too, the scouts in their bone girdles, preparing for their final ordination.

And the Tatar tribesmen came in droves.

Including Jagun of the Kereyit Tatars.

Rushad heard the rumor first, and I prayed it was not true, prayed that Blessed Elua would intercede. 'Twas to no avail. Nariman the Chief Eunuch's face told the tale, his fat cheeks quivering with pleasure as he smiled, his pointing finger summoning Imriel to the festal hall. "*You are to attend the Kereyit warlord,*" he hissed. "See he is well pleased at the banquet!"

Imriel's expression went stony. No one wept for him. I didn't dare.

In the long corridor, he walked like a condemned man going to the gallows, and my heart bled for him. Uru-Azag gave me a sympathetic glance. There was nothing he could do, either.

The festal hall was packed; a full score of us had been summoned. I took my place at the Mahrkagir's side. By this time, it was well established. He kept me next to him as if I were his Queen, even greeting me with a courtly kiss, his eyes mad and adoring. And at his side, I too presided over hell.

The Kereyit Tatars had a place of honor at one of the front tables. I knew Jagun at a glance by the way the others deferred to him. He was resplendent in fur-trimmed armor, broad-shouldered with a horseman's bandy legs, and he shouted his approval when Imriel was sent to attend him, banging a tankard of kumis on the table.

At least, I thought, the Tatars are not willfully cruel—not like the Drujani, who followed the creed of Angra Mainyu. And not, Elua be thanked, like the Mahrkagir, for whom night was day and cold was hot and atrocity was an innocent pleasure. Still, they were fierce and savage, and I saw the tears of helpless rage in Imriel's eyes as Jagun of the Kereyit fondled him, roaring with laughter when he resisted.

"Jagun wants the boy," the Mahrkagir confided to me, watching it. He laughed. "If he will swear allegiance, all the Kereyit will follow, and the Kirghiz and the Uighur will follow them! We will march upon Nineveh!" His eyes shone. "Khebbel-im-Akkad will fall to us, îshta, and it is only a beginning. We will sweep across the land like a dark wind. You will see." He smiled at me. "Your fearful gods are impatient to kneel before Angra Mainyu as you are to kneel at my feet. Tell them

I am coming, îshta. It will not be long. When Jagun and the Tatars agree, I will come for them, and I will make of their destruction a wondrous ill-deed."

"So you will give Jagun the boy, my lord?" I made myself ask him.

"Not yet." He shrugged. "Gashtaham says we cannot move until after the vahmyâcam, anyway. There will be more acolytes, after the offering, and more Âka-Magi will be dedicated, who are worth a thousand warriors each—and something else, he says, something special. I thought I knew, once, but that was before . . . look, îshta!" He laughed again. "See how your D'Angeline lord Jossalin stares at the boy! I think he is jealous, my Bringer of Omens. I knew he would desire the boy if he saw him!"

"Send him to him, then." My voice sounded hollow to my ears. I forced myself to smile at the Mahrkagir. "And then Jagun will be jealous. If his blood is heated, he will be quicker to strike a bargain and be done with it."

"It is a clever thought," he said in approval. "I may do it, soon. Not yet. I want Jagun to keep his hunger. Certain license I have granted him in this hall, but he is forbidden the final prize. There is time, before the vahmyâcam. Then, after it is done, he may possess the boy in full." He caressed my cheek with cold fingers. "See how much you have taught me of desire, îshta! I have grown wise in its ways."

I nodded, closing my eyes against the terrible thrill of his touch. "When is the vahmyâcam, my lord?"

"Oh, that." The Mahrkagir stroked my breast, teasing the nipple to erectness and squeezing it hard, laughing softly as I bit back a whimper of pleasure. It was still a favorite game of his. "Ten days."

The hall reeled in my vision as I opened my eyes, hazed in crimson, the pulse of desire beating hard in my blood. I gripped the tabletop hard, nails digging into the wood. One of the Âka-Magi came to speak to the Mahrkagir, who released me. The Âka-Magus looked at me out of the corner of his eye, a pleased smile hovering about his lips.

And Joscelin was staring at me with no expression whatsoever.

I lifted my hands from the tabletop and spread my fingers. Ten days.

With a brief nod, he looked away.

The remainder of the night is blurred, run together with others, too many others. Nothing was different, save that Imriel was there—and more, more Âka-Magi, more Drujani, more Tatars. What I could not bear to watch unflinching, I avoided. It is a coward's excuse, I know, but I had endured too much to give myself away now. In time, the Mahrkagir led me away to his quarters and I was granted an *anguissette*'s reprieve, forgetting everything in the exquisite depths of pain and humiliation, until it ended and awareness returned in a rush, misery trebled by renewed self-loathing.

I was returned to the zenana before Imriel.

Always before, I would go to my chamber and sleep for some hours when the Mahrkagir had finished with me. This time, I waited, kneeling on my carpet, enduring the dull throb of pain. Rushad and Drucilla hovered alike, both distraught. I kept my gaze fixed on the latticed door and ignored them.

It was over an hour before he returned, Uru-Azag escorting him, and the boy Imriel who returned was not the same I had known, the one who had spat in my face and led me a merry chase about the zenana. This boy walked stiffly, his face blank and dazed, no trace of defiance in his eyes, only uncomprehending hurt. Uru-Azag let him go, bowing imperceptibly as Imriel stumbled with leaden steps toward his couch.

An island of Chowati lay in his path. It is true that Imri had plagued them on more than one occasion, pinching sweets, trading insults. There was no real harm in it . . . but in this place, cruelty bred cruelty. I cannot think why else Jolanta, the most ill-tempered among them, chose to torment him in that moment. I only know that she did.

"Little rooster," she called maliciously to him in zenyan, "little cock, where is your crow? What is wrong, have the Tatars taken your balls?" She threw back her head in laughter at his blank stare. "Come, boy," she said, spreading her legs and rubbing herself, "you'd best use them while you have them, young or no, before you end like the Skaldi!"

"I say he's lost them already," one of the others offered, rising from her couch. Imriel blinked, pushing her hands away as she reached to undo his breeches. Another caught him from behind, pinning his arms. Panicked, he began to struggle, uttering a high, terrible sound. "Any wagers? Is the little rooster's staff still working?"

Light-headed with fury, I did not know I had gotten to my feet. The world had taken on a familiar scarlet tinge. My ears were ringing with the terrible sound Imriel was making, and something else, something that blew through me like a wind, a buffeting bronze-winged storm.

I drew a breath that seared my lungs like fire and shouted. "*Let him go!*"

The words resounded like a whip-crack in the zenana, an echoing silence following. And in the silence, a hundred pairs of eyes stared at me.

Jolanta of the Chowati was no coward. In the silence, she rose from her couch and picked her way across the zenana to confront me. "Why should we? Who are you to order it?"

I held my tongue and did not answer.

"Her name," said a man's voice, cracked and harsh, speaking crude zenyan, "is Phèdre nó Delaunay, and she once walked across a war into torture and sure death to save her country." Erich's lips curled as he pushed himself up against the wall. "From the Skaldi."

"You knew," I whispered, gazing at him.

"I was six," he said. "The defeated always remember."

Jolanta blinked, opening and closing her mouth. Like a dark shadow, Kaneka appeared at her side, sliding an ivory hairpin from her thick, woolen hair. It had a point on it like a dagger, and nearly as long. She gestured with it, smiling pleasantly. "Go back to your island, Chowati."

I started. "Imriel."

"I'll check on him." It was Drucilla, steady and efficient. "There's nothing you can do for him right now. Kaneka, Nariman is coming."

With an unobtrusive motion, the Jebean woman slid the ivory pin back into her hair, and Jolanta sidled away toward her couch. Nariman approached, waddling and officious. "Lady," he said to me in zenyan, breathing hard, dislike in his small eyes, "do not *shout* in my zenana."

The hand of Kushiel had not entirely left me.

"Listen to me, little man," I said in Old Persian. "Whether I like it or not, I am the Mahrkagir's favorite. If you don't stay out of my way, I will ask him for your head on a platter. And if he's in a good mood, he may well grant it to me. Do you think he loves you so well, for opening the door to the Akkadians thirty years ago? Your position here is a bitter jest that has outlived its time."

He blanched. "Favorites change," he hissed. "Or die. Accidents happen, in the zenana."

"Yes," I said, unimpressed. "And if one happens to me, I promise you, you will have a horde of angry Âka-Magi here wondering why."

Nariman went.

Kaneka folded her arms and looked at me.

"Erich," I said, ignoring her. "Rushad said you spoke no zenyan."

"A little," he replied in Skaldic. "No more. I learned to listen, watching you. And I have been here a long time." His gaze was bright and grim behind his tangled yellow hair. "You escaped from Waldemar Selig's steading in the dead of winter. I know. We tell stories about it. I knew you by your eyes, and the scarlet mark. Do you have a plan to escape from here?"

"I might," I said. "Only it will take the zenana's aid to do it."

"Is the sword-priest with you?" he asked. "The one who defeated Selig at the holmgang?"

I hesitated. "Yes."

"Good." Erich smiled, cold as death. "Whatever it takes, I will do it. And don't . . . don't worry about the boy. What happens to him now, he will survive, if his will is strong. Lord Death and his bone-priests, they have told him, if he does what is asked of him, he will keep his manhood. That he is being saved for something special." His mouth twisted. "They won't unman him until he believes it."

I swallowed, tears in my eyes. "I am sorry, Erich."

His shoulders moved in a shrug. "I am paying for someone's sins. Maybe Selig's, who knows? I was six. It does not matter to the gods. If I live, I will ask a priest of All-Father Odhinn why I was chosen for this. If I die . . ." He shrugged again. "Let me do it with a sword in my hand, and I will die with your name on my lips, whether you are my enemy or no. You should go, now, and talk to the tall black one before she throttles you. She could lead a steading, that one. Many women would follow her lead."

I glanced involuntarily at Kaneka, who raised her eyebrows. "I will, Erich, thank you. I swear to you, I am not your enemy. Not here, not in this place—and not after, either. I will not blame the Skaldi for Waldemar Selig's war."

"It does not matter." He closed his eyes. "You sang me songs of home. I would have died blessing you for that alone."

I would have said something else, but at that point, Kaneka's hand closed on my shoulder. "It is time, little one," she said dourly, turning me to face her. "Time we talked."

"Yes." I eyed her ivory hairpins. "It is, Fedabin."

I led her into my chamber and lit the oil lamp, fumbling with the flint to strike a spark. Kaneka drew up the single stool and sat watching, her eyes gleaming in the near-darkness. At last the lamp kindled, a warm glow illuminating the room. I sank onto my pallet with a sigh, raw and aching with pain, unwashed, aware of it in every part now that Kushiel's presence had left me entirely.

"Who are you?" Kaneka asked. "Why are you here?"

I looked squarely at her. "Erich spoke truly. I am Phèdre nó Delaunay, Comtesse de Montrève, Naamah's Servant and Kushiel's Chosen. And I have come for the boy, Imriel."

"The Skaldi knew you."

"His country invaded mine, once. I did somewhat to stop it."

Kaneka showed her teeth in a smile. "Something they tell stories about."

"Yes," I said. "It seems they do."

"You must have been a child at the time." She looked at me, considering. "Do they tell stories of you in your homeland, little one?"

"Some," I said, thinking of my place in Thelesis de Mornay's epic Ysandrine Cycle, of the poems of Gilles Lamiz, of the tales of the Night Court and the gossip of the palace and in the streets of the City of Elua. "Yes, Fedabin, they tell some."

"The boy does not know."

"No." I shook my head. "He doesn't. He was raised by priests, who took care he heard no such stories."

"He does not know you," she said. "And yet you came for him. Why?"

"Because," I said, "I promised his mother that I would. And because my gods required it of me." I permitted myself a smile, tinged with bitterness. "My weak and craven gods."

Kaneka regarded me. "You must love one of them very much," she said. "Either your gods, or the boy's mother."

I laughed, at that—I could not help it. "Fedabin Kaneka," I said, dragging my hands through my disheveled hair, seeking to regain my self-control. "Let us end this dance, because I do not have time for it. In nine days . . . nine days! . . . the Âka-Magi of Drujan will hold their sacrifice, the vahmyâcam. And unless I am very much mistaken, which does not happen so often as you might suppose, I fear it is their intention that the Mahrkagir make me his offering. You see," I said, holding her gaze, "he has learned, against all odds, to love. And if he is allowed to offer *that* upon the altar of Angra Mainyu, he will take on such power as makes everything that came before seem as child's play."

Being dark of skin, Kaneka could not blanch; instead, she turned grey. Still, she did not look away. "You do not propose to let him."

"No," I said, looking at the top of her head. "I propose to borrow your hairpins."

Kaneka's hands, laced between her knees, trembled. "You would kill Lord Death."

I could not say it. I only nodded. At that, Kaneka did look away. Tears stood in the corners of her eyes. "What becomes of us?" she asked. "What becomes of the zenana? What *vengeance*"—the word was a harsh one, in zenyan—"will his followers wreak?"

"None," I whispered, "if they are dead or incapable. Kaneka, listen to me. The power of the Âka-Magi flows through the Mahrkagir. If he is slain, it leaves only the soldiers. And if the zenana helped . . ." I swallowed, ". . . if they did, if they hoarded their opium, if the cook who is enamored of Nazneen the Ephesian rendered it into a tincture, and the women of the zenana served it to the garrison in kumis and beer and wine, on the night of the vahmyâcam, when there is bound to be feasting . . . Kaneka, we could take Daršanga."

"We." She looked back at me, mask-like, ignoring her own tears. "A handful of unarmed women. A boy."

"And Erich. And the Akkadians, who have knives. They will fight, I know it."

"You are so very sure," she murmured. "Little one."

"No." I swallowed again, trying to consume the lump of fear lodged in my throat. "I am so very desperate, Fedabin, because I cannot do this alone, and I think if I fail, we are all dead. You and me and Imriel, and everyone in the zenana, and I do not know where it will end, because if I fail, I will be dead at his hands, and if that happens, I cannot see anyplace on this earth where Angra Mainyu's power will be halted, and I think, although I am desperately afraid I may be wrong, that this is why my gods have sent me here. Fedabin Kaneka, I have told you only true stories. If I place that which I hold dearer than life in your hands, will you lend me your hairpins?"

Kaneka looked at me without speaking, and in a single, abrupt gesture, removed the twinned ivory pins from her hair, placing them in my open hands. I gazed at them, the long shafts tapering to dagger-points, and closed my hands upon them. They retained the warmth of her. It was the one thing I had not been able to conceive—how to get a weapon capable of killing past the guards.

"I was scared," Kaneka said shortly. "Too scared to try it."

I nodded, understanding. "He would have killed you if you had. Fedabin Kaneka, I will keep my bargain. There is one other weapon that we have. They tell stories about him in Skaldia, too."

FIFTY-THREE

THE DAYS that followed were among the most terrifying of my life. As hard as it had been to bear my secret alone, it was worse to have it shared, rendering so many of us vulnerable. The whispering was constant as the conspiracy grew. I was sure, at any instant, someone would speak carelessly in front of Nariman, and all would be lost.

None of it would have been possible without Kaneka. Bullying, cajoling, threatening—it was she who converted the others to our cause, convincing them to surrender their precious allotments of opium. Not all, but many; enough. Drucilla assumed charge of it, carrying the growing ball of resin in her physician's basket. When it was the size of a man's doubled fists, she gauged, it would be sufficient to affect the entire garrison.

Rushad too proved an invaluable ally. Although the prospect of it rendered him pale and stuttering with fear, he nonetheless provided a steady flow of information regarding the dedication ceremony, and the feasting that would accompany it. It was Rushad himself who would bring the opium tincture to the festal hall, late in the proceedings, and see it dispersed among the myriad pitchers of beer and kumis.

I do not think he would have found the courage, if not for Erich. The Skaldi's reemergence into the world of the living filled him with joy, and he held me personally responsible for it. They were an unlikely pair of friends, the young Skaldi warrior and the slender Persian eunuch. Still, Rushad doted on him, and for his part, Erich bore it with a certain fond tolerance.

As for the Akkadians, I told Uru-Azag myself, and not without a good deal of trepidation. He heard me out silently and, for a long moment, only stood and stared, fingering the hilt of his curved dagger.

"Opium alone is not enough," he said shortly. "There will be fighting. And men in the grip of delusion are dangerous."

"But unskilled," I said.

He nodded, thinking. "If we could get to the fishing boats, it might be enough. Drujan has no fleet to give chase. Still. Daggers are of little use against swords. And there will be two guards posted at the upper entrance to the zenana. Even that night."

"The guards will be dead," I said. "You can take their swords, their armor."

Uru-Azag frowned, brows meeting over his hawklike nose. "Who will kill the guards?" he asked. "*You?*"

"No." I shook my head. "The Mahrkagir calls him the Bringer of Omens."

The Akkadian laughed with harsh delight. "*Him!* Ah, then, I see."

"You will do it?"

He stared into the distance over my head, weighing the matter. "You are mad, you know. It is likely that we will all die."

"It is possible," I said. I thought of Erich's words. Like the Skaldi, the Akkadians had been warriors, once. "It would be a warrior's death, Uru-Azag. Not a slave's."

"It would." He looked at me. "Nariman will be a problem. I will kill him myself. It will be a pleasure to slit his fat throat."

I repressed my surge of relief and only nodded. "And the others?"

"They will fight." He smiled grimly. "It would shame them not to. Your god, lady, must be a mighty warrior, to inspire such courage."

A hysterical laugh caught in my throat. "No," I said, half-choking on it. "But he is a prodigious lover. Believe me, Uru-Azag, in this place, it is the more dangerous of the two."

The Akkadian only looked at me askance, and went about his business. It didn't matter. They thought me mad, god-touched. It had made me a pariah, before. Now it made me an icon, a catalyst. The signs had spoken . . . Kaneka's dice, the ringing tone's of Kushiel's presence, the Skaldi's return to life. It was enough. He would fight; they would all fight.

It left Imriel to be told. I had not done it yet.

On the first day, I had gone to see him after Kaneka and I had finished. Drucilla had examined him—this time, he had allowed it. He had been beaten with a lash, and there were marks of branding on the skin of his buttocks; Kereyit runes, indicating possession as one might mark a herd-animal. Prohibited from possessing him, Jagun had none-theless marked Imriel as his own. He was not injured badly, as such things went in the zenana, meaning he would not die of it. She had slathered his welts and burns with Tatar horse liniment and gave him a dose of valerian against the pain, from a store she normally held in reserve for the dying.

Imriel was half-drowsing by the time I saw him, and I hadn't the heart to rouse him. I sat on the end of his couch and watched him.

"Phèdre," he murmured. "Did my mother really send you?"

"Yes, Imri." I stroked his fine blue-black hair. "She really did."

"How did she know I was here?"

"She didn't," I said softly. "But Blessed Elua did."

I thought he might protest it, but his unfocused gaze merely wandered. "When you shouted," he whispered. "When you shouted . . . it made me think of home, and the statue of Elua in the poppy-field . . . one of the goats used to follow me there, Niniver was her name, and she crawled under the fence . . . she was so little and I fed her with a bottle when her mother died, and Liliane helped me, and she would crawl under the fence and follow me . . ."

His voice had drifted into silence and he had fallen asleep. I stayed with him until I was sure he would not awaken, aching with helpless tenderness. I had borne such marks upon my own skin—but I was Kushiel's Chosen, and it was of my own volition. I had entered Naamah's Service as an adult, aware of my own choices. Such a fate was never meant for a child. I waited until his breathing deepened in sleep, and then went at last to bathe.

Afterward, he was fevered—out of trauma, Drucilla said, and not infection, but he talked aloud in his dreams, rambling, and I feared what he might say. "Be glad it's only talking," Drucilla said darkly, and I didn't know what she meant, not then.

It mattered naught to the Mahrkagir, who sent Imriel to attend to the Kereyit warlord in the hall the next night, and the next. The feasting continued, and games of combat, too. Again, Joscelin had to fight. He made it quicker, this time, conscious, I think, of Imriel's fearful gaze. The boy actually shrank back against Jagun when Joscelin passed him. I could have wept to see it, though I understood. Melisande's treachery had taken me thus. For a D'Angeline to betray his country is an unspeakable deed.

After the combat, someone called out for Joscelin to fight Tahmuras, and the shouts of accord rose, wagers being placed. I do not think the massive Persian would have been anything loathe to do it. He glowered under his brows, toying with the haft of his morningstar, a bitter smile on his lips. I had seen him in battle, and I knew enough to be scared. Peerless swordsman or no, it was not a weapon Joscelin had faced before—and the giant was preternaturally gifted with it. Joscelin bowed calmly to the Mahrkagir, awaiting his pleasure, only a faint tightening of his jaw giving any hint of reserve.

"What do you say?" the Mahrkagir asked, laughing. "The Midwife of my Birth-from-Death, my protector Tahmuras, against my Bringer of Omens? It would be a battle to shake the rafters!" He waited for the shouting to die before dashing their hopes of a spectacle, an impish gleam in his eyes. "No. These two, I need. Find someone I do not need to die!"

They did. They found a pair of women of the zenana and made them fight, arming them with daggers and pricking them with spears until they had no choice. One was Jolanta, the Chowati; the other, a Kereyit Tatar, a gift of Jagun, who had very much hoped to be given Imriel in return. I never even knew her name.

Neither of them wanted to do it. They circled one another, skirts knotted for freedom of movement, while the Drujani jabbed at their bare legs. Eventually, fighting to win became preferable to being pierced by a Drujani spear, and they did. Both of them knew how to use a knife. Jolanta knew better.

I saw tears in her eyes as she straightened, the Tatar girl's blood on her gown. If I had hated Jolanta for tormenting Imriel, I pitied her now. She met my gaze briefly across the crowded festal hall, while the Mahrkagir's guests whooped and shouted, pleased at the display. When she looked away, I saw her hand rise. Making a blood-stained fist, she pressed it to her brow, and I knew it for a declaration of loyalty.

"Come," the Mahrkagir said, smiling at me. "It will be an early night. The young men are hunting boar in the morning, for the vahmyâcam."

I went with him.

He didn't know, not yet. Of that, I was certain. I wondered when the Âka-Magi would tell him, and if they feared he would refuse if he had time to consider it. I wished it were true. I was sure it was not. I was his gift, his rare gift, filling him with wonderment and delight, willing to wallow in the vilest of depravity. It would pain him, to lay that gift upon Angra Mainyu's altar. But he would do it, and believe it his finest deed.

The Âka-Magi watched us leave, and they all smiled.

Everyone was returned early to the zenana that night, on account of the morning's hunt. I wished I had known. It might have been better, to plan something when a good portion of the inhabitants were gone. It was how Joscelin and I had escaped from Selig's steading. Still, if we had used the opium that night, they would not have gone a-hunting . . . it does not matter, now. The date was chosen. The vahmyâcam, when they would least expect it, when they would drink deep in celebration, when the Âka-Magi were distracted, and when, I prayed, Angra Mainyu himself would be sufficiently sated with sacrifice that he was slow to take alarm.

I didn't bother to wake Rushad, only gave myself a cursory wash with tepid water from the morning's basin and crawled onto my pallet. There I lay, wakeful, listening to the sounds of others returning. It was not often I had that chance. I knew their steps—the Akkadians' heavier treads; Nazneen the Ephesian, who moved like a weary dancer; the swift, angry pace of Jolanta. I heard Imriel among them, too, his agility gone, his steps stumbling and leaden.

But alive, and walking. I lay down my head and slept.

And awakened to piercing screams.

The sound was indescribable, ear-splitting, deafening. If I had not seen it with my own eyes, I would not have believed a mortal throat, a single boy, could utter such a sound—and I say that as one who endured the mourning wails of La Dolorosa for days on end. There was nothing of grief in this sound, only utter terror. It sent me bolt upright in bed, my heart racing like a distance-runner's, knowing beyond surety it was him.

In the zenana, women groaned, complained, uttered curses and orders to be silent, covered their heads with cushions. Clad only in my shift, I make my way amid the couches.

"Nightmares," Drucilla said in Caerdicci, meeting me halfway. Her shawl was clutched about her, her eyes dull with sleep. "He had them in autumn, too. I have valerian."

"No," I said. "I'll go." After a moment, she nodded and stepped aside.

Shrill and endless, the screams echoed from the walls, until I had to grit my teeth against the sound. Only a few lamps were burning, and by the dim light, I saw Imriel curled into a thrashing ball, his hands fisted, eyes clenched tight, mouth stretched wide in a rictus of terror.

The cords in his throat stood out like cables as he screamed and screamed, never seeming to draw breath.

"Imriel," I whispered, speaking in D'Angeline, kneeling at his side, not daring to touch him for fear of what it might invoke in his dreams, "Imriel, I'm here, it's all right, I'm here."

His eyes flew open, and the sound stopped. He stared at me uncomprehending, then drew in a long, ragged breath and burst into tears.

It was like a dam breaking. His arms came around my neck, chokingly tight, and I held him while he sobbed, raw and gasping, his entire body wracked with the force of it. Tears stood unheeded in my eyes as I murmured meaningless reassurances. His cheek was hard against mine, silky child's skin, sticky and hot with anguish, his shoulders heaving.

He was afraid of anyone seeing him cry.

I am not strong, but I am strong enough; he was only ten years old, and light with it. I picked him up in my arms and carried him to my chamber, the private chamber of the Mahrkagir's favorite, his arms wound tight about my neck, his grief echoing at my ear. And there I lay down with him on my pallet and he clung to me, Melisande's son, burying his face against my throat, still jerking with the force of his misery, soaking my shift with hot tears, until at last his sobbing subsided and his limbs grew still and he passed, grief spent, into the dreamless sleep of utter exhaustion with a child's thoughtless ease, one hand still clutching my shift, the other knotted in my hair.

"Imriel," I whispered, kissing his brow. "Oh, Imriel!"

And I lay for a long time sleepless, aware of the unaccustomed weight, slight though it was, of a child at my side, of his clinging arms. I knew, that night, that my life had changed. I was not sure how, nor why. And since the gods gave no answer—not cruel Kushiel, nor Naamah, nor Blessed Elua himself—in time, I slept.

When I awoke, I knew myself watched.

He sat perched on the stool, heels hooked on the rung, elbows propped on knees, watching me sleep. It was passing strange to wake to that gaze, his mother's sapphire eyes, in a child's considering face.

"Did Elua send you here to die?" he asked me.

Only in the zenana of Daršanga would that question sound so natural.

"No," I said. "I don't think so." And I told him my plan.

He listened carefully, frowning, all traces of the nightmare-ridden child gone. I did not overstate our odds. Imriel had been in Daršanga too long to believe a pleasant fiction; longer than I. And besides, I would not consider it wise, at any time, to mince truths with Melisande's son—nor Ysandre's cousin. I saw it for the first time that day, the lineage of House Courcel in his features.

I hadn't gotten through all of it, only the zenana's part. "Imriel, listen. The Mahrkagir wishes to sow doubt in Jagun, and force him to pledge his oath. I have urged him to play upon the Kereyit's jealousy. Tonight, or mayhap tomorrow, the Mahrkagir will send you to Joscelin Verreuil, the D'Angeline warrior. I want you to tell him—"

No further than that, and his eyes widened, a child's again. "Him!" he spat. "I hate him! He looks at me, and his face never changes. I would sooner go with Jagun—"

"Imriel." I took hold of his shoulders. "He is my consort. He won't touch you."

His face worked; he was trying to make sense of it. "He came here . . . ?"

"He came here with me," I said. "Because I asked it of him, and because he swore a vow, long ago, to Cassiel, to protect and serve me. To damnation and beyond, that is what he swore. And that is what I asked."

"A Cassiline," he echoed. "That's why he never smiles."

I nodded. It was close enough. "Will you tell him what I have told you? On the night of the vahmyâcam, he is to drink no wine, only water. A quarter of an hour after the Mahrkagir retires with me, he is to go to the upper entrance to the zenana, and dispose of the guards. If he can procure other weapons, it is all to the good. If not . . ." I shrugged. "We will do what we can."

"I will tell him," Imriel said. He hunched his shoulders and looked at me. "Do you think we will live?"

"I don't know," I said steadily. "But we will try."

At that, he came off his stool, flinging his arms about my neck and burying his face in my hair. "I am glad," he said in a muffled voice, "that you came here."

"So am I, Imriel," I said to him, meaning it. "So am I."

Fifty-four

On the third day before the vahmyâcam, the Mahrkagir knew.

I did not need to be told. I saw it, the instant I entered the festal hall. His eyes, always bright, glowed like black suns. He was overjoyed. He was transcendent with it. His hands, when they took mine, were trembling; ice-cold and trembling.

"Îshta," he murmured, embracing me. "Îshta, beloved!" He took a step back and gave a radiant smile. "I knew, I knew from the first! I knew that you were special. Such a gift, îshta, such a gift you have given me. I sought, and knew not what I sought. I did not know it had a name, until Daeva Gashtaham told me."

I smiled back, my hands in his. "Everything I have is yours, my lord; everything I am. Of what do you speak?"

He laughed, buoyant and joyous. "Not everything, not yet! Oh, but I cannot tell you. It is a surprise, the greatest surprise." Embracing me again, he nuzzled my neck. These things, these tender niceties, I had taught him. "You will live forever, îshta, through me; for ten thousand years! It is the greatest surprise, I promise."

And so I smiled and smiled and pretended I could not wait for the great surprise, and the Âka-Magi smiled too, Gashtaham most of all, smiling at my innocent pleasure. It was the single greatest performance of my life. Even Joscelin smiled, cool and amused, his arm about Imriel's waist while Jagun the Kereyit gnashed his teeth in fury. Imriel played his part to perfection, resentful and withdrawn, pulling away at every opportunity.

In the Mahrkagir's bedchamber . . . Elua.

Some things are better left unsaid.

If there was anything to offset the horror of it, it was seeing the life return to Imriel's features after the first night he was sent to Joscelin, the spark of defiance rekindled in his eyes. "Even the Drujani are afraid of him," he said, gloating. "No one will touch me while the Mahrkagir has given me to him! And he says he will not let them, ever."

"Did you tell him our plan?" I asked.

Imriel nodded, both feet hooked about the rungs of the stool. "He says you are as mad as the Mahrkagir, and we are all like to die."

I hadn't expected anything different. "Will he do it?"

"Yes."

And so our plan progressed. The palace of Daršanga boiled with activity. A dais was constructed in the festal hall, to the rear of the covered well where once the eternal flame of Ahura Mazda had burned. There were a good many new faces; Âka-Magi, their acolytes and apprentices, and bewildered others—parents, siblings, loved ones, the unwitting victims of the vahmyâcam-to-be. Negotiations continued, too, with the Tatar tribesmen, with a handful of fierce Circassians who arrived unannounced.

The Mahrkagir could scarce contain his glee. If all went as planned, he told me, Drujan would march on Nineveh within the month. And when Nineveh fell . . . they would sweep south between the rivers, and city by city, Khebbel-im-Akkad would be theirs, as it had been in days of old.

"It is a beginning, îshta," he told me. "Only a beginning!" His black eyes shone. "From thence . . . where to go? The Âka-Magi have travelled, these nine years—to Hellas, to Menekhet, to Ephesus, even Caerdicca Unitas! No one can stand against us. And Terre d'Ange . . ." He caressed me, smiling. "Terre d'Ange, I think, will be the greatest prize of all. I have heard stories of your land. It is for this I had the Âka-Magi seek out one of your kind, one without peer, that your gods might know of me and tremble, that I might plant the seeds of death among them, and Angra Mainyu would be mightily pleased." He laughed, soft and delighted. "They brought me the boy, and I served notice upon his flesh at the end of a lash! I marked him well, beloved. And they heard me, îshta, your gods heard me and knew fear. I thought he would serve at the end—but I was wrong, îshta; so wrong. This is more glorious than I could have imagined. Still, it was well that I waited, for his pain carried the message." He smiled at me. "You heard it, didn't you?"

I thought of my dreams, of Imriel kneeling in the *Skotophagotis'* shadow. If we failed, it would be no more than the truth. I could only pray, for all our sakes, that our desperate gamble succeeded. "Yes, my lord," I said softly. "Oh, yes. I heard it."

"As did your gods." He laughed again, caressing my cheek with cold, cold fingers. "And the gods of Terre d'Ange have already given their answer, have they not?"

"Yes, my lord," I said, shivering. "Truly, they have."

Thus, the palace. In the zenana, a grim air prevailed, and our plans continued apace. The lump of opium in Drucilla's basket grew ever larger. The cook had sworn undying love to Nazneen the Ephesian, and promised to aid her in boiling it to a tincture. I had not seen, before, the effects upon addicts when the drug was withheld; I saw it then. They went through agonies, bellies cramping, sleepless and feverish.

"Let them be," Kaneka said when pity weakened my will. "They have endured it before. This time, it is of their choosing. Let them be."

I did. And those who held back, those who hoarded their opium, paid a price as great. The Ephesian boy, the last surviving child in the zenana other than Imriel, died of it. Although I cannot be sure of it, I think that the woman who tended him, lovingly blowing smoke into his mouth, suffocated him with a cushion in the dark hours of night. As for her . . . I do not know how much opium she consumed. Enough to make her dreams last forever.

"Fadimah," Nazneen said in mourning tones, standing over her couch. The dead woman lay slack-faced and still, the boy's limp form clutched to her breast. "It need not have been so." And she looked at me, eyes moist under long lids. "No more. This is why I help you. You see? No more."

I saw, and nodded. Words were not enough for this death.

Words. I lack them; I do not have words to describe the courage of the women of the zenana in this time. So many details! It was hard, so hard, to put together a plan of this scope, of this magnitude, against odds so staggering it dries my tongue to think of it, even now. For most of what happened, I can take no credit. Once the wheels were set in motion, it was a valiant few who executed so much of it. Kaneka . . . Drucilla . . . Nazneen . . . even Jolanta. And the others, the countless others. There are women who died, others whose names I never knew—although I remember their faces, every one—who played crucial roles, overseeing the serving of the opium-laced pitchers. A small role, yes, but a vital one.

Our plans were laid. We could do no more.

I knew a little of what to expect, for the Mahrkagir told me. "Feasting, îshta, such as you have never seen in Daršanga! And you are to attend it with me. And then the vahmyâcam, and the apprentices shall be dedicated, and the acolytes . . ." His lips curved tenderly. ". . . and the acolytes will present their offerings to Angra Mainyu, and the Âka-Magi will deem them fit or unfit. I will present you, îshta, I will present you as my bride." There was no irony in it; truly, he saw it thusly. "This is for you," he said, presenting me with a splendid crimson gown, the edges stiff with gold embroidery. "Do you like it?" he asked in an anxious tone. "It belonged to Hoshdar Ahzad's Queen, my father's first wife. Gashtaham said it would be well to make the most of your beauty for the vahmyâcam."

"It is beautiful, my lord," I murmured.

"It is!" He beamed. "It will adorn you, srîra. And this, and these . . . you will wear these as well." With careless hands, he scooped a queen's ransom of jewelry into my lap—ruby ear-drops, a collar of interlacing gold chains, bangles for both arms. "I, too, want you to be your most beautiful," he whispered in my ear.

"I will try, my lord," I promised him.

I could not have done it alone, when the day came, and fear knotted my belly. For all our preparation, I felt unready, uncertain and horribly aware of the danger.

The women of the zenana helped to dress me, combining their skills and means. A Caerdicci seamstress working with a bone needle and unraveled threads from Drucilla's shawl made cunning alterations to the gown so that it might fit me becomingly. A once-vain Menekhetan girl who had made kohl out of lamp-soot painted my eyes, grave as a squire arming a warrior for battle, while an Aragonian dabbed sandalwood oil at my wrists and throat. Two of the Ch'in, with lovely, porcelain faces, worked my hair into an elaborate upswept coif, affixing it in place with a pair of combs and Kaneka's ivory hairpins.

It was done.

Jolanta showed me my reflection in a tiny hand-mirror she had stolen from somewhere. I did not think Daeva Gashtaham and the Mahrkagir would be displeased. In the dim light of the zenana, the crimson gown glowed, shimmering with gold trim. Rubies shone at my ears, and gold gleamed at my throat and wrists. If my face was pale, my eyes were pools of darkness, the scarlet mote echoing the color of the gown. The ivory hairpins were unobtrusive in the elegantly coiled locks of my hair, mere delicate accents.

"This one," one of the Ch'in women said in her limited, lilting zenyan, guiding my hand to the rightmost hairpin. "You pull. Hair not fall."

"Thank you." My throat was tight with fear.

Uru-Azag, entering the zenana, checked at the sight of me. "It is time, lady," he said as I rose. "Nariman is coming with the summons. You are to attend the feast, and the others to come later, when the wine is poured."

"I am ready." I looked for Imriel. He came forward slowly, dragging his feet, all the fear I felt reflected in his face. "Imriel," I said, stooping to cup his face in my hands. "Whatever happens, stay with Joscelin, do you understand? The Mahrkagir will send you to Jagun, but he will be affected by the wine. Whatever you do, don't leave the festal hall with him. Get away as quickly as you can. Joscelin will do what he can to protect you."

He nodded miserably. I kissed his brow and rose. There was no more I could do.

And so I went to the festal hall for the last time.

There was a little silence when I entered the hall. It seemed to take forever to cross it. They are not used to seeing beauty adorned, in Daršanga, and it was not customary for women to dine among the men. The ancient Magi, the true Magi, were huddled in a group under the shadow of the dais; they drew back in disgust as I passed. The men, Drujani and Tatar, stared. Daeva Gashtaham steepled his fingers and smiled.

"My Queen," the Mahrkagir announced, his eyes shining. "My beloved!"

With that, the feast commenced. I do not remember what was served—fish, I suppose, and boar. There was a good deal of fresh boar, due to the hunt. It might have been sawdust for all that I tasted it. I do not remember what I said, nor how I endured it. Once I caught a glimpse of Rushad lingering inside the doorway leading to the kitchens, and my heart beat so fiercely I thought the Mahrkagir must see it through my gown. I didn't even dare glance at Joscelin.

Dinner lasted an eternity, and when it was done, I wished it had been longer. Servants began bearing wine-jugs from the kitchen, Rushad among them, eyes downcast and humble. The first round would be unlaced; we had all agreed it was safest. Let their palates grow numb before we served the drug. Wine was poured, beer and kumis. The level of noise grew as the men drank, and the women of the zenana entered the hall.

No one betrayed a thing. I, who knew, could see it. The careful pavane of jugs, orchestrated by a terrified Rushad, served by stone-faced women. Imriel was attending Jagun, solicitously filling the Tatar's cup. I gave thanks to Blessed Elua that the Kereyit warlord's attention was fixed on the offering-ceremony. Joscelin, unobtrusive, hovered a few paces away, a thing none of the Tatars had noticed. It was a small thing in which to discern that the hand of Elua was guiding us, but it was all I had.

How long would it take, before the effects of the opium became evident? An hour, mayhap longer. No one knew for sure. Drucilla had calculated it to the best of her ability, but there was no telling. The drug was diluted, and some drank more than others.

And some less. The glowering Tahmuras, for one.

I wondered when the vahmyâcam would begin.

Anywhere else, this would be a sacred rite, with all the attendant solemnities. It did not mean in Daršanga what it meant elsewhere. This profane revelry, held in a desecrated temple—in Angra Mainyu's wor-ship, it was ritual. Not all who were there knew, or cared. It didn't matter. The Âka-Magi knew, and their acolytes. The Mahrkagir knew. And I knew it.

And the god . . . Blessed Elua, the god himself knew it. Living under that dark, ravening *presence*, I had grown half-used to it. I felt it anew that night. Spring had come to Daršanga, and the offering approached the altar. Angra Mainyu was roused, the bottomless maw of hunger yawning open, eager to devour the world. When I blinked, I saw the walls of Daršanga running red with blood. It was in the faces of the men, keen and wolflike. It was in the mad, beautiful eyes of the Mahrk-agir, in the loving smile he bent upon me. It was in the air we breathed, heavy as thunder.

Kill . . . die . . . destroy.

Blessed Elua, I prayed in the silence of my heart, hold us safe in your hand.

"Shahryar Mahrkagir," murmured Gashtaham, bending his head in obeisance. "Angra Mainyu's will is manifest. May we begin the vah-myâcam?"

"Yes!" The Mahrkagir laughed, happy and excited as a boy at his natal festivities. "Go on, Gashtaham, get on with it! I am eager for my gift."

"So be it." The priest glanced at me, his smile hidden in shadows. "You look very beautiful tonight, my lady."

"You are kind." I forced the words through frozen lips. Let him know I was afraid; it didn't matter. Everyone was afraid, in the zenana. I had lived in fear since Nineveh. I couldn't remember what it was like to be without it, except in the Mahrkagir's bed. And that was worse.

Bowing to his lord, Gashtaham walked the aisle and mounted the dais, the other Âka-Magi falling in beside him, bearing shrouded burdens in their arms. There were a dozen, all told. The sullen torchlight flickered on their polished boar's-skull helms, the black robes, the finger-bone girdles. Daeva Gashtaham raised his arms, the ebony staff in his left hand.

In the festal hall, silence fell like a hammer.

"Angra Mainyu," he said, and his voice whispered in every corner of the hall, "we stand before you to profess our faith. Of this world we are created, and in death we are reborn in your name. The works of Ahura Mazda, we abjure! His livestock, we starve and slaughter; his earth, we salt and render barren. We embrace darkness and the lie, abhorring all truths. Your three-fold path, we walk in faith: Ill thoughts, ill words, ill deeds. Let your presence among us be made manifest, and your will spread, until the hearts of all mankind seek only destruction, and brother turns upon brother, and all is laid waste."

There was power in his words, terrible power. And I, who sat next to the smiling source of it, shivered until the bangles on my wrist tinkled sweetly and I had to grip my hands together in my lap to halt it.

"Come." Gashtaham beckoned. "Let those who have made the vahmyâcam and served their apprenticeship come forth to receive their reward."

Nine men came forward, some clad in armor, some in common garb, each with a girdle of finger-bones about his waist. One by one, they knelt before the dais and unknotted their girdles, laying them before them. I saw Arshaka, the old Head Magus, weeping with horror at the side of the dais. As each man approached, the Âka-Magi tended him. Two sheared his hair, letting it fall in careless handfuls. One eased a black robe over his shoulders, and another tied the finger-bone girdle about it. A fifth placed a hollowed boar's-skull helm over his shorn head, and one last bowed, handing the new Âka-Magus an ebony rod, topped with a gleaming ball of jet. When it was done, each new member took his place among their ranks.

It took some time. I scanned the hall, trying to gauge events. The men were rapt, watching the ceremony, and drinking had slowed. Was the drug taking effect? It was too early to say. "Îshta," the Mahrkagir said warmly, stroking my neck. "It will be soon!"

The dedication was finished. Daeva Gashtaham raised his arms once more, now flanked by twenty-one Âka-Magi. "Angra Mainyu," he said. "Destructive Spirit, Lord of Darkness, Demon of Ten Thousand Years! We have quenched the fires of your ancient enemy and plunged the land in terror. With your will to guide us, we will bring more, so much more, to your altar." He raised his voice. "Let those who would make the vahmyâcam come forward with their offerings, save he who is last and greatest among us, beloved of Angra Mainyu!"

The Mahrkagir leaned back, watching; it seemed we were to go last. Seventeen men came forward at Gashtaham's announcement, each bringing a companion. They were the ones I had seen, the new faces— the parents, the siblings, the wives and children. I hadn't seen the children before. A few of the chosen went willingly, proudly. Some went in terror. Each couple mounted the dais to stand before the Âka-Magi. Gashtaham laid his hands upon their shoulders, gazing into their eyes, reading their hearts and the will of Angra Mainyu.

Three were dismissed, the sacrifice found unworthy. It must be love, I thought; truly love. The others were accepted, and to each was given a cord, wrenched from about the waist of one of the true Magi, Arshaka's followers, the priests of Ahura Mazda. Each pair was dismissed, and an Âka-Magus assigned to follow. Where they went, I cannot say. To darkness and death, alone.

So, I thought dully, that is how it is done. I am to be strangled, if I fail. Well, there are crueler deaths.

And then there were no more couples, and Gashtaham raised his arms once more, his face flushed and triumphant beneath his skull-helm. "Angra Mainyu," he crooned, "Father of Lies, I summon your best-beloved, your death-begotten son-on-earth to stand before you and make the vahmyâcam. I summon the Shahryar Mahrkagir!"

The men cheered, shouting and banging their mugs; from the corner of my eye, I saw Jolanta startle and nudge the nearest woman with her elbow, circulating once more with the laced jugs of drink. The other women responded with alacrity, and the warriors drank, Drujani and

Tatar alike, cheering their lord. Jagun the Kereyit was shouting, Imriel's presence at his side forgotten. The Mahrkagir got to his feet, bowing in acknowledgment, savoring the moment, his smile dazzling in its joy.

"Come, îshta," he said to me, extending his hand. "It is time."

I took his hand and rose, and together we walked the aisle to the dais, where Daeva Gashtaham and the others awaited. I would have faltered, I think, if not for his hand on my elbow, a firm cold grip, guiding me as he smiled lovingly down at me.

"So beautiful," he whispered beneath the noise. "You look so beautiful, my Queen!"

Together, we mounted the dais.

Gashtaham laid one hand atop our shoulders, the black rod in his left angling behind the Mahrkagir's neck. I felt a faint surge at his touch and my flesh recoiled; the presence of Angra Mainyu intensified. I felt terribly naked and exposed under the priest's searching gaze, shivering so fiercely I could feel the ruby ear-drops tremble against my skin, terrified that the Ch'in combs would give way, sending my tresses tumbling, the ivory hairpins clattering to the floor of the dais, that any instant Gashtaham would see through my pathetic attempts at deception to the even more pathetic plot they sought to mask.

He didn't. His interest lay in the Mahrkagir, his pride and joy, the gateway of the god.

"My lord," he said, his voice as intimate as a lover's, "is it your will to make of this woman the vahmyâcam?"

"It is," the Mahrkagir replied, squeezing my hand.

"And do you love her?"

He smiled down at my upturned face, a world of adoration in his shining black eyes, all the glory of Blessed Elua. "I do."

"Angra Mainyu," said the priest, profoundly satisfied, "is pleased." He turned to one of his comrades. "Daeva Dâdarshi, bring me the sacred girdle of Arshaka."

The old man struggled, pitiful to behold, as the Âka-Magi cut the filthy cord from about his waist. I had not known, before tonight, that it was a part of their sacred regalia. Gashtaham held the cord in his hands, contemplating it. "I used my own girdle, that you tied about my waist with your own hands, old fool, to string my father's finger-bones," he said to the defeated Magus. "Yours, and your life, I have held in reserve, hoping and praying that this day might come. Now it is here." Raising the cord to his lips, he kissed it, then laid it reverently across the Mahrkagir's outstretched hands. "Take it, my lord, and her life with

it. I will go with you myself, and stand watch outside your door. And
when it is done . . . ah, my lord, you have served your life in apprenticeship to this moment. Angra Mainyu will wait no longer. When it is
done and you have laid open her breast and consumed her still-warm
heart, you will truly be the avatar of darkness." Gashtaham released the
cord and bowed, his face suffused with deep emotion. "And Drujan
shall conquer the earth!"

A roar of approval answered his final words; those, they had heard.
The Mahrkagir accepted the cord. "You see, îshta!" he said, exalted,
letting me in on the glorious secret, taking my face in his hands, the
foul-smelling cord against my cheeks, and kissing me. "It is a gift, the
greatest gift of all! And you have given it to me."

From the corner of my eye, I saw Joscelin take a step closer to
Imriel, hands hovering over the hilts of his daggers. At the side of the
dais, the old Magus Arshaka fell to his knees and wept, his beard trailing
on the flagstones.

It was the last thing I saw as we left the hall.

FIFTY-FIVE

TRUE TO his word, Daeva Gashtaham accompanied us to the Mahrkagir's quarters, along with the hulking Tahmuras. After the noise of the hall, it seemed strange, this silence, the familiar stone walls. All that, I thought, only to end here, where it began; no trappings, no ceremony. Only this, he and I, alone together again as we had been so many times before.

"One lamp," the priest cautioned, outside the double doors. "Enough to find her heart, and no more."

Tahmuras went ahead to make certain that it was so. The Mahrkagir only laughed. "When have I ever needed light, Gashtaham?" he asked, teasing, holding me close to him. "One lamp is enough and more to find my beloved's heart." The priest bowed; the huge guard exited the quarters with a curt nod that all was in order. The Mahrkagir ushered me inside. "I will summon you," he said to the priest, "to see that all was done well."

And with that, he closed the doors.

I reached one hand to my hair while his back was turned, sliding the rightmost ivory hairpin free from my upswept locks and turning it so that the long, daggerlike point lay along the inside of my forearm. My teeth were chattering. I held the hairpin in a death-grip, seeking to keep it from rattling against my bangles.

There was a lamp, the single lamp, burning in an alcove. It was enough, for him, whom the light pained like fire; it must have been as bright as day. To me, it was dark. As it was supposed to be—in darkness and alone.

"Do you see?" The Mahrkagir gestured, sweeping one hand. "It had to be here, where we have known such joy. Such deeds, îshta!" His eyes were bright. "Such ill deeds. I will always think of you, and remember your gift." He came near, looping the cord about my neck, crossing it, drawing it tight across my throat, his lower body firm against mine. "Are you ready?" he asked tenderly. "If you are, we will begin, and I will grant you death when you ask for it. It will be my gift to you, beloved."

"My lord, no." I laid my left hand flat upon his breast. "I beg you not to do this thing. Love is its own reward."

"Yes." He smiled at me, his mad, beautiful eyes shining in the darkness. The cord tightened about my throat. "I know, îshta. I know."

Beneath the splayed fingers of my hand, I could feel his heart beating, a firm, steady pulse. I knew it well. I had felt it against my skin too many times to count, racing with the exertions of cruel desire. I brought my right hand up between us, placing the point of Kaneka's hairpin between my left forefinger and thumb, directly over his heart, positioning it by touch, feather-light. Strong and beating, his life lay beneath my poised hand. If he had looked down, he would have seen it. He didn't. "Gashtaham wishes it," I whispered. "You can say no."

"No." He shook his head gently, tightening the cord, never looking past my face. Why would he? Whatever else was true, he trusted me. "Angra Mainyu wishes it, îshta, and so do you, in your heart of hearts." The cord was cutting off my air, and the darkness beginning to sparkle. The world was fading around me. Only his adoring smile hovered, vivid in my vision. "Your gods sent you as tribute."

The words were uttered in a tone of deepest love.

And beneath my hand lay his steady-beating heart.

"Half right," I gasped, choking. With all the strength that was in me, I shoved the ivory hairpin home into his resisting flesh. His mouth opened wide, his eyes astonished. "My gods did send me . . . but not as tribute."

Silent and shocked, the Mahrkagir of Drujan sank to his knees, the ivory haft of Kaneka's hairpin standing out from his chest. It was a small thing, pretty and decorative. It was enough. The point had pierced his heart.

"I'm sorry," I whispered, miserable. "I'm sorry."

His eyes rolled and his mouth worked. No words emerged. And like that, he died.

I covered my face with my hands and burst into tears.

That part, I told no one, not even Joscelin. It did not last long. He was a monster, and deserved to die. I knew this to be true. But he had been a boy, once; a boy with a dog, a whore's royal get, brought into the zenana, and it was Akkadian atrocities that made him what he was. That, I could not forget.

And he had loved me.

When my tears had done, I gathered myself, kneeling on the floor beside the Mahrkagir's body, listening for signs of disturbance. There were none. I had not known what would happen when I killed him. I had thought, mayhap, that the *Skotophagoti* would know at once, sensing a change in the presence of Angra Mainyu's manifestation. But no; they had grown overdependent upon him, the Conqueror of Death, certain he would not die.

Not at the hands of a D'Angeline whore.

Well and so; they would know it, the first time they reached for Angra Mainyu's power and found it gone, the gateway closed by death. And the next step would be no easier than the last. I hunted through the clutter of the Mahrkagir's quarters until I found somewhat that would serve my purposes—a short spear and a leather bull-whip, en-crusted with old blood. Like as not it was mine.

How long had passed since we left the hall? A quarter hour, at least; mayhap longer. I flung open the doors to his quarters, panic unfeigned. "My lord Mahrkagir!" I said urgently, pointing at the pros-trate figure. "He is having seizures!"

With a muttered curse, Gashtaham shoved me out of the way and hurried into the room, Tahmuras hard on his heels. I slammed the doors closed behind them, shoving the shaft of the spear through the door handles and lashing it in place with the long thong of the bull-whip.

The doors shuddered under the impact of Tahmuras, on the far side, hurling himself against them. The spear buckled, and held. It would not hold him forever. I raced down the Mahrkagir's hidden pas-sageway to the zenana, a path I could trace in the dark. That night, I did.

They were waiting, in the zenana. Nariman the Chief Eunuch lay silent on the floor, his plump throat slit like a pig's. Uru-Azag was smiling with grim pleasure.

"Is it done?" asked Kaneka.

I nodded, not trusting my voice.

If anyone had been listening, the cheering that went up at my nod would have brought the wrath of Daršanga down upon the zenana. No one was. A veritable mob bolted for the latticed door, and only the cool head of Erich, cursing and fending them off, kept them momentarily at bay. "The sword-priest is above?" he asked me in Skaldic, jerking his head at the stairs.

"I'll see," I said. "It was my plan."

Uru-Azag went with me, taking the stairs two at once, dragging me with him, his dagger in his free hand. Behind us, the women of the zenana overran Erich, pushing hard. If Joscelin had not been there . . . if Joscelin had not been there, I daresay they would have torn the guards limb from limb.

But he was there, waiting, wearing a chain-mail shirt over a leather jerkin.

Hordes of women shoved their way into the empty hallway. Two Akkadian eunuchs knelt and began to efficiently strip the slain Drujani guards of their arms and armor. And I ignored it all, flinging my arms around Joscelin's neck, willing, in that moment, to die if only to feel him hold me one last time, chain-mail or no.

"Phèdre," he murmured against my hair.

I said something; Elua knows what. Then, lifting my head, I asked, "Where's Imriel?"

"Safe," he whispered. "Don't worry, I got him out of the hall while the Tatar was distracted. He thinks Imriel is refilling his jug." His arms were strong around me, and I could have wept with relief, but it couldn't last. There was no time, and the crowd was growing. Joscelin turned me loose. Already, we were exposed and vulnerable.

"Lady." Uru-Azag addressed me, clad in an ill-fitting corselet, his dagger in his hand. He'd given the guard's sword to Erich. "We should make for the palace gates, and the harbor."

"Could we make it?" I asked Joscelin.

"No," he said grimly. "Not with this many of us. There are barracks within the walls, outside the palace proper. The secondary garrison would cut us up piecemeal. Our only hope is to take Daršanga and bar the doors."

"*Joscelin!*" It was Imriel's voice, high and piercing, echoing off the walls. He approached at a dead run from the corner of the corridor.

"You had him posted as a *sentry?*" I hissed to Joscelin. "You call that *safe?*"

"It was his idea," he said to me, and to Imriel, "What is it?"

"It's starting." He drew up, panting and white-faced, delivering his words in a breathless mix of D'Angeline and zenyan. "Jolanta . . . Phèdre! . . . Jolanta killed a man, in the hall, and they're . . . they're . . .

and one followed . . ." He turned and pointed. "Behind me."

Someone screamed as the *Skotophagotis* following Imriel appeared at the end of the corridor, near-invisible in the darkness save for his skull-helm and girdle, and his outraged face. He leveled his ebony staff at the assembled crowd, who scattered for the walls.

Joscelin whirled. I never even saw him draw a dagger, only the flash of it as it flew end-over-end, burying itself in the priest's throat. The *Skotophagotis* crumpled.

And that was when all hell broke loose.

I don't know who began it, only that once begun, it was unstoppable as a tide. Angra Mainyu's thwarted rage, deprived of its avatar, found an outlet in madness that night—and madness it was. I had seen truly. The walls of Daršanga would run red with blood. There are people who say women are the gentler sex. They would not say it if they had been there the night Daršanga fell.

It began with a long, ululating cry, and if it was a single throat that uttered it first, it was a dozen in the next instant, and thrice as many after. I could not see who led the mad dash, for it seemed they all went at once, unarmed Furies in ragged attire, running wild for the festal hall, and most of the eunuchs with them.

Joscelin cursed and caught Uru-Azag by the arm. "You," he said in Persian. "Bar the doors. Can you manage it alone?"

"Yes." The Akkadian raised the blade of his curved dagger to his lips and kissed it. "My blade," he said reverently, "is sworn to Shamash. I have consecrated it in blood tonight."

"Good." He turned to me. "Phèdre, take the boy and hide—"

"*Imriel!*" I saw it too late, the fierce glitter of the boy's eyes, his bared teeth. The same feral madness that had taken the others was on him, born of long months of hatred and abuse. Like a flash, he was off, coursing the hallway. "Go," I said to Joscelin, panic-stricken. "*Go!*"

He was already on his way.

Cold with fear, I followed.

ᴊ̇ɪꜰᴛʏ-sɪ̇x

A ɴɪɢʜᴛᴍᴀʀᴇ was taking place in the festal hall.

It was a bloodbath. There is no other way to describe it. And a good deal of the killing had been done by the women of the zenana.

By the time I arrived, the first wave of bloodshed had already occurred. I heard about it, later, from those who survived. The effects of the opium had become evident by the time I had left with the Mahrkagir, and more pronounced with every moment that passed, men growing heavy-lidded with dreams, smiling, talking nonsense. One or two had passed into unconsciousness.

And the Âka-Magi who remained, new initiates for the most part, grew nervous.

It had begun when a Uighur Tatar with a dreamy look on his face put his hand between Jolanta's thighs. It was as Imriel had said. Jolanta had plucked his dagger from his belt and planted it to the hilt beneath the Tatar's ear.

For long moments, no one had reacted. The men gazed stupidly, slow to comprehend. The women stared at one another, unsure what to do. Imriel, lurking outside the door, turned to flee—it was then that one of the Âka-Magi, a *Skotophagotis*, had caught sight of him and followed, beginning to suspect.

What happened to him, I already knew.

After that, the zenana descended in fury.

How many did the women kill, in that initial shock? Scores, at least. It was the sheer unexpectedness of the attack. Seizing blades—daggers, carving knives, swords, even an axe—from bewildered warriors' hands, the women wreaked a terrible vengeance, and the shouts of the Âka-Magi went lost amid their shrieks, empty and harmless as the squawking of crows.

Then the men of Drujan, drugged and dazed, began to fight back.
That was when I arrived.

It was dreadful to behold. Drugged or no, these were trained warriors, many of them clad in partial armor or leather. Such was the
etiquette of the Mahrkagir's festal hall. And under their onslaught, the
women of the zenana died in droves . . . Ephesians, Hellenes, Jebeans—
all nations, blood spattered alike over fair skin and dark, clotted in
tresses of blond and brown, the black silk of Ch'in, the woolen curls
of Jebe-Barkal.

Here and there, some resisted. I saw Kaneka swinging an axe like
a hammer, her teeth gleaming in a warrior's grin, blood splashed to her
elbows. A knot of Chowati fought grimly. The Akkadian eunuchs
stripped armor from dead men and struggled with the living. Across
the hall, Erich the Skaldi held the doorway to the kitchens, Rushad and
a handful of servants behind him, fighting with all the ferocity of his
nation.

And in the center of the hall . . .

Joscelin.

This much I will swear: 'twas not the madness of Angra Mainyu
that drove him. I know. I was with him in the corridor, when it came
upon the others. This was different, untainted, a rage born in the back
alleys of Amílcar where we found the slavers' children, nurtured by
fate, repressed and channeled and honed to an immaculate edge in the
Mahrkagir's service.

It was the most pure and deadly thing I have ever seen.

With his sword in his two-handed grip, Joscelin moved gracefully
through his Cassiline forms, his face as calm and focused as when he
did his morning exercises in the garden. He was smiling, his summer-
blue eyes wide with exaltation, and where his sword flowed, weaving a
silver thread in the dark air, death followed. I daresay the mail shirt
helped, turning a few glancing blows.

Most of them never landed.

He was nigh untouchable.

And they were drawn to him—drawn, like moths to the flame,
Drujani and Tatar alike, abandoning the women and stumbling to the
center of the festal hall to challenge him. Jagun, the Kereyit warlord,
came at him with a cry of fury on his lips, half-stumbling and wild,
only now realizing the scope of the prize that had slipped his fingers.
With a single two-handed stroke, Joscelin cut him down; with a single
stroke, Imriel's torment at the Tatar's hands was ended and avenged.

The Kereyit's corpse measured its length on the floor of the hall. And still others came, flinging themselves against him. It was madness, truly. The dark lord of Daršanga knew, too late, what was in his midst. And Joscelin, Cassiel's servant, my Perfect Companion, danced the blades with the minions of Angra Mainyu, amid a rising circle of corpses, the flagstones growing slick with blood.

"*Imriel!*" I cried, catching sight of him.

There he was, Melisande's son, brandishing a carving knife and snarling, retreating from a lunging Drujani soldier, scrambling onto a bench, a table. The Drujani, sword in hand, pursued him, clambering onto the bench. He had one knee on the table and was jabbing with his sword when I grabbed the bench with both hands and overturned it in a surge of pure terror, toppling it and its occupant with it.

The Drujani fell hard, the back of his head striking the flagstones. "Lady," he said in Persian, blinking at my face suspended above him, Elua knows how much opium coursing through his veins. "Lady."

"The Shahryar Mahrkagir is dead," I said gently. "My lord soldier, it is finished."

"Then . . . this is yours?" He gave me his sword, bemused, still laying on his back, proffering the hilt. Since I did not know what else to do, I took it, the sword awkward and heavy in my hands. He sighed and closed his eyes.

The uproar of battle was subsiding.

It was strange, the dawning silence. Everywhere, people moaned, bleeding and dying, but the clash of arms had begun to fade. Impossible as it seemed, it was ending, combatants slumping in wounded exhaustion, drug-addled and confused. The surviving women of the zenana huddled in groups. I saw Drucilla hobbling around the outskirts, clutching her belly where a dark stain was spreading, tending the injured. The festal hall was a bloody shambles, tables overturned, the trappings on the dais shredded, even the rubble filling the firepit scattered and strewn. Aka-Magi and Magi alike wandered bereft and dazed, powerless. In the center of it all, Joscelin leaned on his sword, breathing hard, encircled by death.

There was no one left alive with the will to continue it.

Save one.

There was no outcry at his appearance, but a deepening silence. It seemed even the wounded held their breath, watching. Tahmuras' shadow darkened the hall. How not, as massive as he was? His shoulders seemed to fill the doorway. Even at a distance, I could see the marks of tears on his face. I daresay in that place, he alone grieved for the Mahrkagir, for the mortal death of a man he had loved. We had that in common, he and I—we alone shed tears. He entered the hall with slow, deliberate steps. No one moved to intercept him. Joscelin's head came up slowly, his weary gaze fixing on the giant warrior.

"You," Tahmuras said to him, his voice taut with pain, pointing with the rod end of his mace. It was as though a mountain had spoken. "You will die." He swung the morningstar, encompassing us all. "You will all die for what you have done!"

Too tired to speak, Joscelin merely nodded, the point of his sword rising from the flagstones as he set himself to meet this last challenge.

It is not a battle I care to remember.

It is not one of which the poets sing.

The morningstar is a deadly weapon, and a difficult one. Few warriors wield it well. Tahmuras of Drujan had a gift. Quicker on his feet than his size would suggest, he came on fast and low, picking his path amid the corpses, the spiked ball whipping at Joscelin's legs. In his left hand, he held a long dagger, using it to make slashing blows as Joscelin whirled in his efforts to evade the mace, disrupting all his careful Cassiline skill.

His patterns broken, Joscelin was forced on the defensive, stumbling backward, tripping over the bodies of his own dead. His parries grew wild, the unpredictable morningstar shattering his guard, the entangling chain threatening to rip the blade from his grasp. Retreating from Tahmuras' onslaught, he gained the dais, careful steps feeling for the edges as his opponent pressed him. I clutched the hilt of my Drujani sword, forgotten in my terror, and felt Imriel's hand close hard upon my upper arm as he knelt on the table behind me.

"Phèdre!" he whispered urgently.

"I know," I said, tears in my eyes, watching the struggle. "I know."

"No!" His voice rose. "Look!"

I followed his pointing finger over my shoulder to see the priest Gashtaham approaching.

"My lady," he said in a hideous parody of courtesy, holding his ebony rod like a club. His steps staggered, but his eyes, beneath the boar's-skull helm, were fixed and intent. "My lady Phèdre nó Delaunay of Terre d'Ange, we have unfinished business."

"Daeva Gashtaham." Remembering the sword, I raised it, gripping the hilt with both hands to keep it from wavering. "Put down your staff. It is over. The doorway is closed."

The priest's smile was a dreadful rictus. "It may be, lady. It may be. But you were promised to Angra Mainyu, and he shall have you, if I must split your skull myself. And afterward, the boy's, and anyone left standing after him." He drew back his staff to swing, heedless of the blade I held, leveling it at my head. "Do you know what you have done?" he shouted, flecks of foam at the corners of his mouth. "Do you know what price I paid? Do you know what you have destroyed, damn your soul?"

"Yes, my lord," I said steadily, keeping the point of the sword trained on his heart, conscious of the weight of it, conscious of Imriel behind me, conscious of a stealthy movement in the shadows of the dark hall and not daring to look. "I do."

"Then *die!*" Gashtaham hissed, his muscles bunching for the blow.

I braced myself for the shock. It never fell.

A strong black hand seized his face from behind, fingers covering his mouth, wrenching his head backward to bare his throat, and I saw Kaneka's smile gleam in the shadows as her other hand rose, the blade of a dagger flashing in the gloom.

A bright spray of arterial blood jetted forth, and I flung myself sideways to avoid it, dragging Imriel with me.

"Well done, little one," Kaneka said complacently, watching the Âka-Magus twitch and die, runnels of blood flowing across the floor and pooling in the spaces between the flagstones. "I was hoping to kill one of his kind."

Ignoring her, I rose to my feet and sought Joscelin.

It was not going well.

Scrambling, he retreated desperately, his sword angled in front of him, driven backward step by step, no longer on the dais, but forced the width of the hall. Tahmuras advanced relentlessly, his morningstar swinging. Each strike, Joscelin deflected more slowly, turning his shoulders into the parry and retreating to resume his guard, his notched and bloodstained sword held ever lower. I could see his arms tremble with the effort of it, his feet seeking purchase on the slippery stones.

And Tahmuras pursued him with implacable vengeance, striking high, striking low, the spiked ball flailing, never losing momentum. It happened; it had to happen. The ball landed, a glancing blow to one knee. Joscelin staggered, dropping his guard, and the mace lashed out again, crushingly hard, against the upper part of his left arm.

I heard his cry of pain, saw his left hand slip nerveless from the hilt, and Tahmuras with his grief-reddened eyes gave a grim smile, swinging the morningstar. The spiked ball whipped around Joscelin's blade, and the chain caught and held.

The Drujani jerked hard on the haft of his weapon and Joscelin was disarmed, the sword clattering onto the floor. I shoved the knuckles of one hand into my mouth, stifling a cry. In a last-ditch effort, Joscelin spun, grabbing one of the hall's few torches from its sconce and brandishing it like a blade, right-handed. Step by step he retreated, thrusting the flames at Tahmuras' face as the giant stalked him, driving him back toward the center of the hall. His left arm hung, dangling and useless. He ignored it and parried one-handed, the torch weaving streaks of light against the darkness, fending off the inevitable final blow.

I had forgotten Imriel.

He was fast; so fast. By the time I thought to halt him, he was already in motion, darting across the corpse-strewn hall, pouncing on the hilt of the Cassiline sword.

"*Joscelin!*" he shouted, his voice high and ringing.

They paused, the combatants, turning. Imriel heaved the sword, and sparks flew as it skittered across the stones. Joscelin cast the torch from him, hurling it point-down like a warrior planting a spear . . .

. . . directly into the uncovered firepit.

With a sound that shook the very rafters, a column of fire ignited, the Sacred Fire of Ahura Mazda, a living, twisting thing of flame, gold and saffron and red, stretching toward the domed ceiling. Tahmuras was a vast shadow before it, stock-still in dismay, his mouth open to utter a cry of repentance or anguish. Joscelin never hesitated, snatching up his sword with his good right hand. With a single lunge, he ran the giant through.

It was ended.

FIFTY-SEVEN

NO ONE could have anticipated the aftermath.

What I remember most, once the column of flame spent its initial fury and sank to a moderate blaze, is the old Chief Magus Arshaka, his rheumy eyes filled with tears, arms outstretched in blessing, his lips moving in prayer as he knelt before the Sacred Fire, bright flames illuming his filthy robes. I remember it because I had no time for it.

I went straightaway to Joscelin, sitting on the bloodstained stones and gasping for air, his right hand clasped loosely about the hilt of his battered sword, his left arm cradled in his lap. He smelled of scorched wool and hot metal. "The boy?" he asked, eyes rolling to meet mine.

"Alive," I said, my voice choked. "Alive, my love."

"See?" Imriel knelt in front of him, his face anxious. "Joscelin, see? I am here."

Joscelin nodded and closed his eyes. "See to the others," he murmured. "I'll not die of a broken arm."

I got to my feet. "Stay with him," I said to Imriel. "Do you hear me? Stay with him, or I swear, I'll kill you myself."

"I will." Imriel's voice broke on the words. Huddled on the flagstones, he looked at me with his mother's eyes, and such an expression in them as hers had never held. "I promise, Phèdre, I will."

It would have to do. While the surviving Drujani and Tatars, addled by opium and terror, made their surrender—some to stunned members of the zenana and some to the Magi, openly weeping before the Sacred Fire—I went to assess the wounded and number the dead.

And outside the gates of Daršanga, the revolution spread.

What stories they tell in Drujan, I cannot say. I did not linger long enough to hear them told, and I have never been back, nor shall I, not while I draw breath. This I know to be true, for I learned it that night:

the fires kindled in the palace ignited in the city and elsewhere. Jahan-adar, the Land of Fires, reclaimed its ancient title, and the hand of Ahura Mazda reached out to reclaim his own.

Well and good; so he might. But it was the folk of a hundred disparate nations, captives and slaves, who paid his ransom.

So many died. So many.

In the doorway to the kitchens, Erich the Skaldi lay dying, his body pierced by a dozen wounds, a sword in his hand and a look of peace on his face. Rushad, a carving knife in his hand, lay slain across his knees, having done his valiant best to defend his fallen friend; gentle Rushad, who was no more a warrior than I. All I could do was to clasp Erich's hand and sing softly to him, cradle-songs, such as I had learned as a slave. Erich died smiling, his hand slackening in mine. And I went on to the next. So many, so many dead. Jolanta, her fingers clutched about a Drujani sword-hilt, stuck together with blood. Nazneen the Ephesian, willowy in death as in life, a Tatar war-axe buried in her skull. Among the women of the zenana, one in three had died . . . Erich, Rushad—two of the Akkadian eunuchs. Gone, all of them.

But there were survivors, too.

Uru-Azag came limping from the inner doors of Daršanga, grey-faced and grim, gathering a contingent to secure the fortress. After the Sacred Fire, there was no resistance. With Kaneka's aid, conferring with Joscelin, who had propped himself on a bench, they got matters well in hand. Here and there, an initiate from the vahmyâcam wandered in dazed shock, having learned too late that their offerings were in vain. Angra Mainyu's reign was broken.

There was one man, with a crimson spill of blood drying on his chin, who took it hardest. I remembered him. He was one who had brought his son to the dais, a boy no older than four or five years. The Mahrkagir's age, I thought, when the Akkadians had taken Daršanga. We had struck too late for the boy; his father had eaten his heart.

Would that there had been another way.

I did what I could, ignoring the thanks-giving prayers of the Magi, calling upon my experience of too many battlefields to help Drucilla, who had bound her own wounds and remained on her feet, trembling. She pressed her fist hard against her belly and gasped orders. The Carthaginian carpenter's daughter was a shadow at my shoulder, aiding without argument, recruiting others. The Caerdicci seamstress who had altered the fit of my gown learned to sew flesh and sinew under Drucilla's tutelage.

Together, we saved a good many.

Until at last it was Joscelin's turn. Removing the chain-mail shirt alone was a torture.

I could not have done it without Drucilla. It was she who instructed me on how to draw his arm straight, pulling by main force until the shattered bones fell into alignment, feeling with delicate fingertips that each was in place. It was a mercy that none had pierced the skin. Cold sweat stood in beads on Joscelin's brow, and he swore a blue streak, using terms I did not know he knew. And then it was done. I bound the fracture as Drucilla instructed, wrapping it firmly with lengths of woolen cloth and securing it with a careful splint.

"A sling," Drucilla murmured, plucking at her shawl. "To keep the arm immobile. Use this. I'll have no need of it."

"No," I whispered, kneeling beside her. "Drucilla, no."

"I'll have no need," she repeated faintly, smiling, reaching up to touch my hair with her maimed hands. "Phèdre. You spoke true, didn't you? An ill-luck name. Still, I will die as I lived, a physician to the end, and not a creature of darkness. You have given me that. It is not a gift I thought to find; not here."

"No." Tears coursed my cheeks, salt and bitter; it seemed unfair that she, who had fought so valiantly to preserve life, to preserve her own sanity, should die. "If you will only tell us what needs be done . . . Drucilla, we can do it, I swear to you!"

Behind me, the Caerdicci seamstress murmured agreement, and other voices echoed it.

"The blade has pierced my bowels," Drucilla said gently, her hand falling away, fingers trailing damp across my tear-stained face. "I feel it, child; the poison in my blood-stream. If you had a chirurgeon's tools and a chirurgeon's skill . . ." She smiled with sorrow and kindness, plucking at the woolen fabric that draped her. "It would still be too late. Take the shawl."

Shaking with grief, I did. It was her wish. She watched the seamstress Helena fold it with care and tie it in exacting knots, making a sling for Joscelin's arm. When it was done, her lashes fluttered closed, and Uru-Azag and two of the Akkadians carried her with all tenderness to the corner of the hall where we had established our infirmary, laying her on cushions purloined from the zenana and heaping blankets atop her.

"Remember this," I told Imriel, who watched gravely. "Remember her courage. Remember them all."

Wordless, he nodded.

It was somewhere in the small hours of the night that Drucilla died, and sometime afterward that the Chief Magus came for me, a lamp in his hand.

"Come," he said in Persian, as I blinked out of a half-waking doze on a makeshift pallet where I maintained a vigil in the infirmary. Somewhere, a clean robe had been found for the old man and the worst of the filth washed from his hair and beard. For all the deep lines that scored his face, he looked stronger than I would have believed possible mere hours before. "We must speak."

"Stay with them," I said to Joscelin, who had come instantly alert, reaching for his sword with his good right hand.

"And let you out of my sight? Not likely," he muttered, levering himself to his feet and calling one of the Akkadians to stand guard over the injured, and the sleeping Imriel. "Now," he said to the ancient Magus, "we will go."

Arshaka inclined his head. "Bringer of Omens. As you wish."

And so saying, he led us through the palace, up a winding stair to one of the lookout towers. There, in a small garret, a Drujani guard lay dead—who had killed him, I do not know—and a shuttered window had been forced open, a square of darkness looking out over the city below and the land beyond.

"Behold," said the Chief Magus. "Jahanadar, the Land of Fires."

In the city of Daršanga, the Sacred Fire burned in the ruined temple. Everywhere there were torches lit, wavering in lines. Voices raised in celebration and prayer floated on the night breeze, crying Ahura Mazda's name. Beyond, across the plain of the peninsula, blazes were scattered like stars emerging from the clouds.

"You cannot stay here," the Magus Arshaka said gently. "The Lord of Light has reclaimed his people. Soon, they will come for Daršanga, and you are too few to hold it."

Joscelin made a sound in his throat that might have been a dour laugh.

"It is ours now, my lord Magus," I reminded him.

"It is," he acknowledged. "This night. You have captives, servants, Magi, all bent to your will. For what you have done, Ahura Mazda permits it. What of the dawn? Will the women of the zenana fight once the madness of Angra Mainyu has passed? Or shall you hold the doors with a handful of eunuchs and wounded warriors? Will Ahura Mazda's grace endure, while you send for aid from Khebbel-im-Akkad and level the Spear of Shamash at our heart?" Slowly, regretfully, Arshaka shook his venerable head. "It will not. Better that you should throw open the doors of Daršanga and go home. Leave us to our own."

I rested my hands on the windowsill, looking at the men of the secondary garrison assembling at the doors below, their hands empty of weapons, pleading for admission that they might be redeemed in the light of the Sacred Fire. "There are a few thousand of the Mahrkagir's men remaining between Daršanga and the border, my lord Magus. We thought to take a sea route."

"You have sailors among you, oarsmen?" He read the answer in my averted face. "If there were such a vessel to suit your needs, I would walk among the people and order it myself, child. But there is not; only such fishing craft as will land you shattered upon the rocks should you attempt such a journey. Your route lies over land. Angra Mainyu's power lies broken, and his former servants will answer to the people of Drujan. If you will give me your word that you will sue for peace on our behalf when you reach Akkad, I will order that your company be allowed to pass unmolested."

"You have the power to order this?" I asked him.

Lamplight lent his creased features a stern dignity. "By the grace of Ahura Mazda, I do."

"Ahura Mazda." My voice hardened. "My lord Magus, I have never wittingly blasphemed the gods of any land, and I do not discount your long travail. But this night . . . *this* night . . . you owe any power you hold to the grace of Blessed Elua and the gods of Terre d'Ange, to Naamah's compassion, to Kushiel's cruel justice, and above all to Cassiel's loyalty."

Joscelin stirred, at that. The Chief Magus never moved. "It may be, Elua's child," he said unflinching, his words an eerie echo of the Âka-Magus Gashtaham's. "It may be. But it is the will of your gods that has freed the Lord of Light, and you are a long way from Terre d'Ange. Heed my counsel, take my offer, and go."

It was too great a matter to decide on my own. Though I was grateful to be alive, I was weary to the bone, exhausted in body and spirit. I did not know, until then, it was possible to know such utter weariness and live. The gods of Terre d'Ange may be merciful, but they use their chosen hard. My head ached from tears wept for the dead, and I had yet to reckon the cost to the living. Ah, Elua! To myself, and to Joscelin most of all. Still, my task was far from done. I owed a debt to the zenana—and there was my promise. There was Imriel. He trusted me. Whatever it took to see him safe, it must be done. Beyond that, I could not think. Turning away from the old man, I leant my brow upon the window-sash, gazing across the dark plain, scattered with fires like distant stars. "Joscelin," I murmured. "What do we do?"

He came to stand behind me, his bound arm clumsy between us. "Love." The broken caress in his voice brought tears to my eyes. "I don't think we have a choice. The priest speaks the truth. Will you order the captives slain, if they chafe at our hold? The servants?" In the darkness, he shook his head. "I couldn't. Neither could you. And the others, were they to do it . . . from what have we freed them, if they become like that which they despised? For good or for ill, Blessed Elua has set free Ahura Mazda. It is his will that led us here. I think we can but trust in it, and pray it leads us out."

I tried to think of another way.

I couldn't.

"I want aid," I said, rounding on the Magus Arshaka. "As much as you can give, whatever you can give. I want horses, mounts for whomever can sit one, and wagons for those who can't. I want armor and arms for whomever will bear them, and supplies, bandages and medicaments, tents and blankets, and provision enough to get us to the border and beyond. I want a mule-train to carry them, and hostlers and bearers. I want four Magi to accompany us, whomever you deem hale enough for the journey. If you have talismans or tokens that will signify the protection of Ahura Mazda, I want those, too."

With every sentence, he nodded, and when I finished, said, "It will be done. All of it."

"It had better." I stepped close to the ancient priest, close enough that he drew back lest my nearness taint him, and I knew that in his eyes, I was still Death's Whore, the Mahrkagir's favorite. "My lord Magus, I swear to you, if you play us false, may Elua have mercy upon your soul."

"I do not lie," Arshaka said stiffly. "Ever."

Thus our fate was decided.

FIFTY-EIGHT

WE DEPARTED before sundown.

It was not enough time to make ready for a journey of such difficulty, not nearly enough, but our skins itched with the presence of danger, and all of us yearned to be free of the shadow of Daršanga.

The Chief Magus Arshaka kept his word. Stores were plundered, stables looted to provide all that I had requested. When the doors of the palace were opened, we braced ourselves to fight or die, but the inrushing guards of the outer garrison hailed the Magi as heroes.

It would have been a bitter irony, had I cared. I didn't. All I wanted was to see us out of Drujan, and safe.

Most of the zenana was going; only the Tatar women took their leave, rejoining such tribesmen as had survived, already preparing a hasty retreat of their own, no longer in favor. It surprised me, a little, that the women were willing to return to the very men who had given them to the Mahrkagir. Not much. The will that had united us had already begun to falter, and the call of blood—and home—is strong.

The others would ride with us to Khebbel-im-Akkad, where I fully intended to prevail upon the ties of House L'Envers and the D'Angeline throne to abjure Valère L'Envers and her husband to see each and every one restored to her homeland.

If we made it.

The dead who remained would be laid to rest in Drujan—with honor. The Chief Magus Arshaka had promised it. I could only accept his word. He had sworn to uphold the truth above all else and revile the dark lie. I suppose that he did, and I am wrong to resent him and his kind after their long suffering. But I am only mortal, and I could not forget the disgust in his face when I drew near to him.

Never, I daresay, has an undertaking been fraught with such chaos. Merely explaining it took the better part of the morning, accomplished in a babble of tongues, with the zenyan argot pervading. Outfitting the carts for the wounded took the rest, and transporting them the afternoon. That part, I supervised, attempting all the while to keep my eye on Imriel. Three times, he went to see the dead to confirm that the Kereyit Tatar Jagun was well and truly slain, which he assuredly was, and once he vanished in search of one of Joscelin's Cassiline daggers, the one that had killed the *Skotophagotis*. One of the women had snatched it up in passing in the wild rush for the festal hall. He found it, too, the hilt jutting from a Drujani soldier's ribs.

"Did you put him up to that?" I asked Joscelin, weary and distraught.

He shook his head. "I mentioned it, that's all. My mistake. Phèdre, are you sure you're fit to ride? You're white as a sheet. We can make room in the third wagon."

"I'll be fine."

Joscelin raised his eyebrows. "Phèdre," he said gently. "I've heard . . . stories."

I looked away. "Yes, well. It doesn't matter. Let me . . . just let me leave as I came. Not . . ." I watched a pair of Drujani servants bring out a young Hellene woman on a litter, careful not to jostle her. "Not like that. A victim."

"All right, then." He gave a wry smile when I glanced at him, shifting his arm in its sling. "Remember, if you faint and fall off your horse, I'm not going to be able to catch you."

"I won't." The words caught in my throat; I couldn't remember the last time I'd seen him smile, except in battle. "I promise. Joscelin . . ." I pressed my fingers to my aching temples, willing the too-ready tears to subside. "We'll put Imri in the wagon."

"He won't like it," he warned.

"Probably not," I said. "But it's the best place for him. You must have seen what Jagun did to him in the hall. The welts are still healing."

It was Joscelin's turn to look away. "I hate this," he said quietly. "I cannot tell you how much I hate this."

"I know." Even if there had been time, it was too enormous to discuss, too immediate. It lay between us, incomprehensible. I touched his uninjured hand. "Joscelin. Let's just . . . let's just get out of this alive, first. The rest can wait. If we can do that, the rest can wait."

After a moment, he nodded. "It will have to."

With a couple of hours of light left to us, we took our leave of Daršanga.

It was an unwieldy, polyglot caravan of riders and wagons and mules, inching and groaning along, flying the pure-white standard of Ahura Mazda and flanked by four unhappy Magi. Still, we were moving, and the grey walls and pitch-blackened roofs of Daršanga palace fell behind us. In the city, people stared open-mouthed, unsure what to make of our company, but leaving us unmolested. No one cringed or fled. In the open temple, the Sacred Fire burned, and a party of workers cleared rubble, cleaning the square, righting the marble benches. The forges had gone cold. We passed through the city and onto the open road.

Joscelin was right; it hurt to ride. If I had willed myself past the endless nights of torment, my body had not forgotten the abuse it had undergone, the ravages of the Mahrkagir's iron rod. I was sore and raw, and the pressure of the saddle made me bite my lip in an effort not to scream.

I rode anyway.

Mayhap it was a punishment, a means of castigating myself for the pain I had inflicted in this god-cursed quest; I cannot say. It was foolish, I know that much, but it was somewhat I needed to do. I had ridden into Daršanga of my own will. I would leave the same way.

And behind me, straddling the saddle with his knees and clinging to my waist with determination, rising with a wince at every bump, rode Imriel. He'd refused the wagon—Joscelin had been right about that, too. I understood it, understood his folly better than my own.

He had his mother's pride, and I could not help but love it in him. How not, when I had loved it in her?

Thus began our long, absurd trek across Drujan, which does not bear telling. Enough to say that we made it, most of us. Betimes we saw soldiers, the wolves of Angra Mainyu, bereft and leaderless. Some of them came to seek the Magi's blessing, penitent. Some saw the white flags and fled. I do not know who ruled in Daršanga, unless it be the Magus Arshaka.

Some of the injured died, despite our best efforts. Wounds took septic, or bled internally; one, with a blow to the head, fell asleep and never awakened. We lost seven in all, leaving scarcely fifty survivors from the zenana.

One was the Hellene girl I'd watched carried out, an islander sold at auction, traded to a *Skotophagotis* for a handful of coin. Ismene, her name was; I knew them all, by then. A sword-stroke had caught her beneath the armpit, and the gash had festered. I stayed with her the night she died, fever raging. Just before dawn, it broke and she grew lucid.

"*Lypiphera*," she said, seeing me and smiling. "I thought it was you."

"Shh, lie still." I removed the damp cloth, feeling her brow as she sought to rise, finding it cool. "Ismene, why do you call me that? I've heard it before."

"It is a story," she whispered, watching me wring out the cloth. "A story that slaves tell in Hellas. Sometimes the gods themselves find the pain of existence too much to bear. Because they are gods, they pick a mortal to bear it for them; a *lypiphera*, a pain-bearer." Catching my hand, she pressed it to her cheek and closed her eyes, still smiling. "Sometimes they take on mortal pain, too. It is a lucky thing, for slaves."

"Ismene." I swallowed my tears for the untold countless time, laying my palm against her soft skin. "Try to sleep."

In the morning, she was dead.

I'd thought the danger past when her fever broke. I sat on a rock and stared at the dawn, brooding. Joscelin had to come find me when camp was struck.

"Phèdre." His voice was cracked with exhaustion; we were all tired, then. "It's time to go. You did what you could."

"If I had studied medicine instead of—"

"You didn't." Something in his tone made me look. Joscelin sighed, dragging his good hand through his tangled, half-braided hair. "Phèdre, let it be. She died in freedom, attended by kindness. It's a better death than any she would have found in Daršanga. Let it be."

Since there was nothing else for it, I did, returning to our campsite. The caravan was waiting. A cairn of stones marked Ismene's final resting place. Imriel, kneeling behind me, turned in the saddle as we rode away, watching it diminish. "Remember them all," he said aloud, echoing my words. "Remember them all."

In the mornings there was no time, but in the evenings, when the tents were pitched, the horses and mules staked and the cookfires burning, Joscelin sought to practice his Cassiline exercises, one-armed and clumsy. All of that flowing grace, all his long discipline, was centered on symmetry and balance—the weaving patterns of his twin daggers, the crossed vambraces forming a living shield, the pivot of his two-handed sword grip. Bereft of it, his movements were awkward. His bound left arm fouled the sweep of his blows, rendering them ungainly, leaving him exposed. Time and again, he stumbled off-balance, losing his form, unable to complete the complex patterns.

It pained me to watch him.

He never complained, not once. And he never ceased trying, pushing himself harder as the bones began to knit. During the first days of our journey, his hand swelled alarmingly. I watched it closely, breathing a prayer of relief when the swelling began to recede. After that, he began to carry a good-sized rock in his left hand as he rode, squeezing it rhythmically for hours on end, trying to keep his muscles from growing slack and useless.

Ten years old, Joscelin had been when he was exiled from the loving chaos of Verreuil to the grim rigor of the Cassiline Brotherhood. I never saw so clearly how it had molded him as I did on that journey, in his unflagging resolve. So young, I thought, watching Imriel; only a boy, wearing the fragile shape of childhood. And I . . . I had been ten when my lord Delaunay took me from Cereus House, beginning the long apprenticeship that had made me what I was.

Imriel had Daršanga.

Remember this.

Twice, he had nightmares, awakening the entire camp with those terrible, piercing screams. The Drujani handlers nearly bolted in terror, and the Magi cringed in fearful reflex, recalling the iron chains of Angra Mainyu. Joscelin, wild-eyed, was on his feet in an instant, sword bare in his right hand, staring about for danger. The Akkadians and the women of the zenana only grumbled. I took Imriel in my arms, soothing him until he awoke and knew me. After that, the tears, and I held him while he shook with them, narrow shoulders heaving.

Joscelin sat with his sword across his knees, watching wearily.

We did not speak of what had happened in Daršanga. It was too soon, too vast. Let us get out of this alive, I had said. What was to become of us afterward, I could not say. There was love, still; that much, I knew. My heart ached at the sight of him. And Joscelin . . . I heard it in his voice, saw it in his wounded gaze, felt it in his touch. Love, broken and damaged, mayhap beyond repair. I prayed it was not so. In the evenings, I watched his halting, faltering exercises, and knew fear. He had survived, and the arm would heal. Whether or not his skills would ever be the same was another matter. Some things, once broken, can never be made whole again.

I prayed we were not one of them.

Halfway through the journey, I found the jade dog, the Mahrkagir's gift, stowed in the bottom of my packs. I sat on the floor of my tent in shock, staring at it. I remembered the Mahrkagir's pleasure in making me gifts, his boyish delight. I thought I had left them all behind. I remembered the nights of anguished pleasure, the exquisite, rending pain and the sound of my own voice begging. And I remembered his eyes, black and shining and mad, filled with adoration, his heart beating steadily beneath my hand as I positioned the hairpin.

"I thought . . . I thought you would want it." It was Imriel, sidling through the tent-flap, wary and unsure. "I didn't know."

"Yes." I longed to hurl it from me. Instead I closed my hand on it, smooth and polished, the jade cool to the touch. "You were right. Thank you, Imri."

I had killed a man, murdered his trust, taken his life. If I had to do it again, I would. I believe that. Still, I could not forget.

Should not forget.

For the others, it was different. They had not chosen their fates, and the shadow of blood-guilt did not lie heavy on their souls. Despite it all, despite the suffering and the madness, the scores of losses, the further we got from Daršanga, the higher their spirits rose. It gladdened my heart to see it, even though I envied them. Uru-Azag and the Akkadians had found in the battle some measure of their lost pride. If they were returning home less than men, still, they were more than slaves.

And the women . . .

At first, I think, a good many did not dare believe. By the time we reached the mountains, guarded fear gave way to hope, and thence to cautious rejoicing. Our company fractured into groups by country, echoing the divisions in the zenana, the zenyan argot fading as women began to speak of home in their own tongues, those who had family and loved ones remembering, speculating on whether or not they would be welcomed back.

Kaneka was one who had no doubts. Fierce and glowing, she took to freedom like a caged hawk to the sky, carrying her purloined battle-axe at her saddle and her dagger stuck through a sash round her waist.

"So, little one," she said to me the day we entered the mountains, our passage slowed by the wagons. "You will go to Jebe-Barkal after all, eh?"

"It seems I will."

"Maybe I will go with you." She grinned, showing her white teeth. "Come with me to Debeho. My grandmother, may she still live, will tell you many tales of the Melehakim."

"I have a guide to Meroë promised in Iskandria," I said.

"Iskandria." Kaneka waved a dismissive hand. "A caravan guide. He will rob you blind, little one. Better to travel the Great River to Majibara, and hire there. With me you will not be robbed."

Our pace was slow enough that a few Akkadians had dismounted to hunt along the way, shooting at rock partridge and the occasional startled hare. I watched Uru-Azag teaching Imriel to draw an Akkadian bow. "Do you mean it, Fedabin?"

"What do you think?" Kaneka touched the leather bag at her throat that held her amber dice. "Your luck . . . your madness. I owe my freedom to it."

"And others owe their deaths," I said.

She shrugged. "Did you kill them? No. Anyway, I am alive. It is enough. You may take my offer or not, I do not care. I am grateful nonetheless."

I looked at her and nodded. "I'll take it."

Fifty-nine

On THE third week of our slow journey, Tizrav son of Tizmaht found us in the mountains.

He was waiting at a campsite off the old royal road, busily skinning a fallow deer. I heard the commotion at the head of the caravan and rode to investigate, Joscelin a few paces behind me.

"Lady." The mercenary greeted me in Persian, grinning behind his greasy eyepatch, his hands messy with blood. "Lordling. You have returned."

"Tizrav!" I was so glad to see him, I nearly kissed him. "Did the Lugal send you? Or Lord Amaury? Are they near?"

"Amaury." He eased a skinning knife a few more inches beneath the deer's hide and separated it with an expert jerk. "He's the one offered a reward. They saw the fires light from Demseen Fort, and the cursed Akkadians are still too scared to go and see. Your Lord Amaury offered gold to anyone who would. That's me."

"You know this man?" Uru-Azag looked down his aquiline nose at Tizrav.

"He is the Lugal's most trusted guide," I said, stretching the truth considerably.

"The Lugal's going to have someone's hide when he finds out the Drujani let you march through with a passel of women and eunuchs, and his men too scared to cross the border," Tizrav said, shifting the flayed carcass. "What happened?"

"It's a long story," I said. "We were granted safe passage. Tizrav, how far are we from the border?"

"At your pace? Two days, maybe three." He eyed Imriel behind me, watching the operation in morbid fascination over my shoulder. "I see you got that boy you wanted."

"Yes. Is the border guarded?"

"By Drujani?" He shrugged. "You could march an army across it untouched, and like as not the Lugal will, when he hears of it. I figured I'd wait. Sinaddan didn't promise gold, not like your Lord Amaury did."

Someone overheard his words, and they passed through the company, translated into a dozen tongues. Cheering arose at the mention of an invading army. I raised my hand. "*No!*" The word came out sharp and forceful, quelling the cheers. I took a deep breath, shifting my mount to address them all, speaking in zenyan. "Drujan wishes to sue for peace, and I gave my word I would deliver the message. Let no one here gainsay it. Is it understood?"

It was, reluctantly.

"And you, son of Tizmaht," I said to the mercenary. "Will you bide your tongue until I have spoken?"

Tizrav gave his crooked shrug. "War, peace; what is it to me? There's more profit in the former, and less risk of dying in the latter. I'll keep silent if you wish it. My father, he'd be glad to see the Sacred Fires lit, devout fool that he was. I reckon I can owe you that much."

And so we made for the border.

On the second day, Tizrav rode ahead to alert the garrison at Demseen Fort of our arrival. Mercenary or no, he'd seen us safely to Daršanga, and I trusted him to keep his word. In that, I was not wrong.

Slowly, creeping along the mountain roads, our company followed.

After so long, it seemed unreal, the grey fortress on the horizon, flying the Lion of the Sun banner of the Shamabarsin, the ancient House of Ur. Some of the Akkadians, Uru-Azag among them, broke down and wept. The reluctant Magi who had accompanied us dug in their heels, deserting us, taking the Drujani hostlers and bearers with them. No one moved to detain them, and the stones rattled with their passage.

Horns rang out from the turrets, clarion calls echoing over the crags. We had been seen.

The garrison turned out to meet us.

Foremost among them was Lord Amaury Trente, disbelief and joy writ large on his features. "Phèdre!" He embraced me, kissed me on both cheeks, then took my shoulders in his hands and shook me. "Name of Elua, I swear . . . Joscelin Verreuil, you mad Cassiline . . ." He embraced Joscelin awkwardly, mindful of his bound arm. "And you—" Catching sight of Imriel lurking warily between us, he paused and executed a courtly bow, his voice unwontedly gentle. "You must be Imriel de la Courcel. My lord prince, welcome back."

"What?" Amid the milling chaos of the reunion, Imriel's voice was lost and bewildered, rising to panic as he glanced from Amaury to me and back. "*What?*"

I closed my eyes and bit the inside of my cheek. I hadn't thought.

"Phèdre." Amaury's hand on my arm forced me to attention. "You didn't *tell* him?"

"No." I shook my head. "Amaury . . . you can't know what it was like."

"*What?*" Imriel's demand rose, strident with fear. In his experience, the unknown was never good. This time, I daresay he was right. "Tell me *what?*"

"Imri." I knelt before him, taking his hands in mine. "I didn't tell you the whole truth. Lord Amaury is right. Your name, your full name, is Imriel de la Courcel, and you are a Prince of the Blood, third in line for the D'Angeline throne."

His face had gone bloodless. "You said . . . you said my father was dead."

"He is," I said steadily. "Your father was Prince Benedicte de la Courcel, the great-uncle of Queen Ysandre. She is your cousin, and she has been praying very hard for your safe return. Lord Amaury here is her emissary. He has come all this way to bring you home."

Imriel tore his hands out of my grasp, clenching them into fists. "You *lied*," he hissed, eyes glittering feverishly in his pale face. "You said my *mother* sent you!"

"Your mother!" Amaury Trente gave a short laugh, and caught himself. "My lord prince, your mother . . ." He looked at my face. "He doesn't know."

"No." Even as I spoke, Imriel spat at me and darted away, running pell-mell for the fortress.

"I'll go after him," Joscelin said quietly, suiting actions to words. I sighed and straightened, wiping spittle from my cheek.

"I'm sorry." Lord Amaury slid his fingers through his hair. "Phèdre, I'm sorry. I assumed——"

"I should have," I said, cutting him off. "I know. Amaury, the boy's spent the past half a year in the seraglio of a madman. Do you see these women? They've been through hell, every one of them. So have I, and so has Imriel. All of us have. So, no. I didn't tell him. And yes, his mother sent me. Ysandre," I said, holding his gaze, "sent you. Melisande sent me."

"Melisande," Amaury repeated doubtfully.

"Yes," I said, weary beyond belief. "Melisande."

We did not stay long at Demseen Fort, only long enough to gather ourselves for the journey to Nineveh. The accommodations were rough, unprepared to handle so many refugees, and we slept crammed on pallets in the main hall. For two nights and a day, Imriel avoided me, clinging fiercely to his sense of betrayal. I let him. Joscelin, somehow exempt from his outrage, shadowed him dutifully, as did Kaneka and Uru-Azag, who had both conceived a fondness for the wayward child.

On the morning we were to depart, Imriel was missing.

"Phèdre." Joscelin found me overseeing the loading of the wounded, helping arrange cushions to bolster the leg of Ursalina, an Aragonian woman whose thigh had been laid open nearly to the bone. Miraculously, it was healing clean, the layers of muscle and skin closed in neat stitches by the hand of the Caerdicci seamstress Helena.

"Did you find him?" I asked.

He nodded toward the far crags on which the fortress perched. "He's up there. I think you should talk to him."

"How is that?" I asked Ursulina in zenyan, testing the stability of the cushions. "Better?" At her grateful nod, I turned to Joscelin. "You go. He's angry at me, and rightly enough."

Joscelin's face was haggard in the morning sunlight. "He knows about his mother," he said, watching my expression change. "Phèdre, he was bound to ask, and bound to find someone who would tell him. It wasn't gently done."

"Who told him?"

"Nicolas Vigny," he said, naming Amaury's right-hand man. "And Martin de Marigot. It's not . . . it's not their fault, either. They only spoke the truth. Vigny fought at Troyes-le-Monte; he lost a brother there. He's reason to be bitter. It was her doing, after all."

"So," I said. "Why me?"

"Because," Joscelin said steadily. "For better or for worse, you understand Melisande Shahrizai. You're the only one who can tell her son she loves him without gagging on the words."

There was so much unspoken between us.

"All right," I said, pushing tendrils of sweat-dampened hair from my brow. "I'll go."

Hoisting the skirts of my riding attire, I traversed the narrow path that encircled Demseen Fortress and found Imriel seated on the farthest outcropping, moodily pitching shards of broken rock into the gorge below.

"Imriel," I said.

His narrow shoulders stiffened, the bones protruding like wings beneath his fine skin; too sharply, I thought, although what did I know of children? Still, he seemed too thin, too frail for his age. The found-lings in the Sanctuary of Elua had been sturdy by comparison. Even Alcuin, the brother of my fosterage, with his slender grace, his milk-white hair and gentle smile, had been hale next to this boy.

I made my way across the crags to join him, sitting without speak-ing. Below us, the forested gorge yawned, a light mist sparkling golden in the morning sun. Imriel kept his face averted, fiddling with a handful of pebbles.

"Why didn't you tell me?" he asked without looking up.

"I was wrong." I kept my tone level. "Imri, I was going to. I wanted to wait until we were safe, that's all. I didn't expect Lord Amaury to greet you thusly. It was stupid of me."

"My mother did something foolish." He drew in a wracking breath, his voice half-breaking. "That's what you told me! Something foolish! My mother betrayed Terre d'Ange to the *Skaldi!*" His head came up, eyes blazing at me. "She married my father for power, and had me as a pawn, a game-piece! She tried to have the Queen *killed!* Something foolish!"

"Yes," I said, unflinching. "It's a lot to bear, isn't it?"

His tears caught the morning light. "You said she *loved* me. You said she sent you."

I clasped my hands around my knees. "She does, Imri. The Queen sent Lord Amaury. Your mother sent me. And I gave her my promise, in Blessed Elua's name, that I would do aught I could to find you and keep you from harm. It wasn't enough. I know that. But it was the best I could do."

"Why would you help her? Why would she ask you?" Imriel looked away, staring into the gorge. "You gave the testimony that condemned her. Nicolas Vigny told me so, and he was there."

"Yes," I said. "He was." I thought about the caravan, near-loaded and waiting. I looked at Imriel's fine-carved profile and thought about all that he had been through, and the life that awaited him as Melisande's son, born of treason twice over, in the court of Ysandre de la Courcel. "Do you want to hear the story? The whole story?"

Without looking at me, he nodded.

And drawing a deep breath, I told him—the story, as best I knew it; his, his mother's and father's, and mine own. I told him of the marital alliances that had bound House Courcel, of my Lord Delaunay's secret vow, and of my upbringing as a pawn, a Servant of Naamah marked by Kushiel, trained in the arts of covertcy and shrouded in ignorance. I told him of his mother's patronage, and how she had freed me, paying the final price of my marque; and I told him without faltering of her betrayal after Delaunay's death—although I spared him the knowledge of how she had questioned me—and how Joscelin and I had awakened to find ourselves in a covered cart bound for Skaldia. I told him of our time there, and what we had learned; I told him how we had escaped, and of our desperate quest to Alba, of the Master of the Straits and Hyacinthe's terrible sacrifice, and then the battle that followed.

Some of it, he knew. Brother Selbert had not kept him completely unaware of history. He knew of the Skaldi invasion, and the Master of the Straits, though not Hyacinthe's name. Of Melisande's role, he knew nothing—nor of the near overthrow of the throne in La Serenissima.

It was hard, telling him that part. He was right. He was a game-piece, gotten for his claim on the D'Angeline throne. I did not deny it, only stressed how his mother had sought to protect him, giving him unto Brother Selbert's keeping. On my own role, I touched lightly, saying only that I had returned in time to give the warning.

And then his disappearance, and his mother's bargain.

Of that, I did not lie or mince words.

"She bought you," he said softly when I had finished, staring at the dispersing mists. "She bought you with knowledge, as surely as with diamonds or gold."

"Imriel." I saw him hunch his shoulders at his name. "Your mother values pride and knowledge above either, and she spent them both to buy my aid. She spent every coin she had."

"What happened to me is because of *her*," he muttered bitterly. "Can you deny it is so?"

"In Siovale, I believed it to be," I admitted. "And I cursed Kushiel's name for it, believing it unjust, that you should suffer for your mother's punishment. In Aragonia, in Amílcar, I did the same. In Daršanga . . . Imri, your mother's bargain and my promise carried me as far as Nineveh. It was the will of Blessed Elua sent me into Drujan to find you, and I swear to you, I'd not have done it for anything less. Imriel . . . I'm no priestess, to reckon the will of the gods. But what do you think the Mahrkagir would have done, if we had not stopped him?"

"Killed a lot of people," he murmured, scraping at the rocky escarpment with a jagged piece of stone. "Conquered the world."

"And laughed." I propped my chin on my hands. "He'd have thought it great sport."

Imriel nodded. "He would have laughed."

"Well." I took a breath. "He's not laughing now. And it's because of you, Imri. Had it not been for you—for who you are, for the terrible thing that befell you—the Mahrkagir would be alive, and laughing. So. I am not so quick to curse the gods, least of all Blessed Elua."

He gazed stubbornly into the chasm beneath his feet. "But it's not *fair*."

"No." My heart ached for him; for me, for Joscelin, for all of us. "It's not. Ah, Imri! Even gods may falter, and I am only mortal. I would have spared you any harm, but I failed to protect you in Daršanga, and I failed here, too. I am sorry. I did my best."

His shoulders twitched. "You were hurt worse. In Daršanga."

"Mayhap." I flinched at the memory, knowing he couldn't see, and made sure my voice was steady. "But it was of my choosing, Imri, and it was worth it in the end. The Mahrkagir is no more. And you . . . you are safe, and will soon be with the Queen, who has yearned these many years to welcome you into her household as kindred. I can ask no more."

"It's still not fair," he muttered.

"I know." Reaching out with one hand, I stroked his hair. "Ah, love! I know."

"I want to stay with you." Abruptly, Imriel lifted his head, his expression at once belligerent and vulnerable. "With you and Joscelin. I don't want to go back with Lord Amaury, to be *her* son and *his*, where all the world will hate me! I don't care about thrones and all that! I don't care about the Queen! I want to stay with you."

"You can't," I said gently. "Like it or not, it is true. You are Imriel de la Courcel, a Prince of the Blood, and you have a future awaiting you. Right now, there is a caravan awaiting your pleasure, and a pony picked out just for you. Uru-Azag saw to the trappings himself. And there are injured women awaiting, who would be better served by the chirurgeons of Nineveh than my poor endeavors. Will you keep them waiting all day?"

"No." Sober at the reminder, Imriel got to his feet at the verge of the yawning gorge. I swallowed my fear and rose, holding out my hand.

He took it gravely, crossing the gap between us. "I'm sorry, Phèdre," he said, looking at me with guilt-stricken eyes. "Will they hate me for it, do you think? Because I am my mother's son?"

"No." I held his hand hard, my heart aching. "I won't let them."

Sixty

Sinaddan-Shamabarsin did not wish us to enter Nineveh with fanfare, and therefore we passed through the gates in the small hours of the night, when the horned moon hung white and distant overhead, diffusing a silver light over the clay buildings, casting odd shadows on the empty streets.

It was the only way. A company of our size, mainly comprised of unveiled women from a dozen nations, would have drawn attention. I was glad of it, for it meant the Lugal had taken the warning I'd sent ahead by courier to heart. He would not act until he had heard me out.

Still, it was strange, everything muffled by night, the faces I'd come to know so well rendered indistinct. And stranger still when we parted ways at the Palace of Nineveh. Valère L'Envers, the Lugalin, had ordered an unused wing of the women's quarters thrown open and made ready for their arrival, and there they would be housed, while their fates were decided.

A different welcome awaited the D'Angelines.

The rest of us—Amaury, Joscelin, Imriel and I—would be treated as royal guests, and Amaury's three comrades quartered within the Palace. And despite the lateness of the hour, we were formally received as such by the Lugalin herself.

"Comtesse Phèdre nó Delaunay de Montrève." Color stood out on Valère L'Envers cheeks as she sat like a gilded effigy on the throne in her private audience hall, and I could not say if she was pleased to see me or not. "My lord Trente, Messire Cassiline." The jewel-bedecked headdress dipped, and her voice changed. "Prince Imriel de la Courcel."

We all made obeisance. Imriel bowed stiffly, wary. "Your highness."

In the cloistered hall, I saw him anew—saw what Valère saw, the gemlike beauty, the blue-black hair of House Shahrizai, his eyes the color of sapphires, the hue of twilight. His mother's face, carved in miniature.

Her mouth twisted as she regarded me. "So again, despite all odds, you return alive, Comtesse. It seems I will not have to undertake the grievous task of composing notice of your death to my cousin Ysandre after all."

"It seems," I said, "that you will not, my lady. We are grateful for your hospitality."

"Yes." Valère contemplated us. "I have arranged for you and Messire Joscelin to share quarters, Comtesse. I trust it will not displease you. As far as the Akkadian nobility is concerned, you may as well be considered wed. And the prince shall be housed in adjoining quarters. I am told you have grown . . . close."

Truly, we were back in the world, and all the politics that it entailed. I remembered the genuine kindness she had shown me before we left; Valère L'Envers, I feared, had liked me a good deal better when she thought I was dead. I made a graceful curtsy, wondering if she'd already written my eulogy in these months gone by. "My lady is too gracious."

She waved a disinterested hand. "It is the least I can do. My lord Sinaddan is eager for your report, once you are rested. My lord Trente, quarters have been prepared also for you. My lords, my lady . . . be welcome in Nineveh."

And with that, we were dismissed and escorted to our quarters. I was bone-weary, too tired to think it through. With Joscelin and Imriel, I followed the attendant eunuch to our appointed quarters, luxuriant and generous. There was a single door dividing our rooms from Imriel's. The last I saw as I laid my head upon soft cushions on a down pallet was Joscelin silhouetted by lamplight, standing in the dividing doorway and asking a question. As I sank into dreams, Imriel's voice followed me, giving an answer . . .

. . . and then I slept, and knew no more.

In the morning, Valère's personal physician, an Eisandine chirurgeon who had travelled with her into virtual exile in Khebbel-im-Akkad, came to examine us. After so long, it was a relief to surrender to his expertise. With careful fingers, he unwrapped the bindings on Joscelin's arm, examining the set of the bone and grunting.

It was something of a shock to see how the muscles had dwindled with disuse, the skin pallid and sloughing. At the chirurgeon's bidding, Joscelin moved his arm, clenched his left hand into a fist. The chirurgeon merely grunted, bathing the injured limb with care and letting it dry before he reapplied bindings of clean white cotton, splinting them in place. Drucilla's shawl, he cast away in disdain, replacing it with an elegant sling of brocaded cloth.

"Will he regain the use of his arm?" I asked.

"Like as not, though he'll favor it all of his days." The chirurgeon shrugged. "It's well set, barbarian work or no."

I gathered Drucilla's shawl, travel-stained and creased into greasy folds, to my breast. Barbarian work. "I set it myself, my lord chirurgeon," I said. "Under the direction of a physician of Tiberium."

"You did well enough." He beckoned. "Come, then, and let me have a look."

Joscelin left the room when the Eisandine chirurgeon examined me. For all his brusqueness, his touch was gentle and impersonal. He kept his head bowed, and made no comment until it was done.

"I saw worse, among the others," he said, washing his hands in a basin. "Her majesty sent me last night. Wouldn't have thought so, if I understood aright what you've undergone. Comfrey, and oil of lavender—I'll have my assistant make a salve. But you're healing anew, where they've scarred. Your tissues . . . Kushiel's gift?"

"Yes." Sitting up, I smoothed my skirts over my knees. "If you want to call it that."

He nodded, an unexpected compassion in his grey eyes. "I've heard. I'll give you a balm, too, to rub on yon Cassiline's arm, when the time comes. Three more weeks, mind, before the bindings come off. It will help the blood flow, and aid healing. Don't tell him I gave it you, or he'll be out of the sling in a heartbeat. I know his kind."

"Thank you," I whispered. "My lord chirurgeon, thank you."

"You needn't. I've taken a vow, like you." He paused. "I saw the boy, earlier."

"And?" Anxiety made my heart beat a little faster.

"He'll heal." The chirurgeon gathered up his things. "The brand will leave a scar, but his welts are clean and he is young, and strong of spirit. 'Tis the bitterness that festers worst. Let him talk of it, if he wishes. As he comes to manhood . . ." Remembering of whom he spoke, he let his words trail into silence. "Well. He'll be cared for, no doubt."

"No doubt," I echoed. "Thank you, my lord chirurgeon. I will take your words to heart, and see that they are passed on to those who need hear them."

The salve came within the hour, and Joscelin's balm with it, stoppered in an earthenware jar and smelling of camphor and wintergreen.

I hid it among my things. Valère L'Envers sent gifts of clothing, gorgeous robes and veils in the Akkadian style, and unguents and cosmetics. After a welcome soak in the waters of the bathhouse, I had myself properly attired. Elua knows, it was strange. My own skin felt unfamiliar to me, clean and fragrant with perfumed oils. The touch of silk against my flesh was unwontedly luxurious.

"My lady." It was one of Valère's eunuchs at the door, eyes downcast. Behind him stood Joscelin, exotic in a long, broad-sleeved tunic of garnet, worn over trousers. He looked manifestly uncomfortable, and not because of the brocaded sling. "The Lugal will see you."

One does not argue, when a prince commands. I donned my veil and went.

"Where's Imri?" I asked Joscelin as we traversed the halls.

"In the zenana." He said it unthinking; the word was the same, in Akkadian. "The women's quarters. Uru-Azag will keep an eye on him."

"Good." I stole a sideways glance at him. His fair hair, clean and braided, hung in a neat cable down his back and the sumptuous attire set off his austere beauty. "It suits you, you know."

The corner of his mouth rose, ever so slightly. "No. It suits *you*."

And then we arrived at Prince Sinaddan-Shamabarsin's private audience room, and there was no time for talk. It was only us and his bride, but nonetheless intense for it. The Lugal paced the room as we entered, black brows scowling beneath his turban of cloth-of-gold.

"Rumors," he said abruptly, fetching up before us. "I hear rumors, Comtesse, rumors of Drujan. From Demseen Fort, they come; from all along the border, from my own lady wife. Rumors that the Mahrkagir's power lies in shards, that his armies have lost their will, that Sacred Fires are alight and the bone-priests of Angra Mainyu run shrieking before the blaze. And in the midst of it you come, alive and unlooked-for, bearing a wagon-train of women and eunuchs, sending word that bids me hold my hand. Well and so, I have done it. Now tell me why."

I told him.

For all that it had taken an eternity to live it, the tale was short in the telling. I had slain the Mahrkagir, and the zenana had overthrown Daršanga. Afterward, the Sacred Fires had kindled, and we had made a bargain with the Chief Magus Arshaka. Such a brief tale, to encompass such suffering.

Valère L'Envers went pale during it. Whether she liked me or no, she was D'Angeline, and guessed better than her royal husband what had ensued, and the cost of it.

"It is for this," I said, "my lord, that I ask your aid in seeing these women restored to their homes. They have suffered gravely and sacrificed much, each one."

Prince Sinaddan glanced briefly at his wife, who nodded. It seemed they were in accord. "It shall be done," he said. "Each one of them. Upon the heads of my sons, I swear it; Khebbel-im-Akkad shall dower each one, fit unto a daughter of the House of Ur. But what, my lady, do you say of Drujan? Your bargain is concluded; you have come safe to Nineveh. You are among friends, and may speak freely. I have a small measure of time before this matter comes to the attention of my father, and pressing decisions to make within it. Do you sue for peace, even after what you have endured?"

Taking a deep breath, I clasped my hands together. "My lord," I said, "I do. It was never the will of the people of Drujan—the farmers, the fisherfolk, the weavers and servants—to follow the worship of Angra Mainyu. 'Twas a few, an embittered few, who grasped power where they found it. And that power, my lord, has its roots in the cruelty of Khebbel-im-Akkad. It is the atrocities committed against the family of Hoshdar Ahzad that gave birth to the Mahrkagir. My lord, I sue for peace on behalf of Drujan that his like may never come again."

"Men have died," he said in a deep voice, "Akkadian men, two mighty armies destroyed. Shall we allow Drujan to surrender peaceably and let this go unpunished? Surely, our weakness will be despised, and Persians everywhere will laugh up their sleeves, encouraged to new insurrection."

"No." I shook my head. "My lord, for eight years Drujani rule has followed the path of Angra Mainyu: ill thoughts, ill words, ill deeds. The land is ravaged, salted and laid barren in many places, the livestock neglected and beaten. The people are starving and weary of living in fear. Ask your scouts, if you do not believe me; ask Tizrav, who accompanied us to Daršanga." I thought of the Persian mercenary, his loyalty sworn to the radiant light of gold. "My lord, if you enter Drujan with vengeance and bloodshed, it will foment hatred. If you enter with order and aid, distributing foodstuffs, restoring trade, they will hail you as a liberator."

"Hmm." Prince Sinaddan studied Joscelin. "What do you say, my silent warrior? You've seen more than the Comtesse of the inner workings of Drujani governance. Are you agreed?"

"My lord." Joscelin inclined his head. He had learned enough of the Akkadian tongue to reply in kind. "The Mahrkagir's army is in disarray, having ever depended on the fearsome gifts of his Âka-Magi. Their power is broken, their allies have fled, and the people look to the ancient Magi to lead them. I concur with my lady Phèdre. The moment is opportune. You will conquer Drujan more thoroughly with compassion than armies."

And the Lugal, the new breed of Akkadian despot, mindful of the responsibilities of power, nodded to himself, his neatly tended black beard bobbing. "It is so," he said, half to himself. "Although my father may not see it. Well, and as he has entrusted me to guard the northern borders, so I may choose. I will dictate terms of a peaceful surrender and send a delegation to this Magus Arshaka. Let us see how he responds."

A profound wave of relief swept through me. "My lord is wise."

"We shall see." Sinaddan allowed himself a smile. "Comtesse, I am mindful of the debt I owe you. You and your consort alone have done what two Akkadian armies could not. Will you not name a reward?"

"Your gratitude is reward enough, my lord," I said automatically. "For the rest, I ask only reparations for the women of the zenana, and mayhap a place of honor among your guard for Uru-Azag and his comrades, to whose bravery we owe our lives."

"They shall form the core of my personal guard," Valère L'Envers announced. "Being eunuchs, they may not serve among whole men, yet I think it shall be honor enough. Phèdre nó Delaunay, is there no reward you will claim for yourself?"

There was a touch of impatience in her voice. I daresay the Lugalin of Khebbel-im-Akkad did not care to be indebted to a D'Angeline courtesan, no matter what the circumstance. "An escort to Tyre would not be amiss, my lady."

"Escort!" Prince Sinaddan laughed. "You'll have that, and more."

And with that we were dismissed, our audience concluded.

When it was done, I felt as exhausted as if I'd fought a second war. Truly, politics is a wearying business, fraught with tension and pitfalls, and so many lives at stake on one man's decision. In our quarters, I went to the dividing door to see if Imriel had been returned to his rooms, but they were still empty. Too tired to move, I simply stood there. Joscelin came up behind me, his good arm resting lightly about my waist. It was enough. As much as I loved him, I couldn't have borne anything more.

"It's going to take me a while," I said quietly.

"I know."

"I'm sorry." I wished I didn't feel broken inside.

"Phèdre." He turned me gently to face him. "I know. You did what you had to do. I would that it had been otherwise, but I don't blame you for it. What you did . . . it was a brave and noble thing, truly."

"Then why do I feel so awful?" I whispered.

Joscelin touched my hair, looking sick. "Do you . . . do you want to speak of it?"

"Of what happened in Daršanga?" I laid one hand on his chest, keeping him at bay, feeling his heart beating steady and strong beneath it. Tears came to my eyes unbidden. "Oh, Joscelin! Even if I did . . . could you bear to hear it?"

His answer, when it came, was rough and honest. "I don't know."

"So." I swallowed hard, nodding. "We'll wait and see."

$\mathscr{S}$ixty-one

İt was Imriel's scream that awoke us both, shattering slumber—short, sharp and urgent, a cry of imminent danger.

"That's no nightmare." Instantaneously alert, Joscelin rolled out of bed and onto his feet, mother-naked, fumbling for a weapon. Struggling into a silk dressing-robe, I followed as he raced into Imriel's room, illuminated by a faint light from the torch-lit hallway.

On his bed, Imriel knelt, white-faced with stark terror, his hands fixed in rigid claws. A figure clad in loose-fitting black clothes, a dark burnoose concealing its face, retreated toward the outer door, which stood ajar.

With a curse, Joscelin hurled his dagger.

It missed, clattering against the door-frame. The figure spun and dashed into the hall, Joscelin hard on its heels. I kindled a lamp with trembling fingers, only then daring to look at Imriel. "Are you all right?"

He nodded, hands unclenching slowly, his narrow chest heaving.

"What happened?" I asked him.

"I woke up and someone was there. I screamed, and—" He mimed striking out with one clawed hand. "Then Joscelin came. Do you think he was trying to kill me?"

I sat down on the edge of Imriel's bed. "What do you think?"

"Yes." His face was still white, but he was calmer. "I think so."

So did I, but I waited until Joscelin returned, grim and empty-handed.

"I lost him," he said shortly. "Or her. I couldn't tell. What do you think, Imri? Was it a man or a woman?"

"I don't know." The boy sounded miserable. "It was dark."

"You did well. You did very well." Joscelin retrieved his dagger and scowled at his left arm in its sling. "I'd have had him, if not for this. It puts off my aim. I can't move as quickly, either. A three-step lead? I should have had him."

Imriel shivered, huddling on the bed and hugging his knees. I stroked his hair. "You must have gotten some odd looks," I said, eyeing Joscelin. Aside from his sling, he was still rather splendidly naked. Imriel peered over his knees and giggled.

"A few." Joscelin raised his eyebrows. "Come on, you. From now on, you'll stay in our quarters."

It took the better part of an hour, but eventually Imriel fell asleep in our bed. Joscelin and I sat up, wrapped in robes and discussing it in low voices.

"It could have been anyone," he said in disgust. "Man, woman, eunuch; Akkadian, D'Angeline—Jebean, even . . . I didn't get a good enough look. He ducked into a side hall, and by the time I'd back-tracked, I'd lost him."

"None of the guards outside saw anything?"

He shook his head. "None would admit it."

"Either they lied, which means likely it's an Akkadian conspiracy, or they saw naught out of the ordinary, which still means it was likely an Akkadian. Not a woman; a woman unescorted would draw notice, at this hour."

"It could be a D'Angeline." Joscelin's voice was quiet. "Valère has D'Angeline servants in her entourage, enough to pass unremarked."

"True." Neither of us needed state the obvious, which was that Valère L'Envers was Duc Barquiel's daughter, and the Duc most assuredly would prefer Imriel dead. "Lord Amaury's men have the run of the Palace as well."

Joscelin sighed, dragging his free hand through his sleep-tangled hair. "Amaury . . . surely you don't suspect Amaury."

"Amaury, no. But the others . . ." I stared at the dancing flame of the oil lamp. "How well do you know them? Vigny, de Marigot, Charves . . . Vigny's bitter, you said so yourself." I looked up. "It would be a stroke of genius for someone who wanted the boy dead to get himself placed on the mission to find him."

"Amaury's company was hand-picked," he said. "Valère's a likelier candidate."

"I agree." I thought of Melisande Shahrizai's description of Lord

Amaury Trente in La Serenissima. *A capable man, it is said, and loyal to the Queen, but not, I think, a clever one.* "Nonetheless, we must consider the possibility."

"So what do we do?"

"Look for scratched faces," I said. "Imri drew blood; there were traces of it under his nails. If it's none of Amaury's men . . ." I grimaced. "All we have to do is get him to Tyre alive."

"With the Lugal's generous escort," Joscelin observed. "Filled with Elua knows how many would-be assassins." He glanced toward the bedchamber. "You know . . . all my life, from the time I was ten, I trained for this, for this very thing—to serve as a personal bodyguard to a member of House Courcel, the finest possible protection against the threat of assassination. And now?" He shrugged, the robe slipping from his bound shoulder. "I'm useless."

"Not useless," I said fiercely. "Never that! I'd rather have you one-handed than an entire company of Black Shields!"

He smiled, but his eyes were bleak. "I can't fight, Phèdre. You've seen it as well as I. Until this happened . . . I didn't mind, not so much as I thought I might. After Daršanga, if I never have to kill anyone again, it will be too soon. But the boy . . ." He glanced back toward Imriel. "He needs a Cassiline, not a cripple."

"Joscelin." Tears stood in my eyes. "Anyone who wants to kill him will have to go through both of us first. And no one's done it yet."

After a moment he nodded, reaching out to brush my cheek. "Go to bed," he murmured. "I'll take the first watch and wake you before dawn."

I slept uneasily and rose when Joscelin, bleary-eyed, awoke me. While they slept, I studied the Jebean scroll which Valère L'Envers had restored to me. I'd learned a good deal more Jeb'ez than I realized, eavesdropping on Kaneka and her companions. I pondered the raiment of the figures, the bejeweled breastplate, the diadem placed upon Melek al'Hakim's brow after he was anointed. I pondered the two figures escaping from the ruin of the Temple, carrying the cloth-shrouded burden between them on two poles. Slowly, the mysteries I had studied filtered back into my mind, the long hours spent with Eleazar ben Enokh, with the Rebbe before him, the many texts I had perused. I thought on Eleazar's parting words. *You must make of the self a vessel where there is no self.* What did it mean, if not what I had undergone in Daršanga? Truly, the ways of gods were unknowable.

A breathless laugh broke my concentration and I jerked my head up, startled.

"You see?" Joscelin said to Imriel. "The Lugal himself could ride past her on a tiger, and she'd not notice."

"I would, too," I said. I don't think either of them believed me.

We spent the day in investigation, as best we might; no easy thing, in unfamiliar surroundings. Joscelin, with Imriel at his side, sought out Lord Amaury's men, examining them for scratches. For my part, I went to the women's quarters where the zenana was housed, hoping to find Uru-Azag. Alas, I was too late—already, Valère had put her plan in motion, and the Akkadians were being fitted for livery and decorative armor suiting their new appointment as the Lugalin's personal guard.

I spoke to Kaneka instead, valuing her wisdom. "Send him here, little one, if you fear for his safety in your keeping. We are enough still to protect one boy." She grinned, hefting her axe. "I have not forgotten how to use this!"

"I will, Fedabin," I said. "Thank you."

Kaneka shrugged. "The sooner we are gone, the better. My feet itch for home."

All was merriment in the women's quarters, aside from the pall my worries cast; Valère and Sinaddan had been generous in their gifts. In that, I could not fault them. New wardrobes, gifts of jewels, visitors coming and going throughout the day, bearing some new tribute. Already the messengers had gone out, and in some cases, among the Persians and Akkadians, negotiations were beginning for their return home.

In Daršanga, someone in the zenana would have known had there been an assassination attempt. Here, they were strangers, more so than I, and Nineveh only a way-station. I had no allies, no Rushad to bring me court rumor. The thought, tinged with a nostalgia that was not entirely rooted in sorrow at the memory of Rushad, was unsettling.

Remember this.

Some things I remembered too well.

After the zenana, I called upon Valère L'Envers. There was, I had determined, nothing to be gained in accusing her, nor in reporting the incident—ostensibly, all she could do was to express deep regrets and offer to appoint us guards, which would put her people even closer at hand. That, I wished to avoid at all costs. Still, I wished to see her, and deliver a subtle message.

Valère received me in her private paradise, which Sinaddan had had built for her. It is not so splendid, I am told, as the famous roof-top gardens of Babylon. Mayhap it is so; since I have not seen them, I cannot say. This was splendid enough, a tiny corner of Terre d'Ange recreated within the red-clay walls of Nineveh.

Fertile soil had been imported, and lush green lawn. The cost of the irrigation system alone must have been phenomenal, creating the gentle brook that wound throughout the garden, crossed by quaint, arching bridges. Flowers bloomed in profusion, quickened by the Akkadian spring—violets, roses, sweet alyssum, jumbled and out of season. Valère L'Envers was picnicking with her ladies-in-waiting beneath a cherry tree, luxuriant carpets spread on the petal-bestrewn grass.

"Phèdre nó Delaunay," she hailed me in Akkadian, lifting a glass of chilled D'Angeline wine. "Pray, come and join us. We are escaping the unpleasantness of the world for an afternoon of leisure."

"Is the world so unpleasant, my lady?" I inquired, kneeling on a carpet and arranging my skirts about me.

"Have you not found it so?" Valère's tone was light, but something in it caught my ear. She smiled blandly, gesturing for an attendant to pour a glass of wine for me. "Given your recent experience, I would have thought you to find it unpleasant indeed."

I sipped my wine. "And which experience would that be, my lady?"

Valère's lids flickered. "Why, Drujan, of course. Surely you've experienced no unpleasantness in Nineveh?"

"No, no." I shook my head. "Nothing of import. I slept poorly last night, is all. I trust it will not happen again. Poor Joscelin was up half the night."

At that, one of her ladies laughed behind her hand, and made a speculative comment about Joscelin's prowess, wondering if his beard-less state indicated he was a eunuch. I assured her that his manhood was intact, and another of the women offered that she had heard he had been seen in the hallways of the Palace last night, in such a lack of attire as made it obvious he was indeed very much intact. This gave way to speculation as to why Joscelin Verreuil was roaming the halls mother-naked, the consensus being that with the exception of the Lugalin, all D'Angelines were mad and unpredictable, but nonetheless pleasant to look at, particularly the spectacularly naked ones, a sight doubtless wasted on the Palace guards.

Throughout it all, the bland smile never left Valère L'Envers' face.

I smiled too, and thanked her when my wine was done, taking my leave.

Well and so; it left no doubt in my mind, although I was sorry for it. She was the Queen's own cousin, and I owed my life to her father. Moreover, she was Nicola's cousin, too—Nicola, to whom I had given a lover's token, and who had taught me once a valuable lesson about my own suspicions. I would far rather, I thought ruefully, have them proved false. Valère L'Envers had done good things in Khebbel-im-Akkad. In my brief time in Nineveh, I had gathered that her influence with Sinaddan was to the good, tempering his Akkadian ferocity and nourishing his forward-looking method of rule, at odds with his father the Khalif's heavy hand. She had borne him three sons, and like as not the eldest would be named Lugal when Sinaddan assumed the Khalifate.

Why did she want Imriel dead?

Loyalty, mayhap; House L'Envers protects its own. It is why they are so fiercely loyal to the code of their password. What plans did Valère have for her younger sons? I could not say; did not know aught of the lads, who had been shielded from our presence here. Loyalty, or ambition? Ysandre was the first member of her House, insofar as I knew, to place the good of the realm above her family . . . but Ysandre, I thought, was a rare being by anyone's terms. I missed her, then; missed her terribly. Cool and calculating she might be, ruled by her intellect, but in her own way, she honored the precept of Blessed Elua to its fullest. *Love as thou wilt.* When it came to it, my icy and precise Queen was willing to stake her life on love. I remembered how she had ridden through the ranks of de Somerville's army, parting them like blades of grass bowing before the wind. And I remembered how she and Drustan mab Necthana had danced together at the fête where we had been honored, their eyes only for each other, smiling, evincing a love so profound it seemed a trespass to behold it.

I'd seen that look in the Mahrkagir's eyes.

I wondered if Joscelin and I would ever look at each other that way again.

And I wondered, deeply, if Valère L'Envers had acted of her own accord, or if she had orders from her father. Lord Amaury Trente had sent word from Menekhet. If Duc Barquiel had learned of it, there would have been time, during the months we spent in Drujan, for him to send orders to Valère. *I'll not pretend I'd be sorry to hear of the child's demise*, he had said to me. Would he contrive it? He had ambitions of his own, and grandsons to fulfill them. He might. And if he did, Imriel was in danger, no less in the City of Elua than Nineveh.

I want to stay with you, Imriel had said. The memory tore at my heart. How much had it cost him to trust Joscelin and me? I wished we could stay with him. Ah, Elua! I trusted Amaury Trente to see him safe, but Imri scarce knew him. He would feel hurt and betrayed, and in truth, I would sooner see him under the protection of Joscelin's sword. Would that we could keep him forever from harm. I wished I were returning home to Terre d'Ange, and not bound for Jebe-Barkal. I could not even make him a promise that we would return. It seemed such a long way, such a very long way.

But I had other promises to keep, and there were fates worse than death.

Hyacinthe.

Sixty-Two

NOTHING HAPPENED that night, nor in the nights that followed, though Joscelin and I traded shifts and remained awake throughout, weary and ragged. My warning, it seemed, had been taken to heart and a one-armed Cassiline was still a sufficient deterrent.

Sinaddan, I thought, must not know. If he did, Valère would not need to rely on stealth—it would have been easy enough, in Nineveh, to kill or poison the lot of us. No, this was a private matter, and not one sanctioned by the Lugal of Khebbel-im-Akkad, who would have been displeased to find Terre d'Ange's most famous courtesan and her consort dead within his walls, along with the rescued prince.

I was glad of that, at least, and glad that Joscelin and Imriel's search had turned up no scratch-marked suspects among Lord Amaury's men. It didn't guarantee there was no danger from that quarter, but it made it less likely.

All told, we remained another week in Nineveh, and it felt like an eternity. There were private fêtes and a public ceremony, all very glorious. Prince Sinaddan heaped an embarrassment of gifts upon us—rare spices, gold jewelry worked in the elegant, flowing lines of the Akkadian style, intricate woven carpets. To Imriel, he presented a curved dagger with a gilded hilt in the shape of a ram's head. Imriel thanked him in zenyan-accented Akkadian, a ten-year-old courtier, his expression giving nothing away.

With no other skills at my disposal, I had begun teaching him the arts of covertcy such as my lord Delaunay had taught me when I was a child: how to observe, how to read expression, tone and posture, how to listen for the unspoken; how to make oneself unobtrusive, and when to watch for what people will reveal when they think themselves unnoticed, and the nine tell-tales of a lie.

Even as a rank novice, he had a knack for it. And why not? He was, after all, Melisande's son—and Melisande was a skilled adept, wedding the art with her gift for manipulation and concealment. My lord Delaunay had taught her, too, in exchange for learning how to bend people to his will as living tools.

Now I taught her son, not for the sake of gaining power, but to safeguard his life.

Keeping watch at night, seeing Imriel warded every waking hour, being careful not to eat or drink anything not already tasted by another . . . in these ways, we maintained vigilance in Nineveh, and all the while, my skin crawled with fearful anticipation. At the farewell fête, I put as good a face on it as I might, thanking Sinaddan-Shamabarsin for his hospitality and generosity. In truth, he had been a gracious host, and I could not fault his sincerity. Valère L'Envers maintained her bland smile and expressed her deep gratitude for our deeds, for the opportunity to meet such august personages.

I couldn't get out of Nineveh fast enough.

And leave we did, with a vast caravan bound for the west, for a good many women of the zenana would be travelling with us. And our escort . . . Prince Sinaddan had kept his promise. It was nearly the size of a small army. The tents, the supply-train, the wagon-loads of gifts and generous dowries; it needed a small army to transport us.

I didn't like it, not one bit. There were hundreds of unfamiliar faces, and hundreds of ways accidents could happen on the journey. And there was not a single blessed thing I could do about it. I'd asked for this escort myself.

For all that, it was a pleasant journey crossing the flood plains between the Great Rivers. The spring floods had deposited a load of rich alluvial soil on the arid plains, and it was farmland as far as the eye could see, fields of wheat and barley waving in the sun, villages flanked by rows of date palms. The days were warm without being unbearable, and the nights pleasantly cool. If not for my fear of Imriel's assassination, it might have been idyllic.

We had told Amaury Trente, of course, who'd heard us out in silence, his shoulders slumping. I pitied him. Unsubtle or no, Amaury was a good man and a loyal one, and he'd undertaken this mission out of regard for the Queen. Already, it had proved harder and led him further astray than he'd ever dreamed possible. This only made his task more difficult. Still, when I had finished, he sighed, squared his shoulders and went about informing his men, whom he vowed were trustworthy. I prayed he was right.

Between us, we kept a guard on Imriel at all times, unless he rode with Kaneka and the Jebeans, betimes joined by the Chowati. He ate no dish that was not from the common pot, and drank no water not drawn by friendly hands.

All went well until the day we crossed the Euphrate.

The floods had subsided, but the river was still swollen to a dangerous torrent. I had not liked the raft-crossing the first time, and I dreaded it no less the second. There were ten passengers on our reed raft—Joscelin, Imriel and I, Kaneka and four others, along with two Akkadian soldiers, who looked no less wet and miserable than the rest, ostensibly placed there for our protection by their captain, Nurad-Sin.

Our unsteady vessel bucked and surged on the raging waters, drawn across by the raft-keepers, chanting and laughing with steady cheer, drawing it hand over hand along one of the massive, water-logged ropes that spanned the river, while a team on the far end hauled on a second rope. Once again, our poor horses had to swim for it, and I feared sorely for there lives. Imriel knelt anxiously at the edge of the raft, watching his Akkadian pony struggle valiantly against the current.

I was watching him. I should have heeded my own teaching, and watched the soldiers.

It happened so suddenly.

At mid-river, the raft was lurching so violently I didn't notice when one of the soldiers rose to his feet, thinking him pitched there by the raft's movement. In a single motion, half-falling, he lurched across the raft, arms extended, pushing Imriel over the edge.

A cry of dismay caught in my throat. Flecked with foam, the roiling brown water swept Imriel downstream into the struggling bodies of our horses, fouled amid their churning legs. With a wan smile, the soldier followed him overboard, letting himself tumble into the raging river. Amid the shouting and panic, one of the raft-keepers somehow lost his grip on the rope, and the force of the river tore it from the others' hands, the raft's surge sending the handlers on the far side staggering and reeling.

What would have happened if Joscelin had not lunged for the rope, catching it in his good right hand, I cannot say. His face was wracked in a grimace of pain, and his arm stretched taut in its socket. I cannot imagine how he held on without being pulled from the raft—but he did. In seconds, the other soldier had grabbed his legs, anchoring him, and the raft-keeper regained the rope with anxious cries. Our craft was stable.

And Imriel had been carried twenty yards, his body now motionless, his head a dark spot on the surging waters.

It may have been hopeless, against that torrent, but he knew how to swim; I knew he did, he'd taught the younger children at the Sanctuary. Why was he not even struggling? I thought of how he'd been tangled amid the horses, their churning hooves, and felt sick at heart. In the raft, Joscelin got unsteadily to his knees, fumbling at the knot on his sling, making ready to go after him.

"Joscelin . . ." I whispered.

He looked as sick as I felt. "I have to try."

That was when we heard the splash, and Jebean voices raised in fierce shouts of encouragement.

Kaneka's form cleaved the waters like a dark spear, long arms flashing in steady strokes, her legs kicking strongly, clearing the line of horses. Where the current was with her, she hurtled downstream; where it eddied and surged, she rode it with skill, drawing ever nearer to her objective.

"Pull," I said to the raft-handlers. "*Pull!*"

They did, at a frantic pace, no longer laughing. I daresay we crossed the Euphrate at record speed. By the time we reached the far shore, Kaneka and Imriel were out of sight. I stumbled onto dry land, ignoring my sodden skirts, and grabbed the reins of the nearest horse, snatching them from the hands of a startled Akkadian soldier.

"Watch him," I said to Joscelin, pointing to the second soldier on our raft. "And get Amaury."

Without waiting for his acknowledgment, I flung myself on the horse's back and wheeled, heading downstream. It was soaked and skittish and unsaddled, but if nothing else, I have become a passing fair rider in my travels, and I clung to its slick hide and urged it onward.

Around the second bend, I came upon Kaneka hauling Imriel out of the shallows.

Water ran off her dark skin in rivulets and she was panting like a distance-runner, her arms trembling with the effort. Imriel was dead weight, hanging limp in her grasp. I drew up the horse so sharply its forehooves sprayed dirt and dismounted at a run.

Together we got him ashore.

"Turn . . . on . . . belly," Kaneka gasped in Jeb'ez, dropping in exhaustion. "Get . . . out . . . water."

Imriel wasn't breathing. Following her instruction, I turned him onto his stomach, pressing rhythmically between his shoulders. A trickle of water emerged from his slack mouth, dribbling onto the soil. I kept pressing. Then, all at once, he drew in a choked breath, coughed, and spewed out half the Euphrate.

I sat back on my heels and breathed a prayer of thanks.

By the time Lord Amaury and the others arrived, Imriel's wracking coughing and spitting had subsided and he was alert, albeit dazed. Beneath the inky tendrils of hair plastered to his brow was a crescent-shaped bruise where a horse's hoof had caught his temple, a deep blue against his bloodless pallor.

"He's all right?" Amaury asked, dismounting and offering his cloak to Kaneka, who'd stripped off her garment before diving.

"I think so." I smoothed the damp hair back from Imriel's brow, shading his eyes to see if his pupils contracted, knowing somewhat of what a blow to the head could do. Elua be praised, they did. "Are you all right, Imri?"

Sodden and shivering, as much with shock as the chill, he nodded. "Kaneka?"

"Here, little one." She answered him herself in zenyan, wrapping herself in Amaury's cloak and laying a hand on the boy's shoulder. "You gave me a fine chase."

"Elua!" Amaury said fervidly, eyeing her. "She swims like a fish. Phèdre, will you convey my thanks and compliments?"

I did, translating them into Jeb'ez. Kaneka laughed, water sparkling like diamonds in her woolly hair. "They call this a Great River?" she said contemptuously. "Let them try the Nahar in flood season, where it passes the cataracts and the crocodiles wait. Now *that* is a river!"

Someone caught the horse I'd borrowed, which had wandered some distance away, and Imriel was bundled in another cloak. By the time we returned to our party, Imriel had stopped shivering and grown excited by the adventure, displaying the bruise on his temple to Joscelin with a boy's pride.

"Very nice," Joscelin said to him, raising his brows. "Phèdre, may we speak?"

The drowned body of the guilty soldier had washed ashore on the far side. Captain Nurad-Sin made profound apologies, swearing up and down that the man was a new conscript, and he'd had no knowledge of his actions, any more than his innocent comrade had had. I heard him out, gauging his words sincere. In the end, I had no choice but to accept them. We were too far outnumbered to do anything else.

"Thank you for your concern, my lord Captain," I said politely. "Her majesty Queen Ysandre de la Courcel is eagerly awaiting the return of her young kinsman, Prince Imriel. She would be most wroth if ill befell him now, after such trials, and I daresay his highness the Lugal would be displeased as well. I pray you ensure your men know this."

He gave a grim nod. "You may be sure of it, my lady."

Mayhap he did, for the next leg of our journey passed without event. I spent the time scavenging paper and ink as unobtrusively as I might, working on various missives by the light of our campfires at night, and during the day, riding among the women of the zenana and conversing with the Ephesians.

They were the first to leave our company, departing with an honor guard of Akkadians and a wagon-load of royal gifts to make their way over land to Ephesium. We made our farewells, and I watched them go, filled with a dour satisfaction.

"Do you care to tell me what that expression betokens?" Joscelin asked.

"Wait till we've crossed the Yehordan," I said.

Once we had, I told him. Joscelin laughed aloud, and went to fetch Nurad-Sin himself. Veiled and proper, seated within my tent while he stood outside it, I addressed the Akkadian captain again.

"My lord Captain," I said to him. "You are aware I have . . . concerns . . . for Prince Imriel's safety."

Nurad-Sin bowed. "My lady, I am. Before Shamash, I pledge you, I have taken every precaution to ensure that no further incidents occur."

"So," I said, "have I. Each of the Ephesian women with whom we parted company a few days past bears with her a missive, addressed in my name to her majesty Ysandre de la Courcel, Queen of Terre d'Ange. These I have instructed to be given to the D'Angeline ambassador in Ephesium city, and thanks to the Lugal's generosity, the women of the zenana shall have the means to accomplish this. In these letters, I have chronicled such events as have befallen us thus far, and laid forth my suspicions as to their cause."

The Akkadian captain went pale. "My lady, the Lugal esteems you above gold. Surely you do not suspect . . . ?"

"No." I said it with a blandness that would have done Valère L'Envers credit. "Not in the least. While Prince Imriel lives, my suspicions will go unspoken. Should any accident befall him . . ." I shrugged. "It is my instruction that the letters be sent. Mayhap, my lord Captain, you might see to it that every man among you—every conscript, every veteran, every hostler and cook and water-porter, for I do not expect you to vouch for every one—is aware of this."

He gave a deep bow. "My lady, it shall be done."

"Well," said Joscelin when he had gone. "You've done what you could."

It didn't feel like enough.

$\mathscr{S}$ixty-THREE

"WHY CAΠ'T you come home with me?"

It was inevitable, I suppose; the only wonder was that Imriel had waited until we were a day's ride from Tyre to broach the subject. I sighed, trying to find the words.

"Imri . . . I made a promise, a long time ago. It's not one I can break."

He lifted guileless blue eyes to mine. "If he loves you, wouldn't he understand?"

"He might," I said, thinking of Hyacinthe, who had never dreamed that the dark road I would travel would prove so very dark indeed, with so many branching forks. "It doesn't matter. That's not the point."

Imriel rode for a while in silence, then, "Do you love him more than Joscelin?"

"No. Imriel, listen. If someone had taken your place in Daršanga, if . . . if Beryl had gone in your stead," I said, recalling the name of the eldest girl in the Sanctuary of Elua, the one who had recited the verses about Kushiel's Dart. "If Beryl had taken your place, and you had the chance to free her, could you go home instead?"

His black brows, straighter than his mother's, knit in thought. "No," he said finally, reluctant. "But . . ."

"But what?"

"*Why* do you have to love him so much?"

I smiled. "Why? I don't know. I've known him since I was, oh, younger than you. Whenever I was upset, or scared, or angry . . . it was always to Hyacinthe that I ran. There was a time, Imri, when he was my only true friend; a long time."

"Was he like me?" he asked. "When he was a boy?"

I considered him. "No. Not much."

"I want to go with you." The words were so soft I could scarce hear them. "With you and Joscelin, to Jebe-Barkal."

"You can't," I said. "Imri, we've talked about this. You've a life awaiting you in Terre d'Ange, and the Queen herself anxious to meet you, to make you a member of her family; of House Courcel, into which you were born."

"And people who want me dead." His mouth was set in a hard, unchildish line.

"Yes," I said. "And that. But Lord Amaury won't let that happen, and neither will Queen Ysandre. And when it comes to it, they're a great deal more qualified for the job than I."

Imriel gave me a look that went clear to the bone. "But you are the only one who is my friend, my true friend."

We made camp that night a few miles outside Tyre, and it was Joscelin who broached the subject while Imriel slept, sitting cross-legged on his blankets before the opening of our tent and massaging his arm with the Eisandine chirurgeon's balm. The bindings and splint had at last come off, and despite his best efforts squeezing rocks and the like, his left arm was pallid and puny, his grip on his dagger feeble at best.

"It's a long way," he said quietly. "And we've been a long time from home. Phèdre . . . I'm not saying we shouldn't go, eventually. But . . . look at me. I'll not be much use, if there's trouble. And you . . . Elua, love! If ever there was a time you needed to heal, it's now."

"I'm fine," I said.

Joscelin merely looked at me.

"All right," I said. "I'm not fine. But I'm well enough to travel, and so are you. Joscelin . . . there's a part of me, a big part, that would like nothing better than to see Imriel restored safely, to deliver a warning in person to Ysandre, to go *home*. But if we do?" I shuddered. "I'm not sure I can face leaving it again. And I can't live knowing that there's somewhat I might do to win Hyacinthe's freedom. Mayhap . . ." I swallowed. "Mayhap it would be best if you went with Imriel."

He flinched. "You don't mean it."

"I don't know." I put my head in my hands. "It's—it's like you said, it's what you trained all your life to do. Not trail around after luckless whores on half-mad quests."

"Phèdre." There was a sound in his voice almost like laughter, although with no levity in it. "If you can't go home while Hyacinthe remains cursed, how can you possibly imagine I could endure letting you go to Jebe-Barkal alone?"

"So you'll go?"

"I swore it to damnation and beyond." He flexed his left hand, testing the muscles. "This would be the beyond."

Our arrival in Tyre was auspicious. The skies were a bright, hard blue above and a good steady wind blew southwesterly. The Lugal's couriers had been there ahead of us, arranging for our varied transports. 'Twas no difficulty for those of us bound for Menekhet, as trade ships travelled regularly, but the longer journeys—Hellas, Illyria, Caerdicca Unitas, Carthage, Aragonia, Terre d'Ange—required special commissions.

His highness Sinaddan-Shamabarsin had been the soul of generosity. The ships were ready and waiting, the finest money could buy, captains and crew hailing the women of the Mahrkagir's zenana as noble-born passengers.

It was a considerable shock, albeit a pleasant one, to some, especially those who had been slave-born. By some means they did not fully comprehend, the horrible dross of their lives, the degradations of Daršanga, had been converted to status. I was glad, for they deserved it. I hoped it would enable some of them to find happiness, or at least contentment. There are many things wealth cannot buy, and most of those are enumerated by philosophers who have never woken wondering if this day would be their last. It pleased me to know that the survivors of Daršanga would, at the least, not have to worry about buying bread.

For the rest, it was up to them. The living must carry on for the dead.

Rushad . . . Drucilla . . . Erich. There was no ship bound for Skaldia. I never even learned his story, never knew how he came to be a Drujani captive. All I had done was hold his hand, and sing him songs as he died. I hoped he'd gotten his answers from All-Father Odhinn.

It was no longer in my heart to hate or fear the Skaldi.

There were tears aplenty upon parting, and if I dared now leave no written trail, I left a good many instructions, whispered in the ears of a dozen women—safeguards, hedged bets, messages for a half-dozen D'Angeline ambassadors. It was the last great conspiracy of the zenana of Daršanga, and every one of them undertook it willingly.

Our ship, set to leave at midday on the morrow, would be the last to leave; the D'Angeline ship would sail at dawn. We passed one last night together in a fine Tyrean inn, which the Lugal had reserved for our pleasure, even ensuring that there would be no fuss about men and women dining in common. The festivities went long into the night, and

I daresay I filled Amaury Trente's ear with more advice than he needed.

At the end of the evening, I bid farewell to Imriel, who would bunk with Lord Amaury's men. "Be well," I whispered, holding him close. "Be safe. Remember what I taught you."

"I will." His voice was muffled, lost in my hair; his arms wound hard about my neck. He let me go, sniffling and blinking at Joscelin, one hand on the prized Akkadian dagger that was thrust through his belt. "Will you teach me to use this, when you come back?"

"I swear it, my prince." There was a strained tone to Joscelin's voice as he bowed, the movement a halting approximation of his old Cassiline grace. He closed his eyes as Imriel hugged him, and I thought I saw tears spiking his lashes. "Ward yourself well until I do."

And then it was ended, and we went to our quarters, which seemed strangely empty without Imriel's presence. There was no need for either of us to keep watch, no need for Joscelin to post himself before the door. It is odd, the things to which one can become accustomed.

"Funny," Joscelin said, unbuckling his vambraces. His left forearm had lost the calluses of a lifetime, and the leather straps had chafed it raw. "I never expected to *like* him."

"Melisande's son," I murmured.

"Yes." He prodded the oozing patches of flesh and winced. "Melisande's son. Do you want to see them off in the morning?"

"Yes," I said. "I'd like that."

And we would have done, had we not slept overlate. Small wonder, I thought, waking to see the first low rays of the sun penetrating our window. It had been—how long?—weeks, at least, since both of us had slept through a night undisturbed. I roused Joscelin, who came awake with customary quickness. Hastily donning our attire, cloaked against the dawn chill, we hurried to the harbor in time to see the anchor drawn, hear the oarsmen chant as the galley turned round in the still waters of the harbor, making ready to hoist sail.

They were there, standing on deck, Lord Amaury's curling auburn hair unmistakably lit by the slanting early sun. He raised one hand in salute, and we waved from the quai. Imriel was a shrouded figure, huddled in a hooded Akkadian cloak and giving no indication of having seen us. Someone—Vigny, I thought—kept a watchful eye upon him.

"Well," said Joscelin. "That's that."

"Did you—?"

"What?"

"Nothing." I shrugged. "One of the men hauling anchor . . . I thought, mayhap, I saw marks on his face. Like scratches. Healed scratches."

Joscelin stared after the receding galley. "Phèdre . . . if you did . . . Lord Amaury knows, yes? You told him about the letters to the Ephesians, about the instructions you gave the others. And he's prepared to make it known to the ship's captain, what repercussions may await if Imriel doesn't make it safe to port in Marsilikos."

"Yes," I said. "Amaury knows."

"Then let it be," he said firmly, tugging my arm. "You're chasing phantoms, now. Valère tried twice; she won't try a third time, and even if she did, there's naught we can do about it. 'Tis Amaury's job, and one to which the Queen appointed him. Let him do it."

Glancing over my shoulder, I went with him. Like as not he was right; even I thought I was imagining things. We returned to the inn and packed our things—vastly reduced from that with which we'd left Nineveh, the bulk of it going westward with Lord Amaury—and went to break our fast and meet with Kaneka and the others.

It was a smallish ship bound for Iskandria; a Menekhetan trader, for which I was glad. It would go unladen, for the Lugal had paid the entire passage, and there were but twelve of us, Jebean, Menekhetan and D'Angeline, with the run of the vessel. When the sun stood high overhead, they cast anchor and in short order we were away, sails hoisting to catch the wind. I stood on deck and watched the gulf of sparkling water widen between us and the coastline of Khebbel-im-Akkad, feeling a giddy lightness as it did.

So, I thought, it is ended. We leave Drujan behind us.

And I prayed the distance would make a difference.

It was a pleasure, after Khebbel-im-Akkad, to go unveiled, to feel the salt spray upon my face. After the zenana, I retained a fondness for open spaces, and there is none so vast as the ocean. We dined together in the mess-hall, attended by sailors glad to have drawn such light duty for full pay, laughing as our plates and cups slid the length of the built-in trestle with the ship's swaying, laughing all the harder when Joscelin, with a peculiar look on his face, excused himself to go above-deck.

"He does not like the sea?" Kaneka asked with a grin.

" 'Tis a long-standing quarrel between them," I replied.

At night, the stars stood bright and close overhead, clustered in diamond swarms against the velvety darkness. Despite the chill, I liked to walk the decks, gazing at them, wondering if such beauty had been created to a purpose. Beauty inspires love; so it is said, in Terre d'Ange.

Was it done that we might find this world worthy of loving? Mayhap it was so. I was no priestess, no philosopher, to find the answers to the world's riddles in the stars. I only know that they were beautiful and stirred my soul.

I was glad I could still be moved by beauty.

By the third day, the heat of noon had grown oppressive as the sun beat down on the wooden decks. Like many of the southerners, I took to my cabin during the worst heat of the day; enclosed or no, 'twas better to be in shade than sun, and our cabin had a portal that admitted a breeze.

I was drowsing on my narrow cot, clad only in a thin linen shift, when the knock came at the door, and I thought it must be Joscelin, unwontedly formal. As always, he had spent a good portion of our first days aft, in the stern of the ship where the clutch and roil of seasickness that gripped his belly would be less troublesome.

"Yes?" I said, opening the door a crack.

It was Kaneka. I had guessed wrongly. "You will want to see this," she said, her expression undecipherable.

I opened the door wide and stared.

There, squirming in her grip, was Imriel de la Courcel.

Sixty-Four

"HOW?"

I folded my arms and glared at him, looking as imposing as I could. Imriel's gaze darted, seeking allies and not finding them. Joscelin, leaning against the door of the cabin, was as grim and stoic as only a seasick Cassiline can be, and Kaneka . . . Kaneka was trying not to laugh, but I do not think Imri knew it. He'd not learned that much, not yet.

"There was a boy," he said defiantly. "At the inn. An Akkadian boy, one of the servants. He wanted to see Terre d'Ange, where the men look like sons of the gods, and the women, the women look like . . . like you. I got him to take my place."

I raised my eyebrows. *"How?"*

"He took my cloak," Imriel muttered. "In the service alley, before the stairs. And I gave him my dagger for it, the one the Lugal gave me. We traded places, when everyone was watching the trunks being brought down. I made as if to sulk, and told Lord Amaury not to bother me, so he would not notice when we changed."

"And how long," I asked, "do you suppose *that* endured aboard the ship?"

"Long enough." He set his chin. "I told him to pretend he was sick, and wanted only to sleep, and to keep his face turned away from the light."

"You arranged this under Lord Amaury's nose?" I said in patent disbelief.

"Lord Amaury," Imriel said stubbornly, "does not speak Akkadian."

I looked at Joscelin. "Would you be so good as to fetch the captain?"

The Menekhetan captain came at once and informed us apologeti-

cally in heavily accented Hellene that there was no question of turning
back to Tyre. The Lugal of Khebbel-im-Akkad had commissioned this
ship to sail directly to Iskandria, and sail it would. Yes, he understood
the development was unforeseen, but the ship's passage was paid, so
the boy's presence was no imposition. Ah, yes, he understood the boy
was a personage of some import in his own country, but this was a
Menekhetan ship, and relations with Khebbel-im-Akkad were ever delicate. Without direct orders from the Lugal himself, he dared not
second-guess his wishes. Surely, we could book passage upon arrival if
we wished to return to Tyre, for the journey was not overlong.

"Well," I said, defeated, when he had left. "That's what we'll have
to do, then."

Kaneka cleared her throat. "Little one . . ."

"What is it?" I didn't like her tone.

"It is not long, no, but . . . if you delay a month, no more, by the
time you reach the south, the rains will come. And then no one may
travel."

I clutched my hair, feeling kinship with Amaury Trente. "Elua!
Imri, why did you do this?"

His face was a study in teary mutiny. "*You* said—you talked about
friends, and honor, and the precept of Blessed Elua! *Love as thou wilt.*"
He spat the words like a curse. "Why am *I* not allowed to choose?"

I sat down on my cot and looked to Joscelin for aid.

"Fedabin." He bowed to Kaneka, crossing his forearms with care,
speaking in the halting zenyan which was our only common tongue.
"How dangerous *is* this trip, anyway?"

"To find the Melehakim?" Kaneka shrugged. "Dangerous, lord.
There is a river greater than the Euphrate, and deserts that kill. There
are crocodiles and lions, and scavengers in between—hyenas, jackals,
even the blood-flies that drive strong men to madness. And there are
tribes, many tribes, in Jebe-Barkal, some of them hostile. But," she
added, a glint in her eye, "none of them will seek to kill a boy due to
an accident of birth. Besides, he could always remain in Debeho, if you
willed it. He would be warded well enough in my village."

Joscelin looked at me. I looked back at him. "You can't be serious,"
I said.

"Phèdre." He sounded eminently reasonable. "Think of it. At least
he'd be safe from assassination attempts. And . . . Name of Elua, the boy
has a point! Is he *never* to be allowed a choice?"

"You weren't," I murmured. "I wasn't. Not at ten."

"And look where it brought us. Still, neither of us had to endure Daršanga."

Some choices must be made swiftly, lest the enormity of them overwhelm the chooser. I pressed the heels of my hands against my eyesockets. "All right," I said. "All right, all right, *all right!* Imriel." I lifted my head. "If we let you stay—if we sanction this—do you swear to me that you will obey us? Joscelin and me both—yes, and Kaneka, too—every word, every whim, as if Blessed Elua himself had crossed the boundary of Terre d'Ange-that-lies-beyond to give voice to a new sacrament?"

Imriel was nodding with every word I spoke, not listening, agreeing to it all. "I swear," he said breathlessly. "I swear, I vow, I promise, Phèdre, every word!"

I spent the remainder of our voyage composing the letter to Amaury Trente.

It was a foolhardy decision, and one I daresay I wouldn't have made half a year ago. Still, great distance and great events have a way of changing one's perspective. As mad as our quest might be, it was nothing to what Imriel had undergone in Daršanga, and Kaneka was right; no one in Jebe-Barkal wanted him dead. Once he set foot on Terre d'Ange, he would always, always have enemies, the shadow of his mother's vast treachery hanging over him, every move watched and scrutinized.

Even so.

"I can't believe you sided with him," I said to Joscelin that night. Imriel was sleeping in Kaneka's cabin, which held a spare cot. After three days of scavenging for scraps and sleeping wedged in a dark corner of the hold, he was grateful for it. If she hadn't caught him at the water-barrel, he might have held out till Iskandria. "Amaury will be like to kill us. And Ysandre . . . I don't want to think of it."

Joscelin shrugged. "You're the one thought you saw an assassin aboard his ship."

"Thought!" I lowered my voice. "Even I admitted it was probably my imagination playing on my fears. It's not like you, that's all. Honor, duty, loyalty—all those Cassiline virtues, that should demand we send him back."

"I'm tired." Lying on his side, he regarded me across the cabin. "Phèdre, all my life, I've had to make that choice, over and over. I'm tired of it."

Daršanga, I thought, had changed him, too; it had changed us all. "Then love is reason enough? Because he willed it?"

"I don't know. Blessed Elua says it is. Imriel followed you—us— out of love. I know that much is true; there's no other reason for it." Joscelin rolled onto his back and gazed at the ceiling. "Phèdre, did you tell him how his mother escaped from Troyes-le-Mont?"

A chill ran the length of my spine. "No," I whispered.

Incredible as it seems, I had not thought, until then, how very similar were the means, even down to the concealing cloak. In Troyes-le-Mont, Melisande had traded places with her cousin Persia and walked out of captivity under the very noses of the men set to guard her. And her son had played nearly the self-same trick. It would not go unremarked, not by the men who'd been duped by it, who were doubtless on their way back to Tyre even as we spoke, taut and furious, holding in custody a disappointed Akkadian serving-lad.

"He did it for love," Joscelin said softly. "That's the difference. And I don't have it in my heart to betray him for it. Phèdre . . . this boy could be dangerous. Or he could be something else. I can't forgive Melisande. But I can forgive her son."

"Someone should," I murmured. "It might as well be us."

"Why not?" He laughed, the sound blending with the rhythmic ripple of waves against the ship's hull. "One way or another, it seems it usually is."

And so our journey passed. In the morning and the evenings, his seasickness faded, Joscelin performed his Cassiline exercises on the foredeck of the ship, sweating under the bright sun as he sought to regain his old balance, the steel daggers weaving intricate patterns—slowly, so slowly. After the first day of his discovery, Imriel joined him, using a pair of wooden practice-blades whittled for him by a bored sailor. With infinite patience, both for his own infirmity and Imri's ineptness, Joscelin taught him the rudiments of it.

I watched them both, stirred by emotions I could not name. In days long gone by, when first he had come to Delaunay's service, I used to watch so, standing upon the terrace while he did his exercises in the garden, and wondered at the Cassiline's patience when he began teaching Alcuin, my near-brother Alcuin, with his milk-white hair and his gentle smile.

In those days, I had despised Joscelin.

Now . . .

I loved him; I loved him still. And when his grin flashed, quick to forgive an error; when he pushed himself tirelessly, silhouetted against the sparkling sea; when Imriel's laugh rang out, surprised and delighted—I loved him all the more, until my heart ached with it, too vast for the confines of my body.

Yet we had not even kissed.

Too many shadows lay between us, and all of them born in Drujan. I am an *anguissette*; I have been so all of my life. Like Joscelin, I had made my way with balance; between the left side and the right, between pleasure and pain, between love and all that it was not. Somewhere, in Daršanga, I had gone too far. And something in me had shattered, as surely as his bones.

I did not know how to find my way back.

And so I watched them and was gladdened, taking secondhand pleasure where I might, in the clean sea and wind, the leap of blood resurgent in wasted muscles and the arc of steel cleaving sky, the sound of a boy's laughter. And I composed, in my head, my letter to Lord Amaury Trente, striving to explain why I believed *this* was in accordance with the will of Blessed Elua.

Thus did we arrive in Iskandria.

I hadn't expected Nesmut.

"Gracious lady!" His voice rang the considerable length of the quai, his sandaled feet slapping the pavings as he pelted toward us, all dignity forgotten. "Gracious lord! You are *alive!*"

"Nesmut." I laughed, my heart rebounding with unwonted joy. "Are you free to take on an old client? There are more of us, this time."

After much negotiation, at once light-hearted and solemn, Nesmut contracted carriages and porters and led us to our lodgings—not Metriche's, these, but a purely Menekhetan establishment, pleasant and modest. The women of the zenana were not like to complain. It was palatial, after Daršanga.

And I did not want us to be easily found.

I obtained parchment and a pen and ink, and spent the better part of a day writing the letter I'd composed—the one to Amaury, and a good many others. When I had finished, I sent a message, via Nesmut, to Ptolemy Dikaios. The lad's status had risen in the world, that such a message might be sent and delivered without question. He preened with it, which I begrudged him not in the least.

Pharaoh's summons came almost immediately.

As I had requested, it was a discreet meeting and not a formal one.

This would all, I thought ruefully, be a great deal easier without Imriel. But the decision was made, and I would do what I could to ensure it done safely.

Ptolemy Dikaios received me in the private reception-hall where we had struck our bargain, and under the impassive eyes of his fan-bearers I gave him a letter from the Lugal which detailed the events that had befallen and requested his aid in seeing the freed Menekhetans restored to their families or housed with honor. He read it without need of a translator and regarded me thoughtfully when he was done, reclining on a couch.

"Bold deeds, Phèdre nó Delaunay, and worthy of honor. Why then do you ask to meet in secret, and not trumpet this victory to your Ambassador de Penfars, to Lord Mesilim-Amurri, the Akkadian consul? I am certain they would wish to arrange for a triumphal procession, if they knew."

"There is a complication, my lord Pharaoh," I said.

His heavy lids flickered. "Indeed? What is it?"

I told him about Imriel.

When I had finished, he laughed. "And what would you have me do about it? By all rights, I should send for de Penfars right now and remand the boy to his custody! It would win me favor with the D'Angeline Queen."

"It would," I said, "until I told her about your alliance with Melisande Shahrizai."

"There is that." Pharaoh rubbed his chin. "What do you propose?"

"We will be gone in several days' time, my lord. If, at that time, I sent various letters to you by messenger, you might see them enacted and dispersed. That, from the Lugal, regarding the survivors of the zenana," I nodded at the letter he held, and produced three more, "this, to be sent to Lord Amaury Trente in Tyre, and this, to be given to Ambassador de Penfars, who will send it by courier to Queen Ysandre. Both detail my suspicions, and give the reason for my actions, asserting that you had no knowledge of my presence and that I relied on your integrity as a ruler to see the missives delivered."

"Sent by messenger, eh?" He thought through the implications. "So it shall seem I'd no idea you were here until you were gone."

"Yes, my lord Pharaoh." I sat straight under his considering gaze.

"You could have done that," he said.

"I could, my lord. But I have an obligation to the women of the zenana. I was entrusted with seeing them restored to Menekhet, and securing your cooperation. I could not leave without doing it."

The fans moved in broad sweeps, stirring the sultry air. Ptolemy Dikaios rested his chin on his fist and stared at me. "You're an odd woman, Phèdre nó Delaunay; beautiful, but odd. For whom is the third letter?"

My mouth had gone dry. "Melisande Shahrizai de la Courcel."

He gave a short bark of laughter.

"My lord," I said. "This I do not ask, but leave to your discretion. Whether or not your communications with her have continued, I do not know, and do not inquire. If they have not . . ." I shrugged, placing the letters on the low table between us. "Consign it to the flames. If they have . . . whatever else she may be, she is a mother, my lord Pharaoh, sore grieved for the loss of her son. She has the right to know he lives."

Pharaoh picked up the letters and studied them, bejeweled rings glinting on every finger of his hands. "Very beautiful, and very odd. You take a risk in coming to me alone, my lady."

"Yes." I nodded. "However, my lord, if I have not returned by sundown, my companions will claim asylum of Ambassador de Penfars."

His eyes gleamed with amusement. "Embassies are vulnerable."

"So are thrones," I said. "I daresay Lord Raife would think to beseech the aid of General Hermodorus if the embassy was threatened, not to mention that of the Akkadian consul. In fact, if I do not return by sundown—"

"Let me guess." Pharaoh tapped two fingers on the thick parchment envelopes. "There are letters already awaiting delivery."

I nodded. "As it happens, my lord, there are."

He laughed and tossed the letters on the table. "Ah, Lady Phèdre! You entertain me; you entertain me greatly. So be it. I give you two days. On the third, I will announce the receipt of great news, and your Menekhetan refugees will be received with much fanfare. Your letters shall be sent accordingly to the Ambassador and to Tyre, and I shall tender my profoundest apologies for my ignorance of your duplicity. I sincerely hope, my lady, that by that time, you are well on your way upriver."

"We will be." I knelt and made a heartfelt obeisance. "Thank you, my lord Pharaoh."

Ptolemy Dikaios waved a jeweled hand. "Go, and be gone."

Sixty-five

OVER THE next two days our arrangements were made, with Nesmut's aid and Kaneka's supervision. We would travel by felucca, the swift, shallow sailing-boats, up the river as far as Majibara, the great caravanserai that marked the end of Menekhet and the border of Jebe-Barkal itself. There our company—seven, all told—would part ways, for two of the women were bound for the western province of Nubia, while the rest of us would strike south across the desert.

Thanks to the Lugal's generosity, we had no lack of funding. On Kaneka's advice, we converted a number of gifts into "trader's coin," heavy chains of soft yellow gold to be paid out link by link. These were given unto Joscelin's keeping, and he wore them about his neck, hidden beneath his clothing.

We spent lightly on supplies in Iskandria, for Kaneka assured us that everything could be had cheaper in Majibara and provisions were ample along the river. We purchased tents of oiled silk, rolled straw sleeping-pallets and a few cook-pots. I bought a broad-brimmed hat to shade my head, and a burnoose of white cotton; for the rest, I still had my Akkadian garb and the celadon riding attire Favrielle nó Eglantine had fashioned for me, which suited the climate well. The other, that I'd worn in Drujan, was long discarded.

New clothing, then, and little more. It might almost have been a pleasure-cruise. We all dined together on our last night in Iskandria, Nesmut included. He regarded Imriel with a certain envy, for having been at the center of great events and embarking on a grand adventure. 'Twas strange, seeing them together. For all that Nesmut was the elder, he seemed the younger of the two, high-spirited and merry.

As before, it made me think of Hyacinthe. *Was he like me?* Imriel had asked, *When he was a boy?* Not much, I had said; 'twas true, when he was a boy. Now . . . I saw the shadows in Imri's eyes, the memory of pain and the burden of his heredity, the hunger that surfaced as he watched Nesmut laugh, eating and drinking with a will, happy in his status. And I remembered Hyacinthe's terrible smile and how *alone* he had been, how profoundly alone.

Truth be told, I was glad Imriel was here.

After we dined, we said our farewells, for we would be off with the dawn.

"I am sorry," I said to Khepri, who was the one I knew best among the Menekhetans, "that it had to be thus. You should have entered the city in procession. It is your right."

She smiled, taking my hand. "Tomorrow is soon enough. We would not be here, were it not for you, and I do not need processions anyway. Peace is all I ask. You have given us that. I hope you find what you need."

"Thank you." I squeezed her hand. "I hope so, too."

Our time together was ended, our numbers dwindling.

In accordance with our plan, we left at sunrise. It is a thing to behold, sunrise upon the delta of the mighty Nahar. Kaneka spoke truly; of all rivers, it is the greatest. In Iskandria, 'tis scarce to be discerned as a river, but an unending series of canals and waterways, placid and calm, winding through a vast expanse of green.

We boarded in the soft hush of dawn, the air still balmy. There were two feluccas, each manned by a single Jebean. Our goods were loaded in short order and we found space aboard the vessels—Joscelin, Imriel, Kaneka and I aboard one, and Safiya and the two Nubians aboard the other. Our erstwhile captain raised a finger to test the breeze, then raised a crude stone anchor.

As the slanting rays of the early sun turned the brown waters of the delta to shimmering bronze, we were on our way.

In truth, the first leg of our journey to Jebe-Barkal *was* nearly a pleasure-cruise. Our feluccas with their lateen-rigged sails tacked back and forth across the sluggish waters, the sailors calling merrily to one another in Jeb'ez. The vegetation was thick and lush, tall papyrus growing along the waterways. Egrets and herons and sacred ibis picked their way along the shores, pausing statuesque to eye us as we passed, long-billed heads poised atop impossibly long necks. A gentle breeze blew at our backs and I felt, for the first time in many months, a touch of my old excitement at beginning a new journey.

To the south of the city some hours later, the myriad waterways gradually converged and the delta gave way to the river proper, broad and stately, flowing between green banks. All manner of traffic travelled the river, from rowboats and fishing vessels to galleys and ox-drawn barges. None travelled so swiftly as the light feluccas, stitching back and forth, triangular sails canted to catch the wind.

All along the riverbanks were villages, interspersed with plantations of wheat and sugarcane, lines of palm trees and tamarisk. We saw caravans, sometimes—camels and donkeys, strung in long processions along the banks. When I realized the speed with which our swift craft left them behind, I was glad I had heeded Kaneka's advice.

For a time, I was apprehensive and craned my neck to look behind us, fearing the Pharaoh would break his word and some pursuit would be forthcoming. It seemed, however, that none was, and after a while, I ceased to worry about it. If it came, it came; there was naught I could do about it.

To my sorrow, we would be unable to see some of the mightiest structures of Menekhet from the river, the Great Tombs of the ancients. Our captain generously offered to halt and guide us overland—for an additional fee, of course—but I deemed it wisest to remain on course, and Kaneka assured me that the temples further upriver would more than compensate.

We made camp that first night near a pleasant village, trading with the villagers for our dinner, roasting chickens which we ate with our fingers, accompanied by melons and sweet dates. The night was velvety-soft, spangled with stars.

"I have to admit," Joscelin said drowsily, lounging before the fire. "This doesn't seem so bad."

"No." I sat cross-legged, combing knots out of Imriel's hair while he gritted his teeth at the pain. "Truly, it doesn't."

The days of that journey blend together in memory, distinguished only by the sights that marked our route. Our first hippopotamus, rising like a colossus from the river, water running in streams down its dark hide; the vast gape of its pink mouth, teeth like yellow pegs. Imriel leapt to his feet, shouting and pointing. Kaneka and the other Jebeans merely laughed. Afterward, we saw many of the creatures, placid and harmless so long as they were undisturbed. More dangerous were the crocodiles, of which there were an abundance. Dark-green and pebbled, they lurked like submerged logs, only the slitted reptilian eyes giving the lie to the illusion. Kaneka assured us that they move with great rapidity on dry land, and we were ever wary about venturing to the water's edge when we made camp.

There is a temple along the way dedicated to Sebek, the Menekhetan crocodile-god, and this we visited at Kaneka's insistence. It is on a bend that juts into the river, and I vow, there must have been a dozen or more of the beasts sunning themselves on the sandy bank. Our two felucca captains picked their beachhead cautiously, leaping ashore with long, hooked harpoons in hand to secure a path to the temple.

Here in the south, the Menekhetan faith has not been Hellenized, and it is augmented by Jebean traffic. I will own, though the temple itself was pleasant, the depictions of Sebek made me shiver. The crocodile-headed man-god is said to have devoured the dismembered pieces of Osiris, the dying-god whom the Hellenes have made one with Serapis, the lord of the dead.

Why they worship the crocodile, I was unsure.

"Lord Sebek has his place, little one," Kaneka told me, seeing my doubtful expression. "Even so, if the Nahar did not overflow its banks to devour the land, the fields could not be reborn. Besides, we have need of his forbearance." And so saying, she laid her offering—a clay figurine painted in bright colors—on the altar of Sebek and backed away bowing.

We had to wait an hour for the crocodiles to clear the sandy beach sufficient for our felucca captains to beat a path to the ships, cursing and sweating with anxiety.

"Some place for a temple!" Joscelin remarked after we had hoisted sail.

"Where else should it be?" Kaneka asked, logically enough. Looking at my face, she grinned. "We will stop at Houba, little one, and visit the temple of Isis. You will like that better, I think."

So the days passed, one like unto the other, and the Greatest River glided between green banks and deep valleys. True to Kaneka's promise, I saw mighty temples and vast tombs along the route, a testament to the tremendous antiquity of this land. The river flowed stronger and our progress slowed, the feluccas needing to tack ever more often across the current, stitching our course upstream. With naught else to do, Kaneka set about teaching Joscelin and Imriel the rudiments of Jeb'ez, singing children's counting songs and the like. It made me smile, thinking how hard I'd fought to get her to allow me to learn. Betimes our felucca captain, whose name was Wali, would join in and their mingled voices would ring across the waters.

Wali, I must say, had developed a prodigious infatuation for Kaneka and thought her the most splendid creature he'd ever seen. Clearly, he regarded her as a person of great stature. Whether or not it had been true in her native village of Debeho, I cannot say, but it had been true in the zenana, and it was certainly true now. Clad in richly embroidered Akkadian robes, she might have been some visiting ambassadress.

It was a source of amusement for the other Jebeans, who watched Wali make cow's-eyes at her around the campfire and laid bets in zenyan as to whether or not Kaneka would acquiesce. Near the end of our journey, she did, laying a hand on Wali's shoulder and beckoning him to her tent. Trembling with disbelief at his fortune, a broad grin splitting his face, he followed her.

I was glad of it, though the noise of their love-making kept us up half the night. There is no privacy in a small campsite. From what I had observed, Wali was a good man—simple and kind, with an abiding pride in his felucca. Certainly he was well-made, with pleasant, open features and broad shoulders and arms corded with muscle from handling the sails.

And Kaneka . . .

Kaneka was smiling in the morning, with the relaxed ease of a woman who has reclaimed ownership of her body's pleasure. I envied her that. There were jests that day, but they were good-natured and affectionate. When Wali sang a Jebean nursery-rhyme at the top of his lungs, everyone in both boats laughed and clapped, cheering him onward.

"Phèdre?" Imriel sat beside me in the prow, dangling his legs over the edge.

"What? Imri, don't do that, a crocodile will bite off your feet."

He drew his legs in and hugged his knees, eyeing me gravely. "Why aren't you and Joscelin like . . ." he nodded at Kaneka and Wali, ". . . like that?"

"Ah, Imri." I smoothed the hair back from his brow. The terrible bruise on his temple was gone, though it had taken forever to fade, yellow traces lingering for weeks after the blow. "You know what I was, in Daršanga."

He nodded, not meeting my eyes. "The Mahrkagir's favorite."

"Death's Whore," I said wryly. "You can say it. You said it before."

"I didn't know, then." His head came up, jaw set stubbornly, that look of House Courcel in his confrontational frown. "It was courage. I know that, now."

"It wasn't all courage." I made my voice gentle. "Imriel, some of the stories . . . some of the stories were true. I am an *anguissette*. Do you know what that means?"

He looked away and nodded again.

"There are places inside of us," I said, picking my words with care, "that are frightening, places no one should go. In Daršanga, I had to go to that place. And . . . Imri, it's hard to find one's way back. I'm trying. But it's not easy. Can you understand?"

"Yes." He swallowed and picked at the cloth of his breeches before looking up at me, his deep blue eyes brimming with pain. "Do you ever . . . do you ever miss it there?"

Ah, Elua! Answering tears stung my own eyes. Not trusting my voice, I nodded. Yes, I missed it. I woke in the night sometimes from dreams of blood and iron, sick with desire.

"I don't," he whispered. "Only . . . sometimes, it was easier, I think."

"Yes," I said, stroking his hair. "I know. But this is better. And it *will* get better, Imri. For all of us. Elua willing, for Joscelin and me, too."

And I listened to Wali's lusty singing, to Kaneka's rich laughter, and willed myself to believe it was true.

Sixty-six

HOUBA WAS the site of the last great temple of the Upper Nahar, a half-day's sail from the caravanserai of Majibara. It is perched on a lush, green island in the broad river, graceful palms waving over its narrow columns, tamarisk clustered thick about the foundations.

We disembarked and joined a line of supplicants awaiting admission to the temple, which did a brisk trade. Outside, under the hot sun, Menekhetans and Jebeans alike mingled in respectful good spirits, sharing gossip and water-skins, glancing curiously at we D'Angelines which is something so common all of us were used to it, even Imriel.

Inside it was as cool and airy as a place could be during early summer on the Nahar. I gazed at the frescos on the high walls, following the goddess' quest to reunite the severed portions of her divine husband Osiris and restore him to eternal life.

At the far end of the temple stood the great effigy, winged arms outspread, her horn-crowned head lowered to her supplicants. I paid for an offering of incense and knelt before the altar, gazing up at the goddess as the blue smoke arose, reminded of Naamah, who had laid down with the King of Persis on Blessed Elua's behalf, of gentle Eisheth, the healer, to whom I had prayed too seldom.

I prayed to them both, now, and to Isis, in whose lands I travelled. Merciful goddess, I prayed, restorer of life, make me whole. Make us all whole.

Whether or not she heard and was minded to grant my prayer, I cannot say; I was a foreigner in her lands, and too far from my own. Nonetheless, my heart felt lighter when I left.

"You see?" Outside the temple, Kaneka smiled at me. "I told you you would like this better."

That night we made camp not far from the outskirts of Majibara.

Indeed, sounds of the city were carried on the night breezes—a skirling sound of pipes, a burst of uproarious laughter, faint and distant. To-morrow, our numbers would dwindle further. Achara and Binudi, the two Nubians, would depart, continuing westward along the Nahar, while the rest of us would strike south for Meroë.

Safiya, who was a native of Meroë, told stories of her city's glory and that of its regent, Queen Zanadakhete, who ruled over all of Jebe-Barkal. Her honor guard, she told us, was two thousand men, none shorter than six feet tall, all clad in splendid embroidered capes and bearing swords and spears and shields made of the patterned hide of the camelopard, tough and light-weight. I was not sure I could credit such stories, but Kaneka assured us they were true.

Thus passed our last night upon the river.

I would be sorry to leave it. It was a pleasant mode of travel, aside from the crocodiles. Wali moped the whole of the way, clearly hoping Kaneka would change her mind and choose to stay with him. As for Wali, I think if he had not loved his boat so much, he might have gone with her, but no craft can navigate the cataracts of the Nahar, which are narrow and strewn with rocks, broken here and there by sharp precipices.

Majibara was vast indeed, a city of yellow sandstone made even larger by the number of caravans camped on its outskirts. We sailed into the city itself and took lodgings at what Wali swore was a reputable inn, hiring porters to bear our goods.

Menekhetans, Jebeans and Umaiyyati dominated, for there is trade overland from the Ahram Sea. Of a surety, there were no other D'Angelines—but nor did I see Caerdicci or Hellenes, or any of the more familiar nations.

And our journey was scarce begun.

What we would have done without Kaneka, I cannot say. She was a shrewd negotiator and wise in the ways of Jebean travel. One camel looks much like another to me. They are odd, ungainly creatures with great, furred humps upon their backs and lambent eyes, with lashes like a woman's. They can bear prodigious amounts of weight and go for many miles with neither food nor drink, traversing the desert sands on broad, splay-toed hooves.

They are also notoriously unpleasant and their shambling gait a torment, but that I learned later.

We spent the better part of a day arranging transport for Achara and Binudi, and that was accomplished in fine form, a train of donkey-porters hired and the transaction registered with Majibara's Master of Caravans. The women were excited, which I was glad to see; I do not think, until then, they entirely believed they would be returning home. I prayed they would find the homecoming they deserved. If nothing else, they were laden with spoil, and greed may prevail where compassion falters.

What stories they would tell their families, I never asked.

Our own arrangements took considerably longer. It would require a forced march of some seven days to regain the river. While this would cut a month or better from our route, it would be grueling. There was only one watering-hole along the route, and that of salt water so bitter only the camels could drink it. The rest, we must carry ourselves. To that end, where we had spent lightly in Iskandria, trusting in the route's rich provisions, we spent heavily in Majibara. Water-skins we bought in abundance, and two great casks to augment our supply; and sacks of sorghum for camel-fodder. For ourselves, we would carry a supply of dried meat cut in strips, dates and a crumbling white cheese made of goats' milk, none of it especially appetizing. Jebeans are great hunters, and where they cannot get fresh game, they make do with scant provision.

Other items as well we purchased: skinning knives, soap, butter, a pair of lanterns, an aromatic unguent reputed to keep lice at bay, satchels, woolen blankets, needles and thread, and bits of hide and thong for patching boots and tack. Joscelin, who'd regretted the lack on the river, bought a set of fishing hooks and sturdy line, which made me laugh, bound as we were for the desert.

We hired four guides and twelve camels, and I cannot count how many Kaneka interviewed before she found a company that suited her exacting requirements. The marketplaces of Majibara are difficult to endure, spread beneath the baking sun and stinking of camel dung. I was glad when it was done and Joscelin measured out five links of chain, prying them loose and paying them unto the guide-master under Kaneka's judicious eye.

"Eat well," she said when the deal was concluded, "drink your fill and visit the baths, for tomorrow we enter the desert."

There was music that night at the inn, a percussionist playing on goat-hide drums to the accompaniment of some wailing stringed instrument, like unto a harp but with only four strings and a looser tone. We sat up for a time and listened, lingering over cups of beer.

"In the Cockerel," Joscelin said, smiling, "there would be dancing."

"And wine." I laughed. "Do you remember the headache I had?"

"The day we set out for Landras? You looked the way I feel at sea."

"We were toasting Hyacinthe," I remembered. "At least I was, and Emile. Imri, I never told you, but if it hadn't been for the Tsingani, we would never have found you." I told him, then, about asking for Emile's aid and how Kristof, son of Oszkar, had brought his *kumpania* to find us at Verreuil.

"Because of Hyacinthe?" he asked when I was done.

"Yes," I said. "Because of Hyacinthe."

Imriel thought about it, frowning his Courcel frown. "Then it is right that I am here, trying to help him. Whether he knows it or not, I am in his debt. It is right and fair."

It would have been humorous, coming from anyone else his age.
This boy could be dangerous. Or he could be something else.

"Yes," I said. "It is right, and fair."

In the early morning, when the sky had lightened to a leaden grey, the stars still visible, we assembled our caravan and set out across the vast wasteland of the desert.

It was my first experience at riding a camel, and I must own, for all I had boasted of my hard-won horsemanship skills, this was somewhat completely different. At the guide's command, my mount lowered itself to its knees, huffing prodigiously. With some apprehension, I clambered into the stiff, high-backed saddle and the camel rose, swaying. I felt very far above the ground, and in no way in control of the strange beast.

"Very good!" said Mek Timmur, our Jebean caravan-guide. "Very good, lady!"

I looked at Imriel, clinging to his saddle and grinning fit to split his face. On the other side of me, Joscelin sat at his ease, wearing a white burnoose with the hood lowered and looking for all the world like he'd ridden a hundred camels. Kaneka and Safiya were as comfortable as if they'd been lounging on couches. Well and good, I thought; if they could manage, so could I.

After the first few miles, I ceased to worry about riding a camel.

The challenge of the desert was overwhelming enough.

For one who has not endured it, it is hard to describe. Words like "heat" and "sun" lose all meaning. The desert was a vast expanse of yellow sand, flat as a board, stretching in all directions. As the sun cleared the horizon and began to climb into the sky, the heat mounted, relentless as a hammer. When it was still, one prayed for a breeze; when the breeze came, it was like the breath of a furnace, hot and parching. I perched atop my shambling camel and withered, feeling my skin, my mouth, my very eyeballs sandy and desiccated.

Here and there, we passed barren hills, pyramids of black basalt jutting forth from the flat sands. At midday, Mek Timmur declared a halt of two hours in the shadow of one such. The respite afforded by the shade was offset by the heat of the stone itself, radiant in the sun. I leaned against an outcropping of rock, fanning myself with my broad-brimmed hat and clutching the cool, sweating bulk of a water-skin.

"You see?" Kaneka said cheerfully. "Safer than Nineveh."

I was too hot to do anything but nod.

The rest of the day passed in much the same manner, and we pushed on into the night. When twilight fell, it was strangely beautiful, the purple shadows lengthening across the endless desert. Nowhere else in the world can one see how far light travels unimpeded, nor darkness. In the absence of the sun, the temperature dropped to bearable levels. Under a canopy of stars, we travelled onward, the spongy footfalls of the camels oddly silent on the desert floor, accompanied only by the rattle of our gear and our own soft breathing.

At what hour I could not guess, Mek Timmur ordered camp made and in short order our tents were pitched, the camels staked for the night, kneeling under the stars and chewing meditatively on their measures of sorghum. I fell onto my own pallet and slept like the dead.

And on the following day, we did it all over again.

Terre d'Ange is a rich and fertile land. While I have travelled to many lands that made me long for home, never had I experienced any place so completely and utterly barren, lacking in all elements that sustain life. If we had not carried our own water, of a surety, we would have died in the first days. The heat and dryness was such that it leeched all moisture from the flesh. On the third day, we entered a sea of grey stone, locked into impossible waves and sculpted by the wind. And here the *simoom* blew, the killing wind of the desert. It was fortunate that we were not in the sands, where we would have had no choice but to wait out the windstorm, crouched beside the bulk of our camels and praying they would shelter us from the suffocating sands. As it was, it was bad enough, but we persevered, wrapping our faces in turbans, reemerging into the airless sea of ochre sand.

Among us all, I daresay Imriel bore it the best, enduring the scorching heat with all the resilience of youth. At the end of the day, he alone had breath left for chatter; even Joscelin, with his Cassiline endurance, looked haggard and weary.

On the fourth day, we reached the watering-hole.

I had expected—oh, I don't know, an oasis of sorts, shaded with palms, a small encampment surrounding it. 'Twas nothing of the sort, but a crater within the desert, flanked by tall cliffs and fantastically hot, lacking the least vegetation. The well was deep and plentiful, but 'twas true, the water was bitter and fit only for the camels, which drank it without harm. All about the floor of the valley, we saw the corpses of camels that had been pushed too hard and sickened and died in sight of water. I understood, then, a little better why Kaneka had been so particular in her choice of caravans. There are no scavengers in the desert—not even blowflies—and the skeletons of the camels were perfectly preserved, sand-colored hummocks, the hides parched and withered onto the bones.

If the water was unsuitable for drinking, at least one could bathe in it, and this we did, filling a large copper basin brought for the purpose. I washed the airborne grit from every crevice of my body, rinsing my sand-caked hair and feeling several pounds lighter for it. Such was the heat that the water evaporated from my skin within minutes of my bath, leaving me cleaner but no less dehydrated for it. My hair, drying nearly as quickly, fair crackled with electric heat.

I remembered ruefully the counsel I'd given Pharaoh's wife, poor, simple Clytemne. Would that I'd had a salve of wool-fat on this journey!

And then we were off again, boarding our lumbering, swaying camels, emerging from the baking shadows of the valley into the blazing wasteland. My lips parched and cracked, and I wet them sparingly with small sips from my water-skin. Only the heaps of dried camel dung at our resting-points gave evidence that anyone else in the world had passed this way—that, and the occasional corpse, the desiccated mounds of fallen camels.

"You are sure," I said to Kaneka at one point, my voice thin and cracking, "that this is the wisest route to Meroë?"

"The wisest?" From under the shadow of her hood she looked at me, eyes dark and amused. "I never said it was the wisest, little one. But it is the shortest."

Yellow sand and basalt hills gave way to granite, grey plains and rugged hills laced with a vein of blue slate, an unexpected gift of color. It fed the imagination until one's mind conjured lakes, vast lakes, blue and shimmering in the distance. The first such vision excited me and I urged my camel onward over the desert floor, imagining the cool depths, plunging my whole head into the waters and drinking my fill, until my parched throat was slaked at last and my belly filled with water, as much water as it could hold.

"No, lady." Mek Timmur held me back, grasping my camel's reins and shaking his head, looking sorrowful. "It is illusion. Only illusion."

I didn't believe him, not at first. After another hour's march, when the shimmering lake remained at the self-same distance, I began to believe. And then he adjusted our course, moving slightly to the east, and the "lake" faded, giving way to barren rock. Then, I believed.

Onward and onward. Our water-skins ran dry, and we had to breach one of the casks, huddling around to share it out among us, lest a drop be spilled. At night, my mouth was so dry I could hardly chew the strips of dried meat. Our camels plodded through deep sand and scree, staggering on the loose pebbles. How long had it been? A week, Kaneka had estimated. It felt like far longer. Despite the best care of the guides—and they were good, if the stories I've heard were any indication—one of the camels foundered, wallowing on the desert floor. Imriel, angry and bitter, would have wept if he'd had the moisture for tears.

And slowly, slowly, the signs of life reemerged.

First were a few stunted mimosa trees, ragged shrubs struggling for life. We hailed them with shouts of joy. On the next to last day, we saw a pair of gazelles, startling and unlikely, bounding southward at our approach.

On the last day, I could smell the river.

One would not suppose, being odorless, that the scent of water could travel so far. In an arid land, believe me, it does. My lord Delaunay trained me to use my nose no less than any other sense, and it was I who scented it first, the sweet, life-giving presence of moisture carried on the air.

We had regained the Nahar.

It was different, far different, from the broad, gracious expanse on which we had sailed upon our feluccas. Here it was younger and swifter, nearer to its source, and there were fewer settlements upon its banks, which were not nearly so lush.

Still, it was water, and life.

We had crossed the desert.

Sixty-seven

ALONG THE banks of the Nahar, it was another several days' journey to Meroë, which lay at the juncture of two Great Rivers—the Nahar, which we had travelled, and the Tabara, which led further south. After the forced march across the desert, this leg of the journey was nearly leisurely. Day in and day out, we drank our fill of water. I never thought it would seem such a luxury.

There were villages along the way, albeit small and struggling. Here we traded for flat-bread and milk, augmenting our diet. And there was game, at last. Mek Timmur and the others hunted, bringing in gazelle, which we ate half-cooked and bloody.

'Twas not to my taste, to be sure. And yet it was better than one might expect. Deprivation is a sharp sauce for hunger.

With our schedule returned to something resembling normalcy, Joscelin resumed the practice of his Cassiline exercises—morning and night, tireless and diligent. It may be that I saw only what I desired, but I thought he was regaining a measure of his old fluid grace. Of a surety, 'twas meaningless without an opponent; and yet the forms were there.

So we made our way to Meroë, and with each mile that passed, Kaneka and Safiya's excitement grew. Their long homecoming was at last becoming a reality.

We had to cross the river to reach the city, a dubious crossing on a vast, swaying bridge that hung suspended over the rapids. I will own, I was nervous, as our camels strung out in a long line, proceeding one after the other, Mek Timmur going first to argue the tarif on the far side. Nonetheless, the crossing was made without incident.

We had reached Meroë, the capital city of Jebe-Barkal.

As the desert has its own harsh beauty, Meroë has its splendor.

Bordered on either side by broad, rushing rivers, it is nearly an island unto itself, afforded natural protection and ready irrigation. On the outskirts of the city lie the royal cemeteries, looming pyramids of reddish mud-brick that challenge the brilliant blue skies, awing the weary traveller. Inside was the city proper, a busy and bustling place, with temples raised to the many gods of Menekhet and indeed, as Safiya told us, to other gods native to Jebe-Barkal, such as lion-headed Apamedek and Kharkos the Hunter, who wielded two bows in his four arms.

At the heart of Meroë lies the royal palace.

It is guarded by high walls, and both the east and west gates are flanked by sculptures of kneeling oliphaunts, massive beasts with trunks upraised, twice as tall as a man. I did not believe a living beast could be so large until I saw one ambling the streets of Meroë, a moving turret in which two soldiers rode affixed to its broad back. Its hide was grey and wrinkled, as thick as cured leather, and its feet the size of serving-platters. I stared, open-mouthed, having only read of such wonders. Its broad ears flapped like sails, moving the hot air. A squadron of soldiers preceded it, chatting inconsequentially among themselves, resplendent in embroidered capes over light mail, carrying the rumored shields of camelopard skin.

"So," Kaneka said softly, watching them pass. "At last you see my land."

I will own, it was humbling. There was so much I had not known of Jebe-Barkal.

'Twas Safiya's turn, in the city of her birth, to play the guide, and she directed our caravan to the finest lodgings in town, which were quite fine indeed. The camels were unloaded, and our farewells said; Mek Timmur and his assistants were bound for an encampment, and thus to seek employ on a return journey. I wished them the joy of it, glad to leave the desert behind. Beyond, to the south, the purple shadow of mountains loomed, the highlands of Jebe-Barkal. It was there that Kaneka's village lay, and there we were bound; south, ever south. For all its splendor, Meroë was but another station on the way.

First, though, we would seek the Queen's blessing and see Safiya restored.

Of Queen Zanadakhete, I knew little; I had not even known, until this journey, that Jebe-Barkal, by tradition, is always ruled by a woman, wed or no. To some extent, her power is largely ceremonial, for there are princes—Ras, is the title—who rule each province. But in Meroë, her role is taken seriously indeed.

We composed our missive over dinner, all of us putting our heads together, and Safiya wrote it out in Jeb'ez, using parchment and ink that I provided. For all that I'd grown proficient at the spoken tongue, the script itself eluded me still. Safiya wrote it with a flowing hand.

"My father was a scribe," she said modestly. "I trained at his knee."

The hotel-keeper was paid, and the message delivered; a full link of gold, it cost us, one-fifth of the cost of our journey from Majibara. One pays, for access.

In the late afternoon of the following day, the reply came. We were summoned to court come morning.

Let Joscelin laugh—and he did, thinking me vain—but I dressed in D'Angeline finery for the audience, hauling my one court gown out of our trunks; the rose-silk with crystal beading that I had worn to meet Pharaoh. I would accord no less to the Queen-Regent of Jebe-Barkal. At Kaneka's insistence, we contracted an entourage and made our way to court thusly, beneath the fringed shade of our hired parasol-bearers.

Queen Zanadakhete received us in her inner courtyard, her august personage concealed behind a curtained alcove while the soft cries of caged birds and the redolent scent of citron surrounded us.

"So," she murmured in Jeb'ez, a half-glimpsed figure, her breath stirring the gauze curtains. "You have come from Khebbel-im-Akkad."

"If it please your majesty." I knelt, proffering the Lugal's letter. A dark arm swathed in ivory bangles emerged to take the letter; an older woman's hand, I thought, the knuckles swollen. There was a stir behind the curtains, and I heard a second voice murmur, translating the Akkadian text into Jeb'ez.

"It is good," the Queen's voice said when the translation was done, soft and satisfied. Behind the curtains, her gauze-misted figure inclined its head. "Although they have not come here, whispers have reached our ears of these . . . these things, these bone-priests, which even Pharaoh in Menekhet feared. It is good they are overthrown, that my people are not in thrall there. The Khalif's son is pleased. Daughters of Jebe-Barkal, you have done well. You shall be rewarded for it, and every honor given unto your families."

Kaneka and Safiya bowed low before her.

"Majesty." I drew a deep breath, redolent with citron. "My companions and I—we seek your permission to travel further south, in search of the descendents of Makeda, the Queen of Saba. Do you grant it?"

There was a pause, and a rustling; a swift exchange of whispers.

The gauze curtains were twitched apart and a bright black eye peered out, set in a wrinkled visage. "You are the chosen of your gods?" the soft voice inquired. "The one who defeated the bone-priests?"

I hesitated, unwilling to make that claim.

"She is, Fedabin." It was Kaneka who spoke, firmly, bowing to press her brow to the earth. "I have seen it. Though she appears weak, the breath of her strange gods blows hard upon her neck."

Another long, assessing pause ensued. I knelt and held myself still, *abeyante*, in the earliest manner to which I had been trained. 'Twas naught new to me, Kaneka's revelation. Hyacinthe had spoken the prophecy for me long ago, delivering it to Melisande Shahrizai in the days when he would not dare bespeak my fate. *That which yields is not always weak.*

Not always, no. I have learned that much about myself.

"So be it," whispered the soft voice of the Queen, the aged hand turning palm-outward, scored with dark lines, ivory bangles clattering. "In the name of Amon-Re, in the blessed names of Isis and Osiris, your request is granted. Such aid as we have will be given. Where the name of Zanadakhete of Meroë holds sway, let these people pass unmolested."

I let out my breath in a sigh. It was done.

Inside, we were met by Ras Lijasu, a grandson of the Queen. He was a handsome young man with his grandmother's bright inquisitive gaze, his ebony skin set off by splendid attire in cloth-of-gold—shirt and breeches, and the togalike *chamma*. I was glad, seeing him, that I'd worn my D'Angeline garb.

"So!" he exclaimed, clapping his hands. "All the way from Terre d'Ange, you have come! And Grandmother likes you, I am told. Such fun! Muni, where are the passage-tokens for our guests?"

His attendant comrade grinned and opened a coffer, and the Jebean prince reached in to grasp a handful of gold cords, each strung with an ivory cylinder that bore the seal of Meroë—Isis enthroned and lion-headed Apamedek.

"With these," Ras Lijasu said, taking my hand and knotting a corded token about my wrist, "you may wander anywhere in Jebe-Barkal, and declare yourself under the divine protection of Queen Zanadakhete." Still holding my hand, he smiled into my eyes. "And everyone you meet will be bound to offer you aid, even Ras Lijasu himself, do you ask him; the moon and the stars, do you ask him for it! Do you speak Jeb'ez, dream-spirit?"

"I do." I laughed. "Though I am more like to ask for maps and guides than the moon and stars, my lord Ras."

He staggered and put a hand to his chest. "She wounds me! Ah, she wounds me, Muni, this one with skin like new cream. What of you, lady?" Lijasu turned his winning smile on Safiya, taking her wrist to bestow a token upon her. "Will you, too, break my heart?"

Safiya stammered and blushed, unprepared for his attentions; I daresay as a scribe's daughter, she never expected to return from perdition to find herself the object of her prince's flirtations. He jested equally with Kaneka, who bore it with amusement, and he treated Joscelin with a warrior's courtesy, according scarce less to Imriel.

I liked him; it was impossible not to do so. For all his flirtatious ways, he took his duties seriously. An escort for Safiya was arranged in short order. In the interim, we adjourned to his study to pore over maps.

"Here, you see," he said, pointing to a broad plain alongside the Tabara River, "is Debeho; your home, Lady Kaneka," he added, sparing her a sly glance. "There is a man, a soldier of my guard, who is from the highlands very near there, and it is he I will release from his duties to guide you. And here . . ." his finger traced a winding route amid the mountains along the river, stopping shy of a vast inland lake. "Here is where our borders end, and the lands of the descendants of Makeda begin." Ras Lijasu tapped the map. "There are bandits along the way, my lady of Terre d'Ange, who will not heed the Queen's seal; highland tribes never brought to heel. Are you sure you must venture thence?"

"Yes," I said. "I am."

He gave a gusty sigh. "And who knows what welcome the Sabaeans will give you! Well." He rolled the map and extended it to me. "Take it."

I did, with gratitude.

We went, all of us, joining the procession to see Safiya restored to her family. Her father fell to his knees, weeping; all told, there was a good deal of weeping on both sides. I had learned a bit, by then, of how she had come to be enslaved in Drujan. One did not ask such things, in the zenana of Daršanga. Women volunteered it or kept silent; one did not ask. Safiya's father had entrusted her unto the keeping of a caravan-guide, to maintain the accounts, on a journey to Iskandria. It was there that the *Skotophagoti* had claimed her.

Queen Zanadakhete had spoken true: the bone-priests had never penetrated Meroë.

Of Kaneka's case, I knew less, for she was reticent on the subject.

We made merry after Safiya's restoration; it had been a joyous homecoming, and we celebrated it into the small hours. I was glad, after all that had transpired, to see with my own eyes a member of the Mahrkagir's hareem returned to the bosom of her family. It felt a victory.

In the morning, Ras Lijasu's guide came for us.

He was mountain-bred, Tifari Amu, with skin the color of cinnamon, keen features and a quiet, capable manner. He and Kaneka conferred at length, arguing over the map, arguing over the number of donkeys required to bear our goods, arguing over everything; Kaneka truculent, the Ras' guide calm and insistent.

"I think she likes him," Imriel observed.

"Yes." I hid a smile. I had taught him well. "I think so, too."

Their arguments were settled, and the matter decided. We would strike south for Debeho, and thence on to the fabled land of Saba.

There were politics involved; there are always politics. It is a fact of life. Relations between Jebe-Barkal and Saba were nonexistent. We would test the waters for Queen Zanadakhete, our embassy owing naught as it did to Jebean politics. It was somewhat they could disown; a favor to the Lugal of Khebbel-im-Akkad, if need be.

I didn't care. Let them use us as they would. I was glad we were going.

Sixty-Eight

OUR COMPANY consisted now of myself, Joscelin, Imriel and Kaneka, with the addition of Tifari Amu and a fellow soldier of Meroë, along with four hired bearers. Leaving the desert behind, we spent now on the purchase of a donkey-train and mounts for ourselves, swift horses of Umaiyyati stock, with arching necks and tails carried at a jaunty angle, flying like pennants.

We followed the Tabara River as best we might, but our journey often took us far afield. Lacking a poet's gifts, I am hard-pressed to describe the terrain we traversed. Such diversity! At its height, the landscape was nearly like unto the Camaeline Mountains that border Skaldi—forested and plunging, dense with pine and sycamore. Here the air grew thin and the nights were cold; so cold we huddled in our tents, shivering and glad of our woolen blankets.

The deep valleys were another matter altogether, green and tropical, filled with all manner of birds, flashing from tree to tree with raucous cries and bright plumage. There were monkeys, too; cunning creatures with bold eyes and scolding voices, agile and long-limbed. Our progress was slow through the valleys, and I was glad of our guides, for we would have been lost on our own, map or no map.

On the eleventh day, we reached the plain where Kaneka's village was located, and it proved yet another new landscape, vast and tawny plains dotted with the gnarled forms of eucalyptus trees. Here we were able to follow the river once more. It flowed at a good pace, narrower and swifter than where it joined the Nahar upstream.

As we drew near Debeho, Kaneka grew moody.

I asked her about it when we made camp that evening, pitching our tents beneath a spreading eucalyptus.

"I quarrelled with my brother, little one," she said, her voice unwontedly somber. "Do you have brothers?"

I shook my head. "Not that I know of."

Kaneka gave a faint smile. "They are a blessing and a curse. We sought, both of us, to be named our grandmother's successor."

"The storyteller," I said, remembering.

"Even so." She nodded. "There was a contest. Each of us was to tell a story, a true story, that had never been told before. Mafud lied. His story, of a magic ring and a spellbound prince—an Umaiyyati trader told it to him. I know, for I overheard it. But my grandmother did not know, and judged him the winner. No one believed me, so I ran away."

"The *Skotophagoti* found you? The Âka-Magi?"

"Not in Jebe-Barkal." Kaneka toyed with a gold necklace she held in her lap, a gift of the Lugal, bowing her head and polishing the gleaming metal. "Tigrati tribesmen found me; highlanders, like him." She jerked her chin at Tifari Amu. "So I was their captive. They traded me to a merchant in Meroë, and there he sold me to a caravan-master, to cook and clean for him." She smiled bitterly. "It is why I know so much about camels, little one. And he, he took me to Iskandria. That is where an Âka-Magus found me, and how I came to Drujan."

"Do you fear the welcome you will receive?" I asked her.

"No," she said shortly, clasping the pendant about her neck, where it nestled against the leather bag that held her amber dice. She looked at me. "Yes. As we draw nigh, I fear."

"Don't." I placed a hand on her arm. "Fedabin, in Daršanga you told us the stories of our fates, and you told them true. Without your courage to follow, the zenana would have faltered. You have lived such a story as your brother can only dream on his darkest nights, and emerged alive to tell it. You will be welcome. I am sure of it."

Kaneka looked at me a long time without speaking, then shook her head. "Would that I could tell your story, little one, but it is writ in no tongue I understand. The gods themselves must throw up their hands in dismay."

"Ah, well." I stood and stretched, watching the purple twilight fall across the plains. Our bearers had a fire blazing, and the spoils of last night's hunt cooking in a stew. Tifari Amu and his comrade Bizan lounged before their tent, whetting their spearheads and conversing. Joscelin and Imriel were returning empty-handed from the river, Joscelin winding the cord of his fishing-line and explaining the finer points of the piscatory arts to Imri. "It is not over yet, I hope," I said, noting absently how the dying sunlight pinned a crown of flame on Joscelin's fair hair.

"No." Kaneka smiled. "Not yet, I think."

In the morning, we rode to Debeho.

By unspoken accord, we rode in procession. Tifari Amu and Bizan took the lead, wearing embroidered capes over snow-white *chammas* and breeches, their horses prancing as if at parade. Kaneka, clad in her Akkadian robes with a dagger at her waist and her war-axe slung across her saddle, paced behind them, and Joscelin and Imriel and I followed. Behind us came the good-natured bearers and the donkey-train, laden with the Lugal's gifts.

Debeho was a collection of thatched mud huts along the river.

But to Kaneka it was home, and home is a powerful thing. We were spotted long before we arrived, and I saw the dark forms of children jumping and pointing, shrill cries of excitement carried on the breeze.

The village turned out to meet us, for good or for ill, weapons and scythes clasped in weathered hands. At Tifari's command, we raised our arms in salute, baring the passage-tokens of ivory and gold cord bound at our wrists.

And they rejoiced.

We were spectators here, all of us but Kaneka, and we hung back accordingly as she greeted her people, majestic as a queen, tears running in rivulets down her stern, dark face as she ordered the treasure-chests thrown open and her goods dispersed. There—that tall man with greying hair and shoulders like an ox; he must be her father. And the young one, who wept and kissed her hand—her brother, I thought. No mother, I noted—but there, a bent figure leaning on two gnarled sticks, her face wise and creased; surely, it was her grandmother.

It must have been, for proud Kaneka knelt. And the woman, the ancient woman, laid her knotted hand upon that bowed head, trembling, tears in her dark eyes.

Kaneka was home.

The celebration lasted for days, and I must own, they were the happiest I had known in longer than I can count. Debeho was a simple village, but I learned great fondness for it. The mud huts I had eyed dismissively were well-kept and clean, pleasantly suited to the hot clime of the plains. The villagers grew cotton and millet and a hardy strain of melon, and kept cattle as well. Wild bees produced honey, which

Jebeans ferment into a heady drink. Spices were prized; some gathered from the fertile mountainous regions, where a particular strain of tiny, hot pepper thrived; others garnered in trade, for Debeho was not so isolated that it never saw traders. There were weavers in the village, and tanners and ivory-workers, for the plains afforded good hunting.

And there was Shoanete, Kaneka's grandmother, the storyteller.

If I had to name her equal, it would be Thelesis de Mornay, who was the Queen's Poet and my friend beside. She had been in seclusion these last few years, her ill health preventing her from carrying out her court duties; it is Gilles Lamiz, her one-time apprentice, who has assumed her mantle. He is gifted, Messire Lamiz—he was the first poet ever to dedicate an epic to me, and I am grateful for it—but the world does not stop and hold its breath when he recites his work. Although she always maintained my lord Delaunay was the superior poet, Thelesis de Mornay had that quality.

Shoanete of Debeho had it, too.

I know, for I spent many hours in that village seated at her feet while she recited tales of the Melehakim, the descendants of Saba, of Shalomon and Makeda and their son, Melek al'Hakim, who was anointed Melek-Zadok. And each one held me spellbound.

'Twas my interest, I will own, that made the subject so compelling; but this did not hold true for the children—yes, and the adults—of Debeho, who gathered round to hear her, listening to her cracked voice give forth the ancient tales. And cracked or no, there was somewhat in it . . . a resonance, a power, that brought her words to life.

"Here," she said, tracing an area along the Ahram Sea on Ras Lijasu's map. "Here is ancient Saba, Saba-that-was. And here is the route along which King Khemosh-Zadok, the falsely anointed, led his people in retreat, weeping and beating their breasts, all the way to the Lake of Tears." Her gnarled finger circled the vast inland lake the Ras had indicated. "It is the source of the Nahar itself, formed by the tears wept by the goddess Isis as she searched for the dismembered body of her beloved husband Osiris."

"And now it is the heart of Saba?" I asked.

"It is," Shoanete said. "The Melehakim hold a secret stolen from their own god, a secret so powerful He would take it back if He could find it. But Isis' tears blind His eyes, and He cannot see it."

My heart beat faster and the small hairs at the back of my neck prickled. "If . . . if it is so powerful, how is it that the Melehakim were defeated?"

"Ah, that." The old woman smiled, deep creases forming in her wrinkled face. "That is the story of King Khemosh-Zadok, the falsely anointed, and how he broke the Covenant of Wisdom. For Queen Makeda herself, you see, was wisdom personified, and her fairness and great learning were renowned throughout the land. It came to her ears that a king far to the north, Shalomon of the Habiru, was similarly lauded for the virtue of his judgement. And so it came to Makeda that she wished to meet this king, and she journeyed with a mighty retinue, presenting him with gifts of gold and ivory and spices, that she might question him."

"So it says in the Tanakh!" I said, excited. "And he answered her questions aright."

"Indeed." Shoanete nodded, unperturbed by my interruption. "And then Makeda told him much he did not know, and King Shalomon bowed down before her wisdom, and gave her the ring from his finger in tribute. And Makeda was moved by his fine form and his grace, and chose to lie with him. 'Because thy wisdom has ceded to mine,' she said to him, 'we have made a covenant between us this night, man and woman. Of it shall come a son. I shall raise him with my teachings, and then I shall send him to thee to be anointed in thine. By thy ring shalt thou know him.' "

"Melek al'Hakim," I mused. "So that was the Covenant of Wisdom?"

"It was," she said. "As equals did they meet, man and woman, King and Queen, and the lesser wisdom did cede to the greater. And thus it was, for many generations. Melek al'Hakim did not steal the Treasures of Shalomon. He was anointed, and they were his by right; his, and the descendants of Khiram the architect and his people, who fled the sacking Akkadians."

"The Tribe of Dân," I said.

Shoanete paused. "It may be," she allowed. "Their name was not known to me. I will add it to the story, little one. Know then that for many generations the Melehakim ruled Saba, a King and Queen ruling together, joined in the Covenant of Wisdom. Mother and son, husband and wife, brother and sister . . . King Tarkhet, it is said, was guided by his daughter, but that is another story. And the shadow they cast over Jebe-Barkal was vast, and all nations and tribes answered to wise and mighty Saba. Until the reign of King Khemosh."

With that she paused, clearing her throat, and one of the listening children leapt up to fetch a cup of honey-mead. Shoanete sipped it and continued.

"There was trouble in the nation, then, for the young Ras Yatani of Meroë had lost his heart to Daliah, the sister of Khemosh. Now, Khemosh was not King at that time, but merely the widowed Queen's elder son; Arhosh was his brother's name, and it was Arhosh their mother chose to be anointed, for he was fair-spoken and wise where his brother was hot-blooded and angry. Arhosh looked with favor upon the union of Ras Yatani and Daliah, but Khemosh spoke against it, saying that Meroë looked to make a claim upon the throne of Saba."

"Did they?" I asked.

Shoanete's dark eyes glinted with mirth. "Perhaps they did, little one. If so, it was a peaceable one—the sword of the loins, and not the sword of steel. However it be, the young men listened to Khemosh and their hearts were stirred to anger. 'Khemosh should be King,' they said. 'Not Arhosh, who will let a stranger reach his hand for the throne.' And in time the elders listened to the young men, and the priests listened to the elders, and no one listened to the Queen, who spoke of the merits of an alliance by marriage to the most powerful of their vassal-nations."

"And love," I murmured, thinking of Ysandre and Drustan. "An alliance of love."

"Yes," she said. "It would have been that. But it was not to be, for the priests anointed Khemosh and raised him up as the King, Khemosh-Zadok, over his living mother and her chosen heir, thus breaking the Covenant of Wisdom. And he decreed the marriage-contract invalid. Now, Ras Yatani's heart was sore within him, and he raised up his army and many allies, and marched against Saba."

"And Saba was defeated," I said.

"Saba was defeated," Shoanete echoed. "It is another story, a long story, that battle. Enough to say that the spirit of the god which had filled the Melehakim ever before, rendering them fierce and invulnerable, filling their mouths with great cries that struck fear into their enemies— it deserted them, little one. On the battlefield, they stumbled and bled, and the only cries they uttered were cries of pain. And so they fled, for by this time, the widowed Queen was dead of sorrow, Arhosh slain in battle and Daliah the fair was dead by her own hand, and Ras Yatani's heart was as a burning stone within him, and he knew no mercy. Under Khemosh-Zadok's leadership, they fled, all the way to the Lake of Tears. And Ras Yatani, who found himself the undisputed ruler of Jebe-

Barkal . . . Ras Yatani swore a vow on Daliah's name that he and his descendants would honor the Covenant of Wisdom that Khemosh-Zadok had broken. It is said, for so long as a Queen rules in Meroë, his line will endure, and so it does, to this day."

"What of Shalomon's treasures," I asked, "and the One God's secret?"

Shoanete spread her hands. "These things the Melehakim took with them and hid, and no one has seen them since."

Thus the stories of Kaneka's grandmother, which I pondered at length. Eleazar ben Enokh had hoped to find that the Tribe of Dân had preserved customs lost by the Habiru, but I do not think he ever envisioned this Covenant of Wisdom. What is truth? History and legend are woven together like a Mendacant's cloak, and when the gods themselves are silent, no mortal may say where truth ends and fabrication begins. I did not think the One God of the Tanakh would bind his people into such a covenant with a foreign Queen—but those stories were written by Habiru scribes. Makeda's people told another story, passed from mouth to mouth.

. . . *great cries that struck fear into their enemies* . . .

Blessed Elua, I prayed, let it be true.

Let it be the Name of God.

Sixty-nine

As PLEASANT as our time in Debeho was, it had to end. There was a great feast on our last day, and no one in the village did any work save to prepare for the festivities, and afterward to eat and drink and make merry for hours on end, with much singing and dancing. Even Tifari Amu and Bizan were made welcome, for they were skilled hunters and contributed much game for the pot during our stay. Kaneka could not entirely maintain her professed dislike of the highland tribesman, and I thought it possible he might return to Debeho to court her.

Imriel was happy in the village.

With a child's quick ear—and his mother's wit—he had become proficient at Jeb'ez, much to the chagrined amusement of Joscelin, who was not much past nursery-rhymes. He made friends easily there, adults and children alike, none of whom knew or cared that Imriel de la Courcel was the son of the deadliest traitoress Terre d'Ange had ever known. And he hadn't had a nightmare since we arrived.

"We should leave him here," Joscelin said, reading my thoughts. "It would be safer."

"Do you think he'd stay?"

"I don't know." He shrugged. "Ask him."

I did, and got the Courcel frown in answer, neat furrows forming between his brows. "You said the Tsingani helped you find me because of Hyacinthe. You said it was right and fair that I should go."

"True," I said, wondering why I'd said somewhat so foolish. "But you could help most of all by remaining safe in Debeho."

That went over about as well as one might expect. "*I* got Joscelin's sword for him in Daršanga!" he reminded me.

"Yes," I said, and sighed. "You did. And if you try anything half so dangerous in Saba, I swear, I'll get Tifari Amu to hold you down and sit on you."

His eyes lit with hope. "You won't leave me?" There was an unexpected plea in his voice.

"No," I said, and this time I sighed inwardly. *Love as thou wilt.* Whether I willed it or no, Blessed Elua's precept had come to encompass this boy, and I didn't have the heart to abandon him. His trust had been violated too many times already. "I promise, Imri. We won't leave you."

After the feasting, Kaneka told the story of Drujan, and everyone fell silent to listen.

She had a touch of her grandmother's gift. 'Twas strange, hearing it told from her perspective. The audience sucked in their breath at the catalogue of the Mahrkagir's cruelties, although she did not list them all, no; not the ones I knew. Nor did she describe the daily squalor of life in the fateful zenana—the factions, the petty hatreds. And I . . . I did not enter the tale as a figure of contempt, Death's Whore, despised by all, but as a cunning trickster, cleverly winning the Mahrkagir's trust. It made me smile, a little bit. But the brooding presence of Angra Mainyu loomed over her tale, terrifying and oppressive, and that much was true.

And the battle in the festal hall, with all its attendant horrors—that, Kaneka told well, much to the Jebeans' shivering delight. They looked in awe at Joscelin as she described how his sword wove and flashed in patterns of steel too quick for the eye to follow, and a ring of the dead rose around him. He smiled quietly, his hands resting on his knees. It was not a thing of which he was proud, nor ever would be.

When she described the column of flame bursting from the well of Ahura Mazda, they clapped and shouted in approval—even her brother Mafud, whose envy and long-born guilt were erased by his relief at her safe return. And thus the story ended in triumph. I looked at Imriel, whose expression was troubled.

"It wasn't like that, Phèdre," he said to me. "Not really."

"I know." I stroked his hair. "That's why it's important to remember. But the stories are important, too."

And we can bear to hear it now, I thought; not the whole truth, no, but Kaneka's truth, the one she will carry to sustain her, that she will weave into legend and one day her grandchildren will tell to their children, holding up an ancient Drujani war-axe and saying, this was hers, and this was her story.

If it is so, mayhap we can learn to endure our own.

This was her land, and these were her people. I envied her that. Her story was done, and I prayed for her sake it was so. Of a surety, she had earned it. Still, mine continued. A sacrifice had been made, and I had allowed another to take my place. I had promised to walk the *Lungo Drom*, the longest road, for Hyacinthe's sake. The end of his story was yet unwritten. I prayed it would find an ending half as meet, in debts forgiven and joyous reunion.

I prayed it would end in love. I prayed we could come *home*, all of us.

In the morning, we departed for Saba. Kaneka held me hard and I returned her embrace, feeling her warm and solid presence. "Take care of yourself, little one," she whispered. "Take care of them all. May your strange gods watch over your every step."

I nodded and swallowed. She had been a good friend, and I was sorry to be leaving her. "And you, Fedabin. I think, after last night, you have a long life as the storyteller of Debeho ahead of you."

"It may be so." Kaneka released me and grinned. "It may be so!"

Onward we rode, turning back in the saddle to wave a half-dozen final farewells. At length, the village faded into the landscape, the mud huts indistinguishable from the tawny plains. Once again, we were on our way.

On the second day, we reentered the mountains, climbing treacherously narrow trails in single file, ascending to dizzying heights with the valley spread below us like a green carpet, deceptively smooth. Our guides Tifari Amu and Bizan relaxed in the mountains, chatting amicably back and forth as they rode. Joscelin too was at his ease, at home in the highlands of Jebe-Barkal as in his own Siovale, and Imriel—I had forgotten that he had been reared in the heights. I watched him scrambling about the crags in the evenings, gathering deadfalls for the fire, agile as a mountain goat.

A lost prince raised in secret by the priesthood of Elua, innocent of his origins. That had been his mother's plan. Watching him in the mountains, I nearly wished it had been so. Too late, now. The goatherd prince was not to be.

Once, a party of Tigrati tribesmen came upon us. For a few minutes, our welcome was uncertain. Hands hovered over swords, and all of us eyed one another. I held my arm out, extended as Tifari had taught us, revealing the Ras' passage-token, and Imriel did the same. Joscelin was tense, his hands crossed low over his daggers; he had not fought since his injury. Then one of the men grinned and made a jest, and Bizan replied in kind, and all was well. *Give every courtesy, and never reveal fear.* We made camp together that evening and shared our goods in a common pot.

I heard the "mountain-talkers" for the first time that night, the speaking drums that Audine Davul's father had studied. The hunters carried a smaller version, a short length of log hollowed and polished, which their percussionist beat on with mallets. It made a sharp, staccato sound, carrying over the highlands in a series of complex rhythms. After a time, we heard the great drums of their distant village boom in answer.

"We will pass undisturbed," Tifari Amu said in satisfaction. "The news has been spread." And it must have been so, for we encountered no one else in the highlands.

After a week, we began to descend once more, following a series of plateaus to rejoin the river. Wildlife abounded in these regions. I cannot even begin to count the species we saw. Antelope and gazelles were plentiful, graceful creatures with russet hides and spiraling, pronged horns. They had a trick of springing straight into the air with all four feet off the ground when startled. Bizan and Tifari Amu hunted them on horseback, with spears. It was an astonishing thing to see the swift Umaiyyati horses keep pace with the fleet beasts, swerving and doubling.

There were camelopards, too, which is another beast I would not have credited without seeing it. They are immensely tall and angular, with legs like knobbled stilts and necks that stretch to the treetops, pale hides covered with a crazed pattern of darker blotches. For all their size, they are gentle creatures and merely watched us pass, wondering.

Of a surety, there were other, less benign inhabitants. At night we heard the roar of lions, a fearsome sound. When we could, we would cut acacia branches, dense with sharp, hooked thorns, and assemble a makeshift stockade around our campsite, for beasts of prey would come for our horses if they dared. There were sharp-faced jackals like great black foxes, and hyenas, the carrion-eaters, with their ungainly bodies and spotted hides. After a successful hunt, one could always hear them, the eerie barking laughter ringing out in the night as they fought over the bones, which they cracked in their strong jaws.

There were scavenger birds, too; the sky would darken with them when Bizan and Tifari made a kill . . . buzzards, and vultures with their vast wingspans and bare necks, and strangest of all, great storks that flew with their long legs trailing and landed to pick their way through the throng of bird-life with long, pointed beaks.

'Twas a beautiful land, that much I will own. I could understand why Audine Davul's father had loved it. I could understand, too, why she longed for home. For all the wonders of Jebe-Barkal—and I am glad, to this day, that I have seen a herd of oliphaunts bathing in the river at sundown—I could not help but think that the lavender must be in full bloom in Terre d'Ange, perfuming the air, grapes beginning to ripen on the vine.

Still, there were far worse places we could be.

I knew. We had been there.

And whether it had been madness to bring him or no, Imriel thrived on the journey. Although the loose Jebean burnoose kept off the worst intensity of the sun, the pallor of the zenana had given way to healthy color. He had lost the skulking wariness I had first known, and the shadows under his eyes were gone. Although he was far from sturdy, his bones no longer seemed quite so frail and vulnerable beneath his skin, and I swear, he'd grown a full inch since we left Daršanga.

"He must be eleven, you know," Joscelin remarked one evening, watching Imriel lay tinder and branches for the campfire in accordance with Bizan's careful instruction.

"Eleven!" It startled me somehow; his age was fixed, in my mind, at ten.

"Do you remember, he was born in the spring? Six months old, when he vanished in fall." From the Little Court of La Serenissima, he meant; he'd been part of that search. "Somewhere between Drujan and here, he would have turned eleven."

"You're right," I said.

Joscelin watched him without speaking for a time. "He'll hate it at court," he said eventually. "They'll watch him like a hawk, every minute of every day, waiting for him to turn into his mother."

"Ysandre won't allow it," I protested.

He gave me a deep look. "Her own cousin tried to have him killed. Elua knows whether or not Barquiel was behind it. What's Ysandre going to do? Bring back the Cassiline Brothers, assign him as someone's ward?"

"If she has to."

"She won't like it." He shook his head. "Not after La Serenissima. And that won't stop the talk. Nothing can stop the talk. He's already pulled one of Melisande's own tricks, eluding Lord Amaury like that."

"He didn't know," I said softly.

"You think that will matter where gossip is concerned?"

I looked away. "No."

"It will make him hard," Joscelin murmured. "I hate to see it, that's all."

"I know." I watched Imriel crouch beside the firepit, coaxing a spark from Bizan's flint striker and blowing softly on a nest of dried grasses at the heart of his arrangement. "Well, we've a long way to go yet, and a longer way back."

"Not as long as it was," Joscelin said. "Not nearly so long as it was."

And I was not sure, then, if we spoke of the journey or somewhat else.

SEVENTY

WE OWED our respite to the rhinoceros.

'Tis passing strange, to owe so much to such a monstrous beast; and yet it is true. We were yet in sight of the river when the creature burst through the dense underbrush of the acacias, the hooked thorns troubling its thick hide not at all. I sat my horse stock-still, feeling it tremble beneath me, staring at the looming head like the prow of a warship, small, maddened eyes set on either side of that great central horn. All I could think of was the Black Boar of the Cullach Gorrym, and how it had emerged from the wood to lead Drustan's troops to victory in Alba. I'd thought *that* was big.

Then Tifari Amu shouted, and Bizan, and both of them wheeled their horses in opposite directions, seeking to draw the beast off. Having none of it, it lowered its head and charged, swerving at the last minute to miss me, scattering our bearers and our donkey-train, scattering all of us. It was fast, faster than one would imagine, and its passage shook the very earth. I heard cries of dismay and a yell of pain as someone was entangled in the thorns.

And then—

"Joscelin!"

Like in Daršanga, Imriel's voice, high and true, rose above the shouting and the drumming of mighty hooves. I saw, and breathed a curse. Joscelin had dismounted and stood between me and the beast as it made its turn, rounding. His sword gleamed, angled in his two-handed grip, and he stood light on his feet, waiting.

The rhinoceros charged.

I did not see, in truth, exactly what happened, for in that instant I dug my heels into my mount's flanks and fought him as he flung up his head in terror, sawing at the reins and wrestling him into a sideways dancing step. I know only that Joscelin whirled out of the way, turning like an Eisandine *tauriere*, both arms extended and the tip of his sword scoring a long gash down the length of the creature's leathern hide.

I will do it, I thought, still fighting my mount and seeing the rhinoceros gather itself, lowering its head, shoulders rising like a hummock on the sea, seeking its opponent. Joscelin moved to intercept it, graceful and sure, Tifari and Bizan returning at full tilt, too far away, the wind snatching their cries from their open mouths. Elua help me, but I will do it, I will ride between him and that monster, if I have to kill my horse and myself.

Why it did, I'll never know, but the rhinoceros thought better of it. It shook itself, for all the world like a massive dog, and turned, trotting toward the river, plowing through the thornbushes and leaving us.

"You *idiot!*" I shouted at Joscelin, finding my voice. "You could have been *killed!* What in Elua's name were you thinking?"

He laughed out loud, spinning in a giddy circle, his blade carving a silver line in the air. "I struck true, Phèdre! Did you see? I can still do it. *I can still do it!*"

I opened my mouth and closed it. "You could have been killed," I repeated with more restraint. "Joscelin, if you need to test your skills, pick something that's not nearly the size of an oliphaunt, with hide like cured leather. You can't kill such a beast on foot, with a naked blade."

"You can if you cut their hamstrings." In a calmer humor, he sheathed his sword behind his back. "Tifari Amu told me; it's how they hunt oliphaunt. It takes precision, that's all. I'm sorry if I frightened you."

I gave him a look and had no time for aught else, for by then, Tifari and Bizan returned, with Bizan's horse pulling up lame, having strained a foreleg, and our bearer Nkuku had to be extricated from the thorns. He was badly scratched and shaken, and two of the donkeys entangled as well, having been scattered by the rhinoceros' charge. Those acacia thorns are like nothing I have ever seen; finger-length and sharper than a fishhook. There were wounds to be tended, human and animal alike, and a pair of water-skins slashed to shreds, good for naught but patch-leather. Tifari Amu opined that the beast must have been ill, and sought only to gain the river. Mayhap it was so, but it wrought a fair amount of damage! 'Twas a mercy Imriel had thought to grab the reins of Joscelin's mount, else we'd have had a job chasing it down, too.

Nonetheless, we needed to regroup, and so it was that Tifari scouted upriver, finding us a pleasant site. Here we would make our camp, until we were fit to travel.

The site was situated at a bend of the river, which flowed smooth over a pebbled bed, swirling and eddying as it turned. At one point a natural spring gave rise to a deep, secluded pool, emptying in a rivulet which meandered off on its own, burbling over rocks to feed the Tabara River. It was a perfect place to bathe or wash clothing without fear of crocodiles or hippopotami intruding, and for that alone I was grateful. We pitched our tents on the grass near the river's bend, lush as greensward and ample fodder for horses and donkeys alike, and Yedo, another of the bearers, carved out a passage through the underbrush to the bathing-pool.

We spent four days there, all told, letting strains and thorn-gouges heal, while Tifari and Bizan hunted gazelle—not only to replenish our supply of meat, but to replace our water-skins, for they used the hides scraped clean and laid to cure, burying them in hot sand and shale away from the green swathe cut by the river. When it was done, the hides would be tied by the four legs and laced tight with leather thong woven from the remnants of the old water-skins, and these, Tifari assured us, would serve us well in the last portion of our journey, where we must depart from the river and again traverse the highlands.

After that, we would reach the Great Falls, and enter Sabaean lands.

I did not know, until we had it, how much we needed that respite.

Thanks to the generosity of the Lugal of Khebbel-im-Akkad and Ras Lijasu of Meroë, while we did not travel in state, we travelled in comfort, as much as one might attain in the wilds of Jebe-Barkal. Millet we had in plenty, for cooking the flat, spongy bread of the Jebeans, and spices as well, and dried dates and figs. Our tents were well made and spacious, and we had all of us adopted the Jebean custom of sleeping on hide cots, stretchers that disassembled easily and raised one off the ground, where scorpions and other insects were wont to be found.

I even had a three-legged stool slung with a leathern seat, and an ample supply of ink and parchment to record our journey. And that I did, sitting before our tent and musing over the activities of our encampment, setting in writing the stories that Shoanete of Debeho had told me; yes, and our own travels as well, and the hunting-songs of Tifari Amu and Bizan, and the workmen's chants of our bearers, that no one had ever recorded. Would that I'd had such luxury in Skaldia! Near as it was, it was a culture no less exotic to those of D'Angeline blood. For a long time, I had wished only to forget it. Now, I thought of the hearth-songs I'd sung to poor Erich in the zenana, and wished I remembered more, and had them written down.

To think, I'd sung the Master of the Straits to calm with such a song.

His mortal mother had sung him songs.

I pondered our neat campsite, the dark skins and exotic features of our comrades, Joscelin and Imriel clad in Jebean attire, the splendid vista of the lowlands flanked by green mountains, the vast blue sky that arched over it all. We were a long way from the grey waters of the Straits, from that rocky, lonely isle.

Hyacinthe. I never forgot.

It was on the third day of our respite that Joscelin caught his fish, although that was not how I would remember that day. To be sure, he'd caught fish before, and a fair number of them, some weighing ten to fifteen pounds. I do not know what species they were—cowfish, the Jebeans called them—but they were a salmon hue, with many-rayed dorsal fins and small heads. When cooked, the flesh resembled trout and was quite agreeable.

Joscelin was after bigger game.

He pointed them out to me, he and Imriel; vast shadows lurking in the pebbled depths of the river. I nodded, listening politely as Imriel explained how they meant to use smaller fish as bait, showing me how the treble hooks were strung. And then I retreated to sit upon my stool and pore over my journal, watching the river's edge with half an eye and thinking about how I was to convince the Sabaeans—the Mele-hakim, Shoanete had called them—that they should reveal to me the Name of God that they had hidden from Adonai Himself.

It was the shouting that caught my ear, and at that I had to go and see.

Joscelin stood knee-deep in the rushing waters, clad only in a pair of white Jebean breeches. Sunlight gleamed on his loose, damp hair, the muscles working in his arms as he played out the line, hand over hand. Downstream, the mighty fish he'd hooked fought him, bucking and leaping, its sides flashing silver. I will own, I gasped when I saw the size of it.

And on a sandbar in the middle of the river, Imriel jumped up and down with excitement, shouting instructions, clutching a stout branch in one hand. His black hair was plastered to his cheeks in coils and he had stripped to his sodden breeches.

I laughed. I couldn't help it. 'Twas an epic battle in its own way, though unfit for any poet's tale. When the line was played, Joscelin began drawing it back in, fighting the fish for every inch of it. And how that fish fought! I saw it when it broke the water, silver-sided with a green back shading to black, fierce and vigorous, a true giant of the river. Imriel floundered into the depths, beating ineffectually at the waters with his club, and Joscelin shouted him back, still hauling on the line. I'd have worried about crocodiles, if I wasn't laughing so hard.

And somewhere, in the midst of it, my heart swelled to aching with love.

Somehow, by main strength, Joscelin hauled the thrashing fish onto the sandbar and Imriel landed it, striking it hard with his club and falling on it, struggling to hook his fingers in its gills. It heaved wildly under him, and boy and fish wrestled in the shallow waters, skin and scales wet and shining. He succeeded, too, though the fish was nearly as large as he was. Once it was subdued, Joscelin had to wade into the river to retrieve it, carrying the massive thing overhanging his arms. It must have weighed fifty pounds. He sloshed ashore, Imriel splashing alongside him, alight with glee.

"What do you think?" Joscelin asked laughing, tossing the fish at my feet where it landed with an audible thud, wriggling and twitching on the greensward.

I took two steps forward, grabbed his hair and kissed him.

For a moment, I think, he was too startled to react, and then—Elua! His arms came hard around me and he returned my kiss, hard, hands sliding along my back, following the path of my marque. It was like the torch igniting the Sacred Fires in the festal hall.

We parted breathless and staring at one another.

"I think," I said unsteadily, "you should bring me fish more often."

"I think I will," Joscelin replied, sounding bemused. He glanced down. "What are you looking at?"

"Nothing." Imriel was hugging himself, grinning fit to split his face, shifting from foot to foot. "You should take a bath, Joscelin; you're all over fish."

"So are you," he said to Imriel, then blinked at me. "And so are you, now. I should . . . I should clean the fish, first."

"I can do it." Imriel wedged his fingers under the gills and dragged the fish a foot, rolling it onto its back to expose the pale belly. "See?" He traced a line with one damp forefinger. "I cut here to begin. You said I made a good job of it, remember? It's bigger than the others, that's all. Yedo can help me."

Joscelin raised his eyebrows at me.

"Well?" I said. "Imri's right, you're all over fish. Go take a bath, Joscelin."

He went, gathering dry clothing, a lump of precious soap and a reasonably clean towel of Menekhetan cotton.

Imriel gloated over his fish, and looked at me sidelong. "I will tell Yedo not to let anyone use the bathing-pool," he said, all innocence. "If you want to go, and wash your gown."

"You think I should?" I touched his river-damp hair. Imriel looked down and nodded fiercely, the matter suddenly too great for words. I wondered why it meant so much to him. "All right," I said. "I'll go."

The passage to the bathing-pool was like a green tunnel, mimosa bushes crowding inward to filter the light, pungent sap weeping from the new-cut branches. Clusters of small yellow flowers brushed my gown as I passed, dusting the fabric with pollen. I felt strange in my own skin, sensitive to every breath of air, my heart beating too fast with uncertainty.

And aching, still.

The passage opened onto the bathing-pool, where Joscelin stood, not quite waist-deep. Since he had not seen me, I went to sit on the sun-warmed rocks at the water's edge and watched him as he dunked his head and flung it back, water spraying in a glittering arc. Dappled light played over his skin, the muscles gliding beneath it. Pale scars marred his flesh and a few new ones, still pink. I knew the old scars by touch. Along his ribs was the curving gash he'd taken in Skaldia. That one, I'd sewn myself, in a cavern marked by the sigil of Blessed Elua, where we'd taken shelter from a blizzard.

And made love, I remembered, for the first time; Cassiline and *anguissette*.

Desire beat in my blood like the distant thunder of drums upon the mountain.

Joscelin saw me and went still, water dripping from him in the sunlight. Even when I'd resented him, long ago, I'd thought him beautiful. He stood patient under my regard. Every one of the scars that marked him, he'd gotten on my behalf. I did not have words to speak to him.

"Phèdre," he said at length, saying my name softly. "Will you join me?"

I nodded without speaking and stayed where I was.

He took a few steps, shadows in the hollows of his flanks, and lifted me from the rocks as if I weighed no more than his enormous fish, lowering me to stand before him. The skirts of my gown floated on the water and I put both arms around his neck as he lowered his head to kiss me.

That kiss, I cannot describe.

It was like a poem, a prayer, a homecoming unlooked-for. It was like dungeon walls crumbling to reveal a glimpse of sky. It shook me to the very roots of my soul.

All I could do was cling to him and gasp.

With infinite gentleness, Joscelin undid the buttons of my gown, sliding it from my shoulders until I stood in its water-billowed folds as at the center of a lotus. What flesh he unveiled, he touched, until I shivered, the tenderness of it nearly unbearable. With cupped hands, he poured water over my head, until droplets clung to my lashes, then followed the water's course with his lips. When he kissed my closed eyelids, I could have wept.

I relearned him that day, with hands, mouth and tongue, tracing the line of his collarbone, the flat planes of his chest that no blade had yet marred, like a blind woman learning sight by touch. Mostly, though, I yielded, and relearned love. He undid my hair, that I wore at the nape of my neck. When his hands rose, dripping, to cup my breasts, I sighed; I whimpered at the touch of his mouth, warm and wet, encompassing my aching nipples.

He lifted me out of the floating lotus of my gown, setting me so that my buttocks rested upon the warm stones to perform the _languisement_, parting my moist nether-lips with a touch delicate as a breath, the tip of his tongue tracing the swollen shape of Naamah's Pearl. And that is where time itself seemed to stretch and flow. I lay open beneath the sky, and everything done by the Mahrkagir was undone, every cruelty, every iron thrust—undone, undone, undone, every kiss, every lick, every stroke, imprinting love upon my flesh, until I shuddered and knotted both hands in Joscelin's hair, calling his name out loud, and my climax followed with the inevitability of the spring-fed waters tumbling over the rocks.

At that, Joscelin lifted his head and smiled.

"Come _here_," I said, drawing him to me.

He did, hoisting himself out of the water on both arms, the left as solid as the right, hands braced on either side of my shoulders. I bit my lip, reaching down to fit him into me, his phallus rigid and hard, the walls of my nether parts still throbbing. Any other man—any one I have known—would have begun, then.

Not Joscelin. He waited, his brow touching mine, sheathed to the hilt in me and our loins enjoined. Slowly, my breathing eased to match his, and our heartbeats synchronized.

In the space between the beating of our hearts, I felt the presence of Blessed Elua.

I'd felt it before, that golden light filling me, the taste of honey in my mouth. I felt it now, and Joscelin's mouth tasted of honey to me, his tongue like nectar as we kissed. I smelled lavender in his damp hair as it fell to frame my face. The world pulsed and surged as he moved within me, and I moved to meet him, hips thrusting, no longer certain where I began and he ended, my fingers seeking the line of his back, the column of his spine, his muscled flanks. His eyes, summer-blue, looked into mine, shining with Elua's tide.

This is how we were made whole.

I cried out, at the end, and whose name it was—Joscelin's or Blessed Elua's—I could not say. It was one and the same, then. And if I had called what had gone before a climax, it was naught to what came after, welling from someplace deeper within me than I knew I had, until I could only cling to Joscelin with all my limbs and shudder at the force of it. And he—Elua! He went rigid against me, within me, and I felt the vibration all the length of his spine before his loins shivered and he spent himself within me.

So it was done.

"I'm sorry," I said when we had finished, and the presence had faded. "Joscelin, I am so, so sorry for what I've done to us."

He brushed my lashes. "For what, love?" he asked, examining my tears on his fingertips. "You did what you were called to do. So did I. What is there to forgive?"

"You know," I said softly. "You heard . . . stories. Some of them are true."

"Yes." He drew a line from the corner of my eye, the left one, with its crimson mote. "Do you wish to speak of them? I swear to you, I can bear it now."

Remembering, I shook my head. "No. Let them fade, and be forgotten. No."

"Then it is what it is," Joscelin said, "And we are what we are. No more, and no less." He smiled. "Never less. Do you agree?"

I did. I demonstrated to him with a degree of ferocity the extent to which I agreed, until he caught his breath and laughed, and then until he laughed no longer, but tumbled me over with keen desire. And if the presence of Blessed Elua was no longer with us, our own presence sufficed.

I asked nothing more.

For once, it was enough.

Seventy-one

THERE WERE jests, of course; Jebeans speak with frank delight about the arts of love, and there are no secrets in a small campsite. But they were good-natured and I did not mind, and Joscelin bore it well. Their great fish had been gutted and cleaned, and strips of flesh hung to smoke over a second fire. We had some of it fresh that evening, fried in an iron pan with coriander and wild onion, and I thought it was the most delicious dish I'd ever tasted. Like as not it wasn't, but it seemed so that night.

After we'd eaten, we sat about the fire discussing plans to make ready on the morrow for the following day's departure. Bizan shared around a skin of honey-mead he'd been hoarding, and the taste of it was sweet and fiery in my mouth. I caught Joscelin's eye and he smiled, lacing his fingers with mine.

"There are thorns and there are thorns," Nkuku said judiciously, noting it. "Some are larger than others, but their prick is more pleasant."

At that, there was laughter; such was the manner of jest we endured. Imriel sat with his legs drawn up and his arms wrapped round them, peering over his knees with scarce-disguised joy. I understood it better, now.

Make me whole, I had prayed in the Temple of Isis. *Make us all whole.*

We had become like family to him.

There are ties that bind more complex than blood. I knew it, who'd been sold into indenture at the age of four; when I think of the family I have lost, I think of my lord Anafiel Delaunay and my foster-brother Alcuin. Of a surety, Joscelin knew it too, he who was an adored stranger in his childhood home of Verreuil.

I'd not thought about the ties we had forged with Imriel, and what they meant to him.

Nor to me.

Well and so; we were a long way yet from home, whatever Joscelin might claim, and our quest was far from over. One day, Elua willing, it would be done and we would be home. Imriel had a destiny that would claim him, with Ysandre's protection extended over him and obligations to House Courcel. And there was Melisande, too. What she would make of this, I dared not think. But I had placed myself in Blessed Elua's hand that day, trusting to his mercy. If it brought love unlooked-for, what right had I to complain? I drew Imriel to join us and he knelt in the firelight between us, leaning against Joscelin's knee, smelling faintly of fish and content for the first time since I had known him.

And Joscelin and I, who had regained the trick of knowing one another's minds without speaking, gazed at each other over Imri's head and wondered.

The next day was a flurry of activity. The new-cured hides must be sewn, the smoked and dried meats gathered, our replenished stores packed, unpacked, rearranged and packed again, boots patched and blades whetted. Tifari Amu showed me on the Ras' map where we would be going, striking out across the mountains to intersect the Great Falls.

"What will happen," I asked him, "when we reach Saba?"

Tifari shrugged, quiet and diffident as always. "As to that," he said, "I cannot say."

So we departed, and left behind our pleasant campsite. I turned in the saddle as we left, watching it vanish behind a bend in the river.

"I never thought," I said to Joscelin, "I would be so grateful to a rhinoceros."

He grinned. "I never thought I'd be so grateful to a fish."

The Jebeans thought we were a little mad, of course, although they didn't mind it. I don't know what Kaneka had told Tifari—during the times she deigned to speak kindly to him, which had been enough to encourage him—but it had got about that we were god-touched, all three of us. That, it was allowed, was why Queen Zanadakhete had blessed our journey, and Ras Lijasu had provided for it. As members of the guard, Tifari and Bizan understood the politics of it better, but they still considered it madness. And Joscelin challenging the rhinoceros hadn't helped. They watched him in the mornings and evenings, performing his Cassiline exercises, and merely shook their heads.

It didn't matter. With each day that passed, we drew nearer.

Once again, we mounted the green heights, wending our way through forests. It was beautiful, untrammeled country, devoid of human inhabitation; too far, Tifari said, from the cities, and too hard to build roads. To be sure, it was hard going, but there were trails carved out by wildlife and these we followed.

"Who do the Sabaeans trade with, then?" I asked Tifari as we rode.

"No one, now." He was silent for a few minutes. "There are other tribes—Zenoë, Shamsun—in this area who owe allegiance to neither Jebe-Barkal nor Saba. But they are hunters, mostly, and bandits. Saba—the Melehakim—have been isolated for a long time, Lady, many hundreds of years. I do not know what you expect, but you may find them otherwise."

I didn't answer. In truth, I had no idea what to expect.

After some days of travel, we reached the Great Falls.

Tifari Amu had described them to me, but he knew them only by legend and nothing could have prepared me for the sight of them. There is nothing in Terre d'Ange to match it; no, nor anywhere else in the world I have travelled.

It was the Nahar river we had regained, and here, near to its source, it was broad and placid once more—until it reached the Falls. Long before we saw them, we heard the tremendous sound. At last we came upon them from above and stood at the edge of the tree-lined gorge, staring in open-mouthed awe; eagles must feel thusly, gazing down from on high. The Falls were as wide as the river itself, far too wide to bridge, and formed a sheer drop of a hundred feet or better. Water cascaded off the edge in a solid sheet, churned white as foam, plunging impossibly far, down and down and farther still, until it plunged into the greenish waters of the basin below with such force as to raise a constant mist, sun-shot and shimmering with rainbows.

"Name of Elua!" Joscelin whispered.

I swallowed and pulled Imriel back from the edge, as he clambered over moss-covered rocks for a better view.

'Tis a poor description I have given of the Great Falls, but it is not something words can compass. The raw force and beauty of it are too great. And so we stood for a time, all of us, drinking in the sight of it, the roar of the falling water filling our ears. Even at this height, wind-blown spray dampened our faces.

I daresay if the Falls had not been so stunning, we would have heard the hunting-party.

They were Shamsun, although I did not know it at the time; Tifari Amu told me, after. There were ten of them, armed with crude bows and javelins; agile and strong to a man, with skin the color of ripening olives and hair braided close to their skulls. Hunters—and bandits. It needed no one to tell me that. I saw it in the way the leader's gaze flicked over our laden mounts and donkeys.

And the way it flicked over me, astonished and avid, his tongue wetting his lips. In a swift motion, he nocked an arrow and drew his bow, aiming at Joscelin, who made the tallest target. The others followed suit, and I drew Imriel behind me.

"Hold," the Shamsun leader said in a recognizable dialect of Jeb'ez, addressing Tifari Amu and Bizan, who'd already begun to fan out. "Let us take what we will, and no one will die."

"What will you have?" Tifari called, his sword half-drawn.

"Your goods. Your weapons. Whatever you have," the Shamsun replied. Let it be that, I prayed; let it only be that. We are near enough now that it makes no difference. There is water, and fish, if we can catch them—surely the Habiru laws of hospitality must hold true in Saba. The leader's gaze slid over me again, and I saw his breath quicken. "And the woman."

Joscelin had learned enough Jeb'ez for that.

It took them by surprise when he bowed, his crossed vambraces flashing in the verdant light. It took them harder when he straightened with daggers in his hands, throwing both in quick succession.

He missed with the left. Not the right, which killed the leader.

Arrows filled the air. I flung myself down on top of Imri scarce in time, feeling a line like a red-hot poker scored across my back. Pain, unexpected, blossomed in me like an old acquaintance come to visit, the scent of crushed ferns filling my nose. Imriel made a muffled sound of protest and I moved cautiously off him, turning my head to see the mêlée.

It wasn't pretty. If the Shamsun had been farther away, they'd have held their advantage, but after the first rain of arrows, it had gone to hand-to-hand combat. Bizan had the shaft of an arrow standing out from his thigh, but he fought undeterred, hobbling fiercely and swinging his sword. One of the bearers had managed to free Tifari's camelopard shield from the baggage, and I got a glimpse, then, of the full skill of Jebean soldiery.

And Joscelin . . . Joscelin had blood pouring in a stream down the right side of his head. For all that, he fought as calmly as if he were at his exercises, wielding his two-handed sword with careful grace. Not like he had before, no. But he was right. He could still do it.

The Shamsun had come prepared for a hunt, not a battle. It was over in minutes. The last one, who tried to flee, Tifari Amu slew with one of his own javelins, picking his mark through the trees and heaving a mighty cast. The man fell, pierced from behind.

"He would have gone for his tribe," Tifari said to my shocked expression, lowering his shield to wipe his brow with his forearm. "And then we would have blood-debt to settle."

To that, I could make no reply. We were alive.

I went instead to see to Joscelin, who winced when I touched him. An arrow had nicked his ear, taking a chunk of flesh from its upper curve. Since it was not a dangerous wound, I washed it and applied a tincture of snakeroot, giving him a clean rag to press against it until the bleeding stopped.

"Well?" he asked.

"It won't show if you wear your hair unbraided," I said. "I always did like it loose."

He laughed, then stopped as I turned to tie up the water-skin. "You're hurt."

"Some." I peered over my shoulder, shrugging at the gouge. "A scratch, no more. I need to see to Bizan."

Over his protest, I went to supervise the extraction of the arrow, which was not so bad as it might have been. The Shamsun were poor. Their arrows were beautifully fletched—how not, with the birdlife that abounded?—but they were only fire-hardened wood, sharpened to a point. If it had been forged steel and barbed, we'd have had to cut it out. As it was, I had Nkuku withdraw it in one swift yank, and clapped a wad of clean cloth in place lest it had pierced an artery. Bizan was lucky, for it had not. I cleaned and dressed it.

"Phèdre." Joscelin had Imriel in tow. He took the jar of snakeroot from my hand. "Sit down," he said, shoving me forcibly onto a rock. "Imri, you're deft. See it cleaned, and put some of this on it."

"A lot you know about medicine—" I began.

"Oh, hush." Joscelin handed a damp rag to Imriel, who moved behind me and dabbed carefully at the graze through my rent gown. "Do you want it to fester?"

"I heal clean," I said, then drew in my breath as Imriel applied the snakeroot. Kaneka had said it was effective; she hadn't mentioned it stung like seven hells. For an instant, my vision was veiled in crimson, and the surge of the Great Falls was like brazen wings buffeting in my ear. "Ah."

When I blinked, the world cleared. Joscelin's expression had changed. "So," he said softly. "That, too, is unchanged."

"Yes." I held his gaze. "So it seems. Are you sorry, now?"

After a moment, he shook his head. "No," he said, stooping to brush my lips with his. "I'll just have to catch more fish, that's all."

I was still laughing when I saw them.

Unlike the Shamsun, the Sabaeans had come ready for battle. They wore armor in an archaic style, or so I thought—bronze corselets over cotton tunics, pleated leather skirts and brightly woven cloaks. At second glance, I realized 'twas not the style, but the armor itself that was old, worn thin and bright with the patina of generations of polishing, traces of gilt lingering in the crevices here and there.

Tifari Amu had spoken truly. No one had traded with Saba for a long, long time.

We sat frozen, all of us, about our makeshift campsite, strewn with medicaments and the corpses of slain bandits. One of the Sabaeans stepped forward, frowning. Like the others, his skin was the hue of polished mahogany, and his bearded face was stern. He wore a helm like a pointed bronze cap, and only the leather straps were new.

"You," he said in Habiru, pointing to Tifari, who had risen, grasping his shield. "What passes here? Who has killed these men?"

Tifari shook his head in a gesture of incomprehension.

They spoke Habiru. After so long, they still spoke it. "Barukh hatah Adonai, father," I said, getting to my feet. "Yeshua a'Mashiach . . ." My voice trailed off. Whatever else these men were, they were not Yeshuite. I cleared my throat and continued in his tongue. "We have come seeking peaceful converse with Saba."

He stared at me unabashed, for which I did not blame him. We made an odd sight altogether, and while he might not know me for the most famous courtesan in Terre d'Ange, I was hardly what one expects to find in a Jebean forest surrounded by corpses. "You," he said slowly. "What *are* you?"

"I am Phèdre nó Delaunay de Montrève of Terre d'Ange," I said. "It is a land very far away, farther even than the homeland of Shalomon.

These are my companions," I added, introducing them. Joscelin gave his Cassiline bow; the Jebeans nodded warily. Imriel kept still, seeking to read the Sabaean's expression.

"From Meroë." The Sabaean captain frowned. "We have no friends in Meroë."

I translated his comment to Tifari Amu, who shrugged. "They have no enemies, either. The quarrel is an ancient one. Our wise Queen would see it laid to rest if Saba willed it. But we are not here to parlay, only to aid you in your quest. It is a favor to the gods, and to the Lugal of Khebbel-im-Akkad, nothing more."

When I relayed his words to the Sabaean captain, he gave a bitter smile. "Our memories are long, foreigner. The quarrel is not ancient to us, and we have no fondness for the Akkadians. As for the gods of Jebe-Barkal, they are foul and bestial monstrosities."

"And yet," I said, "I have heard you use the grief of Isis to hide something from the eyes of Adonai Himself."

He sucked in his breath as if I'd struck him, his bearded cheeks flushing darker. "It is no business of yours, foreigner!" I said nothing. The men behind him stirred. After a moment, he spoke again. "We have tracked these poachers for many days without success," he said reluctantly, nodding toward the slain Shamsun. "For this, if no other, you may claim hearth-friendship. Is it your wish?"

"It is." I inclined my head.

"So be it." His bitter smile returned. "I am Hanoch ben Hadad. I will lead you to the city of Tisaar. Whatever your quest may be, you may present it to the Elders."

Thus did we enter Saba.

$\mathcal{S}$EVENTY-TWO·

IT WAS an uneasy journey, albeit a short one. The Sabaeans were none too glad of our company, and kept themselves separate. The Jebeans, understandably, were nervous and watchful. Joscelin, Imriel and I were subdued.

If Jebe-Barkal was like a land from a fable, Saba was even more so. How many years had they endured in isolation? Between the many calendars involved, I was hard put to do the calculations, but by my best guess, King Khemosh had ruled some two hundred years before the birth of Elua.

The quarrel was more ancient than my homeland.

It was a sobering thought.

Under Hanoch ben Hadad's guidance, we reached the Lake of Tears, which was so vast as to resemble a calm, inland sea, hiding its mysteries. Here at last there were roads and we were able to ride abreast, making our way to the capital city of Tisaar.

'Twas passing strange, in that green wilderness, to see the ruddy stone walls rising around the city by the lake. A sentry looked out from the tower gate, sounding a long blast on a ram's horn. Hanoch ben Hadad raised his hand in acknowledgment and we waited until the wondering guard turned out to question the Sabaean captain.

What he said, I do not know, but it seemed it sufficed. We were admitted to Tisaar.

For near onto twelve years of my life, I had studied the lore and history of the Habiru. Now it seemed as if I had entered one of my own scrolls. Despite the lack of trade, Tisaar was prosperous, the Sabaeans making use to the fullest extent of those resources that abounded in the land. Crops and herds and wild game they had in plenty, and timber and stone. For metal, though, they had only copper and gold.

No iron, and thus no steel; not even tin to render bronze. It explained the great antiquity of their arms, which were handed down from generation to generation, patched and mended, betimes smelted and forged anew, each ounce of metal more precious than gold. What steel there was in Tisaar was a treasured rarity, filtered to Saba through the occasional capture of bandits more successful than the Shamsun we'd encountered. Hanoch's men eyed our weapons with envious wonder. I think they would have seized them if they dared, but the law of hospitality forbade it.

For my part, I stared about me as we rode through the streets of Tisaar, amazed by the sight of wagons built in a style not seen in centuries, the wheel rims made of copper. And the people of Saba stared in turn, their dark faces according strangely with their Habiru tongue and old-fashioned attire, wondering who—and *what*—we were.

There were no inns in all of Tisaar. Sabaeans who travelled from elsewhere in the land stayed with friends or relatives, or camped outside the city, as Tifari and Bizan and our bearers opted to do, granted six-day passes to come and go within the city, provided they left their arms outside the walls. For Joscelin and Imriel and me, Hanoch ben Hadad secured lodging with his widowed sister, gauging us safe enough. Grudgingly, he allowed Joscelin to keep his arms, although he was forbidden to bear them in the city without a Sabaean military escort.

Hanoch's sister's grown daughter had left her for her husband's household and she lived alone on the ground floor of a spacious house with only a cook and an elderly maidservant. The whole second floor was empty and used only for storage.

"A strange place." Joscelin opened a trunk in the room we'd been allotted, sniffing at the linens stored within it. "Smells of mildew. The whole city seems forgotten by time."

"It nearly is. Don't do that, it's rude." I had liked Hanoch's sister, Yevuneh, who bore her sorrow with gentle grace.

"At three links of gold?" Joscelin raised his brows. "We're entitled."

"You could have bought the house for one of your daggers," I noted.

"True." He closed the lid of the trunk. "Our welcome doesn't bode well. I don't imagine they're going to tell us the Name of God and send us on our way."

"No," I said. "I don't suppose they are."

I slept poorly that night and dreamed for the first time in many months—the old dream, the one that had awoken me in our home in the City of Elua, trembling and weeping. Once again I stood at the prow of a ship, clutching the railing in vain as the child Hyacinthe stood on the receding shore, arms outstretched, calling my name over and over, desperate and pleading. Only this time, his cries grew louder as the expanse of water broadened, rising and rising to a shriek of pure, unrelenting terror. In the dream, I clapped my hands over my ears, unable to bear it, and sank to the ship's floor.

And even that did not lessen it. 'Twas so deafening that it wrenched me to wakefulness, and only then did I realize the sound of my dream was real.

"Imriel," I murmured, making my way to his pallet in the darkness. Behind me, Joscelin kindled a lamp. "It's all right, it's just a nightmare."

He came out of it with a start, his body curled and rigid, tears making damp tracks on his cheeks. "I dreamed . . . I dreamed I was in Daršanga, and you were leaving me. Riding away without looking back. And Nariman laughed, and he led me away to the Mahrkagir . . ."

"Hush." I stroked him gently, until I felt his shuddering ease, his rigid limbs loosen. "It was a dream, only a dream. I'm not leaving you anywhere."

After a while, he fell into a dreamless sleep. When I gauged it safe, I went to gaze out the window, which afforded a glimpse of the distant lake. The moon was nearly full in a clear sky, and it glimmered on the dark waters.

"There are over forty islands," Joscelin said behind me. "If that's even where it's hid. One of Hanoch's men said as much."

"I know." Someone was stirring downstairs; Imriel's screams had awoken the household. I should go tell Yevuneh all was well, I thought, but instead I gazed at the lake and wondered.

"Do you think we could find the right one?" Joscelin asked. "If it came to it?"

"I don't know," I said. "But if it comes to it, we'll have to try."

In the morning, the three of us broke our fast with Yevuneh, waiting for word from the Sanhedrin of Elders as to when we might present our case. Whether or no we'd paid dear for the lodgings, she was a kind hostess and gladder of our company than ever her brother had been.

"Tell me again where this land of yours lies," she said, having difficulty compassing the thought. With Joscelin's aid, I turned the dining-table into a map. Saba, she knew, and Jebe-Barkal, as well as Menekhet and the Umaiyyat and Khebbel-im-Akkad; Hellas, she knew by repute. As for the rest, I might have been speaking Skaldic.

"If this is Iskandria, my lady," I said, indicating a pot of honey, "and here lies the ocean . . ." I swept my hand over an expanse of table, "here, this is Hellas, and here the nation-states of Caerdicca Unitas begin, and beyond, here, is Terre d'Ange." I placed a dried fig to mark the spot.

"So far!" she marveled. "Why would you come so far, child?"

"To find the Tribe of Dân," I ventured. "It is said they hold the key to great wisdom."

Yevuneh looked away. "We did, once," she said softly, then shook her head. "You have come a long way in error, if it is wisdom you seek. Do they not tell in Jebe-Barkal how we broke the Covenant of Wisdom?"

"I have heard a story," I said. "I have not heard the Melehakim tell their own story."

"The Melehakim." She smiled at that, gentle creases forming at the sides of her mouth. "Do they call us that, still?"

"Some do," I said, thinking of Shoanete.

"Ah, we've not named ourselves thusly for many generations. We lost the right of it, I fear." Her gaze fell upon Imriel, who was devouring the dried fig that had marked Terre d'Ange. "What do you want to know, child? For a kiss from that dear boy, I will tell you a story."

I translated her words to Imriel, who understood Habiru a little, owing to its similarity to Akkadian, but not enough, yet, to follow a conversation. He met my eyes and nodded gravely, and went to kiss her lined cheek. It was a pretty picture, if one didn't know what it cost him to offer affection to a near-stranger.

"Such a lovely child, like an ivory carving! And charming with it in the bargain." Yevuneh smiled again, caressing his hair. "You are blessed, to have such a son."

Joscelin, who did understand Habiru, made no comment.

"Indeed," I said. "My lady, how was the Covenant of Wisdom broken?"

"Pride," she said. "Pride, and wrath. How else? When Shalomon's kingdom fell, Adonai made us a dwelling-place in Jebe-Barkal, where we might preserve His gifts and keep them safe. Never were they to be used for personal gain, but only for the good of His people—the descendants of the anointed, the Wise Ones, the Melehakim. And the keeping of His gifts lay in the hands of the men, but the passage of wisdom . . . ah! That lay in the hands of the women." Yevuneh turned over her empty hands. "We did not hold it tight enough. You have heard of Khemosh, the falsely anointed?"

I nodded.

She sighed. "We did not act. When Khemosh spoke, the men listened, and began to echo his words. When the Queen spoke, we remained silent in fear. We allowed the chain to be broken, the Covenant sundered. Khemosh was anointed in his wrath and proclaimed King, without a woman's wisdom to balance him; and Khemosh made war upon Meroë. Nemuel, who was the priest of Aaron's line upon that time, brought the Ark of the Broken Tablets onto the battlefield. Always before, in our time of need, the Voice of Adonai rang forth between the cherubim, proclaiming His fearful Name. This time, the Voice was silent."

"And the army of Khemosh was defeated," I said. "This I was told."

"Not that," Yevuneh said. "Not only that. When the Voice was silent . . ." She gazed at Imriel. "Such eyes the boy has! Like sapphires at nightfall. There were sapphires too on the breastplate of Aaron, you know; sapphire and jacinthe and agate, sardius, topaz, diamond . . . I cannot name them all. Twelve stones for the Twelve Tribes."

"The breastplate of Aaron," I mused. "This was taken from Shalomon's Temple?"

"Yes." Yevuneh nodded. "It was one of the treasures. And when the Voice was silent, Nemuel donned it, and the crown, too, wrought with a signet, and 'Holy to Adonai' engraved upon it. In his pride, for he had anointed Khemosh with his own hands, he donned these things to force the will of Adonai. And on the battlefield, Nemuel ordered the cover of the Ark of Broken Tablets to be lifted . . ."

Her voice fell silent. I waited, and Joscelin and Imriel waited with me. After a thousand years and more, these stories were like yesterday to the Sabaean widow.

"It was folly," she whispered, "for Nemuel approached the Ark of Broken Tablets in anger. To think he could contain the sacred Name!" Yevuneh shook her head. "Where there is pride and wrath, there is no room for Adonai. It is death to attempt it. Only in a state of perfect love and trust may such grace be attained."

"To make of the self a vessel where there is no self," I murmured.

"Even so." Yevuneh nodded. "But Adonai was merciful, and withheld the blow of death, for the love he had borne his people. The cover was lifted, and Nemuel alone looked inside and beheld the Name of God." Her expression was sombre. "And when he sought to speak it,

Nemuel was struck dumb, his tongue withering within his mouth like a drought-stricken root. Such was the penalty for breaking the Covenant of Wisdom. And it is as you have said, the army of Khemosh was defeated, and we gathered for flight; fleeing the forces of Meroë, and fleeing moreover the wrath of Adonai, who was at such pains to preserve His people."

"A harsh penalty for one man's transgression," I said quietly.

"No." Yevuneh gave a sad smile. "The sin was shared among us all, for all of us failed in honoring the Covenant. Even now, to this day, the priests of the line of Aaron are born tongueless and dumb, keepers of a useless treasure, which we must hide from the eyes of Adonai, the Lord our God, lest he remember and smite us for our folly. Khemosh himself got neither son nor daughter, and we dare not even raise up a King, but hew only to the ancient laws kept by the Elders, and the women . . . we bear the price still of the power we relinquished. So you see, you seek wisdom in vain."

Joscelin let out his breath in a long whistle, and began the work of translating the story to Imriel. I sat thinking, watching flies circle the honey-pot.

"It may be, my lady Yevuneh," I said at length. "Though I am sorry to hear that the women of the Melehakim do not take up the sundered ends of the chain they let fall. But all knowledge is worth having, and these stories are new to me. Of Moishe's Tablets and the Ark that held them, I have heard. What is this of which you speak, this Ark of Broken Tablets?"

"It is written . . . you know such things were recorded?" she asked me.

I nodded, thinking of the volumes of text I had read, the hours spent at the Rebbe's feet, learning Habiru lore. How could she know? Most of it had been written long after Melek al'Hakim fled his father's land.

"It is written that there were two sets of tablets. The first, that were broken, were written by Adonai's own hand," Yevuneh said softly. "The second, that Moishe chiseled himself—those preserved the law. But the first . . . ah! Those held the Name of God in every syllable."

The hair rose at the back of my neck. "And those are here."

"So it is said." She spread her hands. "I have not seen them, myself. But that is the story for which you asked. And that is the sum of our useless wisdom. One day, perhaps, Adonai will send us a sign to make atonement. In a thousand years, it has not come."

There came a knock at the door; I daresay all of us startled. Yevuneh's maidservant went to see who it was, and came to fetch her mistress. Presently Yevuneh returned, looking grave.

"The Elders will see you."

$\mathscr{S}$EVENTY-THREE

OUR $\mathfrak{m}$EET$\mathfrak{i}$$\mathfrak{n}$G with the Sanhedrin of Elders was long and fruitless.

I told the story well, or so I thought; Hyacinthe's story, the story of the Master of the Straits, the misbegotten son of Rahab, the One God's unrelenting curse, and why I came seeking the Sacred Name. Some of it needed no explanation. Rahab, they knew, and the Book of Raziel, from whence came his powers. But as for the rest . . .

A thousand years and more, the Sabaeans had been closeted in the far south of Jebe-Barkal. Of my own country, of the schism between Terre d'Ange and Alba, they knew nothing, nor what it signified. Of Blessed Elua himself, they knew nothing. And of his begetting—

"You mean to say," one of the Elders frowned, "this man, this Yeshua ben Yosef, was acknowledged the Mashiach and the Son of Adonai?"

"Yes, my lord." I gave him my best curtsy. "So it is said, by the Yeshuites; that is, by the descendants of the other Eleven Tribes. Even now, they undertake to follow Yeshua's will in carving out a new homeland, far to the north even of my home. So many say, although not all believe."

"Adonai!" He breathed the word like a sacrament. "Is it truly so?"

"We hid, Bilgah," another of the Elders reminded him. "Until Adonai Himself despaired of the gifts He had given His people. How not? He presumed us lost. Might He not send the Mashiach to lead those who remained?"

"Say it is not so!" Bilgah the Elder clutched his temples. "I would rather believe Adonai turned His face from us in anger than forgot us!"

So it went, on and on. For Hyacinthe and his plight, they cared little. The news we had brought, a thousand years old, overshadowed aught else. For my own part, I will own, I was shaken. Could it be so, that the birth of Yeshua himself was owed to the folly of the Melehakim, who failed in upholding their Covenant? I do not know. I did not know then, nor ever did I. The politics of gods are beyond mortal ken. In the end, I could only cling to that which I *did* know; that I was D'Angeline, and a scion of Blessed Elua. And no matter how the story is told or who tells it, his begetting was a thing unforeseen, for mortal love—the love of Yeshua ben Yosef and the Magdalene—played a role in it. And that is a thing, I believe, no god may control.

Love as thou wilt.

So I waited, until the Elders of Saba paused in their quarrels, and made another deep curtsy, Joscelin bowing low beside me. "My lords," I said softly. "You have heard my tale, and my plea. Know this. My friend who has taken this sacrifice upon himself grows older with each day that passes—aging, and undying. Now, he is young, still, if one may bear such power and retain youth. One day, he will not be; and one day, madness will come for him. You hold in your hands the key to his freedom. Will you not lend it to me?"

There was a long silence.

"It is not so simple, lady," one of the Elders said into the quiet. "If you speak true . . . and *if*, I say, I grant you nothing . . . Adonai Himself has forgotten us, turning His attention to His Son. What shall become of us, then, if He remembers?" He shook his head. "No, better we remain forgotten."

"For how long?" I asked. "Another thousand years? What I ask, my lords . . . if it be not wisdom, then name it compassion, and forge the Covenant anew."

"It is not," another Elder said, "so simple." He smiled at me with kindness and sorrow. "You see, lady, when Adonai—the One God, you call him—turned His face from us, we lost what we had held sacred. This thing you seek—this key, this Name—there is no one among us with the grace to contain it, with a tongue that may speak it. How long, you ask, does Adonai's wrath endure? That is a thing we may answer. It endures forever, and a thousand years is only the merest beginning."

I thought of the moonlit waters of the Lake of Tears, of Shoanete's story, of Yevuneh's story. And I thought of my dream, and Hyacinthe's pleas mingling with Imriel's screams. "Nonetheless," I said. "I would behold this thing, this Ark of Broken Tablets, and know it for myself."

They voted, the Elders of Saba. And for all that I had told the story well, for all that I had endured—that we had all endured—they voted no. Not happily, not all of them, for there were looks of sympathy, but it is how they decided.

"Whether or not your story is true," said Abiram, eldest of Elders, "we cannot know. It may be so, and this is a thing we may undertake to learn. Perhaps in this news you bring there is a sign, but it will take long study and prayer to determine it. And alas, there is one certainty in all of this. This god you claim to serve—this earth-begotten *Elua*— was never anointed by Adonai. No," he shook his head, "I am sorry. But to allow you to approach the Holiest of Holies . . . no. Even to one of our own, we would deny such a request. It is permitted only to the priests of Aaron's line. What you ask risks greater blasphemy than the Breaking of the Covenant itself, and would end only in your death."

"So be it," I murmured, defeated. "I thank you for hearing my plea."

I was angry, returning to Yevuneh's house. I could not help it.

"It is what you expected," Joscelin said. "No more, and no less. You were warned often enough, Phèdre. Well and so; it has come to pass. The Melehakim have laid wisdom aside, and compassion with it. Although for all we know, they're right and your tongue would shrivel, if you weren't struck . . ." His voice trailed off as he stared at Yevuneh's house. "Name of Elua! Is she holding a fête?"

Dark figures moved to and fro in the windows; women's figures, clad in muted shawls. We were admitted to the house to find a dozen of them, solid Sabaean matrons all past their child-bearing years, engaged in the work of bringing various dishes into the modest courtyard at the rear of the house.

"You've returned!" Yevuneh clapped her hands together, spotting us. The quiet sorrow that had marked her earlier had been replaced by a sense of contained excitement. "Ah, good, we're nearly ready."

"Forgive us, my lady," I said politely. "We did not mean to intrude upon your gathering. We will retire and be out of your way."

"No, no, child; not at all. They are here to see you." Taking my arm, she led me through the house, making introductions: Ranit, Dinah, Semira, Yaffit, a half-dozen others—bewildered, I committed them to memory using the old skills Delaunay had taught me, and all the while they crowded around, murmuring polite greetings, touching my hair and skin in wonderment and exclaiming over Joscelin. We were not only the first D'Angelines they had seen, but the first northerners altogether, and a great novelty as such.

"Wait," Yevuneh told them, "until you see the boy, ah! A jewel in miniature!"

"Where is he?" Alarm rose in me. "He was to remain in our quarters."

"Oh, tcha!" Yevuneh clicked her tongue. "Listen to the young mother fuss over a single chick. Did you bring him this far to fear he would come to harm in Yevuneh's house? Yes, child, he is upstairs, awaiting your return." Her expression turned shrewd. "Not that it will bring good news. So, tell me, did the Elders deny your plea?"

"Yes." The gathered women had grown quiet, waiting and watching with knowing eyes in time-worn faces. I began to understand that this was something like the Elders' Council. "My lady Yevuneh, what passes here?"

"I said that in a thousand years, there had been no sign that the time had come to make atonement." Yevuneh gave her gentle smile, a simple widow bearing her share of her people's thousand-year-old grief. "I spoke wrong. There is you. And that, child, is what we have gathered to discuss."

So it was that I told the story a second time that day.

'Twas different, this time. It was a pleasant courtyard instead of an audience-room, with verdant trellises shading stone benches and comfortable cushions. Dishes of honeyed sweets and melon and sesame balls were passed around, and the strong drink they call *kavah*, beans roasted over a brazier and ground into a fine powder, mixed with boiled water and served with ceremony, hot and bitter. Yevuneh had already relayed to them what I had told her earlier of Terre d'Ange, of the Mashiach and the birth of Blessed Elua.

What they thought of that, I cannot say. The knowledge had dropped like a stone into the depths of their shared story, and what changes it might wreak at that level were beyond my knowing. This much, I know: They wanted to hear more.

And I told again Hyacinthe's story, this time beginning it with the Tsingano boy I'd met in the marketplace, my Prince of Travellers with merry eyes and dark curls, who did not disdain the friendship of an unwanted ward of the Night Court. They sighed over his white grin and chuckled knowingly over his exploits, and nodded approval when he used the hard-won monies from his livery service to buy his mother the lodging-house in which she dwelled.

As for the Tsingani themselves and the fateful folly that had set them on the *Lungo Drom,* the Long Road—this they understood better than anything.

All the while I spoke, Imriel mingled among the women of Tisaar, offering sweets, serving nearly as neat-handed as if I'd taught him myself. They'd not neglected the graces in the Sanctuary of Elua. And the women sighed over him, too, marveling at his fair skin and twilit eyes, seeing in his blue-black hair an echo of the boy Hyacinthe I evoked for them.

Of Skaldia, I told little, save for the threat to our land, and how Hyacinthe embarked with us on a quest to secure the aid of our beleaguered young Queen's betrothed, the exiled Cruithne prince whom she loved. This, too, they understood; and understood the anguished curse of the Master of the Straits, doomed by his immortal father's stricken pride.

"Pride," Yevuneh murmured. "Pride, and wrath. How else?"

I told of Hyacinthe's first sacrifice, how he had surrendered his place among the Tsingani, his rightful role as the heir of the Tsingan kralis, to speak the *dromonde* on my behalf—although I did not speak Melisande's name, for fear that Imriel would hear and understand. It did not matter. They understood, the women of Tisaar, that he had done it in honor of his mother, whose heritage he would not repudiate.

They were mothers, most of them; mothers, grandmothers, wives and widows. I saw the sheen of tears quicken in their eyes as my tale—Hyacinthe's tale—drew near its close on the shores of that stony isle. A lump rose in my own throat. I had to swallow hard to force my voice past it.

Don't you know the dromonde *can look backward as well as forward?*

And I told them, then, how the Prince of Travellers used his gift to take my place, offering himself as sacrifice in my stead, and what had befallen him since.

I thought I had told the story well, before. I was wrong.

There was not a dry eye in the courtyard when I finished, and mine own included. If I'd maintained control of my voice, I'd ceded it to my tears, which rolled unheeded down my cheeks. It should have been me. It should always have been me.

"Oh, *my!*" Yevuneh shook an embroidered kerchief from her sleeve and blew her nose noisily. "Ah, child, such a tale! And you believe—is it so?—that the Sacred Name may break this curse?"

"Yes, my lady." Seated cross-legged on a cushion, I inclined my head. "For ten years and more I have studied the matter. I believe it to be true. The Name of God may force Rahab into relinquishing the long vengeance of his wounded pride. I have found no other way."

"Are your own gods so powerless?" another of the women, Ranit, asked shrewdly. "Why then do you not set aside your heathen ways, and petition the Lord of Hosts with a pure heart? Instead you come like a beggar who dares not approach the door, beseeching alms at the gate."

"Even Adonai Himself uses mortal hands to do His bidding, my lady," I replied.

"You claim your gods have sent you?"

I spread my hands. "I do not have that right, not here. But I am Kushiel's Chosen, and Kushiel was once the Punisher of God. This is a matter of justice, and justice is his province. My ladies, I am D'Angeline. It is bred in my blood and stamped on my flesh. While Adonai grieved for His son, Blessed Elua wandered unheeded, aided only by his Companions. We are his people, their people, born of their seed. When Adonai's attention turned at last to Elua, a new covenant was made, between the Lord of Hosts and the Mother of Earth, and it is by that our lives are sealed. I cannot be other."

Another woman spoke; Semira, with eyes keen and birdlike in a wizened face. "Do you claim, then, that this Elua is the Mashiach?"

"The Mashiach?" The question startled me. "No, mother. No D'Angeline has ever claimed such a thing. Elua is . . . Elua."

"Ah, but your people were barbarians. How could they know?" She nibbled unthinking at her lower lip. "There are those who claimed Melek-Zadok was the Mashiach, and the Covenant of Wisdom the first step toward the great healing of the earth that His reign will betoken, when war shall be no more, and wisdom dwell in every heart."

"There are some," another voice echoed, soft and tentative, "who say Adonai Himself will be reunited with His Eternal Bride when the Mashiach comes, and the union of Shalomon and Makeda was a forerunner of that celebration."

Silence followed on it, and I sensed that this was a women's mystery, written nowhere in the chronicles of Habiru or Yeshuite.

"It did not happen," Semira said firmly. "This we know. Perhaps the fault lay in ourselves, for breaking the Covenant with which we were entrusted. Perhaps it was a false omen, a shadow only of greater things to come, for even in Melek-Zadok's time, there was war. This Yeshua ben Yosef of whom you speak . . . I do not think peace followed in his reign, either."

"No." I shook my head. "The Yeshuites were united in his name, and the Habiru quarreled no more among themselves, but peace—no. Even now, they have begun to divide once more, and the children of Yisra-el seek to carve out a new kingdom with blades." Joscelin stirred at my words, and we exchanged a glance. He had played a role in that matter, though few people ever knew it, nor ever would.

"What *are* you?" It was Ranit who spoke, brows knitting in frustration as she asked the same question with which Hanoch ben Hadad had greeted us. "Unprophesied, unlooked-for . . . you do not *fit!* Elua! Who is this *Elua*, to be born of blood and tears? Who are these angels, these Companions, to defy the will of Adonai and be worshipped as gods? It is evil, I say; vile and foul. How can you say otherwise?"

"My lady." Joscelin's voice followed hers, calm and level as he gave his Cassiline bow. "I can speak to that, if you permit. I serve Cassiel, who alone among the Companions followed Elua out of the purity of his heart." He paused. "Cassiel sought to embody the love and compassion that Adonai, in his ire, forswore. This I believe to be true."

"It is a dangerous heresy." Ranit's words trembled. "Dangerous, indeed!"

"It may be," I said. "Can you be sure, who have been sequestered here for so long? I do not ask for the Sacred Name itself; only the chance to approach the altar. If I am slain or struck dumb for my presumption, so be it. Yet I must ask, and try."

"And we shall be unveiled to the eye of Adonai," Yevuneh murmured.

"So you may," I said steadily. "My lady Ranit accuses us of heresy. Is it meet that the children of Yisra-el should hide their treasures behind the grief of Isis? I cannot answer that, for D'Angelines consider all deities worthy of respect, Elua's children being youngest-born on this earth. It is a question, my ladies, for wisdom to decide; not the wisdom of the Elders, but the wisdom of Makeda's line, to which Shalomon himself deferred. This you hold among yourselves. Is it a thing that may be made to serve base ends?" I shook my head. "I do not believe so."

" 'For wisdom is more mobile than any motion, and extends and moves through all by purity;' " Semira whispered, quoting from the *Chokmah al-Shalomon*, " 'for she is a breath of Adonai's power and an emanation of the unmixed glory of the all-ruling; and because of this nothing tainted steals into her.' "

" 'For she is the brilliance of eternal light,' " I echoed, finishing the verse, " 'and an unstained image of Adonai's mercy and an image of its goodness.' So I was taught," I said, thinking of Eleazar ben Enokh, who taught me the verse, and of my lord Delaunay, who told me *All knowledge is worth having*. "So I believe."

A second silence followed, longer than the first. Yevuneh and the other women looked to Semira, the eldest present. She chewed her lower lip, deep in thought, and looked at me with her keen eyes. "It is a weighty matter. It will need to be debated, and not only among us. Not only among the old, but the young as well, for wisdom takes many guises."

"Of course, my lady." I inclined my head to her.

"Three days." She nodded, then nodded again, satisfied. "We will answer your plea in three days, after the festival of the new moon."

Seventy-four

FOR THREE days, we waited in Tisaar.

We ventured outside the walls of the city to confer with Tifari Amu and the others. Although they were uneasy at their dubious welcome, they had found the common-folk of Saba more accommodating than Hanoch ben Hadad and the guards. For a few scraps of steel—an outworn spearhead, a broken buckle—they had garnered supplies in abundance. And, I daresay, a fair accounting of Saba's readiness for overtures to report to Ras Lijasu.

"Kaneka might welcome me," Tifari said with quiet triumph, "if I became a diplomat."

"So she might," I said, hoping it might prove true, not daring to tell him that if the Women's Council denied us, we would risk the most heinous of blasphemies and the enmity of all of Saba to gain the Name of God.

For so I was resolved, and Joscelin too. Fruitless or no, we had come too far to leave without trying. And for all that had been healed between us . . . it would be lost, if we abandoned Hyacinthe to his fate.

Better we should try our utmost, whatsoever the price.

I wished, in those days, that Imriel was not with us; and I gave thanks as well that he was, for his presence did much to charm the women of Saba, and for that I was grateful. He bore it well. I do not think anyone noticed his inward shudder when an unfamiliar hand caressed his cheek. I knew, and grieved at it. How my lord Delaunay bore it, I will never know.

"You need not endure it, Imri," I said to him. "It is beyond the call."

"No." His brows knit in a familiar frown. Ysandre wore the same look when she quarrelled with Amaury Trente. "I don't mind, not so much. They mean well, and it helps. Even I can tell that much, Phèdre."

He was right. I brushed his brow with a kiss. "You've too much courage for your own good, Imriel de la Courcel. When it becomes too much to bear, tell me."

"Don't call me that!" Imriel drew away from me, his frown turning to a scowl.

"It is your name," I reminded him gently.

He looked away. "They think I am your son, yours and Joscelin's."

We had not disabused anyone of the idea, which was far simpler than the truth and brought with it a measure of goodwill. I understood better, now, why Brother Selbert held that an expedient lie did not violate Elua's wishes. "So they do. It does not change your name, Imri, nor who you are."

"Wish it did," he muttered. "I wish I *was* your son, and not *hers*."

"In the end, what you are is between you and Elua," I told him. "And he would be proud to claim you as his own for all you have done."

And he listened to me, his dark-blue eyes hungering, yearning to believe in some proof of his own goodness. It terrified me beyond belief to think he staked such import on my words. What did I know? Beneath it all, I was still a whore's unwanted get, struggling to make sense of the world and do what was right. To be a parent, I think, must be the most fearful thing there is. I did my best, and prayed it was enough.

One by one, the days passed.

On the third day fell the festival of the new moon. It was unknown to me, being something the Yeshuites no longer celebrate. Many old traditions were shattered with the birth of Yeshua ben Yosef. They are still heeded in Saba. All that day, Tisaar fasted, and we fasted with them out of respect. There had been meetings these last two days, covert and secretive. That much, I knew. Of their outcome, I knew nothing.

The rams' horns blew when the lower rim of the sun touched the horizon, calling the Sabaeans to prayers. Sabaean temples are round, with a square room within—the Holy of Holies—and two concentric circles without, plus an alcove for the altar itself. Although we were not permitted into the temple proper, we were allowed into the outer-most ring which skirts the court of sacrifice.

There was a long procession leading to the temple, winding through the streets of Tisaar. Elaborate parasols were held over the heads of the priests, casting long shadows in dwindling sunlight. The mournful cries of the rams' horns echoed over the city, finding an answer in the rhythmic pulse of two-handed goat-hide drums and the small hand-bells carried by the women. A red heifer was led before us all, lowing softly and adding her voice to the music of their worship.

"Remove your shoes," Yevuneh told us at the temple, "and stand here; no further. That much is permitted."

Most of the ceremony, we could not see, blocked by a sea of bodies, clad in Habiru garb with fringed shawls colored by blue dyes. I heard the prayers offered, and the lowing of the red heifer; I heard her cries cut short, and knew by the reek of blood and the charnel odor that followed that the sacrifice had been offered. Imriel looked ill at it. Then came more prayer in the form of song, and bare feet tramping the temple floor in dance, men and women in counterpoint to one another. Eleazar had been right—here were preserved traditions forgotten by the Yeshuites.

The sky was violet when they spilled out of the temple, the three of us dispersed in their wake, struggling to find our shoes amid the crowd. In the southwest hung the new moon, a slender crescent scarce visible against the darkling sky. The Sabaeans lifted up their hands, praising Adonai for its return.

And I thought . . . Elua help me, but I thought of Asherat-of-the-Sea and her crown of stars. Asherat, who had once saved my life; Asherat, by whose mantle Melisande Shahrizai herself was protected. And I prayed, in that twilight, to the goddess Asherat, to Blessed Elua and his Companions, to Isis who knit the sundered pieces of her beloved Osiris, and to Adonai Himself, the One God of the Habiru.

I do not know which one of them answered.

I know only that when we returned to the household of the widow Yevuneh, the Council of Women had gathered to await us, and a mighty feast had been laid to break our fast and celebrate the new moon. Young and old were gathered alike this time, and the youngest was scarce six weeks old, a nursing babe in the arms of Yevuneh's daughter Ardath. But it was Semira, eldest among them, who was appointed to give us their decision.

"It has been determined," she said in the lamp-lit courtyard, summoning her dignity and drawing her shawl tight across her hunched shoulders. "It has been determined that your presence among us constitutes a sign. And it has been determined that humility is the better part of wisdom. Your case is just. It is not meet that this mortal man—this friend you name *Hyacinthe*—should suffer for the transgressions of

Rahab. This matter must be put to Adonai Himself. This we will help you to do, insofar as we are able."

My head felt light and dizzy atop my shoulders. I sank to my knees in Yevuneh's courtyard, grasping Semira's hand in my own and kissing it. "Thank you, my lady," I said in Habiru, scarce daring to believe. "Thank you!"

"Oh, wait," she said testily, pulling her hand away. "You haven't heard the *how* of it."

The how, it transpired, was complicated.

We sat for long hours that night in the widow's kitchen, poring over maps of the night sky; for that, it transpired, was the only means by which we might find the island of Kapporeth, the fabled land-mass in the Lake of Tears on which the Ark of Broken Tablets was hidden.

"You see, here," said Morit, who was entrusted with our teaching, as she pointed to a scroll. "Nemuel departed from the shores of what would be Tisaar." She was a young woman and grave with her calling, coming from a family that had practiced the art of *Mazzalah* for time out of mind, mapping the night skies and charting time by it. "And here he writes, 'The red planet of war hung low upon the horizon in the tenth degree of the Lion of Judah, and it is toward that I made my way, with the Throne of Shalomon hanging behind my left shoulder like an omen. For five hours we rowed, and came ere daybreak to this isle I have named Kapporeth, that is the mercy seat of the *Luvakh Shabab*, may Adonai have mercy upon us all. And here I shall dwell until the end of my days.' " Morit raised her gaze. "He refers to the Broken Tablets, you understand, and where the temple was built to house them. The location of Kapporeth is known only to Aaron's line and the Sanhedrin of Elders, but a copy of this document was given unto the keeping of my many-times-removed great-grandmother, for the records of the *Mazzalah*."

"Then we have but to follow the red star," Joscelin said, adding wryly, "and row for five hours, I take it."

"No." Morit smiled with kind condescension. "Only the distance remains constant. Nemuel travelled at the end of the rainy season, my lord D'Angeline, and the stars have changed their position from where they were on that night many hundreds of years ago. For two days, I have studied the records. This—" she pointed, "—is a chart of the night sky which Nemuel followed. And this—" she pointed again, "—is the sky as we behold it tonight."

I gazed at the circles inked on parchment, the stars and constellations drawn in with a fine hand. "They're completely different."

"Yes," she said simply. "They are."

For the remainder of the night, into the small hours of morning, Morit taught us to read the charted stars, working out a course that paralleled that by which Nemuel had steered his craft.

Semira was right. It would not be easy.

"The Eagle of Dân is ascendant," Morit observed. "See here, this bright star marks its passage. Do you depart when it is in the tenth degree, and make for the smallest spoke of the Wheel, you will be nearly on course. Keep you the constellation of Moishe's Rod behind your left shoulder, which stands in place of Shalomon's Chair. Do you see, here?" She traced a shape on the parchment. "Moishe holds here the rod which became a serpent when he cast it down, and he seized it by its tail."

"Ye-es," I said, dubious.

"You will see," Morit said, and smiled. "I will show you."

And that she did, for we went into Yevuneh's courtyard and she pointed out to us the myriad stars, naming the constellations and tracing with her forefinger those vast, mighty shapes betwixt the expanse of blackness, the forms of which were echoed in miniature upon her parchments. Over and over she drilled us, a relentless taskmistress, until all of us could name and recite them by rote.

"Now you see," she said, and took us to the second story of Yevuneh's house, where we leaned out the window and gazed at the horizon and Morit showed me how to mark the distance from the horizon to its apex degree by degree.

"So when the Eagle of Dân stands *here,*" I said, squinting down the angle of my raised arm, "we must depart."

"Yes," her voice said from behind me. "I would give you an astrolabe, if I dared. But it was decided. Wisdom only; naught more. Let Adonai and Wisdom decide. If it is meant to be, you will find Kapporeth. And Adonai help you, once you do."

"It is enough." I lowered my arm, having fixed the angle in my memory. Such things are not strange, to one who has been a Servant of Naamah. There are poses in the famous *Trois Mille Joies* that one must remember and hold to an exacting degree, and I have had in my life patrons who required as much of me. "We are grateful, my lady Morit."

Her eyes glimmered in the shadows, dark and luminous, reminding me of Necthana's daughters whom I had met so long ago on the shores of Alba. Morit. *Moiread.* Such was the name of the youngest, who had greeted our arrival; Moiread, Sibeal's sister, whom Hyacinthe might have loved, had she lived. There are omens, if one chooses to see them.

"It is not for gratitude we do this, D'Angeline."

"Nonetheless," I said. "I am grateful."

Morit bowed slightly. "Tomorrow night, if the sky is cloudless, you may go. No more may I say. Adonai grant you a safe journey, and a tongue to speak of it when you return. We will be praying, all of us, that we have not compounded our ancient folly."

With that, she left us.

I tumbled into bed that night in exhaustion, my mind swimming with stars and the vast spaces between them. I slept fitfully and dreamed of piloting a boat across an ocean of night, and woke to remember only fragments, pieces of spangled darkness and an endless journey.

One day, and we would depart.

SEVENTY-FIVE

THAT MORNING as we gathered at the table to discuss the night's doings, yet another of the women of Tisaar came to pay a visit upon the widow Yevuneh, mentioning as she did how her nephew's skiff sat loose-tied and untended along the southeastern reach of the harbor, nearly in the very shadow of the city walls, while he served a turn in the army patrolling for bandits.

Lest we miss the hint, she cleared her throat several times loudly.

"Thank you, my lady," I said to her. "It is a piece of wisdom indeed."

Afterward, we left the city to pay a last visit to the Jebean encampment. And this time, I told the truth—the whole truth—to Tifari Amu and the others. They heard me out with courtesy.

"What happens if you fail," Tifari asked, "or are captured in the attempt?"

"I don't know," I said honestly. "Only that it is unsafe for you to be here if we are discovered. I don't even know what will happen if we succeed. If you leave ere sundown, my lord soldier, you will have a day's lead on any pursuit."

"And your horses?" He gestured. "The donkeys?"

"Yours," Joscelin answered him in his faulty Jeb'ez. "It is the least we can do."

Tifari frowned. "You ask us to abandon you."

"No." I shook my head. "I would have you save yourselves. If all is well, we will follow, and meet you at the place where we made camp, by the bathing-pool." Nkuku laughed, and I colored a little. "That place, we can find, and it is on Jebean soil."

"You would make cowards of us," Bizan said contemptuously. "Fleeing in the night!"

"Queen Zanadakhete and Ras Lijasu did not send you here to die for a D'Angeline cause," I said.

"No," Tifari said thoughtfully. "But our honor is our own. What about the boy? To whom will you entrust his safety?" He looked at Imriel, then; we all looked at Imriel.

"*What?*" Imriel's voice rose sharply. "What is it?"

"Imri." I took care to avoid any tone of placation. "Choose wisely. I promised you I would not leave you, and I will hold to that promise, and Joscelin, too. But our path is fraught with danger. You have done much in Tisaar. Any debt you owed to Hyacinthe and the Tsingani is settled. If you go with Tifari Amu, you are more like to be safe. I can give him letters, to bear to Ras Lijasu, who will see them honored. And I will rest the easier for it."

"You keep offering me the same choice!" Imriel's dark blue eyes welled with tears, which he ignored. "Do you never *listen?*"

Joscelin stirred, adjusting his vambraces, eyeing me without speaking.

"I listen," I said to Imri. "Do you understand what is at stake, love?"

He nodded. "Hyacinthe was your friend. Your one, true friend."

"It's not that simple—" I began, then stopped. It was that simple. "Imriel."

"He didn't care what you were," he said to me. "*Who* you were. That's what you said. That's what you told the women. *Love as thou wilt!*"

"Yes," I said carefully, looking at Joscelin.

"Imriel," he said in soft D'Angeline. "Phèdre is right. It is yours to choose. Only choose wisely, for your life is precious to us."

"Wisdom!" Imriel drew in a harsh breath and hiccuped, coughing. "You keep *saying* and *saying* about wisdom! Look at what the Sabaean women have risked for wisdom's sake. I know, Phèdre. I watch their faces, like you taught me; I listen when they are not speaking. Their people, all their people! What will *you* risk?"

Joscelin raised his eyebrows at me. "He argues like a sophist."

"He argues like his mother," I said, resigned.

"I do *not!*" Imriel said, quivering with fury.

"You do," I informed him. "My lord Tifari, it seems the boy will accompany us, may Blessed Elua have mercy upon us all. Your decision is your own. We will learn it upon our return, one way or the other. I will pray Amon-Re keep you safe."

"Thank you, lady." Tifari Amu bowed from the waist. "I will do the same on your behalf. If you do not find us here . . . I pray we meet again."

Thus did we take our leave of the Jebeans and reentered Tisaar, wandering the city in the midday sun. The quaint lake-front harbor was settling into its noon torpor, fishing boats ashore, the morning's catch netted and weighed. The market-stalls were closed and no women were about. A few children played at the water's edge, and men sat drinking *kavah* and beer in the shade-dim shops, watching with idle curiosity as we strolled. We found the nephew's skiff, a shallow, flat-bottomed craft with a single set of oars, recognizable by its red trim. It was tied to a scrawny palm stunted by an excess of water. We walked casually past it, and in the shadow of the city wall, turned back into the narrow alleys, finding our way back to Yevuneh's home.

Her brother the soldier-captain Hanoch ben Hadad was there awaiting us.

He rose and bowed as we entered the house, and his dark eyes were watchful. "I am pleased you had the chance to observe the festival of the new moon, lady. Shall you be leaving soon, now it is done? The rains will be upon us ere the moon has reached half-full."

"Are you so eager to see us gone, my lord captain?" I asked him, letting a trace of unfeigned bitterness show in my voice. " 'Tis a long journey we face, and all the more arduous without hope to quicken our steps."

It took him aback. "It is but concern that speaks, lady."

I sighed. "Our Jebean guides make repairs upon our equipment, and replace such stores as we will require for the journey. In another day or three, we will depart."

"It is well, then." Hanoch nodded twice, absently fingering the leather-wrapped hilt of his bronze sword. "You would not wish to be caught in the rains."

"So I am told." I stole a glance at Yevuneh, who looked drained and nervous. "Is there a problem, my lord captain? Your sister seemed content with the price on which we agreed for our lodging and meals."

"No." His dark skin grew darker with a flush of embarrassment. "No, of course not. You are strangers here, and welcome; we do not forget, we who were strangers once in Menekhet. Is there . . ." Hanoch cleared his throat, ". . . is there aught you need for your journey? I do but come to offer my aid."

"No, my lord." I said flatly. "We shall have all we need, within a day or three."

"I am sorry your journey was in vain," he said awkwardly. "I am sorry for that."

"Thank you," I said. "We are grateful for your sympathy."

After another uncomfortable pause, Hanoch ben Hadad took his leave, speaking briefly with his sister. Yevuneh sighed when he had gone, nervous and fretful. "He suspects," she said. "I know he does. Oh, I pray we have chosen wisely!"

"So do we all, my lady," I said, glancing at Imriel. "So do we all."

We took to our beds early that night and slept in shifts. It seemed my head had scarce touched the pillow before Joscelin was awakening me, touching one finger to his lips and pointing toward the night sky silhouetted in the window.

It was time.

We dressed in silence and stole out of the sleeping house, onto the quiet streets. The stars were very bright overhead in the black expanse of sky. I thought how Kaneka had told us a delay of a month would bring us into the rainy season, had we returned with Imriel to Tyre. She had been right, which I never doubted; yet I had not known so much would ride upon these clear night skies. Imriel was wide-awake, tense with excitement. I wished I felt the same. We made our way through the winding streets to the harbor, pausing when we heard a watchman giving the all-clear. Even here, the Sabaeans patrolled their streets; but only cursorily, entrusting to their strong walls and long isolation.

The harbor was dark and calm, the distant stars and crescent moon reflected on the still waters. Imriel and I clambered into the skiff, situating ourselves while Joscelin undid the line that secured it to the stunted palm. He was unarmed, his daggers and sword and vambraces rolled into a length of oilskin which I settled between my feet. It would be a long night's row, and these things would only encumber him.

Once the rope was untied, he shoved the skiff free of the bank, feet squelching in the mud. I held my breath as he climbed over the side, the sound of one oar scraping in its lock carrying over the quiet waters. The skiff rocked as Joscelin settled into the oarsman's seat, facing the stern of the vessel where I sat, taking my bearings against the night sky. There was the Eagle of Dân, ascendant in the tenth degree. I raised my arm and sighted along it. Our departure was timely. Joscelin dipped the oars, splashing quietly, maneuvering us away from the bank. Imriel knelt in the prow.

"There," he whispered, spotting the Wheel low on the western horizon.

I aligned my pointing finger with the smallest spoke. "That way."

The oars dipped, and the skiff glided forward. Again, and again, and again. On the shore, Tisaar fell away behind us. When we were well into the open water, I turned to glance over my left shoulder, seeking the constellation of Moishe's Rod. There it was, with the serpent's dangling tail disappearing beneath my line of sight.

"We're on course," I whispered. "Go!"

Joscelin wasted no words, only nodded and began to row.

Swish, dip, pull; swish, dip, pull. Over and over, the sounds a litany unto themselves. How long? Five hours, Nemuel had estimated, marking time by the progress of the stars. By the sound of it, theirs had been a larger vessel, and heavier; but Nemuel had had six oarsmen, two for every oar, trading off in shifts of three.

We had only the three of us.

Truly, the lake was vast. By the first hour, we were altogether out of sight of land, at least insofar as I could see by starlight, which did not avail for distance. There were islands, from time to time, to the north and south of us. We passed them by, and returned to open water. The slow heavens revolved around us. I kept Moishe's Rod behind my left shoulder, my arm upraised and pointing ever westward. Imriel was a shadow in the prow. So bright, the stars! Their light pinned a silvery cap on Joscelin's fair hair, tied in a cabled braid. I could make out the ragged curve of his maimed ear.

And I could hear his breathing grow audible in the second hour.

Swish, dip, pull; a rhythm grown erratic. By the beginning of the third hour, as I gauged it, the skiff moved in steady jerks rather than a smooth glide, drifting ever southward. "Left," I whispered to Joscelin, over and over, correcting our course. "Left!"

He paused between strokes, breathing hard. "My arm," he murmured, apologetic. "It's not as strong as the right, not yet."

Somewhere in the third hour, we traded. It was an awkward maneuver, switching seats in the middle of the lake, hampered by darkness. I showed him our lodestone, the smallest spoke of the Wheel, and how to point the course, keeping Moishe's Rod over his left shoulder. I could see the broken blisters on his palms as he pointed our course.

And then I took my turn at the oars.

It was hard, as hard as anything I have known. At first the well-worn wood seemed silken to the touch, smooth and harmless. I pushed the handles forward, dipping the oars and bracing my legs, and pulled hard against the resistance of the water. The skiff surged forward. Again, and again, and again, until I began to feel the muscles of my shoulders burn with the effort. "Left," Joscelin corrected me, "Left . . . too far! Right, Phèdre, pull right," until I felt the grain of that silken-smooth wood, rubbing and rubbing my sweat-damp palms. It stung like fury. I thought as I rowed about all that Joscelin had done on my behalf—*to protect and serve*—and the sheer physical effort of it, the toll I had never reckoned.

If it were only pain . . . if it were only that, I could endure it. I rowed through the pain, feeling blisters rise and break, the pain so acute it brought on Kushiel's crimson haze. It set my nerves to sing on edge and, for a time, gave me strength. Yet even that waned, and my muscles grew dull with fatigue.

Swish, dip, pull.

The blades of the oars skittered over the surface of the water. The Lake of Tears, they named it; Isis' grief. Why was it always the goddesses who mourned? *Dip.* I willed the oars deeper, pulling hard. My arms trembled. *Pull.* The water seemed as thick as honey, the skiff moving in slow staggers.

"Phèdre. Phèdre!"

I leaned on the oars and stared blearily at Joscelin's face, only exhaustion altering my vision. His expression was fraught with concern.

"Enough," he said softly. "Let me."

"I can row." Imriel turned around in the prow, his face gleaming in the starlight. "For a while, anyway. Let me try."

And so we traded places again, and I resumed mine in the stern, Joscelin going to the prow. Water sloshed along the sides of the rocking skiff. Imriel settled himself in the oarsman's seat, his face grave and unchildish as he took up the cue of my pointing arm. I thought he would spend his strength in a rush, but he started slow and steady, getting the feel of the oars, more patient than any boy his age had a right to be. In the prow, Joscelin tore strips of fabric from the hem of his shirt, binding his raw hands.

Swish, dip, pull; swish, dip, pull.

He did well, did Imriel de la Courcel. He husbanded his strength, rowing at an even pace for longer than I would have reckoned. But the skiff was ideal for carrying two men, no more, and it was heavy work.

I cannot say how long he lasted, before his strength gave out. Between the two of us, I reckon we covered two hours.

Joscelin took over.

Less than an hour to go, by Nemuel's account; but we had not travelled so swiftly. Joscelin resumed his seat, and set to steadily, hauling on the oars. "Left," I murmured as his right arm outdrew its mate, "Left!" He gritted his teeth and adjusted, pulling ever harder. The improvised bandages around his hands darkened with blood. I thought about Kapporeth and wondered if we would reach it in time, and what would happen if we did. Who was I to seek the Name of God? Make of the self a vessel where there is no self, Eleazar had said, in perfect love. Love, I had known; but what is perfection? My lord Delaunay I had loved with a grateful heart, and Hyacinthe with youthful joy and adult sorrow. I had loved Joscelin and loved him still, with a depth and passion that words could not compass. Elua help me, I had loved Melisande Shahrizai, and there was a part of me which ever would.

And in all of these, there was *myself*, bound inextricably into the coils of love—by gratitude, by friendship, by guilt, by passion, by the fatal flaw of Kushiel's Dart. How could one put such a thing as the self aside? I knew only one path, the path I had found in the darkest hours in Daršanga. I did not think it led to the Name of God, and in my heart, I was afraid.

"Phèdre," Imriel called from the prow, pointing. "Dawn is coming."

So it was, the western horizon turning a leaden grey, the spokes of the Wheel paling against it. And in the rising light, I saw a hummock of land to the north of us.

"Look," I murmured. "Do you think?"

Joscelin rested the oars and stared. "Kapporeth?" he said dully. "It could be. It means we're off course. But with my arm . . ."

"It could be." I shuddered. "I don't know. I don't know! Morit was guessing, at best. Let's make for it."

We did, Joscelin rowing with grim determination, the small isle emerging lush and green with the rising sun, exuberant with birdlife; fish eagles and kites and horn-billed ibis. The shores were thick with waving ferns, tall fronds untrodden by human foot. Our skiff edged along them, Imriel standing balanced in the prow, looking for signs of inhabitation.

"Nothing," he reported, gazing inland. "No path, no landing sign . . ." He looked back at me and turned pale. "Name of Elua!"

I turned to look.

It was a ship, of course; what else would it be? Looming in the distance, becoming visible in the dawn. I could barely make out twin banks of oars, four sets rising and falling. Someone had betrayed us, someone's faith had faltered, Hanoch ben Hadad's suspicions had been upheld . . . who knew? It didn't matter. It only mattered that they were coming for us.

"We can hide!" Imriel said, wild-eyed. "Go ashore, and hide! It's all overgrown, they won't find us!"

"No," I muttered. "It's not Kapporeth." Joscelin put up the oars with his bloodstained hands and watched me quietly, waiting. "Elua!" I pressed the heels of my hands against my eyes, thinking and praying. "It's not Kapporeth," I repeated, dropping my hands. "I was wrong, I shouldn't have doubted. We were on course, only slow. Joscelin, can you row?"

"Yes." The red stains spread on his bandages as he regarded me. "Phèdre, the stars have faded."

I stared at the brightening sky. It was true; the stars we had followed all night were paling, lost in the light of the rising sun. The Wheel was fading, its spokes already lost; Moishe's Rod grew invisible. I closed my eyes again, feeling for the direction we had faced. My near-brother Alcuin had been good with maps. I never had, not like him. But Anafiel Delaunay had trained both our memories.

Mine would have to do.

"That way," I said, pointing, not daring to open my eyes.

Swish, dip, pull.

We had to round the nameless island. I felt our course shifting, the skiff moving, and adjusted my arm accordingly. I dared not look, dared not lose the lodestone of my memory; not until I felt the open breezes blow, and our course align with my pointing arm. Then, I opened my eyes.

We were in open water and the skiff leapt forward with each pull of Joscelin's arms, drawing toward an unseen destination, a blur on the horizon. Swish, dip, pull. The rags tied round his hands were crimson with blood, blood smeared on the oar-handles.

It *was* a blur on the horizon. It was land.

"Go!" I shouted. "Go, go, *go!*"

Joscelin's face was blind and unseeing with concentration, his arms moving with relentless precision. I saw the muscles in his shoulders surge, his legs bracing and flexing. The skiff flew over the waters like a swallow on the wing. In the prow, Imriel knelt and looked backward, past Joscelin, past me, charting the progress of our pursuers. I saw the alarm reflected in his face. I did not turn to see why.

Ahead of us, the blur resolved into land; an island, small and unprepossessing, easily missed in the vast Lake of Tears. And it too was green and verdant, but it was marked, stamped by the footprint of mankind. I saw the shallow beach where the underbrush had been cleared, with a fishing boat on the shore and the structure on the hill above it; round, like the temple in Tisaar. I saw the path that cut like a blaze through the green, and evidence of a garden, a sown field, shapes too regular for nature.

"Kapporeth," I whispered. "We have found it."

SEVENTY-SIX

WE SCARCELY beat our pursuers ashore.

Imriel leapt out of the skiff the instant our prow touched land, hauling on it. I scrambled to grab Joscelin's weapons, ignoring the rocking of the vessel as he disembarked. By the time I followed, tossing him the oilskin bundle, the Sabaean craft had landed.

It was a footrace, after that.

I caught a glimpse, as we raced for the path, of the soldiers who emerged from the Sabaean craft. To be sure, their armor and their weapons were ancient, of bronze and not steel, but the edges were no less keen for it, and there were at least twenty of them.

We had steel, yes. We had Joscelin.

He shoved his daggers into the empty sheathes on his belt as he ran, disentangling his baldric and slinging it over his shoulders, his sword jouncing in its scabbard. The oilskin cloth fell by the wayside as he tucked one vambrace under his arm, struggling to force his bleeding left hand into the mesh gauntlet of the other. Leather straps flopped with every stride, impossible to buckle on the run.

And then we were there, in the clearing atop the hill, with the round temple shut tight and slumberous in the early morning light, while twenty Sabaean soldiers fanned out to surround us, their bronze blades drawn and gleaming in the sun.

"I knew it," said Hanoch ben Hadad, jutting his black beard. "I *knew* it! There were too many women paying visits to my sister. I told the Sanhedrin as much."

"How is it, my lord captain?" I asked him softly, watching Joscelin fasten his vambraces out of the corner of my eye. "Is your sister not worthy of company? I found her a gracious hostess."

"Woman's folly," Hanoch said in a hard voice. "Prey to a gentle manner and a sad tale. She is aging, and lonely. It is fortunate for you my niece Ardath thought better of her folly and made confession to her husband Japhet in time for us to pursue. It would go worse if you had succeeded in profaning the temple."

Ardath. Yevuneh's daughter, with the nursing babe in her arms. I felt sick at it, the blood beating hard in my ears. To have come this far! "Ardath knows not what she does," I said, my voice sounding distant and strange. "It is fear that speaks."

"Fear, aye." He nodded. "She fears for her children's future, do we risk Adonai's wrath. Such is wisdom, the truth of women's wisdom; a mother's fear. A pity you did not think to do the same. Your son will suffer for your folly. Give thanks to Adonai that we have halted you in time. If the Sanhedrin is merciful, it may be that you will not be put to death, but only enslaved."

"And how shall you be rewarded, Hanoch ben Hadad, for finding Kapporeth, where Nemuel's shame is hidden?" I asked him, anger flaring. "I tell you this, it is Blessed Elua's will that has led us here, over deserts and mountains and rivers, through dangers that would render you faint to hear told! It is no matter for you to decide, no, nor the Sanhedrin of Elders. It is for Adonai Himself, and it is the wisdom of the women of Tisaar to know it, and hide no longer from the Will of God, who has forgotten you these long centuries!"

It gave Hanoch pause. His dark eyelids flickered, and his men glanced uneasily at one another. "Nonetheless," he said, then, resolve firming. He pointed with the tip of his sword toward the closed door of the temple at our backs. "Therein lies the Holiest of Holies, and the way is barred to you. I am content. Adonai's silence speaks. You will return with us to Tisaar, and face judgement."

Joscelin crossed his forearms and bowed, steel flashing in the rising sun. His daggers rode at his hips, his sword-hilt over his shoulder. Cassiline discipline held immaculate. No one watching would guess the ragged state of his hands, his bone-deep exhaustion. "My lord captain," he said in Habiru. "Do not do this thing. I am loathe to shed blood in this place. Let my lady Phèdre at least seek audience with the priest of Aaron's line."

Hanoch ben Hadad hesitated again, then shook his head. "No," he said, gesturing with his sword, and the line of Sabaean soldiery advanced a step, raising hide shields studded with ancient bronze. "I am sorry, D'Angeline. You are a valiant warrior, if your battle with the Shamsun tells any tale. But the way is barred to you. Adonai's will is clear."

I stole a glance over my shoulder. The temple doors remained adamantly closed.

"As you say," Joscelin said gently, and his daggers sang free of their sheathes, crossed before him and shining like a star, blood trickling down the insides of his wrists. "Nonetheless. I have sworn a vow."

"Not to Adonai," replied the Sabaean captain. "Not to the Lord of Hosts, my friend."

"No." Joscelin smiled, and in the rising light of dawn, his eyes were the blue of summer skies over the fields of Terre d'Ange. "To his once-faithful servant Cassiel, whose memory is more true than God's. And I . . . I protect and serve."

Hanoch ben Hadad shook his bronze-helmed head. "It will be your death, D'Angeline."

"So be it." At the sealed mouth of the temple, birds sang, the sun-warmed foliage released its green scent, and Joscelin Verreuil settled into a defensive stance, sounding almost careless. "It is the death I have spent a lifetime earning."

Something like regret crossed Hanoch ben Hadad's face before he raised his shield and set his sword, its worn bronze honed to a killing edge. "Take them!"

Spreading their line to flank Joscelin, the Sabaeans advanced at his command.

So close; so *close!* I felt the presence of a great mystery hovering near, almost within the grasp of my reaching fingers. Almost. I turned, flinging myself recklessly against the temple door, pounding with my blistered hands to no avail. "Please," I begged; in Habiru, in D'Angeline, in what tongue I could not say. "Name of mercy, let me but *ask!*" But the door remained closed and locked, and no answer was forthcoming. In the background, I heard the terrible clash of battle as Joscelin engaged ben Hadad's men. I had no more gambits to play. It hurt, to come so near and fail. Elua, but it hurt! I sank to my knees, disbelieving my own failure.

"Lady." A hand closed on my shoulder and a Sabaean soldier showed me the sword held loose in his grip. "This is sacred ground and no place for violence. It is over. You will come with us."

"No," I whispered. "Please, no."

And Imriel de la Courcel screamed.

It was the sound that had rent the night in the zenana, in the plains of Drujan, in Yevuneh's house; the sound of terror, pure and unadulterated, shrill and piercing and unbearable to the ear, bone-chilling and awful. His face was white as bleached linen, his pupils black and dilated. Moving with unexpected speed, he put himself between us, wrenched the sword from the startled soldier's grasp and slashed fiercely at him with a two-handed grip. *"Leave her alone!"*

"Adonai!" The soldier took a step back, clutching his thigh where the tip of Imriel's blade had grazed it. Others paused and stared, exchanging glances. Joscelin stood motionless, frozen in the ring of space his sword had cleared, his face a study in horror.

Hanoch ben Hadad grimaced. "Hold him at bay," he ordered the men surrounding Joscelin. He strode toward us, sunlight glinting off the worn, deadly edge of his bronze sword, and anger was like a storm on his face. "Boy," he said grimly, pointing his blade at a defiant Imriel, "the price for the blood you have spilled on the temple's doorstep is death."

It was like a dream, a terrible dream.

As in a dream, I felt here and not here, myself and not myself. Unthinking, I rose from my knees and pushed Imriel behind me, gazing up at the Sabaean captain. "I brought him here," I said, and it sounded to my ears as if a stranger had spoken. "I am responsible." I could hear the din of Joscelin's renewed efforts to break free of the soldiers who surrounded him. It seemed very far away. In all my musings on love, there was one I had not numbered. I had not reckoned on Imriel. There was no god's prompting here; only love, simple and unadorned. I understood, too late, what it meant to put the self aside. Still, there was one way left, and it was a way that ever stands open. It would not gain me the Name of God, but it would gain Imriel's life. "If the price is death, I will pay it."

For a moment, he bowed his head, then straightened and raised his sword. "You are the author of this blasphemy, and it is a dire transgression you have committed here. Better you should die and be shriven of it. I will accept the bargain."

I watched sunlight glint along the blade. "And you will spare the boy?"

Hanoch ben Hadad paused, then nodded. "In Adonai's mercy, I will."

So, I thought, this is how it ends. Hyacinthe, forgive me. I tried my best.

"Phèdre, *no!*"

"Phèdre!"

The first shout was Joscelin's, raw with anguish, searing my heart.

Almost, almost it was enough to sway me from my purpose. It was the second call that did it, Imriel's voice; not terrified, but taut and urgent. Behind me, I heard the clatter of a sword dropping as he grabbed my elbow with one hand, fingers digging into my flesh as he pointed past me at the temple door.

It was open.

The priest of Aaron's line stood in the doorway, silent and watching, with bare feet and a white linen robe trimmed in blue and scarlet and purple, shimmering with gold thread. Hanoch ben Hadad put up his sword, taking two uncertain steps backward, his face blank with confusion. In the silence that followed, all fighting ceased. A few yards away, Joscelin abandoned the scene of battle, walking past the stunned soldiers to join us. We looked at one another, he and I.

"All right, then," he said simply. "Go ask him, Phèdre."

I let out a shuddering breath. "I will."

No one else moved as I approached the priest. He was neither young nor old, but somewhere in between, his closed mouth smiling amid an unruly black beard. A mortal man, no more and no less, a frail vessel to ward such unearthly power and bear the unbroken lineage of the One God's anger. His eyes were dark, like all Sabaeans, and the early heat brought a faint sheen of perspiration to his mahogany skin.

"I am Phèdre nó Delaunay de Montrève of Terre d'Ange," I said to him in Habiru, "and I seek to know the Name of God."

The priest smiled a little more and mouthed a word. *There*, he mouthed, pointing into the shadowy interior of the temple. In the cavity of his mouth I saw the truth of Sabaean legend, the stump of a tongue withered like a drought-stricken root. My skin prickled with nerves, and something else. I turned to face Hanoch ben Hadad.

"My lord captain," I said. "Will you gainsay my passage?"

He had fallen to his knees; all the Sabaeans had, arms discarded, bowing and rocking with murmured prayers. Only Joscelin and Imriel remained standing, watching me. Joscelin's daggers were sheathed and he held Imri close to him with one arm.

"Well," I said to them in D'Angeline, conscious of my own tongue and how it worked in tandem with my lips, shaping words, giving voice to my utterance. If these were to be my last words, I wished they were less banal. "I had better go, then."

Joscelin cleared his throat. "I suppose . . . I suppose you'd better."

"Yes." I nodded like an idiot. "In case I can't tell you afterward . . . well. I love you."

"I know," he said. "I love you."

"And you," I said to Imriel. "And you."

He gave a rough nod, not trusting his voice.

"Well, then," I addressed the priest. "Let us go."

And the priest of Aaron's line smiled and bowed low, indicating the way. I stepped across the threshold of the temple into the dark interior. I heard the door close behind us, blotting out the morning sun. I stood in darkness as he took up a single lamp, kindling a taper and lighting other lamps. My eyes adjusted slowly to the lack of sunlight.

It was a temple, no different in structure from the one in the city, save humbler, wrought of mud-brick. Only the adornments were splendid; fretted lamps, gilded sconces, shedding a rich golden glow throughout the simple interior. The priest pointed at my feet and I stooped to remove my shoes. The floor of the temple was hard-packed earth, dry and crumbling in patches.

"Is it well?" I asked him. "I have brought . . . I have brought no offering, my lord priest."

You, he mouthed, pointing at me, and the shriveled root of his tongue moved within the cavern of his mouth. *You.* And then he pointed at himself, touching his own breast. *Me.*

"Yes," I said softly. "There is that."

And I followed him, then, into the second circle of the temple of Kapporeth, understanding that he was like me; mortal, and marked all unwitting by the touch of a god. Kushiel, Adonai; does it matter, in the end? We pay for sins we do not remember, and seek to do a will we can scarce fathom. That is what it is, to be a god's chosen.

In the second circle there were treasures, more treasures, heaped upon the earthen floor; vessels of gold and silver, tribute dating back to Shalomon's day. And beyond . . . Elua! The Holiest of Holies, Hanoch ben Hadad had called it. I stared at the opening of the inner sanctum, veiled with curtains of scarlet and purple and blue, and shivered.

It was there, I thought. The Ark of Broken Tablets.

The Name of God.

Preserved in silence these long years, a millennium and more, shrouded by a goddess' grief. Who was I to breach it?

Hyacinthe.

Repressing my fear, I followed the priest as he circumnavigated the inner sanctum and approached the altar in its alcove. The altar was of solid gold, and a lamp burned upon it; the Ur Tamid, the light that is never extinguished. Even so is it in Yeshuite temples to this day. A large incensor sat upon the altar, gold on gold, the inner bowl darkened with years of offerings. Mouthing a noiseless prayer, the priest offered a generous handful, lighting the fragrant lumps of resin with a taper. Sweet, pungent smoke rose and hovered against the ceiling in a bluish cloud.

He turned then, and pointed to the sanctum, raising his brows in inquiry.

"What will happen, my lord priest?" I asked him, shivering despite the morning's warmth, the lamp-lit closeted darkness of the temple. "What will happen, if I do?"

He shook his head, his mouth closed on the mysteries of Adonai's wrath.

Hyacinthe.

"Let it be done," I said.

The priest of Aaron's line parted the curtains of the Holiest of Holies.

Seventy-seven

WITHIN THE dim chamber, the Ark of Broken Tablets gleamed like a subtle sun.

The priest moved soundlessly on bare feet, lighting the lampstands about it until the flames were reflected in the gold, sending shifting patterns about the mud-brick walls. I held very still and gazed at it. It was made of acacia wood, so the Tanakh claimed, overlaid with gold, and so I beheld it, still resting on the gilded poles once used to carry it; a mighty chest, that would take four strong men to bear it.

And it was sealed with a lid of gold, that is called Kapporeth, the mercy seat after which the island was named, upon which were two cherubim facing one another—strange creatures, with the hindquarters of a bull, the forequarters of a lion and wings like the eagle, and faces . . . ah, Elua! Faces such as I had seen in the temples of Terre d'Ange, human, and more; stern and serene. There was Kushiel's justice, Naamah's passion, Azza's pride, Shemhazai's intelligence, Camael's ferocity, Eisheth's healing, Anael's bounty, Cassiel's loyalty.

'Twas all encompassed in their carven faces.

The priest bowed low before the Ark, and took from a waiting stand a breastplate of hammered gold, held together before and aft by twisted links of chain. This he donned over his robes, and on his breast winked four lines of gems, three across; sardius, topaz and garnet, emerald, sapphire and diamond; jacinthe, agate and amethyst; beryl, onyx and jasper, each gem inscribed with a name—one each for the Twelve Tribes of the Children of Yisra-el.

And I, Elua's child, watched and trembled.

He took then in his hands a crown, engraved with the words, "Holy to Adonai." And this he placed against his brow, binding it with ties of blue-dyed silk. So had Nemuel done, I thought, on the plains of Jebe-

Barkal. The priest stood waiting, sterner and taller in his regalia. I felt small, and tired. My muscles ached from the ordeal of rowing, and my hands were blistered and sore. There was no voice speaking between the cherubim, no presence of Elua; not even Kushiel to mark the way with his crimson haze.

"I don't know what to do, my lord," I said humbly. "I am only a supplicant here. All I want is to free my friend."

The priest laid his hands on two corners of the massive lid and looked fixedly at me, nodding at the opposite side of the Ark. The silent cherubim gazed at one another.

"The Name of God," I whispered. If it existed, it lay within the Ark. I reached out with trembling hands, curling my fingers beneath the corners opposite the priest. This was the transgression that had blasted Nemuel, and all his descendants. "I am scared, my lord priest."

He made me no answer, watching and waiting, not unkindly. The gems on his breastplate winked, naming the Twelve Tribes, silent prayers and reminders to an unresponsive god. If it was a transgression, this act, it was one for which the priest had already born a lifetime of punishment. Had he tried it already? I could not know. My mouth was dry. Did I transgress here? If Adonai was merciful, I would only suffer the same. I licked my parched lips, thinking of the tongues I had mastered in my day. D'Angeline, Caerdicci, Hellene, Skaldic, Cruithne, all under Delaunay's guidance; Habiru, Illyrian, Akkadian, Persian, Jeb'ez; even zenyan. The argot of Tsingani, the dialect of the Dalriada.

All of this, I stood to lose.

And Naamah's arts, the arts of love. I remembered how Joscelin had kissed me in the bathing-pool. That, I could not even bear to think of losing.

Oh, Hyacinthe, I thought. It is little, so *little*, compared to what you sacrificed. Forgive me my fear, that so ill becomes me. But I cannot help it, for it is so much of what I am, of what I have made myself. And I do not know what will become of us if I fail. With a silent prayer for forgiveness, I set myself and gritted my teeth, lifting with all my might. Terrified of succeeding, terrified of failing, I sought to raise the massive lid, my fingernails digging, bending beneath the weight of it. And on the opposite side, the priest of Aaron's line bowed his head and lifted too, sinews standing out on his forearms, "Holy to Adonai" engraved glimmering on his sweat-beaded brow.

We lifted together, and the lid rose. Inch by strenuous inch, it rose. My arms trembled. It rose. The space between the cherubim lay silent.

538 | JACQUELINE CAREY

The heavy golden lid, the mercy seat, was raised into the darkling air.

Awkward and strained, I dared a glance inside the Ark.

And there I saw the *Luvakh Shabab*, the Broken Tablets; fragments, grey shards of stone battered to gravel, not even a single word of text remaining intact. These were the Tablets inscribed by Adonai's own hand? I would have wept, had I strength to spare. An empty chest with a heap of rubble at the bottom—such was the end of my quest. Such was the mystery Isis' grief had guarded. Such was the secret the Sabaeans had hidden from the Eye of God for more than a thousand years.

The rubble stirred of its own accord.

I caught my breath and held it.

My arms and back and shoulders ached with the strain of holding the lid aloft. Would that Joscelin were here! Truly, I had failed to reckon the cost of his labors. Two-thousand-year-old dust swirled in the gilded depths. The ancient rubble stirred, fragments of stone aligning, letters emerging; the Habiru alphabet, forming before my eyes to spell out the Name . . . Yod, Alef, Quf, Lamed . . . Nun? And, ah, Elua others among them I did not recognize! Kaf, Alef, more—too much, too fast, not even my Delaunay-trained memory could hold it, my facile tongue shaping the letters in vain, too slow, muscles trembling with the strain. Oh, unfair. A lost alphabet, letters I did not know, never etched by mortal hands. Twelve years' of study, gone to no avail. How could I utter a sound I had never heard? I sought to remember their shape, but they were gone, fleeting, before I could capture them. The emergent letters in the golden shadow of the lid spelling out an unpronounceable Name, half-glimpsed. Tears of despair stung my eyes, and I blinked in a futile effort to see.

Dust and rubble spoke; dust and rubble fell silent, returning to its component parts. My fingertips slipped on the corners of the lid, causing the priest's grip to falter. The lid fell with a lurching crash, solid gold. So what? Gold would not free Hyacinthe from his isle, and I did not need to be told that I had spent my one and only chance. I bowed my head and tasted the bitter fruit of failure. The voice between the cherubim had remained silent, but the *Luvakh Shabab* had spoken. Adonai had answered. He would not speak twice. Knowledge had failed me, and it was bitter, bitter indeed.

I should be glad, I thought, that I had tongue left to taste defeat.

I took a deep breath and raised my head to confront my failure.

On the far side of the Ark, his face framed betwixt the silent cherubim, the priest of Aaron's line was smiling. Neither young nor old, he was smiling; smiling, he who had aided me in raising the Kapporeth to no avail. I stared dumbly at him, uncomprehending. A man, a mortal man, with an unruly beard and kind eyes, radiant with joy. Why? His smiling teeth were strong and white, framing the cavern of his shriveled tongue. Such compassion, in his dark gaze; and such joy, such unbearable joy. I wanted to ask why, but fear stopped my mouth. It hurt too much to hope, now.

Silence filled the Holiest of Holies. No stir, no echo, no whisper of sound.

Even the flames stood silent and motionless in the golden lampstands.

And in the deafening silence . . .

Tongueless and unvoiced, the priest spoke the unpronounceable Name of God.

"_____!"

How does one endure a sound not meant for mortal ears to bear? It burst within the confines of my skull like thunder over the mountains, rolling and brazen, setting off clamorous echoes. A word, one word, seared upon my memory. It burned in me like strong wine, like the first taste of *joie* I had known as a child, like Melisande's touch. I knew it all, then, saw my course mapped, from the moment I had glimpsed Anafiel Delaunay, all down the winding path that had led me here— here, to a humble temple on a hidden isle, surrounded by a goddess' grief. Who could have charted this course? The myriad branchings of my fate were foreordained and unknowable. Along dark paths, they had led me here. Here. I understood it all, and grasped at last the whole of the pattern. I gasped for air, feeling my chest like to crack open, streaming flames. The Sacred Name! I was too small to contain it. My knees gave way beneath me and I sank to the earthen floor, curling my body around the space it hollowed within me.

The Name of God.

The Name of God.

Oh, *Hyacinthe!*

How long I laid upon the floor, I cannot say. I would have laid there forever, I think, if the priest had not roused me. His hands were gentle, insistent, shaking my shoulders. His eyes were kind. I could smell the dusty soil of the temple floor, and the pall of incense. I could smell the peppers he'd had for dinner. I was alive, gravid with the Sacred

Name. My body felt strange to me as the priest helped me to my feet. All the space in my mind was taken up by the Name. It swelled the cords of my throat, and I had to clench my teeth to keep from speaking it.

It would have destroyed me had I not found a place within myself where naught but love abided, simple and unencumbered. Only then had the priest, in his wisdom, opened the door. I marveled at the symmetry of the pattern. If I had not brought Imri out of the darkness of Daršanga, this brightness would never have come to pass. Truly, love was a wondrous force, now that I perceived the complexities of its workings.

Everything in the temple seemed distinct, objects standing out bright against the darkness. I had trouble gauging distances. I touched a lamp-stand, marveling at the smoothness of gold. Freed from stasis, the flame in its bowl danced like a little animal, flickering saffron. I put my fingers close to it, feeling its warmth burn. I would have touched it too, if the priest had not put his hand on my wrist, drawing me away and shaking his head gently. He pointed toward the distant door in inquiry. Was I ready to leave?

I nodded my head, not daring to speak. The Name was insistent on my tongue.

He led me into the outer circle, and there I sat upon a marble bench to don my shoes. I felt the cool surface of the marble, the tiny veins and flaws. I gazed at my bare feet, slender and white, engrained with dirt from the temple floor. So many delicate bones, articulated joints! All of that, all for the purpose of treading the earth. I put on my shoes with reluctance, and the priest had to help me with the buckles, for I could not cease marveling at their complexity. I gazed wondering at his deft fingers, at the cords of blue silk that secured his head-piece against the coarse black of his tight-curled hair. "Holy to Adonai." Such contrasts of color, of texture!

At the temple door, he paused and took my upturned face in his hands. I closed my eyes as he kissed my brow, knowing it for kinship, for blessing, for forgiveness. This was not my place, and Adonai was not my God. All of this, I knew.

It was a grave trust I had been given.

I prayed I would be worthy of it.

With that, the priest released me and opened the temple door. Sunlight streamed across the threshold, and the Name surged within me at the sight of so much brightness, ringing in my head with clarion tones.

I shut my teeth hard on it and stepped into the dazzling light. The sky, so blue! And the bushes! Never had I seen such green. I could see every leaf, sharp-edged; I could sense their roots, rustling in the dry soil.

And the people; oh, Elua, the people.

Joscelin, wild-eyed, leapt to his feet. All I could do was stare at him, dumbstruck. Every line, every plane of him was writ in an alphabet of flesh and bone, spelling out love. How had I never seen it? And Imriel, at his side—a tangled knot of fear and need, achingly vulnerable. It made my heart ache to look upon him.

"Do you have it?" Joscelin asked, half-dreading my answer. "Did you succeed?"

I nodded, the Name of God lodged in the throat like a stone.

"Can you . . . can you speak?" he asked.

"I'm not sure," I whispered.

In three swift strides, Joscelin reached me and swept me into a crushing embrace, raining kisses on my face. I clung to him, then kissed him hard, to make sure I still could. Fear left him in a shudder when I let him go. I knelt, then, and opened my arms to Imriel. He flung himself in them and caught me about the neck in a choke-hold, burying his face against my neck.

"I was scared, Phèdre. I didn't know what would happen."

"Neither did I, Imri," I murmured. "Neither did I."

"What happens now?" It was Joscelin who spoke, and it was the Sabaeans he addressed, a hard edge to his voice. I straightened beside him.

They had put off their helmets and laid their shields aside during the long wait—and it must have been long, for the sun, I perceived, was nigh overhead. Hanoch ben Hadad looked at me with a mix of awe and disbelief.

"You have beheld the Sacred Name?" he asked.

"Yes," I said.

"How do we know this is so?"

I had no answer. I merely gazed at him, while the Name of God echoed like thunder in my thoughts, welling up to fill my mouth until I dared not utter a word. Across the clearing, the priest of Aaron's line stood in the temple doorway watching gravely, gems flashing across his gold-plated breast, gold at his brow, bare feet on the earthen floor.

"Hanoch," one of the soldiers said, trembling. "Hanoch, there is a brightness upon her face. I am afraid. Ask no more."

"*Why?*" The Sabaean captain's voice rose in a rage. "After so long, why *you?*"

And that, too, I could not answer. Had I dared, I might have said that it was no curse, no wrath of god that had bound them for centuries, but only fear and guilt. The priest knew it. How many others before him had known? But no one had dared to ask the voiceless. And I— this was not my place, and Adonai was not my God. I could not answer for Him to the Sabaeans. They must ask Him themselves. What was entrusted to me served only one purpose. Aught else would be a transgression.

"Lady." It was a young soldier who stepped forward, his bronze helmet under his arm, his eyes soft and wondering. "I am Eshkol ben Avidan, and I am not afraid. I am sorry we sought to detain you. If you will it, we will take you to Tisaar. And there, I think, you may go free, although it is not my place to assure it."

"Eshkol!" ben Hadad hissed. "It is insubordination you speak!"

"No, captain," the soldier said politely. "It is, I think, wisdom."

In the temple doorway, the priest smiled.

"Yes, my lord soldier," I said, swallowing against the insistent pressure of the Name. "If you will take us, we will go."

SEVENTY-EIGHT

IT WAS a long journey back to Tisaar, and a strange one. I sat silent for most of it, learning how to breathe and think with the awesome presence of the Name of God crowding my mind. Except for Hanoch ben Hadad, who remained sullen and uncertain, the Sabaeans rowed with a good will, trading off in teams, jesting in hushed tones as men will who have witnessed events beyond understanding. Even the soldier Imriel had wounded bore no ill will over it.

The courage of Eshkol ben Avidan had sparked them, and I heard in their voices and saw in their faces the dawn of wonder, of hope. Seeds had been sown here this day, which would bear fruit long after we were gone. Whose tool, I wondered, was I? For so long, I had focused upon my singular quest: To free Hyacinthe.

Now, here, an entire people, whose isolation had lasted longer than the Master of the Straits himself had lived. Whose purpose had I served? Mayhap I was only a small lever in Adonai's plan, serving to set something vast in motion as his slow attention returned to the neglected Tribe of Dân. I could not say.

In the end, it did not matter.

We had what we'd come for.

What transpired after we left Saba was between the Sabaeans themselves and Adonai, the One God, their Lord of Hosts. As for us . . . I shuddered.

I'd never really thought ahead, beyond this point. What remained for us, aside from the dire repercussions of Joscelin and I having taken Imriel de la Courcel with us in defiance of the Queen's will, through myriad dangers to a land that was half-fable even in distant Jebe-Barkal . . .

. . . was between Rahab and I.

Well and so, I thought. This burden I cannot share or pass; it is mine, and mine alone, with the Name of God emblazoned inside my head. And that is as it should be, for it is my place Hyacinthe took. But I have faced death willingly twice today and we are a long way yet from home, and there are bandits and lions and crocodiles in our path, long sea journeys and the anger of Ysandre, which may be no small thing. So I will worry about facing down this angel known as Pride, and Insolence, later, because right now it is too much to fathom.

It was early evening by the time we reached Tisaar, and the harbor was filled with people—men, women and children, silent and watching, awaiting our return. Semira and Yevuneh and some of the others were clustered together under the dour eye of the Elders of the Sanhedrin, looking stubborn and fearful.

"People of Tisaar!" It was Eshkol ben Avidan who addressed them, leaping agilely onto the dock. "Brothers and sisters, Melehakim! We have beheld a mystery this day."

He told them then what had transpired, while the vessel was secured and the rest of us disembarked. My head ringing with the dreadful syllables of the Name, I was glad I did not have to speak. None of us were any too fit. After his long night's ordeal, Joscelin looked exhausted, harrowed with pain, streaks of dried blood on his hands and arms beneath his vambraces, and there were violet shadows under Imriel's eyes. I wondered if the priest would have opened the door if Imri hadn't screamed. Was that the sound, born out of pain and terror in Daršanga, that had moved Adonai's heart to compassion? Mayhap it was so. If it was, he had played a role none of us had ever reckoned.

So I mused, unable to pay Eshkol's recitation the attention it deserved, caught up in the mysteries locked inside my head. But when Eshkol had done, the Elders of the Sanhedrin crowded round, pressing me with questions, anxious and demanding.

"Did the Voice of Adonai speak between the cherubim?"

"What is the nature of the Sacred Name?"

"Did you dare to lift the Kapporeth?"

"My lords." My voice emerged in a hoarse whisper. "It is not my place to answer these things."

"Whose, then?" It was Bilgah the Elder who asked, white-bearded and fierce. "*You* defied our authority to trespass where we said it was forbidden! *You* instigated violence on sacred ground! Who should we ask, if not you?"

"Ask Adonai, old fool!" Semira called from where the women were clustered. "Or ask the priest himself, Aaron's scion and Nemuel's, whose appointment it is to speak for the Lord of Hosts. Have you so forgotten who we are? It is no wonder Adonai has remained silent!" Shaking her head in disgust, she pushed her way through the Elders. I saw compassion writ in the deep creases of her features, and wisdom gained through old sorrow. "Ah, child. It is a mighty thing to bear, is it not?"

I nodded.

"So they say," she murmured. "So they say."

There came more arguing after that—men and women, young and old. I closed my eyes and listened to it, hearing the deep tones of fear and doubt clashing with the clarion notes of hope and faith. It would not be settled this day, nor soon. But it was enough. While they argued the meaning, enough believed. Adonai's incomprehensible will had been made manifest. There would be no punishment, not for us.

"Phèdre." Joscelin's hand was under my elbow, steadying me. I hadn't realized I was wavering on my feet. "Come. Semira says to let them argue. You need rest, and food. We all do." Yevuneh was waiting, Imriel beside her.

"What about Tifari Amu and the others?" I asked with difficulty.

"Alive and imprisoned." He gave a shadow of his wry smile. "They wouldn't flee. Jebean pride, I suppose. Eshkol spoke to the troop-leader ben Hadad sent after them. He said they surrendered more or less peaceably to await our return."

"Can we get them released?"

"Eshkol's working on it."

"Good." I had seen the bright flame of courage in the young soldier, and the trail it would blaze in Saba's future. "Let's go, then, before I fall over."

It was no easy thing to make our way through the throng. People pushed close, wanting to see. Heavy-headed and weary, I pressed onward, concentrating on setting one foot in front of the other, syllables of the Name echoing with every step I took. Yevuneh hovered protectively over Imriel, for which I was glad. Joscelin, steel-clad, kept the worst of the press at bay with warning glances. No one protested the fact that he went armed in the city of Tisaar.

Once, though, he stopped, uncertain.

It was a woman, weeping, who barred our way, placing herself before me. Even Yevuneh faltered, bowing her head. "Ardath," she said in sorrow, acknowledging her daughter.

"Forgive me," Ardath pleaded, tears in her dark eyes. "I was afraid."

I was afraid!" She held up her babe in both hands. "Or let me bear the blame if you must, but I beg of you, spare my daughter its curse and give her your blessing!"

"My blessing?" A strangled laugh caught in my throat, where the Name of God was lodged. "Ardath . . . there is no blame, no curse. If your fear was folly, still, it was born of love. I am D'Angeline. It is not in my heart to fault you for it. Who can say how matters might have transpired, had you not betrayed us? It may be we would never have found Kapporeth."

Her lips trembled. "Then you will not bless my child?"

I gazed at the infant she thrust before me, its crumpled face undecided whether to smile or bawl. "Ardath, it is not my place. I am no priest, to speak for Adonai. I am Phèdre nó Delaunay de Montrève, Naamah's Servant and Kushiel's Chosen, Delaunay's *anguissette* and the foremost courtesan of Terre d'Ange. Is that the blessing you want for your daughter?"

"Yes," she whispered, and I knew she'd not understood a word of it. "Please, lady!"

I looked at Joscelin, who shrugged. "Love as thou wilt," I said in D'Angeline, placing my hand upon the crown of the babe's head. "And may you find wisdom in it."

Ardath's face was transfigured. "Thank you, lady, thank you!" she said with profuse joy, cradling her daughter in one arm and grasping my hand with the other, pressing it to her lips. "Thank you!"

Clutching her babe and bowing, she made her retreat, and Yevuneh, muttering at her daughter's interference, hurried us onward. We did not speak of it then, not until we were safely ensconced within her home, where her cook was waiting anxious in the kitchen, an abundance of food prepared. Tired as we were, none of us had eaten in a full day. The taste of stewed chicken seasoned with hot peppers was a marvel, filling my mouth with rich juices. I swallowed, conscious of the nourishing food travelling to my belly, of strength returning to my limbs. Such a wonder, the workings of the earth, and we mortal souls upon it!

Afterward, while Imriel bathed and Yevuneh bustled about the house, I soaked and unwrapped the makeshift bandages from Joscelin's hands, grimacing at the raw flesh. He bore it uncomplaining, hissing through his teeth as I cleaned the wounds and applied tincture of snakeroot, binding them anew.

"Ought to do the same to you," he muttered. "If you wouldn't enjoy it so."

I examined my blistered palms. "They're not so bad. I've skin left, after all."

Joscelin laughed, but his eyes were grave. "How are you, truly?"

"Truly?" I tilted my head, considering. "All right, I think. Strange. I feel strange. Like myself, only more. I've made a vessel of myself, and the Name weighs heavy within me. It's better, now, than at first. I can learn to carry it."

He nodded. "Can you tell me what happened inside the temple?"

I opened my mouth and closed it, shaking my head. "No. It's too close."

"I didn't think it would be so frightening. I thought the worst of it transpired outside. I may have been wrong." Joscelin gave his faint, deprecating smile. "Funny, isn't it? You setting out to wrestle the Name of God from the Lord of Hosts, and I didn't have any idea."

"Nor did I." I thought of how nearly I'd failed. "It was a gift, you know."

"Was it?" He eyed me. "Well, we'd best use it wisely."

"Wisdom, yes." I made a face. "I spoke bold words about the nature of fear today. Do me a favor, will you, and remind me of them when it comes time."

"To face Rahab?"

I nodded.

"Whatever it is, we'll face it together," he said, taking my blistered hands in his bandaged ones. "You know that, at least."

I glanced toward the back of the house, where the bathing-room was. "All of us?"

"You think we could manage to leave him? You nearly gave your life for his today, Phèdre. If he belongs anywhere, it is with us." Joscelin drew a long, shuddering breath, his fingers tightening on mine. "Bold words, I know. Remind me of them when it comes time."

"To face Ysandre?" I asked.

"Mm-hmm."

And that was all we said, then, for Yevuneh returned, looking tired and drawn, but satisfied. "The lad's asleep, if you don't mind; the bath put him fair under, and I ordered him upstairs. Ah, child! 'Tis a dangerous course you set him, for one so young."

"I know, my lady Yevuneh," I said. "Believe me, the matter is not simple."

"No, I thought not." Her kind gaze was shrewd. "He's not your own, is he?"

"No." I shook my head. "He is another's."

"I thought so." The widow nodded to herself. "He calls you by name, not mother and father. It took me a while to hear it, but tonight I did, when he asked after you. Whose is he, then?"

"It doesn't matter," Joscelin said softly. "Not here. Leave him that."

"Born of sin and folly, was he?"

"He was born," I said. "His nature is his own."

"Like Ardath," Yevuneh murmured. "Like all our children, when they are grown. Ah, child, I do not mean to press. It was a kindness, what you did for Ardath. You have the right of it. As often as not, we forge our own chains. And from those, not even Adonai Himself can free us. We must do it ourselves. You are kind, to encourage her."

With that, she told us to avail ourselves of the bathing-room and bid us good evening, and we spoke no more that night, bone-weary as we were.

Nonetheless, I lay awake for a long time that night, listening to the quiet breathing of Joscelin beside me and Imriel in the next pallet, mercifully too tired for nightmares. My muscles ached and my blisters stung. If it was only that, I could have slept; I have known worse. I lay awake listening to the Name of God, pulsing in my mind with each throb of blood in my veins, hearing the web of debate that spread itself through sleepless Tisaar.

Some chains are forged for us.

Those are the hardest to bear.

Seventy-nine

In THE morning, Tifari Amu and his companions were freed from imprisonment.

They were a little battered, but not the much worse for wear. Tifari grinned in unwonted high spirits when I embraced him.

"Kaneka warned me it would be foolish to desert you," he said, returning my embrace. "Lucky for me Bizan and the others agreed! Shall we go home now, lady?"

Home.

He was thinking of Meroë, I knew; but I thought of Terre d'Ange. "Home," I agreed fervently. "Yes, my lord Tifari. Let us go home."

As always, 'twas a matter more easily said than done. All our goods—our mounts, our donkeys, our gear and supplies—had been seized by Sabaean forces when they took the Jebeans. It was a matter of a day to arrange for their return, effected by shamefaced soldiers under the direction of Eshkol ben Avidan. And it was another day before everything could be inspected, the horses decreed sound, waterskins tight and our stores sufficient.

In Tisaar, the mood was uncertain, fraught with optimism and fear. With my aid as translator, Tifari Amu spoke before the Sanhedrin of Elders, assuring them that he bore no ill-will for the misunderstanding, giving them cordial greetings on behalf of Ras Lijasu of Meroë, grandson of Queen Zanadakhete. The Sanhedrin heard him out, eyeing me all the while.

And he spoke too, he and Bizan, to the Council of Women that Yevuneh had assembled, and that was a merrier affair, for Bizan flirted incorrigibly with the unwed women in terms that required little translation.

Whatever else would transpire in the days to come, Saba would not be the same. The Covenant of Wisdom had been reclaimed, and it had given a measure of power back unto the hands of Sabaean women. I did not think they would hold it lightly. How they would balance this new-found will with the longstanding authority of the Sanhedrin, I did not know, but if there was to be trade with Jebe-Barkal, the Council of Women meant to share in the decision.

"You say they are no enemies, these Jebeans?" Semira asked me, frowning.

"I say Meroë has long forgotten its quarrel with Saba, mother," I said carefully. "As for the rest, it is for your two countries to determine."

"It would be nice," she mused, "to have needles made of this *steel*. Yes, that would be nice, indeed."

We had needles among our stores; I sent Imri running to rummage in my packs. Elua knows I had no use for them. I am as handy with a needle and thread as a camel, and mayhap less so. "My lady Semira," I said, presenting three needles of varying sizes to her. "Pray, accept them with my gratitude."

"My!" She held them with wrinkled fingertips, turning them this way and that to catch the light. Fine-wrought steel winked. I had to blink to keep from seeing the Name of God refracted in the splinters of light. Semira tested the strength of one. "Well-made indeed. These will pierce strong cotton without bending. Thank you, child. This is a generous gift."

"No." I shook my head. "It is naught, to what you have given us."

"And what is that?" The old woman gave a secretive smile. "A chance? We make our own chances, child. We had the wisdom to allow Adonai to speak for Himself. Pray we remember this lesson. You have given us a sign, in turn, and an omen." She held up the needles. "Not swords to cleave, nor armor to turn a blade, nor plows to harrow, but a needle to stitch and bind. Let this mark the beginning of Saba's return to the greater world."

"Elua grant it is so," I murmured.

"Elua!" she said, and laughed. "We may speak more of this Elua one day, yes, and Yeshua ben Yosef, whom the Children of Yisra-el have named the Mashiach. For myself, I think this earth-born Elua who coaxes the angels from Adonai's heaven sounds the more interesting of the two, but perhaps that is blasphemy. I do not know. Perhaps it is a question for my children's children's grandchildren to settle." Semira nudged me. "Do us a kindness, child. If there is trade, if there be routes open to Saba in your lifetime, send us word of how the tale ends."

"The tale?" I asked, confused. "Forgive me, my lady . . ."

"The tale! Your tale, the boy on the island, cursed to live forever."

"Hyacinthe," I said, taking a deep breath.

"Even so. The Prince of Travellers!" Semira said, remembering. "I wept to hear it. It was a true story, was it not?"

"Yes," I said. "It was."

"And you have yet to face the angel Rahab?" she asked shrewdly.

The Sacred Name surged against my tongue. I kept my mouth shut and nodded, afraid.

"Ah, well." She patted my cheek. "We will pray for you, and tell your story."

Although I had not expected him to, Hanoch ben Hadad came to his sister's house before we departed. It was an uncomfortable meeting. We sat across from one another at Yevuneh's table, and Joscelin positioned himself behind my chair, his bandaged hands resting lightly on his daggers. There was no more talk of his going unarmed in the city. Hanoch stared at me with bloodshot eyes. These last days had not been easy on him. I waited him out with a growing sense of pity.

When he broke the silence, his voice was stiff. "I acted in accordance with our law."

I nodded. "That is understood, my lord captain."

"You had no right to do what you did." Anger surged in him, and bewildered frustration. "No right!"

"I know," I said gently. "But I had great need."

He looked away, and there were tears in his eyes. "Do you know how many years we have wasted? How long we have needlessly hidden?"

"Yes." I swallowed. "Hanoch . . ."

Hanoch shook his head. "Adonai's mercy is revealed to us, yet I . . . I have set myself against His will because of you," he said. "I do not understand."

To that, I had no answer, or none he would hear. "I am sorry."

After a moment he rose, issuing a rigid bow. His bronze armor gleamed softly in Yevuneh's lamplit kitchen. "May your journey be swift and your gods protect you," he said tonelessly. "You spoke the truth, lady. I will be glad to see you go."

"Name of Elua!" Joscelin muttered when he had left. "If that was an apology, it was sorely lacking."

"No." Remembering the pattern I had seen in the temple, I knew of a surety that if Hanoch had not sought to prevent us, if I had not been so filled with fear on Imriel's behalf, that I would never have found the place within myself where the self was not. Even in their mercy, gods can be cruel. Hanoch had done what he believed right; no more, no less. "Ah, poor man! He has cause to be bitter."

"I'd spare him more sympathy if I'd not seen his sword at your throat," Joscelin said dryly, taking a seat at the table. "But he's right about one thing. It's time we were gone."

Thus passed our final days in Tisaar, the city beside the Lake of Tears in fabled Saba. On the morrow, the Council of Women gathered at the gates of the city to bid us farewell. Gifts of parting were exchanged on both sides and Yevuneh gathered Imriel in one last embrace, weeping openly. He returned her embrace without fear, pressing his cheek against hers, and despite the sorrow of parting, I was gladdened to see it.

Then it was done, and we turned our faces toward home. We passed through the gate, and in a short time, the city of Tisaar lay behind us. If not for the incessant thunder in my head, our departure was little changed from our arrival, save that it was Eshkol ben Avidan and a company of men who escorted us to the Great Falls, and they were as pleasant as Hanoch had been surly. It seemed a miracle that we were all together, and no lives had been lost.

For my part, I was struggling still to learn to live with the Name of God.

Betimes it was quiescent, a slumbering seed lodged in my brain, and I could nearly forget I carried it. And then something would set it off—the fecund odor of soil, a bird on the wing, or the Falls; Blessed Elua, the Falls! And then it would fill me like the sound of trumpets and I would be lost in reverie, staring, witnessing life as if it were created anew on the instant, over and over. When we reached the Great Falls, I stood on the verge of the opposite cliff gazing down into the roaring, mist-wreathed abyss for ages, watching tons of water moving without cease, seeing the Name written in patterns on the boiling foam.

"Phèdre."

It was Imriel who drew me back, and I saw in his twilight-blue eyes that he was afraid. And then I tried harder to keep the Name from filling me wholly, but it was not easy.

A half-day's ride past the Falls, we said farewell to Eshkol and his men. He wept upon leaving us, too. I watched the tears fill his eyes and overflow his lower lids, trickling like drops of rain on his mahogany cheeks, whispering the Name of God in the path they traced. "You have given me a dream," he said. "I am not sure of what, but it is a *dream*. I never had one before."

"You will know," I said, certain. It was written in the geometry of his bones, the sharp jut of his cheeks and his eloquent hands. It sounded in his voice, and the passion that threaded it. "Whatever Saba is to become, you will help shape it with courage and wisdom."

"I pray it is so," he said, bowing. "Adonai guide you."

"And you," I said, watching them go. "And you."

Mile by slow mile, we began retracing our steps.

It took me sometimes in the highlands, atop the vast mountain peaks where the green carpet of forest spread below us. I watched hawks and buzzards circling over the valleys and grew dizzy at their grace, the gyres etched by their sharp-tilting wings. If the Jebeans had thought I was god-touched before, they were sure of it now; half-mad and blessed with it, but apt to endanger myself. I wasn't, I don't think. I cannot be sure. Semira had spoken truly; it was a mighty thing to bear.

The Yeshuite mystic Eleazar ben Enokh had claimed the Name of God was the first Word spoken, the Word that brought all creation into being. Whether or not it is true, I do not know; no two nations hold the same story as to how it came to pass. We are Elua's children, the last-born, and we took the world as we found it. But I know there was great power in that Name, and when it blazed in my thoughts, I beheld the world through different eyes.

Imriel didn't like it.

I learned why, a week into our journey.

It was the campfire that struck me that night, the glowing orange caverns of embers beneath the stacked branches, the flames leaping above and sparks ascending in a column into the black, black sky. How long did I watch it, marveling? A few seconds, I thought, though I daresay it was a good deal longer, until I realized my arm was being shaken.

"Phèdre!"

"Yes?" I inquired. "I'm sorry, I was thinking."

Imriel shook his head and looked away. "You weren't," he muttered.

"Imri." I waited until he looked back at me. "I'm trying. It's like having someone shout in your ear, can you understand? When it happens, it's all I can hear. I didn't know it would be like this, or I would have told you. But there was no one to ask and no way of knowing."

"You look like you did in Daršanga," he said, half under his breath.

"*What?*"

"You look like you did in Daršanga!" His voice rose, scared and defiant. "When you sat with the Mahrkagir, in the festal hall, your face—you looked the same, exactly the same!"

"Really?" I asked Joscelin.

He raised his eyebrows and shrugged.

It made me laugh. Elua knows why, but it did, and once I had started, I was hard-put to stop. All the absurdity of our long journey, the immensity of our task, the chaos that followed in our wake, the endless variations of the pattern I seemed destined to follow; it all came upon me at once. "Ah, Elua!" I gasped, wiping my eyes. "Well, gods are like patrons, it seems. The shape of their desire may vary, but the manner of possession all comes to the same in the end!"

Imriel regarded my mirth with apprehension.

"She's fine," Joscelin told him.

He looked doubtful.

"Oh, Imri." With difficulty, I managed to gather my composure. "It's nothing like Daršanga, I promise you. Listen, and I'll tell you what happened."

I told them both, then, what had happened after I had entered the temple on Kapporeth, and it seemed my laughter had freed my voice to speak. I told them the furnishings were those described in the ancient writings of the Tanakh, and how the priest offered incense, then led me into the inner sanctum. And I told them of the Ark of Broken Tablets, and the cherubim atop it with faces like those of Elua's Companions. I told how the priest and I had lifted the lid, and the silent rubble had formed a Name I could not read.

And I told them how the tongueless priest had spoken it, and what had befallen me.

They listened, the both of them, and Imriel was wide-eyed as any child hearing a tale of wonder, no longer fearful. What Joscelin thought, I could not say.

"Do I really look like I did with the Mahrkagir?" I asked him later that night, lying against him in the tent with our cots pushed together.

"Mm-hmm." He was half-asleep, his arms around me. "And like you did at the bathing-pool, after I caught that fish."

"Where we made love?" I propped myself up on one elbow to look at him.

"Yes." His eyes opened in the dim light, amused. "And when that arrow grazed you and Imri put snakeroot on the wound, and in Nineveh, when you informed me we had to go into Drujan. Phèdre, I'm used to it. Daršanga was different, but this . . . your wandering around with the Name of God in your head is just one more damned thing to get used to."

"Am I that hard to live with?" I asked.

"Yes." His arms tightened around me. "But it's worth it."

Matters might have fallen out differently that night if Imriel had not been asleep in the tent with us; as it was, it merely made me think— and suggest to Imri with no especial tact that he might enjoy bunking with Bizan or Nkuku the following night, which he did with a good will, for any display of affection between Joscelin and I gladdened him. I may say that we made good use of the time, and I was well content with it. And whether it was the purgative effect of laughter, relating the story or our lovemaking, I cannot say, but the insistent presence of the Sacred Name grew easier to bear in the days that followed.

Like as not, though, it was the rains.

They began two days after our conversation.

After our travels in Khebbel-im-Akkad, I thought I knew somewhat of rain. I was mistaken. The rains that fall in Jebe-Barkal are like naught else, and no one travels in them. We did, though. If I had not seen that landscape once already, I would be hard pressed to describe it, for more often than not, it was a solid veil of rain through which we journeyed. We rode where we could, and walked where we could not, leading our horses through treacherous gullies and over rain-loosened scree. In the plains, we plodded along the banks of a rain-swollen Tabara River, our heads lowered, water running off us in sheets.

In the early part of the day, the rains would cease for a time.

That was when the flies came.

Blood-flies, Kaneka had called them; I remembered that, now. They were black and vicious and their sting hurt like fury. Our animals were half-maddened by them, and we humans were scarce immune. It got so one welcomed the rains. In the evenings, the rain and smoke kept them at bay, when we could muster a fire. Betimes the firewood was so sodden, not even Bizan could coax a flame. We all took to carrying tinder wrapped in oilcloth.

"We can make camp, lady, and wait out the rains," Tifari Amu said to me after five days of misery. "In the highlands, it is not so bad. We can build shelters that will last, and there is easy game."

"How long?" I asked him.

He shrugged. "Three months, perhaps."

It would be winter by the time we reached Menekhet, and too late for any ships. I gazed at Imriel, shrouded in a burnoose; Joscelin, his shoulders hunched against the downpour. Our bearers cursed and pleaded with the donkeys, whose short legs sunk deep in the mire. "What do you say, Tifari?"

"That only madmen travel in the rainy season." He regarded the straggling line of our company. "Madmen, and us. You ask me? I want to go home, lady. If you have the heart for it, I say we press onward."

"Onward it is," I said, thinking, *home*.

ÉIGHTY

IT WAS a miserable journey.

There are no words to describe it. We took to travelling in the morning hours, when the rains had ceased. Once the sun rose, it heated the muddy earth until it was like journeying through a steam-bath, thick and swampy, the air filled with the green reek of rotting vegetation. It was impossible to keep anything dry. Our stores of grain rotted and sprouted in the sack.

We lived, for the most part, on game.

And when we could not get it fresh, we went hungry, for most of what we carried had spoiled. Mercifully, there was water in abundance, and lush grass for our mounts. Would that we could have eaten the same! But Tifari and Bizan brought down game enough between them to fill our bellies two days out of three, and where we followed the river, Joscelin was able to fish. The fish, at least, didn't mind the rains.

Flies continued to plague us, and illness. Yedo, one of the bearers, caught a fever that laid us up for three days. At its worst, he raved incoherently, and his brow, when I felt it, was dry and burning for all the moisture about us. Willow bark might have helped, had we any, but we didn't. I sat with him through the night, sponging his brow, remembering Ismene, the Hellene girl who had died after we left Daršanga.

Ismene died. Yedo lived, the fever breaking before dawn, leaving him wrung-out and sweating freely in the damp air. Who can say why?

And then we broke camp once more, and slogged onward, treading through the sucking mire, making our slow way toward Meroë. The saddles chafed our horses and their proud Umaiyyati heads hung low, sodden manes plastered on drenched hides. It went no better for the donkeys, bearing heavy packs. We treated the sores with powdered sulphur, which turned to a damp paste in the humid air. It didn't help, much. Nothing did. Where there were sores, the blood-flies laid eggs at night. Imriel and I grew deft at picking them out, our fingers smaller than the rest.

"You could have been at court," I reminded him. "Eating poached quails' eggs and sugared violets from a silver platter."

He scowled at me from beneath his dripping burnoose. "I would rather be *here*."

To his credit, Imriel never complained—and he kept up with our company, his boy's hands grown adept at handling the reins of his gelding. The frailty of Daršanga's ravages had concealed a wiry strength and he had, Elua be thanked, a strong constitution. While the rest of us coughed, itched, ached and stung, beset by flies and agues and thorns, Imri remained hale. The worst injury he took was a fierce sunburn from riding bareheaded in the clear morning hours, his sodden burnoose hung from his saddle to dry.

I may say, once again, that without Tifari Amu and the others, we would have been hopelessly lost a dozen times over, wandering the highlands to catch sight of the river where it cut, deep and rushing, through gorges. Despite my best efforts to protect it, Raj Lijasu's map got soaked in the omnipresent rains, the ink running until the markings were blurred and unreadable. In the mountains, Tifari took the lead; in the plains, it was Bizan. And the bearers—Nkuku, Yedo, Bomani and Najja—contributed in no small part.

In this manner did we make our way north across Jebe-Barkal, mile by weary mile. We saw no other human life, which was as well, for our passage-tokens from Meroë were battered and mudcaked and wholly unrecognizable. We saw lions, at a distance, and my heart leapt at the sight. It was in the early morning, across the rain-washed plains, sun-gilded steam rising in the dawning heat of day. They'd made a kill, or found one—lions, Bizan told us, were nothing loathe to scavenge—and surrounded it, five females and a single male.

"Look," he said, pointing across the broad expanse of the river.

We drew our mounts to watch them worry an antelope's carcass, safe on the far side of the Tabara. I marked the awesome power of them, how muscles surged beneath their tawny hides. The syllables of the Name of God tolled within my mind, enumerating them in every part. One of the females lifted her bloodstained muzzle, gazing at us. The male padded to the river's edge, pacing back and forth, shaking his massive mane.

No wonder, I thought, meeting his golden stare across the waters. Ah, Elua, no wonder so many have seen the face of god in such a beast!

"They are lazy," Nkuku offered, grinning. "In his heart of hearts, he is glad we are on the other side of the river. It is the women who do the work, yes?"

After that, the rains began again and we spoke no more, trudging through the endless mud and clambering once more into the green mountains, following the river's gorge. Tifari's mount contracted thrush, a disease of the vulnerable frog of the hoof, and we were laid up a day while Najja brewed a foul poultice of roots he swore would draw out the infection. Our tents leaked, the blood-flies came in clouds and tempers grew surly. What else is there to say? It was a miserable journey.

And like all journeys, it had an end.

I failed to recognize the spreading eucalyptus trees as we descended from the highlands onto another expanse of plains. It was afternoon, and raining, clouds piled in thunderheads as far as the eye could see. We made camp that night and dined on strips of half-smoked gazelle meat from a kill two days old.

And on the morrow, we reached a place where a solidly built village of mud huts stood alongside the swollen Tabara River.

"Debeho," said Tifari Amu, smiling faintly.

It goes without saying that our welcome was a joyous one.

It was a damp one, to be sure; no place is immune from the rains in Jebe-Barkal. But the village turned out as if we were its own. Shoanete herself came out to meet us, hobbling on her sticks. And Kaneka! She looked like a veritable queen, with water streaming down her Akkadian finery. I flung both arms around her, glad of her tall strength, glad beyond words to see her.

"Ah, little one." Her voice rumbled in her chest, and she held me off to look at me. "You found it, didn't you?"

"Yes." I wanted to laugh and cry at once. "I did."

"Well." Her teeth gleamed in a smile as one hand rose to clasp the leather pouch at her throat. "My dice always speak true. I knew you were special. You will have stories to tell my grandmother, yes? I have a vested interest in such matters, now."

"We have stories, Fedabin." I gripped her forearms, smiling. "Oh, yes, you may be sure of it! We have stories."

And we told them, all that day and night, while the folk of Debeho feasted us and the rains drummed on the tight-woven thatch of their central hall, an unwalled building plastered with sun-baked mud. Beneath the roof, it was nearly dry. While communal dishes of spicy stews passed with spongy bread for the dipping, we ate with our fingers and told of the Melehakim, and what had passed in the land of Saba. And old Shoanete listened and nodded her head in approval, watching from the corner of her yellowed eye as Tifari Amu sat modestly beside her tall granddaughter. I made much of his bravery. Kaneka snorted, appearing to be unimpressed, but I saw how she eyed him consideringly.

Love as thou wilt, I whispered, the Name of God throbbing on my tongue.

Imriel resumed old friendships with ease, greeting his playmates in the village. He was half-clad like the rest of them before the night was over, stripped to his breeches and spatchcocked in color, with his face and arms tanned by the sun—although he'd peeled like a snake while he healed, his sunburn had faded—and his torso milk-white. They darted in and out of the unwalled structure, splashing one another, playing some children's game of tag with the veils of water dripping from the eaves, the older taunting the younger, boys baiting the girls. And it was good—ah, Elua, it was good!—to see Imriel de la Courcel at child's play, shouting with laughter like any other boy his age.

"Would that it could remain thus," Joscelin murmured to me.

"I know," I said, leaning into his arm to kiss him. "I know, love."

Kaneka leaned over, hearing us. "He looks well, the boy," she said shrewdly. "Your company suits him, little one. Who would have thought it, when he spat in your face? I myself had wagered he would not withstand the next round of the Mahrkagir's attention."

"You never told me that, Fedabin," I said, stiffening.

She laughed and patted my cheek. "Do not be so quick to anger! Who could have guessed what you were, in Daršanga? The omens were there, but I had lost the will to read them." She felt at Joscelin's arm, then, openly admiring. "And you, lord Joscelin. A leopard among wolves. You have healed well."

"Well enough, my lady Kaneka." He smiled quietly. "Not as before, but well enough to serve."

"Then he serves you well enough, little one?" Kaneka nudged me, lest her meaning be lost. D'Angelines are more subtle in our banter. Her grandmother Shoanete cackled with laughter, leaning over her sticks. "You have no complaints?"

I flushed a bright red. "No complaints, Fedabin."

"Good." Kaneka settled back onto her stool, nodding to herself.

"Good. It is well done, then. The story may end happily after all. It is important, for such a tale."

"There is hope," I said. "For us. Where there is life, there is hope. But the others—they paid the price of our hope. Of our lives."

"Drucilla," Kaneka murmured. "Jolanta, Nazneen, Erich, Rushad . . . yes, and others, so many others. Do not fear, little one. I have not forgotten. I will tell their stories too, and their sacrifices will be remembered. The zenana of Daršanga will live in my stories, in all its desperate courage. And it may be, as Amon-Re wills, that their tales will ensure such a thing may never come to pass in Jebe-Barkal. But it is important, little one, that hope endures. For when it fails—thus are the gates of despair opened, and one such as Lord Death enters the world. Do you understand?"

"Yes," I said, meeting her eyes. "Yes, Fedabin. I understand."

We spent several days in Debeho, and I was as loathe to leave then as I had been before. It may sound foolish, but there are few places I have been happier. What appeared to be mud and squalor to the untrained eye was a community rich in kindness, possessed of a wealth of knowledge. They treated us generously, giving unstintingly of what they had, and we left Debeho with clean, dry garments, our tents patched and oiled, our stores replenished with unperishable goods and our mounts well tended.

And in all these exchanges, I beheld the Name of God, writ in unknowable letters.

"It is the last parting," Kaneka said, embracing me before we left. "I knew you would return. Ah, take care, take care, little one! I will miss you."

"And I, you." I smiled at her. "Be well, Kaneka." I glanced toward our caravan, where Tifari Amu watched our farewell with a hunter's tender patience. "And if any of our number *do* return, I pray you treat them gently."

Kaneka laughed. "Will you never be done meddling?"

"Probably not," I admitted.

"Ah, well." She eyed Tifari sidelong, considering. "If the Ras' highlander guide wished to return, he would not be unwelcome in Debeho. Does that satisfy you, little one?"

"Yes," I said, grinning. "It does."

We left quickly, then, before the rains could begin, before the sorrow could take root. It is hard, always saying farewell. What stories would Kaneka tell as she grew old? I might never know, for Debeho was far away, and Kaneka's stories would likely never be written, but only passed from mouth to ear.

Mayhap, one day, they would filter to Terre d'Ange, carried on some travelling poet's lips, woven of truth and imagination, as fabulous as a Mendacant's cloak, romances and adventures and tragedies stitched through with a gleaming strand of hope, reminding listeners to love truly, to honor the dead, to uphold the covenant of wisdom and to never, even in darkest hours, surrender to despair.

I hoped it might be so.

Éighty-One

WE JOURNEYED to Meroë.

The balance of the journey does not bear telling, for it was uneventful, unless incessant rain may be considered an event. Tifari Amu was glad of heart, for I had related Kaneka's words to him, and he pushed the pace as much as he dared. Nonetheless, it was a wet and arduous trek, and I would be happy when it had ended.

"Remember that," Joscelin commented, wringing out his rain-soaked *chamma*, "when we are in the desert."

By the time we reached Meroë, the rains had begun to ease. All along the flooded banks of the river, village farmers measured the waters and watched, waiting for their retreat. Once the waters had receded, they would plant cotton and millet. The sun shone brightly, longer each day, and the drenched earth steamed.

Meroë.

The city seemed almost like an old friend, after our long journey. Everything I saw—the mighty burial pyramids, the traders' caravans with their long strings of camels, the inner walls of the royal palace, the embroidered capes of the soldiers, even the oliphaunts, whose platter-sized feet lifted from the mud with great sucking sounds—appeared familiar and welcome. Tifari Amu escorted us to the very hotel in which we had first stayed, and bartered with the hotel-keeper to give us the finest suite of rooms.

"Rest here," he said, "and avail yourself of all amenities. I must report to Ras Lijasu, but he will doubtless wish to see you on the morrow."

It was strange, after so long in company, to part; yet another farewell! Tifari and Bizan, we would likely see again, but not the bearers, who would take the Ras' payment and return to their families. I kissed them all in parting, overwhelmed with emotion. Joscelin withdrew the much-shortened chain of trader's coin he wore beneath his *chamma* and gave a gold link to each.

"It is not much," he apologized in his faltering Jeb'ez, "but only for thanks."

The quietest of the bearers, Bomani, tried to give it back. "It is not necessary, lord," he said. "The Ras has paid us. And you have far to go."

"It is necessary," Joscelin said firmly.

"*I* will keep mine," Nkuku said, clapping Joscelin on the back, "and remember the man who would dance with the rhinoceros! No wonder I fell into the thorns!"

There were a good many more jests before we parted—Nkuku had some sly advice for me having to do with snakes and bathing-pools—but in time, they left. And each one made a point of bidding Imriel farewell, treating him as a near-equal.

Well, and why not, I thought; he has earned it.

Our rooms were spacious and pleasant and *dry*. I cannot convey what luxury that was, to one who had not spent countless days waterlogged and sodden. For the first time in my life, I was almost loathe to visit the baths, reveling in the absence of water against my skin. After I did, I was glad of it, and gladder still to be wrapped in a thick cotton robe, clean and blessedly dry.

Most of our clothing, alas, was ruined, save for the peasant garb we had been given in Debeho. The Lugal's gifts; the celadon riding-attire that Favrielle nó Eglantine had designed; the rose-silk gown with the crystal beading—all spoiled, the fabric rotted with moisture. I beheld it with dismay.

"It's only clothing," Joscelin said, shrugging. "You hold the Name of God, Phèdre. Does it matter what you wear?"

A sharp retort was forming on my tongue when a knock came at the door, proving to be a considerable train of servants sent on behalf of Ras Lijasu, who had received word of our return. And they brought with them an array of gifts—sweetmeats, scented oils, sundry fruits, and bolts of fine cloth, with a deferential tailor to take our measurements.

"Yes," I answered him when they had gone. "In Meroë, it matters."

We dined well that night and slept in a proper bed in clean, dry sheets that had been scented with orange-blossom, with a solid roof over our heads to keep out the rains when they began, falling as relentlessly over the city as they had the plains and mountains.

And I slept like the dead until Imriel's nightmare roused me.

It was different, this time; not the inhuman, rending screams of before, but a choked, fearful moaning. "I'll go," I murmured to Joscelin, clambering out of our bed and struggling into my bathing-robe. I made my way to the smaller room we'd allotted Imriel, stumbling over a footstool in the dark. Faint starlight filtered through the unshuttered windows. He was thrashing, entwined in the bedclothes. I perched on the edge of his pallet, keeping my voice gentle. "Imri. Imri, it's all right. It's just a nightmare."

He awoke when I touched him, breathing hard and rubbing his face. "I was dreaming."

"I know." I smoothed his tangled hair and settled myself, tucking one leg beneath me. "Daršanga?"

He nodded. "From before."

I tugged the sheets loose where they'd enwrapped him. "Before what?"

"Before you came." His face was ghostly in the starlight.

"Ah." I got the sheets unwound. Imriel's gaze was fixed on me, his eyes dark as holes in his pallid face. "It's over, you know. It will never happen again."

"I know." He swallowed. "He did things to me."

My hands stilled. "The Mahrkagir."

Imri nodded.

"Do you want to tell me?"

He nodded again, his expression rigid with fear.

"All right," I said gently, my heart an agony within me. "Tell me."

He did.

And I listened as he told me, stroking his brow when his voice faltered, closing my eyes in pain when he continued. If the Mahrkagir had spared him the worst, still, he had been ingenious in his torments, and there are sins against the spirit more dire than those against the flesh. Many of the punishments he described, I have known at the hands of other patrons, and called it pleasure—but ah, Elua! It was Imriel it happened to; *Imri!* A boy, a child of ten, enslaved, and terrified. So I listened, while silent tears stung my eyes. All I feared in a child of my own blood, every pain and humiliation I knew I could bear to endure, but not to behold—it had already befallen him.

At last, he finished.

"Imriel." I cupped his face in my hands, and he watched me fearfully. "It's not your fault, do you understand? None of it. What the Mahrkagir did to you was done against your will. It is a grave wrong, and you were not to blame."

"But he did worse things to others." He looked sick. "Because of me. He told me so."

"No." I shook my head. "He lied, Imri; ill words. He said it only to hurt you."

"There were things he made me do." His voice was faint. "He said if I didn't . . ." He swallowed. "He made me plead for their lives. He promised to spare them, even though he didn't. And I did. I did what he told me."

"And *lived*," I said fiercely. "Never be ashamed of that! Kaneka is right, where there is life, there is hope. You were right, to survive. You did right, Imri. You tried to protect others. It's not your fault he lied. The Mahrkagir did wrong. And he has paid the price of it."

"You killed him." It was not a question, not quite.

"Yes." I nodded. "Blessed Elua set his life in my hand, and I took it. He is dead, Imri. No one will ever hurt you like that again."

"Do you promise it?"

I looked into his haunted eyes and thought about Anafiel Delaunay's vow, that he had sworn to Prince Rolande so many years ago, about Joscelin's vow, and how it had shaped his life; impossible vows, warping the fates of all around them. And I thought about Imriel de la Courcel, who hated for anyone to see him cry, for whom the night held such terrors. In the broad light of day, he would never ask such a thing. "I do," I said, kissing his damp brow. "I promise it."

Imriel sighed and I felt some of the fear leave him. I held him close.

"Imri," I said to him. He lifted his head sleepily from my breast to gaze at me with his mother's eyes. "Imri, if you hadn't acted as you did, on Kapporeth, things would have gone very differently. I want you to know that."

He smiled. It was his own smile. "I didn't want them to hurt you."

"So I gathered." I raised my eyebrows. "Mind, if you ever try the like again, I'll have Joscelin sit on you." It made him laugh. I kissed him again. "It was well done, love. It was a greater gift than I have ever received, and one I pray is never repeated. Now go to sleep, will you? We have to meet the Ras on the morrow."

He did sleep, soon enough, his breathing growing slow and even, his limbs going lax. I lay awake for a long time, gazing into the darkness and thinking. I meant to leave Imriel's bed for my own, but at some point, I passed unknowing from wakefulness into sleep, for the next thing I knew, it was morning and Joscelin was shaking me, Imriel standing behind him, wide-awake and grinning, no trace of the night's fears reflected in his expression.

"Phèdre," Joscelin said, looking amused. "You might want to get up. The tailor is back."

So it was that we were arrayed in Jebean finery when we were summoned back to the royal court of Meroë. For Joscelin and Imriel, that meant breeches and *chamma* of snow-white linen, short cloaks thrown over the top. Joscelin was impatient at it, finding it binding. I had no sympathy for him, for the manner of gown for Jebean women was a tight-wrapped dress worn off the shoulder and secured in place with gold pins, broad bands of color woven in intricate patterns at the borders.

Ras Lijasu, however, approved.

"Ah, lady!" he said, clapping his hands and beaming with delight. "What a pleasure, to see you arrayed in the manner of our people! Nathifa, does she not look lovely?"

"Yes, brother." The Ras' sister smiled at us. She looked much like him, with the same flawless ebony skin and round cheeks, only more solemn.

"My lord is generous," I said, curtsying.

"Oh, it is nothing, nothing. Muni, where are those gifts? Where have you got to?" The Ras looked around. "There you are! You shuffle like an old man, Muni. Come, let me have them." With great ceremony, he bowed and presented a sandalwood coffer to me, opening the lid to show it held six ivory bracelets and six gold, each worked with depictions of the flora and fauna of Jebe-Barkal. "These are from Grandmother, a token of her appreciation. Queen Zanadakhete has heard the report of my men, and she is pleased."

"They are very beautiful, my lord. Thank you," I said.

"Well, put them on! Nathifa, help her, would you? That is not just any ivory, dream-spirit. It is carved from the tusks of Old Mlima, the oliphaunt who bore my great-great-grandfather to war against the Tigrati insurrection. Muni, stop dawdling. Where is . . . ah yes, there." The Ras lifted a startling object from the cushion his grinning attendant proffered: a great collar made entire from a lion's mane. This he draped about Joscelin's shoulders, standing on his toes to reach. "There!" He beheld it with satisfaction. "A fit token for a mighty warrior. Tifari Amu told me how you stood against the Shamsun, and I have heard other stories come out of Khebbel-im-Akkad with you."

I looked at Joscelin and tried not to laugh as he executed a solemn Cassiline bow, his face framed in tawny fur.

"Very nice!" The Ras applauded. "Very good. And for the young lord . . ." He produced a belt and dagger-sheath worked with tooled gold. "Rhinoceros hide, my little man! It will never wear or rot. And see," he added, stretching out the length of the belt, "there is room to grow." He nodded approvingly as Imriel buckled it in place. "You will use that for many years, I think. Well, good, that's done! Come, sup with us, and tell us of Saba."

And we did, seated on cushions around low tables, dining on morsels of spiced chicken, melon and rolled balls of millet flavored with lemon and sesame, with honey-mead and citron-water in abundance. The servants were deft without being particularly deferential, and I had the impression everyone in the royal palace was quite fond of their young ruler. For all his chatter, Ras Lijasu listened attentively, and when he interrupted, his questions were perceptive.

"So change begins with the women, eh?" He glanced at his sister. "That won't surprise Grandmother, will it?"

"No." Nathifa's eyes gleamed merrily, making her resemblance to her brother even more pronounced. "Queen Zanadakhete was quite taken with the three of you. She wishes to know if you are of the opinion that the Sabaeans would welcome a trade delegation. She also wishes to know if the tall one will stay to join her honor guard. She thinks he would make a striking addition."

Joscelin coughed to cover his surprise, and looked at me to make sure he had understood the Jeb'ez correctly. When I nodded, amused, he inclined his head to Nathifa. "Tell the Queen, please, she does much honor to me, but I have duties to my own Queen."

Nathifa laughed. "I will tell her. What do you say of trade, my friends?"

We spoke of the matter at some length. Remembering the gift of needles I had made to Semira, I suggested that a modest delegation was the wisest course, lightly armed enough to constitute no military threat, bearing gifts of domestic and consumable goods such as were unattainable in Saba.

"It will whet their appetites," I said, "and open the doors to peaceable commerce."

"And they have goods in kind?" Ras Lijasu asked. "Such as are worth our while?"

I thought of how gold was held cheaply in Saba, of the abundance of natural resources. "Yes, my lord. Of a surety."

"And no steel." His handsome face took on a speculative cast. "Their army would be ill-equipped, against ours, if it came to it."

"My lord." My mouth had gone dry. I was conscious of my heart beating within my breast, of the Name of God sounding in the blood that throbbed in my veins. "Do you know the old stories of the Melehakim? How their mouths would fill with great cries on the battlefield that struck fear into the hearts of their enemies?"

The Ras nodded slowly.

"Then do not mistake Saba for easy prey."

He regarded me for a long time without speaking. "Tifari and Bizan said you were touched by the gods, lady dream-spirit. I will heed your warning. But remember it is Saba that took arms against Meroë so long ago. I merely think to protect my people."

"So did Khemosh the Accursed," his sister said tartly. "Do not fear, my friends. Queen Zanadakhete is wiser than her impulsive grandson. For so long as Saba is content to let the ancient quarrel rest, so is Jebe-Barkal. There will be no aggression."

"Ah!" Lijasu threw his hands in the air. "Must a man be reviled for thinking? I never proposed war, but only considered the outcome of it. Muni, fill my cup; I am beleaguered by beautiful women."

Thus the moment passed, and my heart beat easier within me. We spoke longer of Saba and other things, and the Ras invited us to remain in Meroë. When we demurred, he insisted on arranging our transport to Majibara. I was grateful for his offer, for in truth, our funds were running short and, too, we would be bereft of Kaneka's expertise in hiring a caravan. It was a pleasant day, all told. Before we left, Nathifa led us to the inner courtyard for a final audience with Queen Zanadak-hete.

The rains had begun, lighter than before. We knelt before the cur-tained alcove, while servants stood at the sides holding parasols of waxed cotton above us.

"Grandmother," Nathifa called. "The D'Angelines wish to give their thanks."

The curtains twitched and I beheld once more a sliver of face, a bright, dark eye peering. On my knees, I bowed low from the waist, hearing the gold and ivory bracelets clatter as I did. Imriel shifted his new belt-sheath as he bowed, and the ruff of Joscelin's lion's-mane collar brushed the moist tiles.

"Please accept our gratitude, your majesty," I said.

"You have done us a service," said the voice of Zanadakhete of Meroë. "Pray, do us another." One hand emerged from the curtains to beckon to Nathifa, who came forward and bowed, accepting a coffer like the one the Ras had given me, only finer. "My grandson tells me you return to your own land. Give this to your Queen, with my greetings. Tell her we would welcome an embassy in Meroë, if she wished to send one."

"I will do that, your majesty," I said, bowing again and taking the coffer.

"It is good. You may go, with my blessing." The curtains fell closed, concealing the veiled figure. We all bowed again, and rose to follow Nathifa. Behind us, I heard a soft voice murmur to an unseen attendant, "It is as I thought. The tall one looks well in a warrior's mane."

"So," Nathifa said to us within the royal palace. "Here are some old friends, to escort you to your lodgings." With a gesture, she indicated Tifari Amu and Bizan, both resplendent in their full soldiers' regalia. "You will want to have a care with that gift."

"What is it?" I asked.

She shrugged. "Look and see."

I opened the coffer and beheld a glittering necklace wrought of gold and gems. The pendant bore an image of the kneeling Isis, her winged arms outspread, a massive emerald between the prongs of the horns that crowned her.

Bizan let out a low whistle.

I closed the coffer. "You want us to carry *this* two thousand miles to Queen Ysandre?"

"From a Queen, fit for a Queen. Why not?" Nathifa smiled and touched my brow with one finger. "You are carrying something more valuable in here, are you not?"

"Yes." I held her gaze.

"This . . ." Nathifa tapped the coffer. "This is only rocks and metal, wrought in a pleasing form. If you can carry the other, this should be no trouble."

"We will try," I told her.

"I know," she said, and smiled again. "Do not fear for Saba, lady. My brother thinks like a man, but he can charm the birds from the sky when he chooses. We have kept the Covenant of Wisdom, here. We will see that it is his charm he wields, and not a sword."

"The gods grant it may be so," I said.

"It shall be," Nathifa promised.

Joscelin, the lion's mane tickling his nose, sneezed mightily.

ƎIGHTY-TWO

THAT EVENING, we said our farewells to Tifari and Bizan.

"Have a care with Kaneka," I said to our highland guide after embracing him. "She is a strong woman, with a strong will."

"I know." He favored me with one of his rare smiles. "It is what draws me to her."

"She is also very handy with an axe," I warned him.

He nodded. He was a handsome man, Tifari Amu, with his cinnamon skin and his dark, patient eyes. "I heard the story, my lady Phèdre. I listened to what was said, and to what was not. I understand a little bit of her courage. I hold it in all honor."

"Good," I said, gripping his upper arms. "I am glad of it."

Bizan made Imriel a gift of his fire-striking kit upon parting, a curved bit of iron and a chunk of flint shaped to fit one's hand, sealed in a watertight pouch with a compartment for tinder. "You were a good companion. You remember how I taught you to lay a fire?"

Imriel nodded, wide-eyed, clutching the pouch to him. "Thank you, Bizan."

"Here, it ties on your fine new belt, like so." Bizan suited actions to words, then ruffled Imriel's hair. Imri not only endured it, but flushed with pride. "There. A proper soldier of the Queen's Guard you'd make, boy."

They refused all gifts in kind, swearing the Ras' commission forbade it. I do not know if it was true, but it was courteously done. Bizan offered to facilitate the sale of our Umaiyyati mounts and the donkeys, his cousin being a horse-trader, and that offer I accepted with gratitude. I daresay he got his cut, but the price was far better than we would have gotten on our own.

Between Bizan's aid and Ras Lijasu's generosity, we were only another day in Meroë, making ready to depart. Once more, as so many times before, we packed our things, items of luxury going at the bottom of our trunks, items of necessity atop. I hid the coffer with Queen Zanadakhete's necklace at the very bottom of mine.

"What am I to do with this?" Joscelin complained, holding up the lion's-mane collar.

"You could wear it," I said, straight-faced. "The Jebeans think it becomes you."

"And you?" He eyed me.

"Truly?" I tilted my head to regard him. "Joscelin Verreuil, missing part of an ear or no, you are one of the most beautiful men I've ever seen. But you look a little foolish with a lion's mane about your neck."

It went into his trunk, rather to Imriel's chagrin.

We departed as we had arrived, crossing the suspension bridge on a long line of camels. Mek Gamal was our caravan-leader's name, and he was a taciturn man, reputed to be one of the best in the business. He took his charge from the Ras with great seriousness, and if he was not the most garrulous of companions, he was assuredly among the most competent.

Perched atop my swaying camel, I turned many times to watch Meroë fall behind us as we followed the Nahar River's course, until only the tips of the burial pyramids were visible. Another parting, another journey.

Another step toward home.

This time, we found the desert in blossom, following hard on the heels of the rains. And if there was anything stranger and more fantastic than that blighted landscape, it was seeing it bedecked with unexpected flowers. How could it be, I marveled, that anything could grow in such a place? And yet it did. On the outskirts, we encountered mimosa in full bloom, shrubs laden with yellow flowers, bright under the hot sun.

Even in the interior, there was life. In the shadow of a jutting basalt formation, we encountered melons growing in the desert, ripening on the vine with unimaginable speed. Mek Gamal called a halt, then, and we ate melons, their fruit faintly astringent, but blessedly moist. Following the Jebeans' lead, we spat the seeds back into the sand.

Truly, the rains had ceased, and at night, the stars were as bright and crowded as I remembered them. I knew them better, now. If no one fetched me to sleep, I would sit for hours, gazing at them, recalling the names Morit had painstakingly taught me. To this day, there are constellations I can name only in Habiru. Hour after hour, they wheeled through the sky in their slow dance. I watched them, and thought about the Name of God.

It was hot, yes; oven-hot, as searing as before. My mouth grew no less parched, my skin no less dry. The endless swaying of the camels was no more comfortable than before. But in the desert, one can observe the dance of the stars, the steady course of the sun across the sky, and the play of light as it crosses the desiccated land. The air was clear, so sharp it cut like a blade. It was in such a place, I thought, stripped to the bare bones of existence, that the Sacred Name was first spoken.

We reached the bitter well that marked the halfway point, and it seemed almost sudden.

I sat on a rock in the baking valley, watching the camels drink their fill, conscious of the heat but paying it scant heed. What a marvel it was, that creatures existed which could endure such conditions! How strange, that we humans needed salt to live, yet would die of its excess. Salt preserves flesh, and yet kills it, too. In saltwater are we nurtured in the womb, and salt runs in the red blood of our veins.

"Phèdre." Joscelin's voice was hoarse as he thrust the water-skin at me. "You need to drink."

I did, tasting the water flat and warm in my mouth, feeling it moisten my tissues, thinking how odd that it should sustain life, and yet death was necessary for us to carry it, the cured leather hide holding portable life within it. How intricate, the working of our world!

"Mek Gamal is waiting," Joscelin informed me. "And you're making Imriel worry."

I got back on my camel, then, and our journey resumed. We entered the sea of grey stone, where the wind had sculpted the landscape into fabulous formations. No winds blew this time, and the only sound for a hundred miles was the rattle of pebbles displaced by our camels' broad hoof-pads. No wonder the Habiru prophets had escaped into the desert to think! I did, on that journey. I thought about Ras Lijasu and his merry good nature, his readiness to consider war a possibility. Was it something intrinsic to mortal kind, that we must always think of killing one another? I prayed it was not so. I had seen too much of death, too much of cruelty.

And yet it is what we do, again and again. And I . . . I was complicit in it, for had I not brought word to Ysandre of the Skaldic invasion, so many years ago? Had I not travelled to Alba, beseeching them to war?

What is our purpose, if not to kill and die?

Love as thou wilt.

'Tis all well and good, if one is a god; not so easy for those of us of mortal kind. Would that there were only that in the world. Were it so, my lord Delaunay would still be alive, and I . . . Elua knows where I would be. Were love enough, if my mother and father could have lived upon it like Blessed Elua, would they have kept me? I hoped it were so.

But even Blessed Elua had his Companions. Where would he be, if Naamah had not given herself to the King of Persis for his freedom, had not laid down in the stews of Bhodistan with strangers so he might be fed? Where would he be, if Camael's sword had not afforded him protection? What of Terre d'Ange, without Azza's pride that staked our boundaries, without Shemhazai's cleverness, that built our cities? Where would we be, without Eisheth's healing skills, without Anael's husbandry? How could we atone, without Kushiel's mercy?

How would Elua have answered the One God, if Cassiel had not handed him his dagger?

We are all these things, I thought, while the sun blazed in the sky and the ochre sands reflected its heat. Pride, desire, compassion, cleverness, belligerence, fruitfulness, loyalty . . . and guilt. But above it all stands love. And if we desire to be more than human, that is the star by which we must set our sights.

It is all we can do to try. It is enough.

Such were the things I thought in the desert, and the journey passed quicker than I believed possible. It was only when we reached Majibara and the vast silences of open spaces gave way to the clamor of the marketplace and the babble of a half-dozen tongues, situated beside the broad expanse of the rain-swollen Nahar that I reckoned the cost of it, and knew myself to be exhausted and half-fevered with thirst, feeling gaunt, scorched to the bone and somehow purged by our desert crossing.

We had reached Menekhet.

"You worry even me, sometimes," Joscelin said to me that night as we lay abed at the inn, listening to distant music from the caravans. "I half thought you might wander off and leave us, if I didn't watch you."

"No." I wound a length of his hair about my finger. "I was thinking, that's all."

"Across a week's worth of desert?" He smiled a little. "About what?"

"Life," I said. "Death, war, love . . . the nature of humanity."

"Did you come to any conclusions?" he asked.

"No," I said, and lifted my head to kiss him. "None I didn't already know." And with that I told them to him, not in words, but in the language of the flesh, of lips and tongue and hands, of quickening breath and the leap of blood in the veins, the salt-slickness of desire. It is the same questions we ask of our existence, and the answer is always the same. The mystery lies not in the question nor the answer, but in the asking and answering themselves, over and over again, and the end is engendered in the beginning.

That much, I had learned.

We had scant difficulty in hiring a felucca to take us to Iskandria. The flood-tides were receding, and trade was brisk all up and down the Nahar. We spent a half-day in the harbor, hiring a vessel, a sturdy craft piloted by a good-natured Menekhetan sailor by the name of Inherit, who spoke a smattering of Jeb'ez and a few words of Hellene. It was nothing fancy, but it would suffice.

After so many farewells, it seemed almost strange to leave Majibara, where we knew no one and had no ties. Our leavetaking of Mek Gamal had been a businesslike affair, the caravan-leader owing allegiance only to Ras Lijasu, pleased at a crossing safely made, eager to strike a deal for a profitable return.

At dawn, we ventured to the harbor, paying bearers to carry our trunks and load them into the hold of the sturdy felucca. The rising sun turned the lake-sized harbor of the river to an expanse of hammered gold. We waited patient on the docks while Inherit offered prayers to the gods of Menekhet and most especially Sebek, the crocodile-god of the Nahar.

Once he had finished, he beckoned us aboard, smiling cheerfully. We situated ourselves about the vessel as he raised the lateen sail. On the docks, a pair of loitering sailors aided him, untying the lines and tossing them aboard. Down the river, the burgeoning green banks of tamarisk and papyrus awaited us.

We were on our way.

ÉIGHTY-THREE

OUR RETURN to Iskandria was swifter than our departure, for we travelled with the current and, although the Upper Nahar was calm, it flowed strongly after the rains. Inherit canted his sail hither and thither to catch the fitful breeze, but whether he succeeded or no, the steady current bore us onward. When the sail's belly did swell with wind, the felucca swooped like a swallow on the broad breast of the river, causing Imriel to shout with glee.

We passed the island temple of Houba, where I had offered a prayer to Isis.

We passed countless plantations, greening in the bright sun, dotted with Menekhetans working hurriedly to make the most of the growing season.

We passed crocodiles and hippopotami, and the many birds we had seen before. On that journey, Kaneka had taught us the names in Jeb'ez. This time, Inherit taught us in Menekhetan, pointing and naming as we went. Imriel played the game along with me, his facile mind quick to grasp new words; Joscelin merely rolled his eyes and took out his fishing gear, trailing a line in the water, catching little in the swiftness of our passage over the waters. In the evenings we made camp on the outskirts of villages, and traded with the villagers for our meals as we had done before.

It was after we had stopped to pay homage at the temple of Sebek—at Inherit's insistence, for I would gladly have foregone the pleasure a second time—that we realized how swiftly indeed this leg of our journey would come to an end.

"Phèdre." In the prow of the felucca, Joscelin set down his neatly wound fishing line. "What happens when we reach Iskandria?"

I glanced toward the stern, where Inherit was teaching Imriel to steer the vessel, both of them absorbed with the tiller. "We present ourselves to Ambassador de Penfars, I suppose. If we're not seized on arrival."

He raised his brows. "You think Ysandre's that angry?"

"No. I don't know. She'll have taken the betrayal harder, coming from the two of us." I thought about it. "We've broken no law in Menekhet. But certainly she would be within her rights to ask Pharaoh for the favor."

"And risk exposing Imriel?"

"Probably not," I conceded.

"I don't think so, either. So," he said. "If we're to be hauled back in disgrace, like as not a delegation awaits us at the embassy."

"Like as not." I looked at him. "I'm sorry."

Joscelin shrugged. "I made the decision first, Phèdre. Have you thought of what you'll say to Ysandre?"

"Yes," I said and swallowed hard.

"She owes you a boon," he said. "The Companion's Star?"

I nodded.

"Aught within her power and right to grant," Joscelin mused. "It is that, although she'll not like it, not one bit. 'Tis your decision to make, love. Is it worth it, to lose the goodwill of the Queen forever?"

I turned to watch Imriel; we both did. Under Inherit's guidance, he held the tiller with both hands, white-knuckled, eyes bright with excitement in his sun-tanned face. Catching sight of us, he grinned with pride.

"Yes," I said. "It's worth it."

In a scant handful of days, we reached the end of the broad, stately river to enter the myriad waterways south of the city. The vegetation was lusher than ever after the rains, the odor moist and rank. Here our course slowed and it took the better part of a day to navigate the swampy delta. The air was unmoving, the felucca's sail hanging slack. We drifted slowly on the sluggish current. Inherit used a long pole to facilitate our passage, humming cheerfully and pointing out black-headed ibis and egrets with their snowy crests, describing how they differed from their brethren further upstream.

"To the market wharf, Kyria?" he asked in a mix of Menekhetan and Hellene when we drew within sight of the city, clusters of palms bowing over the buildings. "You can hire a carriage there, but if you get out before we reach the wharf, there is no toll to pay."

"No," I said. "Take us to the wharf, Inherit."

He complied, poling briskly, then springing to attend the sail as a little breeze arose. I watched the city of Iskandria take shape around us, the familiar landmark of the great lighthouse visible at a distance, the wide, gracious streets and elegant buildings. It was gilded in the evening light, and I could smell the odors that had seemed so exotic upon our first arrival, the scent of oranges and strong spices in the air, and meat grilling for the evening meal.

The market wharf was a busy place, the canal laden with small craft; farmers selling the season's first produce, loading the remnants for departure; fishermen and hunters of waterfowl returning with their catch. There were few travellers such as ourselves, for most went by caravan or caught the larger barges at the port south of the city. We had to wait and jockey for position before we could secure a place and disembark. The tax-collector strolled over as Joscelin and Inherit unloaded our goods, paying us scant attention as he inspected our trunks.

"You speak Menekhetan?" he asked, holding up one of my Jebean gowns.

"A little, only," I said. "Hellene?"

"Do you take me for a farmer or a fisherman? Yes, I speak Hellene." He gave me a brusque nod. "Are these for trade, Kyria, or personal . . . *Serapis!*" The tax-collector's face turned pale as he regarded me for the first time.

"My lord?" I asked, puzzled.

He grabbed my wrist, leaning close. "Kyria, are you . . . *Nesmut's friend?*"

I drew back, seeing Imriel fetch Joscelin. "And if I am?"

"Forgive me." The tax-collector released my wrist and bowed, watching out of the corner of his eye as Joscelin approached, hands resting lightly on his dagger-hilts. "I have been charged with a message for you, Kyria. All of us have, who ward the passages of the city. 'A D'Angeline woman of surpassing beauty, dark of hair and fair of face, with a mark as red as hibiscus in her left eye.' "

"*Nesmut* said that?" I asked.

"No, Kyria." He shook his head. "That was only what I was told to ask. My orders come from Pharaoh."

"And what," I asked, "is Pharaoh's message?"

"He wants to see you," said the tax-collector. "Immediately."

Immediately proved to be a relative term; it took time to settle our accounts with Inherit, and it took time for Joscelin and me to argue the matter to our satisfaction, while Imriel sat on a trunk and watched. In the end, of course, it was a foregone conclusion; a request from Pharaoh in the city of Iskandria amounted to a command. The tax-collector sent word to the Palace of Pharaohs through discreet channels that "Nesmut's friend" had arrived; a covered carriage with a pair of royal guards arrived in short order.

All the while, we stood in plain sight in the marketplace, surrounded by curious denizens. In any other city, I daresay word of our arrival would have reached the D'Angeline embassy before we departed—but this was Iskandria, and those surrounding us were fishers, farmers and hunters, and commonfolk of the city. And Ambassador de Penfars had never bothered to court the Menekhetans, only those of Hellene lineage.

His loss, I thought, and hoped it was not ours.

Our goods were loaded into the carriage, and we ourselves embarked, sitting apprehensively with the curtains drawn.

"Phèdre?" Imriel's voice was worried. "Are we in trouble?"

I shook my head. "I don't think so, love. Ptolemy Dikaios is . . . well, not a friend, but an ally, of sorts. I don't think he would harm us. There's no profit in it."

"Likely he wishes to turn us over to Ambassador de Penfars himself," Joscelin said quietly. "If he lost stature for letting us slip through Iskandria before, this will restore it."

"Oh." Imriel continued to look worried. I didn't blame him.

At the gates, the Pharaoh's guard searched our things, taking considerable interest in the immense, bejeweled necklace at the bottom of my trunk.

"It is a gift," I told them. "From Queen Zanadakhete of Jebe-Barkal to her majesty Queen Ysandre de la Courcel of Terre d'Ange. And neither one, I daresay, would be pleased to find it gone astray in Pharaoh's palace."

"You will get your things back, Kyria," one of them replied. "Do not fear. Kyrios, your weapons, please."

Joscelin disarmed with reluctance, handing over his daggers and his sword. These the guardsmen took, and we were driven around the Palace to a side entrance, one I had entered before. Servants unloaded our trunks, and where they were taken, I could not say, for we were ushered to the self-same reception-chamber I had visited twice before. This time, not even the silent fan-bearers were present.

And here we were left.

For how long? Hours, it seemed. Outside the high windows, dusk fell and the shadows grew long and blue, thickening to darkness. Imriel took out the flint-striker that Bizan had given him and kindled the oil lamps. The frescoed walls leapt to life and glowed, depicting the deeds of the Ptolemaic Dynasty. A servant entered with a tray containing a pitcher of steeped hibiscus-water, set it on the table and departed without a word.

"What do you think?" Joscelin asked in a low voice.

"I think Ptolemy Dikaios is repaying us for forcing his hand," I replying, pouring a cup and tasting it. "If he wanted us dead, he'd have no need of poison."

"I meant the waiting."

I shrugged. "He is Pharaoh, Joscelin. We wait on his pleasure. He means us to know it."

It was another hour before Ptolemy Dikaios arrived, by which time we were tired and hungry. Four guards escorted him into the reception-chamber and waited while we made full obeisance, kneeling and bowing low, then standing with downcast eyes. Imriel followed Joscelin and me, lingering a half-step behind us. I could see the lamplight gleaming from the jewels that bedecked Pharaoh's robes. He waited until his guards had left to address us.

"I rather think we're beyond standing on ceremony, Phèdre nó Delaunay."

I looked up to meet his clever gaze. "As you will, my lord Pharaoh."

He walked over to the low table and smelled the pitcher. "What, no beer? I trust you were well fed, at least."

"No, my lord," I said, watching him. "We have not eaten."

Ptolemy Dikaios made a tsking sound. "My servants misunderstood. I beg your pardon. Well, it will have to be remedied later. Messire Verreuil, it is a pleasure to see you again."

"My lord." Joscelin gave his Cassiline bow.

"And you." Pharaoh turned to Imriel and made a courtly half-bow. "I trust I have the pleasure of meeting Prince Imriel de la Courcel?"

I am given to understand that her son stands third in line for the D'Angeline throne.

Imriel glanced uncertainly at me. I nodded. "My lord Pharaoh," he murmured in schoolboy Hellene, returning Pharaoh's bow.

"A beautiful boy," Ptolemy Dikaios said to me.

"Yes, my lord," I said politely. "My lord, if you will forgive me for being importunate, it is incumbent upon us to report to the household of Comte Raife Laniol, Ambassador de Penfars. Is it your intention to see us delivered there?"

"In gilded chains, perhaps?" Pharaoh chuckled at the notion. "Paraded through the streets of Iskandria, with the rescued D'Angeline Prince carried in a jeweled litter? Yes, that would look well for me, wouldn't it? And I daresay your ambassador would be glad of it. He feels you made a fool of him in more ways than one."

I felt myself blanch, but kept my voice steady. "It is Pharaoh's privilege. Is it his will?"

Ptolemy Dikaios rubbed his chin. "I've not decided. Somehow I suspect your Queen would not be as pleased, after the attempt on the boy's life in Nineveh. Doubtless she would prefer not to have his identity shouted throughout the city, especially given the large Akkadian presence and the fact that no ships are due to sail to Terre d'Ange until spring." He smiled at my expression. "Ah, now, I've my own informants in Khebbel-im-Akkad, my dear. You needn't look surprised."

"Ships can be obtained," I said. "My lord Pharaoh, if you will not deliver us to the embassy, I must ask you to let us go."

"To de Penfars?" He raised his brows. "He *will* clap you in chains, you know. He's of a mind that the Queen should charge you with treason for the abduction of a member of the Royal House."

"It was *my* decision—" Joscelin began, even as Imriel said hotly, "No one *abducted*—"

"Enough." Pharaoh raised one hand, jeweled rings gleaming. "It is not my affair to sit in judgement on your guilt."

"With all due respect, my lord," I said, "nor is it your place to detain us. We are D'Angeline citizens, and whatever else we have done, we have broken no Menekhetan law."

"Always thinking," he said with amusement, "always arguing, Phèdre nó Delaunay. Do you bargain with your own sovereign thusly?"

"No, my lord." I held his gaze. "But Ysandre de la Courcel does not play such games as you."

He laughed. "She might, if she ruled Menekhet and not Terre d'Ange. Those of us whose power rests precariously upon our wits learn to play them early. But you wrong me this time, Lady Phèdre. It is no game I play, but an act of kindness on behalf of an old, dear friend. And where you go when you leave my Palace is entirely up to you, although I might add that there is a very fine trade-ship sailing on the morrow for La Serenissima, and I happen to know there are berths open."

"My lord?"

Ptolemy Dikaios took a sealed letter from the folds of his robe. "The last time you were here, you gave to me letters I would deny receiving from your hand. This time, I have one such for you," he said, and tossed it onto the table.

I didn't need to see the seal. I knew the handwriting.

It was Melisande Shahrizai's.

ÉIGHTY-FOUR

"YOU WROTE to *Melisande?*" Joscelin's tone was outraged. "You didn't tell me *that!*"

"You didn't need to know," I murmured, reading the contents of the letter. Although the parchment was unscented, I swore I could smell her fragrance. The thought of it, combined with hunger and weariness, made me dizzy. And despite it all, her words set my mind to working.

Joscelin took a deep breath and clenched his jaw, mindful of Pharaoh's presence. "What does she want?" he asked, tight-lipped.

I passed him the letter. "To see Imriel."

Imri, looking pale, said nothing.

"Well." Joscelin scanned the few lines and tossed the letter back on the table, shaking his head. "Even if it were possible . . . Elua. But it's not, not with the two of us already standing to be accused of treason."

"No one knows we're here?" I asked Ptolemy Dikaios.

"No," he said. "Not unless your Ambassador de Penfars has had sense to place informants among the Menekhetans, which he has not."

"*Phèdre.*"

"Imri," I said, ignoring Joscelin. "I have an idea. And if it works . . . if it works, it will do a great service for Terre d'Ange. Are you willing to help me?"

Imriel nodded, tears in his eyes. "What do I have to do?"

"See your mother," I said gently. "That's all."

"Will it keep you and Joscelin from being accused of treason?" he asked.

"I don't know," I said. "But it might protect Queen Ysandre and your young cousins, her daughters, from an untimely death."

He swallowed. "I'll do it. Only because you ask."

Joscelin put his head in his hands. "Phèdre. What are you planning?"

"To strike a bargain with Melisande Shahrizai," I said, turning to Pharaoh. "My lord, I think we will be some hours discussing this. Do you grant us leave to go?"

Ptolemy Dikaios nodded at the door. "You will be escorted to quarters within the Palace and awakened at dawn. You will give your decision to the guard posted at your door, a trusted captain of mine. He will escort you to a covered carriage, containing your belongings. And there you will either be driven to the harbor or the D'Angeline embassy, according to your choice. If it is the latter, I will enjoy de Penfars' groveling thanks. If it is the former . . ."

"I understand," I said. "No word of it will ever leave these walls."

"Even so." The Pharaoh of Menekhet reached over to pat Imriel's cheek with his bejeweled hand. "Pity," he said. "I was hoping the young prince would owe me a favor for this, but it seems his gratitude lies elsewhere."

Imriel bared his teeth, eyes glittering with a fury I remembered from Daršanga.

"Imri," I murmured.

Pharaoh snatched his hand back. "Does he bite?" he inquired dryly.

"He might," I said. "His mother does. But I rather suspect you knew that already, my lord Pharaoh."

Thus our final audience with Ptolemy Dikaios, whose cunning made my skin prickle. We were escorted from his presence to generous quarters, wherein we found our trunks undisturbed and apologetic servants brought us a meal of cold bean-cakes and warmed-over lamb stew. And I had guessed aright, for Joscelin and I went sleepless throughout the night, arguing the matter in low voices while Imriel slept, fitful and restless. And all of the points Joscelin made were good and valid, foremost among them that we could easily be walking into a trap.

"We're not," I told him.

"How can you be sure?"

For that, I had no answer save one.

I have no right to see him, and no right to ask it of you. This I know. I can say only that I am willing to place myself in your debt for this, and swear in Kushiel's name that no harm will come to you, nor to him.

I knew Melisande Shahrizai.

Joscelin capitulated in the end, although he looked sick at it. "You know this is like to go unrewarded," he said. "If it even works."

"Yes," I said. "I know."

"Melisande doesn't have the power to threaten Ysandre's life." He sounded uncertain. "Not any more."

I raised my eyebrows. "She has enough to convince the Pharaoh of Menekhet to play messenger-boy, and Elua knows how many agents searching for Imriel before she summoned us. Do you remember what she said to Ysandre in La Serenissima?"

"Yes," Joscelin said. "I remember."

" 'I have always understood, if you have not, that we played a game,' " I said, quoting the words from memory. " 'Do you take my son, we become enemies. Believe me, your majesty, you do not want me as an enemy.' "

"I remember."

"He's third in line for the throne, Joscelin."

He glanced over at Imriel's sleeping form. "And you think you can keep him there. With a promise. From Melisande Shahrizai."

I nodded.

Joscelin sighed. "Tell me at least that this is some prompting of Kushiel's, or Blessed Elua, or the Name of God stirring within you."

"I wish I could," I whispered. "Oh, Joscelin! We're already up to our necks in trouble with Ysandre. As far as she knows, we might be dead in Jebe-Barkal right now, slain by bandits and Imriel with us. Will it really make it so much worse if we return by way of La Serenissima and not Iskandria? For better or for worse, Melisande loves her son, and that's the only cord that will bind her. We only have the chance to try it once."

"Why?" he asked. "Why only once, why now?"

I told him the card I meant to play.

He sighed and rubbed aching temples. "All right. All right. We may as well be hung for a cow as a calf at this point. Ah, Elua, like as not it will be faster, if we're not killed or abducted in the process. I hope Ricciardo Stregazza has kept our horses fit and ready for travel."

"You see?" I said. "We would have had to go to La Serenissima anyway."

One of the Palace slaves awoke us at dawn, and I gave word to the guard on duty outside our doors. He nodded impassively and strode away, returning in short order with porters to bear our belongings back to the covered carriage. No one in the Palace acknowledged our presence as we left. It was a strange feeling. We had to hurry to catch the ship, which was nearly ready to sail by the time we reached the harbor.

"La Serenissima?" one of the guards shouted to a sailor onboard.

"Aye!"

"Hold for three passengers!"

They waited while we were hustled aboard the ship, our trunks loaded. Joscelin snatched his weapons from the guard's hands, slinging his baldric over one shoulder and settling his belt about his waist.

"Come on, then, hurry," the ship's captain said in Caerdicci, hands on his hips. "We're out to catch the last of the autumn winds."

"Autumn," I murmured. "It's autumn?"

"Aye. Nearly winter." He eyed me strangely, as well he might, for I wore one of my Jebean gowns, pinned at the breast, with bracelets of ivory and gold encircling both wrists. I'd meant to have clothing made in Iskandria, or begged some of Juliette Laniol, the Ambassador's wife. "You're D'Angeline, my lady?"

"She is the Comtesse Phèdre nó Delaunay de Montrève of Terre d'Ange," Joscelin informed him, adjusting his baldric.

"Well, she's like to take a chill on the open sea in that attire," the captain said. He eyed me again. "Not that I'm like to complain. Stand by to weigh anchor!"

And with that, we were off.

ᴇ̆ɪɢʜᴛʏ-ꜰɪ̆ᴠᴇ

Iᴛ ᴛᴏᴏᴋ the last of our trader's coin to pay our passage aboard the ship, and the berth was small. By the time we were out of sight of land, the winds turned chilly, and I was forced to barter with one of the Serenissiman sailors for a thick cloak of coarse-spun wool. He'd have given it to me for a kiss—which Joscelin failed to note, being incapacitated with his customary battle with seasickness—but I paid him instead with the crystal beads salvaged from one of my ruined gowns, which was more than the cloak was worth.

At least aboard the ship there was a good deal of time to talk, for we had a good deal of talking to be done, and much of it to Imriel. Ultimately, my plan rested on his decision, and I meant to be certain it was wholly his.

"Why is Queen Ysandre so angry at you?" he wanted to know. "Because of me? But it was my fault—I followed you."

"I know," I said. "But we could have returned you. And that was our choice." And I explained to him once again the long history of his family, House Courcel, and the blood-quarrels that had divided it, and how Ysandre wished to make an end of it by bringing him into the fold. "It's a noble purpose, Imri. You'll like her. You'll like her very much. I do. There is no one I admire more."

He frowned, sitting cross-legged on deck in his Jebean breeches and *chamma*. It was still warm in the sun if one sat out of the wind. "Valère L'Envers wants me dead."

"It may be," I said. "But Nineveh is a long way from the City of Elua."

"Where her father is the Royal Commander."

"Yes," I said. "He is that."

There was nothing childish about Imriel's face as he considered it.

"House L'Envers will not be pleased with the Queen's decision. And they are powerful."

"Not more powerful than the Queen," I said.

He bent his head and fiddled with the pouch at his belt, his voice nearly inaudible. "You said you wouldn't leave me."

"Nor would I," I said gently, touching his arm. "Imri, listen to me. You have strong feelings for Joscelin and I because we found you in the worst of all possible places."

"No." Imriel lifted his head, his expression desperate and stubborn. "You didn't *find* me. You came and *got* me. When the Queen's men did not dare, when the Lugal of Khebbel-im-Akkad did not dare—*you* did! Other nobles foster their children, I know that! Why couldn't I be fostered with you and Joscelin? Because the Queen is angry? Because . . ." his voice faltered, ". . . because you don't want me? I've caused you trouble, I know—"

"*No!*" The word came out sharper and more harsh than I intended. I sighed and ran a hand through my wind-disheveled locks. I was making a mess of this conversation. "Imriel. We love you dearly, Joscelin and I both. If it were only that . . . Elua! We would adopt you in a heartbeat."

He looked at me with the terrible hunger only an abandoned child can muster.

So be it, then. I couldn't bear to leave him in anguish. But I had to be certain. "You remember how you hated me in Daršanga?" I asked him.

Imriel nodded.

"And how the way I was frightened you, after Saba?"

He nodded again.

"Well." I drew a shuddering breath. "It's part of who I am, Imri; of *what* I am. And that . . . that will never change, while I live. The manner of it may, but the nature remains the same. I am an *anguissette*, Kushiel's Chosen. Some of the worst things you have endured . . . those are things I have known freely, of my own will. Do you understand that?"

"Yes," he murmured.

"You've Kushiel's blood in your own veins." I took one of his hands in mine and turned it over, showing him the blue veins that coursed in his fine wrist. "One day, you will know it. And it will make matters more difficult."

"No!" He snatched his hand away. "Never! I am not like that. Like *him*." His face contorted with loathing. "Like *her*."

Like the Mahrkagir.

Like his mother.

"No," I said, "you're not. You are your own. But you're half-Kusheline, Imriel, of one of the oldest and purest bloodlines in the realm. And betimes it will out. Betimes you will despise me, as you did in Daršanga. There was nothing said of me there that was not true. And betimes you may despise Joscelin, who knows it, and chooses to remain. It is a great mystery, Kushiel's mercy. The part I understand is the part that *yields*. Your birthright is the other part."

His face worked. "I don't want it. I don't! Why are you telling me this?"

"Because it is true," I said softly. "And these are things you need to know if it is your wish, truly your wish, to be adopted into my household."

Imriel caught his breath; not daring to breathe, not daring to hope. I knew that feeling too well. "Do you mean it?" The words emerged in a breathless rush.

I nodded. "It won't be easy," I said. "Even if my plan works, and I'm not wholly sure it will, Joscelin and I are going to be in considerable disfavor. But if it means keeping you with us, it will be worth it, love. And that much I can promise. You see, the Queen owes me a favor. A very large favor—"

And that was all I got out before Imriel flung himself on me, his arms in a stranglehold about my neck. All I could do was hold him, not understanding a word of the incomprehensible syllables he gasped into my hair. All the fears I had, all the pitfalls I saw ahead as he grew to manhood—they measured as nothing next to this. All I could do was hold him hard and blink ineffectually at the tears that stung my eyes.

"What did I miss? Has someone died?"

It was Joscelin, emerged at last from his bout of seasickness, standing on the deck and regarding us with perplexity. Imriel relinquished his grip on me to greet Joscelin with a wordless shout of joy, taking a standing leap into his arms. Joscelin caught him and staggered.

"I take it you told him," he said to me over Imriel's head.

"Mm-hmm."

"Well." Joscelin bent his head to kiss Imriel's cheek. "I hope you don't think it's *always* going to be this exciting in our household, love."

And Imriel, overwrought, burst into tears.

It took some time to calm him, and more time to explain the procedures that must needs occur for the adoption to take place. It did not mean, I told him sternly, that he would no longer be a member of House Courcel. If he wished, when he gained his majority at the age of eighteen, he had the right to repudiate his House, although I did not think he would or should. We both of us, I said, stressing the fact, expected him to acknowledge his lineage and become acquainted with his kin and heritage. When his presence was requested at the Palace, we would comply. Whatever terms Ysandre de la Courcel dictated on that score, we would accede to on Imriel's behalf.

"But I can live with you?" Imri asked.

"Yes," I said, my heart swelling absurdly. "You can."

After his first delirious reaction had passed, Imriel settled into calmness. He glowed, though. He glowed with a solemn and private joy. I watched him aboard the ship, and how the sailors taught him their craft willingly, how the other passengers—merchants, for the most part—smiled as he passed. A deep, abiding fear had eased in him, a reserve that held itself half-flinching, prepared for a blow, ready to surface at a harsh word, a hint of cruelty.

"We did well," Joscelin murmured, his arm about my shoulders.

"I know," I said.

"It won't be easy."

"I know." Elua knew, it wouldn't.

"We'll make it work." Joscelin turned me to face him. "We always do."

"I know," I said for the third time, and kissed him. "I know."

There was a good deal more to be discussed before we reached the harbor of La Serenissima, and that we did. Imriel listened gravely to my plan and nodded his consent. I was not worried about his discretion. He had kept silent about the rebellion in Daršanga and given naught away. After that, this was easy.

Except that it involved Melisande.

So we sailed north, and the winds grew cold and cutting, the sea choppy and grey, fraught with unexpected storms. The passengers took to their berths as we sailed northward up the Caerdicci coast, drawing ever nearer to La Serenissima.

We reached La Dolorosa, the black isle.

Joscelin and I stood on deck as the ship sailed past it.

It is all very different, now. The fortress where I was imprisoned stands abandoned and crumbling, and the sailors whistled absentmindedly as we passed, going about their business as they acknowledged the goddess Asherat's awesome grief for her slain son out of habit rather than fear. They tell stories about it still; I know, I have heard them. I am a part of them. This time, no one who would remember noticed, for which I was grateful.

A fraying length of hempen rope, supporting fragments of wooden planks bleached silver-grey with salt spray and time, still twisted in the wind, banging against the basalt cliffs. It had been a bridge, once, swaying over the dangerous sea and crags below. We had crossed that bridge, both of us. I walking it, Melisande's prisoner. And he . . . he, crawling beneath it, inch by torturous inch.

Joscelin reached for my hand and our fingers entwined as we watched La Dolorosa pass.

There were things we spared Imriel, and that was one of them. He had reason enough to hate his mother already; he had no need of ours. My imprisonment in La Dolorosa, the cruel slaying of my loyal chevaliers Fortun and Remy . . . these things were not secret, and doubtless he would learn them, in time. *Now* was too soon.

It is always too soon, with children.

"The Spear of Bellonus!" called the sharp-eyed lookout, sighting the landmark. "La Serenissima lies ahead!"

And it was so.

We entered La Serenissima.

Eighty-six

Cesare Stregazza, the ancient Doge, was dead.

It was not a surprise, since he had already outlived expectations by ten years. What was surprising was that his son Ricciardo had not succeeded him.

"Oh, I daresay he *could* have," his wife Allegra told us after welcoming us to Villa Gaudio with a dozen questions in her gaze, and too much courtesy to ask them. "But it would have been an ugly election, and a divisive one. Sestieri Navis holds a good deal of sway in the city, and after Lorenzo Pescaro concluded such a lucrative deal with the Commander of the Illyrian Merchant Fleet, his supporters doubled. In the end, Ricciardo decided he was content to continue sitting on the Consiglio Maggiore and representing the Scholae. It's all he ever really wanted, anyway."

"The Illyrian Merchant Fleet?" I asked. "The trade restrictions have been lifted?"

Allegra nodded. "Completely, as of this past spring. The Ban of Illyria immediately appointed a Commander and gave him a great deal of autonomy. A clever fellow, they say, and a bold one. Seems there's been a cessation of piracy since his appointment."

"Not . . ." I looked at her sparkling eyes. "No!"

"Kazan Atrabiades?" Allegra laughed at my expression. "Indeed, the very same. I see you remember him, my dear."

In such a manner did we renew our acquaintance and Allegra shared such news as she had heard from Terre d'Ange, none of which, to my relief, was noteworthy. It was not until evening, after we had dined and Imriel had been installed in a bed in one of the villa's many guest rooms, that the discussion turned to our purpose here.

"You must be wondering—" I began.

"Phèdre." Allegra cut me short. "Twelve years ago, your warning saved Ricciardo's life. If not for that . . ." She shook her head. "We are in your debt. If Ricciardo were here, he would say the same. Whatever aid you require is yours. I don't need to know your purpose."

"I think you do, my lady," Joscelin said quietly. "We've incurred the Queen's displeasure, and she may not look favorably on those who aid us."

Allegra Stregazza shrugged. "When has Ysandre de la Courcel ever looked *favorably* on the Stregazza? Not that we haven't given her ample reason. But Terre d'Ange wields less influence in La Serenissima than once it did, and Ysandre has a name for being fair. I do not think we need fear her displeasure for repaying a debt of honor."

"Nonetheless," I said. "Joscelin's right. And if anything goes awry, better you should know, Allegra."

She glanced toward the marble stair leading to the upper floors of the villa. "It's about the boy, isn't it? He's Prince Benedicte's son."

"You knew?"

"Only because Ricciardo saw his mother unveiled in the Temple of Asherat when you . . . interrupted . . . the ceremony of investiture. He described her to me." She smiled faintly. "He said it was as well women's beauty held little sway over him, or he would have feared her even more than he did. I have that, at least, to be thankful for. Are you . . ." Allegra hesitated, ". . . are you planning to return him to her?"

"No!" Joscelin and I said in unison.

"Asherat be praised." She sighed. "I was afraid to ask."

We told her, then, something of our plan, and the adventures that had befallen us since we left La Serenissima a year and more ago to pursue the Name of God in Menekhet. A shortened version, to be sure, but enough to widen her eyes. There are few people in my life I trust implicitly. Allegra Stregazza was not one of them, but she came very close to it.

"You're right to fear Melisande's influence," she said somberly when we had finished. "Cesare never did, and Lorenzo Pescaro . . . well, his interest lies in ships and trade, and little else. No one knows what truly passes in the Temple of Asherat-of-the-Sea; no one except the priestesses and eunuchs, and they're a close-mouthed lot. But I have heard rumors, this year past. You know I continue to work with the Courtesans' Scholae? They hear things no one else does, though I suppose I don't need to tell you that, my dear."

"Rumors?" I inquired.

A servant entered the room to replenish our glasses of rich Caerdicci red. After months without, it was a luxury beyond words to drink good wine. Allegra thanked him graciously, waiting until he left. "Rumors," she said, then. "Of a secret cult of worship."

"Of *Melisande?*" My voice cracked.

Joscelin merely swore.

"She took the Veil of Asherat the minute she entered La Serenissima," Allegra said. "She claimed sanctuary and has endured exile in the Temple without complaint for twelve years. She is a mother bereaved. And though few have seen her face, her beauty is renowned. It takes little more to spark the beginnings of a legend."

"She is also," I observed, "a convicted traitor condemned to execution."

"So Terre d'Ange claims. It is easy for people to disbelieve, here. Whatever allegations have been made of her, nothing was proved in La Serenissima." Allegra's expression was grave. "They are rumors, nothing more. But you are right to fear."

"Wonderful," Joscelin said sourly, putting his head in his hands. "So now we worry that some Serenissiman fanatic will declare Melisande Shahrizai the living avatar of Asherat-of-the-Sea and set out on a holy mission to destroy her enemies?"

"No, love." I smiled at him. "That's why you and I are here."

We talked long into the night, the three of us, and Allegra agreed to the arrangements I requested. I slept poorly and woke early, spending my time composing a reply to Melisande's letter. It wasn't easy. In the end, I kept it simple and to the point.

Swear to me in Kushiel's name that I will have no cause to regret it and you shall see your son.

Summoned by Allegra, Ricciardo Stregazza arrived at Villa Gaudio that morning, and we went through the entire story again. This time, Imriel was present for it, listening with his eyes shadowed and wary, pained at the living reminders of his parents' treason. Not until Ricciardo and Allegra's son Lucio, now sixteen and filled with good-natured manful pride, took Imri to the stables to choose a mount of his own did his spirits lighten.

"He's a good lad, isn't he?" Ricciardo said, watching them go.

"Yes," I said. "That, and more."

My message was delivered by way of an anonymous courier, a stone-mason from one of the Scholae Ricciardo represented. We waited at Villa Gaudio for the man to make his slow return. Allegra took us on a tour of her gardens, where a few late-blooming blossoms lingered.

"I'm sorry," she apologized, glancing at Joscelin. "My lord Cassiline, this must be terribly dull for you."

"No." He gave her his best Cassiline bow. "Not at all, my lady Allegra. I am passing fond of gardens."

I remembered how we had first come here together at Ricciardo's invitation, when Joscelin and I had scarce been speaking to one another. Such a haven it had seemed! We had gardens in Montrève, too, although there are as many herbs as flowers. Richeline Purnell, who is my seneschal's wife, tends them lovingly. Joscelin knelt in one for many hours contemplating his anguish and his Cassiline vows, the day I told him I was returning to Naamah's Service to answer Melisande's challenge.

That seemed a very long time ago.

Ricciardo's stone-mason returned before dusk, bearing a letter with a single phrase written on it.

I swear it.

The handwriting was shaky. It was not noticeable, not to one who didn't know it well, not to one whose own hand wasn't trained in the elegant formal script of D'Angeline nobility and adepts of the Court of Night-Blooming Flowers. I noticed.

Melisande's hand had trembled as she wrote it.

My heart quickened within my breast and my breathing grew shallow. My blood beat in my ears, sounding out the Name of God, while a different name throbbed in my pulse. Blessed Elua, I prayed, let me be strong.

It was a sober meal we passed that night, and much of it due to my own distraction. Ricciardo and Allegra's daughter Sabrina joined us, along with her husband. In the year we had been gone, their studious, even-tempered daughter had surprised them by falling in love with a poet, a minor son of one of the Hundred Worthy Families. They were wed now, and her belly just beginning to swell with their first-born. I noted the tender pride which with she carried herself and thought on the mysteries of life.

"You feel it?" she asked Imriel, inviting him to lay his hands on her. "It will begin to move, soon."

His face was a study in solemn awe. "I helped Liliane to deliver a kid, once," he told her. "It was backward, but it came out all right, because she was there. Brother Selbert always called on her to attend when a goat was birthing."

"Well." Sabrina smiled. "Then I know who to call upon, if the midwife has troubles."

The goat-herd prince. I remembered the stories they had told of him at the Sanctuary of Elua, and the simple-minded acolyte Liliane whom animals trusted, and my heart ached. He should have had that life, should have grown to manhood there in the mountains of Siovale, fit and happy, scrambling over crags.

It should have been so.

But there still would have been Melisande.

We left for the Temple in the morning, travelling by a hired gondola. Ricciardo and Allegra would have gladly given their own vessels, their own guards to attend us, but I preferred it this way. If aught went awry, no taint of it would fall upon them. We travelled the waterways of the mainland and crossed to the islanded city, shivering a little in the cold air. I'd meant to procure new attire, but in the end, some whim made me wear my Jebean garb, Ras Lijasu's finest gift, with a borrowed cloak flung over it, gold and ivory bangles at both wrists. Let Melisande, I thought, remember how far we had travelled.

It was a bright day despite the chill, and La Serenissima shone brightly under the wintry sun, and brightest of all the Temple of Asherat-of-the-Sea with its gilded domes. We disembarked at the bustling Campo Grande, where no one looked strangely at three D'Angelines in Jebean attire. I listened to the merchants' cries as they hawked their wares in a babble of competing tongues, understanding more than I ever had before. In front of the Temple, the eunuchs stood impassive with their ceremonial spears. They had chosen to be unmanned, or so it was said. I thought of Rushad and Erich the Skaldi, and wondered how Uru-Azag was faring in the city of Nineveh.

"Well?" Joscelin laid a hand on my shoulder. Imriel stuck close by his side, unmoved by the marvels of the marketplace of the Campo Grande. The shadow of fear was back in his eyes. "Are you ready?"

"You're sure?" I asked Imri.

He nodded slowly despite his fear, his jaw setting with a familiar stubbornness.

"Yes," I said to Joscelin. "We're ready."

ÉIGHTY-SEVEN

"IMRIEL."

One word, nothing more; half-breathed, a plea, an involuntary prayer. If I could, I would have stopped my ears against the depths of emotion in it—pain, sorrow, remorse and a relief so keen it made my heart ache.

I couldn't bear to look at her.

Imriel stood still and tense within her chambers, his face bloodless beneath its tan. "Mother."

Melisande glanced swiftly at me, and I had to look at her. "He knows," I said. "Ysandre's men told him. One of them lost a brother at Troyes-le-Mont."

The knowledge was bitter to her. I watched her absorb it like a blow, the smooth eyelids flickering. Why was it that nothing on earth seemed to mar her beauty? Time had only burnished it; grief only deepened it. "I am sorry," she said to Imriel. "Believe me when I tell you I am so very sorry for what you have endured."

"Why?" He took a step forward, quivering with rage and tears. *"Why?"*

It was the question, the child's eternal question, directed at last to one who had much for which to answer. Melisande bore it unflinching. "Oh, Imriel," she said softly. "So many reasons, and so few. Would you know them all? It would be a long time in the telling."

"People *died* because of you!" he spat.

"Yes." Her voice was steady. "And people have died because of Ysandre de la Courcel, and because of Phèdre nó Delaunay, too. Messire Verreuil here has dispatched a good many of them himself. Do you despise them because of it?"

"No." Imriel sounded uncertain. Joscelin shot a concerned look at me, and I shook my head imperceptibly. "That's different."

"It's different because you know their story, their *side* of the story." Melisande's face was impossibly calm. "You don't know mine. You have asked. Will you hear it?"

We were standing, all of us, at odd angles to one another, awkward and formal. Winter sunlight filled the marbled chambers and a pair of charcoal braziers provided warmth. In the background, the unseen fountain splashed. Imriel turned to me, tears in his eyes.

"I don't want to know," he said in Jeb'ez. "I shouldn't have asked. Do I have to listen?"

"No." I shook my head. "The choice is yours."

"Is it true?"

I regarded Melisande, whose gaze had sharpened upon hearing her son address me in an unfamiliar tongue. "Yes," I said to Imriel in D'Angeline. "It is true. Every story has two sides, even your mother's."

Joscelin shifted, but offered no comment.

Imriel stared at his mother.

There was no escaping the resemblance between them, nor ever would be. The shape of his chin, he'd got from his father, and the straight line of his brows. Everything else was hers—the elegant bones of his face, the clear brow, the generous, sensual mouth, the blue-black hair that fell in ripples rather than curls. And the eyes, Elua, the eyes!

"No," he said finally, his voice harsh. "I know enough. I don't want to hear more."

Melisande inclined her head. "It is as you wish, Imriel. Remember it is there."

He turned back to me. "Can we go, now?"

"Yes," I said. "If it's what you want."

He nodded, his face sick and pleading.

"Then go with Joscelin," I said gently. "You can make an offering to Asherat-of-the-Sea, who once saved my life. I will stay a moment, and speak with your mother."

They went, Imriel placing his hand trustingly in Joscelin's. Joscelin gave me a dour warning glance as they went, but never spoke a word. And Melisande watched them go, and I felt against my skin the bitter intensity of her longing. When they left, she sat down on the couch with a shuddering sigh, passing both hands blindly over her face.

"How is he, truly?" she asked me.

I remained standing. "Whole enough in body, my lady. He has nightmares."

Melisande lifted her gaze. "Do I want to know why?"

"No." I shook my head. "You don't."

She looked away. "And I am in your debt, twice-over. Do I want to know what you endured to find him, Phèdre?"

"No." I couldn't rid myself of a terrible compassion. "No, my lady, you do not."

"The kingdom that died and lives." Melisande laughed without mirth. "Drujan. Jahanadar, the land of fires. Ptolemy Dikaios feared it, I know that much, and he is a learned man. It lies under the rule of Khebbel-im-Akkad now, had you heard?"

"No."

"It seems they surrendered peaceably." She eyed me. "Passing strange, when even the Khalif's formidable army feared to cross its borders. So, I understand, did Lord Amaury's men."

I said nothing.

Melisande sighed. "What of the men who harmed my son?"

"They are dead."

Her face hardened. "You swear to it?"

"Yes." I thought of Imriel, checking time and again to make certain that the Kereyit Tatar warlord Jagun was dead; and I thought of Mahrkagir's heart beating beneath my hand, his brilliant, trusting eyes as I positioned the hairpin against his breast. "I swear to it."

"You took my son to Jebe-Barkal."

"Yes." I crossed over to the low table where a tray of refreshments sat ignored, pouring myself a glass of wine. My mouth was dry with fear. "I did."

"Why?"

Her gaze was sharper than Kaneka's hairpins. I kept my face neutral as I sat on the couch opposite her and sipped my wine. "Do you know, he followed us? He pulled one of your own tricks, my lady, trading cloaks with a Tyrean serving-lad. Elua knows what Lord Amaury made of it when he discovered it."

"You could have sent him back."

"Shall we play a game?" I asked softly, curling into a corner of the couch. "Yes, my lady, we could have. But it would have cost me a season's wait, while my friend Hyacinthe, my one true friend, descends slowly into madness. That's why I went, remember? That's why I accepted your bargain. And in the end, Imriel too had a part to play."

"You found what you sought."

I gazed at Melisande, feeling the Name of God present on the tip of my tongue, sounding in the throb of my blood. It was there, written in the immaculate geometry of her features, in the framework of bone and the flesh that sheathed it, a fearful beauty. "Yes," I said. "I did."

Never, never show your hand. It is the first law of barter, of games of skill. And it is not my strength, which lies in *yielding*. It was hard, so hard to wait, to hold her gaze. But I did, and it was Melisande who looked away first. "And now you will give my son to Ysandre," she murmured.

I took another sip of wine. "That, my lady, depends upon you."

Her eyes blazed, and the color rose in her cheeks. "What do you mean?"

"I will tell you," I said, "what I offer. And I will tell you what I require in return. I am willing, my lady, to adopt Imriel into mine own household. And as such . . ." My voice caught in my throat. "Ah, Melisande! I can't make him love you. You poisoned that well yourself, long before he was born. But I can promise that he will be left free to make his own choices, and I will not turn him against you, not wittingly. If you wish to correspond with him, I will see your missives delivered. Whether or not he reads them is up to him. One day, he may be willing to hear your story. If it is so, I will let him. I would allow him choice. That is what I offer."

"Ysandre would never permit it."

"She would," I said, "if I claimed it as the boon she owes me. I hold the Companion's Star, my lady. It was seen and witnessed by the flower of D'Angeline nobility. It is the one thing Ysandre cannot refuse."

Melisande studied me. "Why?"

I touched the hollow of my bare throat, where once her diamond had lain. "Why did you pay the price of my marque, so long ago? Why did you set me free?"

A distant smile flickered over her features. "To see what you would do."

"Even so." I nodded. "I would see what Imriel would do, what he would become, were he free to choose. After what he has endured, it is the least he deserves. But I have my own safety to consider, and that of those who are beholden to me."

"The Cassiline," Melisande said dryly.

"Among others," I said. "Yes, Joscelin first of all, but there are others. Ti-Philippe, my chevalier . . . you remember him, my lady? His comrades were slain on Prince Benedicte's orders. And there is Eugènie, my Mistress of the Household, and others, in Montrève . . . my seneschal, Purnell Friote and his wife Richeline, and others, too many to count. I am fond of your son, Melisande; passing fond. But while you plot against the throne, we are all in danger of being accused of conspiracy. I will not jeopardize them on his behalf. I require safeguards."

That was the lie, the bluff. I delivered it unblinking, and Melisande's gaze searched my face. "You said there was a price," she said at length.

It was all I could do to keep from sighing with relief.

"Two things," I said, holding up two fingers. "One: You will swear to me, in Kushiel's name, that you will do naught to jeopardize the lives of Ysandre de la Courcel and her daughters. Two: You will make no attempt to leave this place, but will live out your days in sanctuary, seeking only penitence and not worship."

Melisande laughed.

I waited.

"Ah, Phèdre!" Leaning forward, she brushed my cheek with her fingertips. Her touch stung like a lash, and I closed my eyes against it. "One," Melisande said tenderly, her voice redolent of smoke and honey. "Two conditions have you set me, Phèdre. Do you take my son, and raise him without teaching him to hate me more than he does now, I will grant you one. Only one. And the choosing of it is yours."

It was hard not to lean into her touch. It stirred me, stirred things in me I had not felt since Daršanga. I had thought, after that, I might never yearn for such tender cruelty again. I was wrong. Melisande's scent surrounded me, clouding my faculties. Even the Sacred Name itself blurred under her fingers, turning to incomprehensible syllables, my tongue grown thick with desire. I wanted to touch her, to taste her, to kneel at her feet.

"The first," I said, feeling the pulse beating betwixt my thighs. "On Kushiel's name. Swear you will not raise your hand, nor any other's, against Ysandre and her daughters."

"I swear it." Melisande withdrew her hand. "In Kushiel's name, I swear it."

I stood, feeling giddy. "Then I will raise your son as my own, my lady."

"So be it."

I got halfway to the door before her voice stopped me.

"Why did you do it?" Melisande asked, holding me with her wondering gaze. "Surely, you had done all that was in your power, and more. My oath didn't bind you unto near-certain death. You had your quest, and the key to the Name of God. Why did you abandon it to walk alone, with only that mad Cassiline to protect you, into a land even the most hardened Akkadian warrior feared? Was it only to free my son?"

I paused, and shook my head. "No, my lady. My oath took me to Khebbel-im-Akkad, no further. For the rest, I can say only that it was Elua's will, and part of a pattern more vast than I could have guessed. All of it. There was . . . there was somewhat in Drujan that Ptolemy Dikaios was right to fear, a shadow that might have fallen over us all, had it lived. But it is gone, now. A great ill has been averted. This would not have happened if I had not gone."

Melisande's face was very still. "Then Imriel did not suffer in vain."

"No," I said, and shook my head again, pitying her against my will. "Not wholly, my lady, and not only in retribution for your crimes. There was a purpose to it greater than Kushiel's justice alone."

Her eyes closed, and her lips moved in a prayer of thanksgiving. It was not a thing meant for me to see, and I turned once more to go.

"Phèdre."

After all these years and all that I knew of her, my name on her lips still brought me up short. Melisande might as well have had me on a lead. I stood despairing and watched as she rose from the couch, crossing to approach me. Squares of winter sunlight lay upon the marble floor, and sunlight gleamed on the Veil of Asherat, drawn back to lie in a glittering net on her blue-black hair. Her hands, pale as ivory, with long tapering fingers, rose to cup my face with infinite tenderness and the promise of immaculate cruelty. Caught between the desire to flee and to stay, I caught my breath, my heart beating too fast, erratic.

"Phèdre." Melisande smiled, her eyes as deep blue and fathomless as the evening sky. "You're a dreadful liar."

I drew in a shaking breath, trembling under her touch. "I've never lied to you."

"No?" The corners of her lovely mouth curled with amusement. "Let us say then that there are certain things you failed to mention, such as the attempts upon Imriel's life made in Khebbel-im-Akkad. As for the rest, I will say only this. One day—not soon, but one day— tell my son that this bargain I have made with you today is my gift to him, the only one he would accept from me. And I, I will rest easier in the knowledge that he will be safer with you and your Cassiline than anywhere in the City of Elua, for you will permit no dangerous intrigues under your roof, and the two of you will protect him to the death." She looked at my expression and laughed. "Oh, Phèdre! Did you think

I would not see that he loves you, and is loved in turn? Even Joscelin sought to protect him from me. And you . . . my dear, you could no sooner turn away love than you could erase the prick of Kushiel's Dart from your eye."

Feverish with desire and fear, I struggled to frame a reply.

Melisande ignored my efforts and kissed me.

The Name of God ignited in my skull, blazing under the touch of her lips, her tongue. I saw our paths crossing and recrossing, the myriad paths of *might-have-been*. All the scenarios that might have happened, had events not fallen out as they did. And in each and every one, our fates were intertwined. In one, she joined forces with Anafiel Delaunay and stood *in loco parentis* to me, a relationship as fraught with difficult tensions as the worst possibilities I feared for Imriel. In another, she wed Baudoin de Trevalion, and I served as plaything to both. In another, I stood beside her, gazing at the poisoned corpse of Waldemar Selig, knowing myself the agent of his death.

All of these, and more.

All that might have been.

Melisande raised her head and released me. "Take care of my son."

"I will." How I got out the words, through a throat choked tight with longing and vision and the Name of God, I will never know— but I did. Melisande only nodded.

She had always, always known me better than anyone else.

"Good-bye, Phèdre."

ÉIGHTY-EIGHT

I ENTERED the Temple of Asherat to find Joscelin engaged in describing to Imriel events that had transpired therein some twelve years past, standing in the corner and whispering as he pointed to the balcony opposite the mighty effigy. The priestesses of Asherat frowned visibly behind their veils and muttered, displeased.

Asherat-of-the-Sea, immortal and less easily discomfited, maintained her solemn gaze across the emptiness of domed space, crowned with stars. Like the One God's Sacred Name, her mystery had endured longer than mortal memory, and it would endure too when we had gone, passing to the true Terre d'Ange-that-lies-beyond.

Because I knew it was so, I laughed.

Joscelin lifted his head in answer and smiled at me. And there was no covert message in his smile, no dire knowledge, only simple gladness at my presence. "Did she agree to it?"

I nodded and held out one hand to Imriel.

He came warily, the old fear riding him. "She promised?"

"Yes," I said. "Not all of it. Only the important part."

"Will she keep her promise?" His shadowed eyes searched my face.

"She will," I said. "And we will go *home*."

From the Temple, we went to the Banco Tribuno where I still had notes of promise on record from my factor in the City of Elua, Messire Brenin. His Serenissiman contact there remembered me well, and forbore to comment on the strangeness of our Jebean attire. I signed a scrip for funds sufficient to our purpose, and we went thence to the tailors' quarter and commissioned travelling garb in the Serenissiman style, bright-hued velvets and heavy capes trimmed with ermine. It was overly ornate for my tastes, but far more suitable for the cold Caerdicci winters.

"You didn't have to get the ermine trim," Joscelin observed.

I regarded him over the fur collar of my new cloak. "I am the Comtesse de Montrève, after all. Don't you think I ought to look the part?"

As always, there were other arrangements to be made. Had it merely been Joscelin and I, we would have travelled as before, just the two of us—but there was Imriel to consider, and I had not forgotten the bandits that had attacked us last time we travelled between Terre d'Ange and Caerdicca Unitas. To that end, Ricciardo Stregazza found us an escort, mercenaries he was willing to vouch for personally, sailors out of work until the spring trade resumed. And there were all the usual questions to consider, supplies and routes, water and fodder and the rest.

There was one other matter, too.

I debated it, but in the end, I chose to send a letter to Severio Stregazza, who is the lord of the Little Court, now—the Palazzo Immortali, he renamed it. He inherited it some time after the death of his grandfather, who was Prince Benedicte de la Courcel.

I had known Severio well, once; he had been a patron of mine. He is still the only man who has ever asked to wed me, and I even considered it . . . for a moment. It is as well for both of us that I said no. But he is also the only one of Imriel's Serenissiman kin surviving who has not committed some manner of murder or treason.

Severio's aunt, Thérèse, took part in the assassination of Isabel L'Envers de la Courcel, Ysandre's mother. I will never forget that, for it is the knowledge for which my foster-brother, Alcuin, risked his life— and it was the knowledge Delaunay used to buy a dubious alliance with Duc Barquiel L'Envers.

Barquiel had Severio's uncle Dominic killed for it. I don't forget that, either.

And Severio's mother Marie-Celeste, who was Prince Benedicte's eldest daughter—Marie-Celeste masterminded the plot to have old Cesare removed as Doge, and her husband Marco installed in his stead. Or so they say, in La Serenissima. It was Marie-Celeste who suborned the Temple of Asherat, of that I was certain. Melisande had always been careful to avoid blasphemy.

It is why I knew she would keep her oath.

Even now, if a cult grew around her exile, I did not doubt that she chose her words with care, making no claims that might offend the gods, knowing all the while what effect they might have on Asherat's mortal adherents. And I did not doubt that her genius lay behind Marie-Celeste's treason.

Be as that may; Severio, like his uncle Ricciardo, was one of the good ones, afflicted with the scruples so many of his family lacked. I wrote to him from Villa Gaudio, stressing the need for discretion.

Ricciardo's courier was returned posthaste, in an elegant bissone that bore the Stregazza arms of the carrack-and-tower framed by a pair of the arch-necked swans of House Courcel. A half-dozen noblemen from the Immortali, Severio's beloved club, accompanied it. I recognized their leader, clad in a sweeping cloak of blue velvet, lined with saffron-yellow.

"Contessa," he cried as their helmsman maneuvered the gilded craft alongside Villa Gaudio's dock. "Contessa, come back, and break my heart again!"

"Benito Dandi," I said, smiling.

He grinned, and swept a bow. "You remembered!"

I did remember. The Immortali had saved my life in the Temple of Asherat. And Severio Stregazza had led them to it, intervening even as I held the point of a dagger to my own throat, obedient to Melisande's will, desperate to stop her at all costs.

"Of course," I said, while Joscelin raised his brows. "My lord Benito . . . Severio *did* tell you I begged his discretion?"

"Oh, yes." Benito's grin widened, and he indicated the silk-draped canopy of the bissone. "Under there, no one will see you, but we trusted Immortali will know the pleasure of your visage, which is all the reward we ask. Sir Cassiline, you, of course, are welcome to keep your weapons," he said with a certain deference—Joscelin's duel with the Cassiline traitor David de Rocaille remained legend among those who had witnessed it. "And you . . ." He bowed again, this time to Imriel, his face openly curious. "You must be the kinsman. Welcome, young lord."

We made our way to the former Little Court, entering through the gates off the Grand Canal, where Benito Dandi leapt to the quai to usher us ashore, and the guards waved us through. It was strange, after so long. The air was bright and crisp, reflecting off the water of the canals to cast wavering reflections on the cool marble. Imriel gazed at it in wonderment.

"You were born here," I told him.

He swallowed. "I don't . . . I don't feel a part of it."

"No." I stroked his hair. "I suppose not. Neither did your father, not truly. He wanted a son of pure D'Angeline blood. But it is a part of your history, and you should know it."

"And Severio may be an ally," he said.

Much as I hated to see Imri's face take on that unchildish cast, I nodded. "Politics."

It would be a reality in his life, in ours. Always.

The Little Court had changed. The touches, the D'Angeline niceties, remained; vases in the alcove niches, rich carpets on cold marble floors. These had been augmented by Serenissiman décor—elaborate wooden carvings, inlaid mosaics depicting the exploits of the Stregazza line all the way back to Marcus Aurelius Strega.

Severio received us privately in his chambers, for which I was grateful. I do not have fond memories of the throne-room in that place, which is where Remy and Fortun died.

"Phèdre," he said in Caerdicci, opening his arms to embrace me and give me the D'Angeline kiss of greeting. "It has been too long."

I embraced him in turn. Severio had grown solid with status and contentment, wealthy beyond his dreams with the inheritance he'd earned. He'd had a young man's face when I'd first known him; he was older now, a man grown, lines carved at the corners of his mouth, etched beneath the brown curls that spilled over his brow. "Severio," I said. "It is good to see you."

"And you." He clasped my hands, smiling. "Ah, Phèdre! Time has treated you too kindly. Has it been ten years? Twelve? I would not believe it to look at you. And you, my lord Cassiline." Severio took Joscelin's arm in a strong grip. "My master-of-arms makes me recite your fight in the Temple from memory at least once a year. He's never forgiven me for missing the end."

"Prince Severio," Joscelin murmured, bowing.

"And you." Severio turned to Imriel and gave him the formal Serenissiman bow used among equals. "You are my kinsman, I think; my half-uncle, if I am not mistaken."

Imriel returned his bow, reddening. "My lord, I am Imriel. Only Imriel."

Severio gave me a quizzical look. "It is true," I said to Imri. "Your father, Prince Benedicte, was my lord Severio's grandfather. His mother is your half-sister, though many years removed."

"I'm sorry," Imriel muttered. "I'm sorry, my lord."

"It doesn't matter, little cousin," Severio said, his tone unwontedly gentle. He had matured in more ways than one since I'd met him. "Shall we say that, then? Cousins, and neither of us proud of our heritage. You did not choose the manner of your birth, and I . . . I profited by it in the end. Do you grudge me the Little Court, the Palazzo Immortali? Your father intended it to be yours, you know, once upon a time."

"No!" Imriel raised his gaze, startled. "It is . . ." He looked around him and gestured, helpless. "It is a Serenissiman place. It is meant to be yours, my lord. Not mine."

"Good." Severio smiled. "Then we are agreed, little cousin. Shall we become friends? Your foster-mother Phèdre seems to think it a good idea."

Although I was not, properly speaking, Imriel's foster-mother, there was nothing Severio could have said to gratify him more. We passed some hours in pleasant conversation, giving once again a very abbreviated history of our adventures. Even Joscelin relaxed, forgetting his old resentment. It had been a bad time between us, when Severio became my patron—the worst of times. But we had grown through it and past it, and no one could not deny that Severio too had grown. The rude Serenissiman lordling with royal D'Angeline blood in his veins had become a man whose merit was worth reckoning.

I would have liked to meet his wife. But this was La Serenissima, still, and for all it is goddess-ruled, the role of women does not equal that of men. And too, I suppose, she may not have been as eager to meet me. In the City of Elua, they still speak with awe of the fee Severio Stregazza wagered for the first assignation upon my return to the Service of Naamah.

For all that, Severio was not insensible of how matters differed in Terre d'Ange. "What of his mother?" he asked, nodding at Imriel when we had finished our tale. "She sought once before to set him on the D'Angeline throne. Will she try it again?"

"Not as before," I said. "Not by such means."

"Asherat-of-the Sea grant it may be so," he said.

Thus passed our meeting with Severio Stregazza, and I was glad we had done it. By the time we departed La Serenissima, Imriel was more at ease with the notion that he was indeed a Prince of the Blood and a member of an extended family, not all of whom were traitors and conspirators. Thanks to my folly, the knowledge of his lineage had been broken harshly to him, and the attempts upon his life in Khebbel-im-Akkad had done little to endear his kin to him.

Severio had helped offset that impression, he and his high-spirited Immortali, who ferried us back to Villa Gaudio, all the while serenading us—or me, at least—with absurdly high-flown lyrics, until Joscelin rolled his eyes in mock dismay and Imriel laughed aloud.

For that alone, it was worth it.

&iGHTY-niNE

IT WAS an uneventful journey home, for which I was grateful.

Home. *Home!*

How long had it been? Two years come spring, since I'd awakened in the night weeping and shaking, dreaming of Hyacinthe. It seemed longer, sometimes; sometimes, it seemed the time had gone in the blink of an eye.

A year ago, we had been in Daršanga.

Imriel had grown taller, an inch at least since we had arrived in Jebe-Barkal. In the spring, he would be twelve. What remained of his childhood—what the Mahrkagir had left of it—would pass quickly. I was reminded of it every day, watching him.

Our mercenary escort treated him with good-natured affection, and he was comfortable with that, more comfortable than he was with being treated as nobility. Goat-herd prince, barbarian's slave. These were the things he knew. They taught him how to curse in Caerdicci when they thought I was out of earshot. I smiled to myself and allowed it.

At night, I dreamed.

I dreamed I was alone on a barren island, surrounded by mists, and somewhere on the island was Hyacinthe. I never saw him, although I heard his voice, speaking my name. "Phèdre. Phèdre." And I danced alone on the barren rock, a vast courtly measure, retracing in a circle every step I had taken before. When I came to the beginning, I knew, the mists would clear, and at the center of my circle would be revealed the tower of the Master of the Straits.

Hyacinthe.

Only I never got to the end, in my dreams. I awoke before I could arrive, my heart pounding, the Name of God straining on the tip of my tongue.

All across the peninsula of Caerdicca Unitas, we retraced our steps. How many times had I made this journey? Once, with Ysandre and Amaury Trente—that is the one they tell tales about. Once, there and back, with Joscelin . . . and once, there. That was the last time. We had sailed to Menekhet, afterward.

Now we returned, step by step. Pavento, Milazza . . . we stayed at inns, where we might, and the Serenissiman sailors who escorted us stayed up late, drinking and carousing. I paid the tally unquestioning. When we were caught between towns, we made camp by fresh water. It was at one such site that I told Joscelin while we lingered beside the campfire, Imriel already abed, the Serenissimans passing the wineskin unheeding.

"She knew," I said, gazing into the flickering flames.

"What?" He was slow to understand, not having lived in my thoughts. "Melisande?"

I nodded. "She knew what I asked, and why, and made the bargain anyway. And then she told me."

Joscelin was silent for a time. "Why would she do it?"

"It was her gift," I said, raising my gaze. "Her gift to Imriel, she said. Because of love."

"Love." He repeated the word, and prodded the fire with a long branch.

"Love," I said.

In the embers of the fire, a half-charred branch shifted and fell, sending a shower of orange sparks ascending heavenward. "Can you claim to know the whole of Elua's will?" Joscelin murmured. "Those were the priest's words, in Siovale. If he told me then I would defy my Queen for the sake of Melisande Shahrizai's son, I would have laughed in his face."

I smiled. " 'Tis a dangerous force, this *love*."

One corner of Joscelin's mouth twitched. "That it is."

We crossed the border south of Milazza on a cold, dreary day. The ground was frozen solid and our horses stamped restlessly, hides cooling as we milled and awaited clearance from the Eisandine border-guards. If we had crossed in Camlach, we would have encountered the Black Shields of the Unforgiven, but this far south, they were the Lady of Marsilikos' men, clad in chain-mail with thick cloaks of sea-blue wool to keep them warm, each worked with Eisheth's symbol on the breast—two golden fish, nose to tail, forming a circle.

"Comtesse." The Captain of the Guard approached, bowing deeply.

His face was troubled. "We did not look for you here."

I raised my eyebrows. "Is it ordered that I may not pass?"

"No. No, of course not, my lady. It is only that . . . you were rumored to have disappeared, in a faraway land." His gaze slide sideways toward Imriel. "Who is the boy?"

It was hard to gauge how much he knew; not much, I thought, or we would have been seized upon entry. Ysandre had kept the story quiet, fearing for Imriel's safety. But it was no secret that Prince Imriel de la Courcel had gone missing from the Little Court of La Serenissima ten years and more gone by, and Imri . . . Imri looked like who he was, his mother's son.

The guard along the border of Caerdicca Unitas would have reason to recognize the stamp of Shahrizai blood.

"He is my ward, for the moment." I folded my hands on the pommel of my saddle. "And we do indeed come from a faraway land, much farther than you might imagine. That is all you need know, my lord Captain, and all the Queen would wish known. If it does not suffice, we will travel north and cross into Terre d'Ange at Southfort in Camlach. I am sure the word of Phèdre nó Delaunay de Montrève will be good enough for the Unforgiven . . ."

"No!" The Captain winced, imagining the repercussions of turning away the Queen's favorite confidante and the missing Courcel prince. "Of course not. Passage is granted, for you and your companions. My apologies, Comtesse."

Thus did we enter Terre d'Ange.

It looked little different from the Caerdicci lands we had left behind—hills and low mountains, growing more gentle the further in we rode. Fields lay fallow for winter, dull and grey beneath the lowering skies. Only the cedars that blanketed the sloping hillsides in patches were green. But it was *home*, and I breathed deeply of D'Angeline air. In the towns and villages, I heard nothing but my native tongue. It seemed strange, after so long. Now it was our Serenissiman escorts who were the foreigners, laughing as they struggled to communicate in langue d'oc and sailors' argot.

Imriel gazed about him with new eyes, seeing the land for the first time as both one who stood in line to inherit its rule, and as an exile returning. There were sorrow and hunger both in his gaze. What he thought, he kept to himself, and I did not press him.

At the inns where we stayed, we were recognized by the commonfolk—I by the scarlet mote in my left eye, and Joscelin by his Cassiline arms. It was an occasion for a fête, each time, for our long absence had indeed engendered rumors of our death or disappearance. Wine flowed freely, for which I was hard-put to get them to accept coin, and the finest poets of the village turned out to vie for the honor of singing verses acknowledging our deeds.

Some were heroic.

Some were bawdy.

Imriel listened to both in silent amazement. For a mercy, no one in the villages put a name to his face. Here, in the countryside, the precise nature of Melisande's beauty has been forgotten. All the poems that once bore her name have been changed. At a casual glance, Imriel might pass for our son, the product of our commingled blood. In Saba, they believed it without question. And why not? My own appearance differed from that of my parents, who were dark and fair in turn.

I remember that much about them.

"They write poems about you," Imriel said, the night after the first such fête. "Poems! Why didn't you tell me, in Daršanga?"

"Would it have mattered?" I asked him.

After a moment, he shook his head. "No. Not then."

"I didn't think so, either. Anyway," I added, "they tell a good deal more stories about other people. When we are home, in the City, you will hear the Ysandrine Cycle, which is the great work of Thelesis de Mornay. Now that is a story worth hearing sung, how Ysandre assumed the throne and saved the realm from the Skaldi."

"You were there."

I shrugged. "Only at the end."

"You brought the Alban army, you and Joscelin."

"Well." I thought of Drustan mab Necthana, of Grainne and Eamonn of the Dalriada. "We carried the Queen's plea, yes. But I rather think they brought themselves. And," I said soberly, "it was Hyacinthe who paid the price of that crossing."

"Hyacinthe," Imriel murmured.

"Yes," I said. "Hyacinthe."

They don't tell his story in the inland villages of Terre d'Ange. Hyacinthe, son of Anasztaizia, a footnote in the Ysandrine Cycle. Outside the Tsingani and those who maintain watch along the coast of Azzalle, no one remembers more. A bargain was struck with the Master of the Straits, a price was paid. The mystery of the Master of the Straits, eight hundred years old, endures. An apprentice was taken; the cycle continues unbroken. About me, they tell stories, because I remained, scarlet mote and all, to become the Comtesse de Montrève, the Queen's confidante, the most famous of Naamah's Servants in many generations, who stood upon a balcony in the Temple of Asherat and denounced a vast conspiracy.

Of Hyacinthe—of his quick grin and his irrepressible charm, of his knack with horses and his gift of the *dromonde*—of Hyacinthe, the poets do not sing.

One day, I thought, they will.

I hoped Hyacinthe could still laugh when they did.

Ninety

I<small>T</small> W<small>AS</small> snowing the day we sighted the white walls of the City of Elua.

Our Serenissiman escorts insisted on seeing us into the city, although I would have dismissed them earlier. "Ah, no, lady," their leader said cheerfully. "Lord Ricciardo paid us to see you home, and it's home we will see you, to your doorstep and no less."

The sky was leaden, flakes of snow drifting aimlessly to lie without accumulating on the frozen earth. In the vineyards, the grape vines were desiccated tangles of brown along the fences. At the southern gate, a pair of guards in City livery traded places, sharing a charcoal brazier, stripping off their gloves to warm their chilled hands. The rest were lurking in the garrison.

Joscelin rode forward to announce us. "The Comtesse Phèdre nó Delaunay de Montrève returns," he said in his most inflectionless voice.

There was a brief, stunned silence.

"My lady!" One of the guards stepped forward, bowing low. "Welcome home."

"Thank you." I gazed through the gate, at the familiar streets that lay beyond, the elegant architecture in perfect scale to its surroundings. People strolled the streets, swathed in warm cloaks against the chill, laughing and remarking on the snow. A smart carriage drawn by a pair of matched bays passed; I knew the arms emblazoned on the door, the silver harrow of the Marquis d'Arguil. He had chided Joscelin and me for failing to attend their cherry-blossom fête when last I had seen him, and begged us to attend their next gathering. It seemed a very long time ago. "My lord guardsman," I said, drawing a deep breath. "Pray send word to her majesty Queen Ysandre that I have returned. We will go now to my home, and thence to the Palace forthwith to attend upon her pleasure."

"My lady." He bowed again; his tone had changed. He had seen Imriel. Like the border-guard, he guessed. "It will be done."

"These men," I said, indicating our Serenissiman escort, "are in the service of Lord Ricciardo Stregazza of La Serenissima, and due free passage in the City in accordance with our alliance."

"It is granted." He stepped aside to allow us through, watching and wondering. Half the garrison turned out to watch as we entered the gates; the other half crowded in the doorway of the gatehouse, fighting for exit.

Hearing the whispers, Imriel drew up the hood of his cloak and lowered his head.

"You have nothing to hide," I told him.

He glanced at me from under the shadow of his hood and said nothing, but his bare knuckles were white on the reins.

Behind us, I heard the sound of a mounted guardsman pelting for the Palace.

Joscelin took the lead as we rode through the City of Elua, unperturbed by the whispers. They recognized him, of course. No one else who is not a sworn member of the Cassiline Brotherhood would dare wear the arms—the vambraces glinting steel beneath his sleeves, the twin daggers at his hips, the hilt of his sword riding over his shoulder. And they knew me. Imriel was a slight figure, shrouded and hooded. Our Serenissiman guards pressed close around us, glowering, and I was glad they had stayed.

The whispers followed us. "Phèdre," I heard, my name spoken as in my dream. "Phèdre." And as in my dream, we retraced our journey, step by step, winding our way through the City of Elua in a slow and stately pavane.

In the narrow courtyard outside my house, my stable-keeper Benoit dropped his jaw to see us, a pair of buckets swinging from a yolk across his shoulders.

"Benoit," I said. "We are back. Will you prepare a stall—"

That was as far as I got before the door opened and a young man burst through it, with ruddy cheeks and shoulders on him like an ox. He stared at us in disbelief before shouting at the top of his considerable lungs. "Philippe! *Philippe!*"

I'd gotten half out of the saddle and almost remembered the young man's name by the time Ti-Philippe came at a run, sword half-drawn from a scabbard he clutched in his bare hand. He skidded to a halt on the frost-slick paving stones and let out a whoop of pure joy, tossing his sword aside. "*Phèdre!*" Grabbing me about the waist, he swung me free from the saddle and spun me around. "You're *alive!*"

"You doubted it?" I asked dizzily when he set me down.

"I shouldn't have," he said, and grinned. "I *shouldn't* have. Cassiline!" He turned to Joscelin, who had dismounted, and embraced him hard, thumping his back. "Elua's Balls, it's good to see you!"

"And you, sailor." Even Joscelin was beaming. "And you!"

"And what have you brought home this time, my lady?" Ti-Philippe inquired, surveying the others, still seated in their saddles. "A Yeshuite sage? A Jebean honor guard? They don't *look* Jebean . . ." His voice trailed off as Imriel drew back his hood. "Name of Elua!"

"Philippe Dumont," I said, making formal introduction, "this is—"

"Imriel de la Courcel," he finished for me. "Ah, my lady! You've done it now."

After that, a good deal of chaos ensued, foremost of which was the emergence of Eugènie, who pushed everyone else aside to embrace me and then take me by the shoulders and shake me, weeping, only to embrace me again. Joscelin, she kissed resoundingly on both cheeks, then shook. Imriel watched it wide-eyed. Ti-Philippe saw to the business of dismissing the Serenissimans with thanks and a gift of coin. He spoke Caerdicci and sailor's argot alike, and I've no doubt he instructed them on the best possible places to spend one's coin on dice and wine and pleasure in the City of Elua. I thanked them too, before they left, and promised to commend them to Ricciardo Stregazza. All the while, Hugues—I had remembered his name—toiled to bring our laden trunks inside the house, while Benoit tended to our mounts and Eugènie commenced to turn the entire household upside down to welcome us home.

"Don't," I said gently to her. "We're bound straightaway for the Palace. It's not an occasion to celebrate, not yet. A bath and a bite of food is all."

Her shoulders slumped, then straightened. "Ah, child. It's the boy, isn't it?"

I nodded.

Eugènie patted my cheek. "He needs a bit of tending, doesn't he? And a light touch, I'm guessing. Will you be bringing him home from the Palace, my lady?"

"You know who he is?"

"Shouldn't I?" There was kind wisdom in her smile. "I told you once, my lady: Hearth and home mean love, too. And if ever there was a lad in need of it, it's that one."

I found Imriel in the salon, considering the bust of Delaunay upon its marble plinth. I sat upon the couch and watched him. It seemed strange to be here. The house was immaculately kept, smelling of citrus oil and beeswax. Everything was as I had left it, down to the smallest detail—the pomander ball on the low table, the engraved fire-screen angled just so, the tall vase in the corner with leathery dried flowers that rattled like a gourd when shaken, a gift from a long-ago patron with an interest in botany.

"Who was he?" Imriel asked without turning around.

"That is my lord Anafiel Delaunay de Montrève, of whom I have spoken," I said. "He bought my marque, and adopted me into his household. And he trained me in the arts of covertcy."

"He made you his spy."

"Yes," I said. "He did. But he asked me, every step of the way, if I was certain it was my own desire. I always wondered, Imri, why he kept asking me the same question, over and over, when my answer was always the same. I understand it better now."

Imriel sat down next to me. "Like you keep asking if I'm sure."

On the plinth, the bust of Delaunay watched us both, his austere marble features imbued with all the irony and tenderness of the living man. I rested my chin in my hands and gazed back at him, wondering what he would make of this unlikely turn of events, wishing he was here, as I have wished a thousand times since his death. "Yes," I said. "Like that."

"Were you ever sorry?"

I glanced at Imriel to find him smiling, eyes dancing; he already knew the answer. "No." I smiled back at him. "I may have cursed it once or twice, but I never regretted it. Not in the end."

"I won't either, you know," he said. "I won't."

"I may remind you of that on occasion." I leaned over to kiss his brow. "Come on, I'll show you to the bathing-room so we can get you presentable for court."

"Can I wear my *chamma* and Ras Lijasu's belt?"

"Mmm, better not. It's too cold, and anyway, I'd rather not remind Ysandre—" A pounding at the front door interrupted my words. "Imriel, go into the kitchen with Eugènie. Go!"

He went, the shadow of fear back in his eyes. Ti-Philippe, Joscelin and Hugues were already in the entryway when I arrived. Ti-Philippe motioned for silence, then opened the small speaking-partition in the door, standing well to the side. "Who calls upon the Comtesse de Montrève?"

"Queen's Guard," came the muffled reply.

Ti-Philippe put his eye to the partition, then stepped back, nodding grimly. "There's an entire squadron on your doorstep, my lady."

I sighed. "Admit them."

There were twenty of them, polished sword-hilts at their sides, boots gleaming, in surcoats of deep blue with the swan of House Courcel worked large in silver embroidery. The lieutenant bowed to me. "Comtesse Phèdre nó Delaunay de Montrève?"

"Yes," I said, feeling tired and travel-worn.

"By order of her majesty Queen Ysandre de la Courcel, you are remanded into my custody," he announced in formal tones. "I am ordered to bring you, Messire Joscelin Verreuil and your young . . . companion . . . to the presence of the throne. Immediately." Something flickered in his expression and he added in a different voice, "I am sorry, my lady."

"I understand," I said. "May we have a few moments to change out of this attire? We've ridden hard these last days."

The lieutenant paused, then shook his head. "My orders were to bring you immediately."

I inclined my head. "I will get the boy."

Out of their sight, I hurried to my bedchamber and fetched a couple of other things as well, overturning the trunk Hugues had brought there and turning the neatly preserved order of my quarters into complete disarray. One item, I stowed in the travelling purse that still hung from my girdle; the other, I tucked under one arm. That done, I went to the kitchen to find Imriel.

He was in Eugènie's custody, his face closed and wary.

"The Queen sent an escort," I said. "She requests our presence."

"Do we have to go?"

I nodded. "Do you remember what to say?"

"I remember." Imriel swallowed. "And I'm . . . I'm sorry I caused you so much trouble."

"Don't be." Touching his cheek, I smiled at him. "It was our choice, you know that. And if you hadn't gone with us . . . like as not, I'd still be trying to sweet-talk the women of Tisaar—or at best, pounding on that temple door on Kapporeth, begging the priest to let me in. Remember that?" Too tense to reply, he nodded. "Good," I said. "Just don't scream like that today. I don't think it will have a good effect on Ysandre de la Courcel."

It made him laugh, as I had intended, and he looked less apprehensive as we went to meet the Queen's Guard, at least until they bowed to him.

"Prince Imriel de la Courcel," the lieutenant greeted him, straightening. The genuine courtesy he had shown me had vanished at the sight of Imriel. His face was composed in a formal mask, only a slight twitch at the corner of one eye betraying a hint of disturbance. "I bring you glad greetings from your kinswoman, her majesty Queen Ysandre de la Courcel."

"Thank you." Imriel studied the man's twitch.

"My lords, my lady, you will come with us, if you please," the lieutenant said, attempting to ignore Imri's scrutiny. He put up one hand as Joscelin moved forward. "Forgive me, Messire Verreuil, but you may not bear weapons into the presence of the Queen. Your arms must stay."

Joscelin raised his brows. "I have dispensation from her majesty herself."

"Not any more."

Someone among the Queen's Guard murmured, watching Joscelin methodically disarm. They knew the legend. He did it without complaint, and Hugues stepped forward to accept his well-worn gear with reverence.

"May I ask what you carry, my lady?" The lieutenant indicated the coffer under my arm.

"Rocks and metal," I said, "wrought in a pleasing form."

He made me show him anyway, and when I did, he flushed. "I am sorry. It is my duty, my lady."

"I know," I said. "Shall we go?"

eNinety-one

WE TRAVELLED to the Palace in one of the royal carriages, the Courcel arms on the side. Two guards rode with us inside, and the rest provided a mounted escort. The curtains were drawn. Outside, on the streets, I heard nothing but the usual idle curiosity, passers-by pausing to bow or curtsy, speculating on what royal guest or family member rode within.

That ended when we reached the Palace.

I didn't mind, for myself. I have been a Servant of Naamah for many years now, and I am accustomed to stares and murmurs. And Joscelin . . . Joscelin had endured it before.

My heart bled for Imriel.

Ysandre was done with secrecy, that much was obvious. We walked the wide, gracious halls of the Palace openly, flanked by her Guard. Six of them surrounded Imriel, hands on hilts, tense and alert; the others kept a close eye on Joscelin and me, several paces behind. All I could see of Imri was that his back was very straight, and he did not look to either side.

In the countryside, he had gone unrecognized.

Not in the City of Elua, and least of all in the Royal Palace.

Strolling nobles stopped and stared. One woman clutched the lapdog she carried so hard it yelped in protest. A lordling's attendant bolted down a side corridor—headed, I guessed, for the Hall of Games, where guests of the Palace were apt to while away the hours.

The halls grew lined with spectators, and an undercurrent of venom ran through their whispers. It seemed a very long walk to the throne-room, where we were at last admitted. The doors were closed behind us, the spectators turned away.

Two more squadrons of the Queen's Guard lined the walls, standing at attention. At the far end was Ysandre de la Courcel, Queen of Terre d'Ange, seated in majesty. When I'd seen her thus before, it was as an attendant at her side. She wore a gown of deep violet adorned with a jeweled girdle, and a heavy cloak of forest green, lined with cloth-of-gold. Her fair hair was elaborately dressed, bound with a simple gold fillet. On her left hand stood Duc Barquiel L'Envers, handsome and inscrutable; at her right were her daughters, Sidonie and Alais. They had grown since I'd seen them.

A family affair, then; and one of state, for I recognized a handful of other nobles in attendance, members of Parliament. This was meant to be witnessed.

A short distance into the room, Joscelin and I were made to halt, while Imriel was led to approach the throne. No one spoke. Ysandre waited gravely, watching him approach. She had waited for this moment for a very long time. The guards led him to the foot of the throne and stepped away, leaving him alone before her. Imriel gave a rigid bow.

"Imriel de la Courcel," Ysandre said, and smiled, her features transforming. "Welcome home." Rising from her throne, she descended the step to lay her hands on his shoulders. "We have waited a long time to welcome you to your family, cousin."

"Thank you, your majesty." He got the words out without a tremor, and I was proud. Ysandre turned to face her watching kin and peers, one hand still on Imri's shoulder.

"This is Imriel de la Courcel, Prince of the Blood, son of my great-uncle Prince Benedicte de la Courcel and Melisande Shahrizai of Kusheth," she said firmly. "In the sight of all here assembled, we do acknowledge him and his ancestral claims, and declare him innocent of all crimes committed by his family. Is it heard and witnessed?"

A dozen voices replied more or less in unison, "It is heard and witnessed."

I watched their faces as they responded. Most were schooled to neutrality under the Queen's scrutiny; Barquiel L'Envers looked amused. Amaury Trente was there, and his expression was stony. The Lady Denise Grosmaine, who was Secretary of the Presence and attended all formal functions with the Queen to record what transpired, might have had a hint of kindness on her face. Sidonie, the young Dauphine, regarded Imriel with her mother's cool gravity, and none of the underlying warmth. Only Princess Alais, the younger daughter, considered him with frank curiosity, intrigued by the notion of a new cousin near enough in age to be a brother to her.

"We are pleased." Ysandre inclined her head. "Remember it well, and welcome him into your hearts, as we welcome him to ours. And," she added, "let it also be known: A crime against Prince Imriel will be considered a crime against House Courcel."

"So don't assassinate the little bugger," Barquiel L'Envers murmured.

Someone gasped

Someone loosed a hysterical laugh.

I do not know, to this day, if L'Envers intended the remark to be audible. He spoke under his breath, but the acoustics in the throne-room are outstanding, designed by Siovalese engineers. Surely Barquiel L'Envers knew it. He may have done it for spite, or for a whim; he may have had a deeper purpose in mind. I cannot say.

Ysandre turned pale with anger. She would have turned on him then and there if Imriel hadn't spoken. It wasn't how we had planned it, but he had his mother's fine sense of opportunity and timing.

"Your majesty!" His high, clear voice rang in the throne room. "An offer of two-fold honor has been made. I beg your permission to accept it."

It is the ritual statement that offers negotiations for formal adoptive fosterage among D'Angeline peers—honor upon the House that offers, honor upon the House that accepts.

Ysandre stared at Imriel, as did everyone else. "*What?*"

He flushed, and held his ground, jaw set. "An offer of two-fold honor—"

"Your majesty," I called, stepping forward and ignoring the guards, who looked uncertainly at one another and eyed Joscelin warily. Even unarmed, they feared his reputation. I made a deep curtsy to Ysandre. "Your majesty, on behalf of House Montrève, I make the offer of two-fold honor in the name of Imriel de la Courcel."

"House Montrève?" Ysandre asked in disbelief. "Surely you jest."

I shook my head. "No, your majesty. I am in deadly earnest."

Barquiel L'Envers laughed out loud; after that, it was quiet.

In the silence, Ysandre breathed slowly and deeply, struggling to control her temper. When she spoke, her voice was even. "House Montrève, if I am not mistaken, consists of one highly priced Servant of Naamah, a defrocked Cassiline Brother and a handful of eccentric retainers. Even if you were *not*—" her tone rose sharply "—in danger of being accused of treason for having abducted a member of *my* household, a Prince of the Blood, against my explicit wishes and exposing him to untold danger, what possible merit would there be for House Courcel, inheritors of the D'Angeline throne, kindred by marriage to the Cruarch of Alba and the Khalif of Khebbel-im-Akkad, in accepting your offer?" She drew near, frowning with genuine perplexity. "Have you gone mad in your travels? What possible honor can there be in such an exchange? Phèdre, what on earth makes you think I would *ever* agree to this?"

I gazed at her without speaking, reached into my purse and drew forth the Companions' Star, holding it out on the palm of my hand.

Ysandre went very still. "You wouldn't."

"You owe me a boon, Ysandre," I said softly. "Anything within your power and right to grant. This is both."

"No." Ysandre's chin set with the exact stubbornness of Imriel's. "No," she repeated. "It is a matter of state and crown. Prince Imriel stands third in line for the throne, and I do *not* have the right, as ruler of Terre d'Ange, to place his life in jeopardy. By your own admission, he has enemies who seek his life. How can you possibly claim he would be protected in your household as he would in mine?"

"Will he have a Cassiline Brother vowed to protect him in your household, one you trust unto the death?" I asked. "He will in mine; and defrocked or no, you once awarded him the laurels of the Queen's Champion. I can swear to the loyalty of every man, woman and child under my roof, my lady. Can you do the same?" I let my gaze linger on Barquiel L'Envers, who saluted me with a wry nod.

"Nonetheless," Ysandre said, deliberately ignoring the implication. "It is a small household, and might be easily overwhelmed."

"Not *that* easily." I smiled. "What Montrève lacks in holdings, my lady, it makes up for in friends and allies. How many of the Great Houses of Terre d'Ange can claim a childhood bond with the Master of the Straits?"

It was a telling blow, and I did not deal it lightly, not in front of that audience. I stood unmoving before the Queen, holding the Companions' Star on the palm of my outstretched hand, willing it not to tremble.

Ysandre searched my eyes. "Phèdre, *why?*"

I thought about Imriel in Daršanga, and the night he had wept for the first time. I remembered him floundering on the sandbar, wrestling the immense fish while Joscelin shouted instructions, and how he had beamed when Bizan gave him his fire-striker. I remembered, most of all, how he had flung himself to my defense on the isle of Kapporeth.

"Not all families are born of blood and seed, my lady. You ought to know that much. If Anafiel Delaunay had not loved your father, you would be dead."

Her face stiffened. "You hold that against me at last?"

"No." I shook my head, feeling sad. "I merely claim the price of it."

"And you, Cassiline?" Ysandre turned to address Joscelin, who had come up behind me. "Are you party to this madness?"

He bowed with immaculate Cassiline grace. "Forgive me, majesty, but I am."

"So be it." She took the Companions' Star from my hand, clenching her fist on it as she addressed the dumb-struck watchers. "An offer of two-fold honor has been made," she said grimly, "and a boon requested, which we are sworn to honor by our own word." She turned to Imriel. "Is it your wish to accept this offer?"

"Yes." He quivered with excitement, eyes shining. "Yes, your majesty!"

Ysandre sighed. "Let the registers reflect that this member of our household shall henceforth be known as Imriel nó Montrève de la Courcel, and he shall be fostered at House Montrève until such time as all parties conclude otherwise, presuming we do not cast his purported foster-mother, the Comtesse de Montrève, and her esteemed consort Joscelin Verreuil, in chains in the next proceedings. Comtesse, we have a letter in your own hand, in which you freely confess that you and your consort countermanded my wishes in the matter of Prince Imriel's return. Do you deny it?"

"No, your majesty," I said.

"You pledged to return with all possible speed to Comte Raife Laniol, Ambassador de Penfars, in Iskandria, and yet you did not. Why?"

I cleared my throat. "Because it occurred to me instead to return by way of La Serenissima and strike a bargain with Melisande Shahrizai."

Ysandre's expression was cold. "And what is the nature of this bargain?"

It was hard to hold her eyes, but I made myself do it. "That I will raise her son, and not you. And in exchange, her oath that she will not raise her hand, nor any other's, against you or your daughters."

Whatever Ysandre had expected, that was not it. She looked away. "Hence the offer of two-fold honor."

"No," I said. "I would have made it anyway. What I said before holds true. But this was the only time I could use it as a bargaining chip. I'm sorry, my lady, truly."

"You actually think she will abide by this oath, *anguissette?*" It was Barquiel L'Envers who asked, leaning idly against Ysandre's empty throne, as dangerous as a basking leopard. "What an amusing notion! You are still a touch besotted, my dear."

I didn't answer him, but only watched Ysandre. She had called me mad, once, for what I had believed of Melisande. And after La Serenissima, she had promised never to doubt me again. I knew I was right. I didn't know if Ysandre knew it, or cared.

She eyed me. "Do you have aught else to say?"

"Yes, your majesty." I knelt and proffered the coffer I'd held tucked under my left arm, opening the lid. "Her majesty Queen Zanadakhete of Meroë, who is likewise ruler of Jebe-Barkal, sends her greetings, and wishes you to know that she would welcome a D'Angeline embassy in Meroë, did you wish to send one."

Ysandre removed the necklace from the coffer and held it up for inspection. The necklace dangled from her hand, gleaming gold, the massive emerald betwixt the horns of Isis refracting glints of green light on the walls of the throne-room.

It was worth a king's ransom.

"Queen Zanadakhete of Meroë," Ysandre echoed.

"Yes, your majesty." I'd bowed my head after I gave it to her; I kept it that way.

"*Phèdre.*" Her tone startled me into looking up. Ysandre's face was unreadable. "Did you find the object of your quest?"

We might have been alone in the throne-room, she and I. When all was said and done, we had been through a good deal together, Ysandre de la Courcel and I. My lord Delaunay had pledged his life to protect her, for love of her father. Most of the battles I have fought have been her battles, and if I have regretted any, it was only the means, not the cause.

Our lives too were intertwined.

And that too was the Name of God.

"Yes, your majesty," I said, gazing up at her and feeling unbidden tears prick my eyes. "I found what I sought."

Ysandre nodded slowly and looked about the throne-room, the Companions' Star in one hand, the necklace of Queen Zanadakhete of Meroë in the other. No one spoke; even Barquiel L'Envers did not crack a smile. "In your missive, wherein you admitted your guilt, you cited the rainy season in Jebe-Barkal as a reason you chose not to delay and return Prince Imriel into the custody of Lord Amaury Trente. Is it not so?"

"Yes, my lady," I murmured. "It is so."

"Well and good." Ysandre dropped the necklace into the coffer I held still in my outstretched hands, closing the lid and nodding to a bowing attendant to take it. "Since your guilt is admitted freely, this, then, is my sentence. For the duration of a season, this season you were unwilling to squander for my kinsman's safe return, you and your household will abide in the City of Elua."

Hyacinthe.

"Your majesty!" I gasped. "You can't—"

"_Enough!_" Ysandre's eyes flashed. "How much indulgence will you beg of me, Phèdre nó Delaunay? You were quick to boast of the Master of the Straits' friendship; is it such a slight thing that three more months will jeopardize it? You will abide in the City for the duration of winter, and do you set foot outside the walls, you will be charged with treason. Is that understood?"

"Hyacinthe gave his life for you, my lady," I said. "For you, and for Terre d'Ange, that Drustan mab Necthana might ride to your aid and your side."

"No." Something softened in Ysandre's face. "He gave it for you, Phèdre. And I am not unmindful of the sacrifice he usurped. Nonetheless, you knowingly defied my will, and your transgression carries a price. I regret that Hyacinthe son of Anasztaizia must bear the cost— but it is on your head, and not mine. Will you abide by my judgement?"

I bowed my head, feeling the cold marble beneath my knees. It was bitter—and it was fair. "Yes," I whispered. "I will abide."

Ninety-two

WHEN POETS sing of the Bitterest Winter in Terre d'Ange, they mean the winter before the Skaldic invasion, when sickness ravaged the land, when Melisande Shahrizai and Isidore d'Aiglemort betrayed it, when Ganelon de la Courcel, the old King, died.

For me, it was this one.

It began with Ysandre's dismissal, and the long walk back through the throne-room, through the Palace halls. I had been too quick to boast of my composure under the stares of my peers. These cut hard and deep, and the whispers had turned cruel.

"Phèdre. Phèdre."

No wonder I had been unable to find Hyacinthe in my dream. The way back was longer than I had imagined, and there were more steps to retrace. For Imriel's sake, I kept my shoulders squared and my head high, and blessed for the thousandth time the presence of Joscelin. The whispers ran off him like rain, and he met eyes contemptuous of his downfall with a cool disinterest. He had already lived through his own personal hell. There was nothing with which the peerage of Terre d'Ange could threaten him.

I could have said no.

Ysandre could have clapped me in chains; she would not have done so. I knew that as surely as I knew that Melisande would abide by her oath. If I had gone to Hyacinthe then and there, Ysandre would have allowed it.

Afterward, I would have paid.

And I could not blame her for it. I had defied her, behind her back and to her face, forcing her hand in a state forum. She was the Queen of Terre d'Ange. Such actions could not go unpunished, not without breeding repercussions that would plague her reign for years to come.

In the eyes of the realm, the punishment was a light one. If I had refused to submit, if I had defied her once more, it would have been more grave.

I might have been stripped of my rank and holdings.

I would surely have lost the fosterage of Imri.

It was bitter, and fair. I made my choice knowing it. I wondered if she knew that nothing would grieve me more than knowing Hyacinthe's suffering endured unnecessarily, and I myself the cause of it. Mayhap she did; there is Kusheline blood in House L'Envers, and along with it comes the keen awareness of pain. Mayhap it was Kushiel's will in the end, that I myself might know what it was to have an innocent suffer for my own transgressions, for even Kushiel's Chosen is not immune from his justice.

I do not know.

It was a long and bitter winter to endure.

There were points of brightness in it, and chiefest among them was Imriel. He flourished in our home in the City of Elua. Eugénie doted upon him, as did all the servants in my employ. He studied the Cassiline disciplines with Joscelin in the frozen garden, mimicking his every move; not to be outdone, Ti-Philippe taught him conventional swordsmanship. To the amusement of us all, young Hugues appointed himself Imriel's personal guardian. He was not especially skilled with blades, but he wielded a shepherd's cudgel to wicked effect, and I once saw him give Joscelin a bout that pressed him surprisingly hard. Hugues taught Imri to play the flute, too, finding he already knew the rudiments of it.

My goat-herd prince.

Other things, I taught him—much as Anafiel Delaunay had once taught Alcuin and I. He read well in D'Angeline and Caerdicci, and I gave him histories and philosophies to read, borrowing what I did not possess from the archives of the Academy. I taught him Cruithne, which he had begun to learn in the Sanctuary of Elua. Once upon a time, it was a tongue no one studied, spoken only by blue-painted barbarians on the far side of the divide held by the Master of the Straits. I myself had rebelled at learning it. Now, it is the mother-tongue of the Cruarch of Alba, husband of Queen Ysandre de la Courcel, and D'Angeline schoolchildren study it as a matter of course.

Why? Because of Hyacinthe, who made it possible.

Only they do not say that.

I introduced Imriel to Emile in Night's Doorstep, and through him to the Tsingani population in Terre d'Ange. They did not care whose son he was, but only that he had played a role in procuring the key that would free Anasztaizia's son, the *Tsingan Kralis*, the Prince of Travellers.

Like me, the Tsingani were waiting for spring.

And I introduced him too to Eleazar ben Enokh, the Yeshuite mystic. It grieved me to be unable to share the Name of God with Eleazar, who had sought it for so long—and yet I could not. When I thought upon it, my throat swelled near to closing, and I knew the Sacred Name had been entrusted to me for one purpose, and one purpose only.

"Adonai does as He wills, and none of us may grasp the whole of His thought." Eleazar's words were gentle. "My heart is glad on your behalf, Phèdre nó Delaunay."

If I could not share the Name of God with him, I could tell him of the Tribe of Dân, and that I did, at length—of the union of Shalomon and Makeda and the Covenant of Wisdom, of Khemosh's folly and the flight to Tisaar and the Lake of Tears, of the Ark of Broken Tablets on the island of Kapporeth. These things he recorded eagerly, and his wife Adara looked on with indulgence and interest.

In such ways did my Bitterest Winter pass.

I spent long hours composing letters, replying to a year's worth of correspondence. Although my letters would not go overseas until spring, I wrote to Nicola L'Envers y Aragon in Amílcar, to Kazan Atrabiades in Epidauro, who had written to tell me of his new appointment, to Pasiphae Asterius, who is the Kore of the Tenemos. I studied, obsessively, everything in my library on the angel Rahab, which I had spent ten years compiling, and learned nothing new. I thought about the confrontation to come. Few guests called upon my home and few invited me to theirs during this time. I received several offers of assignations from such people as would never have dared inquire in the past— disreputable merchants, a petty lordling suspected of molesting his household servants. These I burned without deigning to reply.

The City of Elua was waiting to see if Ysandre would forgive me.

Every week, a representative of the Queen came to the house to ensure that Imriel was in good health and good spirits—Cuillen Baphinol, a young Eisandine nobleman who had studied medicine at one of Eisheth's sanctuaries. I treated him with unfailing politeness. At first, he made a show of inspecting the house and assessing its fortitude, testing the bars on the doors with a grave demeanor. Joscelin watched with amusement; Imriel with simmering resentment. Although it is small, my house is as secure as any manse within the City. I have always taken care with such things, ever since my lord Delaunay and my foster-brother Alcuin were slain within their own home. In time, Cuillen warmed to us and I consulted him on such small bits of herb-lore as I have garnered in my travels.

But he never gave any indication of Ysandre's mind.

Not everyone I had known turned their back upon me. Once the gossip reached her ears, I had regular letters from Cecilie Laveau-Perrin, my old mentor in Naamah's arts. Some years ago she had closed her salon for good and retired to her country estate of Perrinwolde, which, alas, lay a day's ride outside the City walls. Nonetheless, it cheered me to receive her letters, and we resumed a lively correspondence.

I received an invitation, too, for all of us to call upon Thelesis de Mornay, the Queen's Poet, and that I accepted, for she was in seclusion at the Palace and I might visit her without breaking my pledge.

It had been mayhap three years since I had seen her last, and I was shocked at her condition. Touched by the fever of that first Bitterest Winter, Thelesis had never recovered completely. Her quarters has always been maintained at a nigh-uncomfortable warmth; now there was a fireplace in every room and multiple braziers and pots of boiling water suspended over the flames added moisture to the air, rendering it as hot and steamy as the plains of Jebe-Barkal in the rainy season. A servant in Courcel livery tended them with quiet diligence.

Thelesis looked older than her years, her hair streaked with grey, her skin grown sallow and loose on her small frame. But if her dark eyes were sunken, they still glowed, and her voice held a ghost of its rich musicality. "Phèdre nó Delaunay," she whispered, giving me the kiss of greeting. "It is good to see you once more."

I leaned my cheek against hers, feeling the frailty of her. "You are kind to do so, Thelesis. Pray, don't let us overtax you."

"Nonsense." She held me off, smiling. "And you, Joscelin Verreuil! Come here and let me feel your strength, Queen's Champion."

"No longer," he said, returning her kiss. "But it is good to see *you*, Queen's Poet. I hope you are keeping yourself as well as may be."

"As you see." Thelesis waved a hand, indicating the boiling pot, the braziers, the eternal disarray of her quarters, which were strewn haphazardly with books and scrolls and fragments of half-finished writing. At the farthest worktable, a young girl in a drab smock sat perched on a stool, grinding oak-galls in a mortar, shards of husks strewn about the floor. In all the time I have known Thelesis de Mornay—which is a good many years, now—she has never been able to work surrounded by order. With her dark poet's eyes, she watched Imriel take it in. "A proper mess, isn't it?" she asked him.

"Phèdre makes a mess of her study when she's trying to find something." He offered the words warily, watching her reaction. "She doesn't think so, but she does."

"Does she?" Thelesis smiled. "I wouldn't have imagined it. I am Thelesis de Mornay. You must be Imriel."

He made a half-bow. "Imriel nó Montrève."

"I know." She touched his cheek lightly. "A fine name you bear, and a noble one. Anafiel Delaunay de Montrève was a friend of mine, and I mourn him still. He would be proud of what Phèdre has made of his name, and as proud again to know you bear it. He never did, you know, not in his adult lifetime. Have you heard that story?"

"Yes." Imriel relaxed, smiling back at her. "We have a bust of him, you know."

"I know." It had been her gift to me. "I'd like to hear your story, Imriel, if you wouldn't mind telling it to me. Yours, and Phèdre's and Joscelin's, too."

So we told our story to the Queen's Poet from beginning to end, and it was a long time in the telling. The quiet servant brought tea sweetened with honey and a plate of small cakes, a warm blanket of fine-combed wool which he settled carefully about his mistress' shoulders as Thelesis sat and listened without interrupting, sipping tea to suppress her cough. From time to time, her dark eyes filled with tears. We told the story in turns, and the only sound save for one voice speaking was the soft noise of oak-galls being ground to powder for ink. In time, even that fell silent as Thelesis' young apprentice ceased her labors to listen, perched on her stool, chin in her hands.

"Oh, my," Thelesis murmured when we had finished. "Oh, children."

There wasn't much more she could say. At the distant worktable, her apprentice picked up her bowl and resumed grinding.

"It's not a tale fit for poetry," I said. "Not Daršanga."

"No." Her gaze rested on Imri, filled with compassion. "But it is a story that must be told, that we might remember and never let such a thing come to pass again. I will think on how best it might be done. I may not live to see it finished, but I daresay I will see it begun."

"You shouldn't say such things," I said, not wanting to hear them.

Her smile was tinged with sorrow. "Ah, Phèdre! You've never shied away from truth. I've lived through such times as poets dream of, and I have no regrets. But don't fear, my dear, I'll not leave yet. To miss the end of the story—ah, now that would grieve me." Her tone changed. "It must be hard for you to wait."

I took a deep breath, and made no reply.

"Ysandre will forgive you, you know." Thelesis read my expression. "You gave her no choice, Phèdre. And I daresay she took it harder, coming from you. But I remember your young Tsingano friend very well indeed, and I suspect he has reserves of fortitude he's yet to tap. Nearly two years ago, you gave him the gift of hope. He'll wait thirty years, if he must; three months is naught to one facing immortality."

My heart rose. "Sibeal delivered my message?"

"No one told you?" She shook her head. "Of course not. Who would dare? Yes, my dear, she did. He permitted the Cruarch's ship to enter the harbor, and she told him. And don't forget, Hyacinthe has the gift of the *dromonde*, does he not? As many unforeseeable turns as the path of your life has taken before, I suspect it lies clear at this point."

"To Rahab." I shivered.

"To the angel known as Pride," Thelesis said, "and Insolence." Her voice was gentle. "Do you know what you will do when you arrive?"

"No," I said. "Not really."

"She'll have a plan by the time we get there," Joscelin said to Imriel. "It will probably involve me swimming three times around the island carrying you on my back, wearing Ras Lijasu's lion's mane on your head and screaming at the top of your lungs and waving a sword. That should get Rahab's attention, don't you think?"

Imriel grinned. "Can you swim when you're seasick?"

"Shhh." Joscelin tweaked a lock of his hair. "You're not supposed to reveal that, especially in front of the Queen's Poet."

I caught Thelesis watching their exchange. She smiled, seeing me take notice. "What was it you said to Ysandre? Not all families are born of blood and seed?"

"She told you that?" I was surprised.

"Even a Queen may recognize Elua's hand at work, Phèdre nó Delaunay. Give her time." Thelesis turned her head away to cough, covering her mouth with a kerchief worked with the Courcel insignia. In the background, the apprentice girl set down her pestle and slipped from the stool, bringing the bowl of fine-ground gall for inspection. "Well done," Thelesis said, regaining her voice. "Thank you, Alais."

Alais? I startled, only now recognizing the dark-haired girl in the drab smock as Ysandre's youngest daughter. So much, I thought, for my vaunted powers of observation. "Princess Alais," I said with alacrity, rising to curtsy.

She peered at me with the violet eyes of House L'Envers and wrinkled her nose. "I'm only Alais, here. Thelesis lets me help, sometimes."

"Now?" I raised my eyebrows at Thelesis.

"She wanted to hear her cousin's story," she said. "Ysandre did not object. Her grandfather Ganelon sought to protect her from unpleasant truths when she was a child. She will not do the same with her daughters. Better they should know the worst, from the beginning, and live their lives accordingly."

"Sidonie didn't want to hear it," Alais said complacently. "She doesn't like to get dirty, either. I do. Will you tell me about seeing lions, cousin?" The latter was directed to Imriel. "I will show you how we make ink."

Imriel glanced at me, uncertain. I shrugged. "Go ahead, if you like."

"Alais, you're not to touch the vitriol," Thelesis called. "Remember last time."

"I won't."

Joscelin, who had risen to bow to the young Princess, laughed aloud as she led Imri away to her worktable. "That one's a handful! I remember, it was Alais who wanted to play with my daggers. How old is she, now? Seven? Eight?"

"Eight," Thelesis said. "She has dreams, sometimes, that hold truths; small things, but accurate. Drustan thinks she may have inherited the gift of his mother, Necthana."

We watched them without speaking, the two heads bent intently over the worktable as Alais explained to Imriel how the powdered galls were mixed with vitriol and gum arabic to make an enduring ink that would not run or smear, even in dampness. At a distance, they might have been brother and sister. She has dreams, I thought, and he has nightmares. I have both, but Blessed Elua willing, that will soon be over. For these two, life is composed wholly of beginnings.

"We speak of stories ending," Thelesis de Mornay said softly, "when in truth it is we who end. The stories go on and on."

I prayed silently that they would not go on without me.

Not yet.

Hyacinthe.

Ninety-three

THE FITFUL winds of early spring came and went.

All across Terre d'Ange, the fields began greening. Shoots emerged from the rich soil, straining toward the sun. Crocuses blossomed in purple, white and yellow, and trees were hazed with leaf-buds. In the mountains, shepherds prepared for lambing. In the countryside, farmers watched the weather and planted seed. On the coasts, sailors gauged the winds and made ready to voyage.

And in the City of Elua, they wagered on the date of the Cruarch's arrival.

I daresay I had never awaited it with such anxiety myself, fond though I am of Drustan mab Necthana. For that was the letter of Ysandre's sentence upon me: When the Cruarch entered the gates of the City, I was free to leave it.

It was Cuillen Baphinol who brought us the news, ostensibly in the form of an official visit. But his horse was lathered when he pulled up in the courtyard and his shouting brought Joscelin at a run, his sword at the ready. Cassilines may only draw their swords to kill, but when it came to Imriel's safety, he didn't bother with his daggers.

"Peace," Cuillen said breathlessly, putting up his hands. "Peace, Messire Verreuil. I've news! The Cruarch's flagship has been sighted!"

Joscelin stared at him, then let out a whoop of joy and embraced the Eisandine lordling.

Cuillen Baphinol grinned, thumping his back. "I thought you'd be pleased, my lord!"

We threw a fête that evening, and the entire household celebrated. Once the preparations were done, I gave everyone, from Eugènie to the stable-keeper Benoit, the night off. The waiting had weighed hard on all of us, and cast a three-month pall over what should have been a joyous homecoming. We celebrated it that night. I do not doubt that among the Great Houses of Terre d'Ange, they would be appalled to know that at House Montrève, the serving-maid was seated with the chevalier, and the stable-keeper dined at the table with straw still in his hair, but it was *my* household, and these were the people who had kept it together in duress. I have been a peer of the realm and a barbarian's slave alike, and I am not too proud to dine with someone with the muck fresh-cleaned from beneath his nails.

Elua grant I never will be.

Although he did smell faintly of the stables.

In the morning, I daresay all of us were a trifle thick-headed. The revelry had gone late into the night and the wine-keg we had tapped was dry. I'd allowed Imriel two glasses, and his eyes had shone with it, color rising beneath his fair skin. He sang a shepherd's love song in his clear, true voice, while Hugues played his flute. How long, I wondered, until his boy's voice broke? It would be soon. His growth had slowed in Daršanga, but he was making up for lost time. "He'll break hearts, that one," Eugènie predicted.

I sent a bleary-eyed Hugues on errands that day, bearing word of the Cruarch's impending return to Emile in Night's Doorstep and to Eleazar in the Yeshuite quarter. It was a courtesy, since both would doubtless have heard the news already, but I had promised to notify both parties when we made ready to journey. When a knock came at the door, I thought it must be Hugues returning.

Instead it was a royal courier, with a summons from the Queen.

"What does she want now?" Joscelin asked, frowning at the missive. "Surely she hasn't changed her mind."

"Did her majesty give any indication?" I asked the courier.

He shook his head. "Only that your presence is requested, my lady. Yours, your consort's and the boy."

Once again, we travelled to the Palace, this time in our own carriage. All throughout the City, people were celebrating the news. The wineshops and taverns were open, markets were doing a brisk business. Wagers were settled, new wagers laid. Students given a day's leave from the Academy thronged the streets, toasting the Cruarch's health, looking forward to three days and nights of revelry when he reached the City. Drustan's return had become a veritable rite of spring. I wished I shared their high spirits, but Ysandre's summons had struck fear into my heart and my joyous mood had faded.

I kept a good face on it as a majordomo escorted us into the Palace, along with a pair of guards. I wondered if we were bound for the throne-room or a private audience. If it was state business, I thought, it will be the throne-room or the Hall of Audience. I feared what Ysandre might declare before an audience of state. What she might say in private, I could not guess, and feared even more.

As it happens, it was neither.

The majordomo brought us to the Salon of Eisheth's Harp, a spacious chamber with elegant frescoes depicting the ill-fated romance of Eisheth and an Eisandine tauriere. It is a place where D'Angeline nobles gather to enjoy pleasant conversation and musical concerts. There was a small crowd assembled, and it seemed a flautist and a lute-player had recently concluded. Ysandre was seated on a couch in the central arrangement, surrounded by courtiers and attendants . . . and someone else I recognized.

"Prince Imriel nó Montrève de la Courcel, the Comtesse Phèdre nó Delaunay de Montrève, Messire Joscelin Verreuil," the majordomo announced.

There was a half-second of silence in the Salon of Eisheth's Harp.

"Elua's Balls, lass, get over here and let me see you!" roared the unmistakable voice of the Royal Admiral Quintilius Rousse as he rose from the couch, opening his arms. "What are you waiting for, an engraved invitation?"

I crossed the distance in a daze to find myself engulfed in a bone-cracking embrace. "My lord Admiral," I stammered when he let me go. "What brings you here?"

Rousse grinned at me. If there was grey in his ruddy hair, he was as hale and hearty as ever, blue eyes bright in his scarred, weathered face. "Oh, I hear we're to fetch that sight-ridden Tsingano lad of yours as soon as Lord Drustan arrives. Sound all right to you?"

I blinked at him, then stared at Ysandre, belatedly curtsying. "Your majesty."

Ysandre raised her fair brows. "Surely you didn't think I'd let you set off unaided on this quest, Phèdre. We have a vested interest in the well-being of Hyacinthe, Anasztaizia's son. It has been arranged over the course of the winter. Lord Rousse has a flagship awaiting at Pointe des Soeurs in Azzalle. Whatsoever you require for this journey, you may arrange with Lord Rousse, who has an open writ with the Secretary of the Privy Purse. I trust you will be ready to depart by the time Drustan arrives?"

"Yes." I swallowed against the tears that threatened to close my throat. It had meant a good deal more than I reckoned, losing Ysandre's friendship, and I would give a great deal to have it back. "Yes, your majesty. We will be ready."

"Good." Ysandre's gaze rested on Imriel. "I suppose you will insist upon going, young cousin?"

"Your majesty." Imriel bowed, expressionless. "If you forbid it, I will stay."

"And what resentments will that breed?" Ysandre smiled wryly, watching Quintilius Rousse gather Joscelin in a pounding embrace. "No, young cousin, I will not forbid it, much as I would like to do so. I have learned somewhat of when to stand in the way, and when to stand aside. Messire Verreuil," she called to Joscelin, who freed himself to approach her, bowing. "In the future, I would appreciate it if you did not accompany Prince Imriel in public unarmed. I was promised, I believe, a Cassiline Brother to attend him? The Queen's Champion?"

"Your majesty." Joscelin bowed again and straightened, grinning. "I will not appear before you unarmed again."

"Good." Ysandre glanced around at the gape-mouthed courtiers. "Is there anyone here who has somewhat to say? No? Well and good. My lord Rousse, I grant you leave to make your arrangements. I expect a full accounting of your plans."

And with that, we were dismissed.

We spent the better part of the day in discussion with Quintilius Rousse, who returned with us to the house. Eugènie nearly tied herself into a knot attempting to stage a fit reception for the Royal Admiral— her kitchens were in complete disarray from last night's revelry. I daresay Rousse never noticed, quaffing wine and eating the savories set in front of him with a good will.

"So you've got the Name of God locked in your pretty head, eh lass?" he asked shrewdly. "Well, it may be and it may not, but either way, I'll take you wherever you want to go. I promised that a long time ago. The question is, what happens when we get there?"

I shrugged. "We try to summon Rahab."

"And if he comes?"

"I speak the Name of God and banish him." I gripped my hands together; they were cold. "My lord Rousse, in ten years, I've learned no more. I cannot tell you what will happen if he comes, nor if the banishment succeeds. Of a surety, it will be dangerous. How much so, I do not know."

"The Lord of the Deep," Quintilius Rousse mused. "I thought it was something, to see the Master of the Straits and live. This will be something, Phèdre nó Delaunay, such as no sailor ever dreamed, whether we survive it or no." He reached over and set a brawny hand on Ti-Philippe's knee, giving it a shake. "You're game, aren't you, my lad? You haven't forgotten how to haul a lanyard, I hope?"

"No, sir!" Ti-Philippe grinned at him. "I'll not be left behind this time!"

"And how about you, you half-mad Cassiline?" Rousse eyed Joscelin. "Still puking over the rails?"

"All the way." Joscelin smiled. "It hasn't stopped me yet."

"And Melisande's whelp." He looked at Imriel and shook his head. "Elua's Balls, boy, but you've a look of your mother! Still, Phèdre says you know your way around a ship, and won't get underfoot. You're bound to do this, eh?"

"Yes, my lord Admiral." Imriel was too fascinated to take offense. Between his blunt speech, his size and the old trawler scar that dragged at half his face, Quintilius Rousse was an imposing figure indeed. He was also one of my lord Delaunay's oldest friends, and one of the few people in the world I trusted implicitly. "The Tsingani helped Phèdre and Joscelin to find me because of Hyacinthe. It's a matter of honor," he added with a touch of defiance.

"Honor, eh?" Rousse squinted at him. "Doesn't *sound* much like your mother."

Imriel's jaw set and his nostrils flared. "I'm not my mother, Lord Rousse."

Quintilius Rousse roared with laughter. "Ah, boy, I should hope not! One's trial enough; the world's not fit to withstand two of the like. Well, for all that she's got a knack for finding trouble like I've never seen, Phèdre nó Delaunay has a gift for choosing friends. And if she's chosen to make you her son, I reckon you'll do."

With Rousse's aid, our plans were made. This would be a larger excursion than the last one. After our meeting in the Salon of Eisheth's Harp, word spread like wildfire through the City. Letters of invitation began to trickle into my home, swelling to a flood. I declined them all with courtesy. It would be different, afterward . . . if there was an afterward. Much as I mislike the hypocrisy of court politics, it is a part of life among D'Angeline peers. For Imriel's sake, it would be a necessity.

Now, I needed to concentrate on Rahab.

By means I did not question, Eleazar ben Enokh found a banned treatise on the summoning of angels, which he gave to me for a promise of discretion. I studied the incantations, committing the formula to memory. As I had never heard of such a thing proving effectual in living memory, I doubted its merit. Still, it was worth trying.

Joscelin was right, though.

A plan was taking shape in my mind.

This plan, I kept silent and told no one. If I had, I think, they might have tried to stop me, to dissuade me. I hoped it would not come to it. If it did . . . well. Until we reached the shores of Third Sister, there was no way of knowing. I had only the Name of God to guide me, syllables beating inside my mind as surely and steadily as my own pulse.

The days passed at a snail's pace. Every day, a courier raced eastward from Azzalle, last in a chain, reporting on the progress of the Cruarch's party. A corps of Rousse's sailors, trained to fight at sea and on land, would accompany us. I was glad it was Rousse's men and not the Royal Army, misliking the idea of travelling with Imriel amid soldiers who owed their allegiance to Duc Barquiel L'Envers.

Our caravan was chosen and outfitted, stores at the ready, horses shod, baggage-train made ready.

We waited.

Drustan mab Necthana entered the City of Elua.

℮Ninety-four

⊙ŋ THAT day, Ysandre staged a meeting in Elua's Square in the center of the City, where four fountains play beneath an ancient oak said to have been planted by Blessed Elua himself. It was there we had been bidden to assemble, waiting for the Cruarch's procession to pass. We heard them long before they arrived, handbells ringing, voices raised in cheers.

It was all very splendid, with Drustan in his crimson cloak with the Cruarch's gold torque at his throat, Ysandre at his side in a gown of spring-green silk, heavy with gold embroidery. Her shoulders were bare and she wore the necklace of Queen Zanadakhete, the massive emerald glinting on her breast. Elua's banner, the Courcel swan and the Black Boar of the Cullach Gorrym fluttered overhead. Alais rode perched on the pommel of her father's saddle, beaming; the Dauphine Sidonie was grave at her mother's side on a matching pony. Twin lines of the Queen's Guard in the livery of House Courcel flanked them, and throngs of people pressed close, throwing flowers.

Petals fell like fragrant rain.

In the shadow of the great oak, we met them, Quintilius Rousse in his finest regalia, standing stalwart to receive the Queen's commendation. I wore a riding-gown of forest-green velvet, the color of House Montrève. Hugues was carrying our banner, looking solemn in his new livery. Imriel had wanted garments in Montrève's color, but I'd thought better of it, and he was outfitted instead in a deep-blue doublet and breeches, giving the nod to his Courcel heritage.

Joscelin, of course, had contrived to secure himself attire in an unremarkable shade of grey, only his Cassiline arms identifying him. I was resigned to it by now.

"My lords and ladies, mesdames and messires!" Ysandre waited until their entourage had halted and raised her clear voice, addressing the crowds. "On this day, we not only welcome our husband and the august ruler of Alba, Drustan mab Necthana, into the City of Elua, but we bid farewell and godspeed to our Royal Admiral Quintilius Rousse, who leads this expedition to the Three Sisters, in the hopes of breaking forevermore the curse of the Master of the Straits. Know that our best hopes go with them." Her mare shifted sideways, and Ysandre settled her, glancing at me. "Phèdre nó Delaunay de Montrève," she said, her tone softening. "On this day, your sentence is ended, and you are free to pursue that which you have sought for ten years and more. Know that we wish you well, and pray for your success."

Standing beside my mount, I curtsied deeply, and my household followed suit.

Drustan mab Necthana dismounted, giving his reins to his daughter Alais' keeping. Heedless of propriety, he came over to greet us all, clasping arms with Quintilius Rousse, embracing Joscelin like a brother. He shook hands gravely with Imriel, who was greatly impressed with the intricate patterns of blue woad that decorated the Cruarch's face.

"Phèdre." Drustan set his hands on my shoulders. We had always understood one another, he and I. "You truly believe you have the means to free him?"

I nodded, unable to reply. The Name of God crowded my tongue. All I could do was gaze at Drustan, seeing in his dark eyes the knowledge of Hyacinthe's sacrifice, the guilt that had plagued him for so long. Like me, he would have taken it upon himself if he could have. He had been there. He knew. I heard in my mind the dry chirruping sound of a grasshopper, and remembered anew what was at stake.

Immortality without youth; an eternity of aging.

That was what Hyacinthe endured, while the rest of us loved and fought and reproduced, carrying on our stories without him.

"May it be so." Drustan bent his head to kiss my brow. "The honor of the Cullach Gorrym goes with you to fight for our brother Hyacinthe. Sibeal awaits you in Pointes des Soeurs, Phèdre. She carries my hope in her heart."

So it was done, and Drustan remounted his horse, securing Alais in the crook of his arm. And the crowds cheered and pelted them with flowers, urging them on their way. In the City of Elua, the revelry would begin in earnest that day, and by evenfall, the salons of reception would be overflowing in the Court of Night-Blooming Flowers, as

D'Angelines sought to celebrate in their own fashion the reunion of their Queen and her husband.

I watched Ysandre ride away, her back straight in the saddle, and sighed.

"Come on, then!" Quintilius Rousse, already mounted, chivvied his troops. "The sooner we're underway, the sooner we're on water, lads! My lady, are you ready? Yes? Then let us be off. The Lord of the Deep is waiting, and I say he's waited long enough!"

Our journey began.

The first thing we noted was the Tsingani. It did not seem strange, at first; there are always Tsingani on the road in the spring, travelling to the horse-fairs. It was Imriel who noted that they were following us. With an entire squadron of Rousse's men accompanying us—most of them drawn from the dedicated corps that still bore the name Phèdre's Boys and held to marching-chants that made me wish to cover Imriel's ears—we were not exactly unobtrusive. In the villages and cities along the way, the Tsingani presence seemed unremarkable. It was when we camped upon the open road that it became obvious.

The Tsingani were following us.

And they weren't the only ones.

The Yeshuite presence was more subtle than the Tsingani, whose brightly painted wagons were unmistakable. But gradually, as we travelled, it became evident that there were Yeshuites among our followers, some on foot, others in wagons, plain and unmarked alongside the gaily painted Tsingani _kumpanias_.

"Elua's Balls!" Quintilius Rousse exclaimed when the truth of it grew apparent. "What do _they_ want?"

"They want to know what happens," I said. "They want to hear the Name of God."

What _would_ happen when I spoke it? I did not know. It was a question too vast for me to comprehend. That which I knew and understood was trial enough. And so we rode across the green-growing land of Terre d'Ange, making for the Pointe des Soeurs, accompanied by our unlikely entourage. And I thought about the Name of God as we rode, and everything I saw was precious in my eyes, from the smallest leaf unfurling on the vine to my own companions. Brusque Rousse, loyal Ti-Philippe, eager Hugues, and ah, Elua! Joscelin, with his drab Cassiline attire covering his many scars, all gotten on my behalf, his hair worn loose to cover his arrow-gouged ear, his one concession to vanity.

And Imriel. *Imriel.*

My heart ached at the sight of him, happy and proud to be embarking once more upon a heroic quest. He rode with his head erect, watchful and sharp, his hands steady on the reins.

A matter of honor.

He believed it.

Oh, Melisande, I thought. You do not know this son of yours; of ours. Brother Selbert was right, he may surprise us all, in the end. Our goat-herd prince, our barbarian's slave. Am I wrong, to risk him thusly? Yet if I did not, if I forbid it . . . Ysandre is right, too. What resentments would it breed? He has your pride, Melisande, and he must be allowed it. Anger would fester too easily in this one. I can only try to offset it, to teach him compassion.

Blessed Elua grant I live to do it.

And so I watched them all, and kept my plan a secret as we made our way across Terre d'Ange, our silent entourage growing.

We arrived to find a Pointe des Soeurs much changed from the lonely garrison it had been, an isolated fortress ten miles from the meanest village. An encampment the size of a small city had grown up around it since I had been there two years past, with lively trade going on to support it. Evrilac Duré, who served the duchy of Trevalion, greeted us and guided us to the fortress. It was he who had brought the news, two years gone, of the passing of the old Master of the Straits, though he had not known it as such.

"It began this winter," he said shortly, in answer to my question regarding the encampment. "Tsingani, mostly. Watching and waiting. I don't know what for, but I have a score of suits pending, begging a place on the Admiral's ship. 'Tis for Lord Rousse to decide, I've told them."

"He's their *Tsingan kralis*," I murmured. "Hyacinthe, that is. They speak his name at the crossroads. They are waiting for him to return."

"Well." Evrilac Duré eyed me. "He may not be what they expect, when he does. I heard the stories, my lady. I saw what I saw. And one who's served as the Master of the Straits has more on his mind than a lot of motley Tsingani. I can tell you, the Cruarch's sister waits here, too."

"The Lady Sibeal," I said.

"The same." He gestured to his guard to raise the portcullis, admitting us into the fortress proper. "And I don't mind telling you, we give a good deal of thought to it, here in Azzalle."

He said no more; he didn't need to. That much I had garnered during my Bitterest Winter in the City of Elua. The question of Drustan's successor remained unsettled. According to the old laws of matrilineal heritage, no child of Drustan mab Necthana's loins could inherit the rulership of Alba. It must be one of his sisters' offspring.

Breidaia, the eldest, had children.

Sibeal did not.

They had given her the best quarters available and housed her honor guard of Cruithne warriors. Ghislain nó Trevalion had sent his own chef and his second chamberlain to ensure her comfort—and ours. This, too, had been arranged over the course of the winter months. Ysandre had not been idle while I brooded.

"Phèdre nó Delaunay." Sibeal's accent had improved. She held my hands in hers. "You have come, as I dreamed you would. Was the journey long?"

"Yes," I said. "It was, my lady."

She nodded gravely and turned to greet Joscelin. "It is good to see you, my brother."

"Lady Sibeal." Joscelin bowed, his vambraces flashing in the lamplit dining hall. "You honor me."

"No." She shook her head. "I speak the truth. So my brother the Cruarch has named you, and so you are. And I . . . I have no place here, who have only watched and waited while others trod the dark path. But here my dream has led me, and I am grateful for your indulgence."

It would have been easier if I could have disliked Sibeal and found it in my heart to resent her. In truth, I could not. She was too like her brother Drustan, with the same grave, dark eyes, the same calm dignity. And she loved Hyacinthe. Could I fault her for that? I loved him too. If I had trodden a dire path on his behalf, still, I had not done it alone.

So we dined together in the wind-battered halls of Pointe des Soeurs, and Quintilius Rousse conferred with his men, plotting our course. Evrilac Duré brought him the petitions to read, pleading for a spot aboard the flagship. Rousse scanned them with half an eye and scowled, passing them off to me.

"Tsingani and Yeshuites, clamoring for a berth! What do they think this is, a pleasure-barge? I've no room for landsmen underfoot. If the Lord of the Deep takes against us, we'll need expert hands on deck, and no mistake."

I glanced at the petitions. "They've a stake in the matter, my lord Admiral."

"Let them get their own ships, if they're so eager." He glowered at me, looking particularly fearsome. "Two. I'll grant you two places, Phèdre nó Delaunay. No more. And you shall have the choosing of it. You let them know at daybreak, for we'll hoist sail soon after."

"My lord." I inclined my head, acknowledging his decision.

Ninety-five

I REMAINED awake long into the small hours of the night. It was not so much the petitions, for those were easy, in the end. The hardest part was deciphering the scribblings of the guards who had accepted them, jotting notes on foolscap. Most of the Tsingani were illiterate, lacking the schooling that is inherent in D'Angeline society. Even the humblest of D'Angeline families see to the education of their children; it is a gift that Elua and his Companions have given us.

We have not shared it well.

Kristof, son of Oszkar. I remembered the name. He had risked his *kumpania* to bring us word of the Carthaginian slavers.

And for the Yeshuites . . .

Eleazar had come. It grieved me that he had not sought me out to ask the boon. We studied together for many years, he and I. After the death of Rebbe Nahum ben Isaac, he was my closest comrade in the Yeshuite community. But I, in favor or not, was the Comtesse de Montrève. I fear he dared not ask.

Well, he would have his chance to hear the Name of God at last. He had earned it, having sought it for so long. I hoped it was a kindness I gave him, and not a death-sentence.

I would know upon the morrow.

Joscelin remained awake with me, long after Imriel had lost the battle and fallen into sound slumber on an adjacent pallet, worn out by travel and the sea winds. I talked over my decisions with him, the wick on the oil lamp trimmed low. And then, at last, there was only one thing left to discuss.

"What happens to us?" Joscelin asked softly, lying beside me. "Phèdre . . . if . . . *when* . . . you succeed in freeing Hyacinthe, what happens to you and I?"

"I don't know," I whispered. A lock of his fair hair lay over his shoulder; I ran it between my fingers. It was easier than meeting his eyes. "Joscelin. You know I love you like my own life. Nothing that ever happens could change that. We *are* a family, you and I . . . and Imri. I would never break that bond."

"But you love him, too."

I did look at him, then; I had to. "Could you ask me not to?"

"No." He shuddered and put his arms around me. "It scares me, that's all."

I felt his strength surrounding me, the steady beat of his heart close to mine, the Name of God sounding in every pulse. "My Perfect Companion," I said, and smiled at him. "Joscelin. We spoke bold words about fear, do you remember? There is no one else like you. No one. We set ourselves in Elua's hand when we entered Drujan. We are there still, and always."

"I pray you're right." He kissed me then, and made no other reply. There was no other to make.

After a time, Joscelin too slept, and I alone was left awake to watch over them. I listened to Imriel murmur in his sleep, too quiet for a full-blown nightmare. I gazed at Joscelin's arm outflung in a patch of moonlight. His hand lay open, the fingers slightly curled. How many times had that strong arm protected me? I could not even count any more. The moon travelled across the night sky, and waves broke on the shore below the fortress.

I wondered what would happen on the morrow.

In time I too slept, and sleeping, dreamed I woke still, watching and waiting. Not until I opened my eyes to the dim grey light of dawn and the sound of seagulls did I realize I had slept. Rousse's men were stirring, making ready for departure. In the fortress, the kitchens were already bustling. Leaving Joscelin to attend Imriel, I rode out to the encampment with Evrilac Duré and a company of his men. There too, life was stirring, cookfires lit, Tsingani and Yeshuites awaiting. They had seen our party enter. They knew it would be today.

"There is room," I called, raising my voice, "for two people, and two people only on the Royal Admiral's flagship. You who have petitioned for this place, know that the journey is dangerous; the end, uncertain. Does anyone wish to withdraw?"

There was a pause as my words were relayed across the encampment. Afterward, silence. In the quiet, a Tsingano babe wailed, hushed by its mother. No other sound answered.

"So be it," I said. "For the Tsingani, to whom he who is Master of the Straits was born, I grant passage to Kristof, Oszkar's son, who gave aid when it was most needed. For the Yeshuites, I summon Eleazar ben Enokh, who has spent his life seeking the Name of God."

And they came, the both of them; the Tsingano *tseroman* bidding his *kumpania* farewell, clad in a shirt of bright yellow, his face guarded as he approached us. Eleazar rode a little donkey, his feet peddling on the ground, a smile of delight splitting his tangled beard.

"You should have asked," I told him.

"It was not yours to grant, before." His smile broadened. "Now, it is."

I sighed, and addressed them both. "You understand we may not return from this?"

Eleazar only beamed, and bobbed his head. I felt a moment's grief for Adara, who had let her husband go to pursue his dream. Kristof gave a brusque nod. "You have walked the *Lungo Drom* for him, lady," he said. "It is fitting one of us should be there to see its end, no matter what it be."

Thus did we make our way back to the fortress of Pointe des Soeurs, and the hungry eyes of those left behind watched us go. Quintilius Rousse had not spoken idly. His flagship, that was named *Elua's Promise,* sat at harbor, ready for departure. A half-dozen pennants fluttered from its mast—the golden lily-and-stars of Elua and his Companions, the silver swan of House Courcel, the Black Boar of the Cullach Gorrym, the crag-and-moon of Montrève, the Navigator's Star of Trevalion, and there . . . a sable banner with a ragged circle of scarlet, crossed by a barbed golden dart.

Kushiel's Dart.

"It is fitting," Quintilius Rousse said somberly. "My lady."

We boarded the ship, all of us. The rising sun emerged from a bank of clouds, laying a cloak of golden light upon the grey waters. The anchor was raised and the sails were hoisted, bearing the silver swan wrought large on a blue field. The oarsmen set to, and their efforts carried us out of the harbor of Pointe des Soeurs.

On the shore, Evrilac Duré and his men cheered. I wondered if they were glad to be remaining behind this time. Another crowd, distant, lined the cliffs above the harbor. I saw the Tsingano Kristof raise his hand in salute, and wondered how many he left behind in his *kumpania*. I was afraid to ask. Eleazar pointed his face into the wind, eager as a lover, his beard blowing in the breeze.

Sibeal stood alone in the prow, swaying with the ship's motion, flanked by her watchful Cruithne warriors. In my dreams, it was always I who stood there.

But I . . . I had Joscelin, looking green and swallowing hard against his illness, standing adamant at Imriel's side, and Ti-Philippe, who looked at home and glad upon the sea, and Hugues, keen as a hound on the scent for adventure.

I was not alone.

Not yet.

The winds blew fair and steady, like a summons. I wondered if Hyacinthe knew, if even now he plied his skills, the Master of the Straits, bringing us homeward. The sky turned into a clear blue vault above us, a few scudding clouds high overhead. Sunlight sparkled on the water, and the gulls circled with raucous cries, hoping we might prove a fishing vessel casting offal from our catch overboard. After so long, the confrontation to come seemed unreal. It was a day for rejoicing, not for endings.

For some hours, we flew over the water. Altogether too soon, the cry came from the crow's nest—the Three Sisters had been sighted. The sun was not yet at its zenith when we drew in sight of the tall cliffs of Third Sister. So close to land; so far from the world! For this short journey, I had travelled to Saba and back. I held my breath as Quintilius Rousse took the helm and shouted orders, maneuvering the flagship around the jutting coast of the island and into the narrow defile that marked the ingress to the harbor.

Between the towering cliffs, it went suddenly wind-still.

"Out oars!" Rousse bellowed as the sails fell slack and empty, the pennants drooping. "Row!"

When first I entered the domain of the Master of the Straits, it was wave-borne; on the second occasion, wind-blown. This time, we glided into the secluded harbor on the effort of mortal labor, wrought of muscle, sinew, bone and sweat.

The water was as flat and calm as a mirror, reflecting the rocky promontory and the carved steps, so that it seemed a second stair led to a temple at the bottom of the harbor, small with distance and impossibly deep, wreathed with clouds on the sea's floor. The advancing ship's prow forged ripples, revealing the illusion, distorting the image of the lone figure who stood upon the promontory, waiting.

Hyacinthe.

The Name of God surged within me, and I yearned to shout it to the empty skies.

He was clad as before, in rusty black velvet in an archaic style, old lace spilling like sea-foam at his cuffs and throat. This time, a cloak of indeterminate color hung from his shoulders, satin-lined. It may have been violet, once; time and sun and salt had faded it to a vague tarnished silver, like twilight on the ocean. As our ship drew near the shore, only a few yards of open water remaining, Hyacinthe placed the palms of both hands together at waist height, then opened them and held them flat to the earth.

I heard Sibeal whisper his name.

The ship halted, oars locked fast in the limpid water. The rowers strained in vain, sinews cracking. Across the distance I gazed at Hyacinthe unspeaking, the Sacred Name locked fast in my throat.

He gazed back at me, unnamable colors shifting in his fathomless eyes, and hope and fear lying distant at the bottom, as tenuous as the temple's reflection. "You've come," he said at last, and his voice sounded odd and unused, not at all like my dream. "I saw you set sail in the sea-mirror of the temple."

"Yes." I swallowed. "Hyacinthe, I have the key."

Fear and hope leapt in his too-dark eyes and the boy I'd loved looked out of the face of the Master of the Straits. He bowed his head to hide it, pressing his fingers to his temples.

"Elder Brother!" Quintilius Rousse made his way to the railing, addressing him with the traditional title sailors accorded the Master of the Straits. "I'm here in the name of her majesty Queen Ysandre de la Courcel, Tsingano. Have you grown too proud to let old friends ashore? We're on the Queen's business, breaking this curse of yours."

"My lord Admiral." Hyacinthe lifted his head, mouth twisting in a smile. "Forgive my manners. It is a pleasure to see you once more. My lady . . . my lady Sibeal." He looked at her for a moment, and what was exchanged in that glance, I could not say. "And you, Cassiline."

"Tsingano." Joscelin bowed, arms crossed. "*Tsingan kralis.*"

Hyacinthe went still, then, seeing Kristof. "Why have you brought him here?"

"The Tsingani await your return, Prince of Travellers," I said to him. "Kristof, Oszkar's son is here on their behalf. Eleazar ben Enokh is here for the Yeshuites, who seek the Name of God. Will you let us ashore?"

He paused, then shook his head, as I had known he would. "I cannot, Phèdre. I dare not." His voice softened. "It would invoke the *geis*."

"And we will break it," I said steadily. "That's why we've come."

"No." His face was set and hard. "It cannot be."

"Then you will have to cross to us," I said.

Something stirred in the depths of his eyes. "You saw what happened before."

I nodded. "Rahab, or an invocation of him. Hyacinthe, it must be. Rahab must manifest to be banished. I will try to summon him if you will try to cross. Will you dare that much?"

His smile was edged with bitterness. "I would risk any part of myself to break this curse. It is innocent blood I will not endanger. Summon him, if you think you can."

"So be it." I turned to Imriel, and bade him fetch my writing case from the stateroom. Everyone aboard the ship was quiet as he did, waiting and watching.

Hyacinthe frowned, perplexed, dark irises waxing and waning. "*Melisande's* son?"

"Ours, now." I glanced at Joscelin, who smiled quietly. Imriel returned with the waxed leather case that contained parchment, pens and ink. Ti-Philippe unlashed an empty water-barrel and rolled it over unasked, making a writing surface. I opened the case and tested the point of a quill, emptying my mind of aught else. Uncorking the inkwell and dipping the pen, I wrote upon a virgin piece of parchment, forming the acrostic square I'd studied in Eleazar's banned treatise.

RAHAB

ABARA

HABAH

ARABA

BAHAR

It was done, and the name of Rahab bounded the cruciform palindrome of Habah—Hu Habah, He-Who-Shall-Come, one of the secret names of the Mashiach. I laid down the quill with trembling fingers and recorked the ink, bowing to the four corners of the globe, acknowledging the One God's dominion. "Rahab do I summon," I cried, giving the Habiru incantation. "As the Hidden Name of the Mashiach does inhabit and summon thee, Rahab who is Lord of the Deep, come thou forth, and answer me, as all spirits are subject unto Yeshua ben Yosef, that every spirit of the firmament and of the ether, upon the earth and under the earth, on dry land or in the water, of whirling air or of rushing fire may be obedient unto the will of Adonai." Leaning over the railing, I let the parchment flutter onto the waters. "Rahab, I summon thee!"

In the depths of the harbor, something stirred. The ship trembled. "Now, Tsingano!" Joscelin shouted.

He tried, Hyacinthe did; tried, as he had before. Trusting, haunted, he took a step onto the now-churning waters, fearless of the depths. And as it had before, the world *shifted*. A maelstrom opened, and something moved within it, something bright and shining and terrible. Squinting my eyes, I saw water surge like a vast wing, green and foam-edged, a roiling eye. I opened my mouth, and the Name of God was there, on my tongue. There it remained, oar-locked and tight as the moment of manifestation trembled on the edge of being. The ship bucked like a restive mount, riding the surge; I fell to my knees and bit my tongue, tasting blood. There was shouting, somewhere, from Rousse's sailors as they sought to steady the craft.

And then it was over, and we were still aboard the ship. The moment had passed, the summoning failed. On the shore, Hyacinthe was doubled and panting, each breath wracked with pain. "Not . . . so . . . easy . . ." he said, forcing out the words, straightening with an effort.

In the prow of the ship, Sibeal wept for the first time.

So be it.

"I'm sorry," I said to Eleazar ben Enokh. "It would have been nice if it had worked." I turned to Imriel. "Remember what I promised," I said. "I would not leave if I didn't believe I'd be back."

He had his mother's eyes. Imri nodded, gravely, understanding, even as Joscelin understood too, already in motion, moving to intercept me, crying, "Phèdre, *no!*"

Placing one hand on the railing, I vaulted over it, my skirts trailing. Even as I leapt, I was aware of Joscelin reaching for me, trying to grasp the merest fold of fabric and halt my momentum.

Too late.

I jumped.

Ninety-six

A MIGHTY gust of wind caught and held me.

I hung suspended in midair, buffeted by gale forces, my hair lashing like a nest of angry adders, skirts snapping and whipping, my watering eyes slitted against the pressure as the winds tore the very breath from my lips.

Behind me, I heard above the roaring wind faint shouts of alarm, the ship creaking, ropes singing taut as the sails flapped and bellied in the fallout from the raging winds that held me. Below me stood Hyacinthe, his arms outspread. The terrible, deadly power of the Master of the Straits suffused his features, and there was nothing in him I could speak to.

Like a great fist, the knotted winds began carrying me back toward the ship.

"*Idiot!*" I shouted, the word lost in the winds. Master of the Straits or no, I'd spent the last two years with Hyacinthe's voice haunting my dreams. "Put me down! I *have* the key! Give me the chance to use it!"

Doubt surfaced in those inhuman eyes. Somehow, in the roaring gale of his own elemental power, he'd heard my shouts. "You're certain of it?"

The words came from all around me, as if the wind itself had spoken. I laughed. How many times had I asked Imriel that very thing? And now the question came back to me. "Yes," I said in the center of my personal whirlwind, trusting Hyacinthe to hear. "I'm sure."

His hands and lips moved and the winds ceased.

I dropped like a stone onto the barren promontory and caught myself on hands and knees, jarred by the impact.

"TSINGANO!"

Joscelin's voice was the first thing I heard when the winds stopped, shouting with fury. I turned my head to see him clambering over the railing, preparing to make the leap even as hands grappled at him, trying to hold him back. The gap had grown wider, the ship blown several yards from shore.

"Joscelin, no!" I cried, getting to my feet. He stared at me, eyes wild and desperate, his fair hair wind-lashed. "Don't do it," I pleaded. "I was the only one who needed to come ashore. Only me. And if I'm wrong . . . there's no need to put the rest at risk."

"You knew." His knuckles were white on the railing, his face taut. "You planned it all along."

"I thought it might come to it," I said softly. "No more."

"Joscelin. Joscelin!" It was Imriel, catching his sleeve, who got Joscelin's attention. "Don't," he said, his voice cracking with fear. "Please don't. Not both of you. You promised."

It was a tense moment. Quintilius Rousse watched with glowering concern, the others with a mix of fear and interest. Ti-Philippe and Hugues stood close at hand, prepared to wrestle Joscelin over the railing if need be. I wouldn't have given much for their chances, if he'd set his mind to it, but Imriel's plea had reached him. Joscelin sighed, defeated, sagging against the railing. "Then do it," he murmured, "and be done with it."

Only then did I fully realize that I stood upon the rock of Third Sister, the isle of the Master of the Straits. I raised my gaze to meet that of Hyacinthe, who stood near enough to touch.

"Phèdre," he whispered.

I flung both arms about his neck and burst into tears.

He felt the same, under my touch. Whatever changes his long ordeal had wrought in him, whatever powers endowed him, beneath it he was Hyacinthe still, my childhood friend, my Prince of Travellers. The scent of his skin triggered more memories than I could count. Before Joscelin, before the Queen, before Thelesis de Mornay, Cecilie Laveau-Perrin, before my lord Delaunay himself . . . before them all, I had known Hyacinthe.

"Phèdre," he said again, drawing a wracking breath, holding me close. "You said you were sure. You said you were *sure!*"

I lifted my tear-stained face. "I am, Hyacinthe; as sure as I can be. You wouldn't risk any of us. Should I risk them, when I am the only one needed?"

His smile was a ghost of its former self as he released me. "You're awfully willful for an *anguissette*, you know. A sickness in the blood, my mother would say."

I laughed through my tears. "I remember."

Hyacinthe shuddered and laid his hands upon my shoulders. "You know I have to ask?"

I nodded. "What is needful to break this curse. I know. I will take your place."

"I could ask more," he reminded me.

"Do I need to say it?" I dashed away the tears with the back of my hand, steadying my voice. "I know the source of your power, that is pages from the *Sepher Raziel*, the Lost Book of Raziel, which Rahab brought forth from the deep. I know that Rahab loved a D'Angeline woman who loved him not, and thus the curse was born. Do you require more? I know more. I can tell you tales of Rahab himself, and how he was punished once before, for failing to part the seas at the One God's command. The *geis* is fulfilled, Hyacinthe. You are free of it."

"The book." He gazed at the stairs. "I shouldn't leave without it."

"Then let's get it."

Hyacinthe nodded and walked to the edge of the promontory, addressing the ship. A dozen faces ranged along the railing, staring back at him. "My lord Rousse," he said in the echoing voice that came from everywhere and nowhere. "We go now to retrieve the one item of value on this forsaken isle. We will return, and attempt once more the crossing. Forgive me, but I must ensure before then that no other disembarks on this deadly shore."

And so saying, he blew out his breath and pushed gently with both hands, whispering unheard words, circling three fingers in the air. The water in the still harbor surged, bearing the ship on a hummock into the center and depositing it there, untouched, while a wall of water circled about it in a contained maelstrom, sea-green and clear, unwitting fish swimming in the limpid barrier.

I heard shouts of dismay and consternation. Even at a distance, I could make out a few reactions. Quintilius Rousse was ordering his men about, rigging the ship with storm-sails, preparing for the worst. Sibeal remained in the prow, clinging to hope. Eleazar looked here and there, visibly exclaiming and beaming at the marvel. Joscelin stood with arms folded, his face a mask of betrayal. And Imri . . . Imri was leaning over the railing, reaching out one hand in an effort to touch one of the circling fish, while Hugues held his legs anchored and Ti-Philippe pointed his efforts.

He wasn't afraid, I thought. Ah, Imriel! Blessed Elua be thanked for that mercy.

"Melisande's son!" Hyacinthe shook his head in wonderment. "I watched in the sea-mirror, so far as I could, but once you passed beyond the waters that border Terre d'Ange, I could see no more. The Master of the Straits' power has its limits."

"And the *dromonde?*" I asked him.

He was quiet for a while, turning and starting up the interminable stairs. "I looked," he said when we had reached the halfway point, me toiling behind him. "The last time I dared was over a year ago. I saw a darkness so profound I feared to look again."

"Daršanga," I said, remembering. "We were in Daršanga, then."

Hyacinthe bowed his head. "You survived it. I wasn't sure, for a long time. After the dire possibilities I saw, I chose to trust to mortal hope and uncertainty rather than the *dromonde*. A few months ago, you reappeared in the sea-mirror, though I could not make sense of all I saw, the boy included."

"We came home," I said. "It's a long story."

"So I believe." Hyacinthe resumed his climb, the cloak of indeterminate color trailing behind him. I gasped after him, muscles quivering. I'd forgotten how long and steep was the stair that led to the top. I was nearly done in by the time we reached the open-air temple.

It was unchanged during his tenure, the flagstones of white marble, marble columns reaching skyward like an unanswered prayer. Far below us, the ship *Elua's Promise* looked like a child's toy, floating in a watery ring. In the center of the temple stood the great bronze vessel upon its tripod—the sea-mirror, Hyacinthe had called it. And beside it, a pair of robed figures bowed deeply before the Master of the Straits.

"Tilian," Hyacinthe said, naming them. "Gildas. You will remember Phèdre nó Delaunay."

I remembered them. Gildas, the elder, had been white-haired when I'd met him before; now, he was ancient. He came forward trembling, one crabbed hand extended. "Thou hast agreed," he said, his voice quavering, speaking in the D'Angeline of the oldest courtly lays. "Thou hast agreed to the sacrifice, fair lady!"

"Not exactly." I took his hand in both of mine. The bones felt bird-hollow, sheathed in skin like parchment. "I have come to break the curse, my lord Gildas. Your long service here is done."

He withdrew his hand with a querulous sound. Hyacinthe merely watched, colors shifting in his dark eyes. Tilian, the younger, bowed to him.

"Wilst thou require the basin refilled ere sundown, my lord?" he asked.

"You heard her," Hyacinthe replied. "Soon it will be ended here, one way or another. I require nothing further."

They remained behind, watching with consternation as Hyacinthe led the way down a second set of steps to the lonely tower that had been his home for so long. It rose, grey and stony, from the rocks of Third Sister, the oriel windows glinting in the sun—rose-red, amber, emerald, a cobalt like the color of Imriel's eyes. I gaped at it now as I had not, then. Hyacinthe paid it no heed. It was his prison, as familiar to him by now as his own skin.

I had forgotten how many of the isle-folk attended upon the Master of the Straits. They bowed low as he entered, watching with curious eyes as we mounted the curving stair, circling to the top of the tower. His attendants, his gaolers. They had been kind to us, long ago. They treated him now with a mixture of awe and fear.

We climbed to the very top of the tower, a level unseen from below. And there, the chamber was set about not with colored oriels, but windows open onto the skies, looking out over the seas in every direction. It held uncountable treasures gathered from the deep—a gilded helmet encrusted with coral, a mottled egg the size of a newborn baby, a marble sphinx, an unstrung harp made from the jawbone of a whale, all things strange and wondrous, salt-pitted and ancient. Hyacinthe stood in the middle of the room and looked about him.

"Here is where he taught me," he said softly. "What I became, I learned in this place. He was not bad, you know; only desperate, and bound by strictures not of his making."

"I know," I whispered.

"It's funny." Hyacinthe turned to a massive bookstand, riffling through the pages that lay spread open upon it, pages of incalculable power. "I never had a father, not really. For a little while, in the Hippochamp, I thought Manoj might acknowledge me. But . . ." He shrugged. "There was the *dromonde*, after all. And in the end, it was this, instead. And *he* is the nearest thing I have known to it. To a father."

I watched him wrap the pages in oilskins and place them in an ancient leather case, bound with straps of bronze. "Are you sorry to leave it?"

"No." He closed the case, and looked at me, swallowing hard. "Yes." He sat down on a low ivory stool that dated to the Tiberian Empire. "It's been a long time, Phèdre. I thought, at first, mayhap I could change this role, this place . . . bring a touch of light, of mirth, cast it in my image instead of *his*." He shook his head. "I was wrong. It was too hard, too long, too lonely. And the power . . . it isolates. It changed me instead. And now?" He gave a bitter laugh. "I've become like *him*. All the servants I thought to befriend bow and fear to meet my eyes. Me, Hyacinthe, who ran a livery stable and told fortunes in Night's Doorstep to drunken lordlings! Who would have believed it? But I have become the Master of the Straits, and I do not know how to be anything else."

"Emile still has the stable," I said, kneeling beside him and taking his hands. "And your mother's lodging-house, and a good deal more. He's made quite a business of it."

"I know." His fingers moved in mine. "I saw it in the sea-mirror. You know I can't go back to that, Phèdre."

"The Tsingani have named you—"

"*Tsingan kralis*." Hyacinthe's mouth twisted. "A *Didikani* half-breed, outcast for wielding the *dromonde*. They let Manoj banish me, and they let my mother live and die as *vrajna*, tainted for her loss of honor, though it was through no fault of her own. Do you think they would name me king if they did not covet the power I bear?"

"Mayhap not," I said steadily. "Do you blame them? For a thousand years, they have been outcast themselves, lest you forget. Even in Terre d'Ange, they are merely tolerated, sometimes despised, left to wander, to fend for themselves. And they are willing to change, for you. Even now, the *Didikani* enjoy greater stature than before. Under your leadership, the laws that condemned your mother, that rendered you outcast, might change."

Hyacinthe withdrew his hands from mine and covered his face. "It's too much," he said, muffled. "You do not know the responsibilities of the Master of the Straits. For eight hundred years, we have protected Alba and Terre d'Ange. Yes." He raised his head at my silence, glaring with unearthly eyes. "*Protected!* For all that the separation was maintained, we protected you! Even now, I keep the bans. No Skaldi ship may sail from the north but I permit it, no Aragonian or Carthaginian from the south. Do you think my responsibilities will end if the curse is broken? They won't, Phèdre. While I live, it is mine to ensure, because it is necessary. Do you suppose I can do that *and* serve to lead the Tsingani?"

"No." I wanted to quail under his glare; I steeled myself instead. "Is that why you're afraid to leave the isle?"

He looked away. "Who says that I am?"

I answered him with a question. "Is it Rahab you fear, or leaving?"

Outside the tower windows, gulls circled, riding the winds. Hyacinthe watched them. "Both," he said at length. "Oh, Phèdre! I want it, I want it so badly I taste it, dream of it. I see my face in the mirror, aging, and I think of nothing else. But it scares me to death." He looked back at me. "I faltered. I was afraid. Would the summoning have worked, if I hadn't?"

"I don't know." I sat on my heels and regarded him. "It will work this time. The *geis* is bound to me, now."

"What happens if you falter?"

I tried to laugh, but it caught in my throat. "I suppose I become your apprentice."

"And I get to die, while you wither into eternity." There were tears, mortal tears, in Hyacinthe's black eyes. "I should never have let you ashore."

I folded my hands to hide their trembling. "I won't falter."

He smiled sadly. "Can you be so sure?"

"No." I forced my tone to remain calm. "But everything I love best in the world, aside from you, is on that ship you bound mid-harbor. And I haven't had twelve years to forget it. What's the cost, Hyacinthe, of pressing forward until Rahab manifests in his entirety? Pain? Fear? I'm an *anguissette*. These are things I was born to endure."

Hyacinthe shook his head. "You never give up, do you?"

"Not yet, anyway." I rose to my feet and extended my hand to him. "Come on, Master of the Straits. There's a ship full of anxious people awaiting us, eager to learn if we're all going to live or die. Let's go find out. You can worry later what to do about the Tsingani." I helped him to his feet, then caught sight of myself in a bronze mirror as I turned to go, stopping me in my tracks. The winds that had born me up had blown my hair into serpentine tangles, wild and disheveled. I raised my hands in dismay, feeling at the gnarled locks, trying ineffectually to unknot them with my fingers. "Name of Elua! Hyacinthe, look what you did to my *hair!*"

"You think it will matter to Rahab?" Hyacinthe asked. I glanced sharply at him, and found him grinning; unexpected, as welcome as light in a dark place, his old grin, irrepressible, white and merry against his brown skin. He laughed at my ire, dodging a well-aimed blow and catching me in his arms. "Ah, Phèdre! You've not changed."

"Neither have you," I whispered, laying my head on his chest. "Not really, not underneath. I still know you, Hyacinthe."

We stood like that for a long time.

"You gave me a gift," he said eventually, his breath warm against my tangled hair. "That last night, on the isle, before you left me here alone . . ." His mouth curved in a smile. "It gave me something beautiful to remember. Sometimes, it was the only thing that kept me going."

"It wasn't a gift," I murmured. "I remember it, too."

"Phèdre." Hyacinthe cupped my face in his hands. "I'm going to miss you."

I met his dark, sea-changing gaze and could not pretend he was wholly unaltered. "You'll go with Sibeal."

He nodded. "She has seen, in dreams, something of what I've become. And I have watched her, too, in the sea-mirror. We understood one another from the beginning, Phèdre, Necthana's daughters and I. Sibeal isn't you. But she's someone I could love. And you . . . I've watched you, too."

"Joscelin," I said.

"Joscelin." His smile was rueful. "That damned Cassiline, yes. Even on Alba, I saw it in both of you. I told you as much. Elua must have laughed when he bound your hearts together. Whatever power I have, it's naught to that. I'll not challenge that bond."

"This is good-bye, then? To you and I?" I asked him.

"To the Queen of Courtesans and the Prince of Travellers." Hyacinthe traced a line along the curve of my left eye, the dart-stricken one. "It's what you became after all, isn't it? And I . . . I will have to acknowledge the claim of the Tsingani. If I cannot rule them as *Tsingan kralis*, still, I shall have a say in the succession, and what we become as a people. That much is owed."

"Then it *is* good-bye."

"Mayhap." Something moved in the depths of his sea-dark eyes, containing something of Hyacinthe's merriment and something of the Master of the Straits' power. "If it came to pass, on the odd year or three, that the night breezes called your name in my voice, Phèdre nó Delaunay, would you answer?"

I put both arms around his neck and kissed him hard in reply.

It was at once familiar and strange, that kiss, and I tasted in it my own lost childhood, the legacy of a whore's unwanted get, raised by a reluctant Night Court, finding friendship for the first time. All of our history was in it, scrapes and mishaps, confidences shared, and the darker shadows of adulthood; the losses of the battle of Bryn Gorrydum, where I had learned there is healing in the sharing of Naamah's arts, and the terrible sacrifice Hyacinthe had made here upon this isle. And I tasted too the strangeness his life had become, the alien knowledge of elemental forces, the salt-surge of seawater, the tidal depths, the roiling clouds and the forked violence of lightning, the pure music of the unstrung winds.

"I was wrong." Hyacinthe laughed aloud, unfettered and joyous. His black eyes danced. "You *have* changed. Is that what it does, to hold the Name of God within you?"

"Yes," I said, and kissed him again.

His grin was pure wickedness when I stopped, and pure Hyacinthe. "And what did Melisande Shahrizai make of it?"

It may be he guessed because he was the Master of the Straits, and privy to arcane knowledge; it may be because he was Anasztaizia's son, and had the gift of the *dromonde*. But like as not, it was because he was Hyacinthe, and had known me longer than anyone else alive. "Oh, shut up." I laughed, sinking both hands into his black ringlets and tugging his head back down to mine. "I'm trying to say farewell, if not goodbye."

That time, he heeded me.

It went no further than a kiss, an unspoken promise, a bittersweet farewell. I would not have repented it if it had. Mayhap, when we were younger, it would have; but there were too many considerations, and we were too conscious of them. I let him go, and watched the solemn mantle of power settle back upon him as he gathered up the case that bore the pages from the Lost Book of Raziel.

"There is nothing else you want from this place?" I asked, glancing around.

"No." Hyacinthe shook his head. "Let it go to the folk of the isles, if they wish it. Those who were born to the Three Sisters have suffered as long as he or I, under this curse." He hesitated. "Is there aught you desire, Phèdre? There is treasure aplenty, and you welcome to it."

"Only the library," I said, remembering how I had passed many hours in this tower reading the works of a Hellene poetess long believed vanished to the world. "There are lost stories in it. I would see them restored."

"Lost stories." He smiled. "They are yours, if we survive this. I will order it so. Well, then, that's it. Are you ready?"

"Are you?" I studied his face.

"Yes." He took my hand, gripping it hard, the colors in his eyes shifting like the changing hues of the night sea when a cloud passes over the moon. "I won't falter if you won't."

He had the power to command the waves to rise and the winds to blow.

The Master of the Straits was afraid.

"I won't," I vowed, and prayed it was true.

Ninety-seven

HYACINTHE CALLED the isle-folk who attended him into the reception chamber in the tower. They crowded around, cooks, scullery-maids, foot-servants, laundresses, servants of all ilk, whose lives for countless generations had been spent doing the bidding of the Master of the Straits, maintaining the tower, purveying food, cleaning and restoring treasures brought forth from the bottom of the sea.

They murmured among themselves in an archaic dialect of D'Angeline, forgotten on the mainland for eight hundred years, stealing fearful glances at Hyacinthe as he stood on the curving stair above them, waiting. Ancient Gildas and Tilian, who was no longer young, were among them; for days on end, they had made the arduous trek down the stone stairs to fill the basin of the sea-mirror at sunrise and sundown. How many years? One might suppose they would be glad of their freedom, but they looked dismayed.

"My people." Although he spoke quietly, Hyacinthe's words encompassed the tower. "This day, I go forth to break the *geis* and leave the island. If we succeed, I will not return. Know that all things in this tower are yours, to distribute as you choose, saving only the contents of the library, which shall be held in keeping for Phèdre nó Delaunay of Montrève. Although this exile has been bitter to me, you have served long and well, and I am grateful for it. I leave you with my thanks."

"Fair my lord!" Old Gildas' voice emerged choked. "Surely, thou hast need of thy sea-mirror—aye, and thine acolytes to attend and fill it!"

"No, Gildas." Hyacinthe shook his head. "It was wrought on Third Sister, and will open its far-seeing eye nowhere else in the world. Elsewhere, I must needs construct a sea-mirror anew, in its own place of vision. Let this one remain here, as a reminder."

"Prithee, how shall we conduct ourselves?" someone said wondering, setting loose a flurry of anxious queries. "What shall become of us? What shall we do?" The questions fluttered around the stone walls of the tower, beating on nervous wings. Hyacinthe's brow darkened, storm clouds gathering in his eyes.

"*Live!*" The word fell like a thunderclap, silencing them. I shuddered at the power that emanated from him in waves, a charged odor like the air after lightning has struck. "Live," he repeated, more gently, in his echoing tone. "Live free of this curse, fish and hunt, grow crops and herd cattle. Build boats and sail to the mainland, trade and prosper. Make music, write poems, dance. Find one another in love, lose one another in sorrow. *Live.*"

No one spoke as he descended the stair, parting to make way for him. I saw how their eyes followed him—fearful, calculating, avid and forlorn by turns. Not until we reached the door did anyone utter a word.

"My lord!" It was Tilian who called after us, daring and defiant. "And if thou dost fail, my lord? 'Tis no secret thou has tried it before; didst do so this very day. We, who have attended thee these long years, know the truth of it. Why shouldst succeed now?"

Hyacinthe turned, staring at the man until he turned pale. "Because this time," he said, "I am not alone. You have served power a long time, Tilian, and come to relish the taste of it. Listen to me now when I tell you: Do not pray for my failure. Because this time, Rahab will come in the fullness of his might and ageless wrath, and my power is to his as a bucket of water is to the ocean. And if we fail, his anger may raise the seas and drown the isles of the Three Sisters, and when the fish nibble at your flesh and the crabs scuttle through your bones, you will not have to worry about how to live without the Master of the Straits to attend."

There were no further protests.

I waited until we were outdoors and the bright sun had chased the crawling chills from my flesh to ask him if he believed it.

"Yes," Hyacinthe said shortly. "Why do you suppose it terrifies me so?"

Well and so; the lives of hundreds of innocent people rested in my hands. I clutched my skirts, concentrating on descending the long stair, my breathing coming shallow and labored—not with exertion, this time, but with fear. Below us, *Elua's Promise* bobbed at anchor in the center of its tame whirlpool, laden with cargo too precious for words.

It would be better, I thought, if they were gone from this place.

"Can you send them away?" I asked him.

"Beyond Rahab's reach?" His mouth twisted. "No such place exists upon the seas."

"Out of sight, then. Surely it would be safer."

We had gained the promontory. Hyacinthe gazed at the ship, then at me, shifting the case he held under one arm, containing the pages salvaged from the Book of Raziel. "It may be so. They will not thank you for it."

"I know," I said. "Do it."

"Quintilius Rousse!" Hyacinthe's voice echoed off the cliff walls, resounding across the harbor. "Raise your anchor! You are journeying beyond Rahab's gaze!"

Across the shining waters, I heard the cries of protest and dismay. Poor Eleazar, I thought; he has travelled all this way to hear the Name of God spoken, and now I send him away. Yet it is better that it is so. I didn't even want to think about what Joscelin would say.

"You're sure?" Hyacinthe asked me.

I nodded. "Now, before I lose my nerve."

Hyacinthe stooped, laying the case upon the rock, then whispered, blowing out his breath. A sharp, stiff breeze sprang up from nowhere, filling the storm-rigged sails of the *Elua's Promise*. Rousse took his warning; I heard the chain clanking as the anchor was raised, a pair of sailors cranking at a furious pace. The sails bellied and snapped as the ship swung around, its prow pointing toward the narrow exit. Hyacinthe circled three fingers in the opposite direction and the whirlpool ceased, vanishing back into the waters.

The green water of the harbor humped and gathered, drawing back against the promontory. Once again, Hyacinthe pushed with both hands, murmuring under his breath. The unnatural wave surged forward, gathering speed, and picked up the ship as effortlessly as a cork. Sails taut, bobbing on the crest, it shot through the passageway and vanished out of sight beyond the cliff walls.

And like that, they were gone.

I sat on the promontory, numb. "Joscelin will be furious."

Hyacinthe continued to concentrate, his black eyes wide and blurred, shifting, seeing something beyond the bounds of mortal vision. "No. He's the boy to think of, now. He'll understand." Satisfied with his efforts, he retrieved his case.

The harbor was as empty and tranquil as it had been when we

entered it. Small figures clustered at the top of the stairs, lining the temple, but dared come no further. It was only the two of us.

"What now?" Hyacinthe asked softly. "We try to cross?"

Still sitting, I nodded. "You can cause the waters to bear us upon their surface?"

"Yes." He sat cross-legged next to me holding the case in his arms, an unlikely figure in centuries-old velvet and lace, a face out of my earliest, best memories and eyes like the bottom of the sea. "Unless we fail."

It had not seemed so fearful when the ship lay anchored just off-shore. I looked up at the bright sky, the wheeling gulls. A day for beginnings, not endings. "We won't fail."

He smiled a bit. "Will you tell me, afterward, how you travelled through darkness and came to find the Name of God?"

"If you like." Our shoulders brushed, barely touching. We used to sit together just so, eating stolen tarts under the bridge at Tertius' Crossing in the City of Elua. "Will you tell me what it's like to command the winds and seas?"

"Yes." Hyacinthe watched the empty harbor. "There's no point in delaying, is there?"

I wished there was, now that it came to it. But there wasn't. "No."

"Then let's go." He rose, tucking the case under one arm; his turn, now, to help me to my feet. I kept hold of his hand as we walked to the very edge of the promontory. Water lapped at the rocks, clear and calm and most assuredly not solid. Hyacinthe released my hand to speak another charm in no tongue I recognized, forming his free hand into a fist and turning it palm-upward, then opening it.

The water continued to ripple gently, looking exactly the same.

My breath caught in my throat; I hadn't thought I'd be afraid to take the first step. "Did I ever tell you how I came near to drowning off the coast of La Serenissima?"

"Phèdre." Hyacinthe touched my cheek. "I am the Master of the Straits, and I have spent the best part of my youth in bondage to Rahab's vengeance taken on a woman long-dead, for the sin of failing to love him. You are my dearest, only hope. As long as your courage holds, I will not let you sink. Do you trust me?"

"Yes," I whispered. "I do."

Closing my eyes, I stepped onto the water.

Ninety-eight

IT WAS hard, harder than I could have imagined, to take that first step off the shore. The *geis* that had bound me to the island struck like a blow the instant my feet left stone, driving the air from my lungs, doubling me over with pain. A yawning void opened in the waters before me, ocean-deep, dark and whirling, twisting my guts with fear. And at the bottom of it, something *moved*, something bright and awful.

All my brave words deserted me.

I forced myself upright and took another step.

The waters were churning, and I couldn't bear to think on what I stood. All around me, the calm harbor was roused to a threatening rage, wind lashing. I wanted to be on the island so keenly it ached, and the fear was like a knife in my belly.

I did turn, then, and saw Hyacinthe behind me, standing on the waters. He clutched the case to him and his face was ashen with terror, eyes stark with helpless power. Only his promise to me held him there.

Fear.

Pain.

Let it come, then. I faced it and let it wash through me, setting my raw nerves to singing with the piercing-sweet, inimitable chords of agony, gradually tinting my vision the hue of blood. I was an *anguissette*. What was this to the Mahrkagir's iron rod, to Melisande's deadly flechettes? No worse, surely. Only pain, only fear.

In a crimson haze, I took another step.

Before me, the maelstrom widened like a maw, and the flickering brightness drove away Kushiel's influence, leaving me with nothing to bolster my courage. What moved at the bottom of the abyss? Angel or monster? I had seen Rahab described as divine messenger and Leviathan alike in the Yeshuite writings. Something surged, a vast coil of flesh, bescaled and gleaming, green as jade. Pain wracked my bones like an ague. I bit my lip and on trembling legs, took another step. The winds rose to shriek past my ears, and I dared not look behind me. It didn't matter if Hyacinthe faltered; only that I didn't. He would not let me sink.

As long as your courage holds . . .

I took another step.

The depths of the maelstrom roiled, revealing glimpses of something changing and unnamable, born of the protean underworld. A tentacle, an impossible slitted eye, a neck maned and arching, a whale's flukes, a sculpted shoulder blade, a mighty wing . . . terrible beauty, formless and shifting, vaster than the mind can comprehend. I cannot say why, but it shook me to the marrow of my soul, filling me with awe and horror.

Still I forced my legs to move, step by trembling step, to the very brink of the maw. And though Hyacinthe's control of the elements was faltering, though the waves raged around me and churned at the cliffs, though the winds flogged me and my garments were soaked, the waters bore my weight.

"Rahab!" My voice was inaudible. I drew a breath choked with salt spray and called again, into the whirling pit. "Rahab, by the binding of your own curse, I summon you here!"

The maelstrom shuddered, and a form arose from it—an outflung fin of water, sea-green and pinioned with foam, pointing to the egress and crashing back into the harbor, spume flying. I looked where it had pointed, and stifled a cry of despair.

There, between the cliffs, came racing the ship *Elua's Promise*, storm-driven, every sail taut and straining, riding like a kestrel on the edge of the winds. Rahab's gaze reached farther than we had reckoned. Somewhere behind me, I heard Hyacinthe cry out with fear, and the churning water that bore me *softened*. I sank to my knees in water and lost my balance, wave-tossed, putting both hands down to catch myself and plunging elbow-deep. The steep walls of the maelstrom canted before me, threatening to pitch me into its maw. Salt water dashed my face and I fought for breath, terrified of drowning.

If I went back all would be well.

If I went back, my loved ones would be safe.

Ah, Elua! It was unfair. I wanted to turn back, wanted it more than anything I'd known. I was afraid, for myself, for Joscelin, for Imriel— for all of us, everyone. But every patron, I thought, has sought to make me give my *signale*. This is no different. If I turn back, what then? I will have surrendered at last. And somewhere behind me, too near to be ashore, I heard Hyacinthe's voice, ragged, chanting the incantation he'd spoken before, keeping his promise. The water grew more buoyant, solidifying. I managed to scramble to my feet, tossing my sodden, tangled hair out of my eyes, taking a deep breath.

"Rahab," I whispered.

The maelstrom ceased its surging and went still, waiting, an impossibly deep well in the small harbor. The churning waves went flat, the winds dropped like a stone. Some thirty yards away, *Elua's Promise* drifted, momentum slowing. The surface of the sea quivered like a horse's flank.

I took another step, edging around the maw. "Rahab."

In the depths, something gathered and flickered, a brightness coalescing. I took another breath, feeling light-headed and strange, walking on water as though it were dry earth. I have only given my *signale* once, and I would not give it now, not to this errant servant of the One God who had brought so much pain to someone I loved.

"Rahab, by the binding of your own curse, I summon you here!"

Brilliance erupted from the sea, gouts of water spewing into the sky, falling in shining cascades to shape a form so magnificent it made me want to weep, vaster and more noble than anything dreamt by mortal flesh. The Face of the Waters shaped by the Master of the Straits was but a pale echo of this form, which towered above the cliffs. Sunlight gleamed on its translucent shoulders as it inclined its massive head, sea-green locks falling about its face like rivers.

Not his true form, not yet.

I swallowed hard. "Rahab. In the Name of God, I summon you here."

And the world . . . *shifted.*

It is said that among a hundred artists who saw them living, not a one captured the beauty of Blessed Elua and his Companions. I did not know, before, how such a thing could be. I have known the Scions of Elua. I spent the earliest part of my life in the Court of Night-Blooming Flowers, where they have bred for beauty for a thousand generations. I understood it, now.

The angel Rahab manifested on the waters.

His beauty was like a sword unsheathed, bright as sun-struck steel and twice as hard. It hurt to behold him. Every bone, every articulated joint, was shaped with terrible purpose. The span of his brow held all the grace of the moon's curve rising above the sea's horizon. In the hollows of his eyes were the shadows of grottos no human gaze would ever behold. Whether he was fair or dark, I could not say, for his flesh shone with a brilliance that owed nothing to our limited understanding of light, and his hair was at once like tarnished water, like kelp, like the corona of an eclipsed sun.

"You have summoned me."

The words rang like silver chimes, piercing the innermost membranes of my ears. If a voice could sound like the dazzle of sunlight on the waters, on all the waters of the world, refracting and multiplying a thousandfold, Rahab's did.

If Hyacinthe had not stood behind me, I would have fled for dry land.

"Rahab." I licked my lips, tasting salt and fear. "I bid you to relinquish your curse."

Slow and inevitable, his head rose like the evening star ascending through twilight, chin raised in defiance. The shape of his lips was cruel and remorseless, formed by the dying utterance of every sailor ever drowned at sea. And his eyes—ah, Elua! They were white as bone, and yet they *saw,* and saw and saw. When the One God ordered the seas to part for Moishe, when the whale swallowed Yehonah, those eyes were already ancient. In those eyes, Blessed Elua was a babe-in-arms.

"My curse."

On the waters, of the waters, the angel Rahab extended his arms. Manacles encircled his wrists, a heavy chain running betwixt them, wrought of granite, it seemed, or more; something more adamant than stone, more dense than any substance mortal hands might wield, each link forged and sealed by the divine alphabet. Rippling and shifting, Rahab's immortal flesh shone against those bonds, the only constraint to his power, confining him to the sea and the One God's will. He held out his hands toward me, showing his chains, the cruel mouth shaping words that rang with beauty.

"For as long as G-d's punishment endures, so does my curse. I have sworn it."

The water grew soft under my feet, and I floundered again, sputtering. The waves rose once more, tall and raging, and seawater filled my mouth, salt as blood and more bitter. I lost my footing, and a great swell swamped me, turning me over until I could not say which way was up and it seemed the ocean would have me, hauling at the water-logged folds of my gown with a tremendous force. Struggle though I would, the water's pull was stronger. My lungs burned, and I could not catch my breath.

As if from a great distance, I heard a voice cry my name, high and clear and urgent. "Phèdre! Phèdre!"

Imriel.

Young and unbroken, his voice carried over the waters, as it had carried over the battle in the Mahrkagir's festal hall, over the thunderous clamor of the rhinoceros' charge, outside the doors of the temple. And I knew, then, which way lay life, and love. I found my feet in the sinking waters, and heard Hyacinthe, repeating the charm like a curse, filled with all the fury and defiance of the lost years of his life.

I stood with an effort, dripping.

"On pain of banishment," I gasped, "I bid you relinquish your curse!"

The seas shimmered about Rahab, rising in columns, in towers, more water than the harbor could possibly hold, rising to threaten the very cliffs. Quintilius Rousse's flagship rode the crests, pitching steeply, drawn toward the epicenter that was Rahab. His bone-white gaze sought mine, and he seemed at once no taller than a man and vast as mountains. "*You dare?*" he asked, bringing his adamant chains taut with a clap like thunder, "*You dare, misbegotten child of Elua?*"

There is strength in yielding. I had gone beyond my own fear.

"Elua understood love," I said to him. "The world may have been better served, my lord Rahab, had you done the same. Will you go peaceably? I offer you that choice."

The seas towered and raged, and Rahab shone like a chained star in their midst, silver-dark, bone-white, kelp-green, cloaked in raiment like water and lit with an inner fire that owed nothing to this world of mortal clay. "*As my heart knows no peace, nor shall yours!*"

So it was to be.

Of a strangeness, I felt calm. The Sacred Name blossomed like a rose within me, swelling to fill every part, until there was no room left for any trace of fear. I saw in Rahab the centuries reaching back untold, the ancient conflict—rebellion, born of pride; subservience, born of adoration. I saw the hatred and bitter envy he bore for Elua and his Companions. All the joy and wonder of the deep seas, I beheld in him, and loneliness, too. And love; ah, Elua! It had hurt, it had cut to the bone. Nothing in the endless centuries of tempestuous service to the One God had prepared Rahab for the vagaries of mortal love, for the pain of rejection.

"In the Name of God," I said with pity, "I banish you, Rahab."

Waves clashed in answer, and Rahab grew terrible with wrath, gathering fury, blue-white lightning flashing in the writhing locks of his hair as the mighty voice chimed. *"You lack the right, Elua's child!"*

But it was there, in every part of me, in every fiber of my being, rising like a tide to overflow me and I would have laughed, if my throat had not been filled with it, or wept, if I could. I had travelled to the farthest reaches of the known world for the Name of God, and walked paths darker than I had dreamed.

All that was left was to speak it.

I did.

"_____!"

If the whole of the mortal world were a brazen bell, and that bell were tolled; that would be the sound of it, as the unpronounceable syllables rolled from my tongue, ringing over the waters, tolling without beginning or end, and it was as if there had never been anything else, not sea nor land nor sky, but only this endless Word, that was before time began. For the space of time in which I spoke it, nothing else existed. Then . . . everything, and I at the center of it, hollow and echoing, my tongue a dumbstruck clapper in the vault of my mouth, while I swayed beneath it, dazed and empty, a sounding vessel whose time had passed.

I had spoken the Name of God.

Ah, *Elua!*

It was done.

Without a sound, Rahab's head bowed, like night's last star vanishing in the dawn. Sorrow, and defeat. One arm rose, sweeping, a plumed wing of water and sea-foam, trailing adamant shackles, passing before his face. Bittersweet, this ending. Even the anger of a spurned heart had held mercy in it. The curse that had divided Terre d'Ange and Alba before Hyacinthe's sacrifice, that had bound him afterward, had held us safe, had protected our shores. Where the One God had abandoned His misbegotten grandchildren, Rahab, in all the anguish of his immortal heart, had not.

Now it was ended.

The brightness that was Rahab sank and subsided, winds dying, towering crests dwindling to ripples, a glimmering on the waters. And then . . . nothing. He was gone, and I, I was a hollow vessel, empty of purpose, the scoured walls of my being forgetful of what they had contained. The flagship *Elua's Promise* bobbed on the waters, momentarily rudderless, thin shouts arising. On the translucent, buoyant chasm of the harbor, I fell to my knees, my soaked skirts floating about me, born on the gentle waves.

"Phèdre."

Hyacinthe's voice; Hyacinthe's hand, upon my shoulder. I gazed up at him, glad of the reminder. Yes, that was who I was, then. Phèdre, Phèdre nó Delaunay, Delaunay's *anguissette;* Kushiel's Chosen, Naamah's Servant. And his friend, Hyacinthe's true friend. His face was gentle, and there was compassion in his changeable eyes, the dark, color-shifting eyes of the Master of the Straits, who had inherited the mantle of Rahab's pain and the twisted love he bore for these lands of ours.

"Look." Hyacinthe nodded across the harbor, to where the ship bore down upon us, sails flapping useless and slack, water dripping from its churning oars as the oarsmen set their backs to the task, hauling hard. "They are coming for us."

With difficulty I rose to my feet for the third time on those waters. I had not faltered.

I saw their faces, as the *Elua's Promise* hove alongside us, dropping anchor; filled with emotion, too profound for words. Quintilius Rousse, with all of a sailor's awe at seeing the Lord of the Deep made manifest. Kristof, Oszkar's son, who had witnessed the end of one Tsingano's long road. Eleazar ben Enokh, who glowed, having heard the Name of God at last.

And the others; the others! Oh, Elua, the others.

Rousse's sailors; Phèdre's Boys. They would retain the name until they died.

Of a surety, Hugues would make bad poetry of it, I saw it in his raptured features, and Ti-Philippe beside him. Were they lovers, then? I'd assumed it, never bothered to ask. I should have done. They were my people. I should know such things.

Joscelin.

There was anger there, in his summer-blue eyes; anger, that I had dared to send him away, that I had dared to send all of them. And there was knowledge—of why I had done it, of what it had cost me. No blame, at the last; only pride, and a relief vaster than the sea. We had gone beyond that, he and I.

In the end, when all was said and done, Joscelin understood.

His hands rested on Imriel's shoulders, and what he knew, Imri knew. I saw it, in the depths of his eyes; as deep a blue as twilight, his mother's eyes, a beauty as indescribable as a nightingale's song, and a faith shining forth in them such as hers had never held.

Imri had never doubted.

Ninety-nine

HOW I got aboard the ship, I cannot say for certain, for it transpired in a confused, muddled mix of efforts; wave and wind lifted at once in obedience to Hyacinthe's murmured command, and then a half-dozen hands grappled for a hold on my sodden gown, unable to wait, and I was pushed and hauled at once, ignominious and dripping, into Joscelin's arms.

It was a good place to be.

If the world had stayed there, unmoving, so would I, until time itself should cease. Since it did not, I let him go and turned to Imriel, a lump rising in my throat. With a sound half shout and half sob, he flung himself at me. I held him hard, pressing my cheek against his spray-dampened hair, tears stinging my eyes.

"Phèdre nó Delaunay." Quintilius Rousse's voice, deep and unwontedly solemn. I looked up to see him sink to one knee before me, bowing his head. "I salute your courage, my lady of Montrève."

"Oh, don't, my lord Admiral," I said, embarrassed. "Please. I hate that."

Laughter rang across the waters, free and unfettered, and everyone aboard the ship turned to see Hyacinthe, standing on the sea. An obedient wave had raised him up to the level of the ship's railing, held him there like a dais. "Let be, Phèdre," he said, holding the case of pages under one arm. "You deserve it." His gaze met mine across the distance. "Thank you."

I nodded, unable to speak. The wave curled over the railing, and, light as a swallow, Hyacinthe stepped off the waters and onto the ship's deck, encountering silence and stares of awe. Now that it was done, no one knew how to address him.

It was Joscelin who broke the stillness. "Tsingano," he said. "Welcome back."

"Cassiline." With a crooked smile, Hyacinthe reached out, and they clasped one another's wrists in a strong grip. "My thanks to you."

Joscelin shrugged. "I had a vow to keep."

"I remember."

No more did they say to one another; I daresay it was enough, for them. There are ways in which men who know one another's hearts and minds may speak without words, and whatever passed between them in that moment sufficed to satisfy both of them. Afterward, Rousse rose to offer a deep bow to the Master of the Straits and welcome him aboard ship, and others pressed close with curiosity, reaching with tentative hands to brush the edge of his sleeve, the hem of his cloak, assuring themselves Hyacinthe was no apparition, but flesh and bone. Imriel stood with me, out of the way, watching as Kristof approached him.

"*Tsingan kralis,*" he said in a husky voice. "You have returned."

Hyacinthe's changeable eyes were cold and dark. "Since when do the Tsingani acknowledge the rights of a *Didikani* gotten out of wedlock, Oszkar's son? Did my grandfather Manoj not have nephews of his blood? Did he name no heir among them?"

"The four families of the *baro kumpai* chose you, Anazstaizia's son." Although sweat stood on his brow, Kristof stood unflinching. "There have been changes. Your mother's name is spoken and remembered."

Something softened in Hyacinthe's face. "Is it? That is well, then."

"Then you will lead us?" The *tseroman's* voice was hopeful.

"No." Hyacinthe shook his head, not without regret. "If the *baro kumpai* wish it, I will meet with them and lend my advice; do they heed it, I will give my protection to whosoever is chosen to rule. But Manoj cast me out, and it is too late for me to become his grandson in deed as well as name. I have become something else instead."

Kristof bowed his head, defeated. "What will you do, sea-*kralis?* Where will you go?"

Hyacinthe gazed across the ship without answering.

In all the commotion, I had nearly forgotten Sibeal; a slight figure, easily overlooked in the prow of the ship, her hands clasped tight in front of her. They stood for a very long time looking at one another, and the air was as motionless as if the wind itself held its breath, and the rest of us with it, aware of the sudden tension. Sibeal's eyes were wide and sombre, only a faint line between her brows betraying any anxiety. The muscles in Hyacinthe's throat moved as he swallowed, seeking his voice.

"Lady Sibeal." He crossed the deck to stand before her, and with a stiff bow, laid the case containing the pages of the Lost Book of Raziel on the deck between them. "Will you share the keeping of this burden with me?"

"Yes." The lines of blue woad dotted on Sibeal's cheeks stood out against a flush of unexpected joy. "I will."

A breeze sprang up, rifling the ship's sails, swirling the folds of Hyacinthe's sea-faded cloak and the strands of Sibeal's shining black hair as he took her hand, momentarily obscuring them. Whatever words they spoke between them were lost in the rustling wind. I turned away that no one might see the fresh tears that pricked my eyes. It was a different pain that stung my heart, one I had never known before. On the shore, the folk of the isle pressed close on the landing, spilling halfway up the steps, pointing and staring in wonder at the wave-locked ship and the Master of the Straits upon it. They will tell stories, I thought, of this day.

"Phèdre." Joscelin leaned on the railing beside me, quiet and undemanding, a presence as familiar my own shadow. "Are you ready to go home?"

Another question underlay his words, and I understood it unspoken. After so long, it hurt to let Hyacinthe go, to watch him join his fate to Sibeal's and to follow a path that diverged from mine. But I was an *anguissette*, and I understood pain. It is the price of living, and of loving well, and I did not doubt, then or ever, that I had chosen wisely. Gripping the railing hard, I took a deep breath. "Yes," I said, lifting my gaze to Joscelin's, smiling at the sight of his beloved face. "I'm ready."

"Good." He smiled back at me, then raised his voice, shouting to Hyacinthe. "Tsingano! Do you wish to linger here, or can you raise a wind to bear us homeward?"

"As you wish, Cassiline." Stepping away from Sibeal, Hyacinthe gave a short bow. "With your permission, my lord Admiral?"

Quintilius Rousse grinned fit to split his scarred face. "Man all positions, lads!" he roared. "Elder Brother's leaving his Three Sisters and blowing us home!"

Cheers arose, Rousse's sailors—Phèdre's Boys—at last giving voice to wild, exuberant relief. I heard, later, tales of exactly how terrifying that day was for them, when Rahab's winds picked them off the open sea, drove them like a leaf before a gale back to the harbor, where the waves rose like towers and threatened to pitch them into the depths of the maelstrom. I heard many tales, later. Then, they merely shouted themselves hoarse with cheers, and Imriel's voice rang high above the rest, whooping as Hugues hoisted him up to perch on his broad shoulders so he might watch the Master of the Straits perform the honors.

With a swirl of his faded cloak, Hyacinthe obliged. His hands gestured, his lips moved, and the wind came in answer like a faithful hound, filling our sails, setting the calm waters to rippling. Hugues, staggering under Imri's weight, set him down with alacrity. Rousse took the helm, and *Elua's Promise* turned her prow toward the egress, then leapt forward on a course as straight and true as a cast javelin.

We were going home.

Now, at last, the bright remnants of the day fit the mood, and my spirits rose as the ship shot out of the narrow passage, canting hard to one side as we tacked with the shifting winds, doubling back past the isle of Third Sister to head for shore. Hyacinthe made his way across the deck, unperturbed by the speed of our passage.

"There is one here I have not met," he said, inclining his head to Imriel.

I stood behind Imri, hands on his shoulders. "Hyacinthe, Anasztaizia's son, Master of the Straits, this is my foster-son and Joscelin's, Prince Imriel nó Montrève de la Courcel."

"*Courcel?*"

The Master of the Straits' sea-mirror was blind beyond D'Angeline waters. I had forgotten. "Prince Benedicte's son," I said, feeling Imriel stiffen under my hands. "Born in La Serenissima, to Melisande Shahrizai. Oh, Hyas! There's a lot to tell you."

"So it would seem." He bowed, bemused. "Well met, Prince Imriel."

Imri bared his teeth. "Imriel nó Montrève," he said, then reconsidered. "My lord."

A glimmer of his old mirth resurfaced in Hyacinthe's sea-shifting eyes. "Forgive me, Imriel nó Montrève," he said, and to me, "I suppose you know what you're doing?"

I shrugged and ruffled Imriel's hair. "Without this one, you'd still be on the isle, and I'd be pounding my hands bloody on the door of a temple of the One God in the farthest reaches of Jebe-Barkal. We owe a good deal to his courage, I daresay."

Imriel looked pleased. Hyacinthe looked nonplussed.

"You *do* have much to tell me," he said.

"More than you know," I agreed. "Will you at least journey to the City of Elua before taking up a life in Alba? It would give us a little time to relive the last twelve years together."

"I fear mine are dull." Hyacinthe turned out his hands, glancing at them with a wry smile. "You have seen the results; the telling doesn't bear hearing, unless you would hear of endless hours of study. But yes, I will come to the City. Sibeal will rejoin Drustan, and we will pass the summer there, returning to Alba in the autumn. And I will speak to the Queen and the Cruarch regarding the safekeeping of our boundary waters, and to the *baro kumpai* of the Tsingani regarding Manoj's successor. And yes," he added, "I would hear of your quest to find the Name of God, and all matters that befell on the way, great and small, and every other thing that has passed in your life since I set foot on that forsaken rock."

"Good," I said, "because I plan on telling you."

With Hyacinthe's steady winds filling the sails, our return journey to Pointe des Soeurs passed swiftly, and as well that it did, for once the shores of Third Sister fell behind us, overdue exhaustion claimed me. I took shelter out of the wind, propped undisturbed against the cabin wall on cushions, and spread my skirts in the late afternoon sun to dry, wondering why I had not thought to bring a change of dry clothing. It seemed impossible that less than a day had passed since I had ridden out to the encampment at dawn.

I felt a different person, almost—empty of the sacred trust I had carried for many months, the Name of God no longer an insistent presence filling my mind, crowding my throat, ever poised on the tip of my tongue. It was written still within me, etched in the deepest layers of memory that we cannot readily summon waking, wrought in bone and sinew and blood. This I knew; and yet I no longer heard it echoing in my skull, drawing me out of myself, immersing me in fearful wonder. In its place, beneath the weariness, beneath the mortal concerns of friends and loved ones, was something that might have been contentment, for I had never known its like.

It was finished.

For twelve years, every happiness, every joy, every pleasure I had known—and despite it all, they had been myriad—had been overcast by the shadow of Hyacinthe's fate. No more. And if he was not as he had been, who among us was? Not I, who had known the lowest depths to which I could sink in the Mahrkagir's bedchamber. Not Joscelin, who had confronted a hell worse than any he could have imagined, forced to stand by and endure watching. And ah, Elua! Surely not Imriel, whose childhood had been shattered in Daršanga, who found himself despised and feared in his own land for the accident of his birth. I grieved for Hyacinthe's lost years, for his lost self. But he would *live*, unchained from a fate worse than death. If the burden continued, still, the curse was broken.

No more could I do.

"You have earned your rest, Phèdre nó Delaunay."

I opened my eyes to see Eleazar ben Enokh seated before me, beaming as if he knew he had answered my unspoken thoughts. I smiled at him. "Eleazar. Are you pleased with this day's adventure?"

"To behold a servant of Adonai Himself in the immortal flesh? To hear the Sacred Name tolling across the waters, such as no one has heard in a thousand generations?" He laughed with delight. "Yes, Phèdre nó Delaunay. I am well pleased."

"You heard it, then." Curious, I sat upright. "Tell me, father. What did you hear when I spoke the Name of God?"

"Ah." Eleazar tugged at his unkempt beard, eyes sparkling. "I heard a Word, of such potent syllables as I could not fathom, sounds I have never heard shaped by mortal lips. Even at a distance, they buffeted my ears with great blows, and my bones felt weak, my knees like water, until I must fall to kneeling upon these boards, while my spirit grew too great for my body to contain, fanned like a mighty fire, and I cried out for joy at it. And yet . . ."

"Yes?" I prompted when his pause lengthened.

"And yet it seemed to me, Phèdre nó Delaunay, that beneath the incomprehensible Word was a root-word which echoed in every syllable, the foundation upon which the Sacred Name was built. And that word, I knew." He folded his hands in his lap, radiated contained joy. "Can you not guess it?"

After a moment, I shook my head. The Name of God was too vast.

"*Awhab* was the word I heard, but . . ." Eleazar lifted one finger, ". . . only I. I have spoken to others. Kristof of the Tsingani heard the echo of a word, too, but that word was *madahn*, and the Cruithne who accompany the Lady Sibeal heard the word *gràdh*. You speak many tongues, Phèdre nó Delaunay." His smile broadened to a grin. "Can you guess what word the D'Angeline sailors heard?"

"Love," I whispered.

"Love!" Eleazar laughed aloud, his beard quivering with mirth. "Love!" His bony knees cracked as he levered himself to his feet, then stooped to kiss my brow with unexpected tenderness. "Though He is slow to acknowledge it, I believe Adonai Himself is proud of His son Elua, misbegotten or no," he said. "Perhaps it took one very stubborn mortal woman to prompt Him to show it."

Caught between disbelief and awe, I watched Eleazar ben Enokh take his leave, a ragged, blissful figure, walking with a rolling gait across the deck as though he'd been born to the sea. I shook my head in bemusement, wondering at the exultation he found in his faith, so strong it could embrace even heresy with open arms. Mayhap it was so; who could say? It is a matter for priests and priestesses to debate, and the gods alone know the truth of it. I had kept my promise and freed my friend, and we were alive, all of us here, to rejoice in it.

It was enough.

I was content.

A high-pitched shout caught my ear, and I rose and glanced about, finding the source at last; Imriel, pointing landward from the impossible vantage of the crow's-nest high atop the central mast, Ti-Philippe holding him fast with one hand.

"He'll take years off our lives, you know."

Joscelin's voice, low and amused, in my ear.

"I know." I reached behind me without looking, catching his arm and drawing it about my waist. Quintilius Rousse was bellowing orders, his men leaping to obey as the shore of Terre d'Ange drew in sight. Hyacinthe gestured gracefully, his expression focused with preternatural concentration as he guided the winds, and Sibeal watched him with the calm certitude of a woman in love. The tattooed Cruithne warriors of her honor guard held his case of pages, proud and apprehensive to have been given such a charge. At the foot of the mast, an anxious Hugues pleaded for Ti-Philippe and Imriel to come down, which made me laugh. "Are you sorry for it?"

"No." Joscelin's arm tightened around me, and I felt him smile against my hair. "Not for any of it. Not for a minute."

Neither was I.

ONE HUNDRED

WORD TRAVELLED before us.

There was celebrating all that night upon our return to Pointe des Soeurs, in the fortress and the encampment alike. By the time we mustered for the journey to the City of Elua, the countryside was alive with the news, word of mouth travelling nearly as swiftly as the royal couriers Quintilius Rousse dispatched to alert Ysandre.

An eight-hundred-year legend had come to earth.

Hyacinthe bore it with dignity, as crowds turned out at every village and hamlet we passed, gaping and whispering to see him . . . a young man of Tsingano descent, quiet and collected, clad in faded velvet attire, only the aura that surrounded him and the sea-deep colors swirling in his dark eyes giving evidence to the tremendous power he wielded.

Once, he would have reveled in the attention; Hyacinthe, my Prince of Travellers, who wore gaudier clothes than half the nobles in the City, whose silver-tongued predictions coaxed coin from their purses and blushes to their cheeks. Now, he merely endured it. I remembered how it had been when we had last travelled together, Joscelin and Hyacinthe and I, and Hyacinthe had played the timbales and flirted with unwed Tsingani women along the road, spending hours teaching a reticent Cassiline Brother how to mimic a Mendacant's flair.

No longer.

Our lodgings were free at every inn, and the inn-keepers vied to serve the most extravagant meals, carrying out the last stores of winter and the first fruits of the earliest harvest. Even the Tsingani who trailed our company were made welcome on the outskirts of town, and villagers who would have hidden their valuables instead brought them gifts of food. The common-rooms were crowded with poets stretching their ears to hear the stories, and Rousse's sailors told them with relish.

From this, I was not exempt; the *anguissette* who banished an angel. Such a thing had never happened in the history of Terre d'Ange. People murmured among themselves and glanced sidelong at me, seeking some stamp of great magic such as Hyacinthe bore and finding none, only the scarlet prick of Kushiel's Dart, a sign grown well-known enough in my lifetime that it held no novelty. And they spoke softly in wonder and doubt.

It made me smile. There had been no magic in my deed save that which the One God had given me to hold in trust. No, Eleazar was right; it was stubbornness as much as anything else, an odd legacy of Kushiel's dubious gift, that taught me to yield without surrendering. Endurance, and love—those things were all the power I'd ever possessed.

Day by day, our journey grew shorter, and never have I known weather so fair, the skies blue and cloudless, the clime temperate. How not, when we travelled with the Master of the Straits? On land or sea, wind and water answered his command, further than the eye could see in any direction. A fearful power indeed, I thought as we passed fields growing ripe with the green and gold of late spring, and more dangerous at loose than it had ever been confined to the isles of the Three Sisters. He could blight the earth itself, did he so choose. It had been folly to imagine Hyacinthe could ever resume his former life.

The pages of the Book of Raziel were never far from his regard, and Sibeal's Alban honor guard was increasingly conscious of the might of what they warded, the Cruithne warriors taking turns among themselves with the case and carrying it as if it might singe their fingers.

"What would happen if someone stole it?" I asked Hyacinthe one day.

"Who would dare?" His smile was bleak, and a small breeze rifled our horses' manes as if in warning. "No, but it would do them no good, Phèdre. No one could read the script who had not been taught, and that was the longest part of my apprenticeship. I spent seven years learning it, for there are characters in it such as I have never beheld and sounds contained in no mortal tongue yet spoken."

My pulse quickened. "So it was with the Name of God."

"Yes." He gazed at me with his sea-shifting eyes. "But that word, I think, was not one ever written, save once. And of a surety, it was never heard on that cursed isle until you spoke it. How you learned it, I will never fathom."

"I was told it by a man with no tongue," I said. Hyacinthe laughed softly, not disbelieving. "Hyacinthe, what will you do with the pages? Will you take an apprentice, or let the knowledge pass with you upon your death?"

For a long time, he did not answer. "I don't know," he said at length. "Phèdre . . . I'm only still getting used to the notion that I am free to wander the earth, that I may live and love, beget children, grow old and die . . . *die*, like any mortal, and not dwindle endlessly into shriveled madness. It is too big to decide at once." He glanced at me again. "Do you wish to learn it?"

"*No!*" I gave a startled laugh. "Name of Elua, no!"

A hint of his old smile lifted the corner of his mouth. "So your curiosity has a limit."

"Yes," I said. "I do believe it does."

Hyacinthe reached over and touched my hand as we rode side by side. "Nor would I wish this on you," he said soberly. "You of all people, for you're wise enough to understand that power of this nature is more burden than blessing. Know this, though. I will never forget what you've done for me, you and Joscelin . . . and the boy. As long as I live, you may count yourself under my protection. Any aid you require is yours, always."

I squeezed his hand. "Thank you."

No more did he say. I had not told him, yet, the whole of our story, nor of what had befallen in Nineveh, where an assassin's blade had sought Imriel's life, but Hyacinthe could guess well enough that Melisande's son would have enemies, and I was truly grateful that he had offered freely the protection I had been so quick to boast of to Ysandre de la Courcel. There would be no guarantees, for Alba's shores lay far from the City of Elua and my estate of Montrève, but of a surety, the friendship of the Master of the Straits was a powerful dissuader.

Imriel.

He rode in the thick of Rousse's sailors, Phèdre's Boys, and one of them had entrusted him with bearing the company standard, the banner that bore the image of Kushiel's Dart. Imri grinned with pride at the honor, but they'd taken to him out of genuine liking, impressed with his unwavering courage aboard the *Elua's Promise*. I swear, it seemed he'd grown another inch on this journey. I thought with rue of Hyacinthe's offer. In truth, it tempted me . . . if only the tiniest bit. Not for the power, no, but the *knowledge*. To master the tongue of Heaven! Ah, Elua, that would be something. Mayhap I would recognize in the strange characters those I had seen forming in the dust of the Ark of

Broken Tablets, that I might record them, writing for posterity the unpronounceable Name of God.

All knowledge is worth having.

So my lord Delaunay used to say, so I have always believed. Seven years, it had taken Hyacinthe to learn it, the tongue and script alone. How long would it take me? Less, I daresay; I had the advantage of ten years of Habiru behind me. That should halve it, at least.

In three years, Imriel would be fifteen.

And not for anything, not for the knowledge of all of the One God's secrets, did I want to miss those years. The furious, terrified child I had found in Daršanga had grown into a boy on the brink of youth, proud and touchy and damaged, but with a streak of courage that awed grown men, a heart capable of love and tremendous sacrifice. While he grew to manhood, it would always be touch and go with Imri, his generosity of spirit at war with the bitter unfairness of the lot he'd drawn, of the horrors that had been visited upon him and the scars they'd left. Love alone could sway the balance.

I touched my bare throat, where once Melisande's diamond had hung.

I had a promise to keep.

Although, I thought, riding under the bright blue D'Angeline skies, it may be that Hyacinthe would be willing to share with me the alphabet alone, and mayhap a phonetic guide to the pronunciation of the unknown characters. After all, I'd done a fair job of teaching myself Jeb'ez from Audine Davul's guide. Kaneka may have laughed at me in the zenana, but she'd understood me well enough, and I'd garnered that much studying on shipboard and over campfires. A few hours here and there . . . I need not devote the last years of my youth to an all-consuming apprenticeship, but a good deal can be accomplished in a few stolen hours over time, if one is determined enough. Who knew what texts might be unearthed if correspondence was established between Saba and Terre d'Ange one day? Eleazar ben Enokh would be glad of the endeavor, of that I was sure. As the schism grew deeper among the Children of Yisra-el, those Yeshuites who sought peace over war were more and more likely to turn to his way of thinking; their presence among us on this journey was proof of that much.

"What on earth are you plotting now?" Joscelin's black gelding ranged alongside mine.

"Nothing." I smiled at him. "Just thinking."

Some five miles outside the City of Elua, the first emissaries met us; a joint party of Ysandre's and Drustan's men, the Queen's Guard resplendent in the blue and silver of House Courcel and the Cruarch's bare-chested in woolen Alban kilts, their elaborate woad markings and copper torques signifying that each was a nobleman's son. They formed an escort around us, leading us through the first of innumerable floral arches built along the way, a court herald calling out the news in stentorian tones to any who had not yet heard it, which I daresay was no one.

From there, our procession grew very, very slow.

I have ridden in a triumph once before, when Ysandre returned to the City after the battle of Troyes-le-Monte, where we defeated the Skaldic army. I remember it well, for it was bittersweet, that occasion; as much as I was gladdened by our victory, I could not help but remember the dead and grieve for our losses.

This time, it was different. For all the terrors that had beset us on the waters, there had been no cost to human life. Hyacinthe was freed, and no one had died for it. As long and arduous as the journey had been, no one else had born the price of it. If I had entered the cavern of the Temenos and undergone the ritual of *thetalos* there and then, the chains of blood-guilt I bore would be no heavier.

I had not realized until then how profoundly grateful I was for it.

There was Daršanga, of course; there would always be Daršanga. None of us who had been there would ever be free of its shadow. But that . . . that had been somewhat *other*, and not the triumph we celebrated today.

Ysandre and Drustan met us at the gates.

How many times had I stood among the throng welcoming Drustan's return? As many years as they had been wed. Now I beheld a like spectacle from the other side, riding at a snail's pace down the packed road, while onlookers shouted and threw a hail of flowers and the harried City Guard sought to keep spectators from spilling onto the road. The white walls of the City of Elua were crowded with watchers. A contingent of Ysandre's ladies-in-waiting tossed sweets and coins to the children, who shouted with glee.

As befitted their status, Hyacinthe and Sibeal rode first, flanked by Cruithne warriors. Behind Quintilius Rousse, I sat my mare and watched as they dismounted.

"Master of the Straits," Ysandre greeted him in her clear voice. "Hyacinthe, son of Anasztaizia, be welcome to the City of Elua." And she made him a deep curtsy and held it, according a Tsingani half-breed, a laundress' son from the gutters of Night's Doorstep, the acknowledgment due a superior, which no ruling monarch of Terre d'Ange has extended to anyone in living memory.

The crowd drew its collective breath, then loosed it in a roar of acclaim.

"On behalf of Alba," Drustan called, "I bid you equal welcome." He too made a deep bow, then straightened, grinning. "And welcome you to my family as well, brother, with thanks for bringing safely to land my sister the lady Sibeal!"

Another roar followed his announcement.

Sibeal merely gave her quiet smile, and went to give the kiss of greeting to Drustan and Ysandre alike, and her young nieces Alais and Sidonie. All eyes remained on Hyacinthe, who stood alone before the joint regents. He bowed deeply, holding it long enough that there could be no doubt he acknowledged their sovereignty. The cloak of indeterminate color fell in immaculate folds as he straightened, his hair tumbling over the collar in black ringlets.

"Your majesties," he said, and although he did not raise his voice, it carried across the crowds, echoed from the walls, coming from everywhere and nowhere. "My lady Queen, my lord Cruarch. I am glad to be here."

That was as far as he got, for the shouting drowned out even him. I daresay the majority of the crowd would have cheered no matter who he was, Rahab's get or laundress' son, for the sheer drama of the Master of the Straits entering the gates of the City of Elua. But there, atop the walls, perched a delegation surely dispatched from the less reputable parts of Night's Doorstep, a handful of young men in their twenties and thirties, Tsingani, half-breed and D'Angeline, who drummed their heels on the white walls of the City and chanted, "Hy-a-cinthe! Hy-a-cinthe!"

He looked around at that, and if I had wondered if the Master of the Straits could still weep, I had my answer. Tears shone on his cheeks as he bowed once more in their direction, swirling his cloak as he rose with a touch of the old Prince of Travellers' flair and sweeping both arms in the air and clapping his palms together.

A ripping peal of thunder split the clear sky.

Hyacinthe was home, if only for a little while.

The roaring din of the crowd eclipsed Quintilius Rousse's salute to Queen and Cruarch, and I had no idea what he said, only that Ysandre raised him up with both hands and kissed his cheek, and Drustan clasped his forearms, grinning. And then it was our turn, and I found my legs trembling as we dismounted and approached the royal pair. To be welcomed thusly after our defiance . . . I had no words for the gratitude in my heart.

It was politics, yes; but somewhat more besides.

Joscelin gave his Cassiline bow, sweeping and precise, sunlight glinting from the battered steel of his vambraces—and the crowd loved that, too. When all was said and done, the Queen had named no other Champion. And here and there, they shouted for Imriel, who still carried the standard of Kushiel's Dart—my standard, the standard of Phèdre's Boys—prompted by the yells of Rousse's soldiers and the pride with which Imri carried it, executing his bow flawlessly without letting the standard dip. He won a few admirers that day on sheer presence alone.

I saw his eyes shine, and knew he did it on my behalf.

And then . . .

"Don't even think of it," Ysandre muttered through stiff lips as I made my curtsy, struggling against the desire to kneel and beg her forgiveness for the enormity of my transgressions against the throne. "I swear, Phèdre nó Delaunay, if you do . . ."

"I'm sorry," I whispered, getting the words out even as her hand grasped my elbow, fingers digging in with painful pressure, keeping me upright. "Ysandre, I'm so sorry."

"I know." Her violet eyes softened despite the pressure of her fingertips, and Queen Ysandre de la Courcel shook her head. "You idiot," she said fondly, then gave me the kiss of greeting in front of ten thousand assembled watchers, restoring my status as her favored confidante, and taking her time in doing it.

This, too, met with considerable approval.

It was Terre d'Ange, after all.

I was flushed when I made my curtsy to Drustan mab Necthana, the Cruarch of Alba. His eyes glinted with amusement and gladness. "So you did it after all."

"Yes." I knew what he meant. Drustan had been there, when Hyacinthe paid the price both of us would have taken on ourselves had it been allowed. I drew a deep breath and loosed it in a tremulous laugh, feeling strange with this unmixed, untempered joy. "We did."

And Drustan too kissed me, and we passed through the gate that the procession might continue, while the cheers rose around us in endless waves beneath the cloudless sky, free of spite or envy, surging in the bright air of the City of Elua, for once celebrating a victory unalloyed with defeat.

I was content.

We were home, all of us.

One Hundred · One

THE SUMMER passed swiftly.

I was visibly and undeniably in favor once more, and the same nobles who had shunned me during the long and bitter winter sent small gifts and jocular invitations to this event and that, most of which I declined, pleading an over-full schedule, which was no lie. At Hyacinthe's word, Ghislain nó Trevalion sent a galley to retrieve the library from the Master of the Straits' tower, and I had my hands full cataloguing some four hundred tomes and scrolls, many of which had been believed lost. Word of this was leaked, and I had to field a half-dozen bids from academies and universities throughout the realm that wished to increase their archives.

Of course, I intended to see first what was there and have fair-copies made.

Hyacinthe, for his part, dwelt at the Palace and spent long hours closeted with Queen and Cruarch and his intended, Sibeal. What transpired in those sessions, I cannot say, save that an agreement was reached and Drustan mab Necthana granted them a coastal territory in Alba, north of Bryn Gorrydum, where the erstwhile Master of the Straits might maintain his vigil. Thence would they travel, come autumn, after plighting their troth before the Cruarch's mother and kin in Alba.

Of a surety, he met with the *baro kumpai* of the Tsingani, the four families who were foremost among their folk, and a successor was chosen among them. This meeting took place outside the walls of the City of Elua, for full-blooded Tsingani who follow the Long Road have ever been uncomfortable in enclosed spaces, and I am told it was the greatest gathering of their kind ever held in the shadow of the City walls.

I missed it, for we were in Montrève at the time, returning to my long-neglected estate.

It was good to visit Montrève. Imriel loved it there; I hadn't reckoned on that. I should have, raised as he was in the mountains of Siovale. The pace of life is slower, there. We found everything much in order, for if I had been two years absent, Purnell Friote and his wife Richeline were capable seneschals, maintaining the manor in impeccable readiness for our return, all the while carrying on effortlessly without us. They had three children between them, Imri's age and younger, and he fell in among them with ease, squabbling and scrapping and jumping out of hay-lofts as a boy his age ought. It did my heart good to see it.

Between them, Joscelin and Ti-Philippe saw to the security of our estate, riding the borders and ensuring that every outlying crofter and free-holder knew the value of what they warded, setting up a system of watchers and messengers to maintain the borders. They are a shrewd folk, the Siovalese—and we had won their loyalty, as much by benign neglect as aught else. Siovalese prefer not to be troubled by their overlords, and I had surely done that much. If they had been uncertain of me at the beginning, they had accepted my stewardship of Montrève over the years. Now it had become a matter of pride, and not a few families sent sons and daughters to the manor to take positions in my household. The garrison, which had stood empty for years, was staffed with some twenty eager young recruits, and Ti-Philippe and Joscelin undertook to train them. By the time they were done, I had no doubts that there were few places in Terre d'Ange safer for Imriel than my lord Delaunay's childhood home of Montrève.

Afterward, Joscelin set about building a mews.

I had promised him that, although I'd forgotten it. Elua knows, he remembered. A bestiary, I'd said, if we returned in one piece. I was fortunate that he sought only a mews; and a kennel, for after the initial word of our return, his brother Luc sent a long, gossip-filled letter and a gift of a hound-bitch from Verreuil ready to whelp, which delighted Imri to no end. As for the mews, Ysandre sent her own Head Falconer to supervise the construction of it, and I must needs be resigned to a portion of my estate being given over to the manly pursuits of hunting and fishing.

If it hadn't pleased them so, I might have minded more.

A lively correspondence went in and out of Montrève all summer long, keeping me abreast of news in the City of Elua and beyond. Nicola L'Envers y Aragon sent a lengthy reply to my own letter, giving a full account of all that had transpired in Aragonia since our visit. It had been a considerable task, rooting out the hidden network of the Carthaginian slave-trade, and her husband Ramiro had distinguished himself in the process, much to the surprise of those who thought him good only for drinking and gaming. I was glad to hear it, although sorry it meant Nicola would not be travelling that year. It would have been pleasant to see her.

Still, mayhap it was as well, for there was much to be done. For all that our surroundings were idyllic, my days were seldom idle. In addition to staying abreast of the changes being wrought in Montrève and continuing Imriel's studies—when I could keep him indoors, which wasn't often—I worked at cataloguing my new-found literary wealth, often lingering over individual texts longer than I ought. Visitors came and went, and our network of watchers in the countryside proved effective, for none came without warning.

Save one.

Hyacinthe.

He came at dusk on an evening when a gathering of storm clouds warred with the setting sun. 'Twas Richeline's cry in the herb garden that alerted me, and I left the manor in time to see him coming, a dim figure on a grey horse, his shape emerging from the veil of low mist that hung in the olive grove, shot through with the last slanting dazzle of the sun's gold before it sank behind the hills. Small wonder that he had passed unnoticed, cloaked in the elements he commanded.

"Phèdre." He smiled at me as the mist dispersed, looming suddenly there and *present*, even as Richeline clapped both hands over her mouth, dropping the herbs she had picked for the evening meal. Droplets of mist clung to his black curls.

"Hyacinthe." I swallowed. "I thought the night breeze was to whisper my name."

"Not that," he said, dismounting; only a man, for an instant, saddle-sore and weary. "Not yet. I have been riding the land, to take the measure of it, that I might know it and remember. And I wanted . . . I wanted to see how you lived, before I left."

There was shouting, then, within the household, and Hugues burst from the rear door with his cudgel upraised, staring to see the Master of the Straits at our garden gate.

"Hugues," I said, "would you see to Hyacinthe's horse?"

Thunder rumbled in reply and Hyacinthe made an absent gesture, whispering an incantation to dispel the clouds.

"Oh, don't." The words came impulsively. "We need the rain."

He smiled sidelong at me and murmured incomprehensible syllables.

A gentle rain began to fall, making a soft, silvery sound in the olive trees. A smell of damp earth arose around us. Such was his power, who was Master of the Straits.

I cleared my throat. "Will you come in?"

"Yes," Hyacinthe said softly. "I'd like that."

We were in the parlour when Joscelin and Imriel returned from their day's long ramble, damp through and through and in high spirits despite it, having found a meadow perfect for the training of hawks. They stopped short, upon finding Hyacinthe there.

How strange, to see them all in the same place.

Adjourning to the dining hall, we passed a pleasant meal together, and Hyacinthe told us of the gathering of the *baro kumpai*, and how he had chosen among the candidates set forth to lead the Tsingani. He had quizzed them all, asking how each would have handled the fate of his mother, Anasztaizia, driven from the Tsingani for having surrendered her virtue to a D'Angeline, the bitter price paid for a cousin's ill-placed wager. All of them knew the answer he sought; only Bexhet, son of Nadja, gave it unfaltering, with all the stammering pride of one raised a widow-woman's son, prepared to challenge the ancient code of the Tsingani that placed such inordinate weight on outmoded rules of honor that valued a woman's virginity above her person.

"You might have chosen a woman to lead them," I said to tease him.

Hyacinthe gave me the ghost of his grin. "I might," he said. "But to force growth is to kill it. Let the Tsingani grow at their own pace. Who knows? They may find the end of the *Lungo Drom* in it."

Afterward, we retired once more to the parlour and Imriel served cordial on a silver tray, taking pride in his role, as deft and neat-handed as an adept of the Night Court, watching and listening with all the acuity I had taught him.

"Melisande's son," Hyacinthe murmured in amazement as Imri left the room.

"No, Tsingano," Joscelin corrected him. "*Ours.*" He drained his glass and set it down with a faint click, frowning. "Forgive my rudeness, for I am glad of your presence. Yet I must ask it: Why have you come?"

"Cassiline." There was an ache in Hyacinthe's voice. "Forgive *me*. Yet I must know it: What is the price you paid for my freedom?"

I sent Imriel to bed, then, before we told the story in its entirety. It was his, yes, and there was no part I would deny him; but he was a boy, still. He would tell it himself in the fullness of time, to those he chooses to trust. Until then, I would protect him from it, from the parts he is too young to understand, from the parts that spark his nightmares anew.

To Hyacinthe, we told the truth.

From Melisande's first bargain, and the long road—our own *Lungo Drom*—it had engendered, we told him all. There were parts where Joscelin faltered, unable to describe what had ensued. I spoke of the zenana and the Mahrkagir's cruelty, the pall of Angra Mainyu, my voice sounding like a stranger's to me. And Hyacinthe wept, silently, tears seeping like slow rain on his brown cheeks as he learned the truth of Daršanga; what I had endured there, what Imri had undergone, and Joscelin, too, whose role in some ways was the hardest of all.

Ill thoughts, ill words, ill deeds.

Even to Hyacinthe, I didn't tell the whole of it.

We told him of Jebe-Barkal, after, and the strangeness that was Saba, in all its attendant terrors and glories, the long effort of our voyage on the Lake of Tears, the awe that befell me upon Kapporeth and the Ark of Broken Tablets. And we spoke of the One God, of Yeshuites and the Children of Yisra-el, of Rahab and the Master of the Straits, of Blessed Elua and his Companions, and where their intertwined paths diverged. At some point, a weary Joscelin rose to bid me good-night, his lips gentle on my cheek. I let him go, and remained awake long hours with Hyacinthe, the both of us quarreling over pronunciation and origins, tracing inadequate ciphers in the lees of our cordial on the tabletop, arguing the Name of God and the alphabet of heaven.

I don't know when I forgot his sea-shifting eyes and he ceased to be the Master of the Straits and became only Hyacinthe once more, my oldest friend, stubborn and clever as my lord Delaunay; as I myself had grown, truth be told.

Somewhere.

We knew, both of us. Hyacinthe bent his head and smiled ruefully, passing one hand over the marble table, the marks of our finger-drawn scribbling erasing with its passage. "I'll do as you asked," he said, hanging ringlets hiding his face. "The alphabet shall be yours, once . . . once we're established in Alba."

An unexpected pain seared my heart. "You and Sibeal."

He nodded without looking up. "She sees you in my dreams, you know," he murmured. "She understands."

"When will you go?"

"A month." He did look up, then, and the Tsingano lad I'd loved looked out of his eyes. "Six weeks, mayhap. No longer."

"Will you go as you came here?" I asked, hating the thought of it. "A mist-wrought shadow crossing the land, your passage unmarked by man nor beast?"

"Mayhap." Hyacinthe shrugged. " 'Tis simpler, thus. Does it matter?"

"Yes," I said. I had an idea. "Yes, it does."

Hyacinthe left in the morning, when the early mists still rose from the fields, blending to surround him and shroud his figure as he departed. My household rose to see him off, watching his mounted form vanish into his surroundings, as the night's rain dripped from the olives and the silvery-green leaves sighed at his passing.

"What are you plotting *now?*" Joscelin inquired, reading my expression with the ease of one who'd had long practice at it.

"Nothing," I said, then amended it. "A fête. I'm planning a fête."

One Hundred Two

THEY ARE still talking of it in the City of Elua.

If it had not been for the aid of a good many people, I daresay I could not have pulled it off; and foremost among them is my old mentor, Cecilie Laveau-Perrin, who gave me invaluable advice. There was my factor, Jacques Brenin, who negotiated the sale of various texts, without which I could not have afforded this endeavor. It was his idea, too, to solicit donations from the many lords and ladies who courted my favor, in the name of honoring the Master of the Straits.

Of a surety, I needed Emile's aid, and that I knew I had. Where he led, Night's Doorstep followed. Hyacinthe's return had only augmented that. And for once, the City would follow the lead of Night's Doorstep instead of the Palace.

That was my tribute to Hyacinthe.

While I have lived, only one thing has brought the City of Elua to a standstill. Fever did not do it, so I am told; I was in Skaldia when it struck. Even Waldemar Selig's invasion did not do it, for he never got this far south. The City halted, they say, when Percy de Somerville assailed its walls, and Ysandre's uncle, Barquiel L'Envers, sealed the gates against him. It halted for a day, they say, before wagering resumed and the Court of Night-Blooming Flowers reopened its doors.

Well and so; it halted for my fête.

I took my time making ready that night; an autumn night, unseasonably warm, winter's chill held in abeyance. Joscelin came into my bathing-room, which was the one chamber of my household I held sacrosanct. He grinned to see me sunk neck-deep in warm water and scented oils. My maid-servant Clory, Eugènie's niece, retreated blushing at his approach.

"It smells like a hot-house in here," Joscelin said, perching on the edge of the tub and dabbling his fingers in the scented waters.

"So?" I raised my brows. "Would you rather we were in Montrève, smelling of sheep?"

"Not exactly." Joscelin eyed me. "I may favor the countryside to the City, but seeing you thus . . ." He shrugged. "It makes me wish I'd a large fish to throw at your feet."

I laughed, and shifted in the tub, making room for him. "Come here," I said as he shed his clothes and climbed in, the light of myriad candles casting into shadow the scars that pitted his body; scars he'd earned on my behalf. I circled dripping arms about his neck as he fit himself beneath me. "Yes, there."

"Imriel," Joscelin murmured, shifting under my parted thighs and gripping my buttocks, "is of the opinion that I should wear the lion's mane given me by Ras Lijasu."

"Is he?" I bit my lower lip as the tip of Joscelin's phallus parted my nether lips.

"Yes."

"Well." Water slopped over the sides of the tub as I impaled myself upon him, inch by delicious inch. "Mayhap he's right."

"Didn't you say I looked foolish in it?"

"Did I?" I locked my legs behind his back, feeling wanton and replete, filled to the core. "I don't remember."

"Yes." Joscelin moved slightly, his fingertips digging into my buttocks. I gasped, and more water slopped over the edge. "You did."

"I must have been out of my mind," I whispered, and lifted my head to kiss him.

It was as well I'd started my preparations early.

It began at sundown, when lamp-lighters moved about the City in teams, kindling torches and the innumerable glass oil lamps strung in dangling lines from tree to tree along the streets and in the squares. At every corner, in every square, musicians assembled, tuning their instruments. Workers hired by Namarrese wine-merchants followed in wagons, grunting as they hoisted casks of wine over the edge, stockpiling them in the squares.

People trickled into the streets, wondering if it were true.

It was.

I had planned a fête for the entire City of Elua; the City of Hyacinthe's birth, the City that had raised him. I had gotten Ysandre's permission, of course. She granted it, though she thought I was mad.

Drustan understood. The City Guard was tripled that night—in part to prevent riots, and in part to allow the guardsmen to work in shifts, giving each time to celebrate. Although the planning had been weeks in the process and a number of people were in on the secret, the broadsides had only been posted that day. I wanted to take the City by surprise—and Hyacinthe.

Night's Doorstep would be the heart of it.

So many memories! I had been seven years old when I'd climbed a pear tree and scaled the garden wall of Cereus House, finding my way to Night's Doorstep where a grinning Tsingano boy taught me to steal tarts in the marketplace. It was the first act of defiance I'd ever undertaken in my young life. And no matter who carted me back home, whether it be the Dowayne's guardsmen or my lord Delaunay's man Guy, I kept returning. It was there that Hyacinthe had grown from a half-breed street urchin to a young man with a thriving trade in information, a livery stable and a boarding-house, the self-styled Prince of Travellers who wielded the gift of the *dromonde* in earnest, my one true friend.

All that he had given up.

They remembered him, there. They had never forgotten him. Not the figure out of legend—for indeed, his legend had begun to spread already, and the tales they told along the coast of Azzalle had reached the City—but Hyacinthe himself, sharp with a jest, shrewd with a bargain, generous with coin, a caring son who had seen to his mother's comfort in her final years. They deserved a chance to bid him farewell.

We all did.

"You're fair glowing, you know," Joscelin murmured as we traversed the already-thronging streets in an open carriage, bending his head so his lips brushed my ear. A group of early revelers raised brimming cups in salute, shouting toasts.

I leaned against him and smiled. "You might have somewhat to do with it."

He'd worn the lion's mane after all; and overmore, he'd conspired with Favrielle nó Eglantine behind my back, planning on it. Ras Lijasu's gift had been sewn onto the collar of a splendid cloak, a hue of red one degree lighter than *sangoire*, that it might complement mine own attire. Pale as wheat, Joscelin's hair spilled over the tawny fur and deep-red velvet alike. Between that and his familiar Cassiline arms, polished to a high gleam, he looked, for once, utterly magnificent.

For my part, I too was clad in Jebean attire—the style of Meroë, as interpreted by Favrielle. It spoke to our journey; the best parts of our long journey. And so I wore a Jebean gown in the blood-at-midnight color of *sangoire*, which only I, as the sole *anguissette* in living memory, was entitled to wear. It left my shoulders bare and wrapped tight about my body, fastened with gold pins shaped like cunning darts. I wore my hair in a coronet of braids, the finial of my marque vivid at the nape of my neck, and ivory and gold bangles—another gift of Ras Lijasu—adorned my wrists.

And if I wore a single ivory hairpin thrust through my braids, who was to ask why?

Oh yes, I had kept it. Kaneka's hairpin, one of a pair. I'd left its mate in Daršanga, piercing the Mahrkagir's heart. Never forget; even here, even now. I kept it, as I kept the jade statue of the dog with staring eyes, that I might always remember. He had trusted me, the Mahrkagir. Even as he'd drawn the cord taut about my throat, gazing at me with love for the gift he thought I'd given him, he had trusted me. And I had murdered him for it.

I remembered.

And I reckoned it worth the price.

Imriel, mercifully, had begun to forget; at least a little bit. Although he had them still, his nightmares came fewer and farther between. Elua knows, I was grateful for it. He wore his Jebean finery, too; had insisted upon it. I let him. The snow-white *chamma* and breeches, the short, embroidered cloak—let him wear them. In six months' time, they wouldn't fit. He wore his rhinoceros-hide belt, too, the one Ras Lijasu had given him. There was room to grow in that gift. His face was bright with excitement, and it made my heart ache to see him so happy.

A cordon of young Siovalese guardsmen in the livery of Montrève surrounded our carriage, chattering among themselves, remembering to maintain vigilance under Ti-Philippe's watchful eye. Our arrival was greeted with cheers, for casks had been breached and the streets of Night's Doorstep were already lively with mirth. Although it is one of the tawdriest quarters of the City, it looked beautiful that night, ablaze with light and merriment. Emile greeted us in the street in front of the Cockerel, sweating in an ostentatious velvet doublet as he bowed.

"Comtesse!" he cried, spreading his arms wide as he straightened. "Kushiel's Chosen, Delaunay's *anguissette!* Welcome to your fête."

It was a glorious thing. I may say so, even if I instigated it, for the sum of its parts was greater than aught I had conceived. A good many noble peers were there already, D'Angeline lords and ladies, clad in fine silks and damasks, glittering with jewels as they mingled with tavern-keepers, merchants and workers of all ilk, delighted at the novelty of it. Some of the more adventurous had been to Night's Doorstep before, titillated by its seedy charms, amusing themselves en route to and from the Houses of the Night Court; many had never been. None would have thought to hold a fête there.

They thought it clever and daring of me, telling me so as I circulated among them, exchanging greetings. Let them. I had done it because it was Hyacinthe's home, and my sanctuary. It didn't matter what they believed, only that they celebrated. And that they did, with a will. The wine was heady and rich on the tongue; I had spared no expense in importing it from Namarre, not trusting to Emile's rot-gut. Musicians played set after set, trading places, and a group of Tsingani fiddlers drew the loudest applause. Squares were cleared for dancing, and nobles and commonfolk elbowed one another to make room, silk gowns brushing breeches of rough fustian. Hired servants flushed and merry from sampling the wine made their way through the crowds, bearing trays of offerings from a half-dozen countries: spicy Aragonian shrimp, Menekhetan kabobs, rice rolled in Hellene grape-leaves, honeyed Akkadian pastries, dollops of Jebean stew on spongy flatbread; too many things to count.

It was a good hour before the guest of honor arrived, and when he did, all of Night's Doorstep fell silent, for Hyacinthe didn't come alone. We heard them coming nearly half the way from the Palace, by the cheering that followed in their wake. I don't think the ruling monarch of Terre d'Ange has ever deigned to visit Night's Doorstep. I know for a surety the Cruarch of Alba has not.

They arrived in a ceremonial Alban chariot, and Drustan mab Necthana himself drove it, the muscles in his forearms working as he held the reins in check, gold torque gleaming at his throat. At his side, Ysandre shone like a flame, tall and bright, a rare awe in her face at the outpouring of love that greeted them. There was no need for the armed escort that surrounded them; the populace of the City adored them.

"They came," Imriel whispered. "I didn't think they would."

"Neither did I," I whispered in reply.

Behind them in the chariot stood Sibeal and Hyacinthe. She was wide-eyed at the scope of their welcome, startled and grave, holding his hand.

And Hyacinthe . . .

"You did this," he said softly as I came alongside the chariot, Imri beside me and Joscelin a protective step behind us. Somewhere, they had begun chanting his name again. Hy-a-cinthe! Hy-a-cinthe! His name; my *signale*. I had only spoken it once. "Why?"

I gripped the edges of the chariot and gazed up at him. "I wanted to say good-bye."

Someone—a daring bit-player from a disreputable theatre troupe—made his way to the chariot, offering a tankard of wine with a bow and a toast to Drustan, who accepted it with a laugh and drank deep before passing it to his Queen. It might have been poisoned, for all they knew. Ysandre poured a propitiatory drop before drinking and the revelers shouted approval, a dozen other hands thrusting forth cups and tankards.

D'Angelines, Tsingani; there were even Yeshuites among them.

"Mont Nuit!" someone else cried, pointing. "Look!"

From the heights of the hill of Mont Nuit, where the Thirteen Houses of the Court of Night-Blooming Flowers were clustered, a torchlit procession was winding toward Night's Doorstep. All of them . . . *all*. I caught my breath to see it. The Night Court had closed its doors. In tribute, they came, in celebration. All of the Servants of Naamah. And Cereus House, that is first and eldest among them, led the way, fragile and beautiful, while the madcap adepts of Eglantine House followed close behind, singing and playing, the tumblers throwing somersaults as they went. Ah, Elua! They were all there: modest Alyssum, gentle Balm, proud Dahlia, dreaming Gentian, merry Orchis, adoring Heliotrope, shrewd Bryony, perfect Camellia, sensuous Jasmine, my own mother's House, and yes—Mandrake too, with its delightful wickedness, and Valerian in all its sweet yielding. And they entered the fête like a stream mingling its waters with a mighty river.

"Did you plan this?" Hyacinthe asked. His voice was shaking.

"No." So was mine. "This was a gift."

"Oh, Phèdre!" The tears shone bright in his eyes; his changeable eyes, still Hyacinthe's beneath it all, my Prince of Travellers. "I will miss you so. I'll miss this all."

An Eglantine tumbler, fresh-faced and merry, evaded the guard and darted onto the chariot to steal a kiss from a laughing Drustan mab Necthana, looping a green ribbon about his neck. Once, in this very spot, a troupe of Eglantine adepts had tormented Joscelin, while Hyacinthe and I had stood atop empty wine-casks and watched, stifling our mirth. The tumbler snatched Ysandre's hand and planted a kiss on it, somersaulting backward off the chariot before the Queen's Guard could stop her. Ysandre was laughing. I saw in the vanguard behind her Duc Barquiel L'Envers, his eyes narrowed with calculating amusement. He saw me watching and saluted. The Dowayne of Orchis House coaxed a Tsingano fiddler into playing a lively tune. Emile's voice was audible above the crowd, roaring about somewhat. No one paid him any heed.

"Miss us later," I said to Hyacinthe. "Tonight is for you."

He nodded, understanding. "Thank you."

Good-bye, I said, only the words came out, "You're welcome."

And the fête, my fête, continued, all throughout the City of Elua. It went long into the small hours of the night, and many stories are told of it, for the City had never seen its like. There was joy in it, and sorrow, for it was celebration and farewell alike. On the morrow, there would be sore heads aplenty, and I would worry anew about Imriel's safety and wonder what message was coded in Barquiel L'Enver's mocking salute, and how long Melisande would remain complacent in the Temple of Asherat-of-the-Sea.

For now, this was enough.

If I did not have everything, I had enough. I had my household to sustain me—there was Eugènie, wading into the fray and hoisting her skirts to dance, unexpectedly nimble. I had the regard of the Cruarch of Alba, whom I esteemed beyond gold, and the forgiveness of my Queen, Ysandre de la Courcel, which meant more to me than I had ever reckoned.

I missed my lord Anafiel Delaunay, more than I could say. And I missed my foster-brother Alcuin, who was too gentle a soul to have died as he did. I missed Kaneka, for whom I had conceived a great respect, from whom I was parted by great distance; I missed Kazan Atrabiades, my Illyrian pirate. I wished I could speak to Pasiphae Asterius, the Kore of the Temenos. And I remembered, and grieved, for those others I missed, those who had died for my goals: Eamonn of the Dalriada, Remy and Fortun, my dear chevaliers, and those brave, doomed women of the zenana. I touched the ivory hairpin thrust through my coronet, remembering Drucilla, fierce Jolanta, so many others. And not just the women, no; there was Rushad, who had reminded me so of Alcuin. Erich the Skaldi, who had died trying to protect him.

So many dead.

So many living.

Hyacinthe, my one true friend. I had given him back his life, and if it was not the one he'd had, still, it was *his*. And he had Sibeal with him, whom I liked and admired, who understood his dreams. And I . . . I had friends everywhere, now. Friends and comrades, patrons and lovers.

I had Joscelin, my Perfect Companion, the compass by which I fixed my heart.

No one could ask more.

Nor had I, and yet it had been given. By Kushiel, who had used his Chosen harder than any in recorded memory? By Naamah, whom I had served long and faithfully? By Blessed Elua himself, whose mercy is beyond reckoning? I do not know. Nor does it matter, in the end.

I had Imriel.

Imri, who'd spat in my face upon our meeting, who trusted me beyond reason. Melisande's son, the scion of my deepest enemy, my darkest desire. Who could have guessed it? Not even Elua's priests, I think. My proud and wounded boy, his heart as vast as the plains of Jebe-Barkal and twice as fierce. I loved him so much it made me dizzy, and if I'd had to defy Ysandre twice-over for him, I would have done it.

Blessed Elua was kind.

The fête, my fête, continued in the City of Elua.

I touched the bare hollow of my throat, and smiled, remembering.

Love as thou wilt.